Three Times As Nauti

Berkley titles by Lora Leigh

COYOTE'S MATE
MERCURY'S WAR
DAWN'S AWAKENING
TANNER'S SCHEME
HARMONY'S WAY
MEGAN'S MARK

NAUTI INTENTIONS
NAUTI DREAMS
NAUTI NIGHTS
NAUTI BOY

Three Times As Nauti

Lora Leigh

Fiction

First Rhapsody Book Club Printing: March 2009

Published by arrangement with
Berkley Publishing Group
An Imprint of Penguin Group (USA) Inc.,
375 Hudson Street, New York, New York 10014, USA.

Visit RBC online at http://www.rhapsodybookclub.com

ISBN 978-1-60751-795-5

Printed in the United States of America.

Contents

Nauti Boy

Acknowledgments

For my CP, you know who you are. Special thanks to my advance readers, Melissa, Annmarie, Shelley, Janine, Susan, Chris, and Marty. Without you guys, I don't know what I would have done. You keep me on track, you keep me moving, and you have my eternal thanks.

Prologue

How had he known she would be waiting on him, here of all places. Rowdy Mackay steered the Harley into its parking spot before lifting his glasses from his face and facing the demon sprite as she moved from the wood bench to stand on the sidewalk in front of him.

She was wearing one of those short, snug little T-shirts she liked so much. At least it wasn't one of his bigger shirts. He had lost two more on this trip home and he knew who to blame. She had been stealing his shirts since she was sixteen—when her mother married his father, bringing his favorite bit of trouble right into his home.

And he had been running from her ever since. Seven years of running.

He turned and tucked the sunglasses into the side of his Marine-issue duffel bag strapped on the back of the Harley before he bent his leg on the gas tank and watched her silently. Dawg and Natches were supposed to be here soon. Dawg was driving Natches over so he could take the Harley back, but they weren't here yet. There was no one to distract him from the hunger driving him crazy.

She was twenty-three and her kisses were soft summer rain. They slid over a man's senses and drew him in, inviting him to get all wet and wild with her, inviting him to give her his worst. And in Rowdy's case, his worst might be a hell of a lot more than she could handle.

She stepped from the sidewalk. The low rise of her jeans didn't even come close to the tempting shadow of her navel. She made him sweat in the middle of damned winter. But it wasn't winter now, it was summer. A hot, Kentucky summer evening, and he was leaving again.

And this time, he knew beyond a shadow of a doubt that he wouldn't be able to walk away again. This was his last year away from home, he figured. Each year without even touching her, without taking her or tasting her kiss, she made him feel things he didn't expect.

His chest tightened at that knowledge. At the effort it was going to take to walk away from her again.

"You left without saying good-bye." She stopped beside the Harley, her dove gray eyes staring back at him with a shadow of hurt. "I didn't even get to see you this time."

No, she hadn't. He had stayed as far away from his dad's home as possible, spending the six weeks he was back on the boat he kept at the marina.

A playful breeze caught at the long curls of her golden brown hair and tugged at the lush waves of silk he dreamed of wrapping around his body. He had dreamed of her while he spent those lonely nights on the boat. Dreamed of touching her, kissing her, dragging her beneath his body, and taking her until neither of them could breathe for the exhaustion filling them.

Other women hadn't even figured into his lust. His stubborn body rejected them. He wanted Kelly.

His mouth was watering. He could feel the need to pull her to him, to wrap himself around her, nearly getting the best of him.

"Rowdy?" Her voice was filled with a young woman's hope, her dreams, and all the passion he knew burned inside her.

"You shouldn't have come here, Kelly." He sighed as he gave in to the impulse to reach out, to use the excuse of pushing her hair back to touch the soft warmth of it.

He really wanted to crush it in his hands, pull her head back, and devour her. Damn, he could do it too. She would let him. He could see it in her eyes.

"You didn't even say good-bye." It wasn't just hurt in her voice then, there was anger.

"If I had to say good-bye, I might not have left," he finally sighed. He was a man; he knew better than this. Kelly might be twenty-three, but she had no damned clue what she was getting into with him.

He'd kissed her three years before. Pinned her against the trunk of a tree and took her lips like the sweet drug they were. He had marked her because he couldn't help himself. He had made certain no one was dumb enough to think they could have Kelly. And his cousins would make sure it stuck while he was gone. While the Marines took their final year of this tour and he decided what the hell he was going to do about Kelly.

"You could have said good-bye," she whispered again.

"I could have been shot by my own father for the things I'd have done to you if I had just a measure of a chance." He tried to smile, but he was too busy trying to keep his hands off the soft curves of her ass instead.

She was making him crazy. But hell, this was Kelly; she had been making him crazy for most of her life in one way or the other.

"I would have come to the boat—"

He laid his finger over her lips when he wanted to lay his own lips over them. Take them, lick at them, feel her open to him as she had that night at the lake.

"No." He shook his head. "You're here now." He had known she would be. Prayed for it.

He lifted his finger from her lips as he lowered his head. He didn't kiss her lips, he couldn't trust himself to rein in his hunger, his lust. It was impossible. He had a plane waiting on him, a job to finish, and he—

Sweet merciful God have pity on him. Her head turned, her lips touched his, and he was a goner. His hands slid over the ripe curves of her ass and he clenched, lifting her into the cradle of his thighs as his hunger overruled all common sense.

His head tilted, his lips slanting over hers, and he swore he saw stars as the sweet taste of her exploded against his senses. Blood began to pound in his veins as his thighs tightened, his dick thickened, and everything but the taste of Kelly receded beneath the force of his lust.

Pure, raw pleasure. That was what she was. She made him hard, made him primal, made him want to show her all the reasons why he should have never touched her the first time.

But she was his. His woman. His sweet, hot taste of paradise, and he could do nothing but beg for more. She was his drug, and God help them both, he was afraid the addiction might well kill one of them. He knew for a certainty it was going to drive him crazy.

Male catcalls and raucous voices had him finally dragging his lips from hers as he glanced up to see several servicemen watching him enviously. *Son of a bitch.* Here he was in the damned parking lot of the airport ready to tear her clothes from her body.

Glancing down, he watched her eyes drift open, saw the passion that clouded her gaze as she stared up at him.

"Don't forget me, Rowdy," she whispered as he set her back from him.

But he couldn't let go of her. His hands clasped her hips as his forehead settled against hers.

"Forget you?" he asked softly. "Baby, you're in every dream that drifts through my head. How the hell am I supposed to ever forget you?"

And that sucked. He couldn't forget her anymore than he could have her. Sweet, little, virgin baby, she had no idea what she was getting into.

One

One Year Later

So that was what had happened to that third shirt. Rowdy Mackay leaned against the kitchen doorway, tilted his head, and watched in amusement as Kelly shuffled over to the refrigerator and opened the door to peer into the interior.

The long, gray Marines T-shirt swallowed her slender frame and hung well past her thighs. A pair of his matching gray socks covered her small feet, and gray sweatpants hung from her hips. Not his, he thought in amusement—obviously hers but loose enough to make a man wonder why the hell she was suddenly hiding that curvy little body he knew she possessed. Especially when she had never bothered to do so in the past.

This outfit was a far cry from the snug shorts and T-shirts she used to don for summer sleepwear. Long, honey brown curls fell from the crown of her head to the middle of her back, the loose ringlets tousled and still a bit tangled from sleep, and damn if she didn't look like she had just dragged herself from a lover's bed.

He knew better, of course. His father's rules were strict. Rowdy might live under his roof during the brief times he was home, but he didn't bring his women here for the night, and he knew damned good and well Kelly wouldn't bring a man here.

The treasured princess of the house might be spoiled beyond bearing, but she respected her mother and stepfather. So dragging herself out of a lover's arms before making her way to the kitchen for a snack wasn't a scenario that was likely to happen here.

It was one of the reasons he had stayed away as much as possible since she had come of age. One of the reasons he had taken that last tour with the Marines. Some things a man just knew he was too weak to resist, and he had accepted long ago that he was too weak to resist Kelly.

That realization had come along about the time she grew breasts and he began noticing those breasts. Somewhere around the time that she started teasing him with innocent smiles and brushing against him, and he began enjoying it.

It was then he joined the service just to get the hell out of the house, to get away from her. College wasn't providing him the escape he needed. She was still there, and so was he, too often. And he was weak. Weak men were dangerous creatures. A twenty-two-year-old man had no damned business touching a sixteen-year-old, and he had known it. The only other option had been leaving. So Rowdy had left.

His time in the Marines had taught him self-control, finished his education, and brought him into manhood. But his greatest weakness was still his greatest weakness. *Kelly.*

"I don't wanna cook."

His lips quirked at the early morning grumpiness in her voice. She was talking to herself. Some things never changed. The sun would rise in the east and set in the west, and Kelly would always mutter to herself when she was irritated.

And the sound of her sweet, husky voice would always make his dick threaten to burst the zipper in his jeans.

"There's cereal in the cabinet." Rowdy expected her to turn with a smile bright enough to rival the sun. His arms were ready to open for the handful of woman barreling toward him. He wasn't expecting what he got, though.

Kelly screamed. The refrigerator door slammed closed hard enough to rattle the contents as she turned to dart through the opposite doorway.

Her face had gone paste white; her wide gray eyes were filled with fear.

Who had she been expecting?

She was poised to run but fighting to stand still. Conflicting emotions ran across her expressive face as her eyes met his, and the room filled with a tension that had never been there before.

Fear filled her eyes.

Rowdy narrowed his eyes on her, his body stiffening. No, it wasn't fear. For a moment, there had been pure, shocking terror. A woman aware that she was alone with a man, that she was weak, that her security wasn't assured. He'd seen it overseas in the eyes of a thousand women, and he saw it now.

"Rowdy?" Her voice was high, thin, her hands bunching in the front of her shirt, fisting the material as she shuddered. "What are you doing here?"

The husky, fear-laden voice twisted at his guts and had pure, unbridled fury simmering in his mind. What had happened to Kelly?

"It's home, isn't it?"

He had been ready to catch her as she ran at him. She always ran to him, throwing her arms around his neck, pressing her tight little breasts against his chest, and slapping a kiss to his cheek. For eight years, he could count on Kelly's greeting. Until today. He wondered in which direction the sun would rise now. Some things should just never change.

"Oh. Yeah." She nodded, her eyes darting around the room before a nervous smile tilted her soft pink lips, trembled there for a moment, then disappeared. "We weren't expecting you. Did you tell Mom and Ray you were coming?"

"No. I never do." His battle instincts were humming now. This wasn't normal. It was so far from normal that he knew with a clench of his gut that he wasn't going to like whatever the hell had been going on here.

Suddenly, nearly a year of his father's discomfort when they talked on the phone rose within his mind. Every time he had asked about Kelly, Ray Mackay's voice had tightened. When Rowdy asked to talk to her, he was given excuses.

The letters he had received from Kelly had changed, too. She no longer sent pictures, no longer filled the exchanges with innuendo or teasing comments. She had still written, but it was different, a difference he couldn't put his finger on, couldn't explain. He had felt it, though.

"No, you're always sneaking up on us." There was that nervous smile again, the way her eyes darted around the room.

Rowdy held himself where he was, leaning against the doorway, arms crossed over his chest. He could be a patient man when he had to be. But he had also learned that sometimes, there was no choice but to forge ahead and confront whatever enemy waited in the dark. He'd learned to forge ahead just as well as he had learned to wait.

"What's going on, Kelly?" He straightened from the doorway, dropped his arms, and tucked his thumbs in the waistband of his low-slung jeans.

His chest was bare, the cooling breeze from the air conditioner drying the sweat that had dampened his flesh. He'd been cleaning the Harley, polishing his baby and getting her ready for her first ride in over a year. He'd dumped his duffel bag in his room and headed straight for the garage, knowing his father and stepmother would be at the marina, and figuring Kelly would be there as well.

The fact that she wasn't was interesting. Her reaction to him even more so.

"Nothing's going on." That damned quick, nervous little smile was starting to get on his nerves.

She was scared of him, and it was eating a hole in his soul. Kelly had never been scared of him, not once, he had always made certain of it. Now she was watching him as though she were terrified he was going to jump her any second.

"You're a lousy liar, baby," he grunted, heading for the fridge and watching as she edged out of his way.

She kept her eyes on him, watching him suspiciously as he opened the door and grabbed a bottle of water. Uncapping it, his gaze locked with hers, he brought it slowly to his lips.

Now there was a glimmer of the girl he had left eight years ago. Shyly watching as he drank from the bottle, her little tongue flicking out to swipe over her own lips, as though she were thirsty. A hungry little gleam filled the soft depths of her eyes, darkening them, making them appear stormy, cloudy as it mixed with the fear.

"When did you get back?" She crossed her arms over her breasts, tearing her gaze from his. "Do Mom and Ray know you're home?"

"Not yet." He recapped the bottle and set it on the kitchen isle as he continued to watch her. "I had Dawg pick me up from the airport this morning. We pulled in here about seven."

She nodded, a jerky little movement that had his fingers tightening as he watched her. The suspicion growing in his mind sent black anger swirling through him. Something had changed her, something dark and ugly, and he could see it in her eyes, in the regret and the anger and the fear that filled her expression.

The girl he had loved nearly all her life was terrified of him. She wasn't wary, or nervous, she was flat out scared. This was the same girl he had held as a child when her father died. He'd been a scrawny teenager, she had been too young to understand the sudden death that had rocked her world, and had sought out the boy who ruffled her hair, teased her about her skinned knees, and protected her from the bullies.

This was the same girl he'd taken to her senior prom when her date had stood her up. The one he had danced with on the dance floor and had to hide his erection from because he knew he couldn't touch her, couldn't have her. The girl he had kissed one night when he'd had too much to drink, the one he had touched too intimately before he headed back to base four years before. She was his girl, and suddenly, she was terrified of him.

"So where's my hug?" He leaned against the middle counter, watching her closely.

What little color had returned to her face, drained. Her eyes jerked to his, then away, her throat working as she swallowed tightly.

"I have to get dressed. I have to get to work." She turned on her heel, moving for the doorway.

"Kelly." Knowing he was making a mistake, feeling that knowledge to the soles of his booted feet, Rowdy reached out to catch her wrist.

His fingers touched her, curled around the bare skin when she shrieked, turning on him with a flash of fear as she jerked away from him, her body tightening defensively.

"What?" She gave it a good fight. She tried to cover her reaction, but the way she suddenly backed away from him and the fear on her face gave her away. There was no hiding the fact that his touch had terrified her. "Kelly, where's Dad?" He kept his voice cool. But fury was racing through him. Only one thing could cause a reaction like this, only one thing would have changed the teasing, tempting little minx he had known into a terrified, scurrying little rabbit.

"The marina." She licked her lips again, her gaze jumping away from him, her expression warring between fear and frustration. "I have to get dressed. I'll . . . I'll be down later."

She ran from him. As quick as that she turned tail in those sloppy, ill-fitting clothes she was wearing and moved from the kitchen to the staircase in the entryway and rushed upstairs.

She left him alone in the sunlit kitchen, his fists clenched, anger surging in his gut, and his suspicions all but confirmed.

He turned abruptly and stalked to the phone, ripping it from its base, and punched in the marina's number.

He waited through four rings impatiently, one hand propped on his hip, the other clenched around the phone with a force that should have shattered it.

"Mackay Marina." His father's booming voice suddenly came over the receiver.

"Hey, Dad, how's it going?" Rowdy kept his voice calm, controlled.

"Hey, Rowdy, not too bad." Ray Mackay chuckled. "How did you get to call so early? That CO of yours sleeping on the job?"

"Hell if I know," he drawled. "I didn't sign up for another tour, Dad." He had planned to, had every intention of doing so until his last birthday passed and he realized that running from some things wasn't working. "I'm home. Showed up about seven this morning." Tension suddenly sizzled across the line.

"You're home?" His dad's voice was deliberately bland, the tone mild. But Rowdy knew his dad, sometimes too well.

"Yep. Saw Kelly too."

He wasn't a fool, but even if he had been the muttered curse that came across the line would have warned him.

"We're on our way home." Ray confirmed his worst fears. "We need to talk."

Rowdy hung up the phone, stared around the kitchen, then breathed out heavily.

Damn. He came home to court his favorite girl, to settle down, to stop fighting what he knew was a losing battle. Had he come home too late?

Kelly let the hot water from the shower flow over her, wash away her tears, though it couldn't wash away the feeling of hands holding her down, of fetid breath on her face and hard, wet lips covering hers.

It couldn't drown out the rage and anger, or the fear. The water turned her skin pink from the heat and stung her tender flesh, but it couldn't ease the need that lay just below the memories of a night she feared had changed her life forever.

Rowdy was home. All six feet, four inches of hard, muscled flesh and teasing sea green eyes. He was home after more than a year away, a man full-grown, mature, and sexy as hell.

She wiped at her tears again, her breath hitching in her throat as she remembered one of the few nights she had followed him to the lake. The houseboat was Rowdy's pride and joy, and it was his escape. And she knew where he would head, to the Point, a serene cove where he and his buddies gathered on the weekends to drink, fish, let off steam, and party out the excessive energy they always seemed to have.

"Dad'll kill me." He had been just a little drunk, and way too sexy. His sea green eyes had darkened, his expression growing heavy with desire as he pressed her against a tree.

They had been hidden in the shadows from the rest of the group, sheltered. The heat of summer and lust had wrapped around them. He had been a man, and she had been too innocent, too uncertain in how to contain the need that pulsed in every cell of her body.

"I won't tell him," she had whispered, her palms smoothing up his chest, feeling the prickle of the light growth of body hair that spread over his torso as his hands gripped her hips, pulling her against his thighs.

"He'll know I touched you." His lips had quirked into a smile. "You're like pure, raw liquor, Kelly. And you go to my head faster."

She had fought to breathe, to contain the explosion of satisfaction and joy that rushed through her bloodstream.

"I'm leaving again tomorrow, baby." At first the words hadn't made sense. "I took another tour. Damned good thing, because sure as hell I'd end up doing this, and fuck us both up for good."

Agony had washed over her body even as pleasure had exploded into fragmented, flickering rays of sensation. His lips had covered hers, his tongue teasing her as he sampled her kiss then tasted the tears that fell from her eyes.

"One kiss, baby. Just this. Damn, you're going to break my heart."

He had kissed her as though he were starved for her. One hand had curled in her long hair, the other had cupped her breast, his thumb rasping over her engorged nipple, their moans blending together as the summer night enfolded them.

The hard length of his cock had pressed between her thighs. Even through the heavy material of his jeans she had felt the throb of his erection, the length of it, the promise of passion and satisfaction.

"Don't leave," she had whispered as he drew back from her. "Don't go, Rowdy."

"If I don't, I'll ruin us both forever . . ." He had set her from him, staring down at her, his eyes raging with lust. "Don't forget me, darlin', because sure as hell, I don't think I'll ever forget you."

He had never touched her again. He had taken her back to the shore and walked her the short distance to the small parking area above the Point. He had put her in her car and sent her home. And the next morning, he was gone. And he had not touched her since. She had lived on fantasy and dreams, because Rowdy made certain there was no chance of a repeat performance. And she had plotted and planned for his return. She had moved out of her mother's home into a small apartment in town. She had begun monthly visits to the local spa where she was plucked, waxed, toned, and lotioned on a regular basis. For too short a time.

Within three months of moving out all her dreams had turned to ashes and fear had taken their place. Her own foolishness had led to her downfall, and pulling herself from the shadows of the terror she had experienced was taking all her strength. She didn't know if she could survive dealing with Rowdy and her need for him, on top of it.

She leaned her head against the shower wall, her breath hitching as she fought back tears. He knew something was wrong. There was no way to hide it. She looked at him now and she didn't just see the man she had been in love with since she was a kid. She saw someone she couldn't fight, couldn't struggle from if she needed to. She saw a threat.

Her fists clenched as she pressed them against the tile, anger building in her chest until she wondered if she would be able to hold back the screams that pressed at the back of her throat.

She loved him. She had loved him forever. Dreamed of him, ached for him, waited for him. And now she was too damned scared to even welcome him home.

Are you my good girl, Kelly?

She flinched at the memory of the scratchy voice at her ear as a hard male body held her down, as the slickened fingers of the other hand probed between her buttocks, ignoring her struggles, her muted screams through the gag over her mouth.

She had been bleeding from the numerous cuts he had made on her body after he tied her spread-eagle on her bed. The wounds had burned like fire as they bled, the adrenaline pumping through her making the blood race and pour from the cuts. It had made her weak, made it hard to think, to work the hastily tied gag loose enough for one piercing scream as she felt him attempt to penetrate her rear.

God, she hated the memory of it. Hated the feeling of helplessness that followed her, even now. She had been unable to fight; unable to protest anything he did to her. And the nightmares that alone brought left her shaking in the darkest hours of the night.

She had been terrified of Rowdy knowing. Fearing he would blame her.

But even more, she had feared *for* Rowdy. He would have never stayed on duty if he knew what was going on at home. He would have left, with or without permission, and returned for vengeance. Rowdy protected those he cared about, and Kelly knew, beyond a shadow of a doubt, that he would have come racing home, even if it meant going AWOL.

But now Rowdy was home. And Kelly knew, once he learned the truth, he would never let it rest. He would find the stalker tormenting her, or he would die in the effort. And the fear of his death overshadowed even the fear of the threat she faced herself. Because life without the promise of seeing Rowdy, of hearing his laughter and the dark promise of passion in his voice, was a life Kelly didn't want to contemplate. A life she knew she didn't want to face.

Two

At fifty-seven, Ray Mackay was still a powerful man, with hazel eyes and hair that still retained much of its raven black color. His weathered face was starting to crease with deep laugh lines at the sides of his eyes. Eyes that were usually cheerful, always warm and friendly, were now somber.

Rowdy was waiting on the front porch of the two-story white and red farmhouse when his dad pulled into the driveway, the dark green Jeep Laredo parking beside Rowdy's Harley.

Maria Mackay was out of the jeep before Ray turned the engine off, rushing up the cement walkway, her gray blue eyes concerned as she met his gaze.

"Is Kelly okay?" Maria Salyers Mackay was still slender for her forty-seven years of age. The summer shorts and crisp, white cotton shirt showed off her tanned legs and arms attractively.

"Why wouldn't she be?" He leaned against the railing, watching her with narrowed eyes. "And why do I have a feeling that if I had warned ya'll I was coming home, that I might have found my way barred?"

He could see it in her face, in his father's heavyset expression. They hadn't expected him, and they weren't comfortable with him being there alone with Kelly. And that just pissed him off. Whatever the hell was going on, one thing should have been set in cement in their heads, and that was the fact that he would die before he hurt Kelly.

"I'd never bar you from your own home, Douglas."

He winced. Maria was the only person who called him Douglas, and the snap in her voice when she said it now was as sharp as a knife. No one called him Douglas, ever. But hell, she had taught him in school and breaking her of the habit wasn't easy.

He crossed his arms over his chest, staring down at her intently as she stepped onto the porch.

"I'm going to check on Kelly." She moved for the door.

"Not yet." He didn't move; he didn't intend for his voice to lower warningly, or his body to tense as he watched a main source of information attempt to escape. But he wanted answers, and she wasn't running off until he had them.

"Go on, Maria." Ray stepped up behind her, his large hands settling on her shoulders as he gave them a comforting squeeze. "I'll talk to Rowdy. We'll be in soon."

She glanced up at Rowdy, worry and regret shimmering in her eyes before she turned to her husband, kissing his cheek gently before moving into the house.

Rowdy's attention fixed on his father, watching as he swiped his fingers through his hair before burying his hands in his jeans pockets.

"Was she raped?" Rowdy lifted the bottle of water to his lips, taking a long sip as he watched Ray's eyes darken with pain.

Ray breathed out roughly, his shoulders shifting as he lowered his head.

"Attacked," he finally muttered. "She wasn't raped. But she was cut up pretty bad, traumatized." He lifted his head and Rowdy wondered if his father could see the pure murder burning inside him now.

"Who did it?" He kept his voice even, cool nonetheless.

Ray shook his head slowly, his expression heavy.

"She didn't see his face; there were no leads on who he was or why he attacked her."

The water bottle crumpled in Rowdy's hand, water sloshing over his fingers before he realized what he had done. Forcing himself to release the plastic, he set it on the railing and focused on his father.

"Where did it happen?"

"She moved out right after your last visit," Ray sighed roughly. "Nice little apartment in town, next to one of her friends. Few weeks later she started getting crank calls. Caller ID couldn't trace them. We put new locks on her doors and windows, but you know how she was." Ray shook his head wearily. "Liked sleeping with her window cracked. She thought she was safe. Thought she would hear it if someone snagged the fire escape ladder. But she didn't. Her neighbor's boyfriend heard her screams and knocked the door down, but he'd already hurt her. The attacker got out the window before the boy could catch him."

Short and to the point. And he was hiding something, Rowdy could feel it. He stared back at his father, silent, probing, knowing he would tell him eventually. Rowdy wouldn't give him a choice.

Ray glanced back at him, then away. His teeth clenched, rage glittered in his eyes.

"It wasn't a normal attack," he finally muttered.

Rowdy felt a chill race up his spine.

"What do you mean by that?" He had to force the words past his throat.

Ray coughed nervously. "He meant to rape her anally. He almost managed it."

"Motherfucker! God. Damn!" Rowdy flung himself across the porch, his hands running over his head before he gripped the back of his neck in fury. "Son of a bitch!" His abdomen tightened as he fought to hold back a howl of pure rage before jerking back to stare at his father. "Why the fuck didn't you tell me?"

"Hell Rowdy, what could you do?" Ray snapped, anger suffusing his face. "She begged us not to tell you. You were clear across the world with no hope of coming home anytime soon. There was nothing you could have done."

"Like hell," he snarled. "They would have let me come home or dealt with the consequences. That's no excuse."

"Exactly." His father's face flushed with anger. "You would have gone AWOL to come home, and caused even more of a mess for that kid. Do you think we didn't know what the hell was going on before you left the first time? You couldn't keep your eyes off her and she was just a fucking kid. Four years later you were back for three months and it was worse. She didn't need that. The attack was too brutal and she was too damned vulnerable. I opted to wait till you returned, and I stand by that decision."

"Damn." Rowdy pushed his fingers through his hair before rubbing at the back of his neck with an edge of violence. "Son of a bitch, Dad. Who would do that to her?"

Ray shook his head. "There was a rash of rapes last summer. Several girls in surrounding counties were attacked, all anally. No one caught the bastard and the sheriff has no leads. She's finally coming out of it, Rowdy, getting a grip on herself. But it was bad for a while. Bad enough that we wondered if she would ever leave this damned house again."

And no one had told him.

"Look, Son," Ray finally breathed heavily. "I know how it was with you the last time you were home. With her." He shifted uncomfortably. "I know about the games you, Dawg, and Natches get up to. And so does Kelly. Don't expect anything from her. You hear me?"

Rowdy stared back at his father in surprise. Damn, this was just what he needed right now.

"What do you want me to say?" he asked his father softly.

Ray shook his head. "I don't want you to say anything, Son. I want you to let Kelly come to you. She's been scared to death of your return, and I don't know why myself. I know you wouldn't hurt her, but I know for a fact she knows about some of those little affairs you and your cousins have participated in."

And his father suspected she was scared of him now. Rowdy could see it in Ray's eyes, feel it in the air around them.

And he was probably right. God help the bastard that touched her, because if Rowdy ever found him, he would turn him into dog meat.

"I'll head to the boat." Rowdy breathed in roughly. He needed time to think, time to figure this one out.

Ray blinked several times, his expression twisting in emotion as he turned quickly away from Rowdy and headed to the house. Pausing at the door, he turned back to his son and said, "Did I ever mention how proud of you I am, Boy?"

Rowdy snorted. "Stop calling me a boy, Pop. You're going to kill my rep, you know."

His throat tightened with emotion as well. He knew what his father was saying.

"I'm proud, Boy," he muttered. "Damned proud."

And Rowdy felt like a failure. He had failed to protect the only woman who had ever held his heart because he was too damned busy running from her. He should have been home, he should have been holding her in his bed, loving the hell out of her.

If he had staked his claim, she wouldn't have been in that damned apartment.

He breathed in roughly before turning to the door himself. His duffel bag was in his old room. Not that he stayed at the house much when he was home in the summers. He had thrown the bag in there for convenience; now he was going to have to collect it.

Rowdy jerked the door open, stalking into the house before coming to an abrupt stop. Kelly stood at the top of the landing, her face paper white, her long, damp hair hanging over that fucking shapeless T-shirt, her hands clenched in front of her.

Her lips were trembling, her eyes big and dark and filled with tears.

Rowdy glanced away, fighting for control before he turned back to her and began to walk steadily up the steps. The tears gathered in her eyes, until one dropped as she stepped back, allowing him to stand beside her.

God, he wanted to wipe that tear away, wanted to erase the shattered pain he saw in her eyes.

"I'm sorry," she whispered, her voice ragged. "I'm so sorry, Rowdy."

"Why?" He asked the question softly, aware of her mother standing farther up the hall, his father in the entryway.

"I wasn't careful—"

"No." She flinched as he snapped the word out. "Don't be sorry for that, baby. That wasn't your fault." His arms hung limply at his side, his own world lying broken at his feet, and he couldn't even hold her. Couldn't comfort her. It was ripping his guts to pieces. "I'll be at the boat if you need me. I'll always be here if you need me."

And for now, that was all he could give her. Right now, it was all he had. He moved away from her, turning and stalking to his bedroom, ignoring Maria's whispered "Douglas?" as he pushed the door open.

His duffel bag was still on his bed, unpacked.

"I'll get the rest of my stuff later." He picked up the Marine-issue bag and turned to face his father as the other man followed him into his room.

"Make sure you're home for dinner," Ray growled, his voice rough. "Don't forget you have family here at the house too."

Rowdy forced a smile to his lips as he jerked the duffel bag from the bed and headed to the door.

"Dinner for sure. Tomorrow." He nodded. "I have things to do tonight."

He paused outside the door, staring at Kelly where she stood on the landing, her eyes wide with pain.

"Come down to the boat whenever you need to," he told her softly. "Anytime baby."

He came back for her. He wasn't hiding that, not from his father and not from her.

A glimmer of surprise filled her eyes as a little flush moved beneath her pale skin. At least she didn't look terrorized anymore. It didn't mean he had recovered though. Rage was eating a hole into his gut and pounding through his bloodstream with enough force to make him wonder exactly how good his control was now.

He wanted to kill the bastard who had hurt her. He wanted to wipe away the memory of her pain and fill it with pleasure. And until he got a handle on himself, he didn't have a hope of doing either.

Three

An hour later, Kelly pulled her car into the parking lot of the marina and stared out at the boats lined at the end of the docks. The Nauti Boys were all there. The *Nauti Buoy*, *Nauti Dawg*, and *Nauti Dreams*. She could see Rowdy on the upper deck, dressed in cut-offs, bare chested and looking like a sun god as he straightened and stared out at the parking lot.

She had to talk to him.

She laid her head on the steering wheel and closed her eyes as she felt her heart thumping erratically in her chest. Fear or excitement? *Both*, she admitted to herself.

The knowledge that he was back sent heat rushing through her even as fear shadowed the arousal. She was a virgin, but she wasn't ignorant. She knew what the tension between her thighs was, and it was stronger than it had ever been. She grabbed her purse before opening the door and stepping out onto the parking lot. She looked around, feeling the snaking fear that always followed her when she left the house. Squaring her shoulders, Kelly turned and headed toward the docks. Her head lifted as her gaze locked on Rowdy. He was watching her, standing beneath the rays of a sun that lovingly painted his hard, muscular body. He made her breathing hard, made her mouth water and her hands shake with nerves.

Pulling her gaze away, she moved onto the floating walkway, heading for the back edge of the docks. There were half a dozen rows of docking slots on this quarter of the marina. They were the least expensive slots, and the farthest away from the marina's office.

Rowdy's, Dawg's, and Natches's boats were in the last three slots, and incidentally where the majority of the ducks tended to congregate. Dawg was notorious for feeding them throughout the day.

As she neared the *Nauti Buoy*, the sliding deck door opened and Rowdy stepped out. Dark gold flesh gleamed with sweat as he leaned against the doorway, his thumbs tucked into the pockets of his ragged cutoffs as he watched her.

"Permission to come aboard?" A nervous smile trembled on her lips.

"Always." His deep voice raced across her nerve endings, sending frissons of heat to lick at her flesh.

He moved back into the interior of the houseboat, his lashes lowering over his brilliant eyes as he watched her.

Kelly stepped onto the small deck, trying to ignore the shaking in her knees as she crossed it and entered the main section of the craft.

She had known for four years that when he came home for good, he would claim her once and for all. She had waited for him like an immature child, weaving dreams and fantasies of what would happen when he came home at last. Somehow she had known that would be his last tour, despite his threats to reenlist. A year ago, she had felt it. Something had changed in him, the way he watched her, the tension that emanated from him whenever they were together.

As it was now. She could feel it tightening in and around her body, reminding her of all the desires and explicit fantasies that had tormented her through the years.

"Thirsty?" He moved to the low fridge, opening it to pull out a beer and lift it to her in invitation.

"No." She shook her head as she pushed her hair from her shoulder and faced him awkwardly.

God, she had no idea what to say to him.

He continued to stare back at her intently.

"I'm sorry," she sighed; she didn't know what else to say. "It was my fault Ray didn't tell you what happened."

His lips quirked as he lowered his head, hiding the hurt she knew he must have been feeling.

He finally shrugged as he lifted his gaze. "Why didn't you let him?"

She blinked furiously at the tears that threatened to fill her eyes.

"You couldn't do anything." She shrugged heavily. "You were a world away, Rowdy. You weren't free. I didn't want you to worry."

He snorted at that. "I would have come home, Kelly. I could have come home without repercussion."

And that was what had scared here.

She breathed in roughly. "I'm doing okay. I've been seeing a therapist and she's really helped. It's just, sometimes, I still get scared." She shrugged helplessly. "I feel like such a wimp."

And she felt watched. Stalked. Not that she had told Ray or her mother how she felt. Her therapist assured her it was normal, under the circumstances. But it eroded her confidence, kept her awake long into the night. His eyes darkened as he moved slowly toward her.

She stepped back instinctively.

"You're scared to death of me," he said softly.

She could hear the dark torment in his voice, see it in his eyes.

"I'm not scared of you." She fought the trembling of her lips as she stared up at him, fought to stand in place rather than running as she wanted to.

"Then what are you scared of?" He reached out, his fingers running down a long curl that fell over her shoulder. "Why are you trembling, Kelly?"

"You've always made me tremble." She bit her lip at the admission. "Now . . ." She stared back at him miserably. "I'm not scared of you, Rowdy, but forgetting . . . sometimes, I can't forget."

His thumb smoothed down her cheek, nearly taking her breath with the latent sensuality of his touch.

"Are you going to keep running, Kelly?" he asked then. "You knew if you told me what happened I'd come home. You knew I would have never stayed away. What couldn't you handle about that?"

"You couldn't come home—"

"Bullshit," he growled. "I would have found a way back to

you, you knew it. But you swore my dad to secrecy and, it seems, my cousins as well. You were scared of me."

"No . . ." She shook her head again, desperate to make him believe her now.

"You knew what I wanted from you, Kelly." He turned away, stalking across the room before turning back to her. "You knew I wanted you in my bed. You knew what was going to happen when I came home. Didn't you?"

"I knew." She couldn't deny it.

"Did you think I'd try to take you while you were raw from an attempted rape?" Disgust filled his voice.

"That's not true." She couldn't let him believe that.

Moving across the room, she gripped his arm, holding him in place when he would have moved from her.

"I knew you wouldn't, Rowdy," she cried fiercely. "I know you would never, ever hurt me. I can't help it. You don't know how long I waited for you to come home, how much I needed you to touch me, and now I don't know what to do. I don't know how to make sense of any of it."

She stared back at him, desperate for him to understand, on the edge of crying and knowing the tears would do her no good.

"What you made me feel has always scared me," she finally admitted, her voice trembling. "How much I needed your touch always terrified me. And now, it's like all the fears are swirling together until I can't make any sense of any of it."

His expression twisted into a grimace of raw pain as his arms came around her. Slowly. Powerful, naked, sun-heated, he pulled her against him as her hands clutched at his waist as the scent of him infused her senses.

"Kelly. God, baby, do you have any idea of what it did to me to realize I wasn't here to protect you?" he whispered against her hair, one big hand holding her head against his chest as the opposite arm wrapped around her back. "If I had been here, I would have been in your bed that night. No one would have touched you."

"This isn't your fault," she snapped, her head lifting, a frown tightening her brow as she glared back at him. "I knew you were going to think that."

"I don't think it, I know it," he growled, holding her tighter, pressing his hips against her lower belly as she felt the breath slam out of her chest.

His erection, impossibly large, hot even through the denim, pressed against her as he stared down at her with heavy-lidded arousal.

"I know, Kelly." His hands moved to her hips as she felt the familiar weakness sweeping through her body. "There's not a damned thing that could have kept me away from you. Why the hell do you think I spent so much time in the Marines? I stayed away because I couldn't keep my hands off you."

His hands were on her now, clasped at her hips as hers flattened against his bare chest and she stared back at him in shock.

"I want you until I can't breathe for it," he whispered then. "But I would never hurt you. And I would never take what you can't give me, Kelly. Ever."

"I know that, Rowdy," she cried, the aching need and shadowed fears that rose inside her clenching in her chest. "I never thought you would."

"I wanted to hold you this morning." His hands smoothed over her back, her hips. "I wanted to pull you in my arms and put myself between you and the world to keep anything, everything, from threatening you ever again."

She shook her head. God, what was she going to do? He wasn't even concerned with what his father had said, the fact that he had been thrown out of his home. He wasn't angry with her or with Ray. He was angry with himself for not being there.

Kelly stared back at him, dazed, uncertain. Rowdy's expression was fierce, arrogant, equal parts frustration and determination mixed with pure, hot lust.

"Rowdy—"

"I want to take all the fear out of your eyes, Kelly," he whispered, his head lowering, his eyes holding hers. "I want it gone. I want to see all that fire and arousal and need that's always been there. That I see now."

She breathed in roughly, fighting to find reality, to make sense of the influx of sensations racing through her body.

"I want to kiss you, Kelly." Her lips parted.

Beneath her hands, his heart raced, just like hers. A hard, rushing throb that transferred to her veins, her nerve endings, and washed through every cell of her body.

"Did you miss me, Kelly?" he whispered.

"Yes." Her vision was filled with his lips. Sensually full, a treat she had dreamed of for too many years, had ached for with everything in her woman's body.

"No. Keep your eyes open." He stopped as her lashes drifted closed. "Watch me, baby. See me. It's just Rowdy. Just my kiss, remember how much you liked my kiss?"

She loved his kiss. Her lips parted in anticipation, but perhaps she hadn't fully remembered what being kissed by Rowdy meant. Somehow, she must not have remembered just right, exactly how it felt that night on the lake.

Because this was nothing like that brief, hungry kiss four years before. This was seduction. It was coercion on its most basic level. The whisper of his lips against hers as his heavy-lidded eyes stared back into hers, darkening, flaming with need as his mouth possessed hers with devastating sensuality. Rough silk caressed her lips, stroking over them as he denied her the deeper, darker possession she was craving. This wasn't a hungry consummation, it was a dream washing over her, easing her from the shadows haunting her and pulling her inexorably into a steadily building whirlwind of sensation.

"So beautiful," he whispered against her lips, sipping at them, making her ache for more. "There you go, just watch me, Kelly. Watch me and feel."

A whimpering moan tore from her throat as she felt his hands lift the hem of her shirt, felt his hands, calloused and hot against the bare flesh of her back. Curling her fingers against his chest she allowed herself to settle into his body, her head falling back as one hand cupped the nape of her neck and his kiss became deeper.

"Keep your eyes open."

Her eyes flew open as he pulled back, her breathing becoming jerky at the hunger in his face.

"Watch me, Kelly."

"I can't," she gasped. "It's too good."

His eyes dilated at the admission.

"Watch me, or it stops," he growled firmly. "See who's touching you, baby. It's me. You've been mine forever, Kelly. We're just going to ease into it now. Let me show you what I've dreamed about for the last eight years."

She was shaking in his grip, but not from fear. Hunger was consuming her as his lips covered hers again, and she struggled to keep her eyes open, to keep her senses from drowning beneath the full-lipped kiss that threatened to dissolve the strength in her knees.

Twining her arms around his neck, she arched against him, barely retaining enough thought to keep her eyes open. If she closed them, then the incredible pleasure tearing through her would be gone. His lips on hers, his tongue stroking along her lips as hers licked back, desperate for more.

Her hips tilted to him, arching as his knees bent enough to tuck his erection at the notch of her thighs.

Oh, that was good. She whimpered as she twisted against him, feeling the heavy rasp against her clit as he lifted her to him, turning her and bearing her to the counter behind them.

"There. No need to worry." He stepped between her spread thighs, pressing firmly against her as her back arched and her hands clenched at his shoulders.

"See how good it feels." His hips moved, dragging a ragged cry from her throat as his lips covered hers again.

Oh yes, it felt good. It felt as though tiny electrical charges were exploding across her flesh, sensitizing her.

His hard, bare chest pressed against her breasts, the lacy material of her bra scraping over her hard nipples, making them ache for a harder, firmer touch. This part of her hunger for Rowdy had always frightened her. The part that refused to accept a gentle touch, that ached, screamed out for more.

Powerful, possessive, Rowdy's kiss consumed her, but his hands didn't touch her. They were flat on the counter beside her, despite her need for them on her body.

"Rowdy," she gasped as his head lifted.

"See how sweet it can be, baby?" he crooned. "So sweet and easy."

"No." She shook her head fiercely. "Touch me. I need you to touch me."

There were no shadows of fear now. The overriding hunger Rowdy filled her with left no room for fear, no room for shadows. There was nothing but the demand for his touch, and that demand was rising by the moment.

"Where?" he whispered the question against her lips. "Where do you want me to touch you, Kelly? Show me, baby."

His powerful biceps flexed at her side as he held back. She

shuddered, realizing the demand in his voice and the fact that whatever she wanted, she was going to have to initiate.

Her lips curled at the corners in amusement.

"You think I won't do it?" Her body was humming with need now.

"I think you could make me lose my mind if you wanted to try." Heavy-lidded eyes, his lips full and sexy, he stared back at her with wicked intent. "But will you?"

The muscles of his chest twitched; the blood pulsed in his neck. A small rivulet of moisture rolled from his neck, drawing her gaze and her hunger. Leaning forward, she moved her tongue against his skin, licking at his flesh and drawing in the salty male taste.

The groan that rumbled from him had a shiver racing up her spine.

"Touch me," she whispered against his neck, her teeth raking over the hard column.

"Show me where." His voice was tight, dark with lust. "It's up to you, baby."

Up to her. She breathed in deeply.

"I want your lips on my nipples." Her breathing grew harder as she let him hear the words, words she had only whispered in her dreams. "Then your teeth—"

"Sweet mercy." The heavy groan tore from his lips. "Oh, baby, the things I'm going to do to those tight, hard little nipples. Lift that shirt for me, baby. Give me those pretty breasts."

Her hands fell to the hem of her shirt, lifting it as she leaned back to stare into his eyes, wanting to see the lust and need flaming in the green depths.

As the shirt cleared her belly and began edging over her bra, a shockingly familiar voice drawled from the doorway. "The door's open; does that mean I can join you?"

Laced with amusement, heavy with interest, Natches's voice had Kelly jerking the shirt down and staring back in shock at the deepened lust in Rowdy's eyes.

There was no anger that Natches had invaded the moment, there was added arousal, a deepening flush of lust on his hard face.

"Ever been watched?" he whispered, his expression heavy with dark desire.

Breathing heavily, Kelly stared back at him. She wasn't shocked, she realized. She had heard too much about the Nauti Boys. Too many tales of their sexual excesses, their uninhibited immersion into their sensual games.

She swallowed tightly, staring back at him as the flames between her thighs began to burn with insistent demand.

"Rowdy . . ." She shook with indecision. She had guessed over the years that the day would come when she would face this choice. That she would run headlong into the hungers the three men shared; she just hadn't expected it nearly this soon.

"As much as I would love this," Natches sighed, "and I surely would love it, I just came to let you know Uncle Ray is headed this way. And he has that bulldog look on his face for sure."

Was it relief or regret that raced through her mind? Whichever it was, there was no doubt her body was howling in protest.

"Well hell." Rowdy dropped a quick, hard kiss to her lips as he stepped back, his hands gripping her waist as he sat her gently on the floor. "Guess the cavalry is going to rescue you, baby."

She didn't need rescuing.

"I'll talk to him," she whispered.

"No talking needed, baby." He shook his head as he sighed wearily and tucked her hair behind her ear, then ran his fingers gently down her cheek. "Go on to the marina. I'll check in later. Okay?"

"He doesn't understand."

"Go, baby." He shook his head. "Me and Dad don't have a problem here. He's just being who he is, that's all. And who he is means he's going to worry about the little lamb staying too long with the big bad wolf." And that was her fault. She had been so hysterical over Rowdy knowing about the attack that she knew Ray was now worrying about her being alone with Rowdy at all.

She had sworn his cousins to secrecy, begging them to hold their silence on the attack, pleading with them not to tell him. Reluctantly, they had agreed. And now Kelly knew why the reluctance had been so thick. They knew Rowdy, and they knew he'd be angry with all of them. And he was. He was hiding it well, but she saw the flash of it in his eyes, mixed with the hurt. Being kept in the dark never had sat well with him. He was the type of man who faced the monsters and fought them back however much it took. He wasn't a man that appreciated being protected or deliberately left out.

"I better go," she sighed, glancing at the door. "Will you be at the house tonight for dinner?"

"Tomorrow," he promised easily, reaching up to tuck her hair behind her ear. "Wear something pretty for me."

Something pretty. She hadn't done that for a year.

"I can do that." She moved away from him slowly. "I'll see you tomorrow."

"Count on it, baby." He leaned against the counter, his gaze heavy lidded, his body hard, aroused as she slid past the doorway.

Her heart was racing in excitement, drumming with latent fear, but for the first time in a year, she felt alive again. Rowdy was home now. A smile edged at her lips. He was home, everything would be fine now.

Four

The Nauti Boys were together again. Rowdy finished off his beer as he stared at the other two men who had followed him topside later that evening.

Natches, the youngest of them at twenty-nine, tossed the pizza box on the table and moved into one of the chairs that set beneath the awning. Dawg, the oldest at thirty-one, flipped on the CD player he had carried up and set it on the spare chair. The better to drown conversation. They had learned young to watch their discussions here at the marina and on the lake. Sound carried on the water, and they had learned more than one secret eavesdropping themselves.

"You're pissed." Dawg sprawled back in his chair as he stared at Rowdy through narrowed, green eyes.

Rowdy took his own chair and stared back at the two men. They had run wild through town and the Marines together, though Dawg and Natches had gone reserves after their first tour rather than staying in longer. Dawg managed the lumberyard his father left him, while Natches had opted to permanently distance himself from his parents' thriving restaurants and owned a garage of all things. His dad stayed elbows deep in flour and Natches was a grease monkey. The family fights over that one had been interesting.

"I'm pissed." Rowdy shrugged, knowing there wasn't a damned thing he could do about it.

Uncapping another beer from the cooler beside him, he stared at his cousins soberly, wondering if he would have made the same choices.

They were the bad boys of the county. The three of them had been the terror of Somerset, Kentucky, when they were young. Fathers locked their daughters up at night in fear of the three of them. They hadn't exactly gained a good reputation where women were concerned.

"Damn, Rowdy, I'm glad you're back." Dawg shook his shaggy head, his raven black hair reflecting the lights of the marina. "Even pissed, it's a hell of a sight better than dealing with this without you."

Natches sipped at his beer, his own black hair not nearly as shaggy as Dawg's but longer. It was pulled back in a ponytail at his nape, giving his features a harder, more savage appearance.

They knew why they were there.

Rowdy turned back to Dawg.

"You could have told me when you picked me up," he informed his cousin, his lips flat, anger tightening his skull.

Dawg shook his head, lowering it briefly before sighing.

"Some things you just don't know how to tell a man." Dawg grimaced. "I figured you'd get a hint soon enough. It's not like she's the same girl she was last year."

Rowdy bit back the angry response burning on his lips, but hell, this was Dawg. When Rowdy hadn't been around to watch out for Kelly's skinned knees and the bullies who liked to pick on her, then Dawg had been there.

"We've pulled all the info on this that we can find, Rowdy." Natches straightened in his chair and reach for the pizza. "We've been working on it since it happened, trying to figure out who the bastard was."

"And?" If anyone could figure it out, it was Dawg and Natches.

"Not much," Natches admitted. "We've had four other rapes in surrounding counties over the last two years. All anal rapes, beatings, cuts, much more severe than Kelly's. She got lucky. Her neighbor's boyfriend heard the single scream she was able to get out. The boyfriend was a tough guy, broke in and tried to apprehend the bastard, but once he caught sight of Kell he let the guy go to help her."

"All this shit going on at home and neither one of you were

good enough to tell me what the fuck was happening?" Rowdy snapped.

He had talked to both of them over the past year and never realized that the distance he had felt had been something they were hiding rather than his own impatience to finish his tour.

"What could you have done, man?" Dawg tilted his head to the side and stared back at him questioningly. "We didn't want the trouble of hiding an AWOL Marine the rest of our natural lives and didn't figure Kelly needed that on top of everything else. We took care of her until you could get home."

"Were there any rapes after Kelly?" He asked.

"Nothing with the same M.O." Dawg shook his head. "It's like the son of a bitch just disappeared. I'm hoping he did."

"Ray keeps us up-to-date on Kelly though," Natches sighed. "And we take turns being here at the marina when she's working. She's retreated so far into herself that sometimes I've wondered if we could find the girl she used to be. The closest I've seen was when you had her backed into the counter this afternoon." Natches's lips twitched at the memory. "She looked real comfortable there, Rowdy."

"Asshole," Rowdy grunted.

Rowdy stared at the other two men as he wiped his hand over his face and considered the situation for long moments.

"He's not gone," he finally sighed. "I want to believe he is, I really do. But I can feel it. He's waiting."

"Are you two free?" He looked at them and knew they would be, whatever it took. "We're free. We made sure of it." Natches nodded firmly. "How do you want to play it?"

"I need one of you watching our back whenever we're away from the house. I can feel that bastard watching her. I felt it today when she was on the boat, like a damned itch just under my skin."

Dawg frowned at that. "There's been no sign of him, Rowdy. We've been watching her every second that we've been able to. No phone calls, no strange accidents. Nothing."

Rowdy clenched his jaw at Dawg's argument.

"Rowdy's right," Natches muttered over the music. "I've felt it all evening, especially since we came up here. That's a feeling you never forget, Dawg. I've had a bead on me in the service enough times to know the feeling."

"Hell, and here I was hoping it was just my overactive imagination," Dawg grunted. "But if he's watching, it's the first time he's watched close. I've only had the willies once or twice since all this hit the fan."

The willies. It was the perfect description for that odd, warning tingle at the back of the neck, the knowledge that something, or someone, intended to take your head off if they had the right chance.

"Dawg and I made sure we were both fairly free this summer," Natches stated. "We're staying on the boats. We'll watch for unusual movement or watchers. We haven't seen anything so far, but with crazies like this, who the hell knows what set them off."

They knew each other too well sometimes, Rowdy thought. His cousins had already anticipated what he would need.

"I've been thinking," Dawg said, his voice graveled, suspicious, "whoever he is, he has to know her. Kelly's not a creature of habit. She's impulsive, unpredictable, and never where you expect her to be. He knew she would be home. He knew she liked to crack her window at night. You can't tell it's cracked from the street. He had to have known."

"He studies his women," Natches said. "Gets to know them somehow. We've been talking about this." He nodded to the others. "Playing it out. I think he's local."

"Why?"

"The rapes are in a four-county radius around Somerset. Until Kelly, Somerset hadn't been hit. She fits the profile of the other girls, though. The others he'll call every now and then from what the detectives on the case told me, and ask if they're being 'good girls,' but he hasn't called Kelly. The only reason he wouldn't call her, is because he's close enough to watch her," Natches pointed out.

"The guy lost it when he was interrupted. The others"—Dawg cleared his throat, fury flashing in his eyes—"he made them beg. First to live, and then for him. Kelly wouldn't beg—"

"And he was interrupted—Shit!" Rowdy ran his hands over his head.

"But she's still a 'good girl,'" Natches pointed out. "When she stops being a good girl, what will he do?"

Rowdy felt his stomach pitch at the thought of that. This was why Ray was so pissed at his son's return. Because he knew

Rowdy had returned to claim Kelly, which was most likely the one thing guaranteed to push her stalker over the edge.

"The redneck code, cowboys," Natches drawled. "You don't fuck the good girls unless you mean it. He doesn't rape them normally, he takes them anally. He's not serious 'bout them. And he's not going to 'dirty' a 'good girl.' "

It was sickening, and the truly horrifying part was it all made sense. There were unwritten rules sometimes, a code, a way of dealing with women. Good girls versus "bad" girls and the rules of engagement. This rapist was twisting those rules. Perverting them in ways guaranteed to give a sane man nightmares. He was targeting good girls, or his perception of a good girl.

And Kelly gave the impression of the perfect good girl. But she was *his* naughty girl. He had seen it in her eyes eight years ago; he saw it there now. She wasn't a fool, and she might very well be a virgin, but Rowdy knew that his naughty girl was in there, waiting for *him*. And he was going to claim her, love her, protect her.

No matter what it took.

"Rowdy, you start fooling with her and the bastard is going to come after her stronger," Natches pointed out. "We can control it if we use it, control him and take him."

"But only if he thinks Kelly isn't a 'good girl,' " Dawg injected. "Good girls can tame the bad boys. Unless he thinks Rowdy is up to his past games with Kelly, it might not push him over the edge in time."

Rowdy stared back at his friends. He heard the question in Dawg's voice, the suspicion. He leaned forward, bracing his arms on the gas tank as he watched them. He ignored the tightening, low in his stomach, the vague disquiet he felt at the thought of sharing Kelly. Of allowing his cousins to touch her, to hold her. He had waited for six years, ever since she turned eighteen, for the chance to show her just how much pleasure he could give her when he took her to his bed. He refused to remember the arousal she inspired two years before that. You didn't lust after babies, and sixteen-year-old, wide-eyed virgins were just that. Babies. But the minute she turned eighteen, he had known his days of freedom were numbered.

"I haven't changed." He stared back at them with an edge of humor, of determination, as he ignored the odd, unfamiliar tightening in his chest. "Have you?"

Snorts of wry amusement met his question.

"Yeah right, and pigs started flying over the lake when it happened." Natches laughed. "We've been waiting on you, Rowdy, you know that. You think that little girl would have stayed unclaimed if any of us had changed over the years?"

They were unique, maybe. Sexual fulfillment and pleasure wasn't a game. It was something they took seriously, something they worked at. They all cared for Kelly, in different degrees. She was Rowdy's life. But the others, hell, they loved her too, and they always would.

Loving Kelly himself didn't change that. He'd kill any other man who dared touch her, but he hoped, prayed, he wasn't wrong about Kelly and the fact that her needs would mirror his own.

The need was an enigma, even to the three men. Maybe they were too close, left on their own too much as teenagers—who the hell knew. They didn't question it, they didn't fight it. If Kelly didn't want it, then it was a no-go, but he had a feeling about Kelly. She was a little sex kitten waiting to purr, and they were ready to stroke her.

So why was he suddenly tensing at the thought of Dawg and Natches inspiring that pleasure, that need within her?

He nodded slowly. She was his; there was no contest there. He would fight any man for her, even a friend. But here, there was no need to fight. Dawg and Natches didn't own her heart, Rowdy did. And the pleasure he knew the three of them could bring her outweighed the subtle warning shifting through his chest.

"Will she agree?" Dawg asked the hardest question to answer.

"Before the attack, I would have said yes." Rowdy sighed roughly. "Now, who knows?" He shook his head before wiping his hand over his face in a gesture of frustration. "We'll see. It will have to be her decision."

They nodded in reply.

"We get her over the attack first, take care of the attacker, then see where we go from there," Rowdy said. "She's not ignorant of the rumors, she suspects what's coming. But"—he swallowed tightly—"she's going to be scared now. And for that alone, I'll kill the bastard."

Five

Ray stepped into the bar the next evening, several hours after Rowdy called to say he wouldn't be home for dinner after all, with the excuse that he had to take care of business. Ray feared that somehow Rowdy felt he couldn't come home. And he wasn't having that. That was Rowdy's home, no matter what was going on, and he needed the boy to know that.

Ray hadn't been in a bar in over ten years. Not since he started dating Maria. He had known her forever. She and her husband had been regulars at the marina, their boat docked close to the office. Hell, during their younger days, when pleasure had been all that mattered, he and James, Maria's husband, had shared Maria at one time. Once, long ago, Maria should have belonged to him, but his own ignorance had been Ray's downfall.

That was how Ray knew his son had come by his darker passions naturally, how he knew what awaited Kelly if she became his son's lover. And yeah, he knew Rowdy would never hurt her, but he also had seen the horror the girl had been through. Kelly was a warm, vibrant girl, just as her mother was, with a capacity to love that would humble any man. The thought of Rowdy tarnishing that love with his games, as Ray had once tarnished Maria's love for him, scared the hell out of him.

Ray's first wife, Layne, had been an aloof woman. He'd cared for her though, loved her in a lot of ways, and the child they had together was a fine man. Ray knew that. But he was a man, in every sense of the word.

Ray stared around the smoky establishment, looking for the boy. Rowdy was sitting alone at a far corner, a beer bottle between his hands, his head lowered. The weight of the world was settled on his son's shoulders, and Ray understood why. Rowdy came home expecting open arms and found a mess instead.

Ray stopped by the bar and purchased a bottle of Jack Daniels, snagged two glasses, and made his way across the room. It was time to talk man-to-man, with no shame. That called for an iron backbone. Or plenty of whisky.

He slammed the bottle on the table as Rowdy lifted his gaze. Deep green eyes spat with fury, blazing from a sun-darkened, roughly hewn face. Yep, the boy was pissed off, clear down to his bones, and Ray didn't blame him.

He pulled out a chair and sat down.

"Some things just call for a good drunk," he said heavily, uncapping the whisky and pouring two small glasses full. "Childbirth. Your son's first date. Your daughter's near rape." His throat tightened with the pain as he tossed back the dark liquid and poured another shot of courage. "And when a man screws up because he feels helpless, and hurts the people he loves the most."

He stared straight into Rowdy's dark eyes, feeling his son's pain as though it were his own.

Ray sighed. "I swore to her I wouldn't tell you. And it's weighed bad on me ever since. While she was all doped up on the pain medication, and hysterical, she told her mom about what happened at the airport with you before you left that last year. She loves you. Always has. We've known that." He swallowed tightly. "And I knew how bad you wanted her." He paused, glancing away for a long second before pulling his gaze back to his son's. "I never told you how much pride I had in you when you walked away, did I?"

He saw his son's surprise.

"I didn't figure you knew why I'd left." Rowdy leaned back in his chair before picking up the whisky and throwing it back. He grimaced but held the burn of it.

"I knew." Ray sighed heavily. "I knew when you were twenty-two and as though overnight, she turned from a clumsy little urchin into a woman-child. I saw your face the day you realized it."

He watched the flush that rose over Rowdy's face, the discomfort.

"She was a kid." He cleared his throat uncomfortably. "She's not a kid anymore, Dad. She's twenty-four, and a grown woman."

"And you were and still are a man." Ray shook his head wearily before sipping at the whisky. "A good man. One any father could be proud of. You didn't touch her, you did what you had to do and didn't make any excuses or cast any blame. Though you could have. You left your home because of the girl—many men would have resented her. You would have been well within your rights to have protested how much Maria and I spoiled her."

"You should have told me that then," Rowdy grunted. "She kept stealing my damned shirts. She still does it. I should have made you throw both Kelly and Maria out."

A grin tugged at his son's lips. Ray shook his head. Rowdy was willing to forgive, no questions asked. And Ray didn't know if he could have been as gracious if someone had hid something so important from him.

Ray cleared his throat again.

"I should have told you." He rolled the glass between his fingers, staring at it rather than his son. "But I knew you'd get home one way or the other and I wasn't sure Kelly could face that. She needed time to put the attack into perspective before she faced what was between the two of you." Damn, he needed another drink.

He poured another, aware of the way his son watched him, his eyes narrowed, his expression thoughtful.

"Hunger like that goes beyond lust, Dad," Rowdy finally sighed. "I've fought it for too long. I don't know what it is yet. I don't know how deep it goes. I know I came back for her." He shook his head when Ray started to speak. "Hear me out. I had no intentions of living in that house, of breaking so much as one of your rules, but that bastard's still out there." Ray's gut clenched. "I'll camp outside her bedroom window if I have to, but you won't keep me away from her."

Rowdy leaned forward, his arms braced on the table, his fists clenched. Ray looked away from his son for long moments, wondering what he was supposed to say. Hell, he felt tired and helpless and not sure how to defend those he loved.

"You've been checking into it?" Ray knew he had. Rowdy had spent the afternoon at the police department before he met up with his cousins.

"I've been checking into it." Rowdy poured himself another shot. "I talked Betty Cline into letting me see the hospital records, and the sheriff gave me everything they had on the other girls. He's calling them. He doesn't call Kelly. He's local, Dad."

For a second, fear sliced through Ray. If the bastard was local, then he wouldn't have to call Kelly. He could watch her. Anytime, anywhere.

Then pride suffused Ray. Hell, that was his boy. Hard-eyed, determined, and ready to fight. He was more man than Ray had ever imagined. Rowdy wasn't drinking himself silly because Kelly had been attacked, but instead, he was plotting and planning justice. It was enough to make a father proud.

Ray breathed in hard. He had discussed this with Maria earlier, knew what he was about to do was hard on her; it would be harder on Kelly.

"Come back home, boy," he muttered. "I'm a damned fool when I get riled and we both know it. That's your home. As much as it is mine. And you're my kid. I want you there."

Rowdy's lips quirked. "The duffel bag is still on the bike. I was coming back tonight anyway."

Ray cleared his throat again. "I trust you, Son."

Rowdy's face changed then. If Ray thought it was hard before, it was more so now. Rowdy leaned forward, his eyes meeting Ray's straight on.

"She's mine, Dad." He kept his voice low, fierce. "Any other time I would have never disrespected your rules or your home. But I won't pull back now. I won't lose her because some bastard tried to destroy her. And I won't play footsie under the table because of your sensibilities. Do you understand that?"

Anger flared in Ray. He rubbed his hand over his lower face before breathing out roughly. "Hell. Fine. Whatever. But"—he glared back at the boy—"you don't play with that girl, Rowdy. You better be damned serious before you end up having sex with her. Son or no son, I taught you respect. She's not one of those little tramps you, Natches, and Dawg screwed with when you were younger."

It was a warning he'd made when he first realized how sexual his son was. Good girls were solid gold. A good girl understood responsibility, values, and herself. A woman like that wasn't a toy, she was a partner.

"I know how to treat a woman, Dad," Rowdy grunted. "All women. Not just Kelly."

Unlike Ray's generation, Rowdy didn't differ how he treated women in regards to their sexuality. One didn't deserve less respect, or more, for the amount of experience they had in bed. Rowdy had argued that with his father many times. But love . . . that made a difference, and Ray knew it. And he knew his son was learning it.

"So you'll come home?" Ray's throat was tight with emotion. Damn, he hated that. Hated knowing there was more he should say and not knowing how to say it.

Rowdy looked over at him, his expression somber, his eyes, that deep sea green, serious and thoughtful. "I missed you too, Dad," he murmured.

If that knot in his throat could have gotten tighter, it would have. Ray swallowed, then tried again. "I love you, boy." His voice was so rasping he was ashamed of it. "And I'm damned proud of you. Damned proud."

"I love you too, Dad." That was his boy. Equal parts hellion and warrior but never afraid to say the words. "And I'm proud of you, too."

He poured the glasses full again; they toasted each other and settled down for a serious drunk. Hell, Ray had been waiting on this day for nearly thirty years. There just wasn't anything like having that first good drunk with your son, and knowing it meant something. Meant something damned fine.

Kelly heard the Harley coming up the drive with her stepfather's truck as the clock flipped over to two in the morning. Her mother had been pacing the house, muttering to herself, worry creasing her brow.

Maria turned to Kelly, her eyes dark as she watched her.

"Are you sure?" Maria asked, her voice soft, uncertain.

"For God's sake." Kelly felt like snarling the words. "Mom, have you and Ray lost your minds?" Sometimes Kelly thought the attack had been more traumatic on them in a lot of ways. Kelly was never really certain how she felt about it. Frightened, yes. Terrified sometimes. Knowing her attacker was still out there kept her nerves on edge.

"He's always wanted you." Maria had never been comfortable with that. Kelly had known it, though they never talked about it. Just as her mother knew Kelly had always wanted Rowdy. It was like some odd fact of life.

"I'm not a little girl anymore," she sighed, curling up on the sofa, watching her mother pace the living room as the vehicles shut off. "You know they're both drunk, don't you?"

One of Rowdy's friends had called from the bar. He hadn't been too sober himself, warning them that the two men were heading home, thankfully being driven by friends rather than driving themselves.

"Ray hasn't been drunk since before we got married." A smile curved her mother's lips, and Kelly swore she looked a little too sensual to suit her. *A daughter shouldn't see things like that,* she thought with a burst of humor.

"Well, he's drunk now." She winced as it sounded like a load of bricks fell on the porch.

"Hell boy, I thought you were holding me up." Ray's voice drifted into the house.

"Thought you were holding me up." Rowdy's laughter was muffled.

Maria moved for the doorway and pulled it open with a quick jerk as Kelly rose from the couch to stand just inside the living room.

The two men were attempting to hold each other up as they paused in the doorway to get their bearings. Rowdy's expression was relaxed, his gaze a little heavy lidded and so darned sexy he took her breath.

As her eyes met his, a slow, sexy smile curved his lips and made her knees weak. He gripped his dad's arm tighter and led him inside the house. Neither of them were too steady on their feet.

"Maria, he's a lousy drunk," Rowdy grunted as his father threw his arm over Maria's shoulder and planted a loud, smacking kiss on her cheek. "He didn't even make it through the first bottle."

Kelly wrapped her arms across her chest, a smile tugging at her lips as Rowdy winked at her.

"He never did, Douglas, you just keep forgetting," her mother chastised him firmly.

Rowdy winced. "That's not my name."

"That's what your birth record has. I didn't see a *Rowdy* there anywhere, Douglas."

Rowdy gave her a mock glare. "You're not being nice to me, Maria."

"That's not my job," she pointed out calmly. "Now move your big feet out of the way so I can get him upstairs. You two should be ashamed of yourselves."

"I can be ashamed later," Ray piped in as she led him to the stairs. "Hell. We had fun, sweetheart."

"I can tell." Maria laughed softly.

Their voices lowered as they moved away, and finally disappeared. A few minutes later the door at the back of the hallway closed and everything was silent.

Kelly watched Rowdy. His hair was still too short. The spiked military cut suited him, but she had loved his long hair when he was younger. The way it framed his face, emphasized his green eyes. He looked like a fallen angel come to tempt mortal women when his hair was long. Short, he looked like the warrior she knew he had to be. A fighter, a Marine. Tall and tough and hard.

He turned to her, placing his hand over his chest, the dark blue material of his cotton shirt stretching across his shoulders.

"Kelly, darlin', you look like an angel standing there." His smile was a tad goofy and too damned sexy.

Unfortunately, she knew better. She was wearing another of his shirts, one she had stolen the last time he was home. A pair of loose sweatpants and socks that bunched at her ankles. She looked messy and frightened, and she knew it.

She licked her lips nervously. Facing him after what had happened at the boat earlier wasn't easy. She wasn't ashamed, but neither was she comfortable with some of the feelings Rowdy caused to burn inside her. "I missed you, Rowdy," she whispered, trying to still the trembling of her lips. "I'm glad you're home."

His expression sobered as he moved toward her slowly. She forced herself to stay still, not to retreat. But he was so big, and powerful. Strong. The memory of hard hands holding her down, a rough voice muttering in her ear as her face was pressed into the pillow, haunted her.

"So where's my hug?" He stood in front of her, his arms at his sides, his eyes dark and glittering with hunger.

He still wanted her. She could see the memories of the heated exchange they'd had earlier in his eyes.

"I . . ." She swallowed tightly, glancing away as her hands tightened on her arms. God, what was wrong with her. She had nearly bared her breasts for him, but now she felt as uncertain, as frightened as she had the moment she stepped into the houseboat.

"Just a hug, Kelly-baby?" He whispered the words, his lips quirking gently. "I dream of your hugs, darlin', just as much as I dream of your kiss."

She stared back at him in surprise.

"You don't believe me?" He reached out, his arm lifting slowly, his fingers reaching out to lift a strand of curls from her shoulder.

She glanced quickly at where he held her hair, biting at her lower lip as she tried to still the pounding of her heart. She had dreamed of his touch for so long, waited for him, longed for him. *Oh God, this isn't fair*, she wailed silently. She had waited for this for so long, now her own insecurities were eating her alive. It didn't matter that her therapist had warned her to expect this. She felt as frightened, as off balance as she had the first months after the attack.

"Rowdy . . ." Her throat tightened as she fought herself, the fear and need warring inside her.

"It's real easy, baby," he crooned, his dark velvet voice washing over her. "You just lift your arms and put them around my neck." He let go of her hair, fingers curling around her wrists as he lifted her arms, urging them up until they curled around his neck. "Then you come up real close to me, so I can hug you back." His arms went around her, slowly, so slowly, pulling her against him until her head rested on his chest.

"There we go."

She was shaking, but was it fear or something more? She didn't know what she was feeling, didn't know how to assimilate the sensations and emotions washing through her.

"I came home for you, Kelly," he reminded her, his breath caressing her ear as she jerked against him. "I came home to touch you, to taste you, to claim you. Do you know what I would have done if I had known you were home when I pulled in yesterday morning?"

She shook her head, a jerky movement as a small whimper

left her lips. He felt so good. A man shouldn't feel this good, powerful yet protective, hot and so blessed sexy.

"I would have come to your room and kissed you awake. I would have seen your pretty eyes opening, knowing it's me beside you, my lips touching yours. I want that real bad, Kelly. Even though I know if Dad caught me he'd skin me alive." He breathed in roughly; the feel of his chest rasping against her breasts sent a shudder racing through her. "Now," he whispered, "I really don't care if he does skin me."

She stiffened against him, needing to draw away, needing to get closer to him. God, she hated this. Hated the fear holding her back, hated not knowing, not understanding the emotions raging through her mind and body.

"Rowdy—"

"Shh." He stilled her protest as he rubbed his head against hers. "Just settle here against me, baby. Let me hold you for a minute; let me know you're okay. Just that."

"But I'm not okay." Her hands clenched in the fabric of his shirt as she finally admitted it to herself. "I'm scared, Rowdy. I'm so scared." She pressed her head against his chest, the words slipping free after nearly a year of burying them. She was terrified.

"I know, baby." He kissed her head, his hands running over her back. "But I won't let you be scared of me."

She heard the pain in his voice, felt it tighten her chest. No, Rowdy would never hurt her, but fear was an insidious disease, and fighting it took more courage than she thought she had.

"We're going to take this nice and easy," he crooned. "We're going to go upstairs and you're going to sleep, baby. I'm going to lie right beside you so you know no one can get to you, no one can hurt you as long as I'm there. Okay?"

"In my bed?" She jerked back, staring up at him. "Ray will skin us *both* alive."

"Dad will deal with it." His expression hardened, determination glittering in his eyes. "He already is. You're not sleeping; you're not eating. We're going to change that, starting tonight."

"Oh, are we now?" The high-handedness in his voice pricked at her.

"Kelly." He tilted his head, staring down at her, a smile quirking at his lips. "Are you going to fight me, baby? Really? Remember the last fight we got into?"

"You put another snake in my drawer, and I'll start calling you Douglas," she sniped. "I can't believe you'd threaten me like that."

He smirked, his gaze drowsy, his expression so sensual it was enough to make her panties damp. And they were damp. Yeah, she was scared spitless at times at the thought of touching him, having him touch her, but he could make her so wet, so fast, that it wasn't even surprising anymore.

"I'm just going to lie beside you, that's all," he whispered. "If you can't sleep, then I'll lie on the floor. But I'll be there, Kelly. Will you trust me enough to let me be there? Remember yesterday morning, baby? You trusted me enough to almost bare those pretty little nipples for me. Keep trusting me, Kelly."

She was breathing roughly; the realization of it forced her to try to regulate it. She hated this weakness, this fear. Even the sessions with the psychologist hadn't been able to erase it.

"I would trust you with my life, Rowdy," she whispered, knowing she did.

"Come on then." His arms wrapped around her as he led her to the stairs. "Let's go on up and see if we can get some sleep. I don't know about you, Kelly, but I'm dead tired."

She hadn't had nightmares in months, she thought as he turned out the lights and led her upstairs. She wasn't sleeping well, but when she did sleep, she wasn't waking screaming as she did in those first months. It should be safe. She could have something she had always dreamed of. Rowdy in her bed, sharing his warmth with her. Maybe even holding her. Surely she could handle that?

Six

Kelly wasn't really surprised when Rowdy stopped at his bedroom to get a pair of soft, gray cotton sweats similar to her own. He slept in the nude, so the concession he was making wasn't lost on her.

"Okay?" He led her to her bedroom door, opening it carefully before stepping in ahead of her.

Kelly drew in a deep, sustaining breath, battling the confusing emotions racing through her. She had waited for Rowdy for so long that she wasn't certain how to adapt to this abrupt shift between his careful distance and his sudden closeness.

"I'm fine," she answered as she stepped in behind him, noticing the tension in his body.

"I'll change in the bathroom." He closed the door behind her.

Kelly fisted her hands in her T-shirt as she bit her lip, fighting to hold back her nerves as Rowdy disappeared into the other room. She gazed around her bedroom, taking in the frilly curtains over the dark shades, the white lace of her comforter. It wasn't exactly a man's room.

Yet, Rowdy hadn't flinched at it. He had filled it, overpowered it, and pulled all focus toward him. Not that she had expected anything less.

She was still standing in the middle of the room when he came from the bathroom long minutes later. She couldn't stop her gasp, couldn't help the leap of her pulse at the sight of him.

He was obviously aroused. In those pants, there was no way to hide just how well-endowed he was either. She swallowed nervously as her gaze moved over hard, flexing abs, sun darkened and powerful, to a wide chest and an expression blazing with hunger.

She took a step back, watching as his eyes narrowed on her.

"Come on, baby. We passed this point." His voice was rough, deep, a rasp of black velvet across her raw senses.

"I'm fine." Her hands knotted in the material of the shirt as she felt the flesh between her thighs heating further, dampening.

And her breasts. They felt heavy, swollen, her nipples almost painful with their sensitivity.

"I don't think I can sleep with you, Rowdy." She fought to keep her breathing under control. "I don't know if I can stand it."

He didn't argue with her. He stepped over to the bed and pulled back the blankets before staring back at her.

"I'd never hurt you," he whispered. "Come on, get into bed. Surely you're not going to let something like a hard-on scare you off, Kelly."

That wasn't just a hard-on. It was Rowdy's hard-on, and she was dying for it with the same intensity that she was terrified of it. Not because she was afraid he would hurt her, but because she was afraid of her own emotions, her own desires.

But when he extended his hand to her, she was helpless. Flushed, uncertain, she moved to the bed, crawling into it stiffly and lying down as he moved in beside her and reached over to turn out the small bed lamp.

And there he was, lying on his side beside her as she stared up at the ceiling, fighting to keep from touching him, from begging him to touch her.

"I told Dad I came back for you, Kelly."

Her gaze flew to his eyes, barely making out the glittering depths in the darkness of the room as she felt his hand move, felt it as it moved gently to her stomach.

"Rowdy . . ." She couldn't breathe. His hands was like a flame through the material of the shirt she wore, pressing against her stomach as she felt her womb spasm with need.

"It's nice and dark," he whispered then. "Like a sweet, warm dream. Your dream, Kelly. What would you do in your dreams? What would I do to you?"

She couldn't help the tiny moan that fell from her lips. She had many, many dreams of what she wanted Rowdy to do to her, with her. The things she would do to him, if she only knew how.

"This is dangerous." Her voice sounded strangled in the darkness around them as her hand gripped his wrist.

"Do you trust me?" The question had her breath catching on a sob.

"With my life," she answered readily. And she did.

"Trust me to touch you. To bring you pleasure, Kelly. Let me touch you."

His hand moved, his fingers bunching in the shirt to drag it over her stomach.

"They'll hear me." Her hands clenched harder around his wrist. "You don't know what you do to me, Rowdy. You can't understand—"

"Do you know what I want to do to those pretty breasts?" He shocked her to silence again. "I want to take this shirt off you, Kelly. I want to bare them and touch your hard little nipples with my fingers, then with my mouth. I want to show you how good just a touch can be."

The material of her shirt began to rise as she tried to draw enough oxygen into her lungs to protect the incredible sensuality of his statement.

"But you might get loud," he whispered with a thread of amusement. "And I think I'd like you loud, Kelly. I want to hear you screaming in pleasure, begging me for more and more until you know you can't take more, but you want it anyway. And that's when you need a harder touch, more sensation. That's when pleasure becomes almost painful and when the pain becomes ecstasy."

She shuddered as his hand moved against bare flesh and the shirt rasped over her hard nipples as he drew it slowly from her.

"Excellent," he crooned. "I'm going to get you naked before the night's out, baby. I'm going to hold you against me and feel the sweet, sleek warmth of your body. Would you like that?"

His hand cupped the hard swell of her breast as her breath rocked from her body and she arched, jerking against the touch as a million sensations began to riot through her.

She had to bite her lip to keep from crying out.

"How pretty," he sighed, looming over her, his gaze on her face despite the warmth of his fingers caressing the globe of her breast.

"What will you do when I get my fingers on those tight little nipples? Or my mouth between your soft thighs?"

"Rowdy, please"—her voice was a breath of sound as she shuddered beneath him—"I don't know . . ."

"Shhh. Just lie here with me," he whispered. "Let me feel you come for me. Just here in a bit, baby. Let me touch your sweet body and show you how good it can feel. Then you can sleep, right here against me."

Let her come for him? He was going to make her come? Here? In her bed?

Then she almost did come. His finger began to circle her nipple, drawing an incredible circle of fire around it as his head lowered, his lips barely touching hers.

"Get ready," he whispered. "Let's see how much you like this."

His thumb and forefinger gripped the violently sensitive peak and exerted just enough pressure to throw her into a maelstrom of sensations. Fire tore from her nipple to her clit, surging to her womb as she felt it flex in hunger.

Her lips parted on a fractured cry that he took into his own mouth. His lips covered hers easily, gently, absorbing her cry as they moved against her with restrained hunger.

His fingers were tugging at her nipples, both of them now, shifting against her until he rose half over her, surrounding her with his heat.

"God, I would have loved to have heard that cry," he groaned against her lips.

Kelly could feel the tremors racing through her body, feel the soft wetness gathering between her thighs. Her hands lifted to his shoulders, her fingers pressing into the hard muscle as his lips smoothed over hers again.

"I just want to feel your nipple in my mouth," he whispered. "I want to slide my hand to your pretty thighs and see how wet and soft you are there. How much could you stand, baby, before you screamed again?"

Not much. She was weak. She was entranced by the pleasure tearing through her body and she could do nothing to stop it.

"I want you naked, Kelly," he breathed against her lips. "Will you be naked for me, baby?"

One hand moved to her hips, curling into the waistband of her sweatpants as he began to push them down her thighs.

"Rowdy . . ." Was she scared? She was terrified, but not of being hurt. She couldn't make sense of the sensations racing through her, pleasure and fear, confusion and dazed hunger. They were flooding her, drowning her with conflicting needs.

"We're just playing, Kelly." He moved back, sliding the pants down her legs before pulling them free of her body.

She was naked now, exposed if it hadn't been for the darkness of the room.

He lifted her hand again, kissing it before he surprised her by laying it over her lips.

"Shhh. We don't want anyone to hear."

She didn't think he really gave a damn if anyone did hear, but she pressed her fingers to her lips, certain she would die of embarrassment if her mother or Ray heard her pleasure.

She saw the flash of his teeth in a wicked grin before his head lowered.

It was a good thing she covered her mouth before his lips touched her aching nipple, before they surrounded the sensitive peak and drew it into his mouth. Because her cry was barely muffled with one hand as the other flew to his head.

Her back arched, and she swore flames burned over her body as he began to suckle at her. He wasn't slow and easy. He didn't ease her into it, he didn't tease her into it, he devoured her, and she was helpless beneath it.

"God. Baby." He buried his head between her breasts then, his breathing rough and hard as his hands moved down her waist, her hips. "You're going to my head faster than the whisky did."

She needed more. She pressed against him, certain she was going to scream for more if he didn't touch her again.

"Easy. Easy." His breathing was a rough groan as his lips moved along her chest, her collarbone. "Come here, baby. Let's ease this fire before I lose my sanity."

He pulled her to him as he moved her hand from her lips and covered them with his own. Then his other hand went between her thighs.

Kelly jerked against him, her hand latching onto his wrist as she felt his fingers part the wet folds.

"Oh God, you're bare." His voice was tortured as his fingers moved over flesh despite her hand gripping him. "Sweet heaven have mercy."

His thumb flicked over her clit as his fingers parted the swollen flesh.

"Easy. We're going to do this quick, baby. If we don't, I'm going to end up taking you here, in your bed, and then we'll both be screaming."

His lips covered hers again as his thumb moved along the outer edge of the sensitive bud of flesh as his fingers began to caress the greedy opening.

She was crying out beneath his lips. One arm latched around his neck as the nails of the other bit into his wrist. It didn't deter him. His thumb caressed, rotated, then pressed against her with diabolical results.

Stars exploded before her eyes as she jerked beneath him, shuddering violently as pleasure whipped over her nerve endings and devastatingly clashed through her senses.

She could feel her juices rushing from her sex, feel his fingers rubbing through them, intensifying her climax as a growl vibrated against her lips, covering her fractured scream.

And she was lost. She was distantly aware of his release, the movement of his free hand, the feel of his semen washing over thigh, which only intensified her own pleasure and egged at her fears. Not her fear of his touch, or the fear of being with him. But the overwhelming fear that there wasn't a chance in hell that she could handle him.

Kelly eased into sleep within minutes of Rowdy cleaning them both up and tucking the blankets around her. He felt her relax against him, felt the soft sigh that left her lips. Moving slowly, he eased the blanket further over her shoulders, feeling her head on his arm, her silky hair against his chest as he held her. It was killing him, the pain, the fear he knew she had to have endured. He could feel his heart breaking in his chest even as a killing rage burned in his soul.

She was his. She had been his as long as he had known her and by God he wasn't letting her go. She knew him, knew he would cut out his own heart before he'd hurt her—that trust was still within her. If it weren't, she would never have been able to climax so sweetly for him, or sleep in his arms, to allow him to hold her, her sweet body tucked so close against his own. Naked.

He stared into the dimly lit bedroom, his eyes narrowed, his mind working. Whoever dared to hurt her, to stalk her, wouldn't be breathing for long. He wouldn't be breathing two seconds past the time Rowdy learned who he was. And that was a silent promise, a vow he made to Kelly. She would never be hurt again.

Seven

Maria opened Kelly's door the next morning, not really expecting what she saw. Ray had warned her the night before, but he had been drunk, amorous, so she hadn't really taken him seriously. Perhaps she should have—the shock wouldn't have been so great.

She was used to coming in to find Kelly napping in the large wingback chair on the other side of the room, the television droning in the background. The room was silent now, and Rowdy was staring at her through slitted eyes from the bed.

He was wrapped around her sleeping daughter like a living vine. Kelly lay on her side, her back pressed against Rowdy's front, her head sheltered beneath his chin. One hard leg lay over her daughter's fragile ones beneath the blankets, his arms surrounding her as her hair tangled over them. He was bent over her, wrapped around her, and Kelly was sleeping peacefully.

It was more than obvious that they both were naked. Kelly was her baby; seeing her sleeping in a man's arms, especially Rowdy's, was disconcerting. She had expected the closeness they had before her marriage to Ray to develop, but not in this way. As siblings, very close friends, but never this. This terrified her.

The sexual tension that vibrated from the two whenever they were together had always worried her, deeply. She had been terrified for years that Rowdy would break her daughter's heart. What she saw now filled her with conflicting emotions. Rowdy would protect Kelly, and, ultimately, that was Maria's greatest wish.

Her daughter's protection. But what he could do to her baby's heart was almost more than she could bear.

As she stared at the two, Rowdy's frown darkened, his gaze narrowing at her. "What?" he mouthed.

Ray had warned her, she had known herself what was coming.

"We're going to the marina." She mouthed the words back at him, hoping her daughter would continue to sleep.

He nodded with a subtle shift of his head, never really moving. Content. That was how he appeared. Content where he was, holding Kelly close.

She backed slowly from the room, her hand lingering on the door panel for a moment as she fought the worry building within her. Maybe Ray was right. Maybe Rowdy was all Kelly truly needed to get past the attack. Maria hoped so. The shadows in her daughter's eyes broke her heart, but even more the worry that whoever had attacked Kelly would return terrified her. Until they caught him, Maria knew she would never sleep easy.

Kelly came awake slowly, her senses alive, her skin tingling at the warmth that surrounded her. There was no momentary fear, no surprise. Rowdy was holding her. She could feel him wrapped around her, spooned against her as though she had been made for the position.

She was aware of something else as well as she lay there, her body tucked into his. He was hard. His erection pressed against the crevice of her buttocks, a thick intruder, waiting. She bit her lip, stiffening in his arms, her muscles tightening. Pleasure and fear combined inside her. And the pleasure was stronger. The culmination of what felt like a lifetime of fantasies and needs rose inside her, blocking the fear, pushing it back until nothing mattered except Rowdy.

"Easy, baby." His voice was drowsy, calm. "It's just a hard-on." He snuggled against her, tucking her closer to his chest as her hands gripped the bedspread and she fought to level her breathing.

"I hate to say this," she wheezed. "That's not a hard-on, Rowdy. That's a baseball bat."

His snorted chuckle vibrated against her back, and only pressed his erection closer against her rear. She stiffened further.

"Want me to move? I'm pretty comfortable right now."

Oh, she just bet he was. She forced herself to breathe deeply, to push back the panic threatening, building in her mind. This was Rowdy and he wouldn't hurt her now.

"You're thinking it to death," he murmured and he rubbed his chin against her hair. "Scared?"

"Of your baseball bat?" She fought for humor rather than hysteria. "I don't know, Rowdy, I hear you're pretty fond of it. Lots of practice and all."

She felt his hand move, his fingers running over hers, sending tingling spirals of heat to build beneath them.

"You're a little minx," he growled at her ear, a velvet-soft sound that rippled through her senses. "That wasn't very nice."

A grin tugged at her lips at his chastising tone. She relaxed against him, feeling her body conform to his, settling against hard muscle and aroused heat.

"I'm not nice, remember?" Her eyes closed as he chuckled at her back. It was an old argument going back years before. It usually occurred whenever she told him what lousy taste he had in women, and pointed out their faults in vivid detail.

"I do remember." His lips smoothed over the top of her head, the caress sending trailing fingers of pleasure to wash through her body. The slightest caress, no matter how subtle, had the power to make her tremble. "You have a mean wit sometimes, Kelly."

She gave an amused snort at that. "I just didn't care to tell you the truth, Rowdy."

His girlfriends weren't exactly the kind of woman he brought home to dinner. As a matter of fact, he had never brought a woman home to dinner. Kelly would never have been able to tolerate that. She wondered if he had known that.

"Do you remember when you were seventeen, and you bought that scrap of material you called a bathing suit?" he mused softly.

She remembered the bathing suit, bought specifically in the hope of teasing him past the control she always hated so much.

"I didn't think you noticed." She turned her head, staring up at him, close.

His eyes were darker, tiny pinpoints of emerald glittered in the sea green iris, mesmerizing her, filling her vision. And his lips. Her eyes darted to his lips, so close. And she knew how they felt rubbing against her own, firm and warm, stoking fires inside her she hadn't imagined existed.

"I noticed," he whispered, his voice rougher now. "All summer. I think my cock still has the imprint of my zipper on it."

His hand stroked up her arm, his palm creating a heated friction that had her nerves prickling with awareness. She could still feel his erection like heated iron resting against the crevice of her rear, but his lips drew her.

"Are you going to kiss me again, Rowdy? Anytime soon?"

"Maybe." The seductive croon had a shiver racing through her.

"When?" *Now would be a good time.*

"When do you want me to?" His hand slid from her arm to her stomach and rested there.

She felt his fingers, long, broad, resting against her, with nothing between them. And they were moving, slowly easing above her hips, passing her abdomen until his hand rested on the bare flesh of her midriff.

"Now." God, if he didn't kiss her she was going to die from the need of it. "You distracted me last night. I didn't get to feel it real good."

"My little Lolita." His lips lowered, brushed against hers. "How long have you been teasing me now?"

"Since I was nine?" She breathed a laugh against his lips.

The first day she had seen him. He had been as handsome as sin and a god in her eyes when he saved her from a bully in that park.

"Hmm. I was fifteen. You were the sweetest little girl. Staring up at me with those big gray eyes so full of tears because that bully had taken your hair bow."

"And you got my hair bow back." She was panting for breath, her lips brushing his with each word.

"I got your hair bow back."

He took her breath. His lips captured hers in an all too brief, fiery kiss. No tongue, no more than a taste of him on her lips before he drew back.

"Rowdy . . ." She reached for him, needing more, aching for more. "That's not fair."

His fingers played against her midriff, rubbing in slow sensual circles, creating little starbursts of sensation that exploded in her sex. Her nipples were on fire, begging to be touched, caressed. His hands were so close, the heat of them warming the tight, aching mounds.

She stilled against him as his hips shifted against her rear once again.

"I'm not scared of you," she whispered, staring into his eyes, fighting to keep her own open. "I've never been scared of you, Rowdy."

"Yeah, you are," he whispered, his eyes darkening. "I can see it in your eyes, in your face." A somber smile touched his lips. "But that's okay, baby, you won't be scared for long."

She opened her lips to speak, then stared at him in astonishment as he rolled from the bed and flashed her a wicked smile. A teasing smile, before bending over and picking up his discarded sweats. He pulled them over his legs, covering his nakedness and the full, engorged length of his erection.

Kelly rolled to her back, propping herself on her elbows and staring at him as he moved to the bottom of the bed. He was so obviously aroused it made her mouth water. His cock pressed against the sweatpants with implicit demand, a thick length of steel-hard flesh that she ached for.

"I don't like being teased like that," she pouted. "Come back here and kiss me properly."

"You don't deserve it yet." His voice was a dark croon, his expression arrogant, certain. Smug.

"I don't deserve it?" Disbelief warred with amusement. "I've been of age for at least six years now, Rowdy. Ready, willing and able. And"—she stretched her legs out slowly, looking at him from beneath lowered lids—"I think I've waited too long. You didn't give me a chance to fully enjoy it last night."

His eyes narrowed, a seductive droop of the eyelids, the exceptional green eyes glittering from between heavy black lashes.

"Oh, I agree." His voice lowered, his hands gripping the railed footboard of the bed, his fingers curling around it, clenching. "We've waited too long, Kelly. Now, let's see how bad you want it." He winked slowly. "Better shower, baby, I think you're due at the marina this afternoon. I'll take you in on the Harley."

And just as easily as that he turned and sauntered to the

bedroom door. He didn't look back, didn't pause. He opened the door and left the bedroom, his broad, bare shoulders straight and strong. Too damned sexy for his own good.

Dammit.

Mackay's Marina was one of the smaller ones, specializing in rentals and mechanical servicing. Some berths were leased out, and the attached restaurant and convenience store added to the overall "one stop" friendly atmosphere of the landing.

Mackay's Marina had begun with Rowdy's grandfather, Joseph Mackay, and then under Ray Mackay's guidance had turned into a thriving, yearlong enterprise. One he wanted to turn over to Rowdy as soon as his son was willing.

The bait shop and sporting goods section of the main buildings were separated from the store and restaurant by the main office. Kelly's mother had put in the convenience store and additional gas pumps after their marriage on the condition that part of the enterprise go to Kelly once they retired. It was an agreement Ray and Rowdy had accepted easily.

Kelly was ringing up the variety of goods that old man Tanner and his son Ricky had picked up, when she saw Rowdy and Dawg walk into the main room. Natches had just left a few minutes ago after spending nearly an hour flirting and straightening the shelves at the side of the room.

She would have been a fool not to notice that the careful restraint in his demeanor toward her had changed. He watched her now with a subtle interest; a promise unique to the Mackay boys. She knew their moves, and knew the instant he walked in the room that he was no longer simply watching over her as he and Dawg had done in the past year. The additional element of desire was no longer hidden from her.

"Kelly girl, you need to put these fishing rods on sale." Ken Tanner's scowl was fierce, his brown eyes eagle-bright. Wisps of gray hair stood on end over his head, and his lined face was normally fierce, though he had a heart of gold.

"I'll tell Ray, Ken. But you know how he is. That will be $14.62."

She took the money from him, ignoring his son. Ricky was a shifty-eyed little prick who took pleasure in poking at others' weaknesses. Thankfully, he reined it in while his father was around.

As she counted out his change, she caught sight of Rowdy moving behind the counter while Dawg started straightening some of the higher shelves across the room. Dawg had spent his summers working at the marina before he left high school. For him, Rowdy, and Natches, it was almost automatic to work when they were hanging around.

"Hey, babe." She stiffened as Rowdy moved behind her, placing a hand on her shoulder as he leaned down to kiss the top of her head. "Tired yet?"

She felt the flush that suffused her face as Ricky's gaze became frankly assessing and old man Tanner grinned in delight.

"Rowdy Mackay. Boy, it's about time you came home. You just visiting or staying?" Ken's raspy voice boomed through the store.

"Hello, Ken. Ricky." He moved to the counter, shaking the gnarled hand reaching out to him. The older man's hand was a pale, weak extension when clasped in Rowdy's strong, darkly tanned hands. "I'm home to stay this time."

"Well, it's about time." He nodded firmly, his knowing gaze shifting to Kelly for a long second, a hint of compassion entering his eyes. "You going to take care of our girl here?"

"Ken!" Her face flamed hotter at the question as she chastised him.

"Like all of us ain't watched you twitching around him since you were too young to know what a twitch was." He snorted, frowning back at her. "Don't you be playing dumb, girl. Just 'cause I'm old don't make me blind."

She ignored Rowdy's chuckle as she quickly bagged the items Ken had bought and handed them across the counter.

"I hope you catch lots of fish, Ken," she gritted out between her clenched teeth, pasting a facsimile of a smile on her face.

She was as fond as she could be of the old man, but he wasn't one to mince words.

His snicker was amused, kindly. "It's all in the bait, girl. It's all in the bait." He nodded to Rowdy with one of the few smiles Kelly had ever seen out of him. "Let's go, Ricky." He nudged at his son, heading toward the lake-side door. "See you later, Rowdy."

"Later, Ken." As he spoke, Kelly felt his hand settle in the small of her back, his fingers rubbing in tiny circles over the loose cotton shirt she wore.

"Stop that," she hissed, turning on him as Ken and Ricky left the building, the glass door whishing shut behind them.

She pushed his hand away, propped her hands on her hips, and glared up at his smiling face as he crossed his arms over his chest and smiled wickedly back at her.

"You're just going to make me pout if you start refusing my pitiful advances, Kelly," he sighed. "And here I stayed awake all night last night with a numb arm just so you could sleep comfortable."

Dawg's snicker was clearly heard.

"Dumb and dumber," she muttered, though she couldn't keep the smile from her face as he reached out to run the backs of his fingers over the side of her neck. Shivers raced through her at the small caress. And it wasn't fear. She could feel the pleasure suffusing her body, dampening the flesh between her thighs.

It was disconcerting. She had spent months with the fear that she would never be able to enjoy Rowdy's touch again. That the desires he had filled her with, the needs and fantasies, would be swamped with the fear. The knowledge that they were coming back, perhaps stronger than ever was at once nerve-racking and comforting.

"It's almost closing time. I thought we'd help you close up. Then we take all that Chinese food I have out in the cycle's saddlebag and have dinner before we head out on the lake." He pushed her hair back from her shoulder as he spoke, his fingers lingering on the shell of her ear for long seconds after he finished.

From the corner of her eye she saw Dawg locking the lakeside doors and hanging up the Closed sign.

"Ray will skin you alive." She shook her head, though she couldn't still the smile on her lips. "Summer hours are longer now, Rowdy. I still have an hour."

"I asked Dad first." He moved back, his expression intent, sexy. "Better yet, Dawg can finish up for you. Come on, Kelly, sneak away with me."

Sneak away with him? How many times had she dreamed of hearing him say those words? She would have snuck out with him, anytime, any place.

"Go on, Kelly." Dawg lent his approval to the idea. "I'll close up shop here and help Ray and your mom outside before I leave."

As Rowdy's first cousin, and the oldest by several months, Dawg had usually led the pranks the Nauti Boys had gotten into. The three men had been hell on wheels through their high school years.

She breathed in deeply, her hands sliding from her hips to her jeans pockets as she glanced up at Rowdy again.

"You know you want to," he whispered with a wink. "Come on, I even spent the day airing out the boat and getting her ready."

The *Nauti Buoy* was his pride and joy, not to mention his weekend home. He and his friends spent their summers on the water, normally in the houseboats they had acquired over the years. Their title, the Nauti Boys, had come as much from the names of their boats as from their sexual practices.

"Okay." She gripped her courage with both hands and gave him a short nod. "I haven't had Chinese in a while."

She hadn't eaten out much period, preferring to stay in the house when she was home rather than forcing herself to pretend a security she didn't feel. It terrified her, not knowing who her attacker was. If he was a friend or a stranger, someone she trusted or would have trusted.

"Good," he said, his voice warm, approving as she moved past him, tugging at the hem of her oversized shirt before one of his big hands caught one of hers.

Warmth surrounded her fingers, fed into her bloodstream, and sent heat surging through her system. Adrenaline spiked the wave of warmth, fed it into her tightening nipples, her swollen clit.

"We'll catch you on the lake later, Dawg."

"I'll give you a call before I head out." Dawg nodded as they moved past him, his eyes narrowed, the brilliant green glittering behind the spiked lashes surrounding them. They held the same teasing warmth and sensual promise that Natches's had earlier.

"Come on."

She followed Rowdy as he moved through the main marina office, waving to her mother as he opened the door and escorted her through it. She wondered if she looked as confused as she felt.

Stilling her emotions and her equilibrium after waking up with him that morning had been hard enough. She had been nervous, her fingers shaking, her stomach clenching each time she thought of waking up beside him, feeling him surrounding her, his erection pressing into her rear. That had been the most disconcerting part. She should have been frightened. The psychologist had told her she would likely be frightened the first time she tried intimate relations after the near-rape. That the intimacy of allowing a man to touch her, to hold her, might be difficult to get through.

It hadn't been. He had made her more aroused than frightened. And in ways, that was more frightening than the fear of his touch. Everyone had told her for months that being touched would be difficult for her, but being touched by Rowdy had been a dream come true.

"You think too much sometimes," Rowdy announced as he collected the bags of Chinese food from the steel saddlebags mounted to the side of the motorcycle.

"I can walk and chew gum at the same time too." She rolled her eyes at him, feeling his hand at the small of her back again.

In the past twenty-four hours he had touched her more than he had in the last ten years. Of course he hadn't been home for the better part of those ten years, but it wasn't as though the opportunity hadn't been there.

"Why didn't you go on to college?" he asked as they moved onto the docks. "I expected you to head off right after high school."

She shrugged at the question. "I took business classes at the tech school. You might get the marina when Ray and Mom retire, but the store and fuel supply are mine," she reminded him. "They'll only grow as the traffic on the lake increases, and I wanted to be prepared for it."

"You say that as though you think I might want to get rid of you." They turned along the plank, heading for the *Nauti Buoy*, the fifty-foot sea green and white houseboat.

"Not get rid of me *maybe*." She stepped onto the wide porch, moving back as he slid open the glass sliding doors before heading into the dim, air-conditioned comfort of the living room/kitchen.

The shades were all drawn, the lights out. As he closed the

door behind them, he pulled the heavy drapes closed over it, sealing them inside the intimate, cool comfort of his home away from home.

"Then what?" he asked as he moved to the small kitchen. "Do you think I wouldn't want you around, Kelly?"

The wheel column sat in the corner in front of the large shaded window beside the glass doors. A six-foot burgundy couch sat to her side, two matching chairs on the other side of the room, behind the wheel. The kitchen was equipped with a mini refrigerator, chest-type freezer, and narrow four-burner stove with an overhead microwave and oak cabinets. The double sink was narrow, but efficient. Across from the work area a circular table with four cushioned captain's chairs sat beneath a stained-glass chandelier. Farther along was a small bathroom and shower, berth bed, and a walkout to the back diving area.

She loved the *Nauti Buoy.* They had spent the summers on it when she was younger. Upstairs was another larger, opulent bedroom, as well as a master bathroom and deck. Before Ray had given it to Rowdy, there had been two bedrooms downstairs. Now, the second one was a drying/changing area for the back deck with a small washer/dryer combo.

"I wasn't sure," she finally answered, staring back at him, her fingers knotting in the hem of her shirt.

"Your mother helped build the marina." He turned to her after setting the food on the table. "I wouldn't take it from you, no matter what happened."

He hooked his thumbs in the pockets of his jeans, watching her with those eyes. Eyes that stripped her defenses, that sent butterflies crashing to and fro in the pit of her stomach.

She licked her lips, staring back at him. The last thing on her mind now was the business. Nerves clashed as her senses became more heightened; the air in the confines of the craft became heavier, dense with the seductive, subtle scent that was unique to Rowdy.

"I know you wouldn't, Rowdy." She cleared her throat, forcing herself to move to the cabinet and the kitchenware there.

As she pulled plates and silverware from where they were held and set the table, Rowdy warmed the food in the microwave, setting it on the table before pulling a bottle of cheap wine from the fridge.

At some point, he had turned on a CD, lowering the volume until the soft, intimate music flowed through the cabin.

"Let's eat." The dark throb in his voice was so sexual that the suggestion took on a whole new meaning.

"Eat." She breathed in slowly. "Okay. We eat."

Eight

As they ate, he told her about the Marines. She knew he was glossing over the harder details, the blood and death he'd seen overseas, the friends he had lost. She knew when he was talking about those friends who were no longer alive to laugh with him. His eyes would darken, his expression becoming reflective.

He told her about the desert, made her laugh at some of the pranks he and his buddies had played on their CO or other soldiers. She saw the beauty of the sun rising over a desert landscape, or the calm tranquillity of the moon rising, with his deep voice and reverent descriptions.

But he had missed home. She heard that in every word. How beautiful the moon glistening off the sand could be, but it didn't compare to the early morning fog that rose from the lake or the moon slicing a path of golden light across the wet surface.

How he would miss the guys he'd fought with, but he dreamed of slipping off into the mountains and making the homemade moonshine he, Natches, and Dawg often made.

The silence of the desert, the symphony of the forest. He saw the beauty of the land he'd been in, but he knew the treasures to be found in the land he'd grown up in.

"What about women?" She asked the question that plagued her most as he stacked the dishes in the tiny dishwasher and turned back to where she watched him from the table.

She propped her elbow on the table, cupping her chin in her hands as she watched him curiously.

"I wasn't a saint, baby." His lips quirked with that sexy little half smile that was trademark Rowdy. "But there was nothing serious. Hasn't been anyone in a while, actually. What about you?"

He was leaning against the counter, his muscular body relaxed. Well, mostly relaxed. He was hard. She could glimpse the bulge in the front of his jeans from the lower portion of her vision and was dying for a full look.

"No one for me," she answered with a self-mocking grimace. "I couldn't get over you. You left and broke my young heart."

"Better your young heart than my neck," he grunted. "I was twenty-two-years-old, Kelly. I should have been shot for even looking at you then." His eyelids lowered. "But it was damned hard not to look. You filled out a pair of shorts almost as good as you fill them out now."

She felt the flush that rose over her face, her gaze flickering away from him for long moments as she breathed in deeply.

"You know, those loose clothes are going to have to go," he sighed. "One of my favorite parts of coming home was watching you run around in those snug little shorts and tank tops. Made my dick harder than hell, but it was a sight I sure as hell miss, Kelly."

Her gaze slammed into his. The green was darker now, his expression heavy with hunger.

"I . . ." She swallowed tightly. "I'm more comfortable—"

"Bullshit." The whispered retort was delivered with a knowing smile. "You're scared. I'm home now, Kelly. Trust me."

He had promised her, so long ago, as long as he was around, no one would hurt her. It was the bully, she remembered. She was terrified of staying in the park after school while her mother worked, after the bullies had started picking on her. Unless Rowdy was there. He had taken care of her. And sometimes one of the others. If Rowdy couldn't be there, Dawg or Natches had been.

"Remember when I promised I'd always take care of you?" he whispered. "You were the littlest bit of thing I had ever laid my young eyes on. Those tears on your face when those bullies stole that frippery in your hair made me madder than hell."

"You saved my hair bows." She restrained her teasing smile. "And saved Mom a ton of extra money. I loved my hair bows."

"You still love your hair bows." He grinned. "I saw them scattered all over your bathroom last night when I got up for a drink. Damned things own your sink counter."

The style of those pretty hair trifles had changed now. Rather than actual bows there were silver barrettes, glittering little bobby pins, and stylish little doodads he had yet to identify.

She lifted her brows. “They’re pretty though.”

He pushed from the counter, moving with a predatory ease, a shift of bone, muscle, and sinew that had her breath catching in her throat as he walked to the table.

“No.” He reached out, the backs of his fingers smoothing over the side of her face. “You’re pretty. Too damned pretty for those loose clothes. Take them off for me.”

Her eyes widened. “I didn’t bring a change—”

“You have on a bra and panties, I presume?” His fingers wrapped around her wrist, drawing her to her feet. “I bet they cover you better than that damned bathing suit did when you were seventeen.”

The air was suddenly too thick to breathe, her sight dazed, filled with the color of Rowdy’s eyes and the desire she could see glowing in them. Her thighs tightened as she felt the tingle of response racing through her womb, rippling through her vagina.

“I’ll head the boat for the cove,” he whispered. “We could do some swimming, watch the moon rise over the lake. Would you like that, Kelly?”

“A bra and panties isn’t exactly a bathing suit.” She drew in a deep breath, moving away from him as she tugged at the large shirt.

“It’s not exactly naked, either,” he said as he moved to the wheel column. “Think about it. So do we go to the cove anyway?” He glanced back at her, lifting a black brow suggestively.

Kelly breathed in deeply.

“The cove sounds like fun.” She finally nodded firmly.

“And the clothes?” His gaze dropped over her body before coming back to her eyes.

She lifted her brow mockingly. “You haven’t done anything to deserve it yet, Rowdy,” she purred sweetly. “I guess I’ll just have to think about it.”

She was going to have to think about it?

As he maneuvered the *Nauti Buoy* toward the hidden cove, Rowdy found a smile tugging at his lips. He might not deserve to see those loose clothes coming over her perky little body, but he was going to. The long, thin, denim shirt fell to her thighs and draped over her slender shoulders. Even her jeans were loose, a protective shell to cover herself with.

His jaw clenched at the thought. Kelly had never had a problem wearing clothes that emphasized her slender body, until now. The attack had changed that; she was nervous now, where before she had been confident of herself as a desirable, pretty young woman.

She didn't tease him like she had for far too many years. She was more contained, quieter. And he realized he missed the spitfire she had been. By now, they should have been arguing loud enough to draw attention, while she drove him crazy with a combination of lust and exasperation.

Instead, she was standing at the glass sliding doors, staring into the distance reflectively as her fingers gripped the drapes at the side.

"I think you're wrong, Kelly." He leaned into the back of the barstool he was sitting in, one hand gripping the wheel as the boat plowed through the water toward the cove.

"About what?" She turned back to him with a frown, her gray eyes twinkling with good humor.

"I think I deserve to see you stripped down to something decent." He scowled. "Stop letting that bastard win."

She rolled her eyes before turning back to the scenery outside the boat.

"You don't know everything, Rowdy," she retorted, but there was no conviction in her voice.

"I know you." He began unbuttoning his own shirt as he glanced at her, his cock throbbing in delight as she glanced back at him, her eyes shadowed with interest.

Within seconds he'd stripped the shirt, tossing it back on the chair behind him as he flashed her a wicked grin.

She turned to him then, crossing her arms over her breasts as she lifted her brow.

"You could at least lose the jeans," he pointed out. "That shirt is big enough to cover two of you. No one would know."

Four years ago she had worn that tiny little bikini all damned day, flipping around him like a wood nymph intent on driving mortal men insane. Now, he couldn't even get her out of her pants.

"You're pushing," she warned, her voice holding a subtle snap.

"You haven't seen me push yet, baby," he growled in return. "Do you think I didn't take the time to find out just how much you've been hiding since that bastard attacked you? You stopped dressing like the girl I knew and started dressing like your damned grandmother instead. You're scared."

"Well, duh!" she mocked him. "Go figure. Maybe I should just prance around naked for you, Rowdy." She wasn't really angry, yet. Her eyes were sparkling though, her cheeks flushing with irritation.

"That would work for me." He grinned wolfishly. "Let's try it and see if it will work for you. Take yours off and I'll take mine off."

"You would take yours off anyway." Her laughter was soft, knowing.

"For you, baby, anytime." He winked.

"A far cry from your answer in the past years." The shade of mockery in her voice wasn't lost on him. "Why now? You come back and suddenly can't wait to get into bed with me? It's enough to make a girl suspicious."

"No doubt," he agreed, grinning back at her. "There's no secret there, sweetheart. I wasn't about to take a kid to my bed. Being a virgin will be hard enough for you, I at least wanted you to be mature enough to know what the hell you were getting into. But I had no intentions of not coming back for you."

Surprise reflected in her eyes.

"And if I decided I wanted someone else?" Her eyes narrowed, her lips thinning at the confidence he knew she was reading in his tone.

"Then Dawg or Natches would have taken care of it until I made it back on leave." He shrugged easily. "I put a claim on you a long time ago, Kelly. You just didn't realize it."

"Somewhere between the little sex games that your buddies shared in?"

Ohhh, now was that just a little shade of jealousy there? He watched her closely from the corner of his eye as he kept the teasing grin in place.

"Sex games are for adults." He scratched at his chin as he glanced back at her. "You couldn't handle them."

"Who says I couldn't handle them?" She frowned back at him

as she straightened and placed her hands on her hips. "You never gave me the chance to try."

He snorted. "Don't let your mouth write checks your body can't cash, baby. Don't dare me."

He gave her a dark, warning look, one she immediately recognized. He wasn't playing here. Not yet. And before he started, he wanted her aware of the rules.

"I'm not stupid." She pushed her hands into her jeans pockets, staring back at him with an edge of anger, of arousal. "I paid attention to your reputation a long time ago."

She wasn't shying away from him. That was good. He didn't want her shying away from him; he wanted her curious, interested. He wanted her horny.

"Did you now?" He ran his hand over his chest as he guided the houseboat into a turn that would take it off the main section of the lake and into a more narrow waterway leading to the cove. "And you still teased me every chance you had. You've stopped teasing me. Maybe you decided you can't handle it."

She rolled her eyes. "You're being a prick."

"I'm being honest, Kelly." He gave his head a quick, negative jerk. "You listened to the rumors, you say. Evidently you didn't listen close enough."

"What does that mean?"

"Exactly what I said," he answered, narrowing his eyes as he glanced back at her. "I'm fine with having the princess. I'll take you to my bed, treat you like crystal, and love you with everything I have to give you, for as long as you can put up with me. But don't tempt the beast, sugar, because when he gets hungry, you might get more than you've bargained for."

He watched her expression go blank.

"You love me?" She blinked back at him, so damned innocent it made his guts clench.

"Kelly, I've always loved you," he told her, meaning it. Knowing he meant it. "In one way or the other, you've always been a part of me. You're old enough to decide if you want to settle in with one man, forever, or not. I figure I can give you this summer to decide for sure if I'm that man. If not, then I'll let you go. It wouldn't be easy, but I'd do it—"

"But, Rowdy, I've always loved you." She watched him in confusion now, hope and fear in equal parts shadowing her eyes.

He tapped his fingers against the wheel, turning it until it swung into another waterway leading to the private cove. Natches's family owned the small property that bordered the bay. It was on the back side of undeveloped land, and completely private.

"Yeah, I know you have," he finally answered as he pulled along the tree-shaded bank and cut the engine.

He didn't say anything more as he moved beyond the sliding doors, throwing out the heavy front anchor weight before moving to the back and doing the same. As he returned to the living area, he paused by the table.

"I came back for you," he said, leaning against the small bar, forcing himself to stand away from her. "That's why Dad was so worried. He knew I came back for you. And the rumors are fact, baby. So don't push me where the games are concerned."

"I don't need you or your dad making decisions for me," she snapped, her gray eyes flaring in defiance. "If we're going to try for a relationship, then we'll meet in the middle. Somehow. But not if you think you can plan my life for me."

His lips twitched. She was a bundle of fire, that was for damned sure.

"Take off the pants," he whispered. "Let's go one step at a time, Kelly. See what your limits are together."

"Our limits," she retorted. "Not just mine."

His lips curled into a frankly sexual, wicked smile.

Kelly licked her lips nervously. The action had the head of his erection pounding with need. Damn, he wanted that little tongue there laving the thick crest, licking around it as though it were a favorite treat.

She bit her lower lip and glanced away before breathing in deeply. Her hands moved, pulling out of the jeans pockets before moving beneath the shirt to unsnap the pants. She kicked off her sandals then pushed the jeans over her hips and down her legs.

Within seconds she was laying them over the chair with his shirt before turning back to him.

"You used to tease me like a brazen little hussy," he whispered, staring at her legs, dying to feel them around his hips. "It was one of the things I looked forward to most when I thought of coming home." He watched her move toward him, her eyes becoming cloudy with passion as he kept his voice low, carefully teasing.

"You didn't act as though you enjoyed it," she murmured as she drew up to him. He jerked as she placed her small hand on his bare chest and ran it slowly down to his tight abdomen. "You stayed away from me."

He lifted his hand, moving it to her arm, feeling the softness of her skin as he ran his fingers to her elbow and back again.

"If you knew the things I wanted to do to you over the years, you would have run screaming." He stared down at her uplifted face, his gaze on her lips. The soft, candy pink perfection of those full curves had him aching. "You're still too damned young for the things I want to do to you. With you."

"What did you want to do to me, Rowdy?" Her hand slid from his abdomen to his chest again as she stared at him, her eyes reflecting the same hungry need she had shown for years, but it also showed a shadow of fear, of hesitation.

"Everything." He wasn't going to lie to her. Now wasn't the time to hide any part of who or what he was, or the hungers he could unleash on her. If there was a time to be honest with her, it was now. Before the emotional connection that had bonded them for so many years deepened, before there was a chance she could be hurt.

Arousal flashed in her eyes as her breathing became heavier, jerkier. "Give me an example."

He ran his fingers down her arm until he found her hand, lifted it, pulling her fingers to his lips as he watched her through narrowed eyes. Her gaze flickered to his lips as he licked over the pad of two fingers, her eyelids drooping, pleasure rather than fear filling her gaze.

"You know what I want," he whispered. "Exactly what I suspect you're most frightened of now." He lifted his other hand, smoothing back her hair from her face, his thumb caressing her cheek. "I want to strip you down, love you from head to toe as often as possible, and sometimes . . . we might not be alone."

Her breath caught in a hard hitch a second before she jerked away from him, moving across the room, her shoulders stiff and straight as he forced himself to relax, to wait.

"And if we weren't alone?" Her voice was thin, breathy. He couldn't tell if it was arousal or fear that inspired it.

"If we weren't alone, you know the only men I'd ever allow around you," he told her softly.

"And if it's not what I want?" She asked, her gray eyes dark, shadowed with indecision.

"Then I won't press you for it." He crossed his arms over his chest again as he leaned against the counter. "That doesn't mean I won't think about it, that I won't fantasize the hell out of it. I won't lie to you, Kelly. Ever. And I won't have things between us that don't need to be there."

"And how do they feel about this?" Arousal lay thick in her voice, as did the fear. "Have the three of you already been making plans to seduce me?"

"There are times when men don't have to make plans, Kelly." He kept his voice smooth, even. "They know me, just as well as I know them. No plans will ever be made outside of your presence."

She breathed in slowly, her nostrils flaring as she watched him closely.

"Which brings me to another point," he continued. "Whether you want to do it or not, you're going to at least have to fake it. Until I catch that bastard who attacked you, I'll let him think it's going on. I'll torture him with the knowledge of it. Because I'll be damned if I'll let him threaten you any longer. So you might want to think about at least enjoying some of the pretense."

As he spoke, he watched her pale, then flush as fury contorted her features with lightning swiftness. A spark was all it took, and he had known he was taking that risk.

"You think you're going to play with me?" she threw back at him, her voice rising in fury. "That I'm going to let you play head games with that sick bastard until he comes after me again?"

Betrayal flashed in her eyes, in her voice.

"Think again, damn you." She stalked over to the chair, yanking her pants from the seat and jerking them over her legs as she cast him a heated glare. "You're a son of a bitch, Rowdy. I can't believe you'd do this." Emotion clogged her throat, the pain in her voice tearing at his chest.

"Hell yes, I'll do it," he snarled, stalking to her as she struggled to snap and zip her jeans. He gripped her arms, staring down at her, rage eating him alive at the thought of that perverted bastard holding her down, cutting her with that knife. "I'll do whatever it takes, Kelly, do you understand me? He's a threat to you. A danger. And that I will not tolerate. If we don't catch him, he's going to rape again, and the next woman might not live to regret it. Is that what you want?"

"You want to use me." She slapped at his arms, breaking away from him as she screamed the accusation in his face, her gray eyes swimming with tears. "You want to pervert what I feel for you, what I've needed for years, and turn it into some kind of damned war game."

"I want you until I can't breathe, dammit," he growled back at her. "I haven't taken a comfortable breath since you developed breasts. But he's going to come after you again, sooner or later. You know it and I know it. What happens if he catches me off guard? If he gets to you again?"

"You can't know that. And I'm careful now."

"I snuck up on you yesterday morning," he snapped. "Do you have any idea how easy it is to get past even Dad's security system? Do you think you could have stopped him even if that window had been closed and locked?" He saw the truth in her eyes. "Forget that, Kelly. The other girls he raped couldn't stop him. He raped one of them while her parents slept only rooms away from her. You can't hide from him, and you can't run."

"Stop yelling at me!" She pushed him back furiously, her hands cracking against his stomach as she slapped against it to forcibly put distance between them.

"You aren't listening to me," he snarled.

"And I *won't* listen to you," she screamed, the tears falling from her eyes, her face pale, her eyes raging with fury and the sense of betrayal he could see tearing through her. "You call this love? Setting me up? Oh God, Rowdy, how could you do this to me?"

A sob tore through her body as she stared up at him, her fists clenched at her side, tears wetting her cheeks and breaking his heart.

"Do what, Kelly?" he finally asked wearily, shaking his head. "Want you safe? Well? I'm telling you who and what I am, and what I am endangers you with this bastard anyway if he's even heard of me. Dawg, Natches, and I have been sharing our women since we were old enough to understand what our dicks were made for. You know that as well as anyone else does. Loving me doesn't mean you have to do shit about it. Loving you doesn't mean it's something I have to have. But we're talking about more than that now. We're talking about your life, and I'll do whatever the hell it takes to keep that bastard from ever touching you again. Ever, Kelly."

"And how do you know it wasn't one of them?" she threw in his face. "It could have been either of them. He tried to rape me anally, Rowdy. And the three of you are considered the ass-fucking kings, so tell me how you know it's not one of them."

"Because they know me," he snapped back. "And they've watched you twitch that little ass at me since you were a teenager. Trust me, baby, if it was one of them, they would have never made the mistake of believing that good girl persona you project to every other man close enough to watch you. You're a good girl to the world, but you, baby, are bad to the bone when it comes to me. I know it, and you know it. You just have to accept it."

"Get fucked!" she screamed back, enraged, her face flushed red, her eyes glittering now with a fury he'd rarely seen in her.

He smiled. A slow, teasing, wicked grin that only fueled her rage as his gaze dropped down her body then back up.

"But, darlin', ain't that what we were talking about?"

Before she could do more than gasp he had her in his arms again, his lips covering hers, his tongue slipping past her lips to taste the wild anger and arousal pumping through her.

She didn't think. She didn't fear. He felt her hands grip his shoulders, her little nails pricking against his flesh as his hand moved beneath her shirt, to her thighs.

"Damn you," he growled, lifting his head to stare into her dazed, stormy eyes as his palm cupped the hot flesh between her thighs, the heat of his flesh searing her even through her jeans. "I bet you're wet, Kelly. So fucking wet it's seeping through your panties."

He pressed closer, feeling her hips buck at the pressure against her clit.

God, he wanted to strip her. He wanted to tear those clothes off her and lay her down on the closest available surface and devour her. He wanted to bury his lips between those perfect thighs, send his tongue searching through the silken folds of her pussy.

And she wanted it, too. She was pressing against his hand, her hips bucking into it as the heat of her filled his palm.

"Feel good?"

"I hate you," she snapped, her breathing rough as a low whimper left her throat.

"No, you don't." He rotated his hand, watching her eyes flare, feeling the heat intensify against his palm. "You love me, Kelly, just like you love this. And you want more. Admit it, baby."

Her thighs parted further as his fingers curved, massaging the sensitive flesh through her clothes.

"I want you, not a game," she cried out, arching to her tiptoes, helpless against him. He liked her helpless against his touch, loved feeling the heat of her against his hand.

"And if the game comes with it?" He watched her intently, his eyes narrowed. "I'll do whatever it takes to keep you safe. And this is what it takes. I won't let him catch us unprepared. I won't let him touch you again."

He released her slowly, hating letting her go as she stared back at him miserably.

"Think about that," he whispered, keeping his voice gentle. "I hate it like hell, and no one wishes I could have seduced you more than I do. I would have loved seducing you, baby. But your safety is more important."

"My safety?" she asked mockingly. "Or your desires?"

Anger flared inside him. "You know me better than that, Kelly." He kept his jaw tensed, his tone of voice low. "Nothing matters as much as keeping you safe."

"But only on your terms," she pointed out, furious, causing him to pause. "On your terms and by your rules. Well, you know what, Rowdy, your rules suck. Maybe I need to decide if playing your game is worth the risk to my heart and to my safety."

Nine

He watched as the Nauti Buoy *pulled into her berth, fifty feet and gleaming beneath the summer moon, her lights giving the craft a soft, romantic look. How he had dreamed of having such a craft, a place he could use to hide, to take his good girls and fulfill the promises he made to them.*

He thought he had chosen so wisely. His perfect girls, pure in heart and in nature, and they loved him. He was their love, but it had taken so long to find the one he wanted for all time. The perfect good girl. So sweet-natured and pure, never dirtying herself or her good name. Despite the brother.

His fists clenched at the thought of the brother. He was depraved, perverted, and he was going to dirty her. Rowdy Mackay was going to shame Kelly, and he knew it. He had seen them today, in the store, his hands on her, his eyes raking over her as though he owned her.

Rowdy Mackay didn't own her. She belonged to the man who loved her, who respected her. And she was going to love him. Just like the others did. They hadn't loved anyone else either. He watched them sometimes, making certain they didn't allow anyone else to touch what belonged to him. Sometimes he called them, reminded them of who they were waiting for. They had promised to wait on him to find his one true love.

Kelly could be his true love. He thought it was possible. Until Rowdy came home.

The Nauti Boys. They were depraved. Perverts. But they had never fooled with the good girls. They left the perfect ones alone, always preferring the tramps, the little whores willing to spread their legs not just for one of them, but sometimes for all three at once. They shared their women all the time, watching and listening to their nasty screams as they begged for more.

His fists clenched, his gut rolling in sick suspicion. Rowdy had taken Kelly away on the houseboat. He had never done that by himself before. In the past, it had always been with her and her friends, never alone.

He shook at the fear that the bastard had dirtied her. He couldn't let that happen. Kelly was sweet and clean, she had never been dirtied by another man's seed, by another's possession of her.

She had screamed for him when he touched her, though. He hadn't had time to hear her beg for him, or to hear her promise to remain true to him. No sooner had he attempted to possess her than that big dumb hick visiting his whore girlfriend had started yelling outside the door. He couldn't get caught. His sweet Kelly couldn't be seen with a man in her bed. It would ruin her reputation and she wouldn't be clean anymore. Her reputation meant everything.

Bastard Rowdy. *Rowdy Mackay thought he was perfect, thought* all *the girls were his. He was going to hurt sweet Kelly, his sister. She was his sister, he had no business touching her. Sisters shouldn't be touched, his father had warned him of that.*

His eyes narrowed as Kelly moved from the boat and jumped onto the narrow floating dock. She was angry. He could see it in her face, in the stiff set of her body beneath the bright lights of the dock.

She said something as Rowdy locked the doors, causing the man to stiffen, to turn to her slowly. He didn't like the smile Rowdy gave her. It was carnal. Dirty.

He watched as she stalked ahead of the other man, her loose clothing demure, hiding the body that belonged to him alone. How perfect she was. His good girl. He had to finish his claim on her. He had to make certain she belonged to him. Not Rowdy. Never Rowdy and his perverted friends.

He watched as Rowdy walked her to her car. He was too close to her, even though she was angry. Rowdy was standing too close. He was crowding her.

She unlocked the door and opened it, then Rowdy touched her. Don't touch her. *He clenched his fists, sniffing miserably, fighting the tears that fell from his eyes. Rowdy shouldn't be touching her.*

But he was. The depraved bastard was touching her hair, her cheek, smiling down at her. Rage shattered in his head, filling his vision with a red haze as he watched another move from the shadows of the dock. Dawg. *The bastard couldn't even use his real name—he used the nickname of the animal he was.*

Kelly started as the other men called out to them, flashed Rowdy a furious look, then got into her car. The car door closed and within seconds she was pulling from the parking lot. She was going home. But she wouldn't be going alone. Rowdy would go as well. He lived in the house with her. His bedroom would be close to hers, he could hear her, smell her, maybe touch her as she slept.

Oh God, don't let him touch her, *he prayed.* Don't let him dirty the good girl. *She was his good girl. And, she just might be his perfect love.*

Kelly forcibly restrained the anger pounding through her bloodstream as she stepped into the house with Rowdy close behind her.

"It's about time you two found your way home." Ray and Maria stepped into the entryway.

Kelly breathed in deeply before turning to them, pasting a smile on her face as she met their concerned gazes.

"Rowdy has a habit of poking along on the way back from the docks." She kept her voice flat and even. "You know how he is."

They weren't convinced.

"She's a lousy liar, isn't she?" Rowdy drawled, his deep baritone still sending shivers up her spine despite her anger.

She glanced over at him. His thumbs were hooked in the pockets of his jeans, long legs stiff and straight as he smiled in open amusement back at their parents. She drew in a deep, hard breath.

"I'm going up to bed." She smiled stiffly. "Rowdy can be a butt by himself. I don't feel like dealing with it."

She raced up the stairs, fearing Rowdy would follow her, grateful he didn't. She slammed the door to her bedroom, twisting the lock on the handle before she stomped to her window and jerked the heavy curtains closed.

"Beg me for it," he panted at her ear, holding her down. "You're my good girl, Kelly. You're mine, it's okay to let me in. Let me in . . ."

She shook her head at the intrusive memory. She had managed to hold back the fear while she was with Rowdy, but now that she was alone, it was sneaking in, attacking her. The feeling of being watched was overwhelming, her skin crawling as her stomach churned with panic.

She had, as Rowdy had argued, essentially been the one who got away. She had escaped the full rape, suffering only some cuts made to weaken her, and a terror that still brought her awake with a cry on her lips.

She didn't wear the clothes she used to because the marks were still there. Shorts and tank tops might reveal the nearly imperceptible white scars that still marred her arms, shoulders, and legs. Nakedness would reveal the ones on her buttocks. Deeper slices had been made there as he held her down, cutting her panties from her.

Her mother swore they weren't noticeable. But to Kelly, they were.

She still remembered the feel of that knife biting into her, razor-sharp, the skin parting as cold pain streaked through her nervous system, and the feel of hot blood as it began to pour from the wounds. The doctor had assured her that within a few years they would be gone entirely. She wondered if the memories would fade as well.

She paced through the dark room to the wide recliner that sat on the far wall, beneath the standing lamp she used to read by. Collapsing into it, she propped her elbows on her knees and dropped her head in her hands. She didn't need Rowdy's arguments earlier to understand that she wasn't out of danger. She knew she wasn't, just as she knew that it was only a matter of time before her attacker made his next move.

She felt stalked. There was no proof, nothing but her own suspicions and her own fears. Shaking her head, she moved to her dresser. She pulled free one of the long sleeveless gowns she slept in and headed for the shower. *A cold shower maybe*, she thought as she adjusted the water. If she didn't get the memory of his kiss, his teasing out of her head, she would go crazy.

But even the cool water did nothing to still the idea he had planted in her head earlier. She was furious that Rowdy would play games to draw the stalker out, but she was smart enough to realize she wasn't safe.

She dried her hair, staring at the thin white scars on her shoulders and upper arms. There were four on one, three on the other. They showed clearly in the bright light of the bathroom, the dark blue gown emphasizing the marks.

At times she swore she could feel the ones on her buttocks.

She shook her head as she turned from the mirror, moving to the bedroom, her hand reaching out to flip off the light. She paused at the switch, her eyes narrowing on the man in her bedroom.

Rowdy had obviously showered as well. Dressed in gray sweatpants, he was propped against her pillows, waiting on her, a scowl creasing his handsome face.

"That expression freezes on your face and you'll be terrifying little kids on the streets," she informed him as she flipped off the light and walked into the bedroom.

"I'm not leaving you alone at night, Kelly—"

"Windows were locked and so was the door," she informed him as she stood by the side of the bed, her arms crossed over her breasts.

"And I got in the door anyway."

She inhaled slowly, her gaze sliding to the shadowed outline of the door as Rowdy reached over and clicked on the dim lamp on the small table beside him.

The lock was in the standing position, still locked.

"How did you do that?" She turned back to him, pretending to ignore the fact that he was mouthwateringly sexy as he lay on the flowered comforter of her bed.

"It's a piece of cake," he grunted. "The window locks aren't a lot harder to release. Until I can get the contractor out here to add to the security, you're stuck with me."

His expression was determined, stubborn. It was easy to tell when Rowdy had made up his mind. His expression went completely bland and his sea green eyes turned as cool as the arctic.

"Fine." She shrugged. "You sleep here and I'll sleep in your bed. No biggie." She moved for the door.

"Open that door, Kelly, and your mom and my dad are going to get dragged into this little disagreement we're having. Is that really what you want?"

Damn.

She stopped halfway to the door before turning back to him.

"Whose side would they take?" She opened her eyes wide, with mocking innocence. "Now I wonder, what will they think about the little proposal you put to me earlier?"

He tilted his head, his eyes glittering with lust, with amused hunger.

"Dad would probably kick my ass out of the house," he growled good-naturedly. "Is that what you really want?"

She turned away from him, restraining the urge to kick his butt herself. He was right. Ray would likely skin his hide if he ever learned of his son's proposal.

It wasn't that she hadn't expected it. She had. She had looked forward to it. How was that for some sick shit? She had actually looked forward to the day Rowdy would return and make good on the promise his kiss had made years ago.

And she had known if he did, the possibility of just such a proposal would come. She had been ready for it. Prepared for it. What she hadn't expected was the cold-blooded intention he had of using it to catch her would-be rapist. As though the act no longer had anything to do with the two of them. As though the desire, the need, and the hunger were a means to an end and nothing more. It was without feeling, without emotion. And God help her, whenever she was around Rowdy, she felt nothing but emotion. Swirls of it. Lava-hot, lightning forks of sensation that rippled over her nerve endings, rendering even the air itself a caress against her sensitive flesh.

And emotions? Oh, she didn't even want to go there. Except she was already there. Arousal, uncertainty, fear of the unknown, and a fear of losing the dream in the face of reality.

He was asking her to choose. She had wanted to be seduced.

She turned back to him, drawing in a slow, deep breath, her head lifting as she stared at the confident, cool countenance he presented to her.

"Get out of my bedroom." She crossed her arms over her breasts, pressing her lips together as she glared at him. "I'm not one of the Nauti Boys' playthings. And I'm not in the mood for games. Not yours or anyone else's."

She watched the surprise gleam in his eyes for just a second. For the first time in all the years she had known him, she had never surprised him, until now.

With a ripple of muscle, he moved from the bed, his gaze

never leaving hers as he rose, coming to his feet and walking around the bed.

He was aroused. The thick length of his erection tented his sweatpants, drew her eyes and made her mouth water. She had fantasized about that erection. About all the things a woman could do with such a prime piece of flesh.

She let her eyes linger on the proof of that arousal before lifting them to his face again. He was close. So close she could smell the clean, male scent of him. Dial soap and heated male arousal.

She stood still as he stalked around her, the movements deliberate, predatory. Suddenly he wasn't the laid-back, patiently amused Rowdy she had always known. She could feel the purpose, the male intent that poured from him.

Her breath caught as he paused behind her, his hand reaching up to allow his fingers to smooth her hair back over her shoulder, to bare the shell of her ear.

"You're mine." She jumped at his whispered response. "And, baby, I do like to play." His hands ran down her arms, creating a friction of heat as she felt his lips at her shoulders. "I guess that makes you my playmate, if not my plaything."

Her eyes widened a second before she jerked out of his hold, turning back to him furiously.

"I don't think so." She gave him a tight, angry smile.

Stupid male confidence, she fumed.

He tilted his head, the beginnings of a smile twitching at the corners of his lips.

"I could convince you."

No doubt.

She snorted as though it weren't possible. Unfortunately, he probably could convince her, but at what cost to her soul?

"Go get in your own bed, Rowdy. Don't make me cause a scene. Ray wouldn't like it." She walked to hers, flipping back the blankets and moving into the comfort of the mattress, ignoring him as though he didn't matter. "Good night."

He chuckled. "You've changed," he murmured as he paced to the other side of the bed, staring down at her, aroused, determined.

"I haven't changed at all, Rowdy." She pulled the blankets to her waist as she sat propped against the pillows. "Perhaps you just never really knew me." She raised her brows in emphasis. "That's always a possibility."

"You enjoyed waking up with me," he accused. "You don't want to throw me out."

That one was a no-brainer. No, she didn't want to throw him out. She wanted to curl against him and sleep as fearlessly as she had the night before and awaken as warm and protected as she had that morning.

She lifted her chin, refusing to answer him, fighting to hold his knowing stare as he watched her from beneath the veil of his thick, black lashes.

"Go play with someone else." She might have to kill him if he tried. "I'm not interested in the games."

"And you think this is a game?" He scowled down at her, his hands bracing on his powerful hips as his eyes began to simmer with irritation.

"I think it is for you," she answered somberly. "And I'm not a game. Don't play games with me, Rowdy. Not now, not ever."

Ten

Rowdy leaned forward, muscular arms propping him up on the mattress as he stared into her eyes. Kelly fought the need to glance away from him, to deny the hold he had on her. There was no turning away from him. He mesmerized her, made her hungry, made her need.

"I'm not scared of you, Rowdy," she tried to smirk back at him. "Don't try to intimidate me."

"If you don't like the games, then don't play them." His voice was dangerously, warningly soft. "You want something from me, then tell me what you want."

Her teeth clenched in anger.

"Fine," she snapped. "I want you out of my bedroom and out of my face. Go away." She made a shooing motion with her hand then stared at him in shock as his hand whipped out, catching her wrist.

Her heart jumped to her throat as he brought her fingers to his mouth, rubbed them against the velvet roughness of his lips before opening them and licking over the pads with a subtle flick of his tongue.

She was helpless. Struck dumb by the sheer sensuality of watching him caress nothing but her fingertips. Feeling the warmth of his lips, the flickering heat of his tongue, the sensual nip of his teeth.

Each caress sent flares of heat exploding with sensual devastation throughout her body. Her nipples were so hard, the nerves there so sensitized, that they were sending rippling flares of response straight to her womb, convulsing it with an erotic punch of pleasure.

"Rowdy . . ." She was shocked at the whimper in her voice, at her inability to pull away from him.

He came closer. Kneeling on the bed, still holding her hand, he pulled her to him until she was on her knees facing him.

He took her other wrist, placing her palms against his chest before his hands smoothed up her arms, over her shoulders, down her back to her hips. She trembled, shuddering at the light caress; it could have been firmer, could have been more destructive. It was subtle instead. Soft. Giving her the chance to break away, knowing she couldn't. That she wouldn't.

"You're mine," he whispered again as his head lowered.

She stared back at him, fighting to breathe, fighting against the desires raging inside her. She was helpless against his touch, against the hunger that gleamed in his eyes.

Just as she became helpless against his kiss.

His lips covered hers, slowly at first. So slowly, too slowly. They stroked over hers, his tongue flickering out to lave them a second before his teeth caught the lower curve, nipping at it as he watched her.

Her breathing hitched as she felt his hands bunch in the material of the gown at her hips. It drew slowly up her thighs, working over her flesh, baring her to his hands.

"Easy," he whispered against her lips. "Just feel, Kelly. Feel for me. Burn for me . . ."

She felt cool air caress her thighs, then his hands against her naked flesh, callused, heated, as his lips slanted over hers and he stole her mind with his kiss.

Deep, drugging kisses. Pleasure tore through her system, consumed her to the point that the knowledge that she was being lowered, laid beneath him, barely registered in her mind. All she knew was the pleasure. The feel of his hard body above her, his hands smoothing over her bare thighs, her hips, then working on the tiny buttons at the bodice while his kisses ravished her lips.

She was drowning in him. The taste of him. His touch. The muted male sounds of hunger and pleasure as she began to touch him. She needed to touch him. To immerse herself in every sensual sensation she could consume. Her nervous system was rioting with the chaotic impulses rushing through them. The air around them became heated, steamy with the desperation that infused each kiss, each touch.

"God, you taste sweet." His lips tore from hers, his breathing heavy, hard, as they moved to her neck.

She tilted her neck, panting for air as she felt his teeth rake down the sensitive column, then felt the brush of cool air over her naked breasts.

As his head lifted, she opened her eyes, staring back at him in dazed fascination as his gaze dropped. He had pulled apart the unbuttoned edges of her gown, displaying the swollen, hard-tipped mounds of her breasts.

The expression on his face was pure, carnal hunger. His eyes heavy-lidded, his lips moist and swollen from their kisses, his cheekbones flushed a brick red.

As though suspended between dream and reality, she watched as his head lowered, her eyes widening, a strangled groan leaving her lips as his tongue covered one spiked, aroused nipple.

Reaction shot through her, jerking at her body as her hands tightened on his neck, her back arching. This was heaven. It was ecstasy. The most pleasure she had ever known in her life.

His tongue lashed at the hard point as he sucked the flesh into his mouth, drawing on her deeply, creating a pleasure–pain sensation that had a startled cry leaving her lips.

Lips he immediately covered, stilling the aroused cries as his fingers replaced his mouth. Tweaking at the tender tips, causing her to writhe beneath him as she fought to get closer, to still the ache burning between her thighs.

"Shh. Easy." His groan was whispered against her lips, his voice dark, desperate. "Damn, Kelly. I can't take you here. Dad will kill me."

"I'll kill you if you don't." His chest pressed against her breasts, rasped her nipples so she fought to breathe. "Don't stop, Rowdy, please."

His hand smoothed down to her thigh, his fingers close, so close to where she needed them. She gazed back at him pleadingly, feeling her vagina ripple with need, the muscles clenching in desperation.

"If I take you, you're going to scream," he whispered, his eyes darkening, a ravenous lust filling his expression. "I want to hear every cry that leaves your lips, Kelly. Every scream as you come around me. I can't do that here. We can't do that here. You know that."

She shook her head, a weak whimper passing her lips.

"I've waited too long, Rowdy."

"Shh." His kiss was gentle and much too short as he eased her gown over her thighs and then covered her breasts once again. "Tomorrow. We'll go out on the boat," he whispered, pushing her hair back before moving slowly to her side and pulling her into his arms.

She laid her head against his chest, fighting to regulate her breathing, to tear herself back from the endless spiral of heat he had thrown her into.

"That wasn't fair," she whispered as he lifted the sheet over them. "You're supposed to be sleeping in your own bed."

She was too weak to make him move now, too desperate for his touch, any touch, to force him from her bed.

"Go to sleep." His arms contracted around her. "I'd be fighting shadows if I slept away from you, Kelly. Let me hold you. Know you're okay."

She pressed her lips to his chest. "It wasn't your fault, Rowdy," she told him softly, wondering at the edge of remorse she heard in his voice.

He was silent, but his hands still stroked her back, soothing now, where seconds before they had been arousing.

"Just let me hold you," he repeated. "Sleep beside me, Kelly. We'll argue out the rest of it later."

"You want me to sleep?" She sighed, shaking her head. "Rowdy, I'm never going to sleep with your hard-on poking at my belly all night."

"Sure you can," he chuckled at her ear. "You need your rest, baby. Because tomorrow night, I really wouldn't bet on you getting any sleep at all."

She was silent then, lying against him, feeling his arms surrounding her, protecting her. God, what was she doing? She had lived and breathed for the day Rowdy would return and see her as more than just a pesky little girl. That he would see her as a woman, as his woman. And here he was, ready to claim her, and she was fighting it, fighting him. Or was she fighting herself?

"This isn't a game, Kelly." His voice was soft, surrounding

her, causing her eyelids to flutter in pleasure as it stroked over her senses. "I'm deadly serious about this. About us. I wasn't joking when I said you were mine. I came home to claim you, if that's what you still want."

"Maybe it doesn't work that way, Rowdy. I want you until I can't think, can't breathe. But you're different now."

"I'm no different than I've ever been and you know it." His voice hardened. "You don't like the fact that I'm willing to do whatever it takes to protect you. You want everything tied up in roses and sweet promises. I can give you that, to a point. But I won't ignore the danger. And you have to accept that. This will be taken care of."

He wasn't angry; he wasn't trying to convince her. He was telling her.

"You're talking about using me. Me and whatever we share between us sexually, flaunting it in front of him to provoke him." That terrified her more than she wanted to admit.

"It's the quickest way to finish this."

"Maybe the quickest way isn't always the best." She didn't know if she wanted to take that step, if she wanted to force a madman's hand.

"Or maybe you think you can hide whatever this relationship brings." His voice hardened. "Do you believe that's possible, Kelly? Whether you make the choice to immerse yourself in everything I can give you, or not, doesn't make a difference. Everyone is going to believe you are. He'll believe you are. My plan will just flush him out quicker, that's all. But we'll play it however you choose."

She didn't like the easy, matter-of-fact way he said that. She could feel a "but" in there somewhere, she just had to find it.

"You could have at least tried to hide that part of your sex life from the world," she finally sighed with an edge of irritation.

"Why?" He sounded genuinely curious now. "Kelly, I'm who I am. I don't hide that, from anyone. I don't flaunt it. I don't advertise it. Others have. What happens between you and me I expect will stay between you and me. You don't advertise yourself, and you won't advertise our relationship. Why should we do without something we might enjoy because of what others suspect, or think?"

She hated it when he pulled logic into his arguments with her. He had always done that.

"Because I'm scared," she whispered, rolling away from him to sit on the side of the bed.

"Of me?"

"Of myself. Of what could happen." She moved to her feet, pacing away from the bed as she rubbed at the chill that rushed over her arms. "You're talking about pushing someone who isn't sane. And in the same breath . . ." She shook her head.

"I'm asking you to make a decision," he finished for her. "Not about your safety but about something much more important to you. Your sexuality."

"I'm still a virgin." Her laughter was self-mocking. "I expected something a little more romantic, Rowdy."

"And you deserved something a hell of a lot more romantic, Kelly." He sighed. "But catching this stalker is more important than romance. And I'm not going to play games with you. From the beginning, we won't be alone. If it doesn't happen for you with Dawg and Natches, then we have to at least give the impression of it. We can't afford to let this guy catch us unawares, I can't afford to let him hurt you again, because God as my witness, my sanity won't survive it, Kelly."

"God!" She pushed her fingers through her hair, turning from him, trying to ignore the fact that she wasn't insulted, wasn't offended or furious. "You're not talking about this thing with your cousins being a one-time deal, are you?" She kept her back to him, kept her expression hidden.

"No. I'm not."

The rumors had started when they were in their teens. Three young men with charisma and sexuality, who had been the downfall of a local divorcée. It had begun then, at an age that none of the three men would reveal. Too young, Rowdy knew. But damn, it had been hot that summer, and not just from the sun. Loren Barnes had been a quiet, schoolmarmish lady on the outside, but inside she had been hotter than fireworks in July.

She had taken three uncertain virgin boys and, in a few short months, taught them to be men well before their time. All together. All at once. One soft female body, her approval and cries of pleasure penetrating their lust-hazed minds as they took her lessons and drove her to the brink of passion with them.

She taught them how to romance, how to tease, how to cajole, how to subtly drive a woman crazy and make her so wet the slick essence of her would dampen her thighs. She had taught them how much more pleasure they could bring together than alone. And to the Mackay boys, that was what it was all about.

Women were treasures, precious gifts of never-ending excitement, sweetly scented flesh, and mysterious motives. They were a challenge and a comfort, a balm to the soul, and an adventure like nothing else ever created. They were infinitely strong, and yet infinitely vulnerable. Rowdy, Dawg, and Natches had realized years before that alone they couldn't give the pleasure they could together, but also, they couldn't protect as well.

Ironically, it was Kelly who taught them that lesson. As a kid, keeping up with her had been practically impossible for just one of them. It took the three of them to keep her safe, to keep her happy as she grew up. Watching for the bullies who liked to pick on her because she was poor, because she was pretty as a picture and sweetly gentle. And they wanted to keep her that way.

She was also impetuous, defiant, and smart as a whip. There had been nothing sexual involved. She amused them, made them laugh, and challenged them to keep up with her with an innocent thirst for life and adventure that appealed to the teenagers. After her mother married Ray, she was then "family," as well.

As she grew older, as they grew older, things had slowly shifted for all of them. Four years ago it had come to a head. She had just turned twenty, hotter than fireworks and as tempting as sin itself. The three of them had been a little too drunk, a little too wild that night. And she had been there.

"Make up your mind, Rowdy. You don't put a claim on her, one of us is going to." Natches's eyes followed her as she laughed and danced beneath the brilliance of the full summer moon.

"She's still too young." He denied the need, as well as the challenge.

"Keeping the local boys off her ass is getting harder," Dawg muttered. "I'm tired of bruising my knuckles on their thick skulls. Make up your mind. If you don't intend to keep her, one of us will."

Rowdy grimaced, finished his beer, then crumpled the can as he fought to hold onto his control. It was getting harder each time he came home, to stay the hell away from her.

"She's too fucking young and the two of you know it," he snapped. "She's not ready for it."

"She's old enough to make the choice," Natches drawled. "You're going back to the Marines and that's fine. But if she's not willing to wait on you, then we aren't either. Claim her man, or one of us will."

She had been like a fire at midnight. He had to make her want to wait on him. He had to ensure her need for him. And he had done that. But in doing it, he had cemented his need for her.

As he held her in the darkness of the night, the soft warmth of her pressed into his chest, he knew her earlier protest was the key to her soul. The romance. She needed the romance, she deserved it, but God knew he had no idea how to make it romantic. He could give her pleasure. Enough pleasure to leave her screaming in orgasm, begging for more. But the heart of the woman needed more. A lesson Loren had taught them, but one they had forgotten over the years.

The women they had drawn to them hadn't been ones to need the romance, or even want it.

For the first time in his life Rowdy felt helpless. Eliminating the threat to her was imperative. And he wasn't going to lie to her. Not Kelly. She deserved more than that.

"You're not asleep." Her whisper was as soft as a breath.

"Neither are you." He sighed, knowing her mind had been running as fast as his.

They hadn't said much since that final question. She had drawn in a deep, hard breath, informed him she was going to sleep then curled into his arms, and turned out the lights. But she hadn't gone to sleep anymore than he had.

"Why do you do it?" she finally asked. He didn't have to ask what she was talking about. It was a question he had hoped she wouldn't ask. Yet he had known she would.

He slid his hand from her hip to her stomach, feeling the muscles flutter beneath his palm.

"A man's pleasure comes from his woman's," he whispered. "Because we learned how much better it can be for a woman when no part of her body is neglected. Because we learned as young men how much easier it is to protect what's ours when we work together. Hell, Kelly, I could give you a thousand reasons and none of them would really make sense. Because it's who we are, what we are."

"Will it end?" He knew where she was going, what she would eventually ask.

"Only if you want it to. My needs aren't more important than yours. It won't be every time. It won't be an either-or."

She was silent for long moments. He closed his eyes, grimacing in painful awareness of the can of worms he had opened.

"And when they find the women they want for their own? What then?"

"It's not an either-or," he repeated. "I'll do nothing you can't live with, Kelly. Ever."

"But you'll want to." Her voice lowered further. "If Dawg or Natches found a woman they wanted for their own, then you'd want to be a part of it, wouldn't you, Rowdy?"

"I wouldn't miss being a part of it, anymore than you would miss their touch after having had it." There was no way to reassure her, and God knew he wanted to.

He felt her flinch against him.

"You would touch another woman?"

"I would never do anything that would jeopardize us." That wasn't acceptable. "Ever. Not at any time."

As he stared into the darkness, he thought of her touch, her kiss. Could he touch another woman? At any time?

"So it would be my choice?"

"It would be your choice."

"But you would still want to." It wasn't a question.

"I don't know." He couldn't lie to her. He wouldn't lie to her, even though he was terrified of losing her.

He caressed her abdomen as he held her, as silence filled the room once again.

"This might not work." Her voice trembled with an awareness of what she might be looking at. "I don't know if I can do that. I don't know if I could handle your need to do it."

He sighed heavily into her hair, drawing her closer, knowing he could be risking both their hearts with the hungers that tormented him. It was the reason he had left four years before, the reason he couldn't begin this relationship with anything less than the truth.

"I can live without it," he told her softly. "I don't know if I could live without you, Kelly. Not now. Not after the years I've spent needing you. I'll give you everything I am, as much as you want. That's all I can do."

She turned to him then, her soft gray eyes dark in the dim light of the room as he stared into the shadowed expanse of her face.

"The first time . . ."

He closed his eyes. "However you want it."

Bonding came in so many ways. He would have had Dawg and Natches there, but he wouldn't push her. He couldn't push her. Not now.

"You want them there."

His eyes flew open at the soft statement.

"I want them there," he affirmed, knowing her safety demanded nothing less. He ignored the possessiveness raging inside him. "Kelly, I want everything for you, and I know that's hard to understand. The first time, it's special for a woman. It begins a bonding with her lover, one that never really dies. It's why I've never taken a virgin, never fooled with a woman who didn't know the score, until you."

He felt the shiver that raced over her, the little tremor of fear, or response, he wasn't certain.

"You want me to have that, with them?" The uncertainty in her voice, the edge of hurt broke his heart.

"Kelly, listen to me." He framed the side of her face with his hand, his thumb smoothing over her cheek. "I'm not going to do a damned thing that's going to hurt you or make you uncomfortable. Baby, it won't be good for me, or for Dawg and Natches, if it isn't something you want with everything inside you. This is your choice. The perception of it isn't."

"But you want it," she said fiercely.

"Don't make excuses." He could feel it in her then, the need to have the choice taken from her, to be seduced. "I'm not making them and I won't let you. Think about it, Kelly. Decide what you want, what you need. I'm not a kid, and you've known me too long to be able to fool yourself about me. You've known, you wanted to sugarcoat it, pretend it wasn't real, but you knew. Now decide what you want, because I won't make that decision for you. Not now, not ever. I love you, baby, but I can't love you enough for both of us."

He felt her then, her fingers moving against his chest, leaving a path of fire in their wake as they smoothed over his chest.

"Can you do anything without your cousins?" she asked. "Or

do you need their help all the time, Rowdy? Maybe you're the one making excuses."

Damn. Her fingers were at his abdomen now, her nails raking over his flesh, tracing the skin above the waistband of his sweat-pants.

Impetuous. Defiant. An adventure. That was Kelly.

His hand trapped hers, holding it still against him, his eyes narrowing on her in the darkness.

"Anywhere but here," he growled. "Now go to sleep, minx. I'll be damned if I'll have our parents hearing us in here screwing our brains out. I'm right fond of keeping my private parts intact if it's all the same to you."

She chuckled, flipped around, then horror of all horrors, because his control was edging toward nonexistence, that curvy little ass tucked into his hips, cushioning the raging fullness of his cock. *Son of a bitch.*

"Good night, Rowdy." Her husky little purr nearly had him coming in his pants. "Maybe tomorrow we'll see what you can actually do without your cousins around to approve of it."

A grin tilted his lips. Oh, he'd show her all right, in ways she could never imagine.

Eleven

Kelly stared at the bed as she came from the shower the next morning. It was perfectly made, the flowered comforter smoothed out, the pillows neatly stacked at the headboard. And lying at the bottom of the mattress was clothing she hadn't worn since the attack.

The low-rise jeans were patched and faded, and she new exactly how low they were. The waistband barely reached her hipbones, with the snap in the front dipping lower nearly an inch.

The white vest-style summer shirt rose above her navel, and would reveal the belly ring that lay glittering on top of the shirt. The brilliant green emerald twinkled and gleamed beneath a shaft of sunlight coming in from the window. She had chosen that particular gem because of its resemblance to Rowdy's eyes.

Kelly drew in a deep breath before turning her head to stare at Rowdy where he sat in the recliner. Leaning forward, his arms resting on his knees, he watched her silently, emotion swirling in his gaze. Compassion, understanding, determination.

She stepped closer to the bed, turning back to stare at the clothes. She had been too scared to wear them before, terrified that how she dressed had somehow caused the attack.

She was still scared, but as she stood there, she realized that the terror that had often filled her before Rowdy's return wasn't there now. Just as he had protected her from those bullies years before, she knew he would protect her now.

She cleared her throat before speaking.

"You're certain you can catch him? That he's watching me? Waiting?" She picked up the belly ring, staring down at it intently.

"I'm certain, Kelly." His voice was dark, deep, confident.

"Do you know who it is?" She knew Rowdy, and his cousins. And she knew Dawg and Natches had been investigating the attack since it happened.

"Not yet. But we will. He's not sane enough to hide for long."

Could she be a woman again, rather than a child hiding? Kelly admitted, if only silently, that the woman had been protesting the baggy clothes and the lack of adventure for a year now. She was ready to return, just as the psychologist had warned her she would be.

She nodded slowly. "I need to go to town today. To the spa." The intimate waxing had been put off too long.

Tension began to sizzle in the room. She knew he would know what it meant. Rowdy was an expert on a woman's body and all the various procedures they used to tempt a man.

"I'd like to drive you in." His voice was hoarse. "We could pick up dinner later and go out on the lake."

She inhaled roughly before nodding. She could feel her insides quivering with the knowledge that once he got her out on the lake, she would be in his bed.

"That sounds good," she said as she turned back to him slowly.

She dropped the towel that covered her, watched his eyes flame, his face flush, and his body come to immediate attention as she stood before him.

"It's hard to put in." She held the belly ring out to him. "Would you help me?"

"Good God!" His gaze moved to hers slowly. "Dad's home, Kelly. If I fuck you here, he'll kill me."

"I didn't ask you to fuck me, Rowdy." She kept her voice low, intimate as she moved to him. "I asked you to put the ring in." She extended her arm, her fingers holding the glittering gem.

She loved teasing Rowdy, always had. The look in his eyes made her breathless, showed his hunger. It was the reason she had always waited on him, always known she belonged to him. For years, every time he looked at her, he ate her with his eyes, consumed her with the hunger in them. Just as he did now.

Without speaking, he moved forward on the chair, spreading

his legs before his hand gripped her hips, pulling her to him. His hands were hot on her flesh, sending sizzling impulses of pleasure raking over her nerve endings.

"Give me the ring." His expression was heavy with sensual intent as he took the ring from her fingers.

Kelly stood still, silent as he inserted the curved metal into the tiny hole before snapping the ball end in place. But he didn't stop touching her there. He positioned the emerald teardrop in place over the entrance to her navel before his fingertips skimmed over her lower belly.

Her womb convulsed beneath his fingers as pleasure tore through her. Lower, she felt the curves of her pussy dampen further than they already were as her vagina pulsed in heavy need.

"Look how pretty," he whispered, his eyes centering between her thighs as her fingers gripped his shoulders and her knees trembled. "You're wet for me, Kelly."

"I'm always wet for you. I've been wet for you for years, Rowdy," she informed him, her voice almost a whimper of hunger.

She realized then the mistake she had made in teasing him. She was too hungry, needed him too much to tempt what she knew she couldn't have beneath Ray's roof.

She stared down at Rowdy in a haze of need as he shifted, his head coming closer, his lips pressing into her lower belly as she gasped at the contact. Long-fingered hands smoothed down her hips to her thighs, nudging them apart gently before raising his head. He stared at the flushed folds of her mound. His thumb caressed over the tattoo just above her pussy. The eagle in flight, one wing dipping toward her damp flesh.

"I want to taste you, Kelly," he groaned, his voice roughening further. "I want to lay you down, spread those pretty legs, and lick all that soft syrup from you."

Weakness flooded her, taking her breath, her senses, and turning them into one hard ache for just that.

"You're so wet." The fingers of one hand trailed around her thigh, then slid slowly, so slowly, but with destructive results, through the thick wetness that lay between the soft folds of flesh.

"Rowdy," she breathed, her fingers sliding to his hair as his head dipped to her belly again. "Please touch me. Please."

She had waited so long, dreamed so desperately of his touch that now that it was happening, she feared it was just another dream.

"I'm going to do more than touch you, baby," he whispered as his lips moved closer to the pounding ache of her clit. "I'm going to touch you, taste you, I'm going to make you scream for me, Kelly. Beg for more."

Okay. She could handle that.

"Now."

She felt his chuckle, the sound rasping, filled with hunger as his fingers circled her clit. Her hips arched forward as a low cry left her lips. Need flamed inside her with an intensity that drove anything else from her mind.

"Shhh, baby," he groaned, his fingers parting her. "Remember Ray."

Ray who?

His breath whispered over the damp, throbbing bud, sending her senses reeling as a knock sounded at the door. Kelly jerked in Rowdy's grip as she felt him tense beneath her hold.

"Rowdy, I'm heading out. I need to talk to you before I leave," Ray called through the thick panel. "Get out here, boy, so I can get to work."

She heard his footsteps retreating as Rowdy's fingers slowly slid from her flesh.

"Damn," he breathed out, moving her back as he lifted his head to stare back at her. "You're dangerous, darlin'."

"Don't stop." Kelly shook her head as he rose from the chair, his hands smoothing up her back, yet holding her from him.

"I'll take you to the spa," he whispered. "And later, I'll show you how much I love having your sweet pussy bare to me. Get dressed, baby, so we can escape for awhile."

His lips whispered over hers, ignoring her silent plea for more as her lips parted.

"Get dressed," he told her again, moving back. "Stop driving me crazy, baby. Let's get out of here."

Okay, two could play this game, Kelly was certain. With narrowed eyes she watched as Rowdy stalked from the bedroom, his body tight with tension and the bulge in his pants so apparent he had pulled the tail of his white cotton shirt free of his pants to cover it. She was sure there was no way Ray wouldn't be aware of his son's problem.

She snickered at the thought of the tough Rowdy squirming beneath his father's gaze. Ray was a good guy, but she knew how he was. He hadn't wanted this relationship to develop between her and Rowdy, neither had her mother, though she wasn't certain why. She had loved Rowdy forever, and despite Ray and her mother's marriage, she had never understood the reasons for their disapproval.

Twenty minutes later, dressed and feeling more feminine and less afraid than she had in months, Kelly picked up her phone and called the spa. Marla Reiner, her favorite technician, was available and eager to see Kelly returning to her regular visits. With a little maneuvering, Marla managed to schedule her right in and disconnected the call with a cheery good-bye.

Drawing in a deep breath, Kelly placed her hand on her stomach to still the butterflies racing through her system before she moved to her bedroom door and headed downstairs.

In the back of her mind was the knowledge that nothing would ever be the same from this day on. Once Rowdy had her, she knew what would happen. Questions still plagued her, as did an instinctive discomfort regarding the idea that Rowdy could ever want to touch another woman, no matter the relationship that developed between her and his cousins.

God, it was so strange having that thought in her mind. It had always stayed distant, an awareness of what could happen if she ever got into Rowdy's bed. There wouldn't be just one man, but three pleasuring her. Now that it could be reality, she found herself both curious and hesitant. Aroused and frightened. But Kelly knew she wasn't willing to draw back. Maybe she was different, maybe she wasn't.

For years rumors had abounded of the Mackay cousins. Women whispered their names with naughty pleasure at the thought of them. Her friends had jokingly informed her that she was insane for not moving into Dawg's or Natches's bed while Rowdy was in the service.

She could have. But deep inside she knew that who her heart belonged to made a difference. Alone, Dawg and Natches held no appeal for her. But with Rowdy . . .

She stepped into the kitchen, watching as he turned to face her, his deep green eyes approving, and hungry.

She belonged to Rowdy.

God, she was gorgeous. Rowdy couldn't keep his eyes off her as he drove the truck into Somerset, listening to her soft voice relating the local gossip.

Johnny Flowers traded wives with his worst enemy, Buck Layne. Crista Jansen was back home and had moved into her parents' home place outside of town. No one knew why she had returned to town after years away, but everyone was gossiping about it. Rowdy bet Dawg was interested in that one. He had been hot as hell for Crista before she ran off to college eight years before.

One of Rowdy's old girlfriends now owned the café he and Dawg and Natches had frequented before Rowdy left, and for the most part, for all the things that had changed, everything was pretty much the same. It was one of the things Rowdy loved about home. It was familiar, endearing.

Lake Cumberland was a place of mystery and beauty, and the small towns that surrounded it were filled with friends and family and memories that had gotten him through the last eight years in the service.

And memories of Kelly.

He glanced at her again, the light reflecting off the emerald at her pretty belly drawing his gaze again. It made his dick hard. Damn, he was dying for her, his cock was throbbing in his jeans and his mouth watering for the taste of her.

He entered the city limits, navigating the summer traffic as he drove to the popular spa the women in town seemed to flock to.

"Here you go." He pulled into an empty space in front of the entrance and turned to her. "I programmed my number into your cell phone; call me before you leave. I'm meeting Dawg and Natches at the café up the street, so I won't be far."

Those kissable lips curved into a slow, promising smile as she leaned close.

"I bet I could walk down the street all by myself, Rowdy," she whispered teasingly, sending a jolt of fear to slice through his soul.

"No!" He hadn't meant his voice to be so harsh, but the slight flinch and the spark of fear and anger that filled her eyes assured him he was much harsher than he intended to be.

Rowdy drew in a quick, hard breath before pushing his fingers through his hair, frustration eating him alive.

"I'm sorry, baby," he growled, his voice still rougher than he wanted. "Don't scare me like that. Give me a while, okay?" He gave her a quick, comforting smile. "Let me protect you, Kelly."

She sat against the door now, her gray eyes quiet, her expression closed until she glanced away and lowered her head.

"I understand, Rowdy," she finally sighed. "But I'm tired of hiding." She turned back to him, a frown edging at her brows. "I'm tired of letting him win."

"Kelly, promise me you'll call me before you leave." He reached out to her, his fingers running down her cheek, feeling the small quiver of response that ran through her. "Don't fight me on this, please. He's a madman—"

"I'm not crazy." She brushed his hand away as she glared back at him. "I'll call you, Rowdy. But I don't think he's going to try anything in broad daylight. It would be too risky."

"Point taken." He nodded. "But we can't be certain, either. Until I know what we're dealing with, we're going to be careful."

"So says the man who wants to poke at the crazy person by letting him think I'm taking on the Mackay cousins all at once," she reminded him. "I think walking down the street is a hell of a lot safer."

"Exactly why you shouldn't be walking down the street alone," he pointed out softly. "He knows I have you now, Kelly. Which means Dawg and Natches aren't far behind, in his eyes. From here on out, we can't underestimate him; we take nothing for granted."

Rowdy forcibly tamped down the violence rising inside him. He knew if he ever managed to get hold of the bastard who dared to touch her, then he would kill him. There would be nothing left for justice to convict.

"Fine. I'll call you before I leave," she snapped with a spark of anger he couldn't blame her for. "But don't take forever to pick me up, if you don't mind. I have a few other things I'd like to do while I'm in town. And I'd appreciate a little less paranoia until he actually shows that he *is* stalking me."

She reached out to grip the door handle. Just as fast Rowdy caught her arm, causing her to turn back to him. His hand moved, his fingers threading through her hair as he drew her head back and captured her lips quickly with his.

Summer heat, lightning, and the sweet taste of a woman's passion met his hunger, tightening his gut with lust. He couldn't wait to get her beneath him. At that moment, nothing mattered except getting through the rest of the day until he could get her to the houseboat and the large bed awaiting them there.

He forced himself to release her seconds later, staring into her dazed features with a satisfaction so intense it caused his balls to tighten.

"That wasn't fair." She smiled despite the chastisement, her cheeks flushed with warmth and her breathing ragged.

"Sure it was," he whispered, pulling back from her, despite the need to wrap her in his arms and run away with her. He wanted to hide her. To make certain no one could ever touch her again. "I need to touch you, babe. That's always fair considering how long I've waited to do it."

She snorted at that before pushing her fingers through her hair and flashing him a disgruntled look. "No one made you wait."

She was out of the truck before he could stop her, tossing him a cheery smile before crossing the sidewalk and entering the spa.

Rowdy breathed out roughly. She was going to be the death of him, there was just no other way around it. With her shining innocence, tempting eyes, and sweetly rounded body, he knew she was capable of making him curse as often as he sighed in need.

He gave his head a quick jerk before reversing from the parking spot and driving farther down the street to the café he had told Dawg and Natches to meet him in.

Reginald's Café was newly remodeled, the inside cool and welcoming as he entered. Dawg and Natches were waiting at one of the back tables, steaming cups of coffee sitting in front of them.

"'Bout time you got here, cuz," Dawg grunted as he slid into the chair across from him. "I thought we were gonna have to come down there and rescue Kelly from your clutches ourselves."

Natches chuckled as Rowdy leaned back in his chair and watched his cousin curiously. Dawg had changed over the years, more than any of them, Rowdy sometimes thought. He was darker, despite the joviality, quieter than he used to be.

Rowdy didn't know what had happened during the years he spent in the Marines, but it had affected his cousin. Natches was just as lazy as always, his smile quiet, his eyes watchful. Of course, none of them were as relaxed, as carefree as they used to be.

There was a darkness in them that had always lurked just beneath the surface. A difference that separated them from other men, made them appear wilder, more dangerous. And in ways they were more dangerous. They had proved that overseas.

"What's up?" Rowdy could tell there was more going on than a general bad mood.

Dawg leaned forward, his eyes narrowed.

"You had company outside the house last night." Dawg's voice was low. "On that little knob above the house that looks into Kelly's room. I was checking it out this morning before heading here. He must have been there all night. The grass was indented where he sat, with claw marks at the side where the bastard dug his fingers into the ground. He's getting pissed."

Hell. Rowdy had known Kelly's attacker was watching, waiting. He just hadn't been certain where, or how.

"Where do we go from here, Rowdy?" Natches watched him with a spark of excitement in his eyes that Rowdy knew was as much to the thought of a good fight as to the chance of touching Kelly.

"I'm taking her back to the boat this evening," he answered. "We'll head out to the cove. We should be staying the night. We'll see how brave he wants to get. We'll have dinner on the boat. Let the bastard think we're all having a fine time. After dark the two of you can slip on shore and I'll pull farther out into the water. We'll see what happens."

Dawg and Natches nodded somberly. They were waiting, watchful, their bodies now on high alert. Not that anyone else would have noticed the change.

They paused as the waitress moved toward them, her steps slow, her head down, waves of burnished chestnut curls pulled into a low ponytail, her classically pretty features stiff and tense.

Rowdy cocked his head at the woman. Crista Jensen kept her head carefully lowered as she refilled the coffee cups before turning to leave.

"You didn't ask me if I wanted anything to eat, Crista." Dawg surprised them all with his mocking drawl. "Didn't Jenny warn you to look after us good?"

"Shut up, Dawg," Natches muttered, his voice low but easy to hear.

Rowdy watched as Crista pulled the ordering pad from the back pocket of her jeans, a pencil from behind her ear and watched Dawg with a spark of anger. Dawg stared back at her expectantly.

"What would you like to order, Dawg?" Her words were gritted, her voice raspy.

"Eh. Nothing right now, but be sure to check back in a few minutes." Dawg's smile was all teeth, a predatory snarl if Rowdy had ever seen one.

"I'll be sure to do that." Crista's smile was no less antagonistic as she returned the order pad to the back pocket of her jeans, picked up the coffeepot, and stalked away.

The minute her back turned, Dawg's eyes narrowed and a flash of anger seared the depths as he rose to his feet, dug into his pocket, and slapped a few dollars to the table.

"I'll see you at the marina," he snapped before stalking from the café.

Rowdy watched, perplexed, before turning to Natches.

"What the hell was that?"

"Dawg in heat," Natches snickered. "She won't give him the time of day."

Rowdy glanced to the woman in question and restrained his smile as he noticed her gaze, centered squarely on Dawg as he stormed from the café. Sad, weary, her expression marked with indecision. Yeah, she was giving him the time of day, perhaps more than the big lug deserved.

Now this was an interesting development.

"So, how are we playing tonight? One on one or is she ready for all of us?"

"Kelly will let us know what she wants." Rowdy shifted his shoulders, a primitive surge of something akin to possessiveness rising inside him as Natches watched him curiously.

That was strange. He was one second from baring his teeth and daring Natches to touch Kelly. He knew the pleasure the three of them could bring her, versus the pleasure he alone could bestow. So what the fuck was his problem all of a sudden?

Shit. He could feel the back of his neck prickling as irritation began to surge inside him.

"Waiting on her has been a bitch," Natches grimaced, his light green eyes gleaming with lustful determination. "She's going to go up in flames—"

"Shut up, Natches." Rowdy lifted his coffee cup to his lips, glaring at his cousin across the table as Crista moved to a table close to them.

Natches watched the woman, his expression considering.

"Something's up with that one," he sighed. "Dawg has been like a bear with a sore tail ever since she arrived back in town. She didn't even let the family know she was coming."

"What about her husband? Didn't she marry some guy from Virginia?"

Natches shook his head. "She was engaged for awhile. Guess it fell through."

Rowdy almost breathed a sigh of relief that the conversation had moved from Kelly. He was going to have to figure this out. Now wasn't a time to be hedging between desires, dammit. But he was hedging, and he knew it.

He glanced at Crista Jansen again, narrowing his eyes. Dawg had had a thing for the other woman for years. She had always managed to resist his charms, his attempts to talk to her, to seduce here.

Rowdy and Natches had watched him attempt to bargain for a single date from her for nearly a year before they joined the Marines, and Natches had related that the first thing Dawg had gone looking for when he came home from the service was Crista. Only to learn she had left Somerset.

Could he fuck her? Rowdy turned his gaze back to the Formica-topped table and sipped from his coffee again. A year ago, he could have, easily. The thought of having her between himself and his two cousins would have had his dick perking in interest.

His dick wasn't interested. He frowned. Hell, there was no excitement, period. He stared back at her.

She was pretty enough. Nicely rounded. She moved a little self-consciously, as though not quite comfortable with what she was doing.

Her face was a rounded oval, her skin clear and silky-looking.

Nice hair. But he wasn't interested. He wasn't aroused. As a matter of fact, the urge to get up and leave the café was so damned strong it was all he could do to stay in place.

He should have been practically drooling at the thought of helping Dawg and Natches fuck her to oblivion. They were sure as hell hot enough at the thought of fucking Kelly.

"Can I get you two anything else?" Crista refilled the coffee cup, her expression resigned for some reason as she glanced at Dawg's chair.

"An explanation would be nice." Rowdy lifted his head, watching her closely as she seemed to pale.

"Excuse me?"

"Dawg's been chasing you for years, Crista. What's up?"

Crista's eyes burned with anger as she slowly tucked the ordering pad into her back pocket and glared at him furiously.

"I'm not a plaything for the three of you," she snarled then, surprising him and Natches. "If you cared for anything past yourselves then you damned well wouldn't expect it. You'd grow the hell up and get over it."

Her voice was hoarse as tears sheened her eyes before she blinked them back furiously.

"Forget it," she snapped. "The three of you might as well be clones of each other. You can't even breathe alone."

Turning, she stalked back to the register where two customers waited, her fingers stabbing at the input keys as she flicked a scornful glance back at them.

"Have I been gone too long?" Rowdy turned back to Natches, gratified to see the same surprise reflecting in his face.

"Damn, and she used to be such a nice, quiet little girl," Natches grumped as he scratched at his chin.

Rowdy snorted at the description. Crista had been anything but nice and quiet and they all knew it.

"I don't have a problem breathing without your help." Rowdy grinned as he finished his coffee.

"Damned good thing." Natches shook his head as he peeked another look back at the little waitress, a frown pulling at his brow. "Hell, you've been gone eight years, Rowdy, and other than a few times you were home, me and Dawg's been pretty damned tame. What the hell has her by the ear anyway?"

Rowdy shook his head as he glanced at his empty coffee cup.

"Do you think she's going to bring us more coffee?" he asked ruefully.

Both men looked back at the woman, estimating their chances for caffeine.

"If she knows what's good for her." Natches's grin was wicked. "Or else, I might have to call Dawg back to sweet-talk her for us."

Rowdy chuckled, though when he glanced back at Crista he could feel the frown tugging at his brow again. The fact that Dawg wanted her should have been all it took to produce a raging hard-on and more than a surfeit of interest. Instead, all he felt was an edge of sadness. Their lifestyle, the very truth of their sexuality stood between Dawg and a woman Rowdy knew had to be more than interested in the other man.

Women didn't get that upset if they weren't interested. If they didn't care. Crista Jansen cared—it had been there in her eyes, in her anger. But he had to agree with one thing. She wasn't the type of woman who would willingly share her man, anymore than Kelly was. And that was the clincher. She was a woman worth keeping, a one-man woman. And she needed a one-woman man.

Twelve

Kelly waited at the door of the spa, watching as Rowdy pulled into the parking area in the pickup. She felt naughty as she waited for him, her body waxed and buffed, smoothed and lotioned.

As he stepped out of the pickup she pushed open the door and moved out to meet him, returning his smile as she felt the flush across her cheeks.

"Ready?" He opened the passenger-side door as she neared the truck, his green eyes intent as he watched her closely.

"All ready." Her voice trembled, dammit. Then she trembled all over as his hands gripped her hips and he lifted her into the seat of the truck.

She could feel the blush deepening in her face.

"Damn, that blush is pretty." Rowdy cupped her face, turning her face to him for a quick kiss and a wicked grin.

"And you're bad," she laughed as he moved back, winking at her before closing the door and heading back to the driver's side.

Within seconds, the interior of the truck was once again filled with his scent. Male. No cologne. Just the scent of primal heat teasing her senses.

"Hungry?" he asked as he slid the vehicle into reverse and pulled out of the parking spot.

"Starved." Her stomach was convinced she hadn't eaten in weeks.

"Why don't we pick up a few greasy cheeseburgers and fries and head out to the boat for awhile?" He suggested smoothly, glancing at her from the corner of his eye as she felt her heart race.

Alone on the boat with Rowdy? And he had to ask?

"Sounds good." She nodded as her thighs clenched and her breasts suddenly felt heavier, more sensitive.

There was something in his expression that warned her he was tired of waiting. A ready stillness, a tension. Rowdy had shown amazing restraint to this point. She had a feeling that patience had come to an abrupt end.

"Will we be taking the boat out?"

"No. The marina is pretty empty today," he said as he made a quick turn into a local fast-food restaurant. "I thought we'd eat, laze around, drink a few beers, and talk."

"Talk," she repeated slowly.

"And other things." There was no smile this time, no teasing, no edging around what they both wanted as he stared back at her. "Still want to go?"

"Yes." Kelly stared back at him, trying to regulate her breathing, to still the excitement climbing inside her.

He nodded slowly before turning his gaze back to the drive-thru he was pulling up beside.

Good to his word, he ordered greasy cheeseburgers, several of them, and masses of fries.

They were silent as he pulled forward, paid for the food, and collected the bag before driving back onto the road. Kelly watched the miles pass, staying quiet. She had waited for this, for too long she sometimes thought. And now, knowing that the waiting was nearly at an end, she could feel her nerves rocketing.

She was a virgin. There wasn't a chance in hell she knew near enough about the male body to please him the first time. Suddenly, she almost regretted waiting. Maybe she should have gone for some kind of experience, but there had been no desire to become intimate with the men she had dated.

Not that she normally dated them long. Dawg and Natches were always too close, always butting their noses into her dates. She had found it amusing over the years, but now she wondered if she should have put a stop to it. Should have at least tried to learn how to please a man.

She wanted to please Rowdy. She wanted to know how to touch him, how to excite him.

"Stop worrying so much," he chastised gently as they neared the marina.

"I'm not worrying." She forced a smile to her face. She was not going to act like a nervous teenager.

He snorted at her denial, his gaze knowing as he glanced at her again. "I know you, Kelly. You're sitting over there biting a hole in your lip. That means you're worrying."

Damn. Busted.

"You don't know everything, Rowdy Mackay." She stuck her tongue out at him as she tossed her head defiantly. "You just think you do."

"I know damned near everything about you," he argued, his lips pulling into a sensual smile as he turned the truck along the lakefront road. "When you're biting your lip like that, you're worrying. And there's nothing that's going to happen between us that you need to worry about. Anticipate maybe." There was that wicked smile again. "But nothing to worry about."

Her face heated again. Damn him. Blushing was not her favorite thing to do.

"What are you going to do if Ray comes out to the boat to check on us?" She leaned back in her seat and regarded him in amusement now. "You know how overprotective he gets."

"Dad had to drive to Louisville this morning." Satisfaction filled his voice. "Your mom went with him. They have the Colberts minding the store and pumps while they're gone."

"So while the cat's away the mouse gets to play, huh?" she asked with a laugh.

"Mouse?" He frowned back playfully. "Sweetheart, trust me here, there ain't no mice on my boat. But the big bad wolf might end up devouring a certain little lamb for sure."

Kelly couldn't help the laugh that bubbled from her throat as Rowdy pulled into the parking slot nearest the entrance to the upper end of the docks. The locked gate was normally for maintenance only, but the Mackay cousins used it rather than walking the distance along the docks to the main entrance.

He laid his forearms over the steering wheel as he turned to look at her then, his green eyes capturing hers as all amusement fled his expression. "Are you ready?"

Kelly inhaled slowly. "I've been ready for years, Rowdy. You're the one that took his own sweet time."

He was dying for her. Rowdy clenched his teeth as he placed his hand at Kelly's back and led her along the floating dock to the *Nauti Buoy*. At this rate, his cock was going to permanently carry the imprint of his zipper. Every step he took the scent of her filled his head; beneath his hand the silken feel of her flesh tortured his senses.

In his other hand he carried the food, which meant he was going to wait to consume Kelly. And waiting wasn't high on his list of priorities today.

The knowledge that the bastard who had attacked her was watching her burned at him. *The son of a bitch.* Rowdy had known he was watching, could feel it, but the proof of it sent fury surging through his veins.

Just five minutes with the bastard, he thought, that was all he needed. *Hell five seconds. Just long enough to relish hearing the son of a bitch's neck break.* Rowdy swore if he got his hands on the man who dared to hurt her, he would die. Never, not ever, would he threaten Kelly again.

"Where are your cousins?" Kelly asked as they neared the *Nauti Dawg*. Rowdy's boat was now sitting between Dawg's and Natches's.

"I didn't ask their schedule." He grinned.

They were around, watching. Seeing who was paying attention to the three boats now parked off to themselves in the temporary docks normally reserved for those boats waiting transporting out of the lake. Later tonight they would be positioned on the hill above the house instead. It was time to catch this bastard, before he went completely off the deep end.

He swore he felt a shiver race up her spine and hid his smile. Kelly was curious, but wary. Until he let her know Dawg and Natches wouldn't be there, she hadn't totally relaxed with him.

"Do you think I would push them on you, Kelly?" He asked softly as they stepped onto the *Nauti Buoy* and he unlocked the glass sliding doors.

"No, I didn't." She shrugged as he glanced over at her. "And I do know how to say 'no,' Rowdy."

But would she say 'no'? It was something he hadn't wanted to think about. He deliberately didn't think about it simply because each time the subject came up he got heartburn. He'd never had heartburn a day in his life, but lately, it was becoming a daily malady.

"Yeah, I know you know how to say no," he grunted as he sat the food on the table and turned back to her. "That's what you told me every time I tried to get you to help me in the yard when you were younger."

"Tried to con me into doing the yard myself." She gave him a knowing look. "Try another one hotshot. I knew your tricks. You would leave me to it and disappear with your buddies without worrying about me following you."

He sighed heavily, but he wasn't fooling her.

"I'm so misunderstood." He shook his head as he neared her, his lashes lowered, his expression just sexy as hell as he passed her.

"Ouch!" She jumped as the palm of his hand landed on her butt before he locked the doors then pulled the heavy drapes over the glass.

"That's what you get for being sassy." He laughed at her frown. "Get over here and eat, woman, then you can show me your wax job."

"I'm not a car, Rowdy." She rolled her eyes despite the flaming awareness sizzling through her body.

She tried not to stare at him, tried not to sink into the brilliance of those green eyes, glittering with hunger and emotion. But it was damned hard not to.

The jeans he was wearing conformed to his hard thighs and emphasized the mouthwatering bulge between them. The shirt he wore stretched across his broad chest and molded to his hard abs. If there was an ounce of fat on his body she couldn't see it.

"Come on, sugar girl." His voice lowered as he moved to the table, turning on the small light hanging overhead. "You empty the bag and I'll get the beer."

Beer and cheeseburgers. Kelly couldn't remember a meal she had enjoyed more as she sat across from Rowdy and talked. They argued. They always argued. Over the weather signs, the best fishing holes, and life in general.

"I think you disagree with me just to have something to do," Rowdy finally laughed as she tossed a French fry at his head.

"Probably. I'd hate for you to confuse me with all those women who swoon at your feet and beg for your attention," she pointed out before finishing her beer and setting the bottle aside. "You're spoiled, Rowdy."

"I *wish* I was spoiled." He sat back in his chair and looked at her. He just looked at her, his gaze intent now rather than teasing or flirting. "I remember the day I realized you were turning into a woman," he finally said softly, his voice deepening. "You were going out with that little prick Charlie Dayne. Your skirt was too short, your legs too tanned and you wearing the necklace I had bought you that Christmas. That damned little heart was laying right on the upper curve of your breast because that shirt was cut too low."

"You tried to get Mom to make me change clothes." She remembered. She remembered seeing his eyes that day, seeing the wild fire in them that nearly stole her breath.

"You were sixteen fucking years old," he whispered. "And all I could think about"—he shook his head—"I should have been shot for what I was thinking, Kelly."

"I thought about you then too." She was mesmerized by the fire in his eyes now. "I only went out with Charlie because I knew you didn't like him."

His eyes narrowed. "Donnie Winters?"

She leaned forward with a little snicker. "He liked you more than he liked me. He thought you were hot, Rowdy."

He blinked back at her before realization dawned in his eyes. "You little minx." He shuddered.

"I had six months of free hand washes for my car at his parents' car detailing shop simply because he got to see you without your shirt on." She laughed, moving cautiously from the table as he leaned forward in his chair, obviously remembering the fact that he had been outside working on his car that day. Shirtless. And the date had been unexpected, a spur of the moment decision Kelly had made.

"You sold my body for a few car washes?" He asked slowly.

Kelly giggled. "A few? Hey stud, one a week for six months. I told you, you were hot."

"I'm going to paddle your ass." He came out of his chair, watching carefully as she backed away from him, trying not to laugh at the outrage in his expression.

"He went on all evening about the sweat dripping down your chest, Rowdy," she snickered. "I think he was more impressed than I was." She shrieked as he bounded over the table, turned, and tried to run.

There was no place to run, and controlling her laughter enough to actually fend him off was impossible, especially once his fingers found the ultrasensitive ticklish areas in her sides and sent her to the floor as she fought his attacking fingers.

"Oh, God. Don't you tickle me," she cried breathlessly, rolling, bucking against him as he came over her, his teeth bared in a laughing growl as he caught her hands, stretching them over her head, and stared her down with mocking retribution.

"You'll pay for that, Kelly," he promised wickedly.

"What are you going to do, stud?" She blew him an air kiss before collapsing in giggles again as he tickled down her side.

"I surrender," she laughed breathlessly, twisting beneath him, desperate to escape the fingers. "I promise. I promise. I surrender."

His fingers stilled, but he didn't move. Her eyes opened, the laughter dying on her lips at the hunger in his face. He was doing nothing to hide it now, nothing to dilute it. And it stole her breath.

"Rowdy," she whispered his name, her heart suddenly slamming against her ribs as his gaze dropped to the buttons of her blouse.

"You were sixteen years old," he whispered. "And all I could think about was doing this."

His head lowered, his lips pressing to the upper swell of one breast as his tongue licked over it. Velvet flames rasped over her flesh as a shock of sensation slammed into her womb.

"And this." His head lifted. "Open your lips for me baby, let me show you why I had to run has hard and as fast as I could run."

He kept hold of her arms, keeping them stretched above her head, helpless beneath him, restrained as his lips lowered and stole her breath.

Heat flamed through her, ripping across nerve endings and destroying any sense of control as his lips slanted across hers in a kiss guaranteed to wipe every thought from her mind except for thoughts of him.

Kelly arched to him, a broken moan leaving her lips as his

tongue laved the lower curve, slipped in to tease hers then retreated as he bestowed a series of deep, short kisses that had her begging for more.

"God, the taste of you," he whispered before licking at her lips again. "You make me hungrier than I've ever been in my life, Kelly. You make me lose my mind with my need for you."

"I can handle that," she panted, breathless, on fire for him now. "Lose your mind some more now."

She arched her neck as his lips slid down it, his free hand moving to the small buttons of her blouse and slowly, too slowly, pushing them through the buttonholes as his lips followed the path he was revealing.

"Oh God, Rowdy," she moaned as his teeth raked over the sensitive chord in her neck as her blouse parted, revealing the white lace bra she had worn beneath it.

Sexy and silky, the bra was bought with Rowdy in mind during his last trip home.

"Sweet Kelly," he groaned as his lips traveled to the valley of her breasts, his tongue licking at the curves as he then flicked open the little closure at the front of the bra.

She was going to explode. She was going to melt. Kelly could feel the perspiration gathering on her body as tension tightened her and arousal prepared her.

"Such pretty breasts. And sweet, sweet hard little nipples." His fingers pulled back the cup of her bra to reveal one swollen curve, peaked with a tight, reddened nipple. "Like perfect ripe little berries."

When his tongue curled around the peak and drew it in his mouth, Kelly was certain she lost her mind. Stars exploded behind her closed eyelids and a whimpering moan tore from her throat as he began to suckle.

It was so good it was killing her. Her head twisted against the carpet as she strained beneath him, desperate to be free as the pleasure began to tear through her body.

She didn't just feel the draw of his mouth on that nipple, but an echo of it in the other nipple. Fingers of sensation trailed to her womb, then ricocheted to her clit and beyond. The slow, sweet suction erupted in pinpoints of flames throughout her body and left her gasping, nearly incoherent beneath the caress.

"God, you're sweet." Rough. Hoarse. The obvious hunger

and need in his voice left her weak even as her nerve endings sizzled with unbearable heat.

This was what she had dreamed of, waited on. Rowdy holding her, his voice husky, his desire for her obvious in each touch, each kiss.

"Don't stop," she begged as he stroked his cheek over the sensitized nipple. "Not yet." She would hate to have to kill him.

"Never," he growled. "Not ever. But I won't take you here."

Before she could catch him, pull him back to her, he was on his feet and lifting her body against his. The room seemed to tilt, the world around her shaking as his lips covered hers again and his hard arms lifted her against him.

Tension radiated in the air around them as she realized the world was tilting because he was lifting her in his arms. It was shaking because he was moving quickly to the steps that led to the bedroom upstairs. Then it stilled, and only the fireworks remained as she felt the mattress beneath her back and Rowdy coming over her.

Her breath caught at the feel of his big, heavy body above her, sheltering her, protecting her. As long as Rowdy was near, then she would always be safe. And warm. Hot even.

She arched against him as he drew the blouse and the strap of her bra from one shoulder, his lips caressing her skin with heated strokes as he undressed her.

"The thought of your soft, waxed flesh has tormented me today," he growled as he lifted her, his hands pulling the clothing from her body as her head fell back on her shoulders to allow his lips to caress her neck.

"Do you have any idea how bad I want to bury my lips between your legs?" He nipped at the rounded curve of her breast as he tossed the shirt and bra to the side and lowered her back to the mattress. "So bad, Kelly, that I stay hard thinking about the taste of you."

His voice was rough, deep. The dark timbre sent shivers racing over her body as she trembled beneath him, her hands reaching up to touch his bare shoulders while his fingers went to the button of her jeans.

Sharp explosions of sensation began to vibrate through her clit, her vagina, as a maelstrom of pleasure whipped through her body.

Finally. God, finally he was touching her as she needed to be touched, holding her, sliding the jeans and thong from her to bare the sensitive, damp folds of her pussy.

"God. Oh hell, Kelly."

Her eyes opened at the serrated sound of his voice, her lashes fluttering over her eyes as she focused on his face. His expression was primal, intent as he stared between her thighs before lifting his gaze to hers.

"You're wet for me." His hand reached out, his fingers running through the drenched slit as she arched, a broken cry leaving her lips at the wake of fire that trailed with his touch.

Then she lost her breath entirely as he brought those fingers to his lips, tasting her, his gaze deepening, his eyes growing brighter as he suddenly moved from the bed, his hands going to his own jeans.

Within seconds he was naked, his hard body gleaming with sweat, the engorged crest of his erection glistening with pre-come.

"I want to taste you," she whispered then, lifting up, reaching for him, desperate for him.

He was hard. Heavy. Her fingers wrapped around the base of his cock and her head lowered, her tongue swiping over the engorged head.

Oh he liked that. The mushroomed head pulsed and spilled a glistening droplet of pre-come. Which she had to lick off. Taste.

"Put it in your mouth." His hands were in her hair now, his green eyes glittering with lust. "Suck it, baby."

Her lips opened slowly as he pressed the thickly flared head against them, cupping over it as it slid into the warmth of her mouth.

A tight grimace pulled at his lips. "Fuck yeah. God, you look pretty. So sweet and pretty."

Kelly swiped her tongue over the throbbing crest, moaning at the dark, erotic taste of his flesh as he began to move, to thrust in small, easy movements against her lips as she began to suck delicately.

It was so good. So sexy. Her gaze was locked on his, her mouth filled with his erection as her hands stroked the straining shaft.

It was the stuff of fantasies. His hands pulling at her hair, burying his cock almost to her throat while his muscles strained from hunger. Hunger for her. For her touch. For her body.

"Not yet, baby. I can't come yet. Oh, God, not yet." He held her back, controlling her needy denial as he pulled his cock from her lips. One hand pressed her back to the bed as he moved between her thighs once again. "Let me have you first, Kelly. Just this once, baby."

His hands restrained her gently, pressing her back to the bed as his head lowered to the wet folds between her thighs, and her senses ignited.

His tongue rasped over the bare, tender flesh with the softest stroke, licking at her, burning her with each touch as she fought to get closer.

It wasn't enough. She needed more.

"Rowdy . . ." Her wail of need tore from her throat as his tongue flickered around her clit, sending pulsating, fiery fingers of sensation wrapping around the tight bundle of nerves. Kelly strained closer, her head thrashing on the bed as her hands dug into his hair and she fought to hold him to her.

Just another second. She knew if he would linger right there, right where the pleasure burned deeper, then the agonizing need tearing through her would ease.

Just another second.

She cried out again as he hummed against her flesh, his hands parting her legs further before she felt the slightest pressure at the entrance to her vagina. A parting, a caress that sent her senses spinning.

"Rowdy, please . . . please . . ." She couldn't hold back the pleas, the need for release.

"So sweet," he crooned against her clit, causing her to jerk, to arch, the terrible need tormenting her only growing by the second now.

Wicked electric arcs of pleasure whipped over her flesh as perspiration began to cover her body and the hunger straining in every cell drove her closer to the brink. She needed. She ached.

She screamed as his lips covered her clit, his tongue flickering as he suckled at her flesh and stars exploded before her closed eyes.

Release was cataclysmic; it erupted inside her, drawing her muscles tight, pulling her upper body forward as she fought for something to hold onto, to find a sense of balance. A balance that couldn't exist within the fiery ecstasy overtaking her.

"Jesus! Kelly." Rowdy rose fiercely between her thighs, a hazy image invading her senses as she stared back at him, dazed, uncomprehending until she felt the sudden, thick pressure parting her, pressing against the convulsing entrance to her vagina.

"Now." She couldn't scream, she could barely speak. "Please. Please . . ."

Her hands gripped his wrists now, her upper body still tense, tight, lifting to him as her gaze dropped between her thighs. There, straining, thick, his cock pressed against her as his hips began to press closer.

"Rowdy." The thin, pleading sound of her own voice was unfamiliar to her ears.

"Easy. Easy, baby." He was panting, his hard abs flexing, thighs tightening.

"No." She couldn't help watching, seeing the thick length of his erection, the heavy veins throbbing, the tight flesh steel hard and iron hot. "Now." She lifted closer, moaning in painful need as her flesh began to stretch.

"Kelly. Baby." His cock slid in deeper, the dark crest disappearing inside her and causing the untouched muscles to convulse as the dampness increased, easing his way.

Her eyes lifted to his, seeing the color blazing from within his dark face, his expression a grimace of painful pleasure.

"Don't wait." She couldn't bear the waiting. "Please."

The sudden jolt of his hips buried him deeper as Kelly shuddered at the tight penetration, her head hitting the mattress as her hips lifted closer.

She was consumed with pleasure. It burned through her nerve endings, clenched her womb, convulsed her vagina, and demanded satisfaction.

"Now." Her hips lifted in a sharp, quick move as he fought to penetrate her slowly, to ease inside her. She didn't want ease. She wanted the burn, the destructive, flaming pleasure she could feel building inside her.

And it came. The sudden upthrust buried his flesh deeper inside her, breaking through her virginity, sending a burst of rapture, sharp and much too short, through her system.

"Fuck! Kelly."

"Oh God. Oh God . . . yes. Please, Rowdy." She twisted beneath him, fighting the tighter hold on her hips, the sudden restraint as he paused above her. "Please. Fuck me. Fuck me now . . ."

She couldn't scream; all she could do was lose her breath as he drew back then filled her, impaled her. Buried the full length of his cock inside her before he came over her, gripping her hair in his fingers as his lips covered hers.

Mindless, rapturous. The sensations blazed deeper, higher; they filled her senses, overcame reality, and sent her spiraling through a star-studded night as he gave her what she begged for.

His cock was a hard, blistering length of iron thrusting inside her, stroking tender tissue, building the tension, the pleasure, to a height that Kelly swore she couldn't bear.

Writhing beneath him, she fought for release, gasping, begging, her hands buried in his hair, her lips open against his, every cell possessed by him, stroked by him, enflamed by him, until she was certain only death could await, because there was no way to survive such pleasure.

"Fuck! There, baby."

She was trying to scream as his lips lifted, one hand gripping her hip, the other her hair as her lashes raised and she fought to plead silently, desperately for release.

"There sweet Kelly," he groaned, the strokes suddenly intensifying, the rapid-fire thrusts pulling the tension tighter. Deeper. "Just like that, baby."

She shook her head as she felt the sudden contractions in her womb.

"There it is sweetheart." His voice was tight, encouraging. "Let it have you, baby. I'll hold you. I promise."

Rowdy would hold her. She wasn't really going to die. She was going to disintegrate.

"Come for me, Kelly. Let it go, sweetheart. I have you. Forever, baby." His voice was guttural, desperate, carnal. It was like black velvet, rasping over her senses, surrounding her, stroking her, filling her.

Her release slammed into her. Kelly felt the sudden implosion, then a heavy gathering, a second before ecstasy exploded violently inside her.

Convulsive spasms of release erupted around his hard flesh, a heavy, wet warmth washing over his cock as her release spilled through her.

Her muscles locked around him, attempting to hold him, to capture forever the rapture radiating through her with such brilliant force.

And she did die, she thought with hazy perception. All preconceived notions of loving Rowdy, died. All her fantasies of what pleasure could be, they died. And they were reborn.

His voice wrapped around her, his arms surrounded her, and he was driving deep, burying himself inside her before she felt the white-hot flames of his release as he began to fill her, spurting inside her with a force that stole any remaining sanity she may have possessed.

Kelly collapsed beneath him, exhausted, fighting to breathe, her strength exhausted as she shuddered in the aftershocks of a pleasure she could have never imagined existed.

This was why women crowded around Rowdy. Why they vied for his attention and begged for his touch. Why she had waited, prayed, and saved herself for him alone.

"I love you." She could barely force the words from her lips as she let exhaustion take her. "Just love you."

Thirteen

Rowdy ordered pizza at midnight and brought it to bed. He fed her bites of pepperoni and cheese and let her drink from his beer. He propped himself behind her, naked, and let her use his chest for a pillow as she acclimated herself from being a virgin to being his woman.

"When were the parents getting home?" The moon had risen hours ago, somewhere around the time that Rowdy was making her scream in the shower.

"They were staying overnight." His voice was low, lazy. It soothed now, reaching into that part of her soul that had been stripped bare by his loving. "I thought we would stay the night on the boat."

Kelly stilled against him. She could feel the tension slowly invading his body now, and it wasn't sexual.

"Why?" Not that she cared to spend the night on the boat, but she knew he worried about vulnerabilities the boat presented if someone were watching it.

His arms came around her, snug, sheltering, and she knew immediately that something was wrong. Rowdy sighed behind her, his muscular arms flexing as he rubbed his cheek against her hair.

"You may as well tell me, Rowdy."

"Someone was watching the house last night," he said softly. "On the hill in front of your bedroom window. They were there for most of the night."

Kelly swallowed tightly as she stared across the room. "He's been watching me." She had sensed it. A part of her had known she was being watched, she just hadn't wanted to admit it.

"It's okay, Kelly." Rowdy's voice lowered as his lips pressed against the top of her head. "It might not even be him. I just want to be certain."

"And how are you going to be certain?" she asked, feeling the fear invade her in a slow, insidious crawl. "Where are Dawg and Natches?"

"They're watching the boat. The sheriff is going to check out the hill tonight. He's ex-Army, he knows how to do it. Besides, there's no way I can make love to you in Dad's house. Every time I think about it, Kelly, my balls shrivel."

He was trying to lighten the mood. She could hear it in his voice. Kelly shook her head as she pulled herself from his arms and moved from the bed, swiping the shirt he had worn earlier from the floor and pulling it on.

"Kelly," he protested softly. "Baby, I'll fix this. I promise."

She held her hand up without turning back to him, hiding her desperate attempt to hold back her screams with sheer force. Shaking her head she moved quickly to the doorway then down the steps that led to the first floor of the houseboat.

Where she was going to go, she didn't know. There was no place to hide, no way to escape.

You're my good girl, Kelly. My good little girl. Tell me you love me. You love me, don't you?

Kelly stumbled at the last step as the words whispered through her mind, the memory of his hissing voice, his hands holding her down, parting the cheeks of her rear as he spread the lubrication there and attempted to rape her.

She had felt him trying to enter her.

She wrapped her arms over her stomach, determined not to throw up, not to scream in rage.

"Don't do this to yourself!" Rowdy's voice was dark, angry, as his arms came around her again, turning her to his chest, pulling her against him as he surrounded her, sharing the heat of his body as she felt ice building in her soul. "Kelly, I swear. We'll catch him."

She shook her head desperately, realizing tears were washing down her cheeks as the sobs clawed at her chest.

She could still feel the cuts the attacker had sliced into her flesh, the blood running over her skin, hot, slick.

"I can't do this," she cried, her fingers curling into fists as he held her to him, refusing to let her go. "I can't do it again." She would never survive another attack and she knew it. "Oh, God, Rowdy. Oh, God. I can't . . ."

Rowdy picked Kelly up in his arms, moving to the sofa, cradling her against his naked body as he held her head to his chest and fought back the intense, primal violence threatening within him.

The bastard had scarred her. Not just her mind with his attempted rape, but her soul. The attack had instilled a fear inside her that he knew she would never fully recover from, and it destroyed him.

"It's okay, Kelly," he crooned at her ear. "I have you, baby. No one can hurt you here, sweetheart. I swear it."

She shuddered against him. The cries had eased, but the trembling in her body hadn't.

"Kelly, baby, you have to trust me." He cupped her chin, forcing her to look up at him, his heart breaking at the sight of her eyes drenched in tears, her face pale from fear. "It's going to be okay, baby."

"It won't be." Husky, filled with fear, her voice sliced open his heart. "I knew he was watching me. I could feel him. God, Rowdy."

She jumped from his lap before he could stop her, stumbling across the floor. She turned on him, her eyes blazing with cloudy fury as she stared across the distance.

"He won't stop. He won't stop until he hurts someone again, and next time, he might hurt you."

What he thought was fury in her eyes was actually horror. He saw it swamp her features, leeching the rest of the color from her face.

Rowdy straightened from the couch, aware he was naked, aware his body was responding to the sight of her, the smell of her. He saw her gaze flicker down, then jerk back up.

"God, Rowdy now is not the time for that." The look of complete female irritation on her face shouldn't have been amusing—he was certain.

He made sure his look was completely wicked. He couldn't

bear to see the fear in her eyes; if he had to replace it with irritation or even anger, than so be it.

"Sweetheart, anytime is the perfect for this when you're around," he chuckled.

"No." She shook her head, pacing back. "We have to talk about this, Rowdy. I have to figure this out."

"Figure what out?" His eyes narrowed at the purpose that began to fill her face.

"I have to leave." Her voice was laden with sorrow, with grief. "I have relatives on Dad's side in Montana. It's a nice little town. I can go there. For awhile." Her voice roughened with the threat of tears.

"No."

"Don't be stubborn, Rowdy." She faced him, determination and grief filling her eyes. "I can't stay here. He could strike at Mom or your dad. Or—you." Her voice trembled.

What the hell was he going to do with her? Rowdy stared back at her somberly, feeling his chest ache with an emotion that so outdistanced love that he couldn't describe it.

"Forget it." He crossed his arms over his chest and frowned back at her. "I'll only follow you, Kelly."

"You can't follow me," she snapped. "This is your home. The marina. The lake. All of it."

"There's lakes in Montana." He shrugged. Arguing over her leaving would only make her more determined to go. He knew Kelly. Once she decided she was right, that was it. It took blood, sweat, and tears, on her part, before she would realize how wrong she was.

She was stubborn, defiant, soft, and loving, but she could drive him crazy in two hours flat if he let her. But he would never be bored with her. Frustrated, yes. Bored? Never.

"You can't leave." She glared back at him. "Your friends are here. Your cousins, your family."

"So are yours." He shrugged. "If you want to leave, fine. Pack. We'll go to Montana. Hell, we'll go to fucking Fiji if you want to and become beach bums, but you aren't leaving without me."

She propped her fists on her hips as her lips flattened.

"So I'm supposed to just sit here and wait on that bastard to attack again? Wait on him to hurt someone else? Maybe you?"

"I can take him." His smile was tight, hard. He would relish it.

"You can't fight a bullet, Rowdy," she argued desperately. "What if he doesn't fight fair?"

"What if you try dropping any idea you have of leaving me," he growled. "It's not going to happen. I didn't go through hell for the past eight years to give you a chance to be certain you want me, just to have some sick bastard fuck it up. You're mine, Kelly."

And if his words didn't convince her, then his cock better, because it was stiff as steel and throbbing with a life of its own.

Her gaze flickered down again, a bit of color flushing her pale cheeks as she licked her lips nervously.

"Put your pants on."

"Why? I'll just have to take them right back off," he promised her. "Take the shirt off."

"No." She crossed her arms over her breasts again. "We're not finished talking."

"Of course we are." He moved closer. "The only thing left is your decision. Do we stay or do we leave? Because whichever, Kelly, we do together."

Before she could evade him he had her in his arms again, ignoring the sharp little nails that pressed into his shoulders as he pulled her hips in against his and pressed his cock against her lower stomach.

"Feel how hard I am, Kelly." He nipped at her ear as she trembled in his arms. "Do you really want to leave me like this? Hot and hard for you? Aching for you every night that you're gone? Like I've ached for the past eight years."

"You survived," she moaned.

"But I hadn't had you then." He licked the shell of her ear before trailing his lips to her throat. "I hadn't felt your hot little pussy wrapped around my cock, milking me dry. I've had that now. I don't think I can live without it."

He watched as heat began to fill her eyes, as the anger in her expression softened, just a little.

"I don't want you hurt," she whispered breathlessly. "He's crazy—"

"Damn right he is," Rowdy bit off the fury that would have filled his voice, barely managing just anger. "He touched you, Kelly. He made the mistake of taking from you, of hurting you. Do you think I'll ever forget that? That he won't pay for it if I ever manage to find out who he is? The son of a bitch would have served himself better to run as hard and as far as he could from me, rather than stalking you. Because I won't rest until I find him."

Kelly opened her lips to speak, to argue he was certain, only to be interrupted by a less than polite pounding on the side of the houseboat.

"Open up, cuz," Dawg called through the sliding doors. "We have trouble, man."

Kelly's eyes widened in alarm as Rowdy stalked to the back of the houseboat, grabbed a pair of shorts, and jerked them on before stalking back to the door.

Dawg and Natches stepped into the room seconds later, their expressions dark, cold.

"He hit the house while we were on the hill, Rowdy," Dawg growled as he glanced over at Kelly. "Kelly's room. He trashed it."

He was going to kill the motherfucker. The minute Rowdy walked into Kelly's room, he made that vow. This wasn't like the promises he had made before to kill a son of a bitch. This was a vow, a soul-deep pledge to kill the sleazy, fucking bastard crazy enough to do this to his woman.

Her room was destroyed. Everything she had was destroyed.

Bits of lace and silk that had once been a treasure trove of frilly feminine panties and bras were scattered on the floor. Her hair bows were broken, ripped, cut. Her bedspread was slashed to ribbons as were her clothes.

Rowdy knelt in front of the closet and picked up the tatters of what had once been a pretty scarlet sundress. Beside it lay a shoe, the heel broken off, the red leather hacked at.

Makeup was smeared, swiped, and dumped over her dresser. Jeans were shredded, frothy nightgowns were unrecognizable, and more than a dozen pair of lace and silk stockings were destroyed.

The feathers from the pillows drifted along the floor, the dresser mirror was smashed, and the padding in the chair had been ripped out.

Kelly was still waiting downstairs to come up and see if anything was missing. The sheriff and his boys had finished dusting for prints, but nothing had been found.

"Someone was pissed." Deputy Carlyle stood in the doorway, his expression curious as he stared around the wreckage.

Rowdy lifted his gaze and stared back at the younger man. Carlyle was new on the force. An unfamiliar face and therefore suspicious as far as Rowdy was concerned.

And Rowdy didn't like the way he was staring around Kelly's room. Curious. A little too interested in the bits of fluff that had once been her clothes.

Carlyle was young, maybe in his early twenties, definitely not long out of the Police Academy, with an ego that showed clearly on his handsome face.

"Did you get any prints?" Rowdy raised slowly, his eyes narrowed as he stared at the deputy.

"Nothin'." Carlyle leaned against the door, his too lean body rangy, his brown eyes surveying the room again. "No prints on the door either. He slid right by the security system, came straight up here, and sliced and diced. Good thing Kelly wasn't here."

Rowdy restrained a growl. Bastard had no right to act so familiar with Kelly.

"Yeah. Good thing," he retorted instead.

"Sheriff contacted your parents, they'll be here soon." Carlyle smiled. "They were upset of course."

His parents? Rowdy frowned at the hint of condemnation in the deputy's voice. As if Kelly were his sister, or some blood relation. The judgment set his teeth on edge.

"Are you finished here?" Rowdy asked tightly. "Anything else you need, Deputy?"

Carlyle lifted a brow. "Nothing, Mr. Mackay. We have everything." He smiled confidently.

"Then maybe you should leave." Rowdy smiled back, all teeth.

"I will." Carlyle nodded. "As soon as we get Kelly up here to see if anything is missing. I need that before I leave. The sheriff insisted."

Assaulting an officer of the law was a very bad thing, Rowdy reminded himself. Kelly would be upset. She wouldn't be happy with him at all.

"She can give her statement tomorrow afternoon, Deputy," he all but barked. "She won't be able to tell you shit tonight."

Carlyle smiled again as he lowered his head and shook it slowly.

"I heard you were a real tough guy," he commented, his voice on the wrong side of mocking. "I'd rein that in if I were you, boy."

Boy? Rowdy narrowed his eyes slowly.

"Get the fuck out of my house," Rowdy growled. "Don't piss me off any further, *boy*. And before you get on your high horse maybe you should call your boss and ask him just how far back we go together. You're risking more than my fist in that smirking face of yours."

Beating around the bush wasn't his style, and he'd just had enough of this little dweeb's sneer.

"Dawg and Natches are still downstairs, Mackay," the deputy said.

"So?" Rowdy snapped.

"Last I heard, there isn't much you boys don't do together. Don't tell me you'd actually fight without them."

Rowdy smiled at that one. The kid was a punk, and he was about to learn a lesson he didn't want right now. "I managed to kill just fine without them for four years, Deputy. Want to test it?"

Carlyle's smirk was going to get him killed for sure.

"I'll just leave you to your business here then," he chuckled. "Bring Kelly into the office in the morning. I'm looking forward to talking to her."

Carlyle turned then and ambled down the hall as Rowdy reminded himself that killing outside the Marines was a bad thing. Very bad. Especially smart-mouthed deputies.

Son of a bitch, when had kids like that decided the job was a power trip? Rowdy had half a mind to follow him outside and show him what real power was. The kind of power that slipped up on you in the dark and left you bleeding.

And he could have, hell, he would have taken him out while he was standing there in the doorway with that sneer, but all he saw was Kelly. She would have been horrified if he had actually hurt that little punk while she was around.

Shaking his head he moved downstairs, mentally gearing himself up to face Kelly. Every little treasure she possessed had been in that room. The teddy bear he won for her at a fair when she was just a kid. The porcelain doll one of her friends had gotten her for a birthday. Her frilly hair bows and her silky clothes.

He stepped into the living room, his gaze connecting with Dawg and Natches as Kelly jumped to her feet from the chair she had been sitting in.

"How bad is it?" Her fingers were twisting together in front of her, her face pale.

Damn, he hated this.

"It's pretty bad, baby," he sighed, moving to her and pulling her into his arms.

She fit against him perfectly. A warm weight he hadn't known was missing in his life until now.

"I'm okay." She shook her head against his chest. "I need to go up there, though. I have to see what's left. The sheriff wants a statement."

And he couldn't keep her from going up there, despite the fact that it was killing him.

He stared at Dawg and Natches over her head and with a small movement of his head indicated that he wanted the area outside of the house checked. The sheriff's boys could have missed something. Something his cousins might identify quicker than the investigative team that had come out could have.

Dawg nodded as he and Natches moved from the room.

"Come on," Rowdy sighed, keeping his arm around her. "Let's go check it out."

There was nothing left, just as Rowdy had warned her. Kelly stared at the mess silently from the doorway and fought back her tears. Even the jewelry box had been destroyed.

"How am I supposed to tell if anything is missing?" The destruction was complete.

"We'll get it cleaned up." Rowdy's arms were wrapped around her from behind, his presence sheltering her. "I'm sorry, baby."

"It's not your fault." Kelly shook her head, trying to hold back the fear growing inside her. "He's angry now, isn't he?"

Always be my good girl. You'll always be my good girl.

"Yeah, he's angry now," Rowdy admitted. "But he's not the only one. Do you want to go through the room now or wait till morning? It might be better to wait."

She had been violated again. Kelly could feel the pervasive knowledge that even though the attacker hadn't touched her again, he had still violated her. He had taken something else from her.

She shook her head. "I need to get this cleaned up. I can't stand knowing it's destroyed like this."

She had to force back her tears. It broke her heart, seeing her treasures destroyed as they were, knowing there was nothing she could do to bring them back. But wasn't that the purpose behind this sort of attack? To take her mementos, the things she loved away from her?

She moved into the bedroom, staring around at the destruction, and wanted to scream. This was her room. She had had all her treasures here. Her jewelry, her stuffed animals, her dolls. And her hair bows. For once Rowdy hadn't been able to save her hair bows.

She bent down and picked up the pieces of a hair comb. The small fake pearls were crushed, the little crystals shattered. It had been one of her favorites.

"We'll replace them, Kelly," Rowdy promised behind her. "All of them."

She cradled the bit of plastic that was left in her palm. They could replace the hair bows, but nothing could replace the sense of security that had been stolen from her.

Fourteen

Rowdy had finally managed to convince Kelly and her mother to leave the bedroom alone until morning. They were both exhausted when he and his father walked into the bedroom at three a.m. to find the two women crying in each other's arms.

Rowdy had taken Kelly to his bedroom where he held her as she slept, and Ray had taken her mother to their bed. Rowdy was certain his father had gotten no more sleep than he had though, despite the fact that Dawg and Natches had slept downstairs until the security system could be repaired.

At eight, Rowdy met Ray in the hallway heading downstairs.

"Kelly still asleep?" Ray kept his voice low.

Rowdy nodded sharply.

"Coffee?" His father's eyes glittered with anger.

"If I know Dawg, it's already on." Rowdy was certain he had smelled it moments before he left his bedroom.

Ray tugged at the band of his jeans and sniffed sharply, his jaw bunching. "Let's go get some. I've had about all I can take of sitting around and thinking."

Rowdy knew exactly what he was talking about.

They met Dawg and Natches in the kitchen. Both men were hunched over steaming cups of coffee, talking quietly as Rowdy and Ray entered the room.

"It's fresh." Dawg nodded to the pot on the counter.

"Did you manage to find anything this morning?" Rowdy asked as he moved to the cabinet and pulled two cups down.

"Nothing." Dawg sighed. "Me and Natches went over this place with a fine-toothed comb. Whoever it was slipped in like a damned ghost and back out the same way."

"Bastard!" Ray snapped. "I'm about tired of this, Rowdy. Maria and Kelly are losing enough sleep. They don't need this."

"I know, Dad." Hell, he didn't need it. He was having nightmares the way it was.

"He was just watching her until you came back, Rowdy," Dawg informed him. "We found several places where he's been watching the house from. The rains have wiped out most of the evidence of someone watching, but he likes to snack while he's watching. A few candy papers, a couple of soda bottles. No prints though. We checked for that. He's watching from points above the house, several different areas."

"She said she knew she was being watched," Rowdy sighed. "She felt it."

"We'll find him." Natches's eyes were flinty, cold. "He'll make the wrong move soon."

Rowdy rubbed the back of his neck as he pulled out a chair and sat. His cup smacked the table as he sat it down.

"He destroyed every fucking piece of clothes she owns. Every goddamned hair bow and frilly girly thing she possessed. He destroyed her."

And Rowdy would destroy him, it was that simple. Once Rowdy got his hands on the bastard, he was dead. Painfully dead. The hurting, screaming kind of dead.

"How do you catch a damned ghost?" Ray snarled as he sat at the other end of the table. "The sheriff has been looking for him, I've been watching out for anyone suspicious, and no one has seen shit."

Rowdy's gaze connected with Dawg's and Natches's. The bastard had come after Kelly again because he knew she was on the boat with Rowdy. He was pissed. He would make a mistake soon enough.

"Don't you three think you're going to keep me out of this," Ray warned knowingly. "You're not as good at those sneaking little looks as you think you are. Tell me what you're up to."

"We're not up to anything, Dad." Rowdy pushed his fingers wearily through his still damp hair. "He's mad. He had to have known Kelly was on the boat with me last night. He considers her his *good girl.* She's not waiting for him, so he's punishing her. He'll make a mistake soon enough."

"Especially if you have your way?" Ray growled. "Be careful, Rowdy. Don't try to play games with this bastard."

"No games." Rowdy lifted his cup to sip at the coffee as he stared back at his father. "I won't have to play any games. He won't be able to stand her being with me. He's trying to scare her away from me with this. When it doesn't work, he'll come after me."

"Or Kelly?" Ray snapped. "What if he goes after Kelly?"

Dawg shook his head at that one. "He'll come after Rowdy. And when he does, we'll all be waiting."

Ray stared at the three of them harshly. "Don't play with Kelly's reputation, Dawg," he warned him. "I won't like that."

Dawg glanced at Rowdy.

"The three of you are going to piss me off," Ray snapped.

Hell, just what he needed, his father getting in on this. If Ray was suspicious, then Maria would be too and then she would start working on Kelly. Rowdy knew what it was going to take to bring Kelly's attacker out of the woodwork. If they didn't push him, then he would strike when none of them expected it. They couldn't take that chance.

"I'll take care of this." He stared back at his father firmly. He wasn't arguing over it. He wasn't debating it. One way or the other, he would make certain Kelly was safe.

"Without hurting Kelly further?" Ray's expression was suspicious.

"There's no way to keep Kelly out of this," Rowdy warned him. "She's the one he's after."

"And she's the one that needs to know how we're going to stop him," Kelly's voice stated from the doorway.

All eyes turned to her. She was dressed in one of her mother's gowns and a robe, her long hair flowing around her, her gray eyes stormy.

She was scared and fighting to be strong. Enduring. Kelly was enduring. He had known that years ago, but he was learning it more now. She wouldn't go down easy. She might have her weak moments, but she would come back fighting. And what he needed her to do now was fight.

He watched as she moved to the coffeepot, filled her cup, then turned back to stare at the four of them in determination.

"Whatever happens, Ray, it's my decision," she stated. "You and Mom can't protect me forever."

Ray's jaw bunched with the anger that acknowledgment brought.

Turning back to Rowdy, his eyes narrowed warningly as he rose from the table. "She better not get hurt," he snapped. "Or the three of you will answer to me."

He stalked from the kitchen then and stomped up the stairs, obviously heading for the bedroom he shared with Maria.

Silent, Rowdy watched as Kelly moved to Ray's chair and sat down gingerly, placing her cup carefully on the table before asking, "What's the quickest way to draw him out?"

Fifteen

Knowing what Rowdy had planned and actually seeing it being put into effect were two different things. Kelly found that watching the men converge on a project was almost scary.

The Nauti Boys weren't known for playing nice, in any way. But seeing the hard, cold men studying the banks as they maneuvered into the wide, deserted cove two days later, reminded her that they had been warriors for years, Marines who had survived a long, bloody war.

The men gathered in the living room. Dawg stood at the sliding glass doors that led to the deck, while Natches watched the back, and Rowdy kept a check on the bank along the side of the river.

Their eyes were narrowed, bodies tense and prepared, and all Kelly could do was worry. And try to stem the butterflies rising in her stomach.

She knew the plan was to make her stalker believe she was playing with all the Nauti Boys at once while protecting her from the three of them. They believed he was unbalanced enough, angry enough to show himself. But there was more. She could feel the tension between the three men, the knowledge that they were waiting on her. Wondering if she would give to the three of them together as she had given to Rowdy.

"You're too quiet, baby." Rowdy's voice was soft, filled with hidden depths as he glanced back at where she sat on the couch, staring back at him.

"There doesn't seem to be much to say," she responded quietly, seeing the shadows that filled his eyes.

She wished he wasn't so handsome, wished he wasn't so male. And she wished his cousins didn't draw her almost as much as Rowdy himself did. It was one of the issues she had struggled with since the attack. Her rapist had called her a good girl, but she knew she wasn't, not really, and that scared her. No woman had ever held even one of the Mackay cousins' hearts—what made her think she could? What made her think she could hold all three?

"I told you, Kelly, whatever happens, it will be just you and me."

Yes, he had. On the way to the marina, his voice quiet and throbbing with lust, but she had heard the tinge of regret as well. As though he were torn in his needs, in his wants.

She was aware of Dawg listening, his back to them, his body tense.

"The Nauti Boys playing separately." She arched her brow at the comment. "That's just about unheard of, Rowdy."

Dawg snorted. Rowdy shook his head, his green eyes chastising.

"Your tongue has grown sharper over the years, darlin'," he growled. "I'm a hungry man right now. It's not nice to tempt hungry men."

She settled into the corner of the couch, lifting her legs to the cushions and stretching them to the side. Rowdy's gaze followed the movement with a spark of interest.

"My tongue has always been sharp, you just haven't been around enough to notice." She shrugged. "Dawg and Natches should have warned you of that. Wasn't that part of their job description?"

Knowing they had been watching her and running off potential lovers hadn't suited her well. It was a damned good thing she hadn't known before Rowdy came home.

"The job was hard enough as it was, brat." Dawg turned his head, flashing her a mock frown over his shoulder. "There was no sense in making it more complicated."

Rowdy chuckled as Kelly glanced back at Dawg archly. He winked with a slow, sensual lowering of one thickly lashed eyelid. And she knew that move shouldn't have affected her; unfortunately, it always did. Dawg was a natural-born flirt.

"You make it sound like I was hard to watch." The pretend pout was aimed at Rowdy. "And here I thought I was being a . . ." The words trailed off as she caught what she was about to say.

She thought she had been a *good girl.*

She jerked from the couch, ignoring Rowdy's soft protest as she stalked through the cabin of the houseboat to the back deck.

For a moment, she wasn't certain she could keep her dinner in her stomach as fear lurched through her. A cold sweat covered her skin and she felt naked, exposed in the tiny bathing suit she had managed to let Rowdy convince her to wear.

Ignoring Natches, she moved to the rail, staring down at the water churning at the hull, and swallowed tightly. She had been a good girl. She had waited for Rowdy, instinctively knowing she belonged to him. She may have moments of insecurity in holding his heart, but she had always known she loved him. Always known that he would be her first. She gripped the rail, forcing back her fears as the remembered sound of her own screams echoed through her head.

"He's won."

The sound of Natches's voice had her breathing in roughly as she shook her head.

"I bet you feel like you're naked, on display," he continued.

"Don't, Natches." She fought back the fears rolling through her. "Please."

"Is your skin crawling, Kelly?"

It was. The feel of him behind her, knowing he could see her bare skin, that he wanted to touch her, was suddenly terrifying.

This was Natches. He was almost an extension of Rowdy, a protector, a friend.

"I don't want this," she whispered. "I don't want to be scared because I'm about to say the wrong thing. I don't want to forget every dream I ever had, or lose the man I've loved forever because I can't control the nightmares."

"You'll never lose Rowdy, Kelly," he spoke behind her, far enough away that she wasn't jumping out of her own skin, but close enough that she could clearly hear him. "He's waited on you for eight years now. You're not going to get rid of him easily."

Her breathing hitched.

"If it doesn't happen tonight, Kelly, then he'll wait until you're ready." His voice was soothing, gentle.

Kelly turned to him, staring into his compassionate expression, ignoring the flame of fury that burned behind the sympathy in his eyes.

"And you and Dawg?"

His lips tugged into a crooked smile as his pale green eyes seemed to darken with a hungry cast.

"You belong to Rowdy, Kelly, and vice versa. If that's what you want, then Rowdy will let us know. Until then, nothing has changed with us. We're no different than we've always been to you, and our feelings for you haven't changed."

His gaze flickered over her quickly, and Kelly remembered that he had looked at her the same way for years. With a tinge of teasing lust that he never allowed free. Dawg had always done the same thing, knowing the day would come that Rowdy would claim her, and possibly they would as well.

She glanced at the doorway as Rowdy suddenly filled it, his green eyes bright as they went over her body. He paused at her thighs, centering his gaze on the black material of the bikini bottom she wore before lifting to the fabric that stretched over her breasts.

"I never mistook you for a good girl," he murmured, his voice deep, rough. "You were *my* girl, Kelly. Always."

His girl. Her breath caught in her throat as she stared back at him. Not his good girl, his bad girl, or his naughty girl. Just his.

"I bet you fantasized about it." Rowdy's voice sent curls of heat whipping through her womb before they struck at her clit, her nipples.

She had fantasized about it. Of Rowdy holding her, whispering in her ear, watching. . . . She bit back her moan at the thought of those fantasies.

"Come back in, Kelly." His voice was a rough growl now, his expression heavy with lust as his eyes darkened to an emerald depth.

She stared at the hand he extended to her before her gaze flickered to Natches. He was watchful, tense, but rather than the driving hunger, his eyes held warmth and desire.

"I'm scared, Rowdy," she whispered.

"We're just going to go in and pilot the boat to the cove, babe. We're going to relax, nothing heavy, no decisions to be made, I promise."

Kelly reached out to his outstretched hand, feeling his heat and strength. Then he was pulling her to him, flush against his body, his hand carrying hers until her arm curved behind her back and she was arched into him. The length of his cock pressed into her belly, a thick wedge of heat and hardness that left her knees trembling.

"Just let me touch you, Kelly. Just me. That's all." His head was lowered until his lips caressed the shell of her ear, sending shivers racing down her spine.

He was seducing her. She lifted her free hand to his biceps, holding on tight as his lips traveled to her neck, smoothing over her sensitive flesh, sending sparks of intense need slicing through every nerve ending.

He lifted his head, a sensual smile curving his lips as he drew her back into the cabin, retaining his hold on her hand as he returned to the wheel.

Dawg moved aside, returning to his post at the balcony doors as Kelly glimpsed the narrow opening into the sheltered cove ahead.

They were staying the night, she knew that. The first step in drawing out a madman. Kelly allowed Rowdy to pull her in front of him, between him and the wheel. Her breath caught as his hand settled on her bare stomach, just over the butterflies beating violently within.

He stood behind her, flush against her, his erection resting in the small of her back, covered only by the thin material of his cutoffs.

"Do you think he knows where we're going?" She could barely force the words from her lips.

"He studies his victims," Rowdy sighed. "He'll know about me, about Dawg and Natches. If he doesn't follow, he'll at least be aware of where you are."

Rowdy's plans were targeted at someone who would be watching, waiting. Which meant her rapist had been watching her more closely than she had ever imagined.

"Kelly, we'll catch him." His hold tightened on her. "I promise you, baby, we'll take care of this. We'll take care of you. I swear it."

"I should have listened," she whispered. "Everyone warned me about the window. I should have listened."

"It wouldn't have stopped him, baby. It didn't help the other women he raped. Women alone, who did everything right. He still got to them. This isn't your fault."

She knew that, in her head. Her fears and her shame told her otherwise.

No. No. No. He crouched on the cliff overlooking the cove, sheltered by the pines and brush that surrounded him, rocking back and forth on his heels as he fought the pain inside his chest.

They were all there. All three of them were there with her. Tears coursed down his face as he watched Dawg and Natches Mackay lower the anchor weights on each side of the boat before returning to the cabin.

The curtains were pulled. Thick, heavy curtains that wouldn't show so much as a shadow once night fell. There would be no way of knowing how far Kelly was allowing those bastards to debase her.

He sniffed, holding back his sobs, and let the rage building inside him burn. He had thought she was such a good girl. A sweet, pure angel who deserved his gentleness and his love.

She was a whore. Just like the other whores who had allowed the Mackay cousins to touch them in the past. There was nothing innocent about her. Nothing good. Nothing pure.

But she was his one true love.

And she was breaking his heart. He had refused to dirty her, had given her his heart, and this was his repayment.

He had treasured her. Had shown her his caring, his respect and consideration.

No more.

A small sob escaped him as he realized what had to be done. She had stolen his heart. The only way to rid himself of the torment was to rid himself of Kelly. She would have to die, but first . . . first he would show her how bad girls were really treated.

She was nervous, frightened. Rowdy wasn't unaware of how warily Kelly watched Dawg and Natches. Equal parts curiosity and fear raged in her eyes. For as long as he could remember he had never had a problem sharing a woman with his cousins. But something made him hesitate now. Held him back from seducing her into the acts that he and his cousins had seduced their women into before.

The more he thought of Kelly's innocence, and the fact that she had saved not just her body, but her heart for him as well, caused something to clench in his chest. An emotion he couldn't name, a hunger, a desire he couldn't define.

But Kelly had always engendered such emotions inside him. She could turn his heart when no one else could, and bring out protective instincts he didn't think he possessed.

As they sat watching one of the latest action-adventure DVDs, he felt her move against his side, drawing closer to him, her mostly bare body tucking closer to his.

Neither Natches nor Dawg were watching her. They had joked through the evening, drank a few beers, and seemed as enthralled with the movie as any man should be. But the tension was rising. Kelly's tension as well as theirs.

He tightened his arm around her, drawing her closer to his chest, and felt the heat rising from her. Her hand flattened on his muscular abdomen, her fingers curling into the flesh as he stared down at her bent head.

He was hard, hurting, his cock throbbing beneath his cutoffs with raging demand.

His breath caught with a shocked hiss as he felt her hand caress the tight muscles of his abdomen. Inquisitive fingers ran along the band of his shorts, sending imperative signals to his overly tight cock.

"You're going to get in trouble," he whispered against her hair as the head of his dick began to throb in demand. If he didn't ease the constriction against his cock, then permanent zipper tracks were a definite threat.

"I'm naughty, remember?" She turned her head, her lips pressing against his breastbone as his hand lifted, his fingers tangling in her hair.

"Don't tease, Kelly," he growled. "I'm riding a very fine edge right now."

She licked him. *Son of a bitch.* He nearly jumped out of his skin as he felt the slow, savoring lick of her hot little tongue.

"Really? Strange, I could say the same thing about myself. Spending the last two nights sleeping with you, without being with you wasn't easy, Rowdy."

No shit. After having her, the hunger for her had only grown.

He wasn't unaware of Dawg and Natches listening closely, or the careful readiness of their bodies. They were as aroused as he was, as hungry.

She lifted her head, her slender, lithe body moving, rising as he watched, entranced. She stood in front of him before gracefully straddling his thighs and lowering herself into his lap.

"Son of a bitch!" His head fell back on the couch, his hands catching her hips as he jerked her flush with the tortured length of his cock.

Her pussy was hot, the heat of it burning through her scanty bathing suit bottom as well as the threadbare material of his denim cutoffs.

"We're not alone, baby." He tilted his head as her lips moved to his neck. Each touch reminded him of her inexperience, or her daring.

She knew Dawg and Natches could hear every move, every passionate sigh.

"I dreamed of you," she whispered in his ear a second later, her soft breath sending pleasure racing over his flesh. "While you were gone, I dreamed of touching you, kissing you, of all the things I knew you enjoyed. That I knew I would enjoy." The hesitant admission had his body tightening further.

He felt the tremor that quivered through her, the hint of fear and of arousal. The soft weight of her body against his was driving him crazy. The need to throw her to her back on the couch and devour her was making him sweat. The feel of her straddling his lap, her hands moving over his chest, her lips at his neck was too much.

She had initiated the contact, had known that Dawg and Natches were in the room. He should leave it at that, he thought. He should seduce her, as he knew she wanted to be seduced. But seduction and the acts he wanted to see her involved in did not go hand in hand. Rowdy knew Kelly's innocence, knew the demons that rode her, and he swore to himself he wouldn't add to them.

If this were her choice, then she would face it. And she would face it from the beginning.

• • •

Kelly felt her head spinning as pleasure washed through her with the force of a sensual tidal wave. She could feel Rowdy's hands roaming over her back, her buttocks, bringing a sense of heat and overwhelming pleasure rather than pain and fear.

One hand moved up her spine, threaded in her hair, and before she could guess his intention he was pulling her head back as he turned, lifting her, pushing her to the couch.

Before she could do more than gasp, he stole her breath with his kiss. Her lips parted beneath his, her tongue meeting his in a duel of exquisite ecstasy. She couldn't help curling her fingers into his broad shoulders, feeling the muscles flex beneath her touch, bunch with power as he buried her smaller body beneath his much larger one.

There was no fear here. There wasn't even the thought of fear. There was only Rowdy's touch, his lips covering hers, one hand tangled in her hair, the other moving inexorably to the rounded curve of one breast.

She fought to breathe, certain there had been enough oxygen in the air before his kiss. And she would have broken away to breathe, but it was so good, so hot, so filled with liquid, carnal delight that she couldn't draw away from him. But she could touch him. God, how she had dreamed of touching him over the years, feeling him against her, possessing her.

"Rowdy . . ." Her cry was instinctive as he pulled his lips from her, her eyes opening to stare into his expression in dazed fascination as he pressed his jeans-clad erection tight between her thighs.

"Be sure." His voice was guttural. "Look around you, Kelly. Be certain of what you're doing. There's no turning back. Ever."

Dark erotic power filled his expression. His brilliant green eyes were moss-dark, his face flushed, his lips heavy with greedy hunger.

"Kiss me, Rowdy." She didn't want to think about what could or would be. She wanted to feel the dreams she had known for so long. Rowdy taking her, his cousins pleasuring her.

"No," he growled, his voice rough, his hands clamping on her wrists as her hands moved for the snap of his cutoffs. "Look around, Kelly. Look at them. Let them know they're welcome or they leave. That simple. Your choice."

"That cold-blooded?" she asked nervously.

"No, dammit." He lifted her from him before she could do more than gasp, striding across the room before turning back to her.

"Rowdy, man, let this go," Dawg muttered warningly as Kelly sat up on the couch.

"You make the choice," he growled, his eyes tormented with need, with demand. "I won't do it for you."

Kelly rose jerkily from the couch, her body on fire, her face flaming with anger and embarrassment, and an instinctive demand that she deny them all. She stared at the three of them, all aroused, all awaiting her decision. A decision that had nothing to do with emotion and everything to do with hunger and their dominance. They wanted her surrender, a complete surrender, and she wasn't certain she could give it.

"All or nothing?" she questioned in reply.

"You know better than that, Kelly." Rowdy sliced his hand through the air with frustrated fury. "Don't play games."

"So I have to say the words instead?" she asked, challenging him, facing him with the same determination that glittered in his eyes.

"Words work." He crossed his arms over his chest as Dawg and Natches slouched in their chairs and watched him, each wearing dark, disapproving frowns.

"Oh, I just bet they would." She flipped her hair from her face before propping her hands on her hips. "Should I just ask you all to screw me, Rowdy? Why don't I just bare it now and let you take turns with me. Hell yeah, make it damned easy on you, wouldn't it? That way, you don't have to feel like shit later because you let another man take what was yours?"

"Do you think for one fucking minute that they don't know exactly who you belong to?" he questioned her with dark intent. "If I didn't care, baby, you wouldn't have been a virgin the other night."

"Says who?" she argued in amazement. "Do you really believe that all it takes is a touch from a Nauti Boy to turn any woman's crank?" She waved her hand mockingly. "Your ego is becoming more swollen than your dick, Rowdy."

Wrong word. All three men seemed to tighten, straighten at the explicit word that left her lips.

"Yeah, just look at the three of you." She rolled her eyes in mocking amusement. "Like little boys waiting for a treat. Well, fuck that. Find someplace else to treat, because I'll be damned if I'm still in the mood."

She stomped across the room, determined to reach the curving staircase that led to the upper bedroom and peace. She passed Rowdy with a disdainful little hiss, so irked and frustrated with his male, redneck attitude that she could have kicked him.

"Oh, no, you don't."

She hadn't expected him to reach for her. But even if she had, she wouldn't have expected him to lift her so quickly into his arms before his lips slammed down on hers.

It wasn't a romantic kiss. It wasn't soft and delving, or deep and passionate. It was hungry demand, carnal intent. It stole resistance and replaced it with pure fiery need, and nothing less.

Before she could protest, before she even processed the information, she found her rear braced on the counter, her thighs spread, and Rowdy devouring her.

She was lost in him, helpless in his arms as usual and loving it. Her fingers speared into his hair as his lips moved over hers, his tongue a restless marauder that conquered hers with inordinate ease.

And his hands weren't still either. Within seconds, the bikini top she wore was tossed aside, the hard tips of her breasts pressing into the fine layer of hair that covered his broad chest.

She shifted against him, her fingernails digging into his scalp as the tender, spike-hard tips burned in pleasure.

Kelly moaned at the loss as his lips pulled from hers, moving to her neck as her head fell back, the whiplash of sensations jerking her against him as his broad palms framed the tender mounds when he pulled back.

"So pretty." His lips were swollen, his eyes heavy-lidded and intense as they focused on the swollen curves. "You have the prettiest nipples, Kelly. As pretty pink as cotton candy. And they taste just as sweet."

Her gaze fell to her breasts. The light pink nipples were straining toward him, diamond-hard and desperate for his touch. No other man had touched her there. No one but Rowdy. She ached for him, needed him, belonged to him.

"I won't stop here," he whispered, his gaze lifting to hers. "Once I sate myself on these pretty nipples, I'm going to go lower,

Kelly. I'm going to strip those damned bottoms off and spread your pretty legs. Then I'm going to lap at every sweet drop of syrup running between your thighs. Are you ready for that? And I won't care who's watching."

"God, Rowdy, I've dreamed of it." She had tossed in her lonely bed as the hunger for it kept her awake night after night.

A primal growl left his throat as his head lowered, his tongue swiping over one tender nipple before he enveloped it in his hot mouth.

His lips closed over the peak, sucking it into his mouth as his tongue curled around it. Kelly jerked violently, the pleasure so strong, so fiery that she could do nothing but cry out in response. Rowdy's hard hands held her in place as his lips devoured her, sending her senses reeling, her pulse rocketing as sensuality wrapped around her.

She heard a male groan, but whose it was she wasn't certain.

"They'll just watch," he whispered as his head lifted. "Watch me eat every perfect inch of your body this time. That's all. No pressure, Kelly."

She arched toward him. She didn't want to hear about it, she didn't want to analyze it. She wanted to feel. She wanted each sensation to rip through her, wanted the pleasure to never end.

And he took the offering. His lips closed on the opposite peak, drawing it into his mouth and setting it aflame as he surrounded the other with his thumb and forefinger. Then, his fingers tightened.

"Rowdy!" The surprised exclamation echoed around her as the fiery lance of sensation tore through her. Not quite pain. Almost, but a fiery kind of hurt that made the pleasure hotter, sweeter.

"God, Kelly . . ." The rough moan was whispered between her breasts as his head moved. He was fighting for breath, his fingers working her nipple, causing her to shudder with each tug at the eager tip. She could feel the hunger blazing out of control now, the need ripping through her, hard, bright, and hotter than a living flame. And she needed more. So much more.

Kelly could feel Dawg and Natches watching as she burned in Rowdy's arms. His lips and hands were never still, caressing over her, filling her senses with the dark taste of passion and the stinging need growing within her.

She was desperate for him. Her legs wrapped around his hips

as she pressed her mound tighter against the rock-hard length of his cock. Her swollen clit was screaming for relief even as her tormented nipples begged for more.

"Come here, baby." Rowdy's voice was a rough growl as he lifted her from the counter, his hands curving beneath her bottom to hold her in place against the straining length of his erection. "I'm not taking you on this counter."

She didn't care where he took her, as long as he did.

"I need you." A whimpering cry whispered from her lips as her arms circled his shoulders, her lips moving to the corded strength of his neck. "Don't make me wait again, Rowdy. I can't wait any longer."

"No more waiting, baby." She felt him moving up the curving steps that led to the upper deck and the large bedroom. She had no idea if Dawg and Natches were following. She didn't care if they were, or if they weren't. Nothing mattered except Rowdy's touch. Except touching Rowdy.

As he lowered her to the wide bed that dominated the center of the room, Kelly twisted, pressing against his broad shoulders until he lowered himself beside her, stretching out beneath her gaze.

Finesse be damned. She wasn't experienced, he knew it and she knew it. But she was desperate to touch him, to taste him. Without thought she scrambled to his side, one hand gripping his shoulder, the other smoothing down his hard chest as her head lowered to the flat male nipples that drew her attention.

If his mouth on hers could make her weak, could she do the same to him?

"Shit! Kelly. Baby . . ." Maybe she could.

His hands buried in her hair, his body jerking against her as she nipped at the little discs before laving them with her tongue.

Hard, growling moans came from his chest as her hand lowered to the band of his cutoffs, her fingers tearing at the snap before he brushed her fingers away to release the material himself.

Kelly contented herself with tasting him. Both nipples, licking and nipping at them with rising pleasure before she began to move lower.

"God, Kelly." Rowdy tightened further as her tongue licked around his navel before heading to the length of hard flesh still covered by his cutoffs.

"I need to touch you, Rowdy," she whispered. "Let me touch you." She parted the fabric, then watched as he gripped the material of the waistband in his hands and shed it with easy grace.

And there he was. Hard, thick, his cock rising along his abdomen, pulsing with life as a small bead of semen collected at the tip. Kelly licked her lips, remembering the taste of him.

She bent, reaching out with her tongue to swipe over the bulging head as she tasted him. A bit salty, bold, wild, like Rowdy. And she wanted more.

A rumbled groan came from his throat as her fingers trailed down the ridged length of his erection, curiously exploring each shift of the bulging veins until she reached the hair-roughened sac below.

"Easy, baby." One hand clenched in her hair as the other cupped her cheek now. "Come down slow and easy. Take me in that pretty mouth of yours."

The hand moved from her cheek as her lips parted. It gripped the base of the hard stalk, lifting it until the head pressed against the damp curves. Kelly whimpered at the heat and hardness before her lips opened, stretching to surround him, to take him into her mouth as her tongue flickered over the expanse of skin that she was able to reach.

"God, yes!" His hips bucked against her mouth, driving his cock in deeper as she tried to lick at each new expanse of flesh.

It stretched her lips, filled her mouth with the taste of sexual intent, a wicked, intoxicating male taste that inflamed her senses. She felt his fingers bunching in her hair as she began to slowly suck at the engorged crest.

"Oh yes, baby," he crooned. "Your mouth is like liquid silk."

The sound of his voice was rough, erotic.

"That's it, baby," he encouraged her as she followed the lead of his hands in her hair, her lips moving up, then down, filling her mouth with as much of his erection as possible as she suckled at the rising flesh, her tongue flickering over it.

He took one hand and caught hers, wrapping her fingers around him, high enough to keep it from going too deep into her mouth before he returned his fingers to her hair. He sifted through the strands before tangling within them and moving more firmly against her, his cock thrusting with slow, easy strokes inside her mouth.

"Damn. You're stealing my sanity, baby," he growled as she felt the bloated crest throb in her mouth. "There you go. Suck it nice and hard. Oh hell . . ." Her lips tightened on him as she lifted her eyes to see the carnal expression on his dark face.

She had never realized how hungry she was for him, until now. Until his cock filled her mouth, the wild taste of aroused male consuming her, driving her past shame to a realm where nothing mattered but touch, taste, desire.

As her mouth moved on him, her hand began to stroke the strong shaft, moving up and down, pumping the hard column as he fucked her mouth with increasingly strong strokes.

At the same time, she felt a touch behind her. Male hands sliding her bikini bottoms from her, smoothing over the rounded curves of her ass. Was it Dawg or Natches? She didn't know, she didn't care.

She watched Rowdy's gaze flare, though, as he stared over her head for a long second. When his eyes returned to hers, they were wild with lust.

Then she felt it. A slow, reverent kiss on one buttock, then the next. A tongue, wicked and alluring, flickering along the top of the narrow crevice that separated the rounded cheeks.

Her head jerked up as a keening moan left her lips, her eyes widening in shocked pleasure. An insidiously wicked caress nearly had her collapsing against Rowdy. Only his hands held her upright, his gaze holding her sanity as she felt the probing tongue gently rimming the ultrasensitive entrance to her anus.

She should be screaming in fear, instead, she was panting with pleasure.

"Oh God, Rowdy . . ." Her voice was weak, questioning. Should it feel so good? Should she be so desperate for more?

"Shh, baby," he whispered gently. "Let it feel good. Just for a minute. Just for another minute."

She cried out as she felt that knowing tongue press against the entrance again. Her head whipped from side to side as she fought to breathe, fought to make sense of the blinding pleasure. When it breached the small hole with a slight pinching sensation, only to pull back, then probe inside again, she shuddered at the intensity of the carnal caress, suddenly terrified. Not of the touch or the man, but of herself.

"It's okay, Kelly . . . easy, baby." The touch was suddenly

gone as Rowdy pulled her to him, his lips covering hers as he bore her to her back.

He kissed her with ruthless demand, leaning over her and working his lips over hers with experienced lust. He ate her kiss, consumed her, and taught her to consume in return.

Rowdy lifted his head from the kiss, his senses drunk with the taste of the woman beneath him, his body aching to possess her.

The soft, dim glow spread over Kelly, clearly revealing bare silken flesh between her thighs, devoid of any sign of feminine hair. He had expected it, had known what awaited him, but the sight of it was a punch of lust to his gut anyway.

He blinked down at the pink, flushed curves as they gleamed with a layer of soft, silky syrup, licking his lips in hunger.

"Baby, you're pushing a man already hanging on the edge," he growled as he watched his fingers move, smoothing over the swollen flesh until they could delve into the rich, dewy slit below.

"Oh God. Rowdy . . ." Her cry pierced through him as he parted her, his gaze drinking in the flushed flesh covered in slick honey as her hips arched to him, her thighs spreading further.

He pressed the pad of his palm over her clit as his fingers found the tender entrance to her pussy and circled it slowly, his mouth watering to taste her. Lifting his fingers he turned his gaze to her again, narrowing his eyes as he moved his fingers to her pouty lips and painted them with her own juices.

Shock widened her eyes as she gasped. His other hand moved to her head, lacing his fingers through her hair as he spread the sweetness over her lush lips.

"Lick it off," he growled. "Come on, baby, see how sweet and hot you're going to taste when I get my tongue inside that hot little pussy."

"Rowdy . . ." He could hear the protest of her innocence, the dark hungers filling her, urged on by his own needs as she hesitated in the face of the unfamiliar intensity of their combined lust.

"Lick your lips," he ordered her again, his voice rough, the need to see her completely immersed in the needs building between them overwhelming.

Her tongue peeked out as the flush deepened on her face. A

grimace twisted his lips as she licked at her own sweetness, tasting what he craved so desperately for himself. Then, her tongue curled around his finger, drawing a hoarse moan from his chest as she sucked it into her mouth.

The feel of her drawing the remaining taste from her fingers broke his control. He pulled from her, moving between her thighs, spreading them further as he lifted her to his descending mouth and buried his lips in the liquid heat flowing from her.

She was more intoxicating than moonshine, sweeter, hotter than life itself, and all his.

Kelly heard her own cries flowing through the night around her and could do nothing to still them, to smother them. Rowdy's mouth was burning through inhibitions, through shyness, and igniting a fire inside her pussy that threatened to consume her. He held her legs wide, his mouth eating her decadently, his whispering murmurs of pleasure and hunger fueling the flames burning through her.

His tongue was voracious. It licked, spread fire through the burning flesh and caressed her with a knowledge and experience that had her gasping. Small, flickering strokes against her clit caused her to arch to him, her hips jerking as sensation raked like talons of need through her nervous system. The pleasure, oh God, the pleasure was too much to bear. Each circular stroke around the hard, pulsing knot of her clit stole her breath. Her womb convulsed with the need for orgasm as the pleasure tore through it before spreading throughout her system.

His fingers weren't still either. One circled the sensitive opening to her vagina, spreading the juices that wept from her aching center before his tongue stroked lower, moving to lap at her, to draw the taste of her into his mouth as she screamed out from the precipice he kept her teetering on.

She was so close. Too close to be held back in such a way. She could feel the sensation burning throughout her body, igniting a firestorm that raced through her bloodstream.

Finally. She writhed beneath him, her head tossing as all the fantasies she had known in the past five years were finally coming to life. Rowdy was touching her, tasting her, loving her.

"Fuck, I could get drunk on your taste." His voice was a

hoarse growl a second before his tongue plunged inside the gripping entrance to her cunt, fucking into her with licking strokes that had a strangled scream leaving her throat.

The tension building inside her was frightening. Control was a thing of the past, as Rowdy was causing the gathering tightness in her belly to deepen, to convulse with each inward thrust of his wicked tongue. Her hands tightened in his hair as she shuddered and the wet heat flowing from her vagina increased.

She was panting for air, sensation racing across her flesh, sensitizing her, leaving her gasping amid the inferno he was creating. His hands weren't still anymore than his tongue was. They smoothed over her thighs, his thumb flicked at her clit, sending sharp sensations of agonizing need tearing through her a moment before it retreated. His hands curled along the cheeks of her ass, and as his tongue plunged inside her again, he parted the soft curves, tugging at the entrance to her ass and sending sharp flares of heat whipping through her system.

"Rowdy . . ." She writhed, beneath him, her head tossing on the blankets as she felt perspiration gathering along her body, trickling down her breasts, her tummy, even as her juices flowed from her pussy. "I can't . . . I can't stand it. . . ."

It was different than the first time. The sensations were harder, fiercer, driving her further from herself as she fought to hold onto reality.

"Make it stop!" She tried to scream, to demand an ease to the pressure building in her womb, her thighs, deep inside her cunt.

He didn't answer. If anything, his mouth became more voracious, his fingers exploring further, pressing deeper against the untouched entrance he was massaging.

"Rowdy . . . I swear . . . I can't stand . . ." She lost her breath as she felt his finger breach her ass, felt it slide slowly inside her as his lips covered her clit, his thumb slipping into the entrance of her pussy and destroying her.

"Oh God!" She fought the lightning surge of almost painful sensation that shot through her.

"The hell you can't. You will come for me, Kelly. Now," he snarled, his finger retreating, gathering more of the silky liquid flowing from her before sliding in deeper, stronger, his thumb pumping into her pussy before his lips covered her clit again. He suckled at the tender bud, his tongue flickering over it as his finger bit into her ass, his thumb fucking her cunt until she felt herself erupt.

Her scream filled the night as she dissolved, saw lights exploding behind her clenched eyes and heard Rowdy's roar of pleasure a second before he was rising between her thighs and throwing her higher.

"Hang on, baby." He gripped her hands, moving them to his shoulders as she felt a thick pressure against the sensitized entrance to her pussy.

She stared up at him, dazed, awash in cascading waves of ecstasy.

"Sweet baby," he groaned, his green eyes darkening as his hands clasped her face. "Hold on to me, sweet thing. I can't wait. Not even another minute."

Her eye widened, fluttered, fought to stay open as she felt his cock stretching her, invading her. Better than the first time, stroking sensitive nerve endings, caressing delicate tissue until she wept with need. And it didn't stop. It went on and on, as though in slow motion, stretching her until she was certain she could hold no more before she found she could.

She jerked in his grip, her nails pressing into his shoulders as she whimpered then screamed as Rowdy settled to the hilt inside her. She could feel every thick inch parting the tender tissue of her pussy, straining it to its limits as fingers of electricity sizzled through and the tension began to increase once again within her.

"God, you're tight." His expression was strained as she stared up at him, fighting to make sense of the sensations ripping through her. "And soft as silk." His forehead pressed against hers.

He grimaced, lifting his head a few inches as he stared down at her, his thumb dragging roughly over her lips as she fought to breathe.

"Lift your legs." His voice was like gravel. "Brace your knees against my hips." He lowered one hand, lifting her thigh as she did as he bid.

"Oh God, Rowdy." He slid in deeper than ever, filling her in ways she couldn't explain. "Oh God, I don't know what to do . . ." She wanted to cry, wanted to ease the furious throb of hunger pulsing in her womb, in her cunt.

"Shush, baby," His voice was strained, his body tight with the effort it was taking as he helped her, positioning her knees against his hips as a ragged moan tore from his chest. "Son of a bitch, you're so fucking tight. I could come just feeling you grip me like that."

The muscles inside her pussy were indeed milking him, rippling around him, driving her crazy with the furious heat building inside them. She stared up at him, feeling the tears on her cheeks, the emotions clogging her throat. She couldn't imagine ever needing anything more than she needed Rowdy.

"Easy now, sweetheart," he warned as she felt his thighs bunching. "If I don't move I'm going to come before you ever get yours. And you have to have yours." A wicked smile crossed his swollen lips as he began to move.

His cock slid slowly from the clutching grip of her cunt as she heard her own desperate groan of pleasure; the thrust back had her crying out in sharp agonizing need, and then there was no stopping him.

He arched back, gripping her legs and pressing them closer to her body as he stared down to where they came together, her gaze following automatically, watching as the slick, glistening shaft of his cock powered in and out of the flattened curves of her cunt. It was mesmerizing, consuming. She could feel raking fingers of pleasure, pain, sharp sensation, and fiery explosions of hunger ripping through her body as she watched him fuck her. Watched his cock thrust in and out, shafting her with furious strokes as the world receded around her.

She came again, screaming through her orgasm, and still he didn't stop.

"Again," he snarled, turning her to her side, her legs bent, pressed to her breasts as he leaned over her, one hand parting the cheeks of her ass as his fingers found the tingling entrance there.

Her back arched, her head falling back as his finger slid inside, pumping in tandem with the thick erection driving inside her cunt, stretching her, burning through her mind as pleasure and pain mixed with the addition of another finger to stretch her tender anus. And still his cock drove into her, stroking furiously over sensitized nerve endings until she was shuddering, convulsing around him, her juices spewing from her pussy as she heard him give a ragged shout and felt his body tighten.

She was still dissolving around him as she felt his release, the hot, furious blasts of semen filling her, burning her, sending her into another quaking paradox of sensation that had her convulsing beneath him as he held his cock deep inside her, shuddering with the pleasure ripping them both apart.

Kelly had lost sanity long before Rowdy's release. She quivered in the aftermath of orgasm, weak, wasted by the emotion, the pleasure that had erupted through her. She felt him collapse beside her, still buried inside her pussy, his breathing harsh, his arms tight as he pulled her to his damp chest.

"Breathe, baby," he crooned in her ear as one hand massaged her chest, reminding her she was holding her breath as it released in a rush, sending stars exploding before her eyes. "There you go, sweet thing," he murmured, his lips at her shoulder as his cock jerked inside her. "Rest for a bit. Just a little bit. Then we'll try it again and see if we can't get it right."

Get it right? Dear God, if that wasn't right then he would kill her if he ever managed perfection.

Sixteen

It was still dark when Kelly awoke, her body pleasantly sore as Rowdy slept deeply beside her, sprawled naked on his stomach.

Heat curled low in her stomach as she stared at his shadowed form, a shiver of remembered pleasure echoing through her womb.

Moving quietly, she slid from the bed, searching until she found Rowdy's T-shirt, discarded on the nearby chair earlier that night, and pulled it over her naked body. She couldn't hear anything below, but she doubted Dawg and Natches were both sleeping.

Making her way down the narrow, curved staircase, the faint glow of the television provided a dim light as Kelly headed for the small refrigerator.

She pulled a bottle of water free, uncapping it as she straightened and lifted it to her lips before she caught sight of Dawg.

He was sitting in the shadowed corner between the table and counter, his eyes gleaming in the darkness as she paused, watching him.

"Rowdy's gonna bitch over you stealing another of his shirts," he drawled quietly as she felt her face flush.

The heat had nothing do with the fact that she was caught stealing more of Rowdy's clothes, it was the sudden question of whether or not his wicked mouth had been the one caressing her earlier.

"He should be used to it by now." She cleared her throat uncomfortably, feeling a tingle of heat curl around her clitoris.

"He's a stubborn boy, though." He shrugged negligently. "You already know that."

Kelly leaned against the counter and watched him curiously. There was a lot she still didn't know about Rowdy and his relationship with his cousins. All anyone seemed to care about was the fact that sexually, they enjoyed sharing their toys.

She ducked her head, knowing she shouldn't have put off learning more about the three men together rather than just focusing on Rowdy. But it was Rowdy who held her heart, not the other two. Though she knew, eventually, they would become a part of the relationship she and Rowdy shared.

"You look like a frightened little doe standing there." His voice was like dark silk. "We've known each other too long for that wariness in your eyes, little girl."

Yes, they had. Dawg and Natches were as much a part of her life as Rowdy was.

"I'm not frightened of you, Dawg," she sighed. "I'm not frightened of any of you."

Maybe she was frightened of herself.

"People make too much out of our little pleasures," he grunted. "As though some insidious evil causes it rather than choice." He chuckled at his own words. "There's nothing evil in it, Kelly. And Rowdy would never press you for what you don't want. So you don't have to watch us as though we're going to jump you at any minute."

"And the three of you think I didn't know what the hell I was getting myself into when I waited on Rowdy." She pressed her lips together as her own frustration ate inside her. "It's not a matter of not wanting it, Dawg, or even if I do want it."

"You want to be seduced into it. You want the choice taken out of your hands?" He leaned back in his chair, watching her intently.

"I don't want to analyze it to death, that's for damned sure," she snapped. "It's a wonder the three of you found a woman to share if you talked her to death first."

"The other women didn't matter, Kelly." He shocked her with his answer. "They were fun and games—you're Rowdy's future. There can be no misunderstandings, no seduction, no hesitations or hiding from the truth if you accept it. If you accept it, then you accept all of it.

Even the fact that eventually, the man she loved would touch another woman, pleasure her, fuck her. She couldn't accept his cousins' touch without that knowledge.

"I love him," she whispered.

"This won't be easy on any of us." He lifted his shoulders heavily. "Natches and I both love you too, Kelly, not like Rowdy does, but we love you. We've been burning along with him to touch you. But the day will come when one or both of us will find the woman we want for our own. The sharing isn't an every time thing, but it would sure as hell be missed if we stopped."

"Has anyone ever asked you to stop, Dawg?" she asked. "Have you ever considered it?"

Something dangerous flashed in his expression before it was gone just as quickly. "I'd stop if someone I loved asked it of me. If I knew the woman I loved couldn't handle it." He shrugged his broad shoulders.

"I don't know if I could bear to see him touch another woman, Dawg." A self-mocking smile twisted her lips. "How's that for hypocrisy?"

"Not hypocrisy, sweetheart, honesty," he told her quietly. "That's what makes a relationship like this work, being honest about it. Being true to yourself and to Rowdy. We couldn't ask for anything more than that."

"I won't do this just for Rowdy," she breathed out roughly. "I won't let him touch another woman just because I know it's what he wants. It has to make sense to me. I have to be able to live with it."

"That's true enough." He nodded in understanding. "Any relationship is give and take. You give a little, Rowdy gives a little, and vice versa." He rose from his chair, moving the short distance to where she stood, towering over her.

Kelly swallowed deeply as she felt him surrounding her, his heat, the sensual hunger building inside him.

"Dawg . . ." There was no way to retreat.

She shivered as he reached out, his callused fingers running down her arm and filling her with conflicting emotions. Could she do it? Fantasizing about it was one thing, and Lord knew she had fantasized about it often. But actually taking that step was another matter.

"I want you," he whispered.

"Stop," she protested, shaking her head as denial began to rage within her. A panicked sense of discomfort began to build. It might be what Rowdy wanted, but this wasn't Rowdy. It wasn't his body heating her, his need surrounding her.

"It's dark and shadowed. A lot of truths can be hid in the shadows." Dawg's voice was darker than the night. "As can lies."

Her breath caught in her throat as his head lowered, his lips too close to her own.

"I could seduce you," he whispered. "I can give you that, Kelly. I don't have to wake up with you in the morning. I don't have to face you knowing I used your body against you. Is that what you want?"

"Moron." She pushed against his chest, her hands smacking into his hard-packed muscles as a shadowy chuckle whispered around her. "Get away from me. You're about as amusing as the flu, Dawg."

"Did I make my point?" His teeth flashed in a smile.

She sniffed disdainfully. "The point wasn't needed. Don't make the mistake of thinking I don't understand his reasons. But I'm also still a woman, Dawg, not a plaything. He can get serious about this, or he can forget it."

"Can he get anymore serious, Kelly? He let one of his cousins lick your ass. That's pretty damned serious to me."

Her face flamed as she narrowed her eyes.

"Was it you?"

He crossed his arms over his chest, watching her with a hint of a smile. "One licked, the other watched in anticipation. I ain't tellin' who did what."

A feeling of denial raged through her at the memory. This wasn't fantasy, it was reality, and she wasn't comfortable with it, no matter how much she wished she was.

"You know, Dawg, one of these days you boys are going to bite off more than you can chew in a woman. What are you going to do then?"

"Looks to me like Rowdy has already managed that one," he chuckled as his gaze shot past her. "And here he is to see how much further he can sink into monogamous bliss."

Kelly turned quickly, barely restraining a moan at the sight of Rowdy, naked, hard, his eyes gleaming with interest as he stood at the bottom of the steps. One thing she could say about him, naked or dressed, confidence oozed from every pore of his body. Confidence and pure, driving lust.

He tilted his head as he watched her, his gaze moving to his cousin, then back to her slowly. There was a challenge there, a knowing glint in his eye that assured her that he was well aware that she was wet and aroused herself.

"There you go stealing my clothes again." He shook his head in mock chastisement. "I was hoping you would learn better, baby."

"I think she needs to be spanked," Dawg murmured behind her, sending her pulse rocketing at the suggestion.

She arched her brow as she held Rowdy's gaze. He was grinning back at her, a crooked, self-assured grin filled with carnal intent.

As she watched him, she was aware of Natches moving from the rear of the cabin, watching the scene curiously. The testosterone swept through the room, heavy with wicked hunger and sinful intent. Three predatory males, no matter how they tried to hide the primal instincts that ran just beneath the surface of their lazy humor.

They converged on her, tall, broad, aroused. Rowdy was the only one completely naked, but the other two were following suit quickly. Natches stripped off his shirt, while behind her she heard Dawg's movements, the rustle of his clothes.

Nerves ripped through her, sending shudders of instinctive response to curl through her lower stomach before burning a path of erotic destruction along her erogenous zones. Her nipples peaked. Her lips ached and her sex wept.

"Take the shirt off, baby," Rowdy whispered as his hands gripped the hem, slowly drawing it upward.

Behind her, Dawg stepped closer. The shock of his bare hands running up her thighs had her tensing at the pleasure. She was so wet she could feel her juices dampening her thighs now, running freely from her weeping pussy as they prepared her for the coming possessions.

"Look how pretty you are . . ." Rowdy whispered reverently as she lifted her arms, allowing him to strip his shirt from her body. "You nipples are so hard, flushed. I love tasting them, Kelly. Feeling them in my mouth, the tight little points throbbing on my tongue."

They were throbbing now at the thought of it.

The shirt was tossed aside, but it wasn't Rowdy's hands that cupped the firm globes, it was Dawg's. They slid around her side until both hands were filled with her flesh, the index finger and thumb of each hand gripping a hard point, playing with them, rolling them deliciously.

Her head fell back against his chest as the fingers moved aside. Rowdy shifted, making room for Natches as both men lowered their heads to the upthrust peaks.

Kelly went to her tiptoes as sensation exploded through her. A ragged cry slipped past her lips as a flood of weakening lust ripped through her.

Kelly lost the ability to speak, to see, to do anything but feel as two sets of hard male lips covered the sensitive peaks. Fire engulfed her as damp, lava-hot tongues begin to whip over the tight flesh, and hard male mouths began to suckle erotically.

"Easy, sweetheart," Dawg whispered at her ear as she began to writhe within the hold the three men had created. The feel of their mouths sucking at her sent arrows of near painful pleasure ripping to her womb, her clit. The aching throb was destroying her. "It's okay, Kelly." His hands moved from her breasts, only to be replaced by Rowdy's and Natches's.

One arm clasped her to him as he slid his hand down her stomach, moving slowly for the tortured flesh of her pussy.

"Rowdy . . ." His name was a whimpering plea as she felt Dawg's palm cup the sensitized folds of her cunt, one finger tucking subtly against the syrup-laden entrance to her vagina.

Rowdy groaned as he continued to suckle her, his teeth raking her nipple, his tongue flickering over it as Natches caught the tip he held captured between his teeth and pinched at it.

Her cry echoed around her as she twisted against Dawg, silently pleading to feel his finger slipping inside her.

The sensations tearing through her body were violent, destructive. Alternative caresses, suckling mouths, hands over her, hot male groans washing over her. And she was in the center of it, weak, helpless against the eroticism of each touch.

She pressed against Dawg's palm, shattering cries passing her lips at the pressure against her clit. It would be so easy to climax, if she could just press against him a bit more, just the barest friction would allow her to ease the hunger beating at her.

"Not yet, baby," he whispered at her ear, nipping her lobe. "Let your body burn for us, get so hungry that nothing matters except the touch, the need."

She was already burning. Her fingers clenched in Rowdy's and Natches's hair as she felt Dawg's fingers moving, felt him spreading her juices, allowing them to coat the tight entrance beyond as his finger massaged the closed portal.

She felt her anal entrance clench at the caresses, felt it open, milk at the tip of his finger as another hand, she didn't know whose, began to play with the swollen bud of her clitoris.

She was trapped between them, in the middle of the kitchen area, suspended within a pleasure, a heat so intense she could barely make sense of it. Pleading, incoherent cries fell from her lips as she arched back, arched forward, so desperate that she no longer knew which touch would send her streaking toward orgasm; she just knew she needed it.

Yet, it was different than it had been with Rowdy alone. She struggled to push aside the vague unease she felt. The lack of emotional warmth, of sharing that had come from being in bed upstairs, just her and Rowdy.

"There you go, sweetheart," Dawg whispered again as she felt the tip of his finger slide inside her anus. "Damn, you're tight, and hot. Your ass is sucking at my finger like a little mouth, needing more. Do you need more, sweetheart?"

At the same time, hard fingers captured her clit and pumped it wickedly. Oh God, she could come so easy, if she could just get closer.

She relaxed her buttocks as flames licked at the little bud. Simultaneously, the little entrance sucked the hard finger deeper as the pressure eased at her clit, causing her to scream in pleasure and frustration.

Her ass felt filled, and yet she needed more. Her clit was pounding with need, her pussy clenching with it until suddenly, sirens began to rip through her head. . . .

"Fuck . . ." Reality slammed through as she was jerked to the floor, three cursing, furious men covering her as blasts shattered the erotic frenzy with cold fury.

"Get her to the side." She was being pulled, jerked to the side, between the heavy cabinets as the sound of pounding feet and raging curses were heralded by return fire.

Shadows flashed around her in the dark as she scrambled to the corner of the cabinets, her hands brushing over fabric as she felt the shirt she had worn earlier beneath her hands.

Pulling it from the floor, she crouched in the V made by the cabinets and pulled it over her head as Rowdy pressed her tight against his side.

She didn't ask questions, she wasn't hysterical. She followed his lead as he, Natches, and Dawg began to work her closer to the back of the houseboat.

"Bastard shot the hull, Rowdy," Dawg hissed as the gunfire eased.

The computerized alarm was still going nuts, the siren shattering her nerves as the sound of the security personnel on the other end demanded an answer.

She noticed no one was answering. Within seconds they were informed that Lake Patrol had been alerted and was now moving for the area.

"The pumps are working." Natches slid in place with them. "We'll be okay until the patrol gets here."

They were dressed. She felt the scratch of Rowdy's jeans on her thigh, Natches at her rear. Dawg had dragged his shorts back on, but where Rowdy had come up with clothes she wasn't certain.

"I think he's on the cliff overlooking us," Natches snapped. "The trajectory of the shots would be about right for that."

"He'll have to cross the point to get back to the road," Dawg growled. "I'll be back. I'm going after him."

"No . . ." The word was a hollow, raspy sound, jerking from Kelly's throat as she caught at his pants.

Dawg brushed her hand aside, moving through the darkness as the pulsing siren continued to echo through the boat.

"Stay here." Rowdy pressed her against the counters before moving for the alarm box and quickly cutting the sound off.

Kelly listened silently as he spoke to the security personnel, his voice hard, dark, furious.

"Don't move from here until Rowdy comes back," Natches whispered in her ear. "I need to check upstairs."

She nodded in reply, her throat tight, fear and fury clogging her voice until she wasn't certain she could speak. This was because of her. Someone had shot into the boat, tried to sink it, to kill them, because of her. She had placed Rowdy and his cousins in danger, had caused a madman to focus on them.

She wrapped her arms around her waist, staying in place, huddled against the counter as Rowdy flipped on a light in the living area.

She looked up as he came around the counter, his expression hard, his eyes gleaming with rage.

"Come on, baby." His voice was gentle as he reached down for her. "Lake Patrol will be here to escort us to the dock in a minute. We need to get you dressed."

She pulled herself wearily to her feet, gazing around at the destruction. The windows were shattered, glass and debris littering the floor, the paneling splintered from the bullets.

"Come on." He lifted her into his arms as she stared around numbly at the destruction.

Despair tightened in her chest as she buried her face against Rowdy's neck. She could feel her stomach cramping with guilt, with fear. One of them could have died. She could have lost Rowdy, or Dawg or Natches could have been hurt, killed.

"Here." He sat her in the middle of the bedroom floor before moving to the small closet and pulling free a pair of her jeans. "Put these on."

She accepted them silently, bending to pull them over her feet and then to her hips before she took the sneakers from his hand. She sat on the bed, slipped them on, then struggled to tie the laces.

"Easy, baby." As Rowdy knelt before her, she realized the small whimpers she could hear were her own.

He brushed her fingers out of the way before tying the laces quickly, then staring up at her. Something twisted inside Kelly at the gentle emotion she saw in his eyes. Beyond the anger, the determination to kill that she could see raging inside him, she saw his gentleness.

"This wasn't your fault, Kelly." He reached up, cupping her cheek in his hand.

Kelly fought the tears that clogged her throat. Rather than answering, she pulled from his touch slowly, shuddering at the thought that his need for her could end in his death.

"Don't even try it." The snarl that twisted his face had her staring back at him in shock. "Don't think I'm going to let you run from me now, Kelly," he snapped roughly. "The time for running was over the minute you let me fuck that hot little body of yours."

She shook her head desperately, pushing against his chest as she fought to jerk to her feet. She couldn't speak. If she dared to attempt to, she knew the screams of rage and fear wouldn't be far behind.

"Stop it, Kelly . . ." He grabbed her wrists, forcing her in place as she heard the first hoarse cry leave her lips. "It's okay to be scared, baby. I swear to you, we're all okay, we anticipated this, we know how to fight him—"

"No," she protested fiercely, feeling the tears seeping past her eyes despite her desperation to hold them in check. "He's crazy. You can't do this. You can't . . ." She wasn't going to let him do it.

She tried to tear herself away from him, to get away from his touch, his warmth. She couldn't live like this. She couldn't live if anything happened to him, or the others, because of her.

"I will do it." He gripped her upper arms, giving her a brief, hard shake as she stared back at him miserably. "Hear me well, Kelly. I will stop him. And when I get my hands on him I'll kill him. Do you understand me? He will never ever touch you or another woman again. Ever."

Death shadowed his eyes as she stared back at him, incredulous. He would kill, and he would do so with no guilt, no second thoughts, she could see it in his eyes.

"He's trying to kill you all. He won't stop." Her voice was shaky, her insides trembling with enough force to make her stomach pitch. "Because of me. What if you're hurt? What if he manages to . . ." *To kill one of you.* She couldn't say the words, was terrified to let the thought pass her lips, as though giving it voice would make it more real than it already was.

"I won't stop either, Kelly," he bit out. "Listen to me, dammit. I will not stop until he's dead. I will not let that bastard terrorize you."

She opened her lips to argue, to beg, only to be cut off as Dawg moved quickly into the room.

"He got away." He was breathing rough, heavy. "Lake Patrol is moving in and Ray and Maria are right behind them. Natches is on the deck waiting for them."

Rowdy turned back to her. "You aren't leaving with them, Kelly. Don't even consider it."

Her breath caught, feeling the shudders in her belly beginning to work through her body. She had no other choice. She had to leave. And soon, she would have to leave Ray's home as well. She couldn't continue to endanger the people she loved.

"Don't make me gag you." She stared back at him in shock as his voice rumbled dangerously.

"What?"

"You're going to try to run from this. I can see it in your eyes. Leaving town isn't the answer Kelly. And if you try, I'll throw you over my shoulder and cart you out of here like a sack of fucking potatoes. Don't push me."

His lips curled back from his teeth in a powerful snarl as his eyes blazed with green fire back at her. Shock whipped through her at the deadly warning she saw in his gaze, as well as the confidence that he would carry out his warning.

"Don't . . ." She tried to protest, to fight against the sheer force she could feel wrapping around her.

"I mean it, Kelly," he growled, rising slowly to his feet as he pulled her after him. "Don't fight me on this. Not right now."

She felt dazed, overtaken, her mind overwhelmed by the danger and the certainty that if she attempted to run from him, then he would chase her down. He wouldn't let her go. Not now, not yet. Not before he shed blood.

Seventeen

Sheriff Ezekiel Mayes had surveyed the destruction of the *Nauti Buoy* after she limped into dock. His deputies were going through the interior as Kelly, Rowdy, Dawg, and Natches sat inside the small employees' room of the marina.

Ray and Maria stood at the side of the room as Sheriff Mayes took their statements. Kelly could see the knowledge in the sheriff's eyes as he questioned her, his gaze flickering to the Mackay cousins, a hint of disapproval lighting the golden brown depths of his eyes.

"You didn't see anything at all?" His gaze went over the four of them once again. "Hard to believe three tough ex-Marines would let a stalker get the jump on them, especially considering those same Marines were well aware of the danger of the situation."

Kelly pressed her lips together as she clenched her hands in her lap. She had to grit her teeth to keep from defending the men. To keep from revealing the fact that she knew Rowdy had planned this. She knew he had, and it infuriated her.

"Come on, Zeke, you know better than that," Rowdy bit out. "Kelly needed some time out. I thought the cove would be safe—"

"I'm not a fool, Rowdy," the sheriff snapped. "I'm not buying that shit and neither is your daddy." He nodded to where Ray was staring back at his son with a heavy scowl.

"I'm old enough that my daddy's opinion either way doesn't sway me, Zeke," Rowdy snapped back. "Now why don't you let me take Kelly home to rest—"

"Kelly, letting these three mix you up in some crazy scheme to catch this stalker is a bad idea." The sheriff hunched down in front of her chair. "Let me handle this. We'll catch him."

"You haven't yet," she whispered, shaking her head as anger and fear collided inside her.

Damn them all. She felt like a bone in the middle of a pack of wild dogs.

Compassion filled the sheriff's eyes. "I'm not a vigilante, sweetheart. When he's caught, I need the law on my side, not his. Kelly, if these boys suspect someone, I need to know."

"If I suspected anyone, you'd know it, Zeke." Rowdy's voice was hard, cold. "Now leave her the hell alone."

"God, stop snapping around me." Kelly jerked to her feet, causing the sheriff to straighten and stare down at her with a heavy scowl. "All of you. I've had enough for tonight. I didn't see anyone. I didn't hear anything. We were on the lake to get the hell away from that bastard. That was all."

She pushed her fingers through her hair, aware of the strained silence filling the room. She glanced over at her mother, and saw knowledge there. They knew why she was at the lake with the three cousins. She and Ray knew, and though Kelly felt no embarrassment, no shame at the knowledge, what she did feel was a sudden certainty that this wasn't a relationship she could endure.

Not because of the knowledge. Not because of morality. Because she didn't love them. She loved Rowdy, and the discontent, the subtle anger building inside her for days now over his expectations were clawing at her heart. The attack had only reinforced it. She was tired of being controlled. Period. First by a damned stalker and then by her need to please Rowdy.

"I'm ready to go home." She shook her head before lifting her chin and staring around the room. "Now. I need to sleep and I need to think."

"You can go home." Sheriff Mayes nodded. "But I may need to ask you some more questions tomorrow."

"Fine. Whatever."

"Just a minute and I'll drive you—" Rowdy began.

"I'll ride with Mom and Ray," she told him, ignoring the surprise that swept across his face. "I need to think, Rowdy. We can talk later."

"Kelly." He caught her arm as she moved to step past him. "We'll be right behind you."

We?

She moved her gaze over his cousins. She had been in their arms, felt their hunger and their lust, and despite the pleasure, she could feel her anger building. They were like little boys desperate to keep their newest toy close to them.

She inhaled deeply. "Whatever you want to do, Rowdy."

She pulled her arm from his grip before moving to Ray and her mother.

"Sure?" Ray asked her quietly.

"I just want to go home," she muttered. "Now."

Rowdy, Natches, and Dawg moved from the store with them. She was aware of how they placed themselves around her, protectively, shielding her. She felt smothered instead as she moved into the backseat of her stepfather's Laredo.

Within minutes they were heading to the house, a fucking convoy of vehicles. Dawg and Natches were in front of the Laredo with Rowdy bringing up the rear.

"Kelly—" Her mother began softly.

"Not now, Mom." She huddled into the backseat, wishing she could make sense of the emotions clouding her heart, her mind. Trying to make sense of her anger.

Rowdy was taking her over. Forceful. Dominant. He was so certain he knew what she needed, but Kelly had seen what she needed, and it wasn't what he was offering.

It was the reason she couldn't make the choice. Why she fought Rowdy every time he pushed for her to make a conscious decision about her needs. It was why she had wanted to be seduced, because she knew that unless the decision was taken out of her hands, she couldn't make it.

And that drove home the sharp edge of knowledge that this wasn't something she could do. She couldn't let this happen, because if she did, it would shadow her relationship with Rowdy forever. It would be better to lose him now than to have to share him later. If any more of her soul became invested in this, then she didn't know how she would bear letting go of every dream she had ever had. Hell, she didn't know how she was going to do it now.

Maybe she just wasn't naughty enough for the man she loved, or his cousins.

He was a fool. Rowdy followed the Laredo, his thoughts as confused as the emotions he had glimpsed raging in Kelly's eyes. He ached, and it wasn't because of the attack. That just pissed him off. No, he ached because the attack had been a diversion he had begun praying for just before it happened. A way to pull Kelly from Dawg's arms, make certain the fingers filling her tight ass were gone, the touch to her clit no one's but his own.

Jealousy had begun to mar the pleasure even before the sounds of gunshots and the whiz of bullets tearing through the cabin had sent them all crashing to the floor.

What the hell was he supposed to do now? Dawg and Natches had protected her for the past four years from the bastards desperate to get into her pants. His two cousins hadn't touched her because of the understanding of the relationship that would evolve later. Even though Rowdy knew they had hungered for her almost as desperately as he had.

Had he not been so intent on running those last four years, of being certain what he wanted, the attack wouldn't have happened. He would have been there to protect her, to keep that bastard from touching her. But what would have happened to the relationship he had always envisioned?

He realized now that the shift in his desires had begun before he returned home. Hell, before he took that last tour in the Marines. He hadn't wanted to face it, and now it was slamming into his face with the force of a sledgehammer.

He was risking everything he had come home for and he hadn't even realized it. His own arrogance, his own certainty that he hadn't, that he couldn't change. That the sexual pleasures that had always been such a part of his life would remain the same.

Kelly was changing the rules. She was changing him.

Rowdy rubbed at his neck wearily, blowing out a frustrated breath as he turned into the driveway of his father's home, his eyes scanning the well-lit exterior. Dawg and Natches had pulled to the sides of the driveway, keeping Ray's Laredo between their vehicles with Rowdy bringing up the rear.

Turning off the ignition, Rowdy opened the door and stepped from his pickup as Ray, Maria, and Kelly slowly stepped from the Laredo.

With a flick of his fingers he sent Natches ahead of them to check out the house before Kelly entered. His eyes continued to scan the exterior, the hairs on the back of his neck tingling as he moved closer to Kelly. He could feel the bastard out there, watching them.

She leaned into him as his arm went around her. Damn, she was exhausted, terrified. What the hell was he going to do about her? As the warmth of her swept through his body, the possessiveness growing inside him seemed to expand, strengthen.

Leading her toward the house, he kept his senses on alert as Natches slipped in ahead of them, with Dawg following close behind.

"Rowdy, we need to talk," Kelly whispered as they stepped up to the porch.

"We will, baby." He bent his head, kissing the top of her head before leading her into the hallway, his eyes finding Dawg as he made his way along the top of the stairs. Natches had moved into the kitchen, each man checking the rooms thoroughly as Rowdy led Kelly, and their parents, into the darkened living room.

"Leave the lights off for now, Dad," he advised his father as he moved Kelly to the wide chair at the side of the room. "There were signs of a watcher on the hill overlooking the house on this side the other night. The lights will pick up shadows with the thin curtains in here."

"Shit," his father muttered, but the lights stayed out. "I need a drink."

As Ray took care of drinks for himself, Maria, and Kelly, Rowdy went through the house again, checking windows, assuring himself it was safe for the few hours of night left. Dawg was currently set up in Kelly's room, armed with a night vision telescope as he watched the hill across the clearing, while Natches had slipped outside to take watch.

Returning downstairs, he escorted Kelly to his own bedroom. She was quiet, withdrawn, and he'd be damned if he knew what to say to her.

"Grab one of my shirts and go on to bed, darling." He couldn't touch her, if he did, he was guaranteed to completely humiliate himself. How could one man be as big a fool as he was? he wondered. And now, how did he fix it?

She was moving for his closet even as he spoke, and pulling free one of his more comfortable T-shirts. He had to give her credit for knowing what she wanted.

As he stood silently watching her, she stripped down to bare skin, then drew the shirt over her head and smoothed it down past her thighs. His clothes hung on her, but they carried her scent for weeks after she wore them. The soft, subtle hint of woman that only he could smell.

"You go ahead and do whatever you have to do," she told him, her voice cool as she flipped the blankets back on his bed and crawled in. "I'm too tired to deal with it tonight."

"Go to sleep, baby." He came close enough to bend, to let his lips caress the still kiss-swollen curves of hers as she stared up at him. "I'll take care of you, Kelly."

"Yes, you will," she sighed heavily, her gray eyes shadowed. "And tomorrow, I'll take care of you."

He didn't think she meant sexually.

"Kelly—"

"Not tonight, Rowdy." She shook her head firmly. "Tomorrow. I'm just too tired to talk tonight."

He could see the adrenaline crashing through her, wiping her out. She was still in shock, fighting the reality of the attack. She would dream later, he knew. And the nightmares could be ugly. He promised himself he'd be back by then, that he would hold her through them, ease her.

"Tomorrow." He smoothed her hair back from her face as she settled into the bed. "I'm going downstairs for a while, baby. I'll leave the door open and I won't be long—"

"I'll be okay, Rowdy," she assured him, a thread of mockery filling her voice. "Go. Just let me sleep."

Rowdy paced the house. Nervous tension was a bitch, and suffering from it wasn't something he normally did. But damn if he wasn't just about to cut his own throat just to ease the thoughts tormenting him.

What the hell had he done?

When he first came downstairs on the *Nauti Buoy*, the sight of

Kelly standing next to Dawg had sent his cock to full erection and the blood racing through his veins. Just as it had earlier when his cousin had moved behind her, his lips moving over her buttocks, spreading them, caressing her.

It had been hot as hell, feeling her pleasure as her hot little mouth surrounded the sensitive crest of his cock. Holding back had been iffy. His balls had drawn up in tortuous need, desperate to explode as the pleasure of it had seared his nerve endings.

He had ignored that unfamiliar tension that began to hover at the back of his mind. Fought with it. Then later, as his lips suckled at her tight nipple his eyes had watched as Natches pleasured the other, and he heard the words Dawg whispered to her. How snug she was, how hot, and the lust that filled his cousin's voice had slapped at Rowdy.

Jealousy. Possessiveness. He wasn't used to those emotions, but now they raged inside him until his fists were clenched and violence simmered just beneath the surface. He prayed for the chance to get his hands on the little son of a bitch stalking Kelly. To take out the fury and aggression rising inside him on someone who deserved it. Neither Dawg nor Natches deserved it, but it was building, growing inside him until Rowdy wasn't certain he could contain it.

Stalking back to the living room, he moved to the small bar Ray kept at the side of the room and poured a measure of whiskey into one of the tumblers sitting ready. The liquid burned going down, but did nothing to calm the beast raging inside him.

"Liquor doesn't help, boy."

He turned, his hand tightening on the butt of the pistol he carried before recognizing his father.

Ray stood just inside the doorway, dressed in a pair of dark cotton pajama bottoms and a faded T-shirt. His expression was sober, lined with worry, and his eyes gleamed with knowledge.

"We'll catch him." Rowdy shrugged. "He's losing focus—"

"I wasn't talking about her stalker." He moved farther into the room. "I was talking about what happened on that boat before he attacked."

Rowdy brought the glass to his lips and threw back the rest of the whisky before grimacing tightly. Damn, he didn't need this conversation with his father.

"Let it go, Dad."

"Doesn't set well, does it, Son?" Ray moved closer to the bar, lifting one of the clean tumblers and pouring his own drink. "It starts eating at your gut first thing, tearing at you, making you wonder where your mind was."

Rowdy narrowed his eyes on his father, hearing the knowledge in his voice, the assurance that only came from experience.

"They didn't take her," he muttered, wondering why the hell he was bothering to explain this to his father of all people.

"Might not have, but something happened. Something strong enough to make you panic, to keep you awake. To tear your guts up with guilt."

Son of a bitch.

"She was shot at, Dad, that's enough to shake any man's insides."

Ray sipped at his drink, staring at him over the rim of the glass. Rowdy couldn't hide from the knowledge, no matter how much he suddenly wanted to.

"I know what's going on, Son," he finally sighed heavily. "You think you and those two hardheaded cousins of yours are the only men in this family to think they know what they want in a woman? And in her pleasure?" Ray frowned heavily, his eyes darkening. "You're not. I've tried to warn you since I first caught wind of what was going on, and you've never wanted to listen."

Rowdy watched his father curiously then. Through the years, there had been whispers that Ray Mackay and his best friend had been up to some sexual little games, but nothing concrete and nothing his dad had ever confirmed.

Ray grunted mockingly. "Your generation thinks they know everything. You don't. Mine knew what a reputation was, and we knew what should be kept private and what should be flaunted. Women like Calista James were steered clear of except for a certain few. We knew our actions would always backfire on us, if not at the time, then later, on our wives, our children. I thought I taught you that, but maybe I failed there too."

Ray shook his head as he nodded to the chairs Maria and Kelly had sat in earlier. "Come over here, Rowdy. Let's talk."

"What's there to talk about?"

"Saving face," his father sighed. "Those two cousins of yours have waited nearly as long as you have for Kelly. They don't love her like you do, but when you yank something like that out of a man's hands, he's bound to get pissed. And you don't want that kind of pissed from men you've been as close to as brothers."

Ray leaned forward in his chair, staring back at Rowdy intently. Damn, that look had the ability to send him right back to his teenage years and the memory of his father's chastisements.

He wasn't a teenager anymore, but at the moment he felt as uncertain as one.

Rowdy turned his gaze to his drink, wondering what the hell he was supposed to say. He'd already figured out the fact that he was making a hell of a mistake—he didn't need his father to point that out to him.

"It's tough, being as close to men as you are to Dawg and Natches," Ray sighed. "You three are closer than brothers, you always have been." He shook his head, staring down at the glass in his hand as he grimaced painfully. "I had a friend like that once, Rowdy." He lifted his eyes then. "A damned good friend."

Rowdy stared back at him, knowing what was coming. Knowing he didn't want to hear it.

"It was before your mother." Ray cleared his throat. "And there was this woman. One that made the blood boil in my veins, made me want forever. But I was dumb. Brick dumb. I thought I'd always be the man I was then. That what I wanted sexually would always be a part of my life. And I shared that woman. Because I thought that pleasure was the greatest gift I could give her . . ."

He tossed back the rest of his drink before meeting Rowdy's eyes once again.

"Kelly should have been your sister, Rowdy. If I hadn't been so stupid, I wouldn't have lost Maria all those years ago. She chose the lover willing to love just her, rather than his own selfishness. Willing to give her all of himself, without the childish need to have it all his own way."

Rowdy's jaw bunched tightly.

"Dad, let it go." Rowdy shook his head sharply.

"You're figuring it out, I can see that in your eyes. The same way I thought I was figuring it out. But I let that bond I thought I had with my buddy get in the way. I was torn between the loss of friendship, and my own wants. And I thought the woman would be there either way. It wasn't the friend I lost, Rowdy. It was the woman. And trust me, when it comes right down to it, Kelly is no different than her mother."

Rowdy breathed in deeply. Damn, he hadn't wanted to hear this. He lifted the whisky before tipping more of the liquor into his glass.

His father was silent then, finishing his drink as Rowdy sipped from his.

"I love her," Rowdy finally breathed out roughly. "I didn't expect this though."

"Love changes us, Son." Ray rose to his feet, crossing the room slowly to set his empty glass on the bar. "Don't make the same mistake I did, Rowdy. Once it's over that first time, once you've let another man claim what's yours and yours alone, you lose a part of your soul. Getting it back is hell. A hell I hope you never know."

Rowdy stared back at his father silently, finally hearing what the other man had always tried to teach him. What was fair, what he wanted alone, wasn't all that mattered. He had begun learning it in the Marines, but it was slapping him upside the head now.

"James Salyers was still a friend when he died, Rowdy. And I grew up and learned some damned hard lessons. Maria gave me a second chance, but that chance came at a cost. A very high cost. The daughter that should have been mine came from another man, and the son I love more than life is about to fuck up not just his own life, but that girl's as well. Watching it and knowing I can't stop it is hell. Remember that while you struggle between what you love and what you want."

As Rowdy watched his father leave the room, a heavy sigh slipped past his lips. Maria's objections to his relationship made more sense now. He shook his head, realizing how well his father, James Salyers, and Maria had kept that secret. Reputations. Theirs was intact, but his wasn't. And now, he was risking Kelly's as well.

Kelly was awake when he returned to the bedroom a little after midnight. Sleep wasn't coming, no matter how hard she sought it. Each time she closed her eyes she saw . . . herself . . . surrounded by the Mackay cousins, their hands touching her as pleasure whipped around her. But it wasn't pleasure she felt in the memory. She felt the dark swirl of shame.

The same emotions she had felt each time she swore she wasn't waiting one day longer on Rowdy and she was going to find someone to love her. To stick around and be with her. Each time she had tried, each time she had attempted to allow another man to touch her, shame had eaten her alive for days later.

The door closed behind him, the click of the lock causing her to open her eyes, to stare through the darkness as his shadow moved toward the bed.

God, she loved him. If she could give him his every desire then she would do it in a second, but some things she knew she couldn't do. Dawg and Natches she couldn't do. And she had no idea how to tell him. No idea how to broach what she knew could destroy the relationship she had dreamed of.

"Everything's quiet," he said softly as he pulled his shirt from his body.

The room was dark, too dark to make out his expression, but she could hear his voice, see the gleam of his eyes.

"I couldn't sleep." She could feel the tension between them.

Rowdy sat at the edge of the bed, pausing before he sighed tiredly and bent to take off his sneakers.

"Rowdy?" She whispered his name, uncertain what to say, what to do as he rose to his feet and shucked off his jeans.

He was naked. As he turned to her she glimpsed the heavy, engorged length of his erection a second before she was suddenly jerked to him.

"Rowdy?" She gasped his name as his lips covered hers, stealing her breath, her startled cry.

And from there, her strength. His hands were hard, dominant as he tore the shirt from her body, tossing it carelessly to the floor before his lips took hers again. Her muted cries built in her head as he bore her to the bed, spreading her thighs, sinking into her.

There were no preliminaries. No foreplay. One moment she was empty, the next she was full, her pussy stretched to its limits as he groaned into her mouth.

She fought to breathe, and she could feel his struggle as well. The harsh sounds that tore from his throat were almost animalistic in their hunger, their intensity. His lips held back both their cries as he began to move, hard, furious strokes inside, sending her nerve endings into shock, the pleasure ripping through her with the same desperation with which his erection thrust into the slick, heated depths of her body.

Her arms wrapped about his neck, fingers pushing into his hair as one hard hand gripped her hip, holding her in place as he moved. The other arm curled beneath her as he supported himself on his elbow.

He surrounded her. He possessed her. Pleasure became a burning, consuming need as he fucked her with a hunger that swept through her soul. She could almost touch his soul. Then her eyes opened, widened, shock and ecstasy exploding through her as the orgasm overtaking her stole a part of her very spirit. Stole it and merged it with his. Melded them together as he stiffened above her, his cock swelling then pulsing as his release jetted inside her. Deep, almost violent spurts of his seed heated her, triggering another, deeper orgasm, sending stars to explode around her as she screamed soundlessly into his kiss.

"Mine!" The hard, throaty growl that left his throat had to have been her imagination. "Mine."

Possessive. Consuming. *His.*

Eighteen

"Rowdy, we're not going to be able to keep her here." Dawg moved through the living room, checking the windows and their latches the next afternoon. "Your dad's security system is good, but it won't stop a bullet."

"Don't know many that will," Rowdy muttered, tamping down his impatience as he pushed his fingers through his hair and surveyed the living room.

He had been through the rest of the house, just as Dawg and Natches had been over the hill above it. The bastard was hiding there at night, watching the house, and he had a clear shot into every room from one point or another, if one of them messed up and didn't close the curtains well enough.

And that didn't change the fact that his dad and Maria were refusing to leave now. As was Kelly.

"He'll come back at us quick enough to keep us from making headway into security here," Natches drawled from the entryway. "He was in that clearing across from her room last night. I never caught sight of him, but I could feel him. He was out there. And he's damn good."

Shit.

"We have to get her out of here, Rowdy," Dawg reiterated. "Now. My gut is going crazy with this. Whoever the bastard is, he's lost his damned mind. He won't care who he kills to get to Kelly."

"Your place?" Rowdy's eyes narrowed on Dawg's expression. He could see the expectation there, the excitement.

Dawg's house was an underground masterpiece built by his parents. The outside was cement and stone overlaid with roughened wood siding. The windows were extra thick and after Dawg's return from the Marines, bulletproof. As far as anyone knew, there was only one way in or out. No one knew about the hidden entrance except for the three of them.

Dawg nodded. "It's the most secure."

Rowdy braced himself. He could feel the sexual tension beginning to heat up in the room. His cousins had waited years for this. Hell, they all had.

"I'm not sharing her." The words were out of Rowdy's mouth before he could stop them.

His head snapped up, his jaw tightening as Dawg and Natches stared back at him in surprise.

"Is that your decision or Kelly's?" Natches tipped his head to the side and watched him curiously.

Rowdy found the look testing his temper. Natches liked to push and he liked to challenge things just for the hell of it. Rowdy hated the thought of fighting his cousin over something that should have been settled years before, but he would.

"It doesn't matter whose decision it is." Rowdy pushed the words past his lips, attempting to contain the anger rising from his cousin's question. "It's not happening. We'll move her to the house, but hands off. Period."

Dawg sighed heavily, a grimace contorting his expression.

"Now, son of a bitch, how did I know you were going to go and get all dog-eared fucking jealous?" he griped, his green eyes narrowed in irritation. "Hell, Rowdy, talk about blue balls going on here."

"Talk about too damned bad," Rowdy muttered as his muscles bunched and flexed beneath his flesh in rising tension. Damn, this shit sucked. As though the possessiveness, the emotions he felt for her were a separate being living within his flesh and bone.

"Hell, we can argue over this later," Natches finally grumped. "After I take out my mad on that son of a bitch stalking her. Then we can fight over sharing rights."

"No sharing rights. Period," Rowdy snapped. The only thing that restrained him from taking his cousins apart limb by limb was the fact that he knew them. They weren't pissed, at least not yet. But Rowdy admitted he was getting there fast.

And it was his own damned fault. He was mad at himself for letting this situation get out of control, for letting his cousins believe there would be more here than he was able to accept now.

"Chill out, cuz," Dawg breathed out roughly. "Hell, it would have been nice, but no one's pushing. Wouldn't be worth a shit if both of you didn't want it anyway."

Rowdy narrowed his eyes on his older cousin. There was a vague restlessness in his voice, and he realized it had been there for a while.

"What the hell do you two think you're doing? Growing the fuck up?" Natches snapped then, disgust lining his voice and filling his green eyes. "If I wanted to grow up I would have stayed in the fucking Marines."

Rowdy rolled his eyes. Trust Natches to get to the heart of the matter.

"I guess it was bound to happen eventually," Dawg sighed. "Come on, let's get the little troublemaker hid out in the house and see what we can do to make her life a little safer before she takes on the resident grouch here." He flicked his hand toward Rowdy.

"This falling in love crap obviously sucks," Natches commented as he turned and headed out of the room. "Remind me to steer clear of it why doncha, guys? God only knows what kind of fool I might end up making of myself if I made that mistake." His mock shudder had a grin pulling at Rowdy's lips.

"Careful, Natches, you know what happens when we tempt fate." How many times had they assured themselves the fun and games would never end. And now look where they were.

"Fate can kiss my ass," he grumbled. "Better yet, she can suck my dick. I'm footloose and fancy-free, my man. And that's how I'll stay."

Rowdy eyed his cousin warily. There was lightning striking somewhere, he was certain, and at that moment he decided he didn't want to be anywhere around when Natches finally did manage to fall in love.

"Think about it guys," he muttered. "Do you think I'd ever be able to touch another woman after Kelly? That she could ever bear the thought of it, even if I could? She's my life—"

"All this sugar is just going to give me a toothache," Natches growled as he threw him a dark look. "Get over it already. She would have gone along with it if she had spent awhile between the three of us. She's a fair-minded person—"

"Well maybe I'm not," Rowdy bit out, his tone guttural. "Keep pushing me, Natches, and you're going to get the fight you're aiming for."

Rowdy was aware of Dawg watching them both warily, sensing the tension suddenly whipping between Natches and Rowdy.

"None of you are going to fight."

Rowdy's head whipped around as Kelly stepped into the room, her gray eyes glittering with temper, her face flushed with it.

She was dressed in a pair of those low-rise jeans he liked so damn well. It was paired with a little cami shirt with tiny straps that flashed abdomen and the belly ring that made his dick jerk in his pants. That curvy little body of hers was going to be the death of him.

Surprisingly, Natches backed down from the look in her eye, not that Rowdy blamed the other man—she looked ready to claw all their eyes out.

"Hell, Kelly, you know us. We fight for the hell of it." Natches flashed a smile at her, one that gave a hell of a pretense of friendly amusement, if you discounted the darkening of those pale eyes.

"Save it for someone you can convince." She frowned back at the other man.

Natches grimaced.

"Kelly, you know"—Rowdy leaned against the bar as he watched her—"I can take care of some things myself here."

She was cute as hell as she watched them with a temper tantrum seething just beneath the surface.

"Where these two are concerned?" She flicked her fingers between Dawg and Natches. "Rowdy, I doubt a whole team of Marines could whip those two in line."

"Several might have tried though," Dawg pointed out, his lips twitching in a grin.

She stared between the three of them before her gaze moved back to Rowdy. He could see it in her eyes, she must have caught part of the conversation, but that didn't mean she liked any of it. He was realizing just how intensely private his little love was, and it shocked him to realize how much that pleased him.

He should have known Kelly would change the rules on him; what surprised him was the fact that she made him like it. It sent a strange little pulse of pride through him, that considering his past, he shouldn't have felt.

"If you're making plans concerning my life or my safety," she said then, crossing her arms beneath the tempting mounds of her breasts, "I think I should be a part of the planning process. Don't you?"

What had made him think she would accept anything less?

"Now, Kelly," Natches drawled then. "We can take care of the detail stuff here. You shouldn't worry your little head about this stuff."

Rowdy and Dawg both blinked back at the other man, wondering if he'd lost his ever-lovin' mind. Everyone who knew Kelly knew you simply did not patronize her, period. She was sharp as a whip and had definite ideas on a lot of things. Pig-headed men being one of those things.

Kelly's eyes narrowed on him. "Just not worry my little head about it?" she asked him gently.

"Kelly . . ." Rowdy cleared his throat, looking for an excuse for his dim-witted cousin.

"More or less." Natches's smile was condescending as Rowdy stared at him in disbelief. When had his cousin decided that women were stupid?

"Kelly, sweetheart, Dad and Maria were supposed to—"

"Don't try to distract me, Rowdy, it doesn't work," she snapped, her dark eyes furious as her stubborn chin lifted, her soft lips tightening in anger as her gaze swung back to Natches.

"Come on, Kelly, we all know Natches can be a knothead," Dawg sighed. "Let's not hurt him too bad here. We might need him down the road later to dig ditches or something."

Natches's lips lifted in a grin as his light green eyes stayed locked on Kelly. And suddenly, Rowdy knew his game. He almost laughed when his gaze went back to Kelly and rather than seeing furious arousal glittering in her eyes, he only saw the anger.

His little spitfire wasn't in the least turned on by Natches's confrontational attitude.

"You know, Natches"—she lifted a hand and surveyed her

nails for a second before lifting her gaze back to the other man—"just because I'm not exactly a part of the upper crust of this fine little town doesn't mean I don't know its little secrets. Don't make the mistake of thinking I'm one of those slow-witted little blondes you and Dawg have been snacking on lately. Because I'm not. And neither am I at all interested in taming that bad boy thing you have going on. And as for you." She turned to Rowdy.

Rowdy lifted his brow curiously. There was the arousal. It glittered just beneath the anger as she raked over his lazy slouch against the bar. "Before making any plans that concern *my* future, maybe you'll be good enough to discuss them with me first. If you don't mind, that is."

Ouch. The lash of displeasure in her voice actually stung.

"And I think that's our cue to go," Dawg stated with a smile as he straightened from where he was leaning against the wall. "Let's go, Natches."

"Like hell," Natches drawled. "Watching her neuter him is way too much fun."

Rowdy straightened as hurt flashed in Kelly's eyes as she stared back at the other man. Natches's tone was bordering snide, and Rowdy was fed up with it.

"Natches, shut the hell up," he warned softly.

"Why?" Natches asked with apparent joviality. "Hell, Rowdy, I'm taking notes here. Watching you get your dick twisted in a knot like this over her is teaching me what not to do."

He was going to kill Natches.

"Kelly, ignore that fool," Dawg drawled then. "He's just pissed as hell that you're not twisting his dick, that's all."

"And he's getting ready to get his ass kicked." Rowdy moved then.

He stalked across the room, ignoring Kelly's flinch as he pulled her against him, his lips pressing to her forehead as he held her to him, his gaze slicing to Natches in warning.

"We're just discussing the best place to protect you, baby." He rubbed his hand down her arm, feeling her tremble against him despite her anger. "No plans are being made without you. I promise."

"I don't need to be babied." She pulled away from him, but the hurt in her voice was easy to hear and Rowdy promised he was going to make Natches pay for that one. "I just thought somehow, plans that included me were my business. Just forget it."

She turned and stalked from the room as Rowdy turned back to Natches. The minute he heard her moving up the hallway, he jumped for the older man.

"Whoa! Hold on there, boy." Dawg jumped in front of him, blocking him with his wider body as Rowdy growled in fury. "You know how he gets. Dammit, Rowdy, you start a fight in here and Maria's gonna kick all our asses."

"Get the fuck out of my face." He jabbed his finger over Dawg's shoulder, glaring back at Natches as his expression darkened with anger. "And so help me God, you treat her like that again and I'll tear your dick off and feed it to you. You want to be a bastard because you're not getting what you want, then you take it up with me."

He knew Natches's problem, and he knew he should have anticipated it. Dawg and Natches both had waited, just as he had, for Kelly. They had hungered, lusted, expected certain things where her relationship with Rowdy was concerned.

This was his fault. As he jerked away from Dawg, he admitted it was his fault, but he'd be damned if Kelly was going to pay for it with Natches's surly attitude.

He paced to the bar, pouring a quick drink and kicking it back as he grimaced at the sting. Natches was damned good at pushing buttons, and, Rowdy admitted, Kelly was a sore spot with him. Hell, he should have known years ago that this wasn't going to work, rather than running from the situation as he had. And he had run. The emotions that damned woman caused to rise inside him threatened his sanity at times.

"I didn't mean to hurt her." Natches cleared his throat uncomfortably. "Hell. I didn't mean anything by it, Rowdy."

Rowdy lifted his gaze. He was so damned close to fighting Natches that he had to clench his fist to hold onto his control.

"She's mine, Natches," he snapped. "I can understand why you're pissed but if you take it out on her again, you'll deal with me. You got that?"

"Yeah, I got that." Natches snorted, though he didn't sound overly concerned at the prospect. "I'm going to go see if I can find a sign of that bastard while you cool off. Hell, son of a bitch needs to die for fucking shit up like this."

He stomped from the living room. Seconds later, the door slammed behind him. Rowdy stared back at Dawg then.

"He'll chill out." Dawg slapped him on the shoulder as he headed from the room. "You take care of Kelly, and we'll watch your back. And when Natches's time comes, we might even watch his."

Nineteen

Kelly was furious. The anger that sizzled through her carried her through the afternoon and into that evening.

It was the fear making her angry and she knew it. It was making her crazy. And Rowdy, Dawg, and Natches weren't helping matters. They were making a target of themselves rather than her, daring a madman to strike out at them. Endangering all their lives, and it scared her to death. And that's where the anger stemmed. Toward the bastard who thought she should belong to him rather than the man she loved. A monster who wanted to terrorize her because she wasn't the good girl he had decided she should be.

She snorted at that thought. The fantasies she'd had over the years where those three men were concerned were anything but good. But they were fantasies for her. She liked the fantasies, she liked pretending she was daring enough, cool enough, to control Rowdy and his cousins.

But the truth of the matter was that she was anything but cool, calm, or collected when it came to Rowdy. And as hot as the thought of having all three men focused on her was, as hot as it had been in the boat, something still held her back. Made her wary.

"I didn't mean to hurt your feelings."

She whirled around with a gasp, wishing now that she had turned the lights on. Natches was shadowed from the hall light, a dark form leaning against the wide entrance into the room.

"You didn't hurt my feelings," she snapped. "You pissed me off."

He sighed. "I didn't mean to piss you off either."

Natches flipped on the light. He grinned at her as she watched him warily.

"Do you remember how Dawg and I rushed to the hospital after you were attacked?" he asked, his voice soft, a bit sad.

And they had. Ray swore the doctors had almost had to call security to get them to leave the hall outside her room.

"I remember."

He brushed back the long hair from his devilishly handsome face. Natches was a charmer, with the face of a fallen angel and eyes that invited a woman to be bad.

"We knew you were ours even when you were a little girl," he said reflectively. "Not in the sense we knew it after you grew up, but we claimed you. Watched out for you—"

"I love Rowdy, Natches," she whispered, halting what she feared was coming. "And don't try to tell me you love me in the same way, because we both know better."

His lips tightened. "We're a set. You're destroying it, Kelly."

He stared back at her, his light green eyes wary and somber but she could feel the anger in him. She was changing the rules and he didn't like it.

"I don't mean to, Natches," she whispered. "I can't be what you want, I can't do what you need."

"You knew that was part of it," he growled. "Everyone knows that's part of it."

Kelly tipped her head to the side, watching him. Of the three cousins, Natches had always been the most alone. Dawg had his sister after his parent's death, as well as Rowdy's parents. Natches's parents were cold, almost inhumanly so. Scions of the county, with more money than they needed and less heart than anyone Kelly had ever met. How a brother of Ray's could have turned out like that, she couldn't figure.

And Natches had always suffered for it, until he was old enough to leave. Dawg and Rowdy were his family. They were all he really claimed. And though she couldn't see him as needy, she could see the regret that egged at him, the fierce determination not to lose that connection he had with the other two men.

"I'm sorry," she whispered. "What Rowdy does when he leaves me—"

"You think he's going to leave you?" Mocking laughter filled his voice then. "Hell, Kelly, what do you think we were fighting over when you walked in? Rowdy gave us the 'hands off.' He's gone all white-knight possessive on us for some damned reason, and it has to be because you refused to do it."

She stared back at him in surprise.

"He did what?"

"You heard me," he grumbled. "Son of a bitch dared us to touch you. You have his dick tied in so many knots he doesn't know what he wants."

Now, that just didn't sound like Rowdy. Rowdy wasn't a man who didn't know what he wanted. And he always meant what he said.

"I didn't know that was what you were arguing over—"

"Because you're not the one who would have problems understanding the concept." Rowdy's deep, angry voice broke in on the conversation as he stepped into the smaller entrance next to the stairs.

He stared back at Natches, his eyes narrowed, his body corded and tense.

"Hell, back down, Rowdy," Natches sighed. "I just wanted to apologize for hurting her feelings, not take you on."

Natches pushed his fingers wearily through his hair. She could feel the sense of resignation moving around him and the sadness of it pricked at her.

Kelly shivered as Rowdy moved next to her, his arm going around her waist, pulling her against the warmth of his body. As he did she caught the look that flashed across Natches's face. It was so quick that she wondered if she imagined it. Envy, regret.

"I accept your apology, Natches," she told him softly. "And I'm sorry, this isn't what I intended."

Rowdy tensed at her side.

Natches's grin was crooked, charming, but the sight of it made her chest ache. It was a ruse. Natches wasn't taking this well, and of the three men, she wondered if perhaps he was the one who needed the sharing the most.

"Time for me to slip out and see if we can catch our evil neighborhood stalker now." He straightened from the doorway, flexing his shoulders as he turned toward the hallway. "Catch ya'll later."

As he disappeared she felt Rowdy's hands slide through her hair.

"Are you okay?" He tilted her head back, staring down at her with a slight frown.

"I'm not an emotional wreck, Rowdy." She grimaced at the concern in his eyes. "You're suddenly treating me with kid gloves and it's getting on my nerves."

"What do you mean by that?" His frown darkened as she moved away from him then turned to face him.

"You told Dawg and Natches to keep their hands off me?" She leaned against the center island and crossed her arms beneath her breasts as she stared back at him. "Why?"

His eyes narrowed. "We'll discuss this later."

He turned away to the fridge, opening it to grab a beer as she stared back at him in surprise.

"Says who?"

"Me." He unscrewed the bottle top with a hard jerk of his fingers.

"And you think that perhaps this doesn't concern me in some way? That maybe I don't have a say in it?"

"Drop this, Kelly," he warned her, his voice grating as his eyes flamed back at her. "This isn't a conversation I'm ready to get involved in where you're concerned, not right now."

"Fine. I'll drop it." She uncrossed her arms, straightened her shoulders, and lifted her chin defiantly. *Drop it*? Oh she could drop it all right. "I'll drop it completely, Rowdy. And you can go to hell at the same time you find yourself someplace else to sleep. If I'm not able to decide for myself whether or not I'll screw another man, then I'll be damned if I have the brains to decide if I want to screw you."

She stalked from the kitchen, fists clenched, her teeth grinding. God, when he had gotten so damned arrogant? So impossible to deal with? She didn't know when it had happened, but where she was concerned, it could stop now.

• • •

When had she become so damned stubborn?

Rowdy watched Kelly as she stalked from the kitchen, then listened to her stomp up the stairs muttering to herself before he moved.

Self-control, he had tried to warn himself. Things weren't exactly stable right now. Between the stalker, his argument with Natches, and his own revelations about himself, he knew his temper wasn't exactly calm. But this was just too much.

Moving quickly up the stairs behind her, he caught the bedroom door as she was attempting to close it, pushing his way in before he slammed it forcibly.

"Did I ask you to follow me?" she hissed, her gray eyes dark and gleaming with irritation as she faced him.

"You didn't have to ask."

Before she could blast him with whatever her lips were opening to say, he jerked her to him, lowered his head, and stole the sound with his kiss.

It was like sinking into ecstasy, fire, all the pleasure he could have ever imagined. He caught her little gasp with his lips, felt her hands grip his shoulders, her nails biting into the fabric of his shirt as he turned and lifted her, pressing her against the wall as he devoured the sweetness of her lips.

Her kiss. He loved her kiss. The feel of her lips softening beneath his, her body straining against him as his hands moved over it, pushing beneath the thin material of her shirt to cup her swollen breasts.

She was ready for him. He could feel it in the way her tongue met his, the hot little moans smothered by his lips. God, he had dreamed of this. Dreamed of touching her. Loving her.

Pulling his head back, he jerked her shirt over her head, staring down at her, fighting to breathe as he watched the heavy lift and fall of the firm mounds.

He loved her breasts. His hands cupped them again, fitting over the fragile lace of her bra, his thumbs raking over the tender tips as he stared back at her.

"You're mine." He could hear the guttural tone of his voice, but he also saw the effect of it in her eyes.

They darkened in hunger as she drew in a hard breath, her tongue licking over her swollen lips.

"I need you," he whispered then, desperately, hungrily. "All of you, baby. Sweet and hot, and crying for me."

He took her lips again before he made a fool of himself. Before he went to his knees and begged her to see, to understand the selfishness rising inside him. It sliced through him like the sharpest blade. The thought of another man touching what was his, taking the innocence, the sweetness of Kelly was more than he could bear.

"Rowdy . . ." She shuddered in his grip as he released her bra, drawing it from her shoulders before his hands went to the clasp of her jeans.

"This is mine." He worked his hand between them to push her jeans roughly over her hips before cupping the hot, wet mound of her pussy.

His fingers delved beneath the silk of her panties, so desperate for the feel of her that taking time to completely undress her was more than he could consider.

His fingers moved through silken heat, parting the bare folds to sink into the sweet, tight depths of her slick core.

She arched into the touch, pressing against him, driving his finger further inside her as she cried into the kiss. The hot little sounds she made as he touched her had his cock throbbing in demand. He needed her. Needed to taste her, to touch her.

Now. He had to claim her.

The sharp knock at the door had his muscles clenching further in denial.

"Rowdy, we have movement out here." Dawg's quiet voice was dark with imminent violence. "You in on this, man?"

"No." Kelly clutched at his shoulders as he moved back.

Son of a bitch, if he caught the bastard stalking her he was going to rip him apart with his bare hands.

"I'll be back." He pulled her jeans quickly back in place.

"Don't go out there," she cried out, her face paling as her fingers gripped his arm. "It's too dark Rowdy, and you don't know where he could be hiding. Wait—"

There wasn't a chance in hell he wasn't going out there.

"You're mine," he snarled, sealing the claim with a hard kiss to her lips. "All mine, Kelly. And that bastard is going to figure that out at the end of my fist or my gun. I don't care which."

He pulled away from her, jerking the door open and closing it before Dawg could see her, her sweet breasts rising over the lace of her bra, her pale face staring back at him with equal amounts of fear and anger.

The fear was going to be gone.

"Let's go hunting." He took the rifle Dawg handed to him and headed downstairs.

Twenty

Kelly waited until nearly dawn for Rowdy, Dawg, and Natches to return to the house. Whatever or whoever had been out there had been determined not to be found. They had disappeared, leaving the three men with a growing, restless anger. And a determination to get her where they felt she would be protected.

Despite her objections, Rowdy packed her clothes and loaded her into Dawg's truck as the sun began to rise beyond the mountains.

She was terrified, she admitted. Whoever was stalking her knew how to hide, which only made him more dangerous. The thought of Rowdy, or one of his cousins, paying for the danger stalking her was eating a bleeding wound into her soul.

Finally, despite her objections and her demands that she simply leave town, the pickup pulled into the graveled road leading to Dawg's house.

Kelly knew the moment she saw the house why they had chosen Dawg's as a secure location. She had forgotten about the house, built by Dawg's parents, and set into the base of the mountain that ran through their property outside Somerset. He spent most of his time on his boat, so she hadn't considered the house.

The huge dwelling was set into the side of the mountain, with only the front left in view. Dawg's father had designed and overseen its building, Ray had once said, claiming that he was determined to have the most unique home in the county. And it was that.

It had been meant to be a vacation home, private, out of the way, and as unique as his parents had been. Though Rowdy had often wondered if Dawg's father hadn't been more than the architect he claimed to be. There were too many secrets in the Mackay family, he admitted, and one of these days, he was going to get to the bottom of them.

The face of the house was warm wood, covering steel and cement, with large windows looking out from the kitchen on the left, and the large living room on the right.

It wasn't opulent, or expensively furnished, but it was a huge dwelling with four bedrooms, accompanied by private baths. There was an exercise room and a basement pantry–wine room larger than some apartments she had been in.

The house was built in three levels—kitchen, living room, and exercise room on the ground level, bedrooms above on the top level, and the basement on a third level. She now understood why Dawg's father, Chandler Mackay, had been considered one of the finest architects in the nation.

It had been surprising when Dawg entered the Army then took over the lumberyard his father had owned. Everyone had expected him to step into his late father's shoes and become an architect instead.

Rowdy led her through the large open living room to the wide hallway that opened at the back of it. There, two sets of curved wooden steps led to the other levels. He moved aside as they reached the stairs that led to the upper level, allowing her to move ahead of him.

The steps were narrow, but comfortable, and led into another short hallway and two open doors.

"The left." He nudged her toward the open door, his voice brooking no argument as they moved into the room.

A huge king-sized bed took up the center of the room, draped with sheer curtains that hung from a steel ring in the center of the ceiling and tied at each corner of the bed.

A dark wood dresser and chest, writing desk, and vanity table sat along the walls. Scenic pictures set in frames that resembled windows on the far side of the bed. Behind it, another door opened into what was obviously a large bathroom.

"Nice," she murmured as Rowdy moved in behind her and closed the door before setting her bags on the floor. He must have packed everything she had before they left his father's house.

"It suits Dawg." He shrugged negligently. "Go ahead and get settled in, take a nap if you need to. We'll go out to dinner later."

"I'd prefer to stay here." She turned to him slowly, keeping her expression carefully bland.

"Too bad." He crossed his arms over his chest as he watched her, the dark gray T-shirt he wore stretching over his rippling muscles. "Dawg, Natches, and I decided we're going to eat out."

"I want to be alone." She pressed her lips firmly together. "I told you that."

The argument had raged for hours. She couldn't believe his complete arrogance and stubbornness. He refused to leave her alone for even a second, and he wouldn't hear of her leaving town without him. At this point, he wouldn't even hear of her leaving town with him. She would have settled for that.

"And I said, you can forget it," he repeated, not for the first time as he dropped his arms and moved closer. Kelly stepped back, ignoring his dark frown. "Kelly, baby, you don't have to worry like this, everything will be okay."

"Sure it will." She smiled tightly. "That's why we're staying in a house that could likely defend against an attack from a foreign government and your cousins are packing in enough weapons to defend against an army."

"They're for looks only," he assured her. "We have a plan, I promise."

"Like you did the other night on the lake?"

"Naw, that was just to see how rock-dumb that bastard could get. He's dumb enough to need help breathing at this point. He won't be that hard to catch."

Confidence gleamed in his eyes, even as dread burned in her belly.

"He would have been caught by now if it were that easy." She pushed her fingers through her hair as she shook her head. "You're underestimating him, Rowdy."

"Maybe you're underestimating me," he grunted as his hands whipped out, pulling her into his embrace before she could avoid him.

Heat instantly sizzled across her body, nearly taking her breath as he pressed the hard length of his erection against her belly.

"Want me to help you shower?" He nuzzled his face against her neck, his tongue licking over her pulse erotically as his fingers clenched at her hips.

Kelly gripped his shoulders, certain the weakness in her knees was going to become a permanent thing if he didn't stop touching her so damned much. She needed to think; she didn't need her mind clogged by his kiss, his passion.

"I can manage alone." Her voice was hoarse, despite the strength she attempted to inject into it.

"Hmm." He lifted his head, staring down at her knowingly before whispering, "I bet you can, but can you manage this alone?"

His lips caught hers before she could do more than gasp, covering them, taking them as his tongue licked at the curves, tempting her to play with him.

How she had always longed to play in just such a way with Rowdy. His lips tugged at hers as he stared down at her, his eyes heavy-lidded and darkening with sexual hunger. His tongue stroked over hers, retreated, then came back for more until she was moaning and reaching for him, desperate for the kiss he was teasing her with.

"Hungry for me, baby?" His voice was dark velvet, rasping against her senses as she arched against him.

"I've always been hungry for you," she whispered, nipping back at his lips as his eyes narrowed, his expression becoming primitive, deepening with sexual energy as her hands smoothed from his shoulders to his chest and lower.

She needed him. She had never pretended otherwise. She needed everything he was, everything he wanted and needed to give her.

She gripped the material of his T-shirt, pulling it quickly from the band of his jeans as she allowed her nails to rake his flesh. The trembling response that raced over his body sent flashes of erotic heat tingling between her thighs.

"Take the shirt off, Rowdy." She pushed the hem to his chest before lowering her head, her lips pressing to the hair-spattered skin beneath the flat, hard male nipple that drew her attention. "I want you naked. I want you against me, inside me."

The shirt was jerked from his body and tossed aside. His expression darkened, his face flushing with hunger as he stared back at her.

Kelly murmured her approval as she bent her head, licking around the tight, hard nipple that fascinated her. How she loved Rowdy's lips on her breasts, his teeth scraping her own hard peaks.

She raked over the tight point with a tentative little nip.

"Son of a bitch." He flinched, his hands gripping her hair, tightening in the strands before pressing her to him again. "Again, Kelly. God, baby, do it again."

She did that and more. She licked, sucked, rasped the point until she could feel a fine sheen of perspiration coating his chest and felt his breath heaving.

She moved her fingers lower, struggling with the metal buttons of his jeans, dragging them free and spreading the material apart. He wore no underwear. Rowdy wasn't an underwear-type man, and she knew it. Which suited her fine. It made it easier for the hard length of his cock to push free, rising nearly to his navel, thick and heavy, the head bloated and damp from the silky precome coating it.

"Suck it." His voice was a hard rasp as she licked a path down his chest to the hardened flesh below.

"Patience is a virtue." She could barely speak for the lust rising inside her.

"Fuck patience," he groaned, his hands tugging sensually at her hair. "God, baby, do you know how often I dream of watching you wrap your pretty mouth around my dick?"

A punch of excitement convulsed her womb and sent a spasm of response trembling through her pussy.

"You should have savored it last time," she panted. "Maybe I don't want to now."

But she did. She grasped the heavy weight of his erection as she used her other hand to push at the band of his jeans. A growl of impatience tore from his throat as he moved, toeing off his shoes before quickly disposing of his jeans.

Each second it took him to undress, her palm stroked his cock, up and down, tightening at the base before loosening and running up the silky shaft once more. Until his hands were in her hair again, clenching in the strands, sending darts of heat to rake across her scalp as lust slammed through her bloodstream. Prickles of sensation, of need, raced across her flesh as emotion erupted through her chest.

Rowdy. She had dreamed of him, lusted for him, waited for him. Now, everything she had ever prayed for was being threatened because of one careless act on her part. Because she had waited. Because she had wanted Rowdy to seduce her rather than take her. Had she belonged to Rowdy before he left last year, then the attacker would have never targeted her. And she could have belonged to him. He would have tried to fight it, but he had wanted her as badly as he did now. He had hungered as much as she had.

She lowered her head the last inches as she bent to him, taking the mushroomed head between her lips as her tongue stroked over the throbbing crest.

"Oh fuck," he growled, his hands tugging at her hair, pulling it just enough to light a sudden blinding flame of need inside her.

She liked the pain. Not true pain, the spark of intensity, the erotic burn that emphasized the pleasure. She liked it, and she wanted more.

Kelly wrapped her fingers around the shaft of his cock, pumping it with slow, measured strokes as she began to suckle the head with a growing hunger she could no longer control. She wanted to take all of him. Wanted to feel his cock pulse in her mouth, feel his semen spilling onto her tongue.

"Here, sweetheart, let me help you take those clothes off." His fingers were pulling at her shirt, tugging at her hands and her head until she released his flesh to have the shirt stripped from her body.

"Come here, darlin', turn right around for me." Rowdy turned her as his hands stripped her jeans over her thighs before tugging them free of her legs as he slipped her shoes from her feet.

His lips touched her thigh as he undressed her, her knee, his tongue licked, his teeth rasped.

It was taking too long and it was taking forever and she was certain she was going to scream from sheer excitement as she felt him push her over the bed, his hard, callused hands parting her buttocks just before hungry lips began to caress the hidden flesh.

She couldn't breathe. Feeling him move, she knew he was reaching for the tube of lubricating gel on the bedside table. Knew what was coming.

Cool lubricated fingers eased into the narrow crevice seconds later, massaged the rippling entrance to her ass as she cried out her pleasure. "There, baby," Rowdy's voice whispered across her senses. "It's just for me. Just feel good, sweetheart. Just for me."

One hand held her in place as the other slowly, methodically prepared her rear.

"I want you there, Kelly," Rowdy groaned as she felt his finger slide fully inside her before retreating. "I need you there. I want to part those pretty cheeks and watch your sweet ass suck my cock in."

She couldn't stop the ragged cry that left her throat, or the overwhelming hunger for him. Rowdy was making her crazy. His fingers were pumping inside her anus now, two stretching her, making her burn in ways she had never imagined.

She could feel the juices weeping from her pussy, thick, silky, soaking the bare curves as he teased her clit with a finger, making her hips jerk and sending talons of need ripping at her womb.

She needed . . . oh God, she needed his fingers pumping inside her pussy, filling her there as the rocketing sensations overwhelmed her body.

She could feel her rear entrance being stretched further, slickened, heavily lubricated as Rowdy kept up the pressure on her clit, kept her begging for more.

Her hips were churning, driving his fingers deeper inside her. He was breathing hard, almost as hard as she was.

"More, baby." Another finger joined the first two, working inside her, stretching her until she was burning alive for more, ready, willing to plead for more if only she could find the strength to speak.

"Oh God!" She shuddered, her back arching at the fullness stretching her.

"Three fingers, Kelly," Rowdy growled as his arm latched around her waist, holding her upright. "Three fingers buried in that tight little ass. When I pull them out, you'll be ready for me." He pressed on her shoulders until she was lying over the bed. Rowdy moved her, arranged her as he pleased, propping her knees on the mattress as he pressed her shoulders down.

All the while he worked his fingers inside her, pulling nearly free, spreading more of the cool gel over them before working them inside her once again.

"Fuck. So fucking pretty"—she felt his hand smooth over her

buttock as he pulled his fingers free of her grip—"so pretty, and so damned sweet—"

"Rowdy . . ." Her fingers clenched in the blanket as she felt the bloated crest of his cock tuck against the entrance.

"Let it hurt, baby," he whispered. "Just a little bit. Let yourself feel how the pleasure and the pain mix, how it can make you fly like nothing else does."

He pressed closer.

Kelly held her breath, feeling the nerve-laden tissue begin to part, to suck him in, rippling around him as it began to burn.

She was fighting to breathe through the pleasure. Through the burn. Through sensations that tore through her mind and left her dazed with the explosions of heat burning through her body.

"Damn. You're tight, sweetheart." He pulled back, pressed forward again, working the thick crest into her further with each stroke.

Below, his fingers circled her throbbing clit, stroked down the parted slit, and massaged the entrance to her vagina. She pressed back, desperate to feel them inside her.

"Rowdy!" She screamed his name as she felt the head of his cock pop inside her. A hard, blinding stretch of tissue that had her arching, had her nerve endings flaming as a finger speared inside the depths of her pussy.

Rowdy slid inside her to the hilt then. His hands were tight on her hips, holding her steady as the hard rasp of his breath echoed in her ears. Part growl, part groan, his pleasure was vocal, physical, wrapping around her as it blended with her own. This was what she wanted. Needed. Just this. Just with Rowdy. He moved then, slowly, dragging his cock nearly free before pressing forward again. The movement sent violent waves of pleasure tearing through her as she begged Rowdy for ease.

"God, yes, baby. You're so sweet. So tight. So hot," he rasped, his voice dark and rough as he began to thrust inside her slow and easy.

"Yes." She reached back for him. "Please . . ." She needed him deep inside her. Needed his erection tunneling into her harder as his fingers teased her pussy. "Now . . ."

He gave her what she was begging for. Slowly. Teasingly.

His fingers caressed the swollen folds of her pussy a second

before his hand retreated, only to return. Her eyes flew open, a startled cry leaving her lips as she felt the buzzing vibration of the vibrator he pressed against her vaginal opening. The thick tip entered her pussy, burning her further. "Damn, you're so fucking tight." She could feel the perspiration that covered her skin, that dripped from his.

Kelly shook her head. "Take me. Please . . ."

She heard him, felt Rowdy press the vibrator upward, working inside her slowly. Her anal muscles flexed around the invading cock as her pussy convulsed around the vibrator filling her. The tapered head of the toy pressed forward, making room for the following shaft.

It was unlike anything she could have imagined. As Rowdy filled her ass with his cock, he filled her pussy, filled her until she was certain she could take no more, only to learn she could take more. Much more.

By the time the toy had seated fully inside her, her screams of pleasure had turned to raspy, incoherent pleas. Sweat coated her body as her juices coated her thighs. She was slick all over, wet and pierced and dying for more.

"How's that, baby?" Rowdy leaned over her, his chest pressing against her lightly as he fucked into her slow and easy. "Can you take it?"

"Please . . ." She was crying, so desperate to come she was shaking from the need. "Fuck me. Please. Please . . ."

He moved. His cock and the vibrator began to power inside her in tandem. The friction, the overwhelming intensity of pleasure consumed her. At first slow, tentative, then faster, harder, he began to thrust inside her with strong, powerful strokes.

Kelly writhed between Rowdy and the toy, the sensations of the dual penetration, of the pleasure flowing between them, just them, no one else, sent ecstasy screaming through her system.

She couldn't survive this pleasure. It was burning, intensifying, stealing her mind, her body. She felt each stroke tightening her womb, pushing her closer, deeper into the maelstrom overtaking her.

She was going to explode. She could feel it, flew closer to it, feeling the rapture build, the pleasure, so deep, so intense, so overwhelming . . .

Rowdy's name was on her lips. A scream of fear, of ecstasy as

Twenty-one

Rowdy walked from the bathroom half an hour later, dressed in fresh jeans and a shirt before moving to the bed and the shoes he had left forgotten beside it. Kelly still slept. A hard, hopefully dreamless sleep. Sprawled on her stomach, one arm tucked beneath the pillow, her cheek rested on, breathing deep. She looked innocent, sweet, and untouched.

It was hard to believe she had been a wildcat less than an hour before. The sweet little kitten sleeping so calmly bore no resemblance to her, he thought with a smile. Rowdy shook his head, the smile creasing his face further at the memory. He had always known she would be a firecracker in bed, ready and willing for any adventure he could give her. She was earthy, lusty, and she liked that sharp little edge of pain he enjoyed giving.

He reached out, smoothing back a thick swathe of hair from her cheek as emotion overwhelmed him, tightened his chest, and reminded him of what he could have lost. If he had given in to the demand that he take her the year before, the attack might have never happened. Hell no, it wouldn't have happened, because he would have demanded reassignment. He couldn't have left her. He had known that then. Once he had her, there was no way he could have walked away.

He was crazy about her. So crazy in love with her that it terrified him clear to the soles of his feet. She was young as hell, and still so innocent it broke his heart.

Leaning forward, he pressed a butterfly kiss against her fore-

she felt the orgasm rip through her. It tightened her body, her vagina, tore through her and flung her into a pleasure she couldn't fight, couldn't resist.

She felt Rowdy stiffen, felt the heat of his release, the hard shudders that suffused his body, and a blinding fiery blaze of emotion that had her screaming his name.

As the hard, wracking shudders eased from her body she collapsed against him, wasted, exhausted, certain she couldn't open her eyes if her very life depended on it.

head before tucking the sheet closer over her shoulders. Minutes later he was striding into the living room where Natches and Dawg waited on him. Natches had his head back on the couch, eyes closed. Dawg just looked grouchy as he stared back from the chair he sat in.

"Bastard!" Dawg grunted as Rowdy dropped into a chair across from him. "Guard duty sucks."

There was a gleam of envy in Dawg's eyes, despite the amusement in his tone.

"Did guard duty pay off though?" Rowdy lifted a brow, staring back at his cousin questioningly.

Dawg grinned in satisfaction. "Guard duty paid. I slipped out the doggie hole and found a nice little perch topside. We had some definite movement."

Natches's eyes opened as he straightened in his seat, his expression going as darkly dangerous as Rowdy felt. Evidently this wasn't information Natches had been given, which surprised Rowdy.

"What kind of movement?" Rowdy asked, paying attention to the dangerous, predatory light that gleamed in Natches's expression as Dawg continued.

"Little fellow, barely taller than Kelly. Dressed in hunting gear with a hooded mask. He was being real careful. Watching the house from heavy cover. I couldn't get a shot."

"Did you recognize anything?" They were getting close. The stalker was losing his grip on reality if he had followed them so quickly.

Kelly's stalker was obviously beginning to crack, and that was what they needed. Just a small fracture in his self-control and they would have him.

Dawg shook his head. "I watched him as best I could. Maybe something will trigger if I see him around anywhere." A grimace twisted his expression. "Catching him might not be easy, but I have a feeling he'll make another move soon."

Of course he would, he considered Kelly his. The fact that the Nauti Boys had her, were possibly sharing her, would be too much for his tenuous hold on reality to survive.

"I'll take guard duty from here on out," Natches spoke up then, his voice bland, unassuming. Dangerous. A good ole boy attitude covering a steel core of determination.

Rowdy stared back at him curiously. Natches had changed in ways that were hard to put a finger on. He had returned from the Marines only months before Rowdy had, quieter and a hell of a lot harder than he had been when he went in. That hardness was more than maturity and confidence, more than a soldier who had seen battle in the sands of another nation. Despite his vow that he had never grown up, somehow, Rowdy knew better.

"Fine." Rowdy nodded slowly. "You take watch. We'll head into town in the morning, take Kelly shopping, do some stocking up. We'll let the bastard see what he's missing. If he's the nutcase I suspect, he'll hit by tomorrow night.

"Are we going to give him an opening?" Natches's voice softened.

"We can't make it look too easy. He has to work for it." Rowdy sat back in the chair, considering their options. "Dawg, weaken the security monitor on the kitchen window, and in the shrubbery beneath it. Make it look natural, something he can get through. He's broken the women's security systems so he's not a stranger to it. Let's see what the bastard's made of."

Dawg nodded sharply as Natches continued to watch them with a hard, merciless stare that assured Rowdy that he wasn't the only one waiting to shed blood.

Rowdy turned his gaze back to Natches, realizing in that second that he had seen the look in his friend's eyes before. He had seen it in another man's eyes, a Marine assassin. He had worked alone, disappearing for weeks at a time and returning with that same dead, cold chill in his eyes.

Hell. He blew out a silent breath as Natches met his eyes, his expression never changing. What the hell had Natches gotten into while he was in the service?

"Go ahead and set up," Rowdy told him quietly. "Let me know before morning how you want to play it."

Dawg's head had lowered, proof that he was aware of a truth that Rowdy hadn't been privy to. A truth he still wasn't certain of the details to.

"I'll go public with you when you need me to," Natches said softly. "I'll use the bolt-hole otherwise."

The bolt-hole, or dog door as Dawg had amusingly named it, was the single, secret entrance into the house from a shrub-hidden door several hundred feet around the base of the hill. Dawg wasn't the trusting sort, and his time in the Marines hadn't helped his trust issues any.

"Boys, we need to talk when this is all over and done," Rowdy sighed, watching the weary resignation in his cousins' eyes. "Keeping secrets among ourselves isn't a good thing, ya know?"

Dawg grunted, a sound of wry amusement that was typical Dawg. Natches's lips quirked into a smile.

"A good drunk maybe," Dawg growled as he rose from his chair and paced across the room toward the kitchen. "Until then, boys, I need food. You want me to take mess duty?"

Rowdy's eyes met Natches's in shock, as his cousin's widened in horror.

"Hell no!" They both came out of their seats, rushing for the kitchen as they heard pans rattling beneath the stove cabinet and remembered Dawg's past attempts at manning a stove. The memory wasn't a pleasant one.

He had checked on his girls. His special good girls. Kelly was weak—she was allowing herself to be degraded, to be taken. Oh, how he had hoped she had been the only one. He had prayed, prayed so long and hard that his good girls were waiting on him.

He curled into the corner of the small dark apartment, rocking himself gently as he stared at the first of his lovers. He had thought she was so pure, so sweet. With her long, silken blond hair, and her innocent blue eyes. She had a soft voice, one that stroked the senses and made him think of his mother before she became a whore. Before she had turned his father away, before his father had stolen him away for his mother's sins. They had to punish her. She hadn't been a good girl.

He sniffed, realizing he was crying. He hated crying. Crying never helped, tears made a man weak, he remembered that from his father's lessons. A man had to do what he had to do. His father had been weak. The old man had cried, he had raged but he had left the depraved creature he had married rather than punishing her.

He should have punished her. If his father had punished his mother, then she wouldn't have been so bad. She would have been the good wife and mother she should have been. If she had been a good woman, then she wouldn't have lost her son.

He flinched at that memory, shaking his head to force it back from his mind as he reached out to touch thick strands of hair that flowed out from his good girl's head.

He touched the silken strands, rubbing them between his fingers, remembering how soft and sweet she had been. Before she had let herself grow weak. Before she had let another man convince her to be bad.

He stared at the man, a tight smile crossing his lips at the sight of the nude man, laying half on the bed, half on the floor. He wasn't dead, but he would soon wish he was.

The girl. He sighed wearily as he let himself stare at the blood staining the carpet. She stared back at him sightlessly, her china blue eyes reflecting the horror of her punishment.

Kelly must have somehow convinced this one that she could be bad, too. How, he wasn't certain. He could have sworn his girls didn't know about each other. He had taken pains to be very careful. But Kelly was so bad, so depraved, that she would have found a way to convince the others that they too could escape him.

They belonged to him. They were his good girls. He wouldn't allow another to touch them, not like his mother had.

He pulled himself to his feet, careful to pick up the knife and clean it of the blood that stained it. Her blood.

"You'll always be my good girl now," he whispered as he stepped around the blood and moved for the spare bedroom.

He had hidden there for hours, waiting for her to come home. Waiting to assure himself that she was a good girl. Only to listen in pain and fury as another man touched her.

He fought back his tears again as he entered the dark room and headed for the window he had used to slip inside the apartment. He had bypassed her security. How easy it had been. She had thought she was safe from him. That she could disobey him as his mother had disobeyed his father. She had found out wrong. Just as Kelly would have to learn as well.

Twenty-two

The next morning, Kelly would have preferred to enjoy the awakening caresses Rowdy was bestowing as she swam toward reality rather than the warm, sensual dreams twining around her. Unfortunately, the moment was interrupted by Dawg's growling message that her mother and Ray were on their way, and they had better get their asses ready before the arrival. His words, not hers.

She had enough time to shower and dress, never realizing the kind of devastating news her parents would bring.

"Her name was Dana Carrington." Ray's voice was low, angry. "She was murdered, and her boyfriend was molested."

Kelly sat in shock, listening as Ray recounted the murder that had taken place the night before. She sat at the kitchen table, her hands wrapped around her coffee cup as Rowdy stood behind her, his hands resting on her shoulders as she felt fear tremble through her.

"Kelly." Her mother leaned forward in her chair, staring back at her worriedly. "I called your aunt Beth in Montana, she wants you to come stay—"

"No." Rowdy's voice was hard.

Kelly's gaze flickered to Ray. He glanced at Rowdy in concern, but said nothing more.

"She's not safe here, Rowdy—" her mother protested.

"She won't be any safer there," he argued as Kelly tightened her fingers on the coffee cup. "At least here, Dawg and Natches and I have a chance of catching this bastard."

"By letting him think she's screwing all three of you?" Maria came out of her chair then, her cry filled with fear as she faced Rowdy. "For God's sake, Douglas, what if using her doesn't work? What if he gets to her—"

"Enough," Rowdy growled warningly.

"Kelly, listen to me, whoever this is has killed now. He won't stop . . ." Her mother stared back at her, her eyes damp with tears, her lips trembling.

"That's enough, Maria," Rowdy protested.

"Let her have her say, Rowdy." Ray shook his head regretfully. "She's her mother."

"All of you stop it!" Kelly's palm cracked on the kitchen table, sending an enveloping silence to fill the kitchen as all eyes turned to her. Ray and her mother, Dawg and Natches, Rowdy, she could feel their gazes boring into her as she lifted her head and stared back at her mother.

Kelly drew in a deep, hard breath. Fear was like a snake coiling in her belly, striking at her chest in an effort to be free.

"Rowdy's right," she whispered. "He won't stop killing now. If I stay here, there's a chance he can be caught—"

"Oh God, Kelly, listen to yourself," Maria protested desperately. "That girl last night is dead. He raped her boyfriend while he was unconscious. He's not sane."

"And I can't run." She shuddered at the thought of being terrified of the dark for the rest of her life, of being terrified of what could happen. But even more, she knew there were a lot of things Rowdy would allow, but he would never let her go. "We have to face it. Now. Here."

God, for a minute she wished Rowdy were less intense, less determined. She wished she didn't know him as well as she did.

"Come on, Aunt Maria," Dawg grunted as she continued to glare at Rowdy. "You know lookin' at him like that don't work. He's just going to get in a bad mood and pout on us all night long if you do."

Maria flashed her nephew by marriage a dark look. Dawg grinned back, flashing strong white teeth through his gaze remained hard.

"You boys are going to get her killed," she snapped. "This isn't a game you're playing here. It's Kelly's life."

"Which makes it my life," Rowdy assured her. "I'll be damned if I'll let this bastard hurt her more. Now stand the hell down and we can talk about this reasonably, or by God we won't talk about it at all."

Ray breathed out wearily.

"He's right, Maria. You know he's right. She can't run all her life," he said, the regret heavy in his voice as Maria gasped in surprise.

"Ray, you don't mean that. She would be safe—"

"She'll never be safe as long as that bastard is on the loose, Maria." He grimaced, shaking his head. "We both know it. She has to make her stand here."

"I won't have it—"

"I said I've heard enough!" Kelly scraped her chair across the floor, coming to her feet and pushing her fingers through her hair with an edge of frustration.

"Kelly . . . I'm scared for you," Maria whispered. "If Rowdy is so determined to stay with you, then the two of you can go away for a while."

"This isn't something I can run away from." Kelly swallowed tightly as she stared back at her mother.

"You mean he won't let you run away," Maria accused. "Don't let him risk your life like this, Kelly."

"I'm letting him save it," she whispered. "Because without him, I'm dead. It won't matter where I go, or how long I stay, he'll find me. Just as he found the other girl. He won't let it go."

"He would have," Maria bit out. "He left that girl alone until she found someone, and he would have left you alone if Rowdy hadn't drawn you into . . . this . . ." Her arm swung out to encompass Rowdy, Dawg, and Natches.

Heat flamed in her cheeks as she breathed in roughly, staring back at her mother, hating what her mother suspected, hating that the danger she was in now was tearing at them all. No explanation would make a difference; her mother would no more believe that she wasn't sleeping with all three men than the stalker would.

"This is my business," she said softly. "Remember that, Mom. And don't forget it. My relationship with Rowdy is my business, and it will stay that way. Period. I love you, but I can't deal with fighting with you right now. I want you to go home."

"No—"

"Mom, go home." She strengthened her voice, fought back her tears, and stared back at her mother firmly. "I'll call. I promise. But this isn't going to help anything, and it's sure as hell not going to make this easier. For my sake, just go."

"Kelly . . ." Rowdy's protest as she moved quickly from the room was ignored, as was Ray's curse and her mother's cry.

She couldn't handle the combined pressure, or her mother's fears. Her own were choking her, strangling her with tightening bands of remembered horror as she escaped the tension building in the kitchen.

She had tried to tell herself that the man who attacked her would go away. That it would stop. That it couldn't be worse than what she had already endured. But now the nightmare was growing worse. Her stalker had become a murderer.

She rushed into the bedroom, carefully closing the door behind her as she capped her hand over her mouth in an effort to hold back her screams of horror. She wasn't the only one at risk now. She had known when the shots were fired into the boat that the stalker was going to try to hurt Rowdy. It hadn't sunk in though, not all the way to the bone, until Ray and her mother dropped their bombshell.

"Kelly, open the door." Rowdy wiggled the doorknob as he spoke on the other side of the panel. His voice was soft, gentle, nearly breaking her resolve to hold back her tears.

Pressing her lips together she turned the lock before moving away, unaware she had locked it in the first place. She moved to the center of the room, wiping her fingers over her cheeks in an attempt to dry the tears from her face.

The door opened then closed as silence engulfed the room for long seconds.

"I don't want him to hurt you," she finally whispered, keeping her back to him as she wrapped her arms over her breasts. "What will I do if he hurts you, Rowdy?"

She heard the male snort behind her, mocking, filled with stubborn pride. She turned to him slowly, wishing, praying, that none of this had happened. That she could have had her dream of holding Rowdy without the danger that surrounded them.

He was staring back at her tenderly, but there was no missing the spark of rage behind the tenderness, or the pure confidence that poured from him.

"What happens if you run, Kelly?" he asked her, moving toward her, a slow, predatory movement that had her heart racing in anticipation even as fear overwhelmed her. "Can you stay one step ahead of him? Can you live your life knowing he can strike at any minute? Knowing that eventually he'll get tired of just watching you, and find a reason to kill you instead? Just as he found a reason to kill that girl last night?"

"I'm not stupid." Her breath caught as his hands cupped her shoulders, his thumbs smoothing over the flesh the straps of her shirt left bare. "I'm scared, Rowdy," her voice lowered. "I'm so scared."

"That's natural," he whispered. "Do you know I'm scared too, Kelly?"

She stared back at him in surprise.

"Scared you won't trust us to protect you. Scared you'll leave, that he'll hurt you in ways you won't be able to come back from. That I'll lose you forever. That's what scares me, Kelly. Hell, it terrifies me."

"Don't . . ." She shook her head, shaking at the throb of emotion in his voice, the pain that threaded through it.

"I'd rather die than see that, Kelly," he whispered painfully, his eyes tormented, dark with emotion. "Don't you understand, sweetheart? I love you until I can't breathe without feeling it move through me, feeling your presence around me. You're my heart. My soul. I won't let that bastard take that from me. If it means I have to lock you up for your own protection and listen to you rage for a lifetime, I'd do it. Anything, Kelly, to keep you safe."

The tears were streaming down her face now, shudders whipping through her body at the sound of his voice. Her big, tough Rowdy, his tone soft, thick with emotion, his eyes brilliant with it.

"I love you so much, Rowdy." Her hands moved from his chest, no longer pressing to hold him back, but moving to his shoulders as he drew her to his chest, holding her close, secure against him.

"It's going to be okay, Kelly." She felt his head lower, felt his lips move over her forehead. "Everything's going to be fine, babe. I'm not stupid, or careless. And Dawg and Natches sure as hell aren't. We're going get through this. All of us, baby."

She lifted her head for his kiss, needing it, desperate to fill the dark places moving through her soul with the fire of his hunger, his need. She could feel his cock straining beneath his jeans, pressing against her stomach as she drew his head down to her.

"Kiss me, Rowdy," she whispered. "Kiss me like I dream—"

His lips stole her words as a hungry groan filled the air. His groan, her whimpering cry of need as she felt the heat and lust moving from him, into her.

Her lips opened as her arms curled around his neck, pulling him closer to her as he tilted her head back, sipping from her lips, licking at them, nipping until they opened as she was crying out for more. Needing more. His tongue was a stroke of fire, his hands were everywhere. Hunger heated the air, filled her body and whipped around her like forked fingers of lightning tingling over her body.

In those moments there was no stalker, no danger, no death or pain. There was only passion. There was only Rowdy.

Amazement flared through Rowdy, not for the first time, at the pleasure he received from just kissing Kelly. Holding her head between his hands, feeling her silky hair fall over his hands, feeling her lips like hot satin beneath his.

And her taste. She intoxicated him. Nothing but Dawg's white lightning had ever had the power to affect him so quickly, until Kelly's kiss. Her touch. Her passion.

He groaned against her lips as he let his tongue dip past them, feeling hers waiting, tangling against him like damp silk and sending his senses spinning.

A man shouldn't be so weak in the face of a kiss, he thought with a sliver of amusement. But damn if she didn't sap his will to resist her, to keep from taking her again and again.

And he was going to have her again. Now. He was going to lay her back on that big bed and sink inside her until she screamed his name.

He backed her toward the bed, keeping his lips on hers as his hands moved from her head to wrap around her back before gripping the hem of her shirt and pushing beneath it. She had the softest skin he had ever touched. Everything about Kelly was different, better, hotter, and sweeter, and with each touch he only wanted more.

"Let's get you out of these damned clothes," he muttered as he tore his lips from hers, his eyes lifting to stare down at her.

Her lips were swollen, cheeks flushed with arousal, and her pretty gray eyes were dark, stormy with hunger. Damn, he liked her hungry. She was like a little tigress, scratching and mewling and uncaring of anything but the pleasure she was attaining. The pleasure he was giving her.

Getting undressed was a matter of a few ripped seams, some buttons popping, and strangled curses as they both struggled with stubborn jeans. But within seconds he was tumbling her back to the bed, his lips zeroing in on her hard, peaked nipples as the taste of her filled his mouth.

God, she was sweet. Arching to him, hoarse cries leaving her lips as he suckled at the tight little points. Her head was thrown back, her hands gripping his head, holding him to her as he went from one swollen mound to the other.

All the while her hot little body twisted and writhed beneath him as her thigh caressed the tight length of his cock. He could feel his balls tightening with the need to fuck and to do it now. It was always like this with Kelly. He couldn't wait to get inside her, to feel her silken heat clasping him, rippling around him as he thrust into the liquid fire of her tight little pussy.

And that heat was so close. He could feel it whispering over the head of his erection, drawing him to her. He wasn't going to be able to wait long, he knew. Long enough maybe, maybe, to ease down her straining body. He did just that, laying quick little kisses down her abdomen, licking at her skin, tasting her with every cell of his body. Just long enough to spread her thighs and settle between them before dipping his head for one quick little taste of her sweet, juicy cunt.

His taste buds exploded as he slid his tongue through the syrupy slit before circling the tight, swollen bud of her clit. Sweet, tart, silken ambrosia that entangled his senses and kept him coming back for more.

Her cries echoed around him as he enjoyed the taste and feel of the slick folds of her flesh. Silken and bare, her pussy flowered open for him. Peaches and cream and soft syrup, and he was a man with a taste for this particular fruit. Especially when those gorgeous legs lifted and her feet propped on his shoulders to allow him maximum access.

He could happily drown in her. He licked at the sweet cream, tasted the hunger and passion that rained from her. His fingers caressed the tender opening to her vagina, teased and tempted her before working inside her. His senses exploded with the heat that surrounded them, with the moist, rich juices that flowed from her.

He ached for her. His cock throbbed like a demon's kiss, but the thought of leaving the succulent flesh beneath his lips was more than he could consider. Not while she burned like this for him. Not while her cries filled the room and her lithe legs spread wide for him.

He licked around her straining clit, grimacing as her pussy tightened further around his fingers. His dick was screaming in pain, begging to push inside her. He pulled his fingers back, pushed inside again and flicked the little nubbin with his tongue as she screamed for more, begged to come.

Not yet. God, the taste of her, the feel of her. He wanted to feel her coming around his cock, not his fingers. He wanted to feel the tight muscles rippling around his erection, sucking the semen from the depths of his balls, and sending his head racing with ecstasy.

He pulled his fingers from her, groaning at the effort it cost to pull back from her, to lift his head from her tender pussy and force himself to rise over her.

He pushed her legs back as he moved, opening her further for him as he pressed the head of his cock against the moist, flexing entrance to her pussy.

She stared up at him, her expression dazed, her eyes the color of storm clouds as her hands lifted to his chest. Her palms pressed against the hair-roughened muscles, her nails biting into his flesh.

"Now," she whispered. "Please, Rowdy, now."

He pressed in the barest fraction, his breath catching at the heat that surrounded the tip of his cock. Looking down, he watched as the smooth, naked lips of her sex parted, glistening with her juices and hugging his cock as he began to work inside her.

Flames traveled from the sensitive crest to his tortured balls as he fought to breathe. Release was an agonizing need that sent fingers of electrified pleasure racing up his spine. He couldn't come yet. Not yet. He thought of baseball, fishing, auto mechanics, and cleaning his gun, but each subject fizzled within his mind as he sank further and further into her heat.

Shaking his head, he plunged in the last inches, growling at the tightness, the suckling heat. He was a man on the verge of madness, control gone, only the wild need to fuck and mate spurring him now.

He didn't stop with one thrust. Pulling back, he began fucking inside her deep and hard, snarling at the pleasure that built with each stroke, at the extreme sensations overtaking his body. His thighs bunched, his balls nearly drawing into his body before he finally felt Kelly explode.

"Fuck. There, baby. So sweet and hot. Come for me, Kelly. Come for me so hard . . ."

Her pussy tightened around his cock nearly to the point of pain as it began convulsing around him. Liquid heat engulfed him, burned him, then sent him careening into a mad, furious drive toward his own pleasure.

"God yes! Sweet baby"—the words ripped from his chest, from his soul—"God help me, I love you."

The release exploded through his body, drawing him tight as an animalistic snarl left his lips. He buried his cock to the furthest depths of her before he felt the harsh, blinding explosions tearing through his scrotum. Pleasure was ecstasy, destructive and consuming as he felt his semen spewing inside the hot depths of the sweet cunt wrapped around him. It held him on edge, milking spurt after spurt of rich seed from his body before the last shudder tore through him and left him wasted.

Rowdy collapsed at Kelly's side, barely retaining enough sanity to keep from falling atop her. He was gasping for air, rippling echoes of pleasure still racing up his spine as he used the last of his strength to drag her into his arms and cushion her against his chest.

"Okay . . . that was wild enough," she panted weakly against him. "You could have warned me first."

"Would have had to suspect first," he mumbled. "Go to sleep or something. Let me rest."

"I'm not sleepy." But her voice was weak, drowsy. "We were going to shop. I heard Mom and Ray leave after we came up here. We could go shopping before they come back for the next round of arguments."

"Nap." He groaned. "Just nap. God, you just killed me. I gotta sleep."

A soft laugh against his chest was the last thing he heard as he sighed deeply and let himself drift off. Dawg and Natches could watch her for half an hour; she had wiped him out.

Kelly rose from the bed, a frown furrowing her brow as she found a loose T-shirt and shorts before heading to the bathroom. She was hungry—breakfast had been set aside because of Ray and her mother's visit, and she was feeling it now.

She forced herself not to think about the reason for that visit. If she thought about it then the fear would take over. The helplessness and overwhelming dread threatening to attack her lingered at the back of her mind, though, shadowing her thoughts.

She cleaned up quickly before dressing and leaving the bathroom. She glanced at Rowdy where he lay facedown on the bed, breathing deeply in sleep, before leaving the room. The beginnings of a smile tipped her lips as the need to curl up against him unfurled inside her.

At the same time her stomach growled warningly. Sex with Rowdy became a secondary need in the face of her hunger. But, she reminded herself, she *had* worked up a bit of an appetite with the sex part.

She moved slowly down the narrow staircase, listening for Dawg and Natches. She couldn't hear either of them, but the television was playing in the living room. She knew Natches had intended to sneak out somewhere, and she wouldn't put it past Dawg to be hiding as well.

She was surprised to see him lying on the couch instead. He was stretched out in what had to be an uncomfortable angle. His head was hanging over the side as he lay on his back and one leg bent at an odd angle, his arm falling to the floor.

Kelly tipped her head, staring at his dozing posture before shaking her head in confusion at it. She had seen some odd sleeping angles, but that one took the cake.

Restraining a soft laugh, she tiptoed through the living room and made her way into the kitchen. Despite the television, there was a heavy silence in the house that bothered her, made her wary. The moment she entered the kitchen she knew why.

She stopped in shock at the sight of Natches, facedown on the floor, a trail of blood oozing from his temple to stain the floor beneath him.

Her heart slammed into her throat, stealing her breath and

the screams that tightened her chest. She gasped for air, certain she was going to smother, knowing the terror filling her would kill her before anything else could.

Rowdy. Oh God, she had to get to Rowdy. She turned, the blood rushing through her veins as her mind screamed at her to run, only to slide to a stop as she moved back into the living room.

Eyes wide, her lips parted in shock, she stared at the form standing in the middle of the living room, a gun pointing toward her chest.

Twenty-three

It took Kelly a moment to realize that she knew him. She blinked in surprise as she recognized the young deputy who had come to the apartment with the police the night of her attack and again to Ray's house the night her bedroom had been destroyed. He had been so quiet she had barely remembered him being there.

"They thought they could catch me." He smiled back at her, his hazel eyes gleaming with triumph as he waved the barrel of his weapon toward where Dawg lay on the couch. "They thought they were better than me because they were big, tough Marines."

His voice was soft, almost girlishly so. His expression was benign, calm, terrifying.

Deputy Carlyle. He hadn't been on the force long, a few years maybe. He was easy to overlook with his nondescript, plain features and quiet voice.

"Deputy Carlyle?"

"Barnes-Carlyle. John," he answered her then. "My mother's maiden name was Barnes, did you know that?"

She shook her head.

"Why are you doing this?" Oh God, had he killed Dawg and Natches? From the corner of her eye she tried to make certain Dawg was still breathing, but she just couldn't be sure. Natches had seemed to be breathing, but was that wishful thinking or had he been?

He sighed as though in regret.

"I didn't mean to make them pay, but I guess the past is

catching up on all of us." He glanced at Dawg before his gaze came back to her. "I lost count of the beatings I took from my father because of what your lovers did with my mother."

"What are you talking about?" She shook her head, confused.

"Loren Barnes was their lover," he snickered. "She was my mother. Dad stole me away from her a few years before she seduced them into her bed. She was such a whore. One man was never enough for her."

Kelly remembered Loren Barnes. She had died several years before, an older woman, perhaps her mother's age. There had been a rumor that the Mackay cousins had been her lovers years before, but Kelly knew none of them had ever confirmed it.

"That doesn't tell me why you've done this." She couldn't breathe, fear was strangling her, weakening her, and she knew right now she couldn't afford to be weak.

He looked at her in surprise, his thin lips curving into a smile.

"You don't know who I am, do you, Kelly?" he asked her.

She shook her head slowly, suspicion and horror beating at her.

"My poor little girl," he whispered, confirming her worst fears. "And you were such a good girl at one time. You know I'm going to have to punish you now. You were supposed to be mine."

Her eyes widened as his finger tightened on the trigger.

"How was I yours?" She was desperate, knowing there was no way to run from that bullet or from him. "You wanted to rape me."

A frown edged at his brows as she fought to remember everything she had heard Rowdy and the others talking about concerning the other rape victims. What had they said? He made them beg for it, made them swear to love him.

"I didn't ask you to touch me." She forced the words past her numb lips. "You know I didn't."

His hand trembled.

"You loved me." She saw the madness light his eyes.

"Did I say I loved you?" She had to buy herself some time. Rowdy would be awake soon, he would know something was wrong. Oh God, where was he?

He blinked at her question before a pout curled his lips. "That stupid neighbor broke in—"

"I never said I loved you, John." She fought to stay in control. "I didn't want you to touch me. I was never yours."

He blinked back at her. "No. You were mine." His voice was almost childlike. "You were a good girl until they touched you. You wanted to be mine, because I knew you were a good girl."

God, he was insane.

"I have always belonged to Rowdy." She kept her voice calm, fought to still the hysteria rising inside her. "You knew I was Rowdy's. Everyone knew. His cousins made sure of it."

Anger leapt to his features.

"They're depraved," he yelled back at her, his features contorting with fury. "They touched my mother. They made my father know what they were doing to her, and he told me about it. How they made her a bad girl. She wasn't supposed to be a bad girl. She was my mother."

"Your father misunderstood." She was shaking, horrified. "They were just boys."

"He didn't misunderstand." John shook his head furiously. "He would sneak and watch them and then he would punish me. He would come home and make me lie down while he punished me with what they were doing to her. He had to teach me not to be bad. Now I have to teach you, Kelly."

Oh God. She felt her stomach pitch with the horrifying knowledge of what he was talking about. How could a father do such a thing? Drive his own son into insanity in such a way.

"John, you have to listen to me." Her fists clenched in her shirt. *Just a few more minutes.* Surely Rowdy would be here in a few more minutes. "You have to leave. If you shoot me, Rowdy will hear . . ."

He smiled then. A confident, mad smile that sent terror racing through her mind.

"I took care of Rowdy already, Kelly. He won't wake up until I'm gone. I'm going to take care of you, then I'll punish him, just like Daddy punished me. He'll learn not to touch what belongs to me."

She was going to throw up. The insanity that spewed from him was the most sickening thing she had ever known. Worse even than the attack she had suffered at his hands.

"Why?" Her voice trembled despite the effort she used to

hold it steady. "He didn't take what was yours. Why should you punish him?"

There had to be a way to get around him, some way to get to Rowdy. She could lock the bedroom door. There was a gun in the dresser, she had seen Rowdy put it in there. A big black pistol that she knew she could use.

"You are mine!" he snarled, his voice rising in fury. "I took you, I marked you. You wear my mark."

"I didn't ask for your mark," she yelled back, fury rising inside her. "I didn't want you, John. Love is given freely. You can't force it."

He shook his head as his eyes glistened with tears, his lips wobbling with some demonic emotion.

"You didn't give me time," he pouted. "You would have told me you loved me."

"I knew I didn't love you." She edged back as his head turned from her. If she could get to the kitchen and he chased her, then she could use the hall exit to get back to the stairs. All she needed was a head start. "I've always loved Rowdy, John. Always."

"No! Mine!" he screamed back at her. "I'll show you, you're mine then I'll kill you."

He lunged for her. Fury lit his expression as rage transformed his face and he rushed her. Kelly turned, sliding on the slick floor as she heard an enraged howl of fury echo through the house a second before the sound of two bodies impacting pulled her up short.

Gripped the door frame, she turned back, shock filling her as she watched Rowdy struggling with the smaller man. Rowdy was bigger, but the blood at his temple showed the earlier blow that was now slowing his reflexes.

The gun John had carried slid across the room as he fought to get to it. Kelly rushed for it, crying out in rage as a hand snagged her ankle, bringing her to her knees.

Her head turned as she saw the knife in John's hand, and Rowdy's reach to grab at his wrist as the other man aimed at her leg. She kicked out, breaking loose before scrambling for the weapon.

Her fingers latched onto the handgrip as she flipped over, bringing it up with both hands as she fought to get a clear shot.

The two men were snarling now, wrestling for the knife as she heard the sounds of sirens in the distance. The gun shook in her hand as she blinked back her tears, terrified that the deputy would manage to actually find a way to wound Rowdy with that knife. There was no way to shoot yet. No way to be certain if she did, that she would miss Rowdy.

There had to be something she could do. But if she did the wrong thing, it could mean Rowdy's life. She prayed, sobbing in terror as she watched the two men grapple until the knife was between them a second before Rowdy jerked the other man closer to him.

They both froze.

A whimper left Kelly's throat as the front door crashed inward, and as though in slow motion, she watched Deputy John Barnes-Carlyle slide slowly from Rowdy's grip to collapse on the floor.

His head turned toward her, his hazel eyes filled with shock and surprise.

"My good girl . . ." he whispered before his gaze dimmed and his body went limp.

Kelly stared back at him, the sounds of police filling the room receding to the background as adrenaline began to crash inside her. She lifted her head as the gun dropped in her lap, watching as Rowdy began to move toward her, only to have the sheriff block him as the room continued to fill up. She could hear her mother, or was it merely wishful thinking? Rowdy was yelling and Sheriff Mayes was barking orders.

She knew she should get up, knew she should do something. But all she could do was turn her gaze back to the dead deputy as she heard his final words ringing in her ears. "My good girl . . ."

She wasn't his good girl. A sob tore from her throat as she pushed to her feet, fighting past the shock winding its way through her. He was dead. He was dead, and Rowdy was surrounded by the police.

"Let him go!" she screamed out hoarsely, fighting past Sheriff Mayes as she struggled to get to Rowdy. She kicked at someone, her fist landed against another, but they parted, staring back at her in shock as she flung herself into Rowdy's arms.

"Thank God! Baby." Rowdy's arms closed around her as his

voice whispered in her ear. "Sweet Lord, Kelly. Don't ever terrify me like that again."

She was crying and couldn't stop. She could feel the sobs shaking her body as her arms tightened around his neck.

She could hear Rowdy explaining the deputy's insanity as he held her close. Somehow, he had managed to regain consciousness and call the police, informing them of who was there and what was going on as he slipped down the stairs.

They were prepared, but questions had to be answered. Dawg and Natches were brought around by the medics and the house continued to fill with people. But Kelly refused to leave Rowdy's side.

She held on to him through the evening, answering questions when she had to, but otherwise remaining silent as the knowledge slowly filled her mind that it was over. The stalker had been John Barnes-Carlyle, and he was gone. He was dead. It was finally over.

Twenty-four

Kelly stared around the living room the next morning, amazed that there was nothing left, not so much as a speck of blood, to prove that the night before had been no dream.

The only proof left was the egg-sized knots that had been left on Dawg's, Natches's, and Rowdy's heads. John Barnes hadn't come to the front door, he had known about Dawg's back entrance through his father, who had spent years spying on the Mackay cousins, and used it to slip into the house.

He had gotten Dawg first, while Natches was outside getting the last supplies from his truck. When he came in, he had seen the same thing Kelly had, what appeared to be Dawg napping on the couch.

He had moved into the kitchen with the supplies, where the deputy had moved in behind him and knocked him unconscious as well. He had waited until Kelly had left the bedroom upstairs, hiding in the other room until she started down the stairs, before he had disabled Rowdy. Or thought he had.

Rowdy had been coming out of his nap as he was struck; the blow had dazed him, taking precious minutes for him to get his bearings enough to struggle from the bed.

The sheriff had called that morning after running a night-long investigation on his dead deputy. He had indeed been Loren Barnes's son, kidnapped by his father several years before the Mackay cousins had become her lovers.

There was a long history of abuse as a child, foster homes,

and disappearances that hadn't been followed up on at the time. As the full story emerged, everyone who had known him on the force had been shocked. His father had molested him for years, punishing him for the supposed crimes his mother had committed. Richard Barnes, the father, had been insane, and his insanity had been forced upon his son until it had warped his view of women.

Four women had paid for that crime.

"Feeling better?" She turned her head as Dawg moved from the kitchen, followed by Rowdy and Natches.

She stared at the three men, feeling the tension that suddenly filled the room, the intensity in their eyes. She had known this was coming, had known Rowdy's cousins would soon put his decision to the test. She could see it in the ready tension of their bodies. There was none of the expected anger in Rowdy's expression though. His body was relaxed, easy, his gaze simmering with amusement.

"Do we have a problem?" She crossed her arms over her breasts and stared back at the three curiously.

"Rowdy's being greedy," Dawg grunted. "How do you feel about that?"

"I'm rather greedy myself, Dawg," she informed him fondly. "I can't do it."

"We wouldn't hurt you." She could see the frustration in his face. "Hell, Kelly, our cousins in Texas have survived just fine."

The Augusts. They didn't even live in Somerset and they had a reputation here.

She breathed in deeply.

"I'm not Marly or their other wives," she informed them as Rowdy straightened, slowly tensing.

Dawg glared back at Rowdy then. "You didn't even give us a chance—"

"You don't love her, Dawg," Rowdy snapped, striding across the room to Kelly's side.

When he turned to face Dawg and Natches, his arm curled around Kelly's back, pulling her closer to his hard body.

"We love her enough," Natches protested, his jaw pulsing tightly.

"Oh give it up!" Kelly stepped away from her lover, staring between the three men incredulously, laughter bubbling from her throat at their fierce expressions. "Geez, do I look like a bone between the three of you?"

They stared back at her in surprise.

"Dawg, how many times did I flirt with you, just for the hell of it, while Rowdy was gone?"

"You did what?" Rowdy turned to her in surprised irritation.

"Save it." She rolled her eyes back at him. "You were gone, so the jealousy is a little late." She turned back to Dawg. "And I'm waiting on an answer, Dawg?"

Dawg shifted nervously, rather like a little boy caught in a fib. He cleared his throat, glancing at Rowdy with a grimace.

"You belonged to him first."

"I'm his always, Dawg," she informed him gently. "Now, forever, and always. And that's my decision. Not Rowdy's. And it's one you won't change."

"I told you she was trouble," Natches griped. "Dammit, Kelly, we didn't ask you to mess things up like this." He cast her a brooding glare.

"You're welcome." She smiled back placidly.

They weren't angry, she could see it in their eyes, feel it in the affection in their gazes.

Natches turned to Dawg and lifted his fist.

"We're the last."

Dawg lifted his fist in return, touching it to his cousin's. "The last."

He appeared firm, decisive. Kelly tilted her head and watched both men curiously. Natches might never let go of the more extreme needs, but there was something there in Dawg's expression. Something hesitant. Something uncertain.

"Let's go." Rowdy's arm hooked around her waist, dragging her toward the stairs.

"Where?"

"To bed," he growled.

"But, Rowdy, I'm not sleepy."

"I promise, you will be. Later . . ."

She was laughing as he swept her into the bedroom.

Nauti Nights

To the proud, the brave, and the daring.
You make the rules, you break the rules,
and you forge the paths
the rest of us only dream of taking.

Prologue

Somerset, Kentucky

Lake Cumberland

Eight Years Ago

Crista Jansen stared at the bed and the man sprawled across it in horror as she stumbled back, the knowledge of the mistake she had made the night before pounding through her head like the strike of a tambourine. Over and over again.

She covered her mouth with her hand, her eyes wide, her stomach churning in sick realization of exactly how huge this mistake was. The mistake and the man. He took up almost every inch of space on the mattress, his powerful legs sprawled, his strong arms moving restlessly as though searching—for her.

And he would be. The man was inexhaustible. A veritable sex machine with no off switch once he got started. And she should know now—she and every other woman he had ever had in his bed.

She could feel the memory of the night before on every inch of her body: her breasts, swollen and sensitive from his lips suckling at the tender tips, her lips abraded and tender from his kisses, and between her thighs—

That memory nearly brought her to her knees as her gaze slipped to his thighs, to the half-erect flesh that appeared threatening and overlarge, even though he wasn't fully erect.

Yet he had fit inside her. Stretching her wide, often in a pleasure bordering pain. He had managed to work every inch of that iron-hard flesh inside her, and he had destroyed her with it. Pounding inside her with a force that shook the bed and shook her senses, throwing her into one orgasm after another, bringing such pleasure that she had been unwilling to deny it. Unwilling to deny him anything, even at the end.

Her hand covered her mouth as tears filled her eyes. Oh God, she hadn't let him do those things to her, had she? Lifted her rear for him and begged for more as his tongue caressed forbidden flesh, then screamed in pleasure and in pain as the head of his cock began to work inside the heavily lubricated little hole.

He had marked her. He had taken her virginity, and he had taken her sanity. When he had finished marking the wet depths of her pussy, he had turned her to her stomach and marked her rear as well. With heated slaps, with diabolically talented fingers, and finally, with the deep, controlled thrusts of his cock.

He had taken her anally, and she had let him. And as she had lain beneath him, fighting for breath, he had told her how much better it could be. How three cocks would take her, move against her, pleasure her.

And with those words he had destroyed a part of her soul. She had dreamed of sweet, gentle words. Endearments. Soft kisses and maybe at least a promise to see her again. She hadn't expected him to tell her that soon, so soon, she would have his cousins as well.

They shared their women; she knew that. It wasn't just rumor, wasn't just hinted at. Alex, her brother, had warned her repeatedly that the stories didn't come close to the reality of the sexual lifestyle Dawg and his cousins lived, and she hadn't heeded that warning.

Shaking in fear, she quickly jerked her shorts and T-shirt on, not bothering to search for her panties and bra. God only knew where they were. She had to get out of there before he awoke, before he realized how incredibly stupid she had been.

He had been drunk. He might not remember. God, he'd been drunk; just getting him back to the houseboat had taken every ounce of strength she possessed. But she had understood the drunkenness. His parents had just died in a horrifying wreck; he had buried them, stood over their graves, and known they were gone from him forever. He deserved a few hours of freedom from the pain.

If only she hadn't been stupid enough to go looking for him when she learned he wasn't with Rowdy and Natches. If only she hadn't grown worried about him, borrowed her brother's car, and gone searching for him.

But she had, and she had known better. She should have sent Alex after him. She should have sent anyone after him but herself. Because she had known how it would end, and she had known where he would want it to go.

Rather than accepting that, she had fooled herself into thinking that taking her, realizing her innocence, her feelings for him, that he would show a spark of possessiveness. Just a moment's hesitancy in sharing her with other men, with seeing another man touching her, taking her.

She was crying as she eased the lock back on the glass door that led to the lower deck of the houseboat. It was still early. The mist was thick on the lake, surrounding the houseboats and creating a luminescent, otherworldly air that cut into her soul. Touching him had been like touching power itself. He was huge, so tall and broad, his body leanly muscled and graceful. His chest lightly furred, the crisp curls had raked her nipples as he thrust into her. When his lips hadn't been suckling them. But it was more than just the physical. That power had seeped inside her, filled her with emotions she had tried to hold in check, tried to protect herself from. She loved him. He made her heart clench and her soul ache. He had the power to bring her to her knees or to make her fly in ecstasy with only a glance from those odd green eyes of his.

And when he touched her . . . When he touched her, he'd had the power to make her forget that she knew exactly who and what Dawg Mackay was.

As she slipped down the docks, she kept her head down, kept her eyes on the floating walkway, and prayed no one saw her. Dawn was barely breaking over the mountains now; most of the inhabitants of the houseboats wouldn't be moving around for hours yet.

She could get lucky. She could escape, and no one would ever know she had spent the night with one of the most notorious sex gods in five counties. One of three.

She swiped at her tears. She hated crying. She had learned years ago that no good came of it. It only succeeded in making her feel worse than ever.

But she couldn't stop the tears any more than she could stop the pain. Dawg had been chasing her all summer. Those light celadon green eyes framed by the thick, inky black lashes, so pale they mesmerized her and pierced into her soul.

His smile was always slow and sexy, knowing. As though he were aware of the ache that centered between her thighs and tormented her long into the night. As though he knew how often she dreamed of feeling him against her, touching him, being touched.

The dream had turned into far more than she had expected. Part nightmare, part temptation. Forcing herself out of that bed had been next to impossible. She had wanted him to flow over her; she wanted to take his cock into her mouth again and practice what he had taught her.

She wanted to hear him moan her name again, watch his eyes darken. She wanted to run and hide and make certain she never let herself become so vulnerable to him ever again.

And it was breaking her heart. Walking away, turning her back on the only man her young heart had ever raced to was killing her. It hurt physically. It made her stomach cramp. It made her heart feel like a raw, aching wound.

She wanted to hide. She wanted to hide and nurse the pain and the fear. She was terrified. Terrified of the things she knew Dawg could make her feel and terrified of the knowledge that she would do anything, commit any act he asked of her, for just one more chance to take another hot, mind-numbing kiss from his perfect lips.

She would become no more than one of a long line of Nauti playthings, and that would destroy her. She could never share him with another woman, and on the same coin, she could not have survived, emotionally, being shared.

As she moved quickly along the floating dock and over the bridge that stretched to the shore, the sound of a motorcycle moving into the parking lot beyond had her heart racing with dread.

She hadn't just destroyed her own dreams but perhaps a friendship as well. Dawg and her brother were close friends. When the Mackay cousins weren't busy sharing their women, Alex had invariably been in their company until he joined the military. And even now, when he returned home on leave, he spent a lot of time with Dawg and the other Mackay cousins.

This could destroy that friendship, and Alex didn't have many friends.

The implications of the past night were racing through her soul with a power that had sobs tearing from her chest. She reached the car she had borrowed at the same time her brother pulled up to the vehicle on his motorcycle.

The powerful throb of the motor eased, then went silent as Alex extended one long leg, bracing his foot on the pavement as the other propped on the foot pedal on the other side.

He wiped his hand over his face slowly before staring out at the houseboats for a long, silent moment. This was her older brother; he had all but raised her. Her parents rarely had time for anyone but the store and themselves and whatever scheme her father had for making more money. It had left Alex with the responsibility of raising the daughter they never seemed to know what to do with.

And now he had to face the fact that his sister had obviously just had sex with not just his best friend but a sexual legend in the county. And Dawg wasn't even twenty-five yet.

She stood still, silent, unable to stop crying as he stared back at her silently. His gray eyes were heavy with sadness, his regal, handsome face drawn into a weary expression.

"Did you tell him no?" he finally asked her gently.

She shook her head. She hadn't even thought to tell him no.

He turned his head, staring toward Dawg's houseboat in resignation. She could see his anger in the tight, controlled line of his lips, in the flash of dark emotion in his eyes.

His jaw bunched with it as the lean muscles in his shoulders and arms flexed warningly.

"Did you want to tell him no?"

She shook her head again, shaking beneath the knowledge in his eyes.

She couldn't have told Dawg no if her life had depended on it. Each touch, each kiss had been a fantasy come to life.

He nodded slowly. "Let's go home then. We can talk about it there. No sense in making things worse by lingering out here long enough for anyone to see you. If you want to keep this quiet, you're going to have to pretend it didn't happen." His gaze sharpened then. "Do you want to keep it quiet, Crista?"

"Yes." She bit her trembling lips as she swiped at her tears. "Oh God, Alex. I just want to get out of here."

"Do you have your keys?"

She dug them out of the pocket of her shorts and quickly unlocked the door before jerking it open.

"Crista." His voice, despite its gentleness, resonated with a dark, hidden fury. "Was he alone?"

Her hand gripped the doorframe as she met his gaze. "It was just Dawg and me, Alex. I swear." This time. She knew if it happened again, if she dared to let it ever repeat, then it wouldn't be just Dawg. And when that happened, Dawg would make an enemy of her brother for life.

"Let's go home, Crista." He breathed out roughly. "I'll follow you."

As they pulled from the driveway, she couldn't help the sob that tore from her chest again or the fear that rolled through her.

She had cried last night when he touched her the first time. Because she had dreamed of it for so long. Because he had stroked more than just her body, kissed more than her lips. He had touched that inner core of her being that she hadn't realized could be possessed. When his fingers had parted the folds between her thighs and his expression had hardened with lust, he had wet his fingers on her juices, then brought them to his lips, his lashes lowering sensually at the taste of her.

A second later he had dipped his fingers between her thighs again and brought them to her lips. And she hadn't been able to deny him. She hadn't been able to deny him a single thing in the hours they had spent touching and tasting each other.

Everything he had asked of her, she had given. God help her if he ever had her that weak again. She would never be able to deny him. Never be able to hold on to her pride or her soul. Because if he shared her, he would break her heart forever. But if he asked it of her, she knew she would never be strong enough to tell him no.

"God! You're so fucking hot. So tight. So tight, Crista. So tight that when Rowdy and Natches get their dicks inside you, you'll destroy us all . . ." She hadn't heard the rest of the statement; her mind had shut down. Her soul had withered in her chest.

She had to get away from Dawg, because if she didn't, he

would own her soul. And that terrified her more than the thought of leaving her home ever had. She would never be able to defend herself. She knew his touch now, knew his kiss, and she knew beyond a shadow of a doubt that she would never love anyone as she loved Dawg Mackay.

One

Somerset, Kentucky

Eight Years Later

It was a nightmare.

No, it wasn't a nightmare, because she was pretty damned sure she was awake. And in nightmares, bullets weren't real. They weren't real, and they weren't exploding around the warehouse like hellish fireflies destroying everything they lodged inside.

Nightmares came with a certain understanding that it was a dream, *not real.* This was definitely real, and if something really good didn't happen very soon, then she was going to have holes in her body that were not supposed to be there.

She fought to hold back her screams as bullets whizzed over her head again, popping in the wood crates around her and sending a shower of wood chips and shattered glass from inside around her head.

This was bad. Very bad. She stared around, wide-eyed and dazed, as she scrambled around more boxes, more crates, fighting for as much protection between her and the bullets as she could find.

Crista Jansen was certain her horoscope hadn't said anything about bullets today. Something about dark knights and ill-advised trips, but there had been nothing in there about bullets.

She would have remembered.

She would have changed her plans.

Oh boy, would she have changed her plans.

Scuttling behind what she hoped was a very thickly packed

crate, she covered her head with her arms as glass sprayed around her.

Those weren't just regular bullets. Those were fast bullets. Automatic? Uzi? Something. The kind that spat fire as they pelleted out dozens of rounds at a time. And she knew because the red flashes of light in the otherwise dark interior of the warehouse were a pretty good clue.

A terrified *squak*, a cross between a squeak and a squawk, fell from her lips as chips of wood exploded from the sides of the crate she found to hide behind.

They were serious out there. People were killing people, and she was caught in the crossfire and wondering how the hell she was going to get out of this one.

She knew this was a bad idea.

She knew. She had felt that sick feeling in her gut the minute she stepped into the cavernous warehouse and realized the lights didn't work. But had she, dumb ass that she was, backed out and left? Oh, hell no, she had just pulled her penlight from her purse and trudged merrily on her way, looking for that stupid box. She told the delivery company to deliver to her home, not here. Yet when she returned home from work, what had she found? An official notice that her package had been dropped off at their local distribution warehouse and why, lookie, there had been the magical key to open the damned locker it was in.

Well, guess what? There's no locker here, she told herself sarcastically. No locker, but plenty of bullets singing a macabre tune through the darkness.

So now, rather than collecting her belongings, she was just trying to stay alive. When did fate decide to bust Crista Jansen's ass? For God's sake, hadn't she had enough bad luck in the past eight years?

This was all Dawg's fault, she decided. Every bit of it. He lived and he breathed and because of it; fate hated her. Fate was female, right? It was probably jealous. There could be no other explanation.

This was so bad.

"Where did the fucking girl go—?" a harsh, accented voice muttered roughly.

Okay she was the only girl she knew of in this stupid place.

She had only heard male orders, commands, and screams since hell had erupted around her.

Crista turned, crawling on her hands and bare knees—she should have worn jeans instead of one of her few good skirts—trying her best to get as far away from the mayhem and bloodshed as possible.

She knew not to come in here, she reminded herself. Remember that sick feeling? That panicked feeling? Hadn't she learned years ago it meant bad things? Get the hell out of Dodge type things?

She had been feeling it more and more lately. And this was just another event in a long string of very odd events. Clothes that would go missing and then turn back up in her closet, freshly washed. The feeling of being watched and strangers who thought they knew her.

Hadn't she told her brother last week that something was wrong? And speaking of screwy brothers, where the hell was hers? Damn it, Alex *would* have to disappear when she needed him most.

Military mission be damned. She didn't need him across the world, unavailable; she needed him here, now, getting her ass out of trouble.

And she hadn't told him good-bye when she talked to him.

Strange that she should remember that as she wedged herself into a dark, musty corner surrounded by crates and backed by a cement support beam.

She hadn't told Alex good-bye when she talked to him last week. She had just hung up on him because he had said something totally idiotic.

Something along the lines of "Call Dawg."

Oh yeah, right. She was going to do that.

He should have known better than to make such an insane suggestion. Where the hell had his mind gone in the past eight years? Had he forgotten how hard it had been for her to stay in Somerset that summer? Dawg had chased her with steady determination for months before the rest of her world had collapsed around her. Even though it was more than obvious that he hadn't remembered that one stolen night she had spent in his bed, he had still chased after her with a tenacity that reminded her why they called him Dawg.

Because he never let up. He never gave up.

She flinched as a projectile tore through the side of the crate that she had hoped was thick enough to protect her. She stared at the hole it made coming out mere inches from her upraised knees and gagged.

It was nearly the size of her fist.

"Get down!"

She heard the male voice screaming from a distance as another bullet ricocheted against the cement beam, inches above her head.

She went down. All the way down. And fought to get through the small crack between the support beam and the heavy crate, wondering how the hell a bullet could penetrate it when she couldn't even move it.

Clawing desperately at the side of the crate, she pressed, pushed, wedging herself into the minute amount of space and almost—almost managing to escape.

She screamed, terror racing through her, freezing her blood to ice as hard fingers grabbed her hair and pulled her back, jerking her back by the thick, dark strands and sending agonizing pain racing through her neck.

Her hands reached back, her nails clawing at the wrist behind her, fighting, struggling as she was dragged from the only means of escape in sight.

"Stupid whore! Where's my fucking money? I teach you to betray me, *puta*!"

She was jerked around, staring back in horror at the dark eyes and pitted face of what she was certain had to be a demon.

Stringy black hair fell over his narrow brow, his flat cheekbones were ruddy with rage, his dark brown eyes lit almost red with fury. And he had a gun.

Crista watched in slow motion. She had heard that expression, events passing in slow motion, and hadn't believed it until now.

Now she was watching it. Tearless. Breathless. Watching in slow motion as his arm raised. One hand pushed her against the cement support, the other was coming up. Up.

But the shot came too soon.

One minute she was watching that black weapon level up to her, the next a shower of red exploded around her as her hands flew to her face and a scream tore from her as his body jerked forward, then fell.

Right at her feet.

"Goddamn you, Crista!"

She recognized that voice.

Jerking her head up from the sight of the bloody mess her assailant's face was now, she stared back at the dark figure, Law Enforcement emblazoned across the bulletproof jacket he was jerking from his broad chest.

"Put it on, damn you!" His voice was a hard rasp, guttural, animalistic, as he jerked her around and strapped her into the vest until the black velco strips were holding it snugly to her chest and back.

"Let's go!" Hard gloved fingers wrapped around her arm as, with a shove, the crate she had been fighting to move was pushed back as though it were no more than a heavy box. "Move it!"

He pushed her through the opening before gripping her arm again and pulling her through the dark.

"What's going on?" She breathed out roughly. She couldn't scream, she couldn't cry. All she could do was follow Dawg.

And she knew it was Dawg. Those brilliant celadon green eyes, that dark, male, honeyed voice. No other man sounded like Dawg. No other man moved like him or smelled like him.

And besides, it was just her dumb luck. He was here. She was here. Hell was erupting around her. Fate was laughing her ass off, and it was all Dawg's fault.

"Shut up!" he snarled, not even bothering to so much as try to explain as he pushed her through the darkness. "Keep your mouth shut, keep your head down, and if God is in a good mood today, I might be able to save your ass."

Save her ass?

"But I was just here—"

"Just fucking save it." He pushed her against something cement, the dim light that spilled in from overhead windows emphasizing the enraged flames in his eyes. "I just killed a man for you, princess. A man worth a hell of a lot more alive than he was dead. Now shut your goddamned mouth and do exactly what I say. Exactly. Or I'll slap cuffs on you and haul you in so fast, you won't have time to twitch that pretty ass of yours."

Before she could process the fact that they were racing from the back of the warehouse, Dawg was lifting her into the backseat of his black four-by-four double cab pickup. He pulled the bulletproof vest from her and jerked it back on, his eyes glowing with rage as his fingers tangled in her hair. He stared down at her, remorseless, before gripping the bottom of her T-shirt and wiping it roughly over her lower face.

Blood. She shuddered at the thought. Someone else's blood stained her now. Then Dawg forced her head back a second before his lips covered hers.

Gunfire receded. Reality dimmed. The world narrowed down to his lips slanted over hers, his tongue pressing between them as hers opened. Electricity sparked, exploded, and sizzled through her head with a dazzling display of color as pleasure tore through her system.

Eight years without him. Without this. Without the hunger that consumed and burned away the ragged wound in her soul that leaving him eight years before had left inside her.

Her hands curled against the bulletproof vest, and a whimper that shocked her vibrated from her throat as he tore his lips from hers as quickly as he had taken them.

She stared up at him, wide-eyed, shocked, as he glared back at her.

"Where did you park?" he snapped out.

Her lips trembled as she fought to drag in enough air to answer him.

"The back lot," she whispered as he jerked her purse open and before she could stop him, pulled her keys from inside.

"You're damned lucky your car wasn't here when this started, Crista," he snarled. "Luckier than you'll ever know. Now, lie down. Don't move. Don't speak. Don't twitch. So help me God, if you give yourself away in here, I'll toss you into a cell so deep and so dark you won't know up or down. Do we have that clear?"

She tried to nod, just as she was trying to breathe. A second later he was pushing her to the seat, pressing her cheek into the fine black leather with a harsh order to "Stay," before the door slammed and he was gone.

And she was alone. She could still hear the gunfire, but it was distant and easing away. It was replaced with shouted orders, vehicles moving, and strident calls.

Inside the truck she shuddered, drew her knees to her chest, and tried to still the shaking in her body.

Shock. She knew she must be having some kind of shock reaction, because it was the middle of the summer. She shouldn't be freezing so much she was shaking; breathing shouldn't be hard. And God help her if she puked in Dawg's truck. He would probably shoot her himself.

She forced herself to breathe slowly, evenly, to draw in the scent of Dawg that permeated his truck and filled her senses with memories. Memories she had fought to forget for eight long years.

The feel of his thighs between hers as he parted them and lowered himself to her. Watching as one large hand gripped the shaft of his cock, nudging it against the hot, wet curls between her thighs.

"Wax your pussy," he had growled, *"so I can see your soft flesh gripping my dick."*

Her womb clenched at the memory, as clear now as it had been the morning after.

And he didn't even remember it. She still had to fight back the rage and the pain of that one. The bastard. He had seen her two days later and had looked right through her as she stood in her parents' convenience store, her heart in her throat, certain that he had come for her.

But he hadn't. He had smiled and flirted, and on his arm hung some stupid twit blond bimbo who cooed over his muscles as he paid for ice and snacks.

He had made some cheerful comment to Crista about her hair, and she glared at him. He had frowned, tried again, and she had turned her back and left Alex to take care of him. Because she couldn't look at him; she couldn't bear remembering and knowing that not so much as a glimmer of that night remained in his memory. Knowing, that if he had her again, they wouldn't be alone.

And then, weeks later, the knowledge that she hadn't escaped that night without repercussions. She had carried his child.

Her initial reaction had been one of anger, of resentment. He was partying, enjoying his life and his women and the dirty little sex games he and his cousins played, and she was pregnant.

But within days that anger had stilled. The knowledge that she would always have a part of him had consumed her young mind, her heart. The heart she had given Dawg on a sultry summer night. And that happiness had built, filling her, glowing inside her.

Until three months to the day after he had taken her. The day she had lost the child she had grown to love so deeply. She had left the clinic Alex had taken her to, packed her bags, and left for Virginia with friends who had been visiting that week.

And here she was, eight years later, her fingers curled into the leather of his truck seat, shaking, terrified as the sound of gunfire finally eased away and shouted commands filled the night instead.

Suddenly, the implications of her very precarious position slammed inside her head. She was at the scene of an obvious raid of some sort. Wasn't that what they called it? A raid? A sting? And she had been right smack-dab in the middle of it.

Which meant she was about to be right smack-dab in the middle of a whole lot of suspicion.

FUBAR. That's what this entire fucking night had turned into. Fucked up beyond all repair, and it was all his own damned fault.

He stared into the shadowed expanse of the warehouse parking lot, his brows lowered, trying to make sense of what he had done and why. The why of it more than anything else.

What had crashed through the hard core of training and beliefs in what he was doing long enough to rush Crista from the warehouse and hide her? What had made him risk his own soul this way for a woman?

Not just any woman though: Crista. The woman that had invaded his dreams for longer than he wanted to admit. The woman who had, somehow, wormed her way into his soul before she left Somerset eight years ago. And the why of that one had no explanation. Just as the dreams of her that had tormented him over the years made no sense.

"I moved her Rodeo," Natches said, sidling up to Dawg as he stood guarding the warehouse entrance. "She was parked outside the range of the cameras, and her head was down as she came through the entrance. With any luck, we can cover her identity."

Dawg glanced at his cousin and best friend from the corner of his eye. He was half tempted to blame his cousin for every second of this madness. Following the vague warning he had given, Dawg had moved to find who they assumed was the female seller who had entered the warehouse. She was the only one unaccounted for now.

Dawg had moved to intercept her ahead of the rest of the team and reacted rather than thinking. If he had given himself time to think, she would be stretched out on the warehouse floor with the rest of the bastards they had arrested in the raid.

They had the buyers, the sellers, four missing experimental missiles, and their guidance chips. It was a damned good haul for the investigation. Except for the fact that the woman who had masterminded the deal hadn't arrived.

That, or she was hiding in the backseat of Dawg's pickup truck.

"Remind me why we're covering her identity," Dawg said softly, his gaze tracking the rest of the combined ATF and Homeland Security team.

Hell, he knew why, but damned if he wanted to admit to it. This wasn't something Crista would do. He knew it wasn't. At least, it wasn't something the Crista he had once known would do.

"Because she's not involved?" Natches hazarded a mocking guess.

"She was here," Dawg pointed out, even as he ignored the hard mental flash of denial that Crista could be involved in this in any way.

"Uh-huh." Natches nodded. "Of which I warned you. You were the one who jerked her out like a wolf protecting its mate, not me, Cousin. I just covered your six. That's my job. Remember?"

Like a wolf protecting its mate. Or a Dawg protecting a bone, he thought sarcastically.

He had taken one look at her, and something inside him had exploded in awareness. He knew damned good and well what would happen if he didn't get her out of there. If she had been caught with the others, with the description of the female suspect they had, she would have never gotten out of the arrest and subsequent imprisonment, involved or not.

And why that should matter to him, he couldn't figure out.

"She's not involved." Natches cradled his rifle in his arms like a lover as he stared back at Dawg. "That's not Crista, Dawg."

Maybe it wasn't. But then again, maybe it was, and he just couldn't see it for his own lust.

Dawg tightened his lips and stared back at the organized chaos inside the now well-lit warehouse. He was a paranoid son of a bitch. He trusted no one but the Father, the Son, and the Holy Ghost, and Crista wasn't included in the Trinity last he checked.

Yet he was risking his own reputation to protect her. Not because of Natches's warning but because his own emotions had interfered with the job for the first time in eight years. And as he stood there, watching the arrests, the recovery of the missiles and their chips, and felt the sense of triumph that the team radiated, he felt disassociated.

He was impatient. Eager to have it over with, because his mind was brewing with all the possibles filtering through it. It was possible Crista wasn't involved. And if she wasn't, then it was possible that for the first time since her return a year ago, he had an edge on her. She couldn't just turn and run, as she was wont to do whenever he came near.

Oh no. Not anymore.

His eyes narrowed, and his lips curled with an anticipatory smile.

He had lived on instinct too damned long to discount it, and instinct was giving her the benefit of the doubt. But he was still a part of the ATF, and she was at the scene of an arms buy. She also fit the brief description of the one female in the group of thieves that had hijacked the weapons and attempted to sell them.

He was going to have to keep an eye on her. A very close eye on her.

"Oh hell, I hate that smile," Natches suddenly groaned beside him. "Dawg, what the hell are you up to?"

Dawg glanced over at him, his brow lifting in mock innocence. "I'm just considering how best to determine who's guilty and who's innocent," he drawled. "Nothing for you to worry about, Natches. Nothing whatsoever."

It was a lot for Dawg to worry about, and even more for Crista.

For Dawg, because Crista made him break his own rules, and that was something he never did, under any circumstances. And for her, because he was going to take payment for those rules out of her sweet little body.

Natches's shoulders slumped. "Hell. Why do I have a feeling now that I should have just played the knight in shining armor myself rather than giving you the opportunity to pull your head out of your ass?"

Dawg snorted at that. "Stop worrying. I have it covered."

"I'm guaranteed to worry at any time that you tell me not to worry. It's a cosmic rule."

Dawg lifted his brows and chuckled in amusement. "Trust me."

Natches stared back at him in worried disbelief. "Man, don't go pulling that kamikaze shit on me again, okay? Four years of it in the Marines were enough. You promised to take it easy once we got home. Remember?" Natches reminded him. "Think about your knee, man. You're only one good accident from being a cripple. Let's not push it, 'kay?"

Dawg let his grin widen. "Take it easy? Easy wasn't what I had in mind, but taking it sure as hell is."

Natches stared at him suspiciously. "Don't do something you're going to regret, Dawg. I don't have time to pull your ass out of any fires."

Dawg clapped him on the shoulder before moving toward the men being lifted from the cement floor and prepared for a nice little trip to the nearest jail cell. "No worries, Natches." He grinned over his shoulder. "No worries at all. Grab her car. Tell the commander we drove in separately; they won't know any better. You were just borrowing a friend's vehicle. And I'll catch ya later."

He had plans to make. Plans that included one sexy little waitress, his bed, and all kinds of wet, hot, nasty sex acts.

The next time she turned her back on him, she would at least remember what it felt like, what it meant to be owned by him. And by God, before it was over, he would own her. Heart and soul. By fair means or by foul. Dawg wasn't playing anymore.

Two

She was still where he left her. Not that he hadn't expected her to be, but it was always comforting to know one was right about these matters.

"Stay put," he told her as he moved into the driver's seat and stuck the key in the ignition. "Wouldn't want anyone to see you as we leave, now would we?"

He flipped the music on. AC/DC rocked through the cab of the truck as he held down the button to the windows, opening them all the way, and peeled from the parking lot like a man on a mission.

He lifted his hand to the state police officers in the front lot, and not for the first time was thankful that he had parked his truck alongside one of the abandoned buildings rather than coming in with the rest of the team later.

He and Natches had been posted to watch the area through the day and give the go-ahead when the team could move in. It was the one thing that had saved Crista's ass. No one would be any wiser when Natches explained that they had come in separately and he pulled out in Crista's Rodeo. They might wonder, until the gossip hit that one Crista Jansen was currently residing with one Dawg Mackay on his infamous houseboat, the *Nauti Dawg.*

As he put distance between the truck and the scene of the arrest, he let the muscles of his neck and shoulders relax before turning down the music and glancing between the seats to the long bench seat in the back.

Something inside him clenched at the sight of her pale face and wide, dark brown eyes. Chocolate eyes. She had big, dark, chocolate eyes, and he was a man that knew how to savor that particular sweet.

"You can come up here now," he told her, turning his attention back to driving as he turned onto one of the curving country roads that wound through the county.

She moved slowly, uncurling from the backseat and moving into the empty passenger seat beside him before settling in and staring out the windshield stiffly.

"Put your seat belt on." Dawg propped his arm on the open window frame and scratched at his jaw consideringly as he drove.

Beside him, Crista clipped her seat belt, moving almost hesitantly, glancing at him every few seconds with silent wariness.

She knew she was fucked. She might not know just how well she was going to be fucked, but she was definitely fucked.

"Let's play a game," he finally drawled in amusement as he glanced over at her.

"We've been playing one for a year," she retorted. "You just keep forgetting to forward the rules to me."

He grinned at that. That was Crista. Never without a snappy little comeback.

"This is an easy game," he promised her. "A guessing game. Tell me, if you will, exactly what the hell you were doing in the goddamned warehouse."

He had to snap his teeth together as anger flamed with each word, overriding the amusement he had previously felt. Once again, he saw her, staring up at that damned terrorist, her eyes wide, her face pale, that gun rising steadily to her face.

She flinched.

"My things," she answered then, her voice haunted. "Mark had the rest of my belongings shipped from Virginia. I have a note. The delivery company said they were at the warehouse in one of the lockers. I have the key here." She was digging in her purse, her voice shaking. "See. I have the key."

She held a key out to him.

Dawg took it slowly, glanced at it, then handed it back to her. It was indeed a locker key with the initials SIY, for Store It Yourself, stamped on it.

"Where's the note?"

She didn't go digging in her purse. Her teeth were biting nervously at her lower lip instead.

"Where's the note, Crista Ann?" he asked her again.

Crista flinched. "I left it in the Rodeo, my car. Back at the warehouse."

Dawg shook his head. "Didn't stick it in your pocketbook, huh?" He glanced at her suspiciously.

"It's there. In the passenger seat." She was gripping her hands in her lap, her fingers twisting together.

She used to do that every damned time she got around him. From the time she was sixteen until just a few months before she left town a little over eight years ago.

"We'll see," he grunted.

"Is this game over now?" she asked him irritably. "I'd like to go back home."

At that point, Dawg grinned.

"Dawg, you are going to take me home, aren't you?"

He heard it in her voice. She was getting a clue.

"Not yet." He flashed her a quick grin, anticipation beginning to build along with the heated lust at the knowledge he saw in her eyes.

"Where are you taking me then?"

"Your new home."

"And that's where?" She pushed the question through gritted teeth. Dawg almost chuckled. Oh yeah, things were changing now.

"We'll play your question and answer game later," he retorted, refusing to answer her for the time being. "For now, let me ask you this: Do you have any clue what the hell was going on in that warehouse?"

She breathed out wearily, leaned her head back against the seat, and said, "Drugs?" It was said with such an air of resignation that he was inclined to believe that maybe she wasn't involved with terrorists.

With her background, it was damned difficult to believe she was. Her brother, Alex, was one of the finest Special Forces soldiers Dawg had ever known, his reputation was solid, and Dawg knew for a fact it had been Alex who had raised Crista.

"Know how much trouble you're in?"

He glanced over in time to see her lashes drift closed, feathering over her cheeks like dark shadows.

"Are you taking me to jail?"

Was he?

Hell no, he wasn't. If he was going to turn her over to the authorities, he would have done so in the warehouse. He was damned stupid was what he was. A horny fool.

"Not yet." He tightened his lips before moving his hand from his cheek and letting his forefinger brush over his lips, remembering her kiss as he watched the road thoughtfully, his elbow still propped on the window frame.

Damn if he wasn't stepping into a mess this time.

"What are you going to do, Dawg?" she asked him quietly.

The sound of her voice made him harder. Not just hard, hell, his dick had been hard since the day he glimpsed her walking down Main Street a year ago and knew she was back, even before he caught sight of her face. No, he was harder. Painfully hard.

A vision of her head lowering to his cock suddenly had his entire body clenching painfully. Wide, innocent chocolate eyes staring up at him as his cock head disappeared into her mouth almost had a groan ripping from his chest.

That vision haunted him; that one and several others. The sight of her pussy, dark curls saturated with her juices as he parted the tender folds with his thick erection. The sound of her cries as he tucked the hungry crest at her rear and took her there, hearing her shock, her pleasure. Dreams that had haunted him for years. Dreams he intended to make reality now that he had her.

"To the boat." His houseboat. The *Nauti Dawg.* His home.

He heard the hard breath she took.

"No."

He glanced at her, seeing the revulsion on her face, and a flare of anger pierced his mind again. She hadn't been good enough to step foot into his home eight years ago, and she still thought she was too good for it.

"You prefer jail?" He eased up on the gas, glancing around as though looking for a place to turn around.

"I wasn't doing anything," she argued desperately then. "You know I wasn't, Dawg. It was a coincidence—"

"I don't believe in coincidence, Crista."

"A mistake then," she cried out as he began easing to the wide shoulder just ahead. "God, Dawg, you know I don't do drugs."

He pulled over and came to a stop. Draping his arms over the steering wheel, he stared back at her silently.

"You can't take me to jail, Dawg. Alex will be home soon, he'll tell you. This is all a mistake."

"Alex can't fix this one, Crista," he told her softly, meaning it. "You're stuck with me." He gave her a minute to process that. "Or jail. Your choice."

She was breathing hard, erratically. If it were only fear that he had glimpsed in her eyes, he would have let her off the hook right then. God knew Alex could definitely deal with this when he got home. But it wasn't just fear; he saw heat there, and something more. Something elusive, a knowledge, a certainty that something was getting ready to rock her little world.

She licked her lips. A quick little flick of her tongue that had his guts tightening in hunger. He wanted that tongue, and he wanted it bad enough to do something so despicable, so dirty it almost, just almost, made him cringe.

He smiled instead, because it was going to be good. So damned good.

"Do I turn around, or do we continue to the marina?" he asked her then. "Your choice, sweetheart."

And if she chose turning around, what the hell would he would do then? He waited, staring back at her, his expression bland, his gaze, he knew, hot and hungry. She knew what he wanted. She knew the price he was exacting for pulling her out of this one.

Her lips trembled before she licked them again. Her gaze flickered with indecision. And he wasn't going to help her. He'd be damned if he would go back to chasing after her like a dog after a bitch in heat and being turned away every time. Not this time. This time, it was his game. His way or jail. Or at least, that was the impression he was intent on giving her.

"Don't turn around," she finally whispered, her gaze dropping, her head turning back to stare stiffly through the windshield once again.

"We go to the *Nauti Dawg*, then?" he asked her.

"If that's my only choice." Her voice was tense, angry.

Fine, let her be angry. He'd been damned mad himself eight years ago, and he could still remember the fury when he realized she had left town with another man. Realized, nothing, he had seen her in the car with the bastard as they drove out of town.

He still remembered that one. Hell, he had nightmares about that one when he least expected them.

"It's not your only choice, Crista Ann," he said softly. "You can go explain to the authorities what you were doing there. That one's real easy."

Of course, he'd have to explain why she wasn't arrested with the rest of the crew, but he was hoping she wouldn't realize that.

"Yeah. I could do that," she snapped back mockingly. "And of course, you would deny to hell and back pulling me out of there. Right?"

He grinned. God love her, he had to give her credit.

Dawg shrugged. "What can I do? I didn't check my backseat until I heard someone move around in it. I can be a bit absent-minded when I'm in a hurry."

"And the reason Natches is driving my Rodeo rather than riding with you?"

Dawg widened his eyes. "You and Natches are friends, Crista. You loaned him the Rodeo."

Okay, he wasn't really that damned dirty. Hell, if she chose jail, he'd take her home and figure something else out. But she should have known that. If she didn't know that, well, that was just her mistake, not his.

"That's dirty, Dawg," she retorted, disgust thickening her voice.

"Sure it is." He nodded in agreement. "But I have a reputation for being dirty. Don't I?" His grin was pure innocence. One of the kind that normally had Natches looking for the nearest escape route.

She rubbed her hands over her face before pushing her fingers through the hair she had pulled back tightly into a long ponytail.

Hair he was dying to loosen, to spread out behind her as he laid her back on his bed. Hair he longed to grip while he rode her hard and deep.

She shook her head before staring straight ahead once again.

"So, we head to the marina, right?"

She nodded slowly. "Fine."

Dawg let off the brake and eased back onto the road before adding speed and heading down the dark highway.

"You act like you're heading to the gallows." He grinned.

She didn't reply.

Dawg glanced at her again, watching as she rubbed at her bare arms and stared out the window, her expression bleak, disheartening.

Damn her. It wasn't as though he intended to rape her. Blackmail her a little bit, definitely. But sex would be only under certain conditions. He'd make damned sure she wanted it as badly as he did, first. He wasn't a complete bastard.

But he was a horny bastard. And a mad bastard.

Eight fucking years she had lived in his dreams, and he couldn't figure out why. She had changed him at a time when he needed to retain that edge of careless unconcern. She had pricked his emotions, filled his head, and he couldn't make sense of it.

She tormented him. It was that damned simple, and it was time the torment eased.

"Don't worry, darlin'. It won't be so bad," he assured her, reaching over to pat her knee in a totally false gesture of comfort. "We used to get along good once, remember?"

Once.

Crista turned her head slowly and stared at his profile. Once, she had loved him with all the passion and innocence of a young girl who revered the town's baddest bad boy. But she wasn't a girl anymore; she was a grown woman. She was well aware of just how easily he could destroy her life again.

"I remember how stupid I was," she finally answered him with a measure of self-disgust at the memory. "And I remember learning my lesson. I don't really remember much other than that, Dawg. Perhaps you could remind me of a time that we actually got along."

He didn't remember that night. Crista knew he didn't. And she knew Alex would have never told him what happened. He had promised her.

Dawg tapped his fingers on the steering wheel. "You ran from me every chance you got," he growled back at her.

Not every chance. Not one dark night when she had found him too drunk to drive and helped him home. And then helped him break her heart.

"I was smart then," she said, feeling the regret that welled inside her. If only she had been smarter. If only she had faced the truth then, and what had happened. Maybe the past eight years would have been different. If nothing else, she might not have been tormented with so many what-ifs and the fact that she had been a coward.

Dawg grunted at that. "Too bad you weren't smart enough to stay out of dark warehouses at night. If you had, you wouldn't be here now."

Too bad she hadn't been smart enough to stay in Virginia to begin with. But no, she had to come home. She missed being home. She missed the mountains, the lake, and home. And she had known it was time to lay old ghosts to rest. She had come home to make peace with the memories and with herself. And with Dawg. She just hadn't expected to make peace with him in quite this way.

Instead, she found more demons. She found herself in the untenable position of relying on Dawg for something as imperative as her freedom. And there wasn't a doubt in her mind exactly how he intended to manipulate this one.

He had been after her ever since she had returned to Somerset a year ago. He hadn't stalked her. He was just always around. Always smiling that rakish grin of his, giving her that mocking once-over, that invitation to play. If he wasn't doing that, he was glaring at her. And he filled her dreams. Heated dreams, memories of one unforgettable night and the consequences of it.

She watched the miles pass by, feeling his hand on her knee when he wasn't shifting gears in the powerful pickup, and feeling the warmth of his touch burning through her skirt.

At least he wasn't groping her. Her body was so hyped on nerves right now that she wondered if she could bear that. If her heart could bear it.

She thought she had learned her lesson before leaving Somerset. After all, she knew what Dawg was, she knew what he intended, and she knew she could never live with it.

The Nauti Boys were legendary in Somerset and the surrounding counties. Their prowess, dedication to a woman's pleasure, and insistence on sharing those women had been well-known. Her brother, Alex, had warned her about Dawg repeatedly.

Her head had warned her about Dawg, but her heart hadn't wanted to listen. She could tame the bad boy, she had assured herself. Love would make him possessive. All she had to do was touch him, love him, and he would realize he loved her.

She snorted silently as she peeked a look at his hard profile.

What a fool she had been. Naive, impossibly innocent, incredibly foolish. And she still hadn't learned her lesson, not all the way to the soul. Because a part of her had never forgotten that one night. That sultry summer night when he had taken her with singular determination and fiery lust. When he had taught her the true depths of carnal pleasure and the ultimate despair.

"This isn't going to work." The words tore from her lips as he pulled into the small marina his uncle Ray Mackay owned.

She could feel the panic building in her chest now, the certainty that the *Nauti Dawg* was going to hold more memories and more heartache than she could bear.

"I can't do this." She was shaking as Dawg pulled the truck into the private parking slot in front of the marina.

He turned off the motor. Pulling the key from the ignition, he turned and stared at her silently.

Him or jail. She could see it in his expression.

Crista shook her head slowly before swallowing tightly.

"I'm not one of the Nauti Boys' whores," she whispered harshly. "I can't play one to stay out of jail, Dawg. I'd rather rot in prison than buy my freedom at the expense of my soul."

He stared back at her, his light green eyes icy, unemotional, as he watched her. His expression was as dark as the shadows around them and as still as death.

This wasn't the man she had known eight years ago. Charming, though brooding, James "Dawg" Mackay had had a will of iron, but he hadn't been cold. He'd been hard but not unemotional. Not as he was now.

He had joined the Marines just after she left town; she knew that. He'd spent one tour, when he had been shipped home because of a wound that shattered his kneecap. Not that she had seen any sign of an injury in the way he moved.

But right now, he was rubbing his knee almost absently as he watched her.

"We'll talk about this on the boat," he finally said warningly. "Not here."

"No, Dawg." She reached out, gripping his arm as he moved to open the door. "Not at the boat. I won't go out to that boat, and I won't spread myself for the Nauti Boys. I wouldn't do it when I was too stupid to know any better, and I sure as hell won't do it now. You're fooling yourself if you think you can convince me to do otherwise."

"And if going to that boat didn't mean spreading yourself for anyone but me, Crista?" he asked her. "Would you go then?"

Three

Eight years ago, she had slipped from Dawg's upper-deck bedroom and stolen from the *Nauti Dawg* like a thief in the early morning mists. But she had left something behind that morning, a part of herself she had never regained.

Now Crista stepped back through the reinforced French door that led into the living room and stilled herself against the memories that threatened to overwhelm her.

He still left a low light shining on the small table that sat beside the couch. It was a maroon plush couch now, where before it had been black leather. A matching recliner sat by the side of the same table.

The television was now mounted on the wall on the side they entered, and across the room on the opposite side sat a small dining table and four chairs.

A teak bar separated the dining area from the kitchen, two captain's barstools placed under it.

The rug was a rich, thick forest green. Eight years ago it had been a dark tan. The living room and kitchen were more refined now, stating a mature taste in furnishings but still a broad male influence. Dark woods and few frills.

A picture of his Marine Corps unit sat on the table by the couch alongside a picture of the Nauti cousins in camouflage greens and a picture of Rowdy and his fiancée, Kelly Salyers.

There were no pictures or prints on the wall. There was nothing to decorate the rooms. Beyond the kitchen was another large bedroom and small washroom as well as an extra bathroom. From where Crista stood, she could also see the curving staircase that led to the upper deck and master bed and bath, as well as the steering controls.

She flinched as the door closed and locked behind her.

"I need a beer," Dawg announced. "Want one?"

Crista shook her head as she gripped her purse and watched him move across the living room, then into the kitchen. He pulled a beer from the refrigerator before unscrewing the cap with a quick twist and tossing the cap beneath the bar, where the garbage can must have been hidden.

He moved to the sink first, pulled a dish towel from a small stack on the counter, dampened it, then tossed it to her.

"Clean your face."

She felt her stomach heave at the thought of the blood that had sprayed over her. It was on her face, her clothes. She scrubbed at her flesh quickly, harshly, hoping she managed to clean it away as he stared at her.

He tilted the bottle of beer to his lips and drank deeply, his gaze never leaving hers.

He had stripped the bulletproof vest, but he still wore the shoulder holster and weapon. His black T-shirt stretched over his wide chest and thick biceps. Black jeans rode low on his hips and outlined long, muscular legs and a more than impressive bulge.

"You're clean," he announced, holding his hand out. "Give me the towel."

Her gaze jerked from that area. It was more than obvious he was aroused, ready for her. And she hated admitting that her body had been ready for his since the moment he asked her if she was willing to spread herself for him alone.

She tossed the towel back to him, ignoring his mocking grin as he caught it and dumped it in the sink.

She was insane. She should have run from him while she had the chance.

"One night," she whispered. "That's all."

The bottle was smacked on the bar top so hard beer sloshed from the top, and Crista jumped at the sound.

"You aren't making the deal here," he informed her, his expression hardening. "You didn't catch me possibly breaking the law and consorting with criminals, Crista. I caught you, remember?"

Her fingernails dug into the leather of her purse.

"And I know what you want in exchange for my freedom," she snapped back. "Fine, you want to fuck. You want something you haven't been able to con me out of this year: my body. You can have it. For one night."

"And if I want more than one night?" The black velvet tone of his voice had a tremor quaking through her womb, clenching at the muscles of her stomach as she stared back at him in shock.

"Why would you want more than one night?" She shook her head in confusion. "How many women have you kept more than one night, Dawg?"

She still had friends she had kept in Somerset, and they liked to gossip. Dawg was as newsworthy now as he had been eight years ago.

"You aren't every other woman, Crista," he drawled. "I've never had to chase one for eight years before. It's built up a hunger. One that I doubt one night is going to sate."

She blinked back at him in shock. She had expected what he wanted, but she hadn't expected this. One night she could handle. More than one night?

"How many nights?" She kept her voice from trembling, barely.

Dawg's expression hardened further. "I haven't decided."

"You haven't decided? So I'm supposed to just be ready and available for you whenever you get a hard-on?"

Mocking consideration filled his face then. He nodded slowly. "That would work for me."

Crista clenched her teeth and calculated how long she still had to wait before Alex returned. He had been gone three months. Her last conversation with him, he had indicated that he could return within the next few weeks.

Could she handle being Dawg's lover that long? Could she walk away with her soul if she did?

"Don't think about it too damned hard," he bit out irritably. "I might change my mind."

Crista wrapped her arms over her breasts and stilled the anger beginning to rise inside her. She couldn't afford to be angry at this point; she had to think. Dawg always managed to mess up her mind. She couldn't afford to let him do it this time.

"You're being a bastard," she told him forcefully. "You know I wasn't involved in whatever you were doing there. I don't deal with drugs, I never have."

He shrugged easily as he propped himself against the bar. "I haven't seen you in eight years, Crista. People change in that time."

"Oh yeah, and people dealing in drugs work as waitresses at crappy little diners where they don't even make minimum wage, too," she snapped. "Don't play with me; I don't like it. At least admit that you're using this to force something out of me that I wasn't willing to give you."

A frown snapped between his brows, causing her stomach to clench nervously. "I wouldn't force you."

"Then what do you call it? I can fuck you or I can go to jail? Hell of a choice there, Dawg," she sneered.

Crista watched the muscle at his jaw tighten, a heavy tic rippling through it as he watched her.

"I thought I was being rather charitable," he growled. "Deny you're interested in being in my bed."

"I have. Every time I've ignored your petty little efforts at flirtation. Or didn't you notice?"

"I noticed that kiss earlier, too." Black velvet seduction. His voice raked over her nerve endings and reminded her just how good it had been. "That wasn't force, Crista. Stop fooling yourself. You loved it."

Okay, he had her there. Her stomach tightened at the memory and at the knowledge that she had no defenses against him.

"I agree to one night—"

"And I said one night isn't enough. I want the summer. All summer."

Crista froze. Three months? Summer had just begun, and he wanted the rest of it.

"Why?" She forced the word past her numb lips as she stared back at him.

"It takes time to determine guilt or innocence, Crista Ann. I want you close while I figure which one to attach to you. If you're really innocent, then at the end of the summer, you're free to go. I find out you're guilty, and your ass heads to jail. Consider it your trial period. Except instead of sitting in a jail cell, you're enjoying all the comforts I can provide you."

His smile was dangerous, sensual. It curved like a predatory smirk that had her heart racing in her chest.

And he was messing with her head again. Her mind filled with memories, the touch and the taste of him. How the slightest brush of his fingers could steal her defenses and leave her shaking in his arms.

His kiss. It was drugging, fiery. And what he could do to her heart, her emotions, should be illegal. He could tie her up in so many knots on the inside that she wondered if they would ever be untangled.

Crista swallowed tightly against the onslaught of remembered sensations and pleasures.

"You keep thinking about it." He shrugged easily. "You can take a shower, rest a bit before you decide. I'll loan you a clean shirt." He smiled again. "You won't need it for long."

"You've changed, Dawg," she whispered then. "You didn't used to be such a cold-blooded bastard."

"Sure I did," he drawled. "You were just one of the few that hadn't recognized it. Didn't you hear all about that nasty little court battle after my parents died? Hell, honey, even my parents knew I was a lost cause."

She had heard about the court battle. How his aunt had tried to take the entire estate his parents had left him based on a few letters his father had written to his aunt. Letters that were filled with disgust over his son's lifestyle and his belief that Dawg didn't deserve to share his name.

It had lasted for years. Even after he was in the Marines, he had been plagued with legal conflicts and the fight to hold on to his inheritance. It had finally ended after his return home four years ago, but he had lost tens of thousands of dollars in the fight.

"No." She shook her head. "You weren't like this before. You would have never forced this on me then."

"But I am now. You can make your choice while you're cleaning up. But when you step back into this room, you damned well better have made your mind up. You're mine for the summer, or you can belong to the federal government, it's all up to you."

Dawg didn't let out a relieved breath until Crista disappeared into the lower bathroom long minutes later, one of his T-shirts clenched tightly in her fingers, her large brown eyes watching him warily as she closed the door behind her.

Minutes later he heard the shower running and ran his fingers through his hair as he blew out another hard breath.

For a while there, he honestly thought she was going to choose the alternative. When she had finally headed for the shower, he had to force himself to hold back, to keep from assuring her that nothing in hell could convince him to turn her over to the authorities. To just let her go.

He rubbed at the back of his neck as he grimaced at the thought. Eight years he had dreamed about her. When he least expected it, when he was weak, tired. Dreams so blistering hot he would wake up pumping his own dick like an adolescent and moaning her name.

The past year had been worse. He was like a damned love-starved teenager going out of his way just to see her. Hoping to catch her smile, craving the sound of her voice.

Damn, he had missed her after she left town. Not that he had stuck around for long. He had signed up with the Marines before his parents' death, and he shipped out just months afterward. Long-distance court battles and the hell of trying to hold on to his parents' estate had consumed him, but through it, he had thought of Crista.

She had left so suddenly, before he had the chance to gather up his nerve and do more than flirt with her a little bit.

When she returned to Somerset the year before, he thought maybe, this time, he could make it work. Until she stared at him like a slug crawling out from under a rock.

Why the hell did he even care? It wasn't like she was the only game in town. He could have his pick from dozens of women. One night, one week, one month, one whole fucking year if he wanted to keep one that long.

Instead, he was blackmailing a woman who clearly had no interest in doing a damned thing about the attraction burning between them like wildfire.

And it was there. It sparked and exploded every time they were within seeing distance of each other. He could see her response to it. The widening of her eyes, the accelerated breathing, her hard little nipples pressing beneath her clothing and a wild flush to her creamy cheeks. She wanted him almost as damned bad as he wanted her, but she was denying it, fighting it with everything inside her, and Dawg wanted to know why.

He knew women. They didn't fight something that strong without a damned good reason. Now, he just had to figure out the reason.

Breathing out roughly, he moved upstairs to his own shower and quickly stripped before stepping beneath the spray.

He showered quickly. He didn't want to give her time to run. He wanted to give her time to think, though—to consider her options as they stood.

She wanted him, that much he knew. Wanted him enough that the whole time she was arguing the deal, her nipples were pressing harder beneath her shirt and her gaze was flashing with a subtle spark of lust.

Dawg had made it a point to know women before he had any business knowing them. Too young and too dumb to even understand why, he had been drawn to their softness, their veneer of sweetness. The dark undercurrents of passion, power plays, and feminine wiles.

Women who were the exact opposite of his cold-blooded, crazy mother. Women who gave soft touches and whimpered for the pleasure he gave them. Who reached for him, who whispered his name in ecstasy rather than cursing it in hatred.

He knew how to read them, how to pleasure them.

And he knew that look of veiled hunger they gave to indicate their willingness to be pleasured.

Oh yeah, Crista wanted him, but for some reason she wasn't willing to accept the fact that he was there for the taking.

Dawg grinned at the thought as he quickly toweled dry and dressed. The cotton briefs and sweats did nothing to hide the hard-on raging beneath the soft material. Pulling on a clean T-shirt, he moved back downstairs, his gaze roving around the dimly lit room as he searched for her.

And there she was. His T-shirt draped past her thighs as she sat nervously on the couch, her long hair still a little damp. She had obviously made use of the blow-dryer he kept in the guest bathroom.

Beautiful long, thick, dark chocolate hair that fell to the middle of her back and gave her a waiflike appearance.

Damn, she was small. Barely five feet six inches tall in her bare feet, with delicate bones and a nicely rounded figure. She wasn't stick skinny, and he liked that, though he was well aware of the delicacy of her body in comparison to his.

Her face was still pale, her eyes too dark, but she looked composed. Hell, she looked like she was heading to the gallows rather than his bed.

"You aren't the best salve to my ego, fancy-face," he told her as he moved through the room, watching her with an edge of amusement.

She rose slowly to her feet.

"I wish you wouldn't call me that."

She had never liked being called fancy-face, but that was how he saw her. Her face was a little irregular, her lips pouty and winsome, her nose pert with the slightest little tilt, and high, glorious cheekbones.

She was different in a way that stood out. She wasn't beautiful in the acceptable sense of the word, rather she was eye-catching, mysterious. Unique.

"Why?" He glanced at the clock and almost winced. Damn, it was nearly two in the morning; no wonder she looked like she had been run over by a truck. She was exhausted. And so was he.

Now, if he could just convince his cock how tired he was.

"Because I hate nicknames," she retorted.

Dawg shook his head. "Look, it's damned late. I just had a killer day, and from the looks of it, yours wasn't any better. Let's sleep on this, then we'll see how things look in the morning."

She licked her lips warily. "In separate beds?"

"In your dreams," he grunted back. "Damn it, Crista, stop waffling like a damned little sissy. Either you're going to fuck me or you're not. Let's get this over with now so we can both get some sleep."

"I haven't decided yet." Crista narrowed her eyes on Dawg, considering the irritation in his expression and the flash of lust in his gaze.

She was trying to keep her eyes off the erection clearly displayed beneath his sweatpants. Okay, she had already made her decision. Sort of.

She was furious over it. It wasn't enough that she had tried to stay out of his way, that she had rebuffed every overture he had made. Now he had to take the decision away from her, force her to risk her heart to him again, knowing the outcome.

As the minutes had ticked by, she had only become angrier as she showered. It had taken her years to put him behind her enough to even date another man. And still, when the nights were the darkest, she felt the same ragged pain and loss that she had felt that summer, as clearly as she had felt it then.

He crossed his arms over his chest. "You haven't, huh? What are you waiting for?"

Crista clenched her teeth in anger. "I'll sleep with you."

His brow arched.

"But I won't just spread myself for you, Dawg. I can't just fuck you like that."

"Spread yourself?" he asked softly, his voice dark as his gaze narrowed back at her. "Like what, Crista?"

"Like one of your damned playmates," she bit out.

The more he stared at her like that, the more angry she became. Nerves, exhaustion, and the fallout from terror were crashing through her system. On top of that, she had to deal with blackmail by a man she could have never expected blackmail from.

"You are my playmate now." He grinned back at her, his expression becoming one of intense satisfaction. "And I do like to play, Crista. You should be aware of that by now."

"Aware of it!" The anger snapped through her then. "Dawg, I was aware of it eight damned years ago when you decided you were drunk enough and horny enough to fuck me without your cousins standing by to join in. I'm not the one that forgot that fucking night; you are."

Horror slammed through her. Her hand clapped over her mouth, and the breath stilled in her throat as his expression slowly stilled from amusement, then shock, then outright fury.

She had never seen Dawg mad. Few people had ever seen Dawg really mad. Crista had only heard of it, and she had decided long ago she never wanted to see it.

"You're lying." Cold, brutal certainty filled his voice.

She was already too pissed off to take that one silently. Her hand lowered from her lips as her gaze raked over his body with heated memories and fiery anger.

"You know better," she sneered. "You were falling down

drunk outside of town the night you buried your parents, Dawg. How do you think you got home? I brought you home, and you spent the night screwing me. All night," she cried out. "Before you told me exactly how those Neanderthal bastard cousins of yours were going to fuck me. Where and how, and how long."

She hated the fear and the pain and the fist-sized lump that tore at her chest every time *she* remembered. By God, if he was going to blackmail her into his bed and sneer at her attempts to protect her heart from him, then he could hear the truth.

"Don't worry, Dawg," she spoke in ragged bursts now, just trying to find the breath to sustain her through the rage. "You don't have to worry about the one that got away. Because she never got away from anything but the foursome you seemed determined to force her into."

She stepped back, fear and panic raging through her body with the same force, as eight years of pent-up anger finally flowed free.

Escape. She needed to get away from him. She needed to run, just as she had before, just as far away from him as she could get.

"Touch that fucking door, and I'll have you arrested in an hour flat." His gaze smoldered with anger now.

Oh, this wasn't the Dawg she knew. The Dawg she knew was unaffected, playful, cynical. He didn't become enraged, and he sure as hell wasn't tormented. Which was exactly how he seemed now.

He paced into the kitchen, jerking another beer from the fridge before uncapping it and tilting it to his lips. In two long draws, he emptied it. A second later it shattered as it hit the wall.

Crista flinched violently, staring at the dark paneling across the kitchen, bits of glass clinging to the dampness a small amount of the liquid had left. Dawg rubbed his hands roughly over his face before pushing them through his hair and dislodging the leather thong that held the loose ponytail at the nape of his neck.

"Did I rape you?" His voice was unemotional, but his eyes weren't. They seethed, darkening in spots, lightening in others as he stared at her from across the room.

"You didn't rape me," she gritted out, there were times when she wished she didn't have such an aversion to lying.

"What happened?" His lips were a thin, furious line, his expression rigid.

Crista shook her head wearily. "Dawg—"

"What. Happened," he bit out again, his voice harsher, icier.

"You were drunk. I brought you home. We had sex. End of story."

"How?"

"What?" She watched him warily now, her stomach knotting in tension at the tone of his voice. It was hoarse, brutal.

"How did we have sex?" he repeated, his chest moving harshly, nostrils flaring as his expression seemed to grow colder.

"The usual way?" She retreated an additional foot.

His gaze sharpened at her movement as his lips twisted in contempt. "I didn't rape you then; I won't do it now," he rasped. "Now answer me. How?"

"I answered you." Her fingers tugged nervously at the bottom of her shirt as the air filled with dangerous tension.

"You were a virgin." It didn't sound like a question.

Crista nodded slowly.

"I took you." He swallowed tightly at that point. "I took you hard."

Did he remember? He didn't appear to, yet he was right. He had taken her hard, and she had loved it.

Crista nodded again. She began to shake.

"I fucked your ass!" His lips curled back in an enraged snarl as his hands curled into fists and the muscles beneath his T-shirt rippled and bunched tensely.

She didn't shake her head, she didn't answer him. She stared at the phenomenon that she was certain no one else had ever seen.

Dawg enraged. She had only rarely heard of him appearing truly angry, let alone enraged. Even drunk, he had been playful, mocking, a little silly, but never angry.

"Answer me!" he shouted, causing her to jerk violently.

"Why should I answer you?" she snapped back. "It's obvious you've remembered it. Why pursue a piece of ass you've already had? And why the hell would you be stupid enough to blackmail me into giving you more? You didn't think much of it the first time, or you wouldn't have wanted to give it away."

She watched him cautiously, rather like watching a rabid bulldog straining at a chain.

Dawg saw the wariness in her dark eyes. He dreamed of those

eyes. Dreamed of being mesmerized by the chocolatey color, drowning in them, burning in them.

And her face, a flush of arousal burning across her cheekbones, her lips swollen from his kiss, and her voice whispering across his mind. Begging for more.

It hadn't been a dream. The words crashed in his skull. The dreams that tortured him for eight long years had been insidious memories that had managed to survive the drink-induced haze his mind had been in. He had had her, and the memory of it, so dim and shadowed, had haunted him ever since.

Four

Dawg shut back the rage and the fear that he had somehow hurt her and she wasn't admitting it. No doubt, this changed things. Son of a bitch, he couldn't blame her for staying as far away from him as possible all these years. But that didn't mean he was willing to let her go.

He would have been inclined to doubt that he could forget a night with her, but there were too many dreams, too many indications that she was right.

He had taken her virginity. He had taken her without consideration of her innocence, her youth. He had taken an eighteen-year-old virgin to his bed and done things that even mature women would blink at being asked to do.

He cleaned up the glass from the broken bottle carefully, aware of her watching him now with quiet concern. Fuck that; he didn't need her concern. He wanted her. He wanted her hot and wild, all that hunger and passion he had glimpsed in her burning for him.

She would have loved him, he thought, to have followed him into his bed all those years ago. It made him cringe, wondering what he had done to her, how he must have hurt her to make her run before he even awakened.

And he deserved it even less now than he had eight years ago.

"This deal. It involves us only," he told her as he threw the glass in the garbage and kept his back to her. "No one else."

When she didn't speak, he turned and stared back at her.

What the hell had been wrong with him the night he had taken her? He had known that Crista wasn't the sharing kind. She was a one-man woman, just like Kelly.

"Why can't you just let me go? You owe me that, Dawg."

Yeah, he owed her. If his dreams were anything close to what had actually happened, then he owed her a hell of a lot more than he could ever repay.

"You owe me as well," he told her coolly. "All I have are fragmented dreams that drive me fucking crazy. Whatever we started eight years ago, we'll finish this summer. One way or the other."

Nothing on earth could convince him to let her out of his sight now. Possessiveness, desire, and emotions he hadn't felt in so many years he barely remembered them rose to the surface of his consciousness. Emotions he felt in those dreams. Something softer, more tender, and yet a thousand times hotter than lust alone. He wouldn't call it love; he had assured himself years ago that love didn't exist. Besides, this went deeper than anything he had heard love described as.

"Just like that." Bitterness curled at her lips. "As though the fact that I don't want to finish anything doesn't matter."

"It wouldn't be blackmail if it did." He shrugged, fighting back the guilt he could feel building in his gut. "If you wanted to pay the price, then it wouldn't be such a dirty word, would it?"

She stared at him with big dark eyes filled with hurt and made him wish he were someone other than who he was.

"Tell me something," he asked her then. "That night we had, did you at least enjoy it?"

Her gaze flickered away as sharp heat filled her face.

"That's not the point."

"If my dreams are anything to go by, you were just as hot for it as I was. Tell me I'm wrong, Crista. Tell me you hated it."

He moved toward her then, watching as her head snapped back and her eyes tracked his progress across the room.

She didn't retreat; she couldn't be frightened of him. She stared back at him defiantly, her hands clenched at her sides, her expression mutinous.

She wanted to say she hated it, but she couldn't. She hadn't been able to lie worth a damn when she was younger, and she couldn't do it now.

"It was hot, wasn't it, Crista?" He stopped within inches of her, his hand cupping her arm, smoothing down it to her wrist before he lifted her hand to his shoulder and gripped her waist. "So hot we burned down the night. That's what I dream. That you're wet and wild, screwing me with the same crazy lust I'm screwing you with."

Her face flamed brighter.

"And you slipped out on me that morning, didn't you? Just ran away, like the scared little girl you were."

Her eyes flashed with anger.

"I'm not a plaything for the Nauti Boys. Not then and not now."

"And you were too scared to stick around and fight for the singular position, too, weren't you, Crista. What happened, baby? Did it get too hot?"

"Fight for Dawg?" She widened her eyes as though mocking him. She tried to mock him, but he saw the pleasure she was fighting to hide as he drew her closer, nudging his cock against her lower belly and feeling the muscles clench. "Why fight over something every other woman in the county had already had?"

Dawg smiled. "You were scared."

"I was disinterested." She couldn't lie. He heard the tremor in her voice, saw her grimace as she acknowledged it.

He shook his head at her as he allowed the fingers of his free hand to twine into those long, silky strands of hair. Soft, fragrant hair. In his dreams it had twined around him, snaring him, binding him to her. And it had never let him go.

"Are you more interested now?" The hand at her waist bunched the material of the shirt in it.

He was going to have her. He was going to touch her, taste her, feel her come apart in his arms.

"Dawg please . . ." Her voice trembled then.

Dark eyes stared back at him almost pleadingly as the shirt cleared her thighs and rose higher.

"Please what, Crista Ann?" He lowered his head until he could inhale the scent of her. Sweet vanilla and wild roses. She always smelled of vanilla and wild roses to him.

That elusive little scent wasn't enough though. He had to taste her. His lips touched the silken flesh of her neck, his tongue tasting her flesh, and he swore he saw stars as the taste of her exploded against his tongue.

His arm came around her back, lifting her to him as primal hunger replaced the careful seduction he had intended.

He pulled her head back, covered her lips with his own, and found the fiery heat he had been searching for, for eight damn years.

And son of a bitch if it wasn't worth waiting for. She exploded in his arms. A shudder rushed through her, then her hands were twining in his hair, pulling at the thick strands, and pulling his lips harder against hers.

God, she made him feel. Made him feel things he couldn't remember ever feeling, except in his dreams. Dreams of her. Dreams of heat and primal pleasure and sensations he couldn't have imagined really existed.

But they existed here with her in his arms, her body straining toward him, her whimper of pleasure and distress filling his ears as his tongue parted her lips and delved inside.

Fiery sweetness. Spicy ice. She was every contradiction in the world, and his blood raced at the defiance, the challenge, and the sheer response he felt radiating from her.

Crista tried to tell herself she could fight the attraction, the pleasure. Before he touched her, she tried to convince herself she could hold herself aloof from him.

Until his eyes had dilated with pleasure and he had pulled her to him. Until his lips touched her neck; then that hungry moan had left his lips a second before his kiss rocked her mind.

This was a very bad thing. Starbursts of pleasure were exploding inside her bloodstream as she fought herself, fought her response to him, and failed.

Oh how she failed. She was trying to climb into his body instead, to burn in the center of a sensation so hot, so dark and heated she was lost beneath it.

"Off!" His lips lifted from hers only long enough to whisk the shirt from her arms and over her head before she could react. Before she could stop him. Then he was bending to her, his lips moving unerringly for the tight, too-sensitive nipples lifting to his lips as though they had craved this caress for eight years.

And they had.

"Oh God. Dawg." She arched in his arms as he sucked her nipple into his mouth.

And it was as good, no, it was better than before. His lips

drew on the tender tip, his thigh pressed between her legs, and within seconds she was pressing the aching flesh between her thighs into the heavy muscle of his leg and riding it almost frantically as he sucked at her.

"Yes." The word hissed from between her lips. "Oh yes. Do that. Just like that."

Just as he had that night years before. His teeth raking over her nipple before he sucked it back, hard and hot, his tongue lashing over it like a fiery whip.

She was falling. Dizzy. Off balance. And before she knew it, stretched out on the couch with Dawg's lips still ravishing her tender nipples, first one, then the other, growling with hunger and heat as his hand cupped between her thighs.

Finesse was forgotten, but it wasn't finesse she wanted. Dawg was rumored to be smooth, practiced, deliberate in every touch. But there was nothing deliberate or practiced in his touch now.

Experienced, yes. Confident and too damned experienced.

His fingers parted the curl-covered folds between her thighs, and a second later, one broad, male finger was piercing her core.

Crista froze. Heat exploded in her vagina, tore through her bloodstream and into her womb as she felt the tender muscles clenching desperately around his caressing finger.

"So hot." He was panting as his lips lifted from a reddened nipple, and his eyes, darker now but still mesmerizing, almost hypnotizing, stared into hers. "So tight and hot, Crista."

Her hips jerked as his finger pulled back, then stroked inside her again. One long thrust that had her gasping and arching in his arms, her thighs falling farther apart, her hips lifting for a deeper, wilder penetration.

"You'll destroy me," she cried out, her fingers digging into his scalp as his tongue licked over her nipple. "Again. You'll destroy me again, Dawg."

He had to understand. He couldn't do this to her again. She could easily give herself to him, just like before.

"It's okay, Crista. I won't hurt you, baby," he groaned. "It's just us. See? No one else is here. Ever. God, I'd kill the man that tried to touch you now."

She cried out as another finger joined the first, thrust inside her, parted flesh that had never known another man's touch, never clenched, never became slick and hot and achy as it did for Dawg.

"Mine." His snarl shocked her.

His lips covering hers again fed the hungers rising sharp and deep inside her.

Her hips lifted, arched as she bucked against him, writhing beneath his larger body as his fingers fucked into her, sent a firestorm of sensation raging through her.

She had sworn she would never let this happen again. But here she was, naked, hot, wet, and begging for more.

Her lips were wild beneath his, taking kiss for kiss and returning it with another. Her fingers held him to her. Her thighs tightened on the cloth-covered leg between her knees, and she fought to hold his fingers inside her.

She was falling. Just like she had before. Losing her common sense, her heart, and her soul to this man.

Dumb. Caution was screaming through her brain.

"Now this is a pretty sight. Damn, Dawg, you started without me. I'm hurt."

Like a slap of cold water, Natches's voice tore through her head as Dawg's head lifted, and Crista swore she heard him curse.

Anger. Pain. Fear. It lashed through her as she stared up at Natches, fighting back the wave of sickness as his gaze flickered over her with amused lust. He was leaning against the bar, thankfully dressed, grinning, and the epitome of every reason why she should have fought harder, should have remembered why she couldn't let Dawg have another part of her soul.

"Let me go!" She slapped at his shoulders. "Get off me."

"Damn it, Crista. You're naked," he snarled the reminder.

"Get off me!" She kicked at him, jerking out of his arms and rolling from beneath him.

"Look your fill, asshole," she told Natches as she grabbed Dawg's shirt from the floor. "Because it will be the last damn look you ever get the chance to take."

Clasping the material over her breasts and making certain it covered her thighs, she tore from the room, rushed past him, and ran for the stairs.

Fine, she was flashing her ass. Let them both look. One last damned time.

"Natches, you're a bastard," she heard Dawg curse.

Natches was laughing, and Crista felt like crying.

Because for a few precious moments, she had believed.

She was a fool for it, she admitted to herself. A fool for Dawg. And seconds later, staring around the opulent bedroom, the monstrously large bed, and the drape-shrouded windows that surrounded it, she realized what she had done.

She had run straight to his bedroom rather than the spare room. Straight into Dawg's private lair.

Dawg stared at Crista's perky little butt as it disappeared up the stairs and sighed heavily.

"What the hell do you want, Natches?" he asked his cousin wearily, turning to him and watching as Natches grinned back.

The other man hadn't watched the charming display of flesh; it was the only reason he still had all his teeth in his head.

Natches shook his head. "You and Rowdy. Man, you two are so possessive it's enough to make a man's stomach turn. And here I thought I could depend on you to hold out."

Dawg grunted at the comment. "You didn't answer my question."

"I brought her Rodeo back. I thought I'd drop in and see how you two were doing before heading to bed." His grin was pure evil. "And I thought I'd give you this. It was in the passenger seat."

Dawg took the slip of paper. Express Movers. The letterhead and address were legit. The scrawled handwriting assured Miss Jansen she could now pick up her items in Store It Yourself, and enclosed in the envelope she would find the key to the indoor warehouse locker.

"I hacked the company computers before coming over here. They don't have a record for the delivery. Someone set her up."

Dawg tucked the note carefully into the pocket of his sweats until he could lock it in the upstairs safe later.

"Looks like you were making progress, anyway," Natches smirked.

"We were doing fine until you opened your mouth. But I think you were aware of that."

Natches glanced toward the stairs then. For a second, regret sliced across his features, then his ever-present mocking smile was back on his face.

"One-man woman, huh?" he asked, though from his look, it was more a statement.

Dawg stared back at him, seeing the flash of loneliness, of knowledge that filled his cousin's dark, forest green eyes.

"She's not as agreeable to being my woman as I would wish, though." Dawg raked his fingers heavily through his hair as he glanced at the stairs again. "I blackmailed her."

He glanced back at Natches in time to see his cousin shaking his head.

"I knew you were going to do something dumb like that." He chuckled, though the sound carried little amusement. "Good luck on that one. I just stopped by to drop these off." He dropped Crista's keys on the counter. "And to tell you Cranston wants our final reports in his office by the end of the day. Oral and written. He's still a little upset over losing the woman. But he seems certain the men he captured will talk."

"They probably will." *But who would they identify?*

If Crista had been led there, then it was for a reason. The thieves would spill their guts in a heartbeat, either way.

"I don't know." Natches shrugged. "I followed them to the van when they were loading them up. All Cranston got from them were vague looks when he was questioning them. They might not know."

Dawg stared at him in complete disbelief.

"Hey, we can hope," Natches snickered, holding his hands up in surrender before straightening from the bar and heading for the door. "I came in the back, I'll leave through the front. Give the gossips something to crow about. While you're having fun, I'll see what I can find out, see who's too interested in the setup you have going on here. I don't like this a damned bit, Dawg, I'll tell you. She shouldn't have been there tonight. It's a setup."

Dawg couldn't agree with him more. "Let me know what you find out."

As Natches left, Dawg relocked the doors behind him and reset the alarms. But he didn't immediately follow Crista to the bedroom on the upper deck. He stared around the lower level instead, seeing more than the crisp, clean lines of the interior and the nice furnishings.

He'd been living on the *Nauti Dawg* for years. Only through the coldest months did he leave the marina and stay in the small apartment he had above the lumber store. He rarely stayed at the underground home his father had built before his death.

He sat down slowly on the couch, leaned back, and breathed out wearily. God, he was exhausted. Tired and horny and conflicted. It was a hell of a state to be in at three o'clock in the morning.

His silent laughter was bitter and mocking. Hell, he was turning into the bastard his father had always predicted he was. Maybe he was more like his grandfather, Nate August, than he wanted to admit. The son of a bitch had left three bastard sons and a daughter in Somerset before returning to his Texas home more than fifty years before. Of the four children, Dawg's father and his uncles and aunt, only Ray Mackay, Rowdy's father, had shown any sort of decency to his wife or his children. His aunt didn't count. She worshipped the ground her son, Johnny, walked on, but many suspected she had driven her husband, Ralph, to his grave.

Dawg rubbed at the ache in his knee, feeling every steel pin that held the joint and kneecap together. The weather was getting ready to turn damp; he could predict it within days now. And he'd been on his leg too damned long. He was riding close to twenty-four hours without sleep, and Cranston wanted him in to give his final report.

And upstairs, Crista was waiting in his bedroom. Pissed off and probably feeling just as betrayed as she had every right to feel.

He should just let her go. He owed her that much. But he couldn't do it. Everything inside him howled in protest at the thought of letting her go. He had a hold on her now, a way to keep her in his bed if nothing else. A chance to figure out why she had haunted him for eight fucking years.

She wasn't the only woman he had fucked in his life that he couldn't remember. For a few years there, there had been more than a few. But she was the only woman who had ever lingered in his head to the point that the thought of her nearly drove him insane.

Seducing her wasn't going to be easy. He didn't just want her body; he wanted more, and he was man enough to admit to it. Just fucking her would never be enough. He needed to capture the elusive sense of something more that was so much a part of her.

He rubbed his jaw as he considered that one. Hell, he had

never courted a woman a day in his life, especially not one he knew he could fuck. He could walk upstairs to that bedroom and within a few hot kisses, have her ready and willing. For the moment.

But she would resent it. She would eventually hate him for it, and that wasn't what he wanted. He wanted her sweet smiles, her soft touches. He wanted her to be his lover, not just a bedmate.

He'd never really had a lover.

Dawg frowned at that. He was thirty-two years old, yet he had never had a steady lover, a woman he wanted in his bed for more than a night or two. And he couldn't figure out why.

Oh, he had considered it once. Eight fucking years ago. When he had been trying to get Crista into his bed, he had known then that he wanted more than a few nights with her. A few weeks, a few months, maybe.

Something tightened in his chest at the thought, something akin to regret, a knowledge that even a few months might not be enough.

One step at a time, he thought tiredly. Tonight, he'd just sleep with her. Just hold her. See how that went. That was something else he had never done, just held a woman through the night and felt the warmth of her against him.

Rowdy swore that some nights, it was better than sex, just having Kelly next to him, soft and sweet.

Would it be like that with Crista?

He glanced back at the stairs, his mind filling with the memory of her sweet scent, the warmth of her delicate body. Maybe, for one fucking night in his life, he could sleep without dreaming, if he were holding her.

He pushed himself to his feet and moved through the houseboat. He checked the windows, the back deck door, and the security alarms before moving up the stairs. When he stepped into the bedroom, he stopped in surprise.

He expected her to be awake and ready to shoot him. She had been madder than hell when she flew up that metal staircase. Instead, she was curled beneath the blankets of his king-sized bed, the covers pulled up to her nose, sleeping like a baby.

And she wasn't just on the edge of the bed. She was in the middle, where he slept. A slow smile curled his lips as he stripped silently, leaving the small, dim light, which sat on the corner table on the far end of the room, turned on. He moved around the bed, slid beneath the blankets, and carefully, very cautiously, he eased in beside her.

She muttered something not so nice. A drowsy little comment about cold feet, but she settled back to sleep as his arm came over her and he drew her against him.

She didn't awaken.

His frown deepened. A woman who slept alone was always aware when a man slid into bed beside her.

Crista was used to sleeping with someone.

Had that someone held her through the night and kept dreams of Dawg at bay? The bastard. He gritted his teeth at the thought of any other man holding her like this.

She belonged here, curled against his chest, snuggled into his body, keeping him warm.

It was . . . interesting.

He was still harder than hell. Hornier than he could remember being in years, but there was no need to hurry. No race to satisfaction so he could be alone.

His eyes closed as she muttered something again. Something about Alex and the electric bill, and he grinned. Female fluff stuff that Rowdy always teased Kelly about.

Hell, this was nice.

His eyes drifted closed, his arousal pounded between his thighs, but the edge was tempered with exhaustion and a slow easing of the tight sense of cold anger that had gripped him for years.

He buried his face in Crista's hair, breathed out slowly, and let the darkness have him, for a few hours at least.

Five

Some days, it just didn't pay to wake up. Waking up in Dawg's bed had been bad enough, but thankfully he had been gone. She'd been able to steal a shirt and someone's smaller-sized sweatpants, call a cab, rush back to her brother's house to shower and change, and arrive to work on time.

Only to be fired.

Fired from a crappy waitress job in a diner that obviously didn't have enough help to begin with. And it had been more than clear that the owner was reluctant to fire her, which led Crista to only one conclusion. Dawg had influenced the owner.

He had her fired.

He wasn't even decent enough to stop at just blackmailing her when she knew he had to know she was innocent. But now she was out of a job so he could have his little plaything close by.

She stood by the register as the manager wrote out her final paycheck and sighed wearily.

"Thanks, Madge," she said quietly when the other woman, concerned and clearly upset with the orders to fire her, handed over the check.

"I'm sure sorry 'bout this, Crista." Madge sighed, her hazel eyes compassionate. "Owner just called and said do it. Nothing I could do."

Crista shrugged. The owner was friends with Dawg, she knew that, she knew how it happened.

Turning from the register, she tucked the check in her purse and made her way across the floor. There were few customers at this time of the morning. Some coffee drinkers, an early rising tourist, and Johnny Grace, her next-door neighbor and Dawg's cousin. Though Dawg admitted to the relationship only when he was forced.

He sat at the back table, a heavy frown on his brow as she moved toward him.

"Crista." He stopped her before she could make it to the door. "Is everything okay?"

"Fine." She gave him a stiff smile. "Cutbacks, I guess."

She liked Johnny. He ran a bakery from his house beside hers and often brought her over fresh bread and sweets on baking days, free of charge, just because, he said, they were neighbors.

His gaze flicked to the manager, the frown still darkening his amazingly clear, soft brow. Dark blond curls framed his face, giving him an almost feminine appearance.

"Is there anything I can do?"

Anything he could do? She had a feeling there wasn't a damned thing anyone could do. She shook her head, forcing a stiff smile to her face.

"I'll be fine, Johnny. I have to go now, though. I'll catch you later."

Johnny was a good neighbor, but not a confidant. Right now, she couldn't handle discussing this with anyone.

Her hand tightened on her purse as she stepped from the diner, her gaze swinging unerringly to the big black pickup across the street.

How the hell had she known he would be there? What instinct possessed her that she could feel him watching her, wanting her?

He was a dark shadow behind the tinted windows, until the passenger side window rolled smoothly down, revealing his unsmiling countenance and the dark glasses shielding his eyes.

His overlong black hair was tied back at the nape of his neck, revealing the strong line of his jaw and the arrogance that permeated his expression.

His hand lifted from where his long arm was stretched along the backseat, and his fingers beckoned her to him with regal confidence that she would come. Like a damned pet.

Her eyes narrowed on him as she turned and stalked down the sidewalk to the side of the diner where her Rodeo was parked.

She had packed a suitcase that morning before heading to the job she didn't have anymore. She had actually given Dawg the benefit of the doubt that he would at least trust her to work while he was playing the high-and-mighty blackmailer from hell.

But could he do that? Hell no. He had to have it all.

She jerked her keys from her purse as she heard the powerful motor moving behind her. She threw a glare over her shoulder before striding furiously across the parking lot.

She had bills to pay, a college loan to honor, not that she was using the damned degree at present, but there was always the potential of getting a decent job. Now she was going to go job hunting again and pray there was someone willing to laugh in his face when he ordered her fired.

God, he hadn't changed. In eight years, most people managed to mature a little bit, but Dawg was still Dawg. Just a little darker, a little more dangerous, but still determined to have everything his own way.

"I don't think so." His big hand shackled her wrist as she moved to shove the key into the lock of the Rodeo.

Crista stood still, freezing as anger threatened to overwhelm her.

"I can't believe you." She tried to jerk her arm back, then stared at his fingers as he refused to release her.

They were shackled on her wrist like irons, snug enough to hold her in place, to remind her that he was bigger, stronger, harder than she was.

"What can't you believe about me?" he asked, drawing her along with him to the truck where it sat, driver's side door still standing open, a few feet behind him.

"Let me go, Dawg! I have to go job hunting," she sneered with false sweetness. "Someone cost me this job."

Mocking disbelief filled his face. "No! Someone got you fired? Shame on them."

Wicked amusement filled his eyes, almost playful, inviting her to share in the fun when he had just taken her only means of support.

When she jerked her wrist back this time, he let her go.

"Tell me, Dawg, how do you expect me to support myself? To pay my bills? To keep my car? I don't have a job now because of you."

"You have a job." The playful amusement left his expression.

"I have a job?" she jeered bitterly. "Let me guess, you're going to pay me to play your whore?"

His expression stilled then. "Get in the truck."

She should have been nervous. She had seen that expression on her brother's face before, and it was one that was best avoided. One she would have avoided if she weren't so damned mad.

She knew what he expected, and it enraged her.

"Not on your egotistical little life!" Her hand slapped against his chest as she felt anger engulf her. "I have a job to—"

The breath rushed from her chest as he jerked her to him, her breasts flush against his broad chest, the fingers of one broad hand tangled in her hair as he pulled her head back, his gaze imprisoning hers as she stared back at him in shock.

"We made a deal." His voice rasped with something akin to anger, and yet it went deeper than anger.

Crista trembled as she stared into the light green eyes and the determination that glowed inside them.

"That deal didn't include stealing my job and my life. You had no right to do this."

"My bed, or jail. My terms. And my terms say that while you're sharing my bed, then by God you'll share when I want you there, not when you have time for me."

Shock filled her, and not for the first time. This wasn't the Dawg she had known eight years before, but he was the man who had taken her that night so long ago.

The veneer of teasing charm had been stripped away, and in its place was a man she wasn't certain she could handle.

"You won't arrest me." Her voice trembled. "You know I wasn't doing anything wrong."

"We have a deal," he repeated. "Now get your ass in that truck. We'll discuss the terms of it back at the houseboat, but we will not discuss them here, in the middle of a goddamned parking lot."

He didn't give her time to argue. He picked her up by her waist, turned, and pushed her into the vehicle.

"My clothes . . ." She tried to scramble back out, only to come face-to-face with eyes that began to become turbulent in their color. Light greens, sparks of darker color, a swirl of chaotic shades that had her suddenly stilling.

His jaw bunched with tension, the muscle in his cheek twitching twice before he managed to control it.

The keys were plucked from her fingers.

"Don't move. So help me God, you come out of that truck, Crista, and you'll regret it. Because I'll turn you over my knee and paddle your ass here and now. Do you understand me?"

She stared back at him warily.

He stomped, literally stomped the short distance to her Rodeo, unlocked it, and dragged her suitcase from the front seat.

"My flowers." Her voice gained strength. If all she was risking was a spanking, then he could damned well get everything she had packed. "And the box in the back."

The suitcase thumped on the ground as he turned and stared back at her broodingly.

"Surely I can at least have the few things I need." She smiled back at him tightly. "Even condemned prisoners get a few personal articles, Dawg."

His eyes narrowed before he locked the driver's side door and slammed it closed. He paced to the back of the vehicle, unlocked the hatchback, and jerked it open. The box of extra clothes, makeup, and personal items was set out, then the miniature rosebush and flowering cactus that sat in the corner.

Slamming the hatchback closed again, he locked it and packed her items in the backseat of his truck.

"Move over." His voice was harsh as he stepped to the opened door once again.

"I need my car."

"I said move over."

"You can't just leave my car sitting here, Dawg, I need it." She forced herself not to scream in complete frustration. "This is going too damned far . . ."

He gripped her waist, and before Crista could fight him he had lifted her over the console and dropped her into the passenger side seat before climbing in.

Damn him. She gripped the door latch with every intention of throwing herself from the truck and reclaiming her precious Rodeo.

"Open that door, and so help me, you'll regret it."

She stilled at the sound of his voice, turning to glare at him furiously as he put the truck in gear and turned the monster vehicle around.

"I need my car."

"Natches can collect it later." One hand tightened on the steering wheel, the other on the gearshift that rose from the floor as he drove from the parking lot and turned back onto Main Street before heading for the interstate.

"That's not fair. None of this is fair, Dawg," she yelled. "You stole my job. That's the same as stealing everything I own."

And that wasn't much, admittedly. Mainly the Rodeo, but it was the thought that counted.

"I'll take care of your bills," he bit out.

"Why not just stamp whore on my head," she sneered.

The truck was jerked to the side of the road, rocking to a hard stop as he turned to her, the effort to control whatever rose inside him visibly apparent on his face.

"Call yourself a whore again, and I'll make sure that spanking you have yet to receive is nothing pleasant," he snarled between clenched teeth.

"What do you call it then?"

"I call it a deal you made and agreed to." He spoke with hard deliberation as his eyes speared into hers. "And I make the rules. You don't. Now sit back, fasten your seat belt, and stop arguing the point with me before I do something guaranteed to show everyone who passes by this truck just how little I care about propriety or their fucking opinions of either of us."

Which amounted to nothing, and Crista knew it. Gritting her teeth against the furious words rising to her lips, she slammed the seat belt latch in, crossed her arms over her breasts, and stared straight ahead.

She admitted to being slightly nervous. Not exactly frightened of Dawg, but warier than she would have been even two days before. There was a glow of lust, of hunger in his gaze that had the feminine core of her shaking in trepidation. And it had her mind spinning.

Dawg had always been so fiercely controlled. He never showed anger, at least that was the rumor. He was a get-even rather than a get-mad kind of man.

It wasn't anger she saw in him now but the dark, primal core of a man who was no longer hiding who or what he was. And the savage hunger that glowed in his eyes aroused her more than the false charm ever had.

This was the Dawg she had always sensed lurking beneath the surface. The one who had held her back when she was younger, who frightened the immature sexuality she had possessed then.

It was that inner man he had let loose on her the night she had spent with him. The drunken charm had evaporated once he had her in his bed, and though he hadn't been rough, he had been determined, hungry.

"What happened that night?"

His voice had her stilling, her heart beating faster in her chest. She didn't want to talk about that night. She didn't want to relive it any more than she already had.

"We had sex. Period."

"We had sex, so you ran out of town with another man, stayed away seven years, and now you're fighting something between us that threatens to burn down the county once we get back into bed. Sorry, fancy-face, that one doesn't go over so well with me. You're lying."

She remembered, this was how he got his name. She'd heard Ray relate the tale, how even as a child he would get something in his mind and wouldn't let it go. Like a dog with a bone. Dawg. He hadn't changed much.

"What happened eight years ago doesn't matter, Dawg." She shook her head tiredly. "What's happening now does. I can't afford not to work for three months, and I won't accept money to sleep with you. I have to have a job."

"We're not talking about that right now." His voice rumbled with displeasure.

"And we're not talking about what happened eight years ago, either," she retorted. "Actually, that night is really pretty fuzzy in my head. I've all but forgotten it."

And that had to be the biggest lie she had ever told in her life.

Crista glanced over at him, satisfied and yet more nervous than ever once she saw the dark, brooding intensity of his expression.

"It just pisses me off when you lie to me, Crista Ann," he growled, glancing at her over the top edge of his dark glasses as he came to a stoplight.

The vehicle rolled to a stop as Crista stared out at the town that stretched on each side of the highway running through it. It had grown in the years she had been away from it, but it was still filled with the same qualities she had missed.

There were no high-rises here, no frantic rush of people walking down the sidewalks, fighting to get from office to office and ignoring everyone around them. She could walk into any store and see someone she knew or had known from her childhood.

She had friends here, distant relatives, and history.

She was aware of him glancing back at her as he put the truck into gear and accelerated through the green light, gathering speed and heading to the marina outside town.

"How long have you been working undercover against the drug dealers around here?" she asked him then. "I know Alex said the problem had grown, but I didn't know it was bad enough to warrant late-night raids."

"They're rare." His voice was clipped, the message clear. He didn't want to talk about it.

"It must be getting pretty bad. The guy who caught me in the warehouse looked like one of the monsters television portrays. If the Latin factions have moved into Somerset, won't it be hard to weed them out?"

His fingers tapped against the steering wheel as he glanced at her.

"Doubtful." He was determined not to discuss it with her, that was more than obvious.

"Do you know who the woman was who was supposed to be there?"

At that question, he froze. "Not yet."

Crista bit at her lower lip nervously. "You've questioned the other men though, right?"

"This morning."

"Did you find the money they were missing?"

His head swung around briefly, his gaze hidden behind the dark glasses now.

"Not yet." Clipped, dark, his voice sent a shiver down her spine. "Why?"

"He seemed to think I had it. That was what he said to me: 'Where's my money, *puta*?' Evidently, he's not the only one that considers me a—"

She swore he growled. Crista compressed her lips at the silent snarl that pulled at his lips.

"What else did he say?" he snapped out.

"He didn't have time to say anything else. You splattered his blood all over me less than a second later."

"It beat seeing your fucking blood staining that damned warehouse." Violence filled his voice before Crista watched him forcibly rein it in with a tight grimace. "Did you hear anything else? See anything else?"

She shook her head slowly, feeling the terror that had risen inside her the night before beating at her head again. Dawg had relieved the horror of the event the night before, strangely enough, with his obnoxious blackmail demand. But now it was beginning to set in. The fact that she had nearly died. That if she had just gone to Dawg before, this might not have happened.

She licked her lips nervously. "Look, this is probably totally unrelated, but before this, weird things were happening anyway. So weird that when I told Alex about them, he just about ordered me to call you."

"What things?"

She went through them briefly: missing clothes, the feeling that someone was following her, watching her.

"Do you think it had something to do with last night?" she asked as she finished.

Dawg didn't think; he knew. He could feel it burning in his gut and itching along the back of his neck. Primitive possession roiled through his mind as he glanced at Crista and realized that somehow, for some reason, someone among the crew they had rounded up last night had known to use her.

It was far-fetched; he would do better to suspect her of being involved to begin with, but his unruly dick refused to let him consider it.

But, if someone had been trying to throw her into the mix, then it was because they knew of his obsession for her. And there were very, very few people who knew that Dawg couldn't forget one Crista Ann Jansen.

He wiped his hand down his face and considered his options. They hadn't caught the one female of the group who they knew had been involved. The mediator between the buyers and sellers had been a woman; the vague description the team had of her resembled Crista. And if she was telling the truth about the buyer, Aaron Grael, then the woman had made off with half down on a two million dollar deal.

He blew out a rough breath as he glanced over at her. She was watching him worriedly, her chocolate eyes filled with indecision and a hint of fear. But there was no guilt. Over the years, hell, even before he joined the Marines, he had been able to spot most lies a mile away. He couldn't see anything in Crista's gaze but her worry and her discomfort.

"You haven't answered me." There was a snap to her voice that assured him that she wasn't frightened enough to have forgotten her earlier anger with him.

"Let me check into a few things and talk to Natches about this," he finally said, his voice rough. There was too damned much money missing to discount any of it. "But my best guess is that it's all connected. Somehow. I just have to figure out how."

"If you're undercover, as I assume you are, because I haven't heard anything about you working with the DEA, then someone would have to know the truth to know to use me," she said hesitantly.

He had to give her credit for being smart. No one had ever accused Crista of being without her own sense of intuition.

Too bad he wasn't really working with the DEA; his problems might be easier at the moment.

"Natches and I both are undercover," he finally said. "The deal we broke up last night had been in the works for over six months. We pulled in everyone except the buyer I killed and one more player. We're looking for the other person now."

She didn't say anything for long moments.

"The other player is a woman," she finally guessed, her voice trembling. "And she resembles me, doesn't she?"

Dawg made the turn into the Mackay Marina in silence before he glanced over at her again.

"The description we have of her resembles you," he admitted softly, seeing her flinch from the corner of his eye. "She's the only one missing; she has the money. There's no reason for any focus to linger on you."

"Unless one of the men you captured saw me? Or recognized me from town? Or someone associated with them sees me now?"

"Let's not borrow trouble, Crista." But they were thoughts

brewing in his own mind. "You concentrate on the here and now; I'll concentrate on the rest of it."

"Just concentrate on your little blackmail scheme?" she retorted acidly.

"Make happy with my dick, and I'll be a happy little camper." He said the words for shock effect. He hated seeing the fear in her eyes, in her expression. And that took care of it nicely.

"Has anyone ever told you what a bastard you are, Dawg?" Hostility radiated from her now.

Dawg let his lips curl into a mocking grin. Oh yeah, he knew what a bastard he was. His father had made certain he had known at a very early age.

"You're telling me now." He pulled into his parking slot close to the docks, his gaze moving carefully around the area as he shut the pickup off before turning to face her. "You ready to make nice and go to the boat yet? Or do we need to sit here and have a screaming match instead?"

"I don't have screaming matches." Her expression lit with offended anger.

"You'd be the first woman then," he grunted, moving from the vehicle. "Let's go. I need a cold beer."

Summer had just started, but it was already warming up with a ferocity that sent waves of heat curling up from the asphalt.

He pulled her suitcase from the backseat as well as the box and tucked it under his arm as she rounded the front of the truck.

"I'll get the flowers." Her expression was anxious, as though she couldn't trust him to take care of two damned pots of flowers.

But hell, why should she? She couldn't even trust him to help her when Alex advised her to.

Son of a bitch. Missing items from her home, a feeling of being watched and followed. She had all the signs of a stalker at the very least, and she hadn't contacted anyone. If she had contacted the sheriff, Zeke Mayes, he would have let Dawg know.

Dawg let her gather the two oversized pots in her arms. The red miniature rosebush with its pot was nearly as tall as she was. The flowering cactus was smaller but no less bulky.

"I can have Natches come back for those," he told her doubtfully.

The glare she gave him had his lips tightening in annoyance.

"Fine." He slammed the doors closed as he turned back to her. "Let me carry one of them before you topple over."

"I have them." She peeked between the branches of the rosebush. "Just lead the way."

"If you fall in the lake because you can't see over those damned pots, then I'm going to let you drown," he warned her.

He knew better. He was so damned stupid where she was concerned, he'd save her and the fucking plants.

"I know what I'm doing." Dark brown eyes narrowed on him. "Just go on. I'll be right behind you."

"After you." He smiled tightly. "And watch where you're going, if you can. Don't walk off the side of a dock. Please."

As she moved ahead of him, Dawg stayed close to her, just in case. She was so damned stubborn she would probably kill herself rather than see a single rose damaged.

He frowned at the small roses topping their green branches. He had given her a rosebush once. He wondered what had happened to it. On her seventeenth birthday, an attempt to sweeten her toward him. He had arrived at her home, endured Alex's glare, and given her the plastic-wrapped little bush for the tiny rose garden she had behind the house. He had noticed that. How much she liked roses.

She'd probably tossed it out just like she had tossed out the memory of them together.

Memories that were still foggy to him. At twenty-four, he had drunk too much, partied too damned hard, and had no sense where women were concerned. But he had been smart enough to think Crista was different. Special.

Hell, she was special, and so different from any other woman he had ever known that it was like night and day. The leading difference being the fact that Crista had never been bowled over by the famous Mackay charm.

At least, not until he was too drunk to remember what had convinced her to sleep with him in the first place.

Now, he had to deal with a hard-on that made common sense iffy at best and the knowledge that someone had been drawing Crista into this game between the agents looking for missiles and those involved in the buying and selling of those missiles.

Damn. He knew the only missing component to this case was the woman who had escaped with a million dollars in unmarked bills. He prayed she was running far and fast and was the only person aware of Crista. Not that he could get that damned lucky, but he could hope.

Unlocking the glass door that led into the houseboat, Dawg checked the security monitor as he entered the living room before setting the suitcase and box on the couch and watching as Crista stood hesitantly in the room, looking around.

"Can I put the flowers upstairs?" she asked. "There's more sunlight there."

"Set them down. I'll take them up later." He strode across the room to the refrigerator and the cold beer inside.

Twisting the cap off the bottle, he took a healthy drink as he stared at Crista through the dark glasses he wore. Better to hide his eyes, to hide the emotions he knew he wasn't holding back very well. Even Natches had watched him in concern during the meeting with the joint ATF and Homeland Security task force that had been working the investigation.

Something about Crista made him dangerously hungry. Knowing he had had her and being unable to remember anything but the dimmest events made him crazy.

"You have a choice." He set the beer on the counter with enough force to cause her to jump.

"Do I?" She was watching him nervously.

At least it wasn't in fear.

He pulled the sunglasses from his nose and tossed them to the counter before turning his gaze back to her. Immediate. Her response came as fast as her gaze took in his.

He watched her breasts begin to rise and lower with her quicker breathing, watched the little points of her nipples tighten beneath her shirt and a softening in the defiant stance she had adopted.

His hand went to his belt, loosening it slowly as her eyes began to widen.

"Dawg." She swallowed tightly. "I'm not ready for this yet."

At least she hadn't said no outright.

The belt came loose. Moving toward her, he tore the metal button open, then rasped the zipper down. Her eyes became wider, darker, and sharp little teeth bit at her lip.

"I dreamed." The rough sound of his own voice surprised him. "I dreamed of your mouth taking me. Sucking me into a pleasure so hot I nearly died from it."

Her eyes seemed to glaze; her face flushed heatedly as he pulled her to the couch. Dragging his jeans down his thighs, he sat down, removed his boots, then kicked the material free as she watched in shock.

He was desperate. So fucking hard he was dying from the hunger crawling through his system.

"Say no, and it stops," he bit out. "Just say no."

"And go to jail?"

He clamped his lips shut. He had one advantage over her, and that was it. She very well might not be ready for the rest of it yet, but he had to have this, or he was going to die.

"Your choice."

Six

Her choice.

Crista stared down at him, feeling every cell in her body reacting to the sight of Dawg, leaning back on the couch, his devil's black hair mussed around his face, his light green eyes darkening, and she felt her vagina flood with the response.

She was dampening her panties. Growing so sensitive that even the air from the air conditioner was a caress against flesh still covered by her clothing.

"Dawg—" She could hear the plea in her voice.

"You're so pretty, Crista," he whispered. "I dreamed of it last night. Your sweet mouth moving over my cock, driving me insane. Give me that. Just that. We can wait for the rest of it."

Wait for the rest of it?

Was this his idea of seduction? If it was, then she was weaker than she could have ever imagined, because it was working.

"Come here, baby." He gripped her wrist, drawing her to her knees as he leaned forward.

As she settled before him, his hands gripped the hem of her shirt and drew it upward, drawing it over her head, then her arms, until he tossed it away.

"Sweet God have mercy," he groaned, his eyes like brilliant pinpoints of color in his dark face as he stared at the white lace covering her breasts.

"Dawg, this is too soon." She had to force the words past her lips. "You have to let me—"

One hand cupped around her neck, tilting her head back as the other touched her lips.

"You have the memories of this," he said, his voice rough. "Give me one now. Just one memory, Crista, instead of a dream that tears my guts to ribbons with hunger."

One hand gripped her wrist as he settled against the back of the couch once again and folded her fingers partially around the width of his cock. They wouldn't surround it.

The hard flesh throbbed beneath her hand, silky and ridged with heavy veins, the bloated head darkened as a drop of pre-cum beaded at the tiny slit.

She knew what he tasted like. Like a storm coming in from the mountains. She knew what was going to happen the minute she took him into her mouth. She was going to lose herself in the sensuality he wrapped around her.

He terrified her. The knowledge of what he could do to her had her shaking before him.

"There, Crista." His hand tangled in her hair, cupping the side of her head as he drew her forward. "Just a little bit, fancy-face. Suck me just a little bit."

Just a little bit?

Crista whimpered as the thick crest touched her lips, parted them, slid inside.

She couldn't help herself. Because she did remember that night, and she knew exactly what he had taught her. She knew what he liked then, but would he like it now?

Tentatively, she swirled her tongue over the engorged head, feeling his thighs clench, hearing the ragged groan that rumbled in his chest. His hand tightened in her hair, pulling at the strands and sending a tingling heat through her scalp.

His chest was moving fiercely, rising and falling quickly as her own breathing became labored, and she let her mouth fill with the head of his cock and the few inches beyond that she could manage.

"Sweet God. Crista. Sweetheart. Ah God yes, suck my dick, fancy-face. Hard and deep . . ."

Dawg felt his head fall back against the cushion behind him and fought to breathe. Her mouth was hot, tight, drawing over his cock head, her tongue rasping the ultrasensitive flesh beneath it. His balls drew up painfully tight as her fingers were tucked beneath them, cupping them, massaging the taut sac with such wicked caresses that he had to clench his teeth to hold back the brutal pleasure tearing through him.

He struggled to open his eyes, to stare down at her. God help him, she was gorgeous. Long hair flowed around her flushed face, her lips stretched wide around his dick, her dark eyes almost black.

Delicate fingers gripped the shaft, working it slow and easy as she drew on the pleasure-tortured crest. She sucked it, tongued it. Her cheeks hollowed and her eyes glowed, and he swore he saw the same needs in her eyes that he felt ripping through his guts.

Hunger like nothing he had ever known before.

"Ah yes." He hissed out on a hard breath of pleasure as she worked the head of his cock with strong sucks and fast, flickering lashes of her tongue. "That's good, baby. So good."

He pulled at her hair, drawing her head back, feeling her fight the tug at the strands and watching the pleasure that consumed her expression.

He pulled at her hair again, his teeth gritting as her lashes fluttered and she took his cock deeper into her mouth.

"Like that?" He was almost shaking with the pleasure.

"Hmm." She lifted her lips from his aching flesh and raised her eyes.

"Do you?" she asked him a second before her tongue took a lingering taste of the underside of his cock.

"Oh hell yes," he groaned, sending a surge of pleasure racing through her. "It's so damned good I'm about to burn alive with it."

His abdomen flexed and rippled with tension. His scrotum was tight as she cupped and caressed it in the palm of her hand, and heat radiated from him.

Crista took him into her mouth again, holding his gaze, sucking him deep and hard as she remembered, licking the underside and feeling her own edge of ecstasy twisting inside her at the pleasure she was bringing him.

She knew better than this, better than to allow herself to be affected by his pleasure. But she couldn't help it now any more than she could have done anything to stop it eight years before.

She loved giving Dawg pleasure. She loved watching his expression tense as he fought for control, how his body tensed and a sheen of sweat slicked his muscles.

Her mouth moved on his cock, taking as much as possible, holding it deep and then retreating to suckle at the head with loving greed. She moaned at the taste of pre-cum that whispered over her taste buds and teased more to her hungry mouth as his hands tightened in her hair.

Fingers tugged at the long strands, pulled it forward, drew it over his taut abdomen, and a whispered male groan filled her ears.

"Ah, Crista. So sweet and good." His voice was low and tight with lust. "Perfect, sweet mouth."

She tongued the underside of his cock, licked and probed and gloried at the shudder that traveled through his heavily muscled body.

She wasn't as hesitant as she had been eight years ago. She knew what he liked then, what he still liked now, and she applied the lessons he had given her through the long, dark hours on an unforgettable summer night. Lessons she had dreamed of, fantasized about using on him once again.

"Crista, sweetheart." Dawg could feel the sweat building on his flesh, the heat rushing through his body.

His head fell to the back of the couch, his eyes closed, and memory slammed into him.

Innocent brown eyes staring at him from the same spot where she knelt now. She had helped him into the houseboat and then to the couch, and there he had pulled her to his lap, kissed her, caressed her, and teasingly convinced her to go down on him.

"Suck my dick, baby," he whispered now as he had whispered then. "God, your mouth is killing me."

She had been more shy then. Hesitant. A bit of fear in her wide eyes, but mixed with that fear had been immeasurable excitement.

He forced his head up, his eyes to open, and he stared at her now. Not that much had changed. She was still shy, a little afraid, but the hesitancy was gone. And the pleasure was starker, clearer.

The sight of that pleasure nearly destroyed his control. That coupled with the heat of her sucking mouth, the tempting touch of her fingers on his shaft and his balls, and her moan, and Dawg knew his control wouldn't last much longer.

"Sweet mercy," he groaned, arching, driving his cock deeper in her mouth as she began to lengthen and quicken her suckling strokes. "You're destroying me, Crista."

He hadn't expected this. He had expected a fight. Hell, he halfway wanted a fight. Anything to give him an excuse to escape the hunger that dug into his guts like a dull knife.

There was no escaping it with Crista's hot mouth wrapped around his dick, though. No escaping the pleasure or the pain. Each time he stared down at her, past and present merged. What he had believed were dreams swirled alongside reality.

His chest clenched at the sight of her, emotions held so closely in check for most of his life swirling inside him, confusing him, multiplying the pleasure until he was pulling at her hair, his hips lifting to her, his cock flexing, tensing.

"Crista. Sweetheart." He could barely breathe. Sensation tore through, wrenching at his muscles and stealing his control. "Ah God. I'm gonna come, baby."

He couldn't stand it. His balls were so tight they were torturous, the seed boiling in them, building, breaking down the walls of his restraint as easily as a hammer against sandstone.

Crista's lips, mouth, and tongue were destroying him. Giving more pleasure than he had ever known. How could it be so good? How could one woman, one sweet, shy little mouth rip his control to shreds?

"Ah, God. Crista." His voice was rasping, guttural. "I can't hold back. Ease up."

She didn't ease up. Her mouth was hungrier, her moans hotter, her fingers . . . hot, wicked fingers playing with his balls while the fingers of her other hand stroked his shaft. Her mouth sucked, her tongue licked, her teeth scraped with delicate greed, and an edge of fire ripped through his balls and tore the choice from him.

The first explosive spurt of semen had a strangled cry tearing from his throat. His body tightened to breaking point, his hands gripping her hair, holding her in place. Praying . . . "Oh hell. Tongue it. Suck it. Fuck. Yes."

His head slammed back to the cushions, and light exploded in front of his eyes as pleasure became a fiery, torturous ecstasy unlike anything he had experienced in his life.

He filled her mouth. Forced her to take his release. Held her head in place and nearly writhed with the sensations burning and twisting through his body. His hips lifted from the couch, and her hungry moans rippled over his cock until finally, blessedly, the hot fingers of electricity eased from his spine, and he slumped back to his seat, fighting just to breathe.

Dawg forced himself to release his fingers from Crista's hair, and despite the shame that raged through him, he made himself stare down at her.

Shock wound through his consciousness at the sight of her. A temptress's smile curved her plump, swollen lips as she licked down the shaft of his cock in soothing motions, easing the sharp, heavy contractions in the still-hard flesh. Her eyes were nearly black with her own arousal, her cheeks stained with a flush of lust and shyness.

"Come here." He caught her arms as she moved to distance herself, ignored the flash of hesitancy in her expression, and lifted her to him before bearing her back on the cushions.

Moving over her, Dawg didn't give her time to argue or to protest. His lips covered hers, and for once, his distaste at kissing a woman who had just consumed his seed was absent.

He needed her kiss. The sweetness of her response. Her arms twining around his shoulders and her body softening beneath his.

Her lips parted for him with a gasp, and he nipped at the swollen lower curve before sinking into another, different whirlpool of arousal.

The past few years, sex had been rare. Even the desire for it had been rare. But now, as though fighting to make up for lost time, his body went into overdrive. His cock thickened back to full strength, and the need began to whip through his system once more.

Because of Crista. Because there was something about her that made him hungry. Hell, made him ravenous for the taste of her. For her touch, her breathy little moans and the kisses that burned through his soul.

He tore his lips from hers a second later, turned to her jaw, nipped and licked, kissing his way down the graceful arch.

"Dawg. Wait," she gasped, her voice thick with arousal.

He could hear the hunger in her tone, feel it in the heated silk of her flesh. His hand flattened on her upper stomach, slid down, his fingers gripping the metal button of her jeans.

"Wait for what?" Damn, he was nearly shaking. Every cell in his body was in a frenzy of need to mate. To fuck. If he didn't bury inside her, he was going to go crazy.

"Dawg, please." Was it a protest or need?

His hand flattened on her abdomen, beneath the loose material of her jeans, and felt the muscles there flexing, spasming.

He needed her. Sweet heaven, her womb was clenching for release; her pussy would ripple and contract around him. It would hug him like a hot little fist and welcome him more eagerly than her mouth.

His lips moved to the swollen, flushed mounds of her breasts above the lace of her bra then. Her nipples were hard and pointed beneath. With his free hand, he drew the material over the flushed mound and stared in rapt attention a second before the overriding need to taste her had his head lowering.

Dawg groaned at the feel of her nipple against his tongue, the taste. The acceptance she allowed when his lips closed over one hungrily.

She jerked as though jolted with a hard surge of electricity. Her nipple tightened further, fit perfectly against his tongue, and drew him into a heated intimacy he had never known before.

He had never known, never understood how intimate this act could be. How it could feed his arousal, feed that deep, uncharted core of emotion he kept trapped in his soul.

It wasn't trapped any longer. It spilled from inside him, filling him with blistering pleasure and acceptance. She was accepting him. Giving to him. Letting him inside her soul as he drew the tender bud farther into his mouth.

He drew on the hard, silky flesh, lashed it with his tongue, and felt his own body tighten in pleasure as her thin, sensual wail filled his ears.

Her fingers pulled at his hair, her nails kneaded his scalp, sending tiny pinpoints of fiery pleasure to erupt through his head before it exploded straight to his dick.

Dawg lifted his head, tore his T-shirt from his shoulders, and stared down at her for a long, intense moment.

As her lashes lifted, he watched the pleasure rising inside her, the hunger and needs, and keeping a rein on his own was almost impossible.

"Now," he growled. "I need you now."

Crista stared up at Dawg as his fingers hooked in the loosened waist of her jeans and began to draw them, along with the thong she wore beneath, slowly over her hips.

Naked, aroused, his eyes glowing with unsuppressed hunger and raging need, he looked like a vanquishing conqueror. All the warriors and warlords that the best romances wrote about.

But this wasn't a story. It wasn't a book, and it wasn't fiction. It was the man blackmailing her into his bed and stealing her soul with his touch.

"Dawg." Trembling fingers slid over his shoulders as she tried to force strength into her arms to push him away, to push herself away from the temptation.

"I dreamed of you, Crista." The material slid over her thighs as he drew back. "I dreamed of your kiss, your taste. I dreamed of every wicked fantasy a man could have about his woman for eight years." His voice strengthened as he tossed the jeans and panties to the floor, and his eyes sharpened with angry desire. "Eight years, damn you. One fucking night, and you didn't give me a chance to make up for it. You didn't give me a chance to prove you're fucking *mine*!"

The snarl that drew his lips back held her mesmerized. Possessive, dominant. His eyes slid over her naked body, heating her insides and sending her juices spilling between her thighs.

Crista felt her head shaking, felt the denial born of a sudden knowledge that Dawg wasn't what she expected. This wasn't going to be an affair she could walk away from. Dawg wasn't a man she could watch walk out of her life a second time and survive it.

"Yes, damn you," he cursed, calloused hands pressing her legs apart as he slid deftly between them.

His lips lowered, stealing her protest and replacing it with passion and fire, with a whipping hunger she had no defenses against. As his tongue entered her lips, she felt the blunt pressure, the heated head of his cock pressing against the swollen folds of her pussy.

Tingling fingers of sensations began to play across her flesh. She froze beneath him. She remembered this part. Clearly, so clearly.

Her eyes struggled to open as she felt Dawg lever up, looking into his absorbed expression before she followed the point where his gaze had locked.

There, between her thighs. Her legs were draped over his thighs, spread wide, her hips angled to the thick spear of flesh pressing into her.

Crista watched as the wet folds parted, separating for his cock, hugging the wide crest as he pressed closer, penetrated the tender opening, and he groaned with hoarse male pleasure.

"So sweet. So hot."

Crista whimpered as her body began to stretch to accommodate the impalement. She shook her head against the cushion she lay on, dazed by the pleasure beginning to build inside her.

No, this went beyond pleasure. It went beyond words that Crista could compare it to. It was like being the center of a flame. It was burning in rapture.

"Dawg . . . It's so good." She watched. Watched as the wide crest disappeared inside her. As aching pleasure-pain began to fill her.

"Easy." He held her as her hips twisted, as she fought for more. A deeper stroke, a hard, filling thrust. "You're too tight, Crista. We'll go slow. Easy."

"You didn't before," she whispered feeling the agonizing need clawing through her system as her gaze lifted to his. "Like before, Dawg. All of you. All over me."

His hips bucked, piercing her another inch before he controlled the impulse. She didn't want his control. She wanted his hunger. As frightening as it could be, as dominant and possessive as it was, she wanted it all.

Her hands lifted from the cushions her nails had been digging into. Lifting her arms, she arched them behind her head, stretched, lifted, then lowered them until her hands could cup her breasts, and her fingers could play erotically with her nipples.

"You were wild that night," she whispered.

She had seen his desperation to separate dream from reality, and now some wicked imp insisted that she help him remember.

"How wild?" His gaze blistered her with erotic hunger.

"You didn't hesitate." She brought a finger to her lips, dampened it, then painted her hard nipple with the moisture.

His gaze sliced to the motion before pulling back to her eyes, hotter, darker than before.

His breath was sawing in and out of his chest; moisture clung to his forehead, his shoulders.

"It might hurt," he groaned, easing back.

"It destroyed me," she assured him. "Pleasure and pain." Her breathing hitched at the memory. "And you were wild and hungry . . ."

Her head tipped back as a ragged, strangled scream left her lips at the penetration.

Halfway. He was buried halfway inside her, but he pulled back quickly, his muscles bunching as he gripped her hips and plunged inside her again.

All the way.

Crista arched to him, her hips jerked, writhed, undulated to the fiery stretching, the pleasure-pain and ecstatic sensations whipping through her like wildfire now.

"Like that?" He spoke, but he didn't stop.

Hard hands held her beneath him, his hips thrust and churned, his erection plunged inside her, spreading the fire and sending it burning through her body. Across sensitive nerve endings, through her pleasure-dazed mind and back to the clenching, spasming muscles of her vagina as it struggled to hold him inside, to hold on to the sensations that built to cataclysmic proportions.

"Is that what you want?" he snarled, fucking her furiously now, building sensation on top of sensation.

Her hands latched onto his wrists as he held her hips, her gaze locking with his as she felt perspiration begin to roll off her body.

"Like this," she panted, shuddering beneath him, her hands sliding up his arms, reaching for his face. "All of it. Like before. Just like before."

Before, his lips had been at her nipples, his lips, teeth, and tongue ravaging the tips as his cock ravished her pussy.

And he knew. A hollow groan left his throat as he came over her, his lips covering her nipple as Crista became lost in the eroticism of being possessed by Dawg.

Hard plunging hips, the thick length of his cock, his lips suckling at her nipple, his hands latching in her hair and pulling at it sensually.

The band of tension in her womb began to tighten. Her hips flexed beneath him, arching to him as he fucked her with mindless hunger, took her with dominant strength.

She was possessed. Taken. Fingers of fire rippled and burned beneath her flesh, and within seconds the conflagration overtook her. The orgasm that tore through her had her crying out at the intensity of the pleasure that rushed through her system. It exploded through her; it ripped through the few remaining defenses around her soul as it released more than just the sexual tension.

She held onto him, her arms tight around his neck as she shuddered through each spasm of pleasure, felt his release tearing through him, and whimpered at the remembered sensation of his semen pulsing inside her.

The man was known for his paranoia with condoms, and twice he had forgotten while taking her. It was enough to terrify a woman.

As he collapsed over her, Crista let a weary breath leave her throat and felt her muscles become relaxed, slack. Weariness washed over her, and she gave in to it. Because it was better to give in to it than it was to think about exactly what had happened. Because if she had to think, then she had to remember. And if she had to remember, then fear was going to overcome her. The fear of losing her soul once again.

"Crista," he whispered her name against her ear then. "Did I make it better this time?"

"What do you mean?"

"Tell me the truth now." He kissed the shell of her ear gently. "That first time, did I hurt you?"

Silence filled the room. Memories and regrets clashed inside her, tearing at her soul.

"More than you'll ever know, Dawg. More than you'll ever know."

Seven

Dawg had learned years before how to read between the lines when it came to women. The survival instinct was strong, and as a boy he had learned that a soft smile and a gentle voice didn't always mean a gentle heart. Just as he had learned that there were often a dozen different definitions to any one comment that a man could garner when it came to difficult questions.

Had he hurt her? He heard the flash of remembered pain in her voice, but the memory wasn't of a physical hurt. He hadn't forced her, he hadn't taken her so roughly that he had destroyed girlish dreams of a first time. If her response to him in the living room was anything to go by, then she had hungered as much for him as he had for her over the years.

No, it hadn't been her body that he had hurt. It had been something far more delicate. He had hurt her young heart and possibly scared the hell out of her when he spoke of bringing his cousins to their bed.

As he lay in his bed the next morning and stared up at the ceiling, he would have snorted at that thought if he weren't more concerned about waking the woman now sleeping next to him.

Share her? He couldn't imagine it. Even then the thought of sharing her had sent a spike of denial tearing through his chest, despite his stubbornness to remain dedicated to the extreme, raunchy pleasure to be had in the act.

And now? Hell, he hadn't shared one of his women in years,

despite Natches's obvious dissatisfaction in his cousin's recent lack of desire to participate in the games of their youth.

The truth had become obvious when Rowdy returned home from the Marines last year to claim his stepsister. Even as the sharing had begun to wane, Dawg and Natches both had been certain they had known what was coming. That when Rowdy returned, the need for the fun and games would return.

For Dawg, it hadn't returned, though. He had seen the possessiveness his cousin felt for Kelly immediately. He had been amused. More understanding than Natches had been, but privately relieved. As much as he had once desired the little vixen that Rowdy was now engaged to, he found that over the years that desire had slowly changed. Affection and protectiveness had replaced the lust.

But the need for Crista had only grown over the years. Maybe he had understood Rowdy more than Natches did because Crista had been back in town when Rowdy returned, and Dawg had been fighting the demons that came with her return: the knowledge that he was missing something with her, that something had been taken away from him. And now he knew exactly what he had lost.

A night of memories. The knowledge of how she smelled, how she tasted, the sounds of her cries and the whisper of her desire as he took her. All the things he cherished about the sex act were missing from the night he had spent with her in his bed.

All he had were the dreams. Fragmented, broken, more tease than knowledge of an event that threatened to take his head off with the pleasure.

Oh yeah, he remembered that much. In his dreams, he remembered being consumed by a fire so overwhelming it had been all he could do to survive it. The same fire had ripped through him the day before when he took her downstairs on the couch, pushing into her, possessing her.

He should have known, he told himself as he turned his head to stare at her. All these years, he should have known that something had happened that night. If not because of Crista's abrupt change, then because of her brother Alex's.

Alex Jansen had become more mocking, if possible, and even more critical of the cousins' lifestyles the same week Crista had gone from an emerging sex kitten in her flirtatiousness with Dawg to a cold, frightened woman running from a nameless terror.

Too young and too dumb, Dawg thought now. That was what he had been.

Which made him an even bigger bastard now in her eyes. His lips twitched at the memory of her fury the previous day as soon as she realized exactly how damned sexy she had been when he took her.

He couldn't believe he had dared to blackmail her into his bed. He could still remember the shock in her eyes, the disbelief, the way she had watched him through the day as though expecting him to suddenly smile and declare it had all been a joke. Right up until she had opened her eyes, stared into his, and realized there was no chance to escape now that he had had her.

She was dreaming if she thought that was ever going to happen. Dawg had learned a lot of things in the four years he had been in the Marines and then the last four years training and working with the ATF. He had learned how to be hard. How to kill. He knew how to assess a situation in a single moment and make lightning-fast decisions that had saved his life on more than one occasion.

And he had known, standing outside that warehouse with Crista safely hidden in his pickup, he had known there wasn't a chance in hell she was going to come to his bed in any conventional manner. No, he would have to take the choice from her first, then work on making her forgive him for it.

He turned his head and looked at her now, a smile playing at his lips. It had taken hours to get her to try to sleep. She had spent the day pacing the downstairs section of his houseboat, railing and arguing and coming up with some damned good arguments as to why he was a class-A bastard and a disgrace to the human race.

Her last argument still had him holding back a chuckle.

"Alex is so going to kick your ass!" she had raged as he finally grew tired of the arguments, picked her up, and carried her to his bed. "He'll have your balls for this, Dawg."

As though she would tell Alex.

Alex most likely knew about the night they had spent together, but he didn't know enough to want to kill Dawg. Eight years ago he could have done it. It would be a little harder job now, however.

She was in his bed, though. Still wearing her T-shirt and panties, but minus the jeans that had covered her slender legs when he pulled her up here. She might have been too angry to give him another taste of the heated arousal he knew she felt, but the knowledge that she felt it was still there.

He drew the sheet from her legs slowly, ignoring her mumbled little protest as she shifted on her back, one leg bending at the knee, the other stretched out along the bed.

A soft cotton thong covered her pussy, the material shaping itself over her mound and revealing the soft curls beneath. Dawg rarely liked that silky growth on a woman's mound. It hampered his dining pleasure when he was going down on a woman. He wanted to taste her flesh, feel the responsiveness of each soft fold that hid the treasure beyond.

Those curls would have to go. Binding Crista to him wasn't going to be easy. She was stubborn as hell, and she had already made up her mind that Dawg and his sex games were too far out of her league.

Because she was scared. He had seen that flash of fear in her eyes. That feminine knowledge that she had come up against something or someone that she wasn't certain how to handle.

She would learn how to handle it, how to handle him, because the bottom line came down to the fact that he couldn't risk letting her go.

The information they had on the female within the group of thieves that had stolen that arms shipment en route to the U.S. Army garrison in Fort Knox was too similar to Crista's description. There were no photographs yet, no one had managed to identify her, and Dawg was going to make damned sure that Crista didn't get identified in the criminal's stead.

He didn't like the pinch in his gut that warned him that some bad shit was coming down the road. He could feel it, like a premonition. An instinctual warning that danger was moving in on his position like a bird of prey gliding over the valley searching for food. And Crista was sitting smack-dab in the middle of that valley, a tasty little morsel just waiting to be plucked into the jaws of whoever or whatever was moving in.

It had to do with these missiles; he could feel it. It wasn't a coincidence that she had been there, but he couldn't convince himself she was involved, either. He had found something else in the small house her parents had left her and Alex, though.

The freshly swept carpet had shown signs of traffic. He knew Crista; like most women she did things in a certain way, and he remembered Alex bitching years ago about how she always swept the floors before they left the house. She would sweep back to the front door, storing the sweeper in the hall closet before they left and leaving the carpet pristine and devoid of tracks.

Crista's carpet had tracks in it. Tracks just slightly too large to be hers. Or so he tried to convince himself. They were subtle; he gave credit to whoever had made them, someone had tried to wipe them out, but they hadn't completely managed it.

The tracks had started in the living room, just off the small foyer. They had walked through the living room, gone up the steps, and moved into her bedroom to her dresser, then to her closet. While there, Dawg had found the address to the warehouse tucked into a dark bronze blazer that had been hung haphazardly in the closet. There had been nothing else. Not a scrap of paper, not a stash of money, nothing to tie her to the theft of the weapons, other than that address. There had been just enough of a disturbance to allay his conscience in lying to his superiors.

Not that he needed to excuse that very often. He had a very high respect for the chain of command, there was no doubt; he was, after all, a Marine. But he knew that sometimes, some things needed a little closer investigation before he reported them. Crista was one of those instances.

Soft, warm, hotter than hell, and fighting him tooth and nail. But she was back in his bed and sleeping next to him.

How many times had he awakened over the years, certain he would find her next to him, knowing that the dream that had haunted his sleep had to be more than a dream. And each time he had awakened alone, until now.

Hell no, he wasn't letting her out of this one. He would blackmail her a thousand times over if that was what it took to get her into his bed and to keep her there.

He watched her carefully, reaching out with his hand, his fingertips only touching the silky flesh of her thigh.

Damn, she was soft. Like the finest silk. The most expensive satin. Warm and sweet.

She shifted again, a muttered little moan slipping past her lips as he let more of his fingers experience that heated sensation, caressing the rounded flesh gently.

She whispered a sigh, her thighs falling farther apart, giving him a clear view of the sweet flesh covered in cotton.

Was she wet?

His fingers paused on her thigh, only inches from what was paradise.

"Does this deal include molesting me in my sleep?" Her half-drowsy exclamation of contempt was punctuated by a quick jerk at the sheet to draw it back over her thighs.

He grinned. Damn, she was going to be a challenge, maybe more than he anticipated.

"I think I should start a list," he murmured lazily, drawing the sheet back toward him. "Keeping your little butt off the firing line could get complicated. I'll need compensation.

She didn't let go of the covering. Her fingers tightened on it, her chocolate eyes glared back at him.

"Now, Crista," he chided her gently, though his gaze was anything but gentle as it met hers. "Let go of the sheet. Let me see what I'm lying for today."

"You wouldn't turn me in."

He could see the bravado in her gaze now. She was well-rested and feeling more confident, better able to handle him. Let's see if she could.

He pushed back desire, need, temptation, and gave her the steely eyed look he had perfected in the Marines. The one that assured those both above and lower in rank that he was someone to be reckoned with.

Her eyes flickered with indecision.

"It's like this, fancy-face." He smirked. "When Alex returns, he won't be able to do a damned thing about what's happened here, right now. If my superiors connect you to this case, then you're gone."

"Over drugs?" She snorted. "I don't think so, Dawg. Drug dealers are not terrorists."

"Unless terrorists are dealing in drugs." He shrugged, omitting the fact that his case didn't have a damned thing to do with drugs.

She blinked back at him silently again. Damn, that little mind was quick. He could see it working in her expression, the play of emotions that crossed her face finally settling into lines of resentment and anger.

"Stop doing this," she finally pushed out between clenched teeth.

"Why?" If she had a good reason, he might relent. For this morning.

"Because I don't want it." He could feel her tensing as he drew the sheet fully away, his gaze going to the mounds of her breasts beneath her shirt.

Didn't want it, his ass. He restrained a knowing smile. He knew women, and he knew body language, and if he wasn't totally wrong, she wanted it just as bad, maybe worse, than he did. Though he couldn't imagine her wanting it worse. He swore his cock would rupture with the need to burrow into the tight, heated confines of her pussy.

"Your nipples are hard." And he was going to taste them soon. "Is your pussy wet? Sorry, baby, but if you didn't want it, then you did a damned good imitation of it on my couch yesterday."

Shock, arousal, it filled her face as surely as the blush that began to work up along her neck and into her face. And it was damned enchanting. He hadn't seen a woman blush in years.

But she wasn't ready for another round yet, and Dawg could sense the uncertainty in her. If he weren't careful, she could choose prison over him. Crista could be incredibly stubborn as he well knew. She wasn't above cutting off her own nose to spite her face.

"No answer, huh?" He let an amused grin quirk his lips.

Hell, Crista was fun. Even with her back up and her mad on, she was fun.

She licked her lips, and his gut clenched. He wanted that tongue on his dick again. If she didn't decide on his course of action pretty damned soon, then he was going to have to play another very delicate card in the hand he had dealt himself.

Yep, blackmail was a very dirty word, and a man had to have some way of backing up his threat.

"I have to meet with my team this afternoon." He rolled away from her, stretching lazily as she seemed to freeze beside him. "We have bad guys—and girls—to catch." He threw her a careless smile as he untangled his legs from the sheet and rose from the bed.

Her eyes were narrowed on him, but her fingers had a death grip on the sheet as she held it over her.

She was thinking, though. He could always tell when she was

rolling something around in her head. He remembered before she left, catching that look on her face and wanting to be so deep inside her that she couldn't hide anything from him. That need had only grown. Right now, he would give his eyeteeth to be buried so deep inside her that even their cells would bond.

"So what am I supposed to do now that you've had me fired from my job?" she snapped back at him irately. "I'm going to assume that during this game you're playing, I'm not allowed to work."

Dawg scratched at his chest, feeling a surge of satisfaction as her gaze licked over him. He was naked, aroused, and he would be damned if he was going to try to hide it from her.

"You have a job," he assured her, turning to the low chest of drawers on the other side of the room and pulling out clean clothes.

"What kind of a job?" The low, wrathful tone had his lips twitching again.

"Fucking me. I'm fairly high maintenance, Crista. You won't need another job."

Then he ducked to avoid the alarm clock that came sailing at his head, then to avoid the picture frame that held a picture of his Harley. But he felt a swell of joy rise inside him as he jumped for her, gripping her wrist as she reached for the lamp, pulling her under him and holding her to the mattress as she bucked and writhed and cursed with all the exuberance of a damned sailor.

Crista couldn't remember ever being so furious. A haze of red distorted her view, and a mix of murderous, adrenaline-crazed fury pumped through her veins.

"You bastard!" She tried to scream past the tightening in her chest, her throat. "Do I have *whore* written on my forehead? Do I look like one of your sex-starved little bimbos?"

She cringed from his body lying atop hers now, from the heavy, naked thighs pushing between her own and the powerful arms that held his body just far enough above her to allow her to breathe.

She wasn't unaffected. Arousal pumped side by side with the fury, bringing angry tears to her eyes as she collapsed beneath him, exhausted, panting as she glared up at him.

"I hate you," she hissed, feeling the first tear fall from her eye and track down her cheek. "I can't believe what a bastard you've turned into."

His gaze lightened, then became shadowed as he held her wrists in one hand and the other came up to touch the tear on her face.

"You cried then, too." His voice was soft, brooding. "Didn't you? When I kissed you, you cried."

Oh yeah, she was going to answer that one for him. Not. Not in a million years would she ever tell him what he did to her then, and now.

"You told me you dreamed of me." His jaw tensed as a flash of lust lit up his eyes like lightning.

"I wouldn't dream of you if you were the last man on earth," she scoffed, panting at the effort to force him to release her. "Get off me. I don't want you anywhere near me."

She didn't want the blood pumping to her nipples and her clit with a force that had them straining, tight and engorged, against the material of her clothing as he covered her.

She didn't want her skin so sensitive she could feel the hairs on his chest, even through her shirt. And she didn't want the pleasure that was building, burning through her as he held her beneath him, restrained. Helpless.

"I thought of that all night as you slept," he said guardedly. "Taking you again, having you beneath me. It was better than the dreams, Crista. They didn't even compare."

His voice dropped to a guttural whisper as his gaze flared with carnal heat. It was mesmerizing, watching his gaze flare, then lighten with sexual need.

"Get off me, Dawg." It was all she could do to push the words past her lips. "I won't let you turn into me a whore for your own amusement."

"Say that word again, and I'll make you regret it, Crista." The order was clipped and filled with menace. "I haven't called you a whore, and I never believed you were one."

"Don't you? Evidently you do, if you think my only job is fucking you." She strained against him again, only to still as she felt the broad head of his cock butt against the crotch of her thin panties. Too thin, because she could feel the heat of his thick flesh pressing against her.

"Until I figure out what the hell is going on, that's exactly what your job is. Because, make no mistake, fancy-face, I'm not a very charitable person anymore. Just because you're not guilty doesn't mean you don't look guilty. You need me so you can stay out of jail. And you know the price for my help."

Was he serious? And did it really matter at this point if he was or not? Her senses were suddenly rioting at the feel of his cock head pressing against her, causing her to grow wetter, her flesh more sensitive.

She didn't want this.

Crista shook her head as she felt Dawg's lips at her cheek, rough velvet, sliding over her flesh as her breath hitched in her throat.

"Nothing matters to me but fucking you." Self-disgust filled his voice. "Being so deep inside you that this hunger that's eaten at my gut for eight years dissolves." His head lifted as he glowered down at her from between sensually narrowed eyes. "Make no mistake, Crista, you will spread those pretty legs for me again, and you'll give me what I want. Because it's the only way I can keep your ass out of jail. Walk away from me, and I won't lift a finger to help you when they slap the cuffs on your wrists and you disappear. Because, baby, it will so be out of my hands then that I couldn't help you if I wanted to."

"But you can if I'm sleeping with you?" Disillusionment, disappointment, he heard it all in her voice.

Quite simply, as he said, unless he relented, she had no choice.

"Of course." His smile was tight and hard. "I'll know where you are. I'll know if you're playing dirty or playing nice, and then putting my neck on the line won't feel like a fool's fucking errand to me. Now make your choice."

Crista stared back at him, finally admitting that the man she had dreamed of for eight years was gone, in more ways than she had imagined.

"It's the same as rape," she whispered, then bit back a moan as his free hand reached down, pulling her panties aside and allowing the heavy crest of his cock to slide through the juices gathering there.

"Do you enjoy lying to yourself, Crista?"

Dawg was breathing harder now, and Crista found it nearly

impossible to draw in enough oxygen herself. The air was ripe with steamy carnality, her body so sensitive now, her clit so swollen, she wondered if she could survive if he didn't fuck her.

"Damn," he suddenly groaned, his hand gripping her hip as he let his cock slide through the heavy moisture until the feel of it rasping over her clit had her jerking in his hold and whimpering in heat.

"Your pussy's so hot I'll burn to ash," he muttered, lowering his head again, his lips brushing over hers, though he ignored the parting of her lips to move to her jaw. "Like hot silk, molten silk. Let me have you again, Crista. I'll take you so easy this time." His lips caressed the shell of her ear now. "I'll slide inside you slow and sweet, darlin'. And I promise, I'll make you scream again with pleasure."

As he had the first time and again yesterday. But then, he had pounded inside her both times, rocked her. Impaled her. He had taken her with a force that had left her shaken, not just from his possession, but from her response to it.

As he spoke, his free hand slid beneath her T-shirt. Broad and calloused, it rasped over her sensitive flesh, sending brilliant spears of pleasure exploding through her system.

"Dawg, don't you think—"

"I never think around you," he muttered as his lips moved back along her jaw. "All I do is feel." His hips moved, dragging his erection down, the thick head sliding through saturated folds, then with wicked effectiveness, pressed into the clutching entrance of her vagina.

Crista stilled. She stared up at Dawg as his head lifted, his eyes nearly colorless, the green so light that the pupils of his eyes were stark in the center.

"Are you protected?" His voice was tortured.

"Fine time to ask that question." Her fists clenched, her wrists straining against his hold.

Of course she was protected. She had learned her lesson. She stayed protected.

It was too much pleasure. She could feel it rising forcefully inside her, tearing at her senses, dissolving her objections. Just as he had the first time, he was ripping her from the moorings of her own common sense.

"Answer me!" His lips were tight, his body straining.

"Yes—" The cry that tore from her was a mixture of pleasurable agony and bitter realization.

The heavy, hard thrust that sent him tunneling through unused muscles and slick, heated flesh was almost as painful as it had been the first time. And it was definitely more pleasurable than it should have been.

Crista stared up at him in shock and surprise, uncertain, confused. This wasn't supposed to happen. Not like this. Not this fast. Not at all, if she hadn't been so weak, so wet.

"Dawg." She would wince at the beseeching tone of her voice later. For now, all she could do was lie there, feeling the muscles of her pussy ripple, clench, and struggle to accept the flesh impaling it.

Little darts of sensation were racing over her body, detonating with trembling force in erogenous zones that she didn't know were erogenous zones.

"Do you know"—a heavy grimace contorted his expression as his hips flexed against her, causing the head of his cock to stroke the deepest part of her vagina in a way that had her breath catching violently—"know how tight and hot your pussy is? How you feel wrapped around me?"

She shook her head. She couldn't do this again. Hear his voice, his words causing her to grow wetter, hotter. She couldn't let him steal her mind or her heart again. But he was, stealing it all as the pleasure began to tear through her senses.

"Here. Come here, darlin'."

She nearly wailed at the feeling of his cock shifting, stretching her farther as he lifted her enough, just enough, to pull her shirt free of her body, baring the lacy bra she wore beneath. A bra that did nothing to hide the straining nubs of her nipples.

"This is so—so not a good idea," she panted as the front clip of the bra released, and her breasts spilled out to his waiting palms.

"Did I suck these pretty nipples that first time?" he asked then, his voice a hard, rough rasp. "I dreamed I did. I dreamed I dined on them. Fed from them."

Her head tossed on the mattress as her hands gripped his wrists. To hold on or to protest his fingers caressing the swollen mounds, his thumbs brushing over her tight nipples, she wasn't certain.

"Dawg, think—" She needed to think.

"Don't think." He pulled the bra free before tossing it away. "You think too much, Crista."

A second later her panties were ripped from her hips, the scraps tossed to the floor as she stared down her body. Straight to where they were joined.

Dark brown curls glistened with moisture and pressed against his pelvis. Her legs were spread wide to accommodate his powerful thighs, her knees bent and hugging the outside of his legs.

"See how good we look together." His voice was an insidious murmur of heated lust and pleasure as he flexed inside her again. "Let me show you, sweetheart. Look at this."

Eight

"Let me show you . . ."

Crista couldn't help but watch. Dazed, mesmerized, even more than she had been yesterday. She watched as Dawg shifted his hips back slowly, his erection pulling free of her inner grip as a whimper of denial left her lips.

The thick, hard flesh was flushed a ruddy red, his cock head purpled and throbbing and wide enough to make her swallow tightly at the sight of it.

It glistened with her juices, shimmered in the afternoon sunlight spearing into the high, narrow windows over the bed.

It was powerful, iron hard, and hot, and within seconds easing inside her again. Crista watched that, too. She couldn't help it. It was so sexy, erotic. Inch by inch, it disappeared inside her until once again his pubic hair was tangling with hers as a low groan fell from his lips.

"I've dreamed of this," he rasped. "Watching my dick fill you slow and easy. Watching you take me."

She was caught in a whirlwind, sensations piling atop each other, pleasure ripping through her as the stiff length of his cock stretched her, sending a burning ecstasy roiling through her system.

How was she supposed to deny him now? How the hell was she supposed to survive again once it was over and Dawg went on to the next conquest? Because this—oh Lord—this could become addictive.

Her gaze moved from where he was buried inside her, lifting over the flat, rippling planes of his abdomen to his fiercely set expression. Light green eyes glowed in the dark expanse of his face; long, sooty lashes were lowered to half-mast; and a flush of erotic pleasure stained his cheekbones.

He was a warrior, a conqueror, and he was stealing her soul.

"You like this." He shifted, moved, drawing free of her body slowly before pushing heavily inside her once again.

Mercy. It was too good. Her back bowed as she arched to it, driving him inside her as she felt the muscles of her pussy stretch again. Burning, searing pleasure.

"Tell me you like this, Crista." His voice was filled with wicked knowledge as he began a slow, heavy rhythm, fucking her as though he had all the time in the world when she knew that if she didn't orgasm soon, she was going to die.

"Come on, honey," he urged, his voice insistent, almost gentle. "Tell me you missed feeling me inside you, fucking you slow and easy, making you burn for me."

Her head shook desperately. She couldn't miss what she hadn't had, could she? He had taken her hard, fast, in a variety of ways and positions, but he hadn't taken her like this. Like the act mattered. Like she mattered.

"Look at me, Crista. Come on, open your eyes, honey."

His voice was too gentle, too rough with passion. Her eyes opened, and she felt the first tear fall. A stupid tear, because he was taking her too deep, stealing too much of her.

Dawg almost stopped at the sight of that single tear easing down her cheek. And he would have, if he hadn't seen much more than that in her eyes. Shimmering damply, they were filled with such tormented need, a hunger that he recognized, one he knew went clear to the soul.

It was a hunger he recognized because it was the same hunger that had tormented him for too long. So many years dreaming of her, and she was better than the dream. Sweeter than passion, hotter than lust.

Silky wet with the juices gathering inside her, coating his dick with syrupy heat and lubricating each heavy thrust inside her.

Delicate muscles clamped on his cock, stroked over him with a tight-fisted grip, and nearly destroyed his determination to go slow. To take her easy. To relish every fucking minute inside her when he wanted nothing more than to pound into her pussy with greedy, harsh strokes.

He was a hard lover. He had always known that. Sometimes, he hated that part of his sensuality, because going slow and easy had always taken thought. He had to think his way through each thrust to keep his head. Until Crista. Taking her slow and easy was—damn, it was easy. He wasn't thinking, he was relishing, enjoying, burning alive in her heat.

"I shouldn't have taken you so hard yesterday," he crooned, suddenly wondering if he had been too rough with her after all, if he had hurt her.

She was delicate, tender. Not like the other women he had been with, women who knew and anticipated that hardened side of his sexuality.

"Dawg." She was panting. Those stiff little nipples were pushing closer to his face as her lips parted to drag in more air. "Please . . ." her head tossed on the pillow. "Not like this."

Not like this?

He pushed inside her, deep, forcing himself to stop, to make her *feel* as his dick throbbed inside her.

"You're wrapped around me like a fist," he gritted out. "Feel it, Crista. I can. Your pussy is working over my dick like a hot little mouth starving for satisfaction. Deny you want this. Just like this."

He flexed inside her again, feeling the head of his cock stroking her, the crown positioned just right to notch the flared, stiffened edge into her G-spot. He stroked her internally, watching her eyes darken, her face flush a delicate pink as the pleasure began to build higher, hotter.

Damn, she was making him high just from the feel of her. The blood was pounding in his head, adrenaline and lust clouding his vision as he shook his head and breathed in roughly.

Just a few more minutes. God, he had to feel her just a few more minutes. He couldn't come yet, not yet, not until those little ripples around his dick began to clench and spasm in release.

Crista felt her legs lifting, felt her body melting, and she whimpered at the surrender that rushed through her mind. She couldn't fight this. He was buried inside her, fiery hot and thick, pulsing and stroking internal muscles that even after all this time hadn't forgotten the pleasure he could give her.

She bit her lip as she stared up at him. Her wild man. That was what he was, a wild man. Maybe not hers, but here, buried inside her, for this moment in time, he was hers. And he was every inch a primal, sexual male.

His eyes were so light now they seemed to glow within his face, his lips tight with the fight for control. She didn't want his control. She wanted what she had before. Wild, primitive. Maybe, just maybe she could survive the fallout later.

As she watched, a smile tugged at the taut line of his lips, and he began to move again. That slow, destructive rhythm that forced her to feel every blazing inch of his cock.

Oh, that was good. Her breath hitched; a hard, jerking shudder tore through her body as her hips jerked upward to hold him inside her as long as possible.

"Oh yeah, you like that," he muttered, his voice becoming thicker, rough. "I like it, Crista. I like it a lot."

Of course he liked it. He was winning. Triumph glittered in his gaze as her hands tightened on the wrists beside her head.

"Let's see if you like this."

The rhythm stayed the same, but his head lowered, his lips surrounding a hard, sensitive nipple and drawing it into his mouth.

"Oh, God. Dawg, please, don't . . ." Don't make her feel this. Don't make her lose her senses to him.

Her head twisted against the mattress, though she arched closer, pushing the peak deeper into his mouth.

His lips, teeth, tongue. They all played with the hot nerve center of her nipple. Licking, nipping, suckling with male greed as he continued to thrust inside her slow and easy.

Her pussy was clenching around the length of his erection, spasming with brutal need and desperate lust. Her hands moved from his wrists to his head, trembling fingers sinking into his long hair, holding him closer as her hips moved beneath him.

"Harder." The cry shocked her. It came from her in a voice strangled with furious need. "Fuck me, Dawg. Please. Please, like before."

The desperation rose inside her. The need for more, the need for racing bolts of electric ecstasy tearing through her rather than zipping teasingly around her.

"How was it before, baby?" he whispered, his voice a guttural rasp now. "Tell me what I missed, Crista. Tell me how I took you."

"Hard." She was panting, shaking. Sweat dampened both their flesh now as her juices built along her thighs, easing from around Dawg's cock with each movement inside her.

She was so wet, so hot, and becoming violently sensitive to each touch of his mouth against her nipples, each stroke inside her.

"How hard?" He nipped the sensitive curve of her breast before stroking his stubbled cheek against it.

Crista felt the breath tear from her throat.

"So hard. Please, Dawg."

"Did I pound inside you?" Tortured, hungry, his tone stroked her senses just as his cock stroked inside the burning center of her body.

"Yes," she hissed, writhing beneath him.

Crista could feel her response blazing out of control now. Her senses were overwhelming her common sense. She knew it; she couldn't stop it. She couldn't force it back inside her now that Dawg had released it.

"Do it!" She jerked beneath him, her legs rising, her ankles clasping at his hips as she shoved upward, then cried out at the feeling of him delving deeper, stretching her farther.

A hard male groan tore from his chest then. Hard hands pulled her legs free, pushed them back as he rose to his knees in front of her and gave her what she demanded.

Just as he had the first time.

He rose over her like a sex god come to life. Hard hands held her behind her knees, forcing them to bend, forcing her legs back as his hips began to move.

A bed pounder. The headboard would have been striking the wall behind them if it weren't attached. The mattress shook, and Crista felt the tender tissue of her sex quaking in rapture as he began to fuck her with hard, driving strokes.

Burning strokes.

Pleasure and pain that combined inside her and had starlight bursting in front of her vision as she exploded beneath him.

Lightning tore through her veins. It licked over her nipples, her clitoris, then ruptured forcefully inside her womb as she felt the wet, hot force of her orgasm frothing inside her, around Dawg's pounding erection.

Within seconds, it was joined by his release. His teeth clenched, his lips pulling back as his gaze caught hers, held it, and the feel of his semen spurting inside her triggered another forceful, screaming, sheet-clawing orgasm inside her.

"Fuck yes!" he snarled. "Come for me, Crista. Like that—fuck yes, milk me with that sweet pussy. Take it. Take it all." He jerked spasmodically inside her before his head tilted back on his shoulders, and a harsh tremor shook his hard body.

He released her legs slowly. They melted back to the bed as he came over her, still buried inside her, his cock jerking weakly now as he covered her.

"I came like that inside you the first time," he panted at her ear. "I remember that, Crista. Over and over again I came inside you."

He had. Her lashes lifted to stare at the ceiling, to force back the bitter memories.

"Tell me." His voice was insidious, low, dangerous. "Were you pregnant when you left Somerset? And don't bother lying to me." His head raised, his gaze spearing into hers. "Did you have my baby?"

She stared back at him, the bitterness rising inside her like a cancer she couldn't rid herself of.

"There's no baby," she whispered harshly, wondering why the hell she even bothered. "I didn't have your child."

His eyes narrowed as fury began to light the depths.

"Did you abort my baby, Crista?"

God help her if she had. Crista could see the murderous rage lurking in the depths now.

Her lips twisted mockingly. "There was nothing to abort, Dawg. And if you can ask me that question, then you have no business coming inside me. Tell me something now. How many of your bimbos have you double-fucked with your cousins and not worn a condom? Maybe I should be checked for STDs rather than a pregnancy."

A snarling smile pulled at his lips now as he leaned close, nearly nose to nose, his gaze flaring, heating, lightening, then darkening again.

"I marked your pussy eight years ago, and I marked it today. And trust me, sweetheart, no other has taken my seed. I've made damned sure of it."

Her eyes widened in a parody of joy that didn't hint at the anger running through her. "Oh wow. Dawg gave me his seed three times now." She fluttered her lashes. "How lucky am I? Well, just let me up right now so I can jump for joy and tell the world my accomplishments. I have finally arrived in life."

A grin quirked his lips. Bastard that he was, he was amused.

"There you go, sugar, you're getting the idea," he murmured as a slight grimace twisted his features as he pulled free of her.

And her stupid, traitorous body tried to hold on to him. Clenching around his flesh, her hips jerking upward as though to relish that final stroke of heat and pleasure.

She flung the sheet over her as he rolled from the bed, pushing his fingers through his hair as he glanced back at her.

"You're a smart-ass," he grunted.

"Just figuring that one out? And here I thought I was being less than subtle for the past year."

Twelve months of trying to keep him at arm's length, of trying to hold back the bitterness and the memories that tormented her, and what had she done? She'd twisted and mewled beneath him like a bitch in heat. Apt, considering his nickname, she told herself cruelly.

She was setting herself up for heartbreak again, and Alex wasn't here to save her. Mark wasn't here to comfort her, and his lover wasn't here to make her laugh and help her rebuild herself once Dawg was finished with her.

For the first time in her life, Crista could feel how very alone she was.

"At least you were smart enough to use protection that first time." He sighed, though she fooled herself into thinking she heard an edge of regret in his tone.

Fooling herself. Just as she had fooled herself those months before he took her to his bed that first time. Fooled herself into thinking he cared about her, that she mattered.

"Yeah, that's me, intelligent to a fault," she bit out as she wrapped the sheet around her and moved from the bed. She needed to find her clothes. She needed to shower and wash the smell of Dawg from her body. The scent of sunrise and a storm. Wild and hot. He should bottle it. He would be a millionaire. Hell, she should bottle it, but she would be too stupid to sell it. She would hoard it all for herself.

That was her. Greedy as hell when it came to Dawg.

Too greedy, she imagined, for the lifestyle he had chosen years before.

"I need a shower," she told him, furious with herself and her emotions.

It had been eight years since she had left Somerset. Eight long, exhausting, completely unproductive years, because all she thought about was coming home, returning to the mountains she loved and the man she couldn't forget.

And he had forgotten her so easily.

"Go ahead. I'll hop downstairs and shower. The two bathrooms have separate hot water heaters. You'll have plenty enough for a bath or a shower."

The *Nauti Dawg* had all the comforts of home, she remembered. Including a sinfully deep tub large enough to hold even Dawg.

The thought of soaking in that tub, easing the aches and pains from her still-bruised body, was almost irresistible. Almost. Unfortunately, she had things to do. Things like finding a newspaper to begin job hunting. Again.

It was Friday, so actually hunting up a job wasn't going to happen today. But she needed to return to the house and get organized.

The waitressing job had been okay for a while. It kept her going while she finished the tests for her business degree, but she had no intentions of staying there, anyway. She had been marking time since completing her advanced degree three months before. Something she had put off when she had landed the office manager job in Virginia.

It had been a good job. Until her boss married, and the wife decided she could save her husband's money by doing the job herself. Crista had received two weeks' notice and a very small severance package, and then good-bye.

"I need a ride back to the restaurant to pick up my car," she told him as she gathered her clothes from the floor and headed to the bathroom.

"I'll drive you back," he said behind her. "Then we can go to the house and collect the rest of your things. Did you have any furniture you have to bring back with you?"

Crista froze at the bathroom doorway before turning back to him slowly.

"Why would I need to bring my furniture? You just said until the end of summer." She kept her voice calm. When dealing with Dawg, one had to learn to stay calm, or he would drive one insane.

He pulled a pair of shorts over his naked hips before straightening without answering.

His gaze pierced hers. His arms crossed over his chest in a stance of pure power, and he looked straight down that arrogant nose of his as though he were lord of all he surveyed.

Her calm slipped, just a little bit, as she stared back at him incredulously, her fingers fisting in the sheet she held around her. "Have you lost your mind?"

"Do you have furniture that needs to be moved?"

"No, I don't," she replied with sugary sweetness. "Because I'm not moving in here with you indefinitely. As soon as I can, I'm returning to the house."

The house she shared with Alex was small and located farther outside of town than she liked, but it was nice. It was home.

It was nothing like the nice apartment she had shared with her roommate Mark and his lover Ty: the two-bedroom, ultramodern, brightly lit apartment with a balcony that overlooked the beach. It hadn't been home, though. Somerset was home.

"Tell me, Crista, do you *want* to die?" he asked her then. "Because you will. Those men at that warehouse weren't playing games with those bullets, fancy-face. They were serious. And now, someone else could possibly believe you have their money. How long do you think it will take them to find you and slit your throat in your sleep?"

Crista felt the color leech from her face.

"But I didn't have anything to do with that," she argued weakly, feeling the stupidity in her response even as it came out of her lips.

"You were there."

"Accidentally." She shook her head at the futility of her own argument. "Money's involved, right? They won't just kill me."

"No. They'll torture you first." He nodded with mock sobriety. "They'll tie you down, cut you a little, let you bleed some. Rape you, most likely." His gaze flickered over her with a flare of inner rage. "And when they realize you don't know anything, they'll really start having fun. You'll pray to die before they finish. Is that what you want?"

She was shaking by the time he finished, knowing he was right, knowing her life had just taken a very serious turn for the worse.

She breathed out wearily. "I don't have furniture. Just some clothes." And not a lot, at that. Most of her stuff she was still waiting for. Mark and Ty had been good enough to hold it for her until she had a place for it. She just hadn't found a place yet.

The same furniture and small items that she thought had been waiting for her at that warehouse. They hadn't been there. Her earlier call to Mark had confirmed that he hadn't sent anything.

A year.

Had a year really gone by since she left Virginia?

A year that she had been steeped in the memories she had deliberately pushed behind her when she left home. Memories that had the power to break her if she didn't get a handle on them. Getting a handle on them hadn't been easy.

He nodded abruptly. "Get your shower and get dressed. We'll pack the rest of your stuff and bring it here. You can keep your car in the private marina parking that Uncle Ray lets us use."

"I still need a job." Her chin lifted defiantly.

"I can put you to work at the lumber store." He shrugged. "I hear you're pretty slick in the office."

Crista's eyes narrowed. "I applied there months ago. There were no openings."

"I'm the boss; I'll make an opening," he gritted out.

"And you couldn't make one before I had to take that job at the diner?"

He grinned, devilry glittering in his gaze then. "I didn't have enough incentive then. Maybe I do now."

If she had something to throw at him, she would have given a pitch worthy of a baseball player at that moment, just to wipe the smirk off his face.

"You're a real ass, Dawg," she sneered instead.

"So I keep hearing, fancy-face. So I keep hearing."

Nine

Aaron Grael was dead, and no one else was talking. As far as the thieves and the buyers were concerned, there was no one missing from either little group. And that was bullshit. They already knew that, a million of the two million dollar price tag on the missiles had been paid to a middleman, or woman as the case may be. And Dawg knew Grael had been convinced Crista was that woman two seconds before Dawg killed him.

Dawg's report was turned in. He had seen Grael firing at the team; he had wounded several of them. Dawg had made the shot and taken him out. It wasn't exactly a lie, of course, but it wasn't the truth, either.

Now they had to figure out where the missing middle person was, where the money was, and how it affected the case.

The four experimental, newly designed Sidewinders could be launched from greater distances and carried an explosive weight nearly double their predecessors. And they could be nuclear-armed.

They were built with detonation chips, a safeguard that disabled the missiles entirely and effectively halted any chance of detonation or guidance of the weapon without them. They were to have been transported to Fort Knox without those chips before heading to another base. But, somehow, the Army fucked up. The missiles were shipped with their safety chips, and the shipment was hijacked.

Fortunately for the task force, it seemed the hijacking was done by a group with little or no experience in the stealing and selling of the Sidewinder missiles.

A Swedish mercenary had negotiated the buy for a Middle Eastern terrorist with fingers in damned near every conflict in the world. The Swede, alias Akron Svengaurrd, had contacted Aaron Grael for the exchange of half the money down and two of the safety and guidance chips. The rest of the money would come once the chips were authenticated—and the Army had made certain they were authenticated—and the missiles were in place for the Swede's team to pick up.

The operation the combined ATF and Homeland Security task force were working netted not just the thieves but the Swede as well. And it was the Swede they had wanted most. Him and the missiles.

The thieves might not have had much experience in the stealing and selling of weapons, but they were damned smart. And they had the contacts imperative in such a sell. It had also made them harder to catch. They were paranoid, and they were damned careful. And the only man they had a chance of getting any information out of was dead.

Because Dawg had a hard-on for Crista.

"The woman was there." Timothy Cranston wiped his hand over his balding crown in a sign of disgust as he handed out the reports to be passed around. "No one identified her; no one saw where she went."

"Do you think she killed Grael?" Greta Dane, a grimly determined agent at Dawg's right spoke up.

"Why would she kill him?" Natches snorted. "That's her money man. She would want him alive."

"He could identify her," Greta pointed out with a snide look in Natches's direction. "And he would have known there would be plenty of his guys left alive when the smoke cleared. Someone could have talked."

"She didn't kill our man," Timothy assured them all, glancing at Dawg. "Shot came from the back of the head and from Dawg's weapon. Autopsy confirmed it this morning. The camera's put our lady in front of him. After she disappeared behind those crates closest to the wall, she disappeared from sight completely. All we have on the outside cameras is some erratic shadowing too large to be a woman."

Dawg sat back in his chair and kept his mouth carefully shut. He didn't give a damn that Grael was dead, but he knew Cranston was pissed. Ultimately, it would work for them rather than against them. The Swede was a major player in several conflicts; just catching him had been an incredible coup.

Which was pretty much Cranston's opinion. But it also left the team with a contact they had been lusting after, a potential double agent.

And that was too bad. That contact was a dead end, and Dawg's lust had come first. He had dibs on it.

"I want to know who that woman was," Timothy barked in irritation. "Come on, boys and girls. All we have is brown hair, brown eyes, slender, and pretty. That's a third of the fucking women in this state or any other. If we get her, we get the money and hopefully break the silence among the thieves. This is the weak link, or they wouldn't be so nervous they're pacing their cells. She's our weak link. I can feel it."

Dawg almost grinned. Timothy's fat little hands were rubbing together in glee.

He was the most unlikely looking OHS agent that Dawg had ever seen. Portly, grandfatherly, the crown of his head shining, and the short gray hair around it standing out in spikes, he looked more like an accountant or overworked executive than one of the sharpest minds in Homeland Security.

"Dawg, have you or Natches heard anything new?" Timothy barked then.

The lumberyard and Natches's garage were two of the gossip points in the county. Information on the theft had come to Dawg's lumberyard before news of it had made the agency channels. Considering the fact that so far, news of it hadn't hit the television or radio stations, they were fairly certain it had to have leaked from the thieves themselves.

"Johnny's come up clear on involvement." Dawg grimaced at the thought of his estranged cousin, who raked on his nerves worse than nails over a chalkboard. The news of the hijacking had first come from Johnny when he stopped by the lumber store to buy shelving materials for the bakery goods store he owned outside of town. "We can't place him anywhere with our buyers or sellers, and according to the agent that questioned him, he overheard it at the store. But he gets a lot of customers, especially out-of-towners and soldiers from Fort Knox, so that makes sense. He could have just heard about the hijacking. And he likes to gossip about everything he hears."

Asking Johnny where he heard it hadn't worked out, and Dawg and Natches both knew better than to push it. The snaky little bastard would immediately see a weakness and strike.

"Would you know it if you even heard anything?" Greta suggested snidely, her honey-colored eyes gleaming with bitterness in her pale, freckled face.

It was rumored that she had lost family to a terrorist attack, and Dawg had always tried to temper his sarcasm toward her, for that fact alone, but her own bitterness was beginning to create a sense of tension in the team whenever she was around.

"Meaning?" He arched his brows mockingly.

"Meaning these are your people." She waved her hand to the files and reports. "Whoever stole the missiles knows this area like a native. Which means the woman is probably a native. You wouldn't suspect a friend or an ex-lover."

He heard Natches snort mockingly at that statement.

"Sweetheart, I live for paranoia. I suspect everyone but the Father, the Son, and the Holy Ghost." He gave her a toothy grin and watched as irritation thickened in her expression. "Are you in that group?"

"Dawg." Timothy's voice was a warning little snarl. He was always snarling when he wasn't rubbing his hands in glee.

Dawg turned back to him, his brow lifting in question as Natches smirked behind him.

"Don't you two get on my nerves." He pointed his finger back at them demandingly. "I won't be nice."

Bald and portly he might be, but he could put a hurtin' on the ego if a man wasn't careful.

"Go over that information, and we'll meet back here tomorrow afternoon," Timothy finally ordered with an edge of frustration. "Keep your eyes and ears open and hope we get something before the week is out, or my boss is going to rip all our asses. Boys, we don't want that."

Dawg flipped open the file, his gaze running over the pages in a slow scan. He was more concerned about finding any incriminating evidence that could have come up against Crista than he was information he had already read. If she was guilty, now was the best time to know. If she wasn't, then she would gain the benefit of the doubt until he saw otherwise. But not a lack of suspicion.

They were lucky. Crista had been in the shadows the entire time she had been there when the agents moving into the warehouse had assumed she was with the buyers. They had swarmed the back end of the cavernous building and worked their way forward.

Dawg had gone after Grael when the other man had sprinted for the shadowed, crated area in the front of the warehouse. Grael had gone after the woman he believed had betrayed him. If Dawg had been a second later, Crista would have died.

No one could possibly know Dawg was involved in this investigation. Other than the task force members, no one else could have known. And they were die-hard agents. It would shock him to his back teeth to find out one of them was a traitor.

But hell, he had been wrong before. And as he said, trust wasn't one of his virtues. If he even had a virtue. He was a vices type of guy, virtues weren't his strong point.

The file was empty of any incriminating evidence against Crista, which meant he didn't have to tell Cranston she was involved. At least, not just yet.

Slapping the file closed on the desk, Dawg rose to his feet and glanced at Natches. His cousin was rising from his own chair and snagged the dark glasses he had left lying on the table.

"Ready to roll?" Natches smirked, his dark, forest green eyes gleaming with amusement.

He knew Crista was waiting for them at the lumber store, safely ensconced in Dawg's office and going over his paperwork. Her eyes had gleamed in joy the minute she saw the mess his personal office had become over the past year. A man would think she was staring at diamonds rather than the paperwork from hell.

And Natches, being Natches, had found no end of amusement in the sight of Crista's curvy little ass plopping in Dawg's oversized chair as she told him, none too politely, to just get the hell out of her way while she organized his mess.

"Do you think I have an office to return to?" Dawg sighed the question in resignation.

"Think smelly candles and vases of flowers." Natches lifted his head, his nostrils flaring as though testing the air for a sweet scent. "I'm betting vanilla and roses," he said then, looking back at Dawg.

Hell, if all it took was the scent of vanilla and roses to keep her tight ass out of trouble, then he was all for it. He was to the point that he was ready to pull his hair out. He hadn't had her in his life forty-eight hours yet, and she already had him on such a tight edge that explosion was imminent.

Explosion of the sexual sort. He was so damned hard he was about to rupture his jeans with his erection. Or choke said erection with the confinement.

He hadn't had enough of her that morning. Hell, he had a feeling he could take her for hours and still not have enough of her.

As they left the small downstairs office Cranston had taken in the London, Kentucky, courthouse, Dawg stayed carefully on guard for watching eyes. Exiting the lower level, they were able to stay out of the main portion of the courthouse. The other agents used other exits, other hallways.

Paranoia. It had been bred into him by his coldly suspicious parents long before he ever joined the Marines and then the ATF. Even as a kid, too damned young to know what the word meant, he had begun to develop a suspicious nature.

Of course, with two cold, selfish egomaniacs as parents, how could he help it? His mother saw shadows in shadows, and everyone was out to get her. Emotions were her worst enemy, and she had fought against them tirelessly. And his father. Hell, his father had been as much a bastard as Natches's father was. Sometimes Dawg wondered how Rowdy had hit it so lucky. His father, Ray, had been tough but caring. And Rowdy had never suffered a beating in his life.

Until Dawg was old enough and big enough to fight back, his father had taken great delight in making his son cower.

Dawg hadn't inherited his father's habit of striking first, but his mother's insidious paranoia was a part of him.

So much so that he couldn't get out of his head the look in Crista's eyes when he asked her about a pregnancy. For a second, pain and fear and sorrow had flashed in the chocolate orbs. It had been so quick he couldn't even be certain it had been there. Paranoia or fact?

He shook his head as he and Natches moved toward their Harleys. Dawg pulled his dark glasses from his shirt pocket and placed them on his nose as he stared around the sunlit courthouse parking lot.

"Stop worrying so much," Natches murmured as they straddled the bikes. "We have any number of reasons for being here."

Dawg glanced over at him before turning the key and starting the cycle. The rough, dangerous rumble of the motor ignited beneath him. The relaxing sense of freedom it normally gave him was absent now.

He had found a new freedom. A new peace. That of being buried so deep inside Crista that he could feel her heartbeat.

Agonizing arousal clenched his cock and balls at the thought of taking her. The shock and surprise that had at first filled her eyes had been followed closely by desperation, desire, and emotions he didn't want to even think about. But she had burned him alive.

There had been more pleasure in her arms than he'd had in a lifetime of sexual acts, and that was damned scary.

Because he wasn't a fool. He knew what they were facing. One little slipup, one agent remembering the wrong thing, and he would be revealed; Crista would be betrayed. And, hell, that would suck. Because there wasn't a chance he was going to let Homeland Security get their hands on her.

If he was paranoid, then Homeland Security was over the limit. Even Cranston, as much as Dawg liked the special agent in charge of the investigation, was more paranoid than anyone Dawg had known before or since. He would jerk Crista out of Somerset and send her straight to a detention center out of the country. And once there, she would be buried in so much fucking red tape and shadows that he would never find her again.

Once they were far enough from London to find a relatively secure spot to pull into, Dawg and Natches turned their Harleys onto a secluded lane and pulled into the small, deserted clearing hidden from the road.

Cutting the motor, Dawg bit off a curse and stared around the clearing before turning his gaze to Natches.

"What did you find out?"

Natches had talked to the agents last night, subtly questioning them and covering Crista's ass.

"No one saw anything but me," he drawled. "I reported that you came in before me, and I borrowed your girlfriend's car to drive in. I was point, remember? No one can question me, because no one else knows any different."

Natches had indeed had point outside the front of the warehouse, communicating with the rest of the team that had been in place as the interested parties drove in. He'd announced the arrival of the woman, and in his voice Dawg had heard something the others hadn't. A warning.

"Watch the front, Dawg," Natches had drawled. Not because Dawg had been closest, as Cranston had reminded him sharply.

"My mistake," Natches had murmured into the communications link.

Dawg had known then. Natches didn't make mistakes, not like that. Whoever the woman was, something was wrong, and Dawg had moved to intercept her.

The agents assigned to this case were wild-eyed and bitter, paranoid and determined. And it didn't help one damned bit that Crista so closely resembled the superficial description they had of the woman acting as a contact point between the buyers and sellers.

"If someone set her up, then we need to know why." If someone set her up. Son of a bitch, he was aching so bad to fuck her that he was trying to find excuses where he knew he should be finding handcuffs instead.

"Someone's setting *you* up," Natches grunted as he stared at Dawg over the rim of his glasses. "And that's not a good thing. Who could know you're on the team?"

Dawg shook his head. "Better yet, who would know to use Crista if they did?"

Natches gave him a long, mocking look then. "Dawg, Cuz, who *doesn't know* that Crista Jansen is your weakness? You've been dogging her ass like a stray mutt for months now." Natches smirked at his own puns.

"Ha-ha," Dawg sneered.

Then he rubbed the back of his neck. Hell, had he been that transparent?

"Even Johnny noticed." Natches was gleefully snickering now. "And he just can't understand the attraction, doncha know?"

Dawg grimaced. Johnny Grace. He was a lousy damned excuse for a cousin. When Dawg's parents had been killed in an auto accident, Johnny's mother, Dawg's aunt, had decided to attempt to claim part of the estate Dawg's parents had left him. Dawg had spent a year protecting the inheritance that amounted to the only damned thing his parents had ever willingly given him.

And there had been Johnny, standing in a court of law, reciting his father's complaints against Dawg and swearing that his parents had meant to leave the better portion of their estate to his mother.

And through it all, Johnny had sneered and snidely reminded Dawg over and again that his relationship with Dawg's father had been much deeper than that of his son's.

Because Johnny was an ass-kissing little bastard that played up to Dawg's father's opinion of himself.

"Old man Thompson was by the garage this morning," Natches said then. "He was bitching about the lights moving back along the mountain last night behind his house. We could check it out again."

Again. That about summed it the hell up.

Dawg rubbed his hand over his stubbled cheeks before making a mental note to shave before rubbing on Crista again. She had razor burn on her neck that morning after her shower.

"Someone knows something, Dawg," Natches said softly. "They know enough to throw Crista at you to distract you. Give you someone to suspect."

Dawg shook his head. "I know better than to be distracted that easily. Besides, we have everything but the money and the woman. How am I a threat to either, as things stand now?"

"This is someone who doesn't know you heed your common sense when it's important," Natches pointed out. "This is someone who only knows the fact that Dawg distrusts everyone but the Father, the Son, and the Holy Ghost. Which could be just about everyone you've met in this country and a dozen others.

And it could be someone who is afraid one of the men we captured will talk. If he talks, who says they won't name Crista?"

Dawg wasn't known for his trusting nature.

"We'll let them think they've succeeded then." He smiled slowly, watching as Natches grimaced. "And Crista has an alibi. You were using her Rodeo; she was at home."

"Man, I hate that smile." Natches sighed, resignation glittering in his gaze. "What are you going to do?"

Dawg leaned forward, rested his forearms on the handlebars of the motorcycle, and let his grin widen.

"I'm going to let Crista distract me, of course. Why fight it? And while she's distracting, I'm going to see who's watching and what happens later. If she was thrown into my path to catch me off guard, then they threw her in for a reason. Let's see what they intend to do with it now that they have her there. And why it's so damned important that she be there. They couldn't have expected the raid. So their plans are going to be off balance."

"They expected her to be arrested, shipped off, and you running at her heels," Natches bit out. "Be careful they don't catch you in that little net, and you and Crista get shipped off together."

Yeah, that one had occurred to him around midnight.

"I guess I'll just have to take my chances. Hell, I've already broken more laws than I want to think about just getting her out of there. They told us to use initiative, but I don't think that's exactly what they were talking about."

"Sure it was," Natches drawled. "We knew she wasn't involved, so we evened the playing field with no fuss and no muss. Its redneck code. That's what we'll tell 'em." The laid-back country-boy drawl wouldn't fool anyone who happened to know Natches. There was pure bloodthirsty redneck bloodletting in that tone, and it was something Dawg knew he could count on. Natches would watch his back.

His and Crista's.

And that thought opened a whole other can of worms. One he wasn't ready to empty right now. He knew Natches hadn't taken Rowdy's defection from the ménages very well. He had waited, anticipated Rowdy's return and the slow seduction of his fiancée, Kelly. When Rowdy had put the skids on that idea, Natches had been downright pissed.

Hell, the sharing had been a part of their lives since their first sexual encounter as teenagers.

The widow Barnes. She had been soft and sweet, older, more experienced, and lonely enough to take three young boys to her bed.

At the time, no one knew she was also hiding from her psychotic husband, a man who had been watching the teenage Mackay cousins slip into her house, and through the window he had watched the sexual antics they had gotten up to.

That first foray into the dark sexuality of a ménage had come back to haunt them last year when the lady's son, warped beyond belief by his father's molestation of him and the beatings he had endured, had begun raping the girls he claimed as his own.

Then he had targeted Rowdy's stepsister and the woman that held Rowdy's heart, Kelly Salyers. The bastard had nearly killed them all before they stopped him.

And now, Natches was in the cold again, and Dawg knew that was how he had to be feeling. And he was withdrawing. Dawg had been feeling it for a while now. Natches was drifting away from them; the connection that had held him with his cousins all these years was gone now. The ménages, the emotional bond they created, Natches didn't have that anymore.

"Come on, Dawg, stop wrestling over it," Natches advised somberly. "Let's play this out and see what the hell happens. I have an SOS out to her brother, Alex. The minute his head pops out of whatever hole the government sent him to, then he'll come running with backup."

"We'll play it out." Dawg breathed out roughly before pushing his sunglasses back up his nose.

There wasn't much more they could do. Someone else, someone who knew too much, had dealt Crista into a very deadly game. To save her now, Dawg was going to have to risk everything and pray to God they caught the thieves before the Swede pulled in friends or the task force learned she was at the warehouse. If that happened, all shit was going to hit the fan.

"Look, man, we're backup mostly. The majority of the investigation is being handled by those HS tightwads. They won't call us until something gets ready to go down anyway. We just lie back and keep watch on Miss Crista's tight little rear, and we'll do fine."

Dawg's gaze sharpened on his cousin. "*I'll* watch her rear."

It came out harsher than he had meant, a snapping reply he would have never intended.

Natches's lips quirked mockingly, but Dawg saw the knowledge in his eyes. He also saw a vague edge of distance settle over the other man's face as he nodded slowly.

"You watch her ass. I'll just watch. Whatever." He turned the switch and kicked the Harley's motor in gear before pulling out without saying anything more and leaving Dawg to follow.

Damn it to hell. Dawg hit the ignition and gunned the motor, feeling an edge of anger beginning to burn inside him. It wasn't supposed to be like this, was it? He, Rowdy, and Natches had been closer than brothers all their lives. They had fucked the same women, loved the same women, until Kelly, and now Crista.

Dawg wasn't a fool. He might not love Crista, but that edge of possessiveness had been there, even eight years before. Growing up was hell. Maturing was even worse. Three men who had been as close as ticks to a hound dog eight years ago were fading apart and, Dawg admitted, sometimes it sucked. And sometimes, like now, there was an edge of relief.

But a part of him knew that Natches was being affected worst by the maturity of his two older cousins. For Natches, the sharing had never been a game; it had just taken Rowdy and Dawg longer to see it. For Natches, it was a part of who he was, and losing that connection was starting to affect the other man in ways Dawg hadn't anticipated.

Damn, he would have ripped his own arm out to have kept this from happening. He and Rowdy had always gone out of their way to protect Natches, even as a kid. And maybe as an adult, too.

Somewhere along the way, they had all grown up, though. Even Natches. To the point that the other man had become even harder, darker, than Dawg or Rowdy. Which explained how Natches had stepped into the role of an assassin that last year he had been in the Marines. An assassin the military had been loath to lose when Natches had taken a bullet in the shoulder during a skirmish in Iraq on his off time.

Natches had stepped out of the Marines darker, harder, and more dangerous than he had been when he, Dawg, and Rowdy had stepped into basic training.

Yeah, they had all grown up. But sometimes Dawg wondered if they had grown up for the better.

Ten

She was making headway. Crista stared at the top of the surprisingly nice desk. Walnut, if she wasn't mistaken, and rather old with deep drawers on each side. The middle drawer had been removed; in its place was a keyboard shelf where the computer keyboard rested.

She hadn't powered up the computer; she had to clean it first. There was so much dust gathered around the tower that she had been half afraid to turn it on.

It didn't make sense. The houseboat was spotless. She hadn't seen so much as a dish or an article of clothing out of place. But the office was a war zone. Scattered files and papers, miscellaneous receipts—receipts for God's sake; how the hell did he pay his taxes?—and a variety of other papers, files, and memos that she knew had to be important.

Those scattered on the desk were now neatly filed. Of course, that was after she had spent hours straightening out his filing system. Not that she was finished with that chore. Last year's files were mixed with this year's files, and the aging metal file cabinet was was about to give its last groan of effort and collapse into the floor.

She glanced to the glass door, looking onto the floor from the view the office commanded. She had sent two of the stock boys for the nice wooden file cabinets she knew sat in the office supply section of the lumber store.

Dawg was smart. He had taken ideas from several smaller

chains and incorporated them into Mackay's Lumber, Building and Supplies, the business his father had left him.

There was every manner of appliance, office needs, paints, and hobby supplies as well as a mix of seasonal items that added to the sales from the lumberyard.

It was a thriving business if the customers below were anything to go by. Yet, from what she had seen in this office, Dawg rarely made the effort it took to keep everything together.

She knew a manager had overseen the business while he was in the Marines. A man Dawg had promptly fired when he returned home to learn the manager had been systematically embezzling from him.

According to the floor manager, Dawg had nearly gone bankrupt that first year after his return, despite the steady business that came through the large double doors.

There was no danger of bankruptcy now. An audit, maybe. Terminal mismanagement of his office for certain. But not bankruptcy, because despite the "hellhole," as she had called it, there had been a very weird sort of system that Dawg had going on. Just not a system that anyone else could have worked with.

Shaking her head, she moved from the now-cleaned desk to the stack of files, folders, papers, books, and every manner of receipt awaiting her stacked on the other side of the room in front of the large, overstuffed couch.

Evidently Dawg also liked his creature comforts. The couch was long enough and most likely wide enough for him to sleep on. There was a plasma television off to the side, a microwave, and mini refrigerator stocked with beer. Just beer.

It was too bad he didn't like a neat office to go with his creature comforts. But, to be on the fair side, the seating area was ridiculously neat until Crista began stacking the slush inside the area.

She wiped her palms down her jeans and glanced at her watch before breathing out a weary sigh. Dawg was supposed to have picked her up thirty minutes ago to collect her car and her clothes.

He had stashed her in his office with a firm warning to stay put, then headed out with no more information than the approximate time he would be back.

And while he had been gone, she had been thinking.

What happened at the warehouse made absolutely no sense whatsoever to her. The fact that the note from the delivery company was missing from her car made even less sense. About as much sense as the other items that had come up missing over the last few months, just to turn back up days later. She had meant to look for the note. It must have slipped onto the floor or between the seats, but Dawg hadn't given her a change to search for it.

She propped her elbow on her knee and cupped her fingers in her hand, a frown tightening her brow as she tapped her lips with her fingers.

Why would she be deliberately drawn to the warehouse?

Unless someone wanted to mess up something Dawg was doing. It wouldn't take a rocket scientist to figure out he had been chasing her ever since he had learned of her return to Somerset.

And in doing it, they had given him the perfect opportunity to blackmail her.

Would he really turn her over to the authorities? Damn, he had looked serious, sounded serious. And he warned her in no uncertain terms not to discuss the other night with anyone.

She jerked to her feet and paced to the wide door with its tinted window to stare at the busy floor below. She was in trouble, and she knew it. She had known it even before she bumbled into the warehouse; she just hadn't wanted to admit it. Even Alex had had enough sense to know something was wrong. He would have never told her to call Dawg otherwise. Because he must have known that Dawg was some kind of agent. Alex would have known that Dawg would have the means to find out what was going on.

But Alex couldn't have known the fee Dawg would require: her body.

She shivered at the memory.

He had caught her off guard, she assured herself; otherwise, she would have never given in to him. He had been inside her before she could assimilate the change from anger to passion, even within her own body.

And her body had betrayed her. She had been so slick, so wet, that even now her face flamed in mortification. Even as she grew wetter.

She was going to have to buy more panties at this rate.

She glanced at her watch again. Nearly an hour late. If she didn't pick up her car, it was going to be towed.

What would it have hurt to let her go ahead and pick up the rest of her stuff and then meet him here? It was broad daylight. She didn't exactly live in the boondocks, and she had neighbors.

Besides, other than Dawg, Natches, and that insane person who tried to shoot her, no one knew she was at the warehouse. Except whoever sent her to the warehouse to begin with.

She shoved her hands in the pockets of her jeans and continued to stare into the sales floor. She would give him a few more minutes. If he wasn't back in a few minutes, then she would catch a ride from here to the diner where her Rodeo was still parked. It was no more than a half dozen blocks. Broad daylight. She could have her car back and her meager belongings packed and waiting in the front of the store before he returned.

It wasn't like there was much to pack.

As the thought zipped through her mind, her gaze landed on the short, leanly built man moving through the register counter below.

A smile lit her face.

Johnny Grace owned the little bakery store on the land next to her and Alex's house. The scent of the delicacies wafting through the air nearly drove her crazy on her off days.

He was obviously ringing up his purchases, flashing a smile to the checkout boy and flirting easily. Johnny wasn't deterred when it came to his sexual lifestyle. He enjoyed men more than he did women, and he saw no reason to hide it.

She glanced at her watch. She could be back before Dawg ever knew she was gone.

She grabbed her purse from the table next to her, opened the door, and hurried out before locking it as Johnny headed for the automatic doors.

"Crista." He stopped and blinked quickly as she moved around the registers and called out his name. "What are you doing here?"

She flicked her fingers to the upstairs office. "New job." *Or something.* "Look, I left my car at the diner. Could you give me a ride?"

He was maybe a quarter inch taller than she was, but she wasn't betting on it. He glanced to the door, then smiled again.

"Are you sure you want me to give you a ride? Dawg and I aren't on the best of terms. If you two have something going here, then he's liable to be a tad upset if you go anywhere with me."

She flicked a glance to the doors. Nope, no Dawg in sight.

"Dawg is always upset over something." She swallowed back her own trepidation at the thought. "And I promise, I won't tell him who offered me a lift."

She smiled back at him with an edge of desperation.

Johnny chuckled in amusement, shaking his head at her, his dark blond curls tumbling about his face. He really should have been born a woman, she thought. He had a soft, feminine air about him, an almost gentle demeanor. And he was nice. He shared his baked delights with her on her off days when the store below was closed and he was alone putting together the next week's confections. And it wasn't as though Dawg could be jealous.

"Come on then." He nodded toward the doors. "I'll give you a lift. Are you coming back here or heading home?"

"I'm going home." She neglected to mention why she was going home. That was a subject she didn't want to get into just now.

Following Johnny through the doors, she glanced around quickly, expecting any minute to see Dawg bearing down on her like some avenging angel.

Yes, he had told her to stay put, but he was late, and the precautions made no sense. By his own report, the man who saw her was dead, and the other suspects had been arrested or were dead. No one else but Dawg and Natches could know she was there. No one was going to step out from behind a vehicle or a building and start shooting anyway.

Were they?

"When did you start working for Dawg?" Johnny drew her attention away from her morbid paranoia as he glanced behind his shoulder to show her a warm smile.

"Just today." She drew level with him, gazing around in front of her. "How far away did you park?"

Johnny laughed. "The far end. This is how I work off all those calories I add into my body on baking days."

The other side of the parking lot was no joke.

The early June heat was bearing down on them, causing a

fine film of perspiration to break out on Crista's face as they reached the late-model Taurus Johnny drove.

He unlocked her door with a florish. "Roll down the window," he advised. "The air conditioner went out last week, and I haven't had a chance to get it fixed yet."

She rolled down the window before closing the door and snapped her seat belt in place.

Still no Dawg.

She was tired of waiting for Dawg. The danger he kept harping on couldn't be too high, or he wouldn't have left her alone for hours at the lumber store.

She was really rethinking this whole danger and blackmailing business. She was starting to wonder if the danger wasn't more in Dawg's mind than in her life, and was just a ready means of getting her into his bed. After all, they had arrested those guys at the warehouse. And whoever got away with the money was probably spending it right now in the Bahamas or something.

And why hadn't she thought of that one before now? she asked herself as Johnny moved into the driver's seat and started his car.

"Where were you the other night?" he asked, startling her out of her thoughts. "I was at the store until late, and you still weren't home."

She glanced at him, surprised he had noticed. "I was, uhh, with Dawg."

And Dawg was making her paranoid, because suddenly she felt nervous, uncertain. Why would Johnny care where she was? Why would he check to see that she wasn't home?

Johnny faced forward as he started the car and brushed back a curl from his cheek.

"With Dawg, huh?" he asked curiously.

Technically. For a little while. "Yes," she answered carefully.

His lips turned up into a grin as he glanced over her and put the car in gear. Driving from the parking lot, he turned onto the interstate that led back to the main street of Somerset before flicking her another look.

"Be careful, Crista." He finally sighed. "You know, we call him Dawg for a reason, right?"

The gentleness in his voice had her hackles rising. She could feel the judgment in his tone and she didn't like it. She wasn't a child anymore, and she had endured enough lectures eight years before. She didn't need any more.

"Because he's stubborn?" she batted at him sweetly. "Come on, Johnny, I'm a big girl here. I can handle Dawg."

She heard lightning struck in cases of whopper lies like that one. She looked up at the clear blue sky. Not a cloud in sight, thank God.

Johnny only chuckled. "So, did he bring along the rest of the team, or was he solo?"

She nearly gaped back at him. "That's a rude question, Johnny." And it made her more nervous, more uncertain, and even more aware of the enmity that existed between Johnny and Dawg. Leaving with Johnny hadn't been a good idea.

"And entirely qualified." Johnny rolled his eyes. "Darling, despite Kelly's determination to hold out, its more than obvious those three have been working her for years. They saved her for Rowdy, and he will share her eventually. It's a delicate little seduction technique they use. How delicate the seduction determines how serious they are about the prey."

"Oh Lord, you make them sound like wolves."

"Very well-bred wolves, I'm certain." Johnny laughed. "And you didn't answer my question."

"Dawg was traveling alone that night," she assured him. "Otherwise, I wouldn't have been with him." Was that a cloud overhead? A rumble of thunder maybe?

Okay, no thunder. But there were two Harleys behind them, the smooth rumble of their motors reminding her of Alex.

"Interesting," Johnny murmured as he flicked on the turn signal and pulled into the turn lane to head into the smaller road that led into the old center of the city.

"Just interesting?" She smothered a yawn, wishing he would hurry.

"Dawg never seemed the possessive sort to me." Johnny shrugged. "But as I said, it's usually a seduction technique. He has any number of interesting games he's played over the years. He does give the family plenty to gossip over."

Suddenly, being here just didn't feel right. It was obvious that despite their familial connection that Johnny liked Dawg even less than he claimed Dawg liked him. Not that she figured the whole family feud thing was any of her business, but right now, it paid to be just a little wary of Dawg.

"And we're definitely in trouble," Johnny suddenly claimed morosely, his lips pursing into a pout as he glanced at the rearview mirror.

Crista twisted around in the seat, her eyes widened, then she flopped forward again and crossed her arms over her breasts.

Dawg and Natches were riding behind the car like denim-clad motorized warriors. Their expressions were stony, and the smile Dawg had flashed her was anything but friendly. It reminded her of a shark.

"Just drop me off in front of the diner, Johnny." She sighed. "I'll be okay there."

"Are you sure?" A delicate frown formed between his brows. "I feel a little funny just leaving you with him like this. Dawg isn't always predictable."

She snorted. That was an understatement if she ever heard one.

"I can handle Dawg." She hoped.

She waited as Johnny pulled to the curb several minutes later and stopped the car. She didn't give him time to say anything. She stepped quickly from the car, slammed the door, and then turned her back on all of them and moved for the narrow alley that led to the back lot.

Dawg was right behind her, and so was Natches. Opening her purse, she pulled her keys free, refusing to glance around. He had no right to intimidate her. And if she let him keep doing it, then it would never stop.

As she reached her car and unlocked it, she turned back then, lifting her brows at the two men watching her with equally fierce expressions from the motorcycles that pulled in behind her little red Rodeo.

Déjà vu. She wondered if she would end up leaving with her car this time.

The engines were cut, leaving the parking lot strangely silent, as though even the breeze itself were wondering what they would do now.

"I see you've been out having fun." She flicked a glance to the motorcycles.

"Get on." Dawg jerked his head to the side, indicating the back of the motorcycle.

"I don't think so," she said brightly. "I'm going to go home, pack the rest of my stuff, and I'll meet you back at the boat later. Why don't you and Natches there go take the edge off your tempers somewhere? I'm not in the mood to deal with it."

He swung his leg over the seat of the motorcycle as he rose, clad in faded jeans and a white, short-sleeved, buttoned shirt, he looked like the ultimate bad boy. A ravisher, a modern-day warrior.

The sight of his black hair blowing in the breeze and his light green eyes glittering in his dark face had a rush of damp warmth spilling from her vagina.

As though she hadn't been wet enough to begin with.

"Dawg." She sighed. "Don't start trying to intimidate me, okay? We both know damned good and well no one but you and whoever left that notice knew I was there last night. You're trying to control me, and a good blackmailer sticks to the main object; he doesn't blackmail for the air a person breathes. Okay?"

His eyes narrowed. "You have it all worked out, don't you, fancy-face?"

"Stop calling me that." She hated the nickname he had given her as a teenager. It had caused her no end of teasing for years. "Now, you can follow me to the house and help me finish packing, or you can go back where you came from. Your choice."

She lifted herself into the driver's seat, closed the door, and shoved the key into the ignition. She gave it a quick turn, and nothing happened. The starter clicked hollowly, but the motor didn't turn over. Frowning, she released it, then moved to turn it again.

Before she could complete the motion, the door jerked open, and she barely had time to gasp before Dawg was pulling her free of the vehicle, his expression fierce as he all but lifted her off her feet and rushed away from the vehicle.

"What the hell are you doing?" She tugged at the arm latched around her waist and stared back at her Rodeo. It was sitting there, door open, deserted, as Dawg pushed her to the motorcycle and turned back to the vehicle.

"Dawg. I'm tired. I'm dusty. And I need the rest of my clothes. If you don't have a really, really good reason—"

A loud, wrenching pop jerked her gaze back to the Rodeo. A Rodeo whose little red hood was tossed into the air like a Frisbee. The front of the vehicle suddenly shot up in flames.

Lots of flames. So fast and so hot that within a second the interior was a red, furious blaze as she stood in shock, trying to comprehend exactly what had happened.

The hood landed on the other side of the parking lot, the crash of metal to asphalt barely registering as she watched Dawg and Natches tearing toward the vehicle, the fire extinguishers they carried in the saddle packs of their motorcycles gripped in their hands.

Diners came running from the back door. The cook lugged out a larger extinguisher, and someone yelled that the fire department was on their way. And all Crista could do was stare at the driver's seat, engulfed in flames, and feel the ice moving through her body.

It appeared that Dawg had been right after all.

Eleven

"I hope the three of you have some damned good explanations, because I'm not really happy with you right now."

Sheriff Ezekiel Mayes, Zeke to his friends, didn't bother glancing at Crista or Kelly Salyers, who had arrived at the diner with her fiancé within half an hour of the initial explosion. He trained his light brown eyes on the three cousins instead, a hard frown pulling at his forehead.

"Don't look at me, Zeke." Rowdy shook his head, his short black hair gleaming beneath the bright overhead lights. "I just came by to make sure they were still alive." He nodded toward his cousins, a friendly smile on his lips, though his gaze was cool and warning.

The three cousins sat at the large, round table in the back of the dining room. Kelly was placed between Rowdy and Natches, and Crista between Dawg and Natches. The scene couldn't have been more incriminating, considering the Mackay cousins' reputations.

"Zeke, you keep forgetting they've grown up." Kelly leaned forward, propping her chin on her hand as she braced her elbow on the table and grinned back at the sheriff with a winning smile.

"And you used to be such a sweet, honest little thing." The sheriff clucked in disapproval. "Lying for these boys only gets everyone in trouble, Kelly. Remember?"

Kelly grimaced. "They caught him."

She was obviously talking about the stalker who had nearly killed her and the three cousins last summer.

"I could have caught him faster if these three yahoos had told me what the hell they were doing," he grunted, eying the yahoos in question. "Am I going to get any better answers this time?" His gaze finally moved to Crista. "Alex asked me to watch after you before he left, Crista. Are you going to help me out?"

She tried to smile, but her face felt frozen. "Zeke, if I knew anything, I promise I'd tell you. I don't know myself what happened."

Zeke grunted at that. "You have a homemade detonation device set in your vehicle that created enough heat to burn your flesh off your bones, and you don't know why?"

Crista's stomach rolled threateningly.

"Hell, Zeke, go a little easier on her," Dawg bit out. "She doesn't know what the hell is going on, and neither do we. I heard the ignition click and jerked her out of the vehicle in time. It was that simple. I do have a bit of experience with these things, you know."

Zeke's gaze lingered a little too long on Dawg before he turned back to Crista. "I'm going to have to start warning the women around here about getting mixed up with these boys. Bad things seem to follow them nowadays." He took the remaining chair, straddling it with an easy motion and leaning his darkly tanned forearms on the table as he stared back at Crista. "Why does someone want to kill you, Crista Ann?"

She felt the color leech from her face as Dawg's arm suddenly came around her shoulders, his chair moving in closer to hers.

"For God's sake, Zeke," he snarled. "Have a little compassion here."

Zeke didn't take his eyes off her. "Crista, you're a smart girl," he said softly. "Alex raised you to think on your feet. Let me help you."

She shook her head. She had already ignored Dawg once by leaving the store and coming out on her own. She had almost died because of it. She was too stunned now, too frightened, to consider ignoring him again.

"I don't know why." Her lips felt numb, her body cold.

"Any strange goin' ons?" Zeke's gaze sharpened as Dawg's hand tightened warningly on her shoulder.

She could feel his heat surrounding her, but it wasn't touching the core of ice that seemed to solidify inside her chest.

She shook her head. Lying. She was lying through her teeth to friends now, covering up something that Zeke should know about.

"If nothing's going on, then why did Alex call me last week and ask me to keep an extra eye on you?" he asked her then. "He said you had mentioned some strange things then, Crista." His voice was gentle but firm. He knew she was lying.

"I'm not used to living alone," she whispered. "I was a little freaked out when I talked to him. The house sounds funny sometimes."

And it did. Sometimes, she could have sworn someone was moving around the house at night, though she had never been able to find any proof of it. That wasn't a lie, but it felt like one, because she wasn't telling Zeke the whole truth.

He sighed then. "Anyone from Virginia that you think might want to hurt you? What about that guy Alex said you were living with? Mark?"

"Mark Lessing." The tension around the table was suddenly thick enough to cut with a knife. Dawg tightened subtly, his body seeming to shift with dangerous force.

She looked at him in confusion, seeing the glitter of an inner flame in his eyes that had the blood suddenly rushing through her body with dizzying force. She swallowed tightly before forcing her gaze back to Zeke.

"Mark wouldn't hurt me. He has no reason to want to hurt me."

"So your relationship with him ended amicably?" Zeke asked curiously. "That's a little unusual. Relationships don't just end with no anger on either side."

"Nothing ended." She shrugged. "I came home. Mark agreed it was time. End of story."

Zeke glanced at Dawg. "You believe that?"

"What kind of game are you playing, Zeke?" Dawg asked then.

Zeke blinked with a look of studied male mockery. "Just trying to figure out the rules of the game you're playing, Dawg. Leave me in the dark, and that's what I tend to do."

"He's not playing any games." Crista clenched her fists in her lap as she fought to control the shaking of her limbs. "Nothing has been going on. Mark wouldn't hurt me, and neither would anyone else I know. I don't know what happened out there or why anyone would want to hurt me."

And she was a lousy liar.

Zeke breathed out wearily as he leaned back in his chair and regarded them all cynically. "When you think you can tell me the truth, Crista, you know how to get hold of me," he finally said, then stared back at Dawg. "You know what Alex will do if she gets hurt, right? He'll come down on the three of you like a wrecking ball. It won't be pretty."

"Come on, Zeke, threats don't work." Dawg rose from his seat before gripping Crista's arm and drawing her up with him. "If you have any more questions, she'll be on the boat with me or working in my office."

Zeke's gaze flicked to the hold Dawg had on her before his eyes lifted back to hers.

"If she's not in trouble, then why isn't she staying at her place?"

"Because she moved in with me yesterday," Dawg answered coolly. "We were heading to her house to pack her stuff when this happened."

Crista was suddenly aware of the other diners packed into the restaurant, their curious gazes following them, even though the table had been moved far enough away to give the sheriff the privacy he needed to question them.

And those curious diners couldn't have helped but overhear Dawg's little announcement.

"Well, I know where to find her then, that's all that matters." Zeke moved smoothly to his feet, his leanly muscled body flexing in frustration as he glanced around the table again. "Natches, Rowdy, next time I have proof you're pulling ops behind my back, I'm going to arrest every damned one of you. I'm giving you fair warning now."

Ops. Operations. Crista knew that word, she had heard Alex use it often enough.

"Save it, Zeke." Natches followed Rowdy and Kelly as they rose from their seats as well. "We're not running ops on you. And if we were, we would know how to cover our asses."

Zeke breathed out in exasperation. "Unfortunately, that's too true." He stood as well, his gaze coming back to Crista. "Have you talked to Alex yet?"

She shook her head. "He's out of the country."

Zeke nodded. "I put out a call to his CO, and he told me the same thing. Any idea when he'll be back?"

"When he gets back."

Zeke's questions were beginning to grate on her nerves, especially when it was more than obvious that he knew the answers before he did the asking.

Zeke nodded again, his gaze going over the five of them before it landed on Kelly once more. "You're letting them get you in trouble again, Kel. Not a good idea?"

At that, Kelly's laughter whispered around the table. "Zeke, they are trouble, remember? But in this case, I promise you, I'm innocent as a babe."

His lips twitched at that, and an edge of amusement filled his gaze. "Course you are, Kel." He chuckled. "And it's more than obvious that fiancé of yours is a damned bad influence. Not that I expected anything less. You, my girl, are a little too easily taken in by that rogue's smile of his."

"Ease up, Zeke." Though his voice was amused, there was an edge of steel in Rowdy's voice. "We need to get Crista back to the marina and let Dawg get her settled. Her nerves are raw, and so are ours. Like you said, you know where to find her if you have any more questions."

Crista let Dawg lead her from the diner then, aware that the sheriff watched them leave, suspicion shadowing his gaze. Not that he didn't have a damned good reason to be suspicious. She knew Zeke, and knew, from the conversations she had with her brother in the past, how seriously he took his job and the protection of the county. And suspicion meant a challenge to Zeke. He wasn't going to just let this go.

"Just hang on." Dawg's voice was a whisper of sound as he led her from the diner. "We're almost clear." He turned to Rowdy. "Did you bring the pickup?"

"Dad drove yours in," Rowdy answered softly as they moved toward the parking lot. "He's waiting to take your Harley back to the marina. We sure as hell didn't want to leave it here."

Crista wrapped her arms across herself as Dawg led her to the big black pickup truck that she had ridden in the day before.

Her life had definitely gone beyond Mercury in retrograde. Car bombs were major catastrophes, not fate fucking with you.

"We'll meet you back at your place," Rowdy told him as they neared the pickup, and Ray Mackay opened the door and stepped from it.

Rowdy's tan pickup sat beside it, and Dawg's and Natches's cycles on the other side. Ray lifted the rifle he carried from the seat, unloaded it, and calmly reached in to hang it on the gun rack that stretched across the back window.

"Few curiosity seekers and that rabid little twit Johnny," he grunted as they neared him. "Little bastard. His daddy would roll over in his grave if he knew how that boy turned out."

Crista stared at Ray in surprise. "Johnny Grace?"

"Grace my ass," he muttered. "That bitch that spawned him had to have gotten the sperm donor from someone other than Ralph. Ralph was a fine man. Ain't none of him in that boy."

"Easy, Dad." Rowdy's voice was clearly warning. "Johnny probably just wanted to check on Crista. They're neighbors. Kind of."

Ray's eyes speared into her then. "Don't tell me you befriended that little shit?"

"Johnny's always been kind to me, Mr. Mackay," she said, wishing she didn't sound so weak, so tired. "He wouldn't have meant any harm."

She was aware of the gazes now trained on her in disbelief. Her chin lifted. She didn't base her opinions or her friendships on others' opinions, and she wasn't going to start now. "Fine. For some reason you don't like Johnny, and from what he said earlier, there's not a lot of love lost. That's none of my business, and it has nothing to do with me." And she was too tired right now to make sense of any of it.

She respected Ray Mackay, trusted him. The fact that he so intensely disliked his own nephew was telling. But until Crista understood why, she wasn't going to automatically dislike him herself. She would definitely be wary, but she would reserve judgment.

Ray turned his gaze from her to Dawg as he rubbed his hand over is face in agitation before he and Dawg seemed to share some private communication. Crista hated private communications between men. She wasn't a male mind reader, so she didn't consider it fair in her presence.

"I'll take care of her, Ray," Dawg finally murmured.

"You know, you could get on my nerves fairly quickly," she told them with no small amount of her own irritation. "If you want to take care of me so damned bad, take me to get my clothes, and then leave me alone to shower and sleep."

"We'll stop on the way to the marina and buy you a few more things," Dawg told her firmly, causing her to freeze and stare back at him in disbelief.

"You said we could pick up my stuff from the house. Damn it, Dawg, I can't just go out and buy more clothes."

"And that was before someone decided to turn you into a piece of charcoal," he snapped back. "I'm not even attempting that house with you along. I'll go check it out myself in the morning and get your stuff. Until then, we can stop on the way home and buy you a few extra things."

She was aware of the interested gazes on them. The men were watching with expressions varying between amusement and wariness, and Kelly shook her head back at Crista warningly from Dawg's side.

The men she could have ignored, but there was something in Kelly's eyes that warned Crista that now wasn't the time to push Dawg. And that sucked. Because she wanted her own clothes; she didn't want to have to spend the small amount of savings she had on clothes she didn't need.

"I'll just use your damned washer tonight," she finally retorted. She wasn't about to end up more in debt to him than it already appeared she was going to be.

"Just get in the truck." He didn't wait for her to follow the harshly worded order. Dawg gripped her waist and lifted her in before crowding in beside her and forcing her to climb over the console to the passenger seat.

As she faced forward and stared through the windshield, she was faced with her poor little burned Rodeo. She had loved that little SUV.

The engine flared to life. As it did, Crista glanced over to see Dawg's hands wrapped around the steering wheel with a white-knuckled, furious grip.

"Is Lessing who you left here with?" His voice was cold, furious.

"Yes." She kept her voice soft, kept it calm.

Mark and Ty had come from Virginia that week eight years ago to inform Alex, their former Special Forces commander, why they were discharged from the Army. She had left with them when they returned home. It was supposed to have been a temporary thing. Instead, they had all become friends, family in a strange kind of way, and she hadn't moved out until returning home the year before.

"You left me for another man?"

She stayed silent, despite the shaking in the pit of her stomach. She could lie to the sheriff but not to Dawg, not about this. The words would choke her to death.

"Crista, so help me God, you better answer me now." His voice was a graveled, curt sound that had her flinching imperceptibly.

"I didn't leave you for another man," she finally answered evenly.

She had left him because of two other men, the men he had been intent on sharing her with. Then she had left town because she couldn't bear the hollow pain that burned inside her months later.

"But you went with another man?" His voice was harsher, if possible.

"I left Somerset with Mark. I moved in with Mark. I lived with him for seven years. Is that what you want to know?

He turned his head toward her, his eyes glittering back at her with burning male lust and anger.

"No. What I want to know is, did you sleep with the son of a bitch?"

She drew in a slow, deep breath. "I slept with him often."

Three hours later, Dawg pulled Crista inside the dimly lit houseboat where Natches waited silently, jerked the door closed, and locked it, before tossing the handful of plastic shopping bags filled with clothes to the couch.

His fingers were latched around her wrist, where he had learned fast to keep them as he forced her through the store and chose the clothing himself.

There were some panties in there that had his dick throbbing at the thought of pulling them from her body. Lacy little push-up bras, skimpy little pj's, some low-rise jeans and high-rise shirts that were guaranteed to make his blood boil if he caught another man staring at her.

As he released her, Natches uncurled his body from the deep shadows in the corner of the room, rising from the recliner and watching them expectantly.

"What is he doing here?" She flicked Natches an irritated glare.

She was irritated, and he was still so damned mad he was wearing his back teeth down.

"He," Natches drawled, "is being a Good Samaritan. I brought the rest of your thirsty plants." He indicated the freshly watered greenery sitting on the dining table. "And your personal stuff." He grinned as though proud of himself. "I knew Dawg was buying you new clothes, so I didn't bother with those."

Dawg watched Crista carefully. He could see the mad washing over her expression, the light flush that stained her cheeks, and the glitter of it in her eyes.

"Of course you didn't bother," she muttered through her teeth. At least Dawg wasn't the only one gritting his molars. "Wouldn't it just suck to spoil Dawg's fun?"

"Hell yeah." Natches breathed as though relieved that she understood some complicated dilemma. "We're real careful not to spoil Dawg's fun. That could get bloody."

As Crista swung around, Dawg ducked his head, hiding a grin that tugged involuntarily at his lips. Natches could play the fool better than anyone Dawg knew. He could be playful, teasing, almost innocent. As long as one didn't make the mistake of staring into the cold depths of his frozen green eyes.

As Dawg glanced down, he got a generous view of her well-rounded breasts heaving beneath her T-shirt and her fists clenching at her side.

"You have your clothes." He jerked his head to the bags. "You can take a shower now and change. I'll order something to eat."

"Shove it," she snapped.

"Don't tempt me, sugar girl." Tension fairly snapped through him, he was so damned on edge, so horny and pissed off that he didn't know if he could trust himself to keep his hands off her or not. "Because shoving it is something I could do real easy right now."

He watched her eyes widen in shock and surprise before the glitter of anger increased.

"You are not intimidating me, Dawg," she retorted.

And she looked serious.

Dawg grinned. A slow, easy curve of his lips as he let his hands move to his belt, jerking the slack through his belt loops and pulling at the buckle. Her eyes widened. Her lips parted. Dawg watched as her gaze jerked to Natches before she grabbed the bags and ran like a rabbit that just caught sight of the wicked wolf.

Natches was chuckling as she sprinted up the curving stairs, never pausing to look back.

"Man, she should have gotten a clue with the smile," Natches snorted as he turned back, his gaze smug as Dawg readjusted his belt.

Amusement lingered in Natches's expression, but there was regret lurking in his eyes.

Dawg knew where the regret stemmed from. He wouldn't be sharing in this relationship between Crista and Dawg. As fiery, as problematic and irritating as it was shaping up to be, he would be on the outside looking in. And that was a helluva place to be.

Dawg shook his head. "What did you see after we left?"

Natches pushed his fingers through his shoulder length, straight black hair as a grimace contorted his rough hewn features.

"I saw Johnny. He was watching you and Crista like a beady-eyed little snake from the corner as you drove off. You could see his brain just calculating ways to use this. The little twit. Other than that, all I saw were the customers from the diner. There were no unknowns."

No unknowns. No one unfamiliar.

"Where could they have hidden?" Dawg wondered curiously, mentally laying out the area in his head.

"Too many places." Natches shrugged, mirroring his own thoughts. "Sheriff Mayes is having the Rodeo impounded, though. He's *investigating* the crime."

Dawg grimaced.

"Uh-huh," his cousin breathed out sharply. "My opinion of it as well."

Dawg tightened his lips as he strode over to the fridge and

jerked out two bottles of beer. After handing one to Natches, he twisted the cap off his own and took a long, fortifying drink.

"This is turning into a fucking mess," he bit out. "How the hell did she manage to get herself mixed up in this?"

Natches twisted the cap off his own beer as he shook his head and paced over to the glass sliding doors.

"That's not all I found out." Natches turned back to him slowly, his gaze brooding, hooded. "When Crista left here eight years ago, she didn't just leave with Mark Lessing. Following them was Tyrell Grayson. Both men were once a part of Alex's spec op team, though they were discharged a month or so before for medical reasons. They all moved into Lessing's apartment on her arrival there, and she lived with them the whole time she was there. Rumor has it, both men were her lovers."

Twelve

Dawg froze at that information. He remembered Tyrell Grayson, though he had never met Mark Lessing. Tyrell had been a medic in the small Special Forces team Alex fought with at one time. Leanly muscled, blond-haired, and charming as hell.

"She had two lovers," he said quietly.

"That's the rumor." Natches shrugged. "I called a friend of mine who lived in Virginia Beach, not too far from where she lived with the two men. He did a little poking around yesterday. Lessing comes from money, and his position in his father's law firm obviously pays well. The penthouse apartment he still owns is supposed to be sweet. Lots of windows and space with a view of the beach. Lessing and Grayson still share the apartment, but a few of the neighbors say she broke their hearts when she left. My contact there believes differently. He talked to Lessing, posing as a potential employer who had heard about Crista's references and her lack of a job. Both men sang her praises and seemed fairly upbeat about her move."

She had two lovers. Two men. Ex–Special Forces. Hard men. And yet she had run from him and the fear that he wanted to share her with his cousins?

It didn't make sense.

"Any rumors of drugs or illegal activities?" Dawg asked.

"She's clean as a whistle there." Natches shook his head.

"But she could have made the right contacts to learn about the missiles and possible movements, as well as those needed to sell them." Dawg didn't want to believe that. He could feel everything inside him rejecting the idea that Crista could have possibly been involved in that.

"Initial reports say no." Natches shrugged. "Lessing and Grayson didn't associate with the military or former friends. But my contact is checking into it further."

Dawg felt his jaw tightening with fury.

"See what else you can find out," he ordered harshly. "And while you're at it, find out why she left town to begin with. Somehow, I doubt it had anything to do with avoiding a relationship with me."

Why should it have? She hadn't worried about moving in with two other men. Why run from him?

"What about the explosive device in that Rodeo, Dawg?" Natches said then. "We have the buyers and sellers, and not one of them has mentioned her name. Who struck at her, and why?"

Dawg shook his head. That question was still eating away at his brain.

"Whoever made away with the money set her up as well as the buyers and sellers for the missiles. Whoever the woman was, she knew we'd be there. She knew how to get Crista there. Why would she want to kill her now? She obviously set Crista up. Why wait till now to get rid of her?"

"Are we certain we got all the players?" Natches asked. "The buyers could have had a man on the outside. That's what I would have done."

"Why try to kill her without trying to find the money first?" Dawg asked. "Better yet, what's the point in killing her until they get the money?"

Natches stared back at Dawg silently, his expression still, calm.

"I'll watch things from the *Wet Dreams*," he finally said softly, referring to his own houseboat, the *Nauti Wet Dreams*. "The Rodeo, I think, was more of a warning. Otherwise, it would have gone up with the first turn of the key. Someone wants the money, and they're warning her that they're not letting it go. We need to go to Cranston, pull him in on this. Show her picture to the players and see how they react."

"I don't trust Cranston that far," Dawg muttered.

"You don't trust anyone that far, but Cranston has a good

grasp of how things work. We don't tell him Crista was at the warehouse. We explain about the Rodeo, our suspicions that Crista might resemble the money-girl, and go from there."

"And if they identify Crista?" Dawg asked dangerously. "Cranston could decide to go with what he can arrest and forget the rest."

Natches shook his head. "He's too good for that, Dawg. He'll want to use it, and we can use the team this way. Let's see how it works. What do we have to lose? We're her alibi, remember? Who can fight it?"

The shower shut off upstairs. Dawg turned his head and gave the stairs a long, hard look.

"Talk to Cranston," he said. "We'll see where it goes."

He was walking a damned tightrope, and he knew it. If the players arrested at the warehouse the other night identified Crista as their go-between, then all the suspicion would fall on Crista.

"Cranston's smarter than to believe it would be this easy," Natches assured him as he headed for the door. "I'll head in first thing in the morning to talk to him. I'll flash the pictures to our boys in the cells and see what we get. We could get lucky, and they won't recognize her."

Dawg grunted at that. "Don't bet on it."

He let Natches out of the houseboat and locked the door behind him before resetting the alarms and heading for the stairs.

Crista was up there. Showered, soft, and warm. And he hoped ready to give him the answers he needed. Because the thought of her living with one man had rage eating into his soul. Surprisingly, the thought of her living with two men, sharing in a relationship that his women had always shared with him and his cousins, was like an acid to his soul.

Because Dawg couldn't imagine sharing her, not eight years ago and definitely not now.

He headed to the stairs, moving up them with slow anticipation as his body tightened with the thought of her wearing the clothes he had bought her, the lacy panties he had picked out or the brief pajamas he had imagined seeing her in. The image was tightening through him with the same force as the knowledge of her lovers.

Her lovers.

God help him if that was what she needed now. Once, the thought of sharing her with his cousins would have had his cock pounding in glee. Now, he had to shake back the jealousy, fight to hold back his outrage that she would leave him for not just one man but two.

She had taken from others what she had refused to consider taking from him? He had always thought she had run because of his reputation, because of her fear of the ménages. To find out she had run straight into another one had his temper riding a thin, sharp line.

When he entered the upper-level bedroom, he came to a hard stop.

She was sitting on the bed, wearing one of his large shirts rather than her new pj's, slowly spreading some kind of lotion over her legs, which looked silky, rounded, and too damned tempting to believe.

For a moment, memory flashed through his head. Those silky legs spread, his mouth buried between them. His senses erupted with the remembered taste of silky, sweet feminine cream and hot, rich, satiny flesh. He could remember being as drunk on her as he was on the whiskey, as her fingers clenched in his hair and she whispered. His teeth clenched. She was a vocal lover. Begging, pleading, urging him on.

She set aside the lotion, her hands gripping the shirt where it covered her abdomen and glancing down at it as she rose nervously to her feet.

Oh, baby, it would pay for you to be nervous, he thought with a mix of lust and anger. Because there were so many wild, wicked things he intended to do with that hot little body.

"You have lousy taste in pajamas." She finally glared up at him. "There's not enough material to them to cover a postage stamp, let alone me."

He glanced over at the chair where some of the articles lay. The snug boy short panties and camisole tops would have covered more flesh than he liked, actually.

It wasn't the pajamas he wanted to discuss, though.

"Tell me something, Crista." He began unbuttoning his shirt. "When did you intend to tell me that you didn't have just one lover but two? Lessing and his friend Ty Grayson?"

Her gaze flickered, her eyes narrowing back at him as the

buttons released from his shirt and his flesh sensitized with the need to touch her.

Then, a slender brow arched tauntingly. "Why would I tell you anything, Dawg? It was none of your business. And that's beside the fact that they weren't my lovers. I simply lived with them."

"You slept with them," he snarled. "You admitted to sleeping with Lessing."

She shrugged. "I slept with them occasionally."

"Both of them?"

Her arms crossed over her breasts then. "Both of them," she agreed.

"At the same fucking time?"

Her lips thinned, irritation sparkling in her eyes then. "At the same time."

Crista had never considered herself to be the type of woman who walked heedlessly into danger, but she admitted to herself that right now, that was exactly what she was doing.

She would have thought that suspecting she had two lovers would have pleased him. She had expected him to suggest blackmailing her to sleep with Natches as well. Instead, he seemed angry.

"You ran away from me, by your own words, because I said I wanted to share you with Rowdy and Natches, yet you leave my bed and move in with two other men?" Incredulity filled his voice, causing it to rise as she stared back at him in surprise.

"What I did after I left you is none of your business." She stepped back as he threw his shirt to the side of the room.

He looked enraged. Dark brows were lowered heavily over brilliant, light green eyes that seemed to glow in his dark face. His lips were a flat, thin line, his shoulders bunched with tension.

He wasn't frightening; he was sexy. He should have been frightening. Instead, she could feel a sense of overwhelming eroticism, anticipation. She should have been enraged, at least as angry as he was. But she was seeing so much emotion in his face, something besides the mocking amusement or cynical awareness he normally displayed.

He was—jealous.

Dawg, jealous?

She felt her breasts become more sensitive, her nipples beading impossibly harder against the material of the T-shirt that she wore, and it made no sense. He had no reason to be jealous; she didn't want him to be jealous. But he was.

Dawg had never been jealous about another woman. Never possessive. That possessiveness had every cell in her body hypersensitive and screaming for his touch.

Her clit was swollen, the folds surrounding it heated and wet. She stared at him, mesmerized, watching as his hand went to the wide leather belt cinching his waist, seeing as though in slow motion the loosening of the leather, the way he left it hanging to jerk the snap of his jeans free.

"What are you doing?" The words rose unbidden. He was furious with her; she could see it. Furious and aroused and so possessive she could see the emotions blazing in his eyes.

"You agreed." His lips twisted, lost their flat, furious line, only to appear fuller, almost swollen, hungry.

The metamorphosis was hypnotizing. Watching anger fall beneath hunger, suspicion beneath possessiveness, and need overtaking his expression.

"You agreed," he repeated as he toed his boots off and tossed them aside, "to sleep with me. To fuck with me."

She flinched at the sound of his voice, not his words. It was rough, guttural, filled with lust. And it struck a chord inside her own sensuality that had her womb clenching violently.

"That's my shirt," he rasped when she continued to stare back at him. "Take it off!"

Crista shook her head slowly, watching as he advanced on her, as muscles rippled across his chest and shoulders, along his tight abs.

Below, pressing hard and tight against his jeans, his rampant erection demanded freedom.

She knew what Dawg was like when hunger beat him. She had seen him drunk and aroused but never sober and hungry. Not like this. Powerful, intent, focused only on the lust burning inside him. Burning inside her.

Even before, the one night she had spent in his bed, she hadn't known the powerful draw he could be. Tanned and hard, strong and dominant. The determination glowing in his eyes was like chains, holding her still, silent, as he advanced on her.

Her head tilted back as he came within inches of her, her gaze locked with his as his hand lifted, thumb and forefinger gripping the material between her breasts.

"Eight years it's tormented me," he murmured, his voice a dark velvet rasp over her senses. "Dreaming of it. Aching for it to the point that some nights, I couldn't even touch another woman because I ached for you to the point of pain."

He couldn't have ached more than she had. Couldn't have known the brutality of remembering a touch that ruined her for any other.

"But you still took them," she whispered hoarsely, trying to fight past the thickening eroticism building between them. "Alone. And with your cousins."

"And you went to another man." His lips drew back from his teeth in a hard snarl. "Two men."

He moved closer, pressing her against the dresser behind her as she caught her breath at the savage lust rising between them now. "Did they hold you? Did my name scream in your head each time they touched you, as yours screamed in mine?"

"Don't." Show no weakness. She had learned that so many years ago. Show no weakness, never let him see the hunger or the need that ripped through her.

And yet she was showing exactly that.

Her hands gripped the edge of the dresser behind her as she strained away from him, knowing she couldn't fight the hunger if he didn't stop touching her.

And he wouldn't stop. His hands gripped her waist, lifted her to the top of the dresser, then slid to her knees to draw them slowly apart.

"Dawg. Dawg, you don't want to do this." She was panting, certain she couldn't breathe through this. He was stealing the oxygen between them, making it thick and heavy with lust.

"I don't want to do it?" He drew the shirt up her waist, pulling it over her breasts, then forcing her arms up to tug it free of her body.

The cool air of the air conditioner washed over her nipples, sending a talon of sensation raking down her spine.

When he tossed the shirt aside, he didn't release her wrists. They were bound in one large hand, stretched above her head, lifting her breasts high as he stared at her.

"I should have tied you to my bed that night," he whispered

hoarsely. "I would have kept you with me, rather than allowing you to escape."

His other arm wrapped around her waist as he moved between her thighs, forcing them to part as he jerked her to him. A hard, quick motion that buried her nipples against his chest.

Sensation tore through her nerve endings. Crista felt her back arch, a shuddering breath ripping from her lungs as fire and ice seared her nipples, then tore a ragged, ecstatic path to her womb and the hungry depths of her pussy.

Before she could gather her breath to protest, before she could form the protest, his head lowered, his lips stole hers, and for the first time in eight years, Crista relived that first fiery kiss, that first trembling knowledge that every part of her, heart and soul, belonged to Dawg.

Thirteen

Crista wasn't aware of when he released her wrists; she was only aware that the second his lips parted from hers, the velvety texture and flaming heat were gone.

Her hands tightened in his hair, she lifted closer, a keening cry leaving her throat as her nipples raked over his chest, and the denim-covered heat of his erection pressed against the saturated flesh of her pussy.

"You like that, don't you, Crista?" He shifted against her, raking his chest over the sensitive tips, watching her face as she fought to hold back another cry.

"I like that," she admitted, shivering violently as his calloused palms rasped down her naked back. "I always loved your hands, Dawg. Always loved your touch."

She arched, her head falling back against the mirror behind her as his hands lifted her closer, his lips moving to her neck, his tongue licking her flesh before his teeth rasped over tender nerve endings.

"I dreamed of this." Her breathing faltered as her eyes drifted closed. "So long. I dreamed of this."

And she had. During those first pain-ridden months away from Somerset, through the loneliness of the years she had spent away from home, she had dreamed of him and his touch.

"Did you dream of this, sweetheart?" Rasping, rough, his voice was but a breath ahead of the silken rasp of the beginnings of a beard along his cheeks and jaw.

"I dreamed of this." Her thighs lifted along his hips, clutching at him as her arms moved from his shoulders, moving between them, searching for the zipper of his jeans, for the fierce, thick flesh beneath.

His chuckle was a low breath of arousal and denial.

His hands caught her wrists, dragging them back up his body. "This time, I get to savor you."

"No. Dawg." She shook her head, moaning at the thought of what she knew he intended. What he had done that first time before taking her.

"Yes. Crista," he growled.

Then he was drawing back from her, lifting her before turning and stepping to the bed, tossing her to it before he followed.

He didn't give her time to protest what she knew he wanted, what she wanted. His hands immediately spread her thighs, pushing her knees up as his head bent to the wet flesh aching for his touch.

"Oh God. Dawg." She arched, she moaned, as his tongue licked slowly through the saturated folds. "Yes. Oh yes, I need this."

She needed. She hungered for it.

He growled against the swollen curves, licked, his tongue moving with velvet roughness around her swollen clit as she stretched beneath him, arched to his mouth and did nothing to hold back her cries.

"You taste like fucking summer." His voice sounded angry. Harsh. But she knew that voice, it wasn't anger that drove him, it was a surfeit of lust that poured from every cell of his body.

Dawg couldn't believe how sweet and hot she tasted. Smoother than whiskey, yet more potent. Sweeter than candy and more addictive than drugs.

He buried his tongue in the sweetness, licked and sucked at it, tried to draw enough of the creamy syrup into him to sate himself on the taste of her.

If he could ever sate himself. With each lick, each taste, he only burned for more.

"Dawg." She twisted beneath him as he drew the fragile bud of her clit into his mouth in a long, firm kiss. A tiny suck, a flick of his tongue before he released it.

"More," she whispered breathlessly. "I like that. Oh I like that so much."

"How much do you like that, sweetheart?" He was dying for more of her. He smoothed his fingers along the saturated curls, feeling her syrup cling to them, tasting the sweetness of her against his tongue as he licked around the swollen little bud of her clit once again.

"I love it," she whimpered. "Oh God, Dawg. I love it."

Her clit throbbed against his tongue, almost as fiercely as his cock was throbbing in his jeans. He was wild for her, driven by a hunger that made no sense to him, that had his senses consumed by her, his muscles tight with the need to taste her, touch her, fuck her.

She belonged to him.

And where that thought came from he had no idea.

But it was there, suddenly so much a part of him that it sent a hard shudder racing through his body.

"I can't breathe," she panted, arching, writhing beneath him as his hands held her still. Her voice was soft, light, echoing with her own hunger.

Dawg lapped at her; his tongue slid through the soft folds, ached for bare, creamy flesh all around. She would be visiting the spa soon, he assured himself. He needed her soft pussy bare to his lips, so sensitive that his breath washing over it would send her to the brink of climax.

As he moved lower, the snug little opening that drew him clenched and fluttered against his tongue. Sliding his hands under her hips, he lifted her higher, closer, then sent his tongue burrowing into the sweetest flesh he had ever known.

Crista knew she was losing her mind beneath his touch. Stars exploded against the backdrop of her closed eyes and sent her arching closer, desperate for more. She fought the hands holding her, the broad shoulders that held her legs wide, and pleaded for more.

"Damn, you're sweet," he muttered as his head lifted just enough to allow his tongue to lick back to her clit. Not that it brought her any semblance of control, because his fingers were moving in to replace his tongue, sliding inside her, first one, then two, stretching her with exquisite heat as she undulated beneath him.

"I could eat you for hours." His voice was a rumbled vibration against her clit. "So creamy and sweet."

His voice stroked over her senses, drawing her farther into the maelstrom of sensation tearing through her body. She was helpless against it, helpless against him.

His fingers moved inside her, fucking her with long, smooth strokes as she tightened around him and begged for release.

"Your pussy's so tight, Crista." He lodged his fingers inside her. Just his fingertips, rasping inside her, bringing to life nerve endings she couldn't have possibly known existed.

"Stop teasing me," she gasped, shaking in his hold, her hips lifting to his hot mouth as he licked around her clit with gentle strokes. "Please Dawg. Let me come. I need to come."

"Just a little longer." His breathing was harsh, the strokes of his fingers inside her pussy were deeper now, stronger.

Crista felt her pussy clenching, felt the wash of her juices and his tongue licking, stroking her.

"I want your pussy waxed," he groaned. "All sweet and soft and sensitive. I want to lick your juices from every sweet inch of this hot little pussy."

Her fingers tightened in her hair as a shaft of white-hot heat seared her womb. Perspiration gathered on her flesh, ran in rivulets across her chest and breasts. The air became heated despite the air conditioning, and Crista could feel her own body unraveling as Dawg's lips surrounded her clit, suckled, licked, and gave her release.

She wondered if he gave her death along with it.

She was barely aware of her own screams, hoarse and broken, as he fucked her with hard thrusts of his fingers and sucked at her clit with deep, hungry draws of his mouth.

She twisted beneath him, fought the explosions of rapture, and finally fell beneath the force of pleasure overtaking her. Beneath the force of Dawg's hungry touch.

There was no chance to gather herself for the next attack against her soul. How he had managed to shed his jeans so quickly she would never be certain, but before the last tidal wave of ecstasy had dissolved, he was on his knees, fitting his cock between the swollen folds of her pussy and pushing inside her.

Crista stilled, froze. Her eyes jerked open to stare in his piercing gaze as he rested on his knees, his eyes lowered to where he was slowly, oh God so slowly, penetrating her.

Inch by torturously pleasurable inch. Burning because the fit was so tight, because the width of his cock stretched her to the point of pleasured pain as it stroked inside her.

"This is what I've dreamed of." His breath was sawing, his voice guttural. "Watching you take me, hug me. Feeling your pussy tighten around me like a fiery fist."

Her hips jerked upward, and between one broken breath and the next, his erection plunged forcefully inside her, and with the surge of sensation came a surge of primal ferocity she hadn't known she possessed.

Her legs lifted, wrapping possessively around him, angling her hips up to him, taking all of him, deeper than before, harder than before.

Her nails raked over his hair-spattered chest, combing through the sweat-dampened black curls before skimming along his abdomen and back again. Just to touch him, to feel the shudders racing through his body.

Then she was moving beneath him, fighting for dominance as she watched his eyes narrow a second before he gave her what she wanted.

Surprisingly. He moved, going to his back as he lifted her above him, never dislodging from her, thrusting deeper as she settled astride him and began to move.

The feel of his cock moving inside her was exquisite. The way he stretched her, burned her. The throb of blood pounding into the shaft and rippling against her sensitive inner walls drove her crazy with need. She wanted more sensation, harder strokes, a deeper burn.

"Slow down." His hands gripped her hips as she began to impale herself on him.

"No." Crista shook her head wildly. "Not yet. Let me—"

"You're not coming yet, Crista." His voice was forceful. Dominant. As dominant as the hands that restrained her hips and kept her from riding him as she needed to.

"I need to come again, Dawg." She would be embarrassed over the whimper in her voice later. "Just one more time. Just now."

She flexed above him, straining as his cock stroked her internally.

"Soon, sweetheart." He grimaced. "Soon . . . Ah fuck!"

She lowered her upper body, her lips moving to a flat, hard

nipple that she nipped at gently, then licked, tasting the salty male taste of his flesh and the heat of his lust.

His hips jerked beneath her, his cock plunging heatedly inside her, just once. Just once when she needed so much more.

"Easy, fancy-face," he groaned, allowing her to move by the smallest degree, to work herself on the thick, stiff flesh impaling her with the smallest strokes.

"Dawg, please. I need—" She wasn't certain what she needed. Wild. Hard. God yes, she needed hard. "Hard. Fuck me hard. I can't stand this."

His hips jerked at her shattered plea. Dawg could feel his balls drawing tight, his dick flexing, jerking inside her with the need to come. And a part of him needed to savor. To hold her back, to draw out the exquisite torment to the point that when the explosion came, she would know, to the depths of her soul, exactly who she belonged to.

One hand moved from her hip as the other restrained her, forcing her to the slower pace he wanted. To the long, gentle thrusts that forced her to feel every inch of his cock taking her, possessing her.

Just for a moment longer.

His free hand snagged in her hair, pulling her head up as he moved into position for her kiss.

"Come here, Crista," he whispered. "Kiss me, darlin'. Show me how you need me."

She didn't hesitate. Passion and hunger darkened her chocolate eyes and flushed her cheeks. Her head lowered, her lips meeting his eagerly as he rolled her to her back, moving between her thighs, feeling her pussy tighten on him as he retreated, then clench again with need as he thrust inside her once more.

Sweat slicked both their bodies as her legs twined around his hips and his tongue sought the heated depths of her mouth.

He was lost inside her.

Dawg groaned, growled, slanted his lips over hers and gave his cock the freedom to take her as he needed to. Deep. Hard. He began rocking inside her, fighting for the control to hold back, fighting to torment them both just a little while longer.

But the pleasure was too deep, too hard. Within seconds he was fucking her with a primal hunger that should have made him wary. As though he had never fucked before, never known a woman's touch before.

Crista could feel herself screaming into his kiss. Her hands stroked over his shoulders, his upper back. Her nails scraped and raked, her palms begging for the touch of his skin.

His kiss was like wildfire.

The feel of his cock shafting hard and deep inside her added to the surfeit of sensation. Each plunging stroke, each forceful thrust threw her higher, drew her deeper into the vortex sweeping through her.

Until finally, her senses exploded beneath the impact.

Her orgasm tore through her, swept through her mind and left chaos in its wake, detonated through her flesh and spasmed through her womb until her broken screams were joined by Dawg's hard, male cry of release.

She felt the fiery blasts of his semen filling her, sparking another explosion, another wash of ecstasy. It lasted forever; it didn't last long enough.

She collapsed beneath him, fighting for breath, certain she could never draw in enough air, when he began moving again.

"Dawg." Her voice was small, not really a protest, perhaps a question of sanity.

He was still hard, still hungry, and within seconds, she could feel her own pleasure building again. This time, when he rolled to his back and drew her above him, she didn't have the strength to fight the slow, languorous thrusts he demanded. She needed hard and fast, but her muscles were lax, too worn and drained to draw the energy for it.

She lifted herself above him, her hands braced on his chest, feeling his palms stroking over her back, her hips, and moved on him with building pleasure.

"How pretty." His voice was tight, hungry. "That's the way, sweetheart. Ride my cock. Ride it like you love it."

Like she loved it? She had loved him all her life, and he hadn't known it. He couldn't know it. And her body ached for him. Lonely nights curled into a ball because the ache was so bad. Dreams and fantasies had sustained her. Until now.

Her back arched as she lifted, her hands gripped his powerful arms now, using them to steady herself as she began to raise and lower herself, feeling him sink into her, rasping delicate nerve endings, stretching tender tissue until the world was spinning around her, and she knew nothing but his touch, but the feel of him invading her body. Her soul.

Her vagina pulsed around him, tighter for the orgasm that had filled it minutes before, swelling the muscles that surrounded his shuttling flesh and sending an agony of pleasure to wash through her system.

The release that overtook her long, long minutes later was lazier, slower, but no less intense.

And after that, long into the night, each release slammed harder inside her soul. This wasn't like the first time. He had been drunk, a little clumsier, and had taken her with haste rather than finesse.

Dawg didn't have that problem tonight. There was no hesitancy, no clumsiness; there was only hunger, intensity, and strength. Eroticism filled each touch, and his voice, guttural and rasping, explicit and dominant, filled her head.

By the time he collapsed beside her and dragged her against his chest, she was soaked with sweat, immersed in the scent of their lust, and on the verge of complete exhaustion.

His hand curled around a breast as his chest heaved for breath behind her.

"Mine," he reminded her, his voice hoarse, exhausted. "Remember that, Crista. You're mine."

Mine. Not theirs. Not one of the Nauti playmates. Just Dawg's.

Fourteen

"So tell me about your lovers?"

Crista's gaze jerked from the last of the full breakfast she had made while Dawg was in the shower the next morning to his icy light green gaze. She had really hoped he was going to forget about that.

"I didn't say they were my lovers. You did," she pointed out as she laid her fork on the plate and finished the last of her coffee.

He didn't deserve explanations, and Mark and Ty's relationship was their own. She wasn't going to make him feel better or ease his little mind by giving him explanations he should never be asking for.

"You slept with them. You admitted it." He scowled back at her.

"So?" She rose from the table, collected their plates and cups, and paced to the sink. "Do I ask you about your past lovers, Dawg? How many you shared? How many you didn't? Have I asked you to explain those choices to me?"

She turned back to face him, bracing her back against the counter and watching as his jaw bunched with angry tension.

"I didn't walk away from you because of the sharing," he said harshly. "You did."

"Mark and Ty never, at any time brought another woman to their bed, or another man. Would Rowdy and Natches have loved me enough to give up other women? I don't think so."

Mark and Ty had never been her lovers. They were each other's lovers. Sometimes though, when the nights were too dark and the pain followed too closely, they would draw her to their bed much as parents would a child. There, they sheltered her between them and gave her the warmth she needed to hold on to at the time.

His eyes narrowed as his expression turned stony.

"I'm not going to argue with you over this." She finally shook her head as she glanced at her watch. "The lumber store will be open in half an hour. We should go."

"I never open." He shrugged.

"Which is a lousy way to promote a locally owned business," she informed him. "And I know you know better than that, Dawg. You're more of a businessman than this. Besides, I have work to do, and I do my best work in the morning."

"My business." His smile was tight and hard. "Not yours."

"As long as I'm getting paid to organize and manage that hellhole of an office, then I have a vested interest in your business," she told him sweetly. "And holding me hostage here because you don't like my answers is not going to get you what you want."

He uncoiled from the table. Despite his size and the obvious power in his body, he moved silently, gracefully. Like a panther on the prowl, his predatory green eyes narrowed and glittering behind pitch-black lashes, his body tense but prepared. As though she would attempt to run from him.

Crista stood her ground instead, her arms crossing over her breasts as she stared back at him guardedly.

"That store could burn down around its foundations for all I give a fuck," he sneered, shocking her with the latent fury in his voice. "I keep it to piss off the holier-than-thou relatives who tried so damned hard to take it away from me, period. Its success is due to nothing more than luck."

And she didn't believe that. She knew better. He wanted to pretend he hated it, but the stories related to her the day before by the employees showed something totally different.

Dawg did care about that business, but for some reason he refused to admit it.

"It was your father's business." She tested the waters gently. "I know your relationship with him wasn't close, but surely you don't hate him enough to let the store suffer."

"I bet he's spinning in his grave." Dawg's smile was tight and vicious. "I've hired people from the families he hated the most, and I've made certain people he would never give credit to, have it. The fact that that damned place makes money never fails to amaze me." He shook his head as though he truly couldn't make sense of it.

Yet, when he had fired the manager that had been cheating him, the current floor manager had told Crista that Dawg practically lived in his office until he had the books and the store straightened out.

He had an instinct for what people needed and what they wanted, and he hired people who could provide it. And every employee hired had been hired by him personally.

"Well, I need your help anyway," she told him firmly. "Your manager, Layla Matcher, has a pretty good handle on things, but I was going through some of the more recent catalogs gathering dust in the office and noticed you hadn't ordered for the Christmas season yet. You need to get that in."

"It's in." His lip curled in disgust, self-disgust. She could tell by his expression that admitting it didn't set well with him.

"Then I need the order log." She turned and rinsed their dishes. "We also need to get a stack of files taller than I am filed. The stock boy I sent for the file cabinets yesterday hadn't arrived by time I left."

"They're waiting in the office." If his voice could have become shorter, it did.

Crista hid her smile as she stacked the dishes in the dishwasher.

"Good; then you check the problem Layla told me was building in the lumberyard behind the store. For some reason, orders were missed with surprising regularlity last week. Several of your best contractors have threatened to use the chain lumberyard rather than Mackay's because of the mess-up."

She turned in time to catch the narrowing of his eyes.

"Why didn't Layla report this when it began?" His lips flattened in irritation.

"Check your cell phone messages." She shrugged. "She left several texts."

A heavy grimace tightened his expression then. "I had a problem with the phone last week."

"There you go then." She moved across the kitchen where her purse sat on the far counter.

Before she could make it halfway across the room, Dawg caught her arm and turned her firmly back to face him.

"Don't start trying to run my life, Crista. You're the one being blackmailed here, not me. There's only so much I'll let you get away with."

She restrained her smile; gloating wasn't the best way to handle Dawg.

"Keep telling yourself that," she told him instead. "And while you're at it, ask yourself the same question I had to answer sometime last night when I was still trying to catch my breath. You wouldn't blackmail someone you believed was a criminal, Dawg, and we both know it. No more than you would see an innocent person imprisoned. No matter the cost. So what are you doing in this relationship?"

"Getting the fuck of my life," he snarled.

Her lips did twitch then. "So you are," she agreed, pulling her arm from his grip before moving back to her purse, then turning and glancing at him over her shoulder. "Now, the question is, what do you really intend to do with it? Or me, as the case may be. Because we're both smart enough to know that the thing you're not going to do is turn me over to Homeland Security. Fuck me to death maybe, but you wouldn't turn me in."

"Are you betting your life on it?"

"Yeah." She nodded slowly. "I'm betting my life on it."

It was a damned good thing her brother had raised her, Crista thought later as they pulled into the parking lot behind the lumber store marked Employees Only. Because Dawg was snarling and growling and being a general pain in the butt just for the hell of it. From her experience with Alex, she could tell the male irritability factor was in full swing here.

But he hadn't called his agent-in-charge, and she was fairly certain there were no agents en route to slap restraints on her. She might get lucky, and the worst she would have to deal with was a snarling Dawg.

Not that answering her own question in the middle of the night had been easy. Because Crista had known from that first night that Dawg wouldn't arrest her, and he wouldn't see her arrested. He knew she wasn't involved.

So why was she letting him blackmail her?

She had to fight to keep from laying her palm against her abdomen as they drove from the houseboat to the store. That was why she was letting him blackmail her. Because nothing had been finished when she had left Somerset eight years before. But everything had been lost.

Her dreams. The man she had loved for what seemed most of her life. And the child she had carried from that night.

The miscarriage had destroyed something inside her, something she hadn't been able to recapture after leaving town. And she had never forgotten Dawg: his touch, his kiss, or the pleasure that had filled every cell of her body.

"You're making me look bad," he snapped as he jerked the vehicle into park and turned his head to stare at her over the top of the dark glasses he wore. "I never open."

"You never hire one of your lovers to work here, either." She shrugged.

"For a woman who was supposed to stay locked in the office, you managed to filter through a lot of gossip."

"I'm good at that." She nodded benignly as she opened the truck door and stepped out of the vehicle, leaving him to snarl and curse behind her as she slammed the door closed.

She was moving around the edge of the building when he finally drew up beside her.

"You're working on a spanking," he warned her.

Unfortunately, the idea of that shouldn't have been titillating.

"Am I?" she asked sweetly. "I hear you're particularly good at that little disciplinary act. Before I left Somerset, all the girls were talking about it."

She had to force those words past her lips. Just as she'd had to force back the jealousy at the time.

He grunted. An irritated sound of male displeasure.

Crista shrugged. "You and your cousins aren't exactly good at hiding your lights under a barrel, so to speak," she told him, casting him a disapproving glare. "Really, Dawg, it's a little late to worry about gossip."

She should have known better than to dare him. She really should have.

Before she could do more than gasp, he had pushed her against the chain-link fence and stole her lips in a kiss that had her system rioting with conflicting emotions.

They weren't on the houseboat, in his bed. They were in full view, and she was very well aware of what he was doing. Marking her as his. As another woman in the very long line of women who had shared his bed.

"Stop, Dawg." She tore her lips from his, panting with the effort it cost her.

His hands were on her back, holding her against him, the length of his erection pressing into her lower stomach, as his big body seemed to surround her.

"Don't push me, Crista." He stared down at her, his light green eyes practically glowing with an anger held closely in check. "I've never given a damn about gossip or others' opinions of me, and I won't care about it now. Remember that when you're twitching that tight little ass around me and trying to convince yourself what a good guy I might really be underneath it all. I'm a son of a bitch, darlin', and one you really don't want to cross."

No, he was one she wanted to soothe, because she could see the pain in his eyes, in the mockery of his expression. She could see it in the anger he was holding back, despite his words.

"Are you going to hurt me, Dawg?" she asked him then, reaching up to touch his jaw before he jerked away from her.

"Get your ass in the store, goddamn it," he cursed, stepping back and gripping her arm to lead her to the front doors where Layla was unlocking the employees' entrance.

She cast them a curious glance, her dark hazel eyes concerned as Dawg approached.

"Good morning, Mr. Mackay. Crista," she greeted them with an attempt at brightness, despite Dawg's heavy scowl.

"If you can call me Mr. Mackay, then you can call her Miss Jansen," Dawg told the manager brusquely as Crista sighed behind him.

"Call him Dawg, Layla. Maybe he'll stop snarling at us because he had to come in so soon." Crista tugged at his grip. "And he's really not dragging me along behind him like a recalcitrant child. I get off on dominance."

Layla coughed as she turned her back on them quickly, and Dawg stopped and stared back at her in surprise.

She lifted one brow curiously. "What? I wasn't supposed to tell?"

They both knew she hated being dragged around like a favorite puppy, and she was certain that was exactly why he made a habit of doing it.

Spanked. He mouthed back at her before turning back to Layla.

Crista smiled serenely back at the other woman as she finished unlocking the door.

"Layla, follow us to the office, I want to know what the hell is going on with the lumberyard. I thought Bedsford had a handle on that?"

"He was working out great, Mr. . . . uhh Dawg," she stuttered as she relocked the door, then followed behind them. "He's been with us ever since he was discharged from the service. I don't know what happened."

Crista glanced behind her at the manager, winking as Dawg continued to drag her behind him as he mounted the steps to the office.

"When did it start?"

"Last week." They paused as Dawg dug the key to the office out of his jeans pocket, still holding onto Crista, and inserted it into lock, turned it, then stopped.

"Dawg?" Crista tried to stare around him. "What's wrong?"

"You didn't lock up last night." His voice was carefully restrained.

"Of course I locked the office before I left." Crista frowned. "I know I did."

"I also checked it before I left Mr., umm, Dawg." Layla cleared her throat again. "I always check the office doors before I close up at night."

Dawg stepped back, his keys still hanging in the lock.

"Crista, I want you and Layla to go back out front. Use your cell phone and call Natches. I programmed his and Rowdy's numbers in last night."

"Why?" Crista could feel the dread rising inside her now.

"Layla, does anyone know you check the offices at night?" Dawg asked then.

"I don't know, Dawg." There was an edge of fear in her voice. "Jamie and the boys always go through the store with me at night when they pick me up, just to make sure everything is okay. I check all the office doors then."

"Get out front and call Natches, Crista." Dawg turned back to her, his expression closed, dangerous. "Now."

"Not without you." Her hands gripped his arm, tugging at him. "You can call him yourself. He'll come faster if you call him."

Surprise tightened his features. "I know what I'm doing, Crista."

"I don't care." She wasn't leaving him here alone. Only God knew what was behind that door. "You can come with us."

"Mr. Mackay, we should all go out front. What if whoever was in the store, if anyone was, is waiting outside?"

That had murderous fury lighting in his eyes. Dawg's gaze sliced to the tall, wide windows of the front of the store as his expression became cold, dangerous.

"Come on." Thankfully, he turned, moving them down the metal steps and headed for the entrance as he pulled his cell phone from his pocket.

Punching in Natches's number, Dawg stalked away from the women.

"It's early, Dawg," Natches mumbled into the line.

"Get to the store. Someone was in the office last night. I'm calling the sheriff to dust for prints, but I need someone to watch Crista while I'm taking care of Mayes's questions. After last night, this could get ugly."

"Shit!" He could hear Natches moving. "Bastards moved fast."

"Makes me wonder if the car going up in flames wasn't more of a distraction than an attempt. Just hurry. I'm calling Sheriff Mayes now. And you know Layla, her husband and sons are going to come down here like a pack of ravening wolves intent on protecting her. I'm going to need help here."

Natches snickered.

Jamie Matcher and his brood of overgrown sons had come to the store and stayed with Layla every day for the first damned year she had worked for Dawg. And Jamie, all six feet five inches of him, had towered over Dawg and warned him what would happen if his little Layla got smeared with gossip because of games Dawg might want to play in the privacy of his office.

As if he played games in his office. Damnit, he liked a bed for games. The office was work. Paperwork. Something he didn't handle well, despite Crista's certainty.

"Just get your ass down here." Dawg closed his eyes and rubbed at his forehead, anticipating the headache he knew was well on its way.

As he flipped the phone closed and turned back to the two women, he sighed again. Layla was looking decidedly nervous. Crista was defiant and suspicious.

"Layla, call Jamie and the boys," he told her. "I have to call Sheriff Mayes, and once the call goes out on the radio, Jamie will blow a fuse."

"He worries, Dawg." But she was pulling the phone from the case she wore on the slim leather belt that cinched her crisp tan slacks.

"He worries," Dawg muttered. "I worry." Then he turned to Crista.

She was leaning against the block wall like she didn't have a damned care in the world. Concerned but amused. She was amused at him, and that one was biting his ass. He was blackmailing her, but damned if he didn't suddenly feel like she had the upper hand.

"Layla, why don't you and Crista go to the lounge and get some coffee on. The employees will be showing up about the same time the sheriff and the state boys do. If they have their coffee, they might not make too much of a mess investigating this."

He could hope. But he wasn't betting the houseboat on it. By the time he got off the phone with Sheriff Mayes, he could feel the headache beginning in his temples.

Good old Ezekiel Mayes. The son of a bitch. Dawg swore he was going to vote against him each election, but he always managed to vote for him. Better the devil you knew . . .

He stood and stared around the store. It was just as huge now as it was each time he found himself doing this. The first year out of the Marines he had nearly gutted the place. His knee had ached like a son of a bitch that year, but he had nearly tripled the size and added to the layout. Not that he cared one way or the other about the business, he reminded himself. He had been bored.

Fuck that. Even Crista knew better. And he was kidding himself. He had been kidding himself for eight years. The estate his parents had left him was riddled with so much guilt, resentment, and bitterness that sometimes he wished he'd sold it all that first year after their death, while he was in the Marines and worrying his ass off over it.

The house especially. Where he had never lived. His father had finished it after Dawg had bought the *Nauti Dawg* from an inheritance left to him by his mother's mother. He had never spent a night in that house until after their deaths.

His father had hated the lumber store, too. But he had kept it anyway. He had always said it was the only thing Dawg was smart enough to actually make a living with. And maybe the old bastard had been right.

He had a knack for it, unlike his knack for warfare. He tended to get his knees blown off there. The ATF assignment wasn't a bad one, but the restrictions pissed him off. Answering to other people wasn't his strong suit.

Unfortunately, Sheriff Mayes liked a lot of answers to his questions.

"What the hell are you involved in, Dawg?" Zeke kept his voice low as they stood back from the state police unit now inspecting his office.

There were no prints, no hint of anything disturbed, though it was impossible for Dawg to tell if anything was missing. He glared at Crista where she stood in the open door of the lounge beneath the office. He hadn't even recognized his damned office.

And she smiled.

That smile lit a fire inside him he didn't even want to understand. A fire-charged electrical arousal and a brooding anger, in equal intensity through his body.

Because he knew she was holding back. Some part of her didn't yet belong to him, whether it was her honesty or something deeper, he didn't want to delve into at the moment. But she was holding back. And that just flat pissed him off.

"What the hell is she involved in, then?" Zeke asked.

Dawg glanced at the sheriff before leaning against the floor-to-ceiling shelving that ran the length of the aisle they were in front of.

"Nada," he answered shortly.

"Your *nada*s are getting on my nerves," Zeke warned him.

"It's going to get on your nerves worse when I campaign for

your opponent next election," Dawg pointed out irritably. "Leave it alone, Zeke."

"You're going to get her killed, Dawg," Zeke said quietly. "Whatever you're doing, it's going to backfire on her."

"Then you'll have bloodshed to clean up, Zeke." Dawg's smile, he knew, was a shark's glare. "Anyone even thinks about hurting her, and they'll die. Expect that. Count on that. Now get the hell out of my way. I have a business to run."

Unfortunately, Zeke was right. Whatever the hell was going on, someone was intent on not just drawing Crista into it, but of striking out at her.

As Zeke headed back toward the small crowd of investigators and officers, Natches moved up to him.

His cousin's dark green eyes were like flinty ice in a stone-cold expression.

Dawg crossed his arms over his chest and stared around the crowd intently, making certain no one came close.

"The investigators want to think she deliberately left the door unlocked," Natches muttered. "The scrapes on the lock are being brushed aside because there are no prints. Someone wants you to think she's incompetent at the least, using you at the worst."

Dawg nodded slowly.

"They struck after you were seen arguing with her. After the Rodeo went up in flames. None of it makes any sense or ties in. Threaten her, and you're only going to cover her closer. So why attempt to search your office?"

"Unless the point was to plant something against her," Natches said softly. "Thankfully, I was able to get in there with the first investigators. There was a map of the warehouse, the address, and a detailed list of the missiles and their chips, along with about twenty-five thousand in cash in an envelope tucked into the file cabinet. Someone's setting you up with her."

"Did you get the envelope?"

Natches nodded slowly. "Taken care of. Security tapes were fuzzed, bad. Both the outside and inside monitors were affected. There was so much static on them there's no way to tell who it was or what they were doing."

"They know my system." His was state-of-the-art with a few additional devices that should have made it impossible for the average thief to bypass.

"They know you," Natches pointed out. "I'm going to head to town, spread a little trash, and see what happens."

"What kind of trash?" Dawg stared at his cousin suspiciously.

"Well, you hired a new manager, and look what happened." Natches nodded to the officers and agents milling around. "What if, after they leave, I overhear you and Crista arguing about it? Maybe she's called her good friend Mark, and she's heading back to Virginia. Whoever's involved with this is trying to lay the money at her feet to keep suspicion off them. If she's arrested, Dawg, with the pictures they have of the woman resembling her, then any testimony the thieves give that she wasn't involved won't matter. She'll take the rap, and someone else gets away with the money."

"Do the thieves know for certain it's not Crista?" Dawg asked then, remembering the interrogation of the men they had arrested. "If they knew, why not take the deal Cranston offered them for the woman? From all reports, she was the mastermind behind this."

"Maybe they don't know who she is," Natches suggested. "They were a few good ole boys contacted because of their knowledge of the military and their ability to pull this deal together. Someone else was the brains."

"Someone who knows my security system," Dawg mused.

"Close the store down for the rest of the day. I'll hang around until everyone has left, check things out, then head to the diner with Rowdy and Kelly. We can get the information that Crista is heading to Virginia where I think it needs to go. Whatever's going on, that diner seems to be the center of it."

"Or someone who hangs out there too much." Dawg nodded.

"Wait till after dark to leave, and when you do, take the back roads to the marina. Stay in the houseboat tomorrow; keep the windows and doors closed and Crista hidden. Let's give them time to take the bait."

Dawg nodded. It could work. At the moment, it was the best chance they had at flushing out the culprit.

"Keep me up-to-date," Dawg ordered. "And watch Cranston. He's making me nervous."

The agent was watching Crista too closely at the moment. Standing back, his head tilted to the side and his eyes narrowed on her as she and Layla kept the officers supplied with coffee.

Natches nodded sharply. "I'll be around the houseboat later tonight and let you know how things are going."

Dawg nodded again as he watched the crowd. One of his employees had to be involved; there was no doubt. But which one? And why?

He watched them milling around, gossiping, chatting, filled with curiosity. One of them had betrayed him and threatened Crista. Which meant one of them had a death wish.

Fifteen

Eight years before, Crista had lived for the moments she could bask in Dawg's smile. His flirting had turned her heart over, filled her with a wild, reckless joy, and made her dream of being in his arms.

She had ached for him even before she knew what the ache was. His charm, his lazy humor, and that shadow of pain that haunted his eyes drew her. And in her deepest fantasies she eased that shadow away and saw his odd, light green eyes fill with joy.

When she had first realized she was pregnant, she had been furious, resentful. Then the knowledge of that life she held stilled the anger. His child would never know loneliness, never lack for love. She would never see that shadow of hurt in their baby's eyes. She would love it, protect it. Their baby.

The day she had lost that child something inside her had died, only to be reborn when she returned and realized that that silent draw between her and Dawg was still there.

She had fought it. She had thought she could protect her heart and live on the periphery of his attention, warmed yet protected from the heat she knew could destroy her.

What a fool she had been.

Crista watched Dawg as they finished the office arrangement, going through files, searching for a reason why his office had been breached.

He was silent, angry. Determination sharpened the lines and angles of his face, giving him a warrior's appearance, a savage aura that turned her on more than it had a right to. He made quick work of hefting the furniture and sliding it into place as Crista cleaned. He helped go through files, helped pack them to the new cabinets and load them, his celadon eyes sharp and intent as he went over every inch of the office to track anything that had been bothered or searched.

As he moved, the sunlight spearing through the wide office windows on the other side of the room worshipped his raven black hair and sun-kissed flesh. It slid over his broad shoulders and emphasized his muscular arms as the short sleeves of his black T-shirt stretched over them.

Jeans molded to his powerful hips and thighs, and those boots he wore made his legs even sexier. Not to mention how the denim of his jeans lovingly cupped his muscular ass.

He was enough to steal a girl's breath, and Crista admitted to having a lot of breathless moments. And perhaps she had been wrong before when she thought he hadn't matured from the self-centered determination he had possessed in those days.

Dawg had changed over the years after all. He was harder. Still just as sexy, but more dangerous than he had been before he joined the Marines and definitely more mature.

He had proven that today. Crista had watched as he moved through the office after the sheriff's men had finished dusting for prints, and the state police had finished their questions.

They could find nothing moved, nothing bothered. The only proof there was that there might have been a break-in was the suspected tampering with the security cameras and the lock on the office door.

And Crista felt sorry for the culprit, because Dawg looked mad enough to draw blood hours later. He had sent the employees home after the police left and locked up behind Layla before leading Crista back into the office.

She stared at him from the other end of the large room as she straightened the lamp on the table by the couch and he stored the last of the files. His eyes were narrowed, his expression brooding as he turned to her.

"Do you realize you just destroyed years of deliberate chaos?" Dawg asked as the last of the files were stored away and she gave the furniture a final buffing with the polish she used. Everything gleamed, even the hardwood floor beneath their feet.

She turned and looked around, realizing how large the office was. There was plenty of room for the other file cabinets she wanted as well as the extra desk Dawg had ordered one of the stock floor boys to put together for her in the morning. A nice miniature version of the huge walnut desk he was using himself.

Deliberate chaos he called it. A slap at the father that would have taken even this from him, if he could have managed to do it without looking like the monster he had been.

"Chaos doesn't beat success." She shrugged. "Organization can raise productivity and profits. The way it is, the chain lumber stores are still running ahead of you in profits and customers. We want to pull those customers to Mackay's."

He leaned against the file cabinet and regarded her quizzically. "It makes enough money. Even with the court battle Johnny and his mother waged against me those first years, I came out of it a very rich man, Crista."

"And that's enough for you?" She knew Dawg better than that.

"It's more than most have." That irritable frown was on his face again, the one that encouraged the person he was talking to, to go straight to hell.

Crista shook her head. "It's not enough for you, Dawg."

"Says who?" He threw himself in the large leather chair behind his desk and stared back at her broodingly.

Crista rolled her eyes as she stored the polish and rag in the bottom drawer of one of the file cabinets before straightening to face him.

The look on his face was sexy and scary at the same time. Intent, brooding, dominant, and aroused.

"Stop being an ass," she chided him. "You know you love this store. You pretend you don't. You want people to think you don't. But I know better."

He folded his fingers together over his tight abs as he leaned back and let his gaze rake over her.

"And how do you know so much about me?" he drawled with a hint of anger. "It's not like you try to get close to me."

And there he was wrong. Even in the past year, Crista had soaked up every hint of gossip she could about him. She had watched him, let others talk about him, and found herself looking for excuses to be in places where she knew he would be.

She knew the lawsuit that his aunt had brought against him just after he joined the Marines had ignited a fury of controversy through the town at the time.

All the cousins—Rowdy, Natches, and Dawg—had been in the service, leaving no one in Somerset to protect his interests other than his uncle Ray. Ray Mackay had held that front line like a bulldog holding onto a bone, though.

He had hired the best lawyers, paid them himself, and kept Dawg apprised of each step of the battle. He had managed to get court dates delayed until Dawg had leave, and had stood beside his nephew, against his sister, and shed a tear on the stand as he related the times he had been forced to protect Dawg as a young boy from the father who would have abused him.

Dawg's bitterness went clear to his childhood, and it had created a man who, even at twenty-four, had been hard and shadowed with distrust. Four years in the Marines and four years working for whatever government agency he was a part of hadn't helped.

"Getting close to you would have been hard, Dawg," she finally answered him. "Your groupies stood layers deep and jealously hoarded that hard body of yours."

It wasn't far from the truth.

"Or you were just too scared to take what I was offering." He leaned forward, bracing his arms on the desk as he stared back tauntingly.

And maybe he was right there, too.

Crista shrugged. "I was young. Ages younger than you in experience."

"But not anymore, are you, Crista? Seven years in bed with two lovers at the same time? Your experience definitely matches mine now, wouldn't you say?"

Crista felt her heart pause, then race viciously in her chest. She didn't want this conversation with him now.

"My life after I left Somerset is none of your business, Dawg," she finally said, aware of the defensive sound of her own voice. "I've already explained the distinction to you."

She didn't want to explain Mark and Ty; they were none of his business. And he hadn't begun this relationship with her because of an overwhelming need or rousing love. She was the one that got away. She was smart enough to admit that to herself.

"So, if the three of us had been willing to be faithful to you, you would have considered it?"

She didn't like the look on his face as he posed that question. It was suggestive, dark, and warning.

"No. I wouldn't have." She tucked a lock of hair behind her ear before crossing her arms over her breasts and staring back at him candidly. "Come on, Dawg, it was eight years ago. You weren't in love with me. I was a nice little one-night stand that you were too drunk to remember, that's all. Now, I'm just the woman you're blackmailing. Let's not start dragging the past into it."

"Just the woman I'm blackmailing," he murmured then, his voice deepening, becoming harsher, hungry. "My own little sex toy, right?"

Crista didn't let her lips twitch or her amusement show in her eyes. She had a feeling he wouldn't appreciate it in the least.

She shrugged her shoulders negligently instead. "Do you have a better description?"

He rose from the desk abruptly, startling her enough to cause her to jump a step backward. Smiling in satisfaction, he moved to the tinted windows that looked out over the floor of the lumber store.

Layla had closed up nearly an hour ago and left with her husband and sons, leaving the floor eerily quiet below them. Still, Dawg jerked the shades closed and locked the office door.

Crista licked her lips nervously, feeling the ever-ready heat that lingered beneath her flesh building then. As though every cell of her body was so attuned to him that it knew the moment he decided it was time to begin playing again.

"Fine, I feel like playing then. Take your clothes off."

Instantly the air was redolent with arousal and hard, male domination.

Crista had already decided that rather than fighting the sensuality and Dawg, she would instead allow herself to enjoy. To revel in the carnal intensity that was so much a part of him and to allow herself this one moment in time to enjoy his taste, his touch.

There was no other man like Dawg, and there never would be.

She couldn't fight him today. Not right now. She needed his touch as much as he evidently wanted to give it.

She toed her sandals from her feet as her fingers went to the narrow leather belt that cinched her jeans. Her heart was racing in her chest as she flicked the metal button loose and rasped the zipper down. His gaze never left her hands, following each movement as she skimmed the material over her thighs and pushed it down her legs. Stepping out of the jeans, she tossed them to the leather visitor's chair that sat in front of his desk.

She was left in the snug, narrow-strapped camisole top, lacy white bra, and matching thong she wore. Dawg's eyes darkened, dilated, as he moved slowly back around the desk and lowered the shade behind the desk.

His expression was pure lust. Dark, overwhelming, tight with hunger, and blazing with arousal. It sent a shaft of fiery sensation streaking to her womb, clenching it violently before snapping to her vagina and spasming through the tender muscles there. Silky wet heat spilled from her as the outer folds became swollen and heavy, so sensitive she had to bite her lip against the whimper that would have escaped her throat.

Dawg disposed of his T-shirt before bending and pulling his boots from his masculine feet. Stripping his white socks off next, his head lifted, his eyes spearing into her.

"You're not naked," he reminded her gutturally. "Take the clothes off, or I'll rip them of you."

"This is your office." She was breathless, teasing him even though she knew better.

His lips tightened in a feral smile. "And you're my sex toy. Office hours are over, and I'm ready to play, Crista."

Oh Lord, was he ready to play. The T-shirt was tossed in the corner of the room; the muscles of his chest and abs rippled with power and tensed with determination.

"Take the shirt off."

She gripped the hem of the shirt and pulled it off slowly, her thighs weakening at the sound of his harsh, indrawn breath. Tossing it to the chair with her jeans, she faced him with nothing but a few scraps of lace and a hunger she knew was as naked as his.

"Fucking beautiful," he growled, his hands loosening his belt slowly. "Now the bra. I want to see those pretty tits. Your sweet, hard nipples."

Her hands were shaking as she gripped the clasp between her

breasts and loosened it. Drawing it from her shoulders, she allowed it to drop, forgotten, to the floor at her feet.

Dawg's jaw clenched. He pushed his fingers through his long black hair, pulling back the thick, silky strands from his face.

He looked like a savage. Tall, hard, intent on claiming what he believed was his, for now.

Her hands went to the band of her panties.

"Leave them," he rasped. "Come over here. Right here." He patted the top of the desk in front of his chair.

Crista felt a shudder work over her body as she moved to him slowly. Wariness had her watching him closely. This wasn't a hunger that burned hot and fast. She could see that. It was simmering just beneath the surface, a banked, furious blaze that he ruthlessly controlled now.

"Absolutely beautiful," he crooned in that husky, dark voice as she moved around the corner of the desk.

Sliding in front of the chair, she began to lift herself to the walnut top when he stopped her.

"Not like that." He gripped her hip with one hand. "Turn around and lean over it."

She fought to breathe. Turning, she flattened her hands on the desktop and, with his hand on her back, let him guide her into position.

Her breasts flattened against the dark wood, her nipples tightening against the cool desktop as she felt him move behind her.

She remembered, so clearly, just how much he enjoyed playing with that particular portion of her anatomy.

"The prettiest ass in the state." His hand smoothed over the rounded globes revealed by the thong.

His hand, calloused and warm, stroked with subtle destruction, his fingers lifting the small scrap of material that slid between the cheeks before replacing it gently.

"Did I spank you that night, Crista?" He leaned close, his lips at her shoulder as he posed the suggestive question.

"No." She was panting for air now.

There hadn't been so much as a second of foreplay, and already she could feel her juices dampening her panties.

"I fucked this pretty ass and didn't spank it?" His hand clenched on one curve as his lips began to trail down her spine. "How neglectful of me. I should rectify that, don't you think?"

She did whimper then. She had cleaned his office; she knew damned good and well that his desk held exactly what he needed to take her in any way he pleased. The new tube of lubrication he had placed there earlier hadn't gone unnoticed. And she had found the packaged sex toys herself the day before. Toys that he had opened as he grinned wickedly and washed in the attached bathroom.

He was fully prepared for any sex games he may want to play in his office. And she was no more experienced now than she had been eight years ago.

Feminine fear and nerves raced through her mind, her body. She shuddered beneath him as his lips tracked each vertebra of her spine until he reached the narrow band of the thong she wore.

"I noticed how pretty your ass was at a time when I should have been whipped for noticing." He drew the band over her thighs, his lips tracking down the side of her buttock as he disposed of the lacy material. "So soft and silky looking, and delightfully curved."

Crista fought back her cry as his teeth raked over the flesh.

She felt him move, heard the creak of the leather behind her, and knew he had sat back down in his chair. The scrape of the chair wheels over the wooden floor had her flinching as his knees bracketed her legs.

"Perfect position." Both hands gripped her rear then, spreading the cheeks gently as she felt a soft puff of air against the hidden entrance there.

"Don't do this," she suddenly begged, her nails scraping against the top of the desk as her nerves got the best of her. "I can't stand it, Dawg. Don't tease me. Just do it."

She couldn't bear it. He had already stolen too much of her. Recovering from this episode of her life would take years. What he was doing now she might never recover from.

"You're the toy, remember?" His voice was harsh with lust now. My toy. Mine to play with, to touch and to taste." His voice sounded tortured. "Sweet heaven, Crista, how I've dreamed of this. Just like this." He parted her farther a second before his teeth gripped the side of the inner flesh and his tongue flickered over it heatedly.

She tried to jerk upright, to escape the lash of sensation that exploded through her body.

"Stay put," he ordered forcefully, one hand pressing into the small of her back a second before his tongue swiped through the narrow cleft.

Crista lifted to her tiptoes. The sheer eroticism of what he was doing would brand her soul forever. His tongue flickered along the narrow valley, found the tiny, forbidden entrance, and lashed against the nerve-ridden flesh with destructive strokes.

"Damn you, Crista, you make me wild for you," he snarled behind her as his head lifted.

His head lifted, and his hand landed on one rounded cheek in a forceful caress that sent a bolt of pleasure ripping through her nerve endings.

She jerked, shuddered, and tried again to lift from the top of the desk.

"Don't move. You owe me this. Eight fucking years of dreams, and you owe me this." His hand landed on the opposite side of her rear, sending heat blazing through her in a pleasure-pain that bordered orgasm.

Crista heard her own moan of surrender then. Her rear lifted to him, and a cry escaped her lips as his hand landed again. And again. Sweet God.

"Again." She heard herself cry out the word, knew she was bucking, pressing back, begging for more of the sweet pleasure-pain. And he gave her more.

"Do you like that, Crista Ann?" He groaned behind her, his hand smoothing over her rear before another heated caress landed on her flesh. Never the same place often enough to draw her from the sensual haze he was building in her mind. Never hard enough to bring her down from the erotic high whipping through her veins.

"Yes," she cried out.

And she did. Too much. A distant part of her brain connected the dots. She knew what each touch was doing, what each fiery slap against her ass was creating. It was drawing her deeper into the web he was weaving around her soul. Making certain she belonged to him forever. That her soul always followed him, whether his followed hers or not.

Dawg watched as Crista's ass turned a pretty, heated pink. It mesmerized him. Seeing her body accept each delicately placed, heavy caress. Never too hard. Always just enough to heat rather than burn.

And it was heating her. Not just her flesh, either. Her legs parted farther, mindlessly following the direction of his hand beneath her knee as he lifted her small foot to the desk drawer he had pulled free. He propped it on the edge, watching as her rear parted, as the soft curl-laden folds between her thighs were revealed.

Dew glistened on those folds. Sweet, soft little droplets that had his mouth watering to taste, to lick. He parted the soft swells of her rear once again and leaned forward, groaning as his tongue found the heated core of her pussy and the hot syrup filling it.

Crista flinched, cried out his name, and pressed back, giving him more, begging for a deeper caress.

Not yet. Hell no, not yet. When he finished, he wanted to be certain that not so much as a hint of her former lovers remained in her dreams. He intended to brand her body and her mind with his touch, his possession. When the summer was over, leaving him would be like tearing out her own soul. He'd make certain of it. He had to make certain of it, because he couldn't imagine losing her.

He nearly paused at the thought. Dawg, getting possessive. It was damned unheard of, but he was. So possessive that he growled, nipped at her smooth rear, then stiffened his tongue and drove inside the liquid hot depths of her pussy as he slid from his chair to his knees behind her.

Sliding the sweet, slick juices from her pussy back to her ass, he lubricated the little hole enough to take the tip of his finger. She flinched, cried out, then drove back, burying the digit to the first knuckle as he fucked his tongue hot and deep inside her.

She was like a fire, burning in his arms. Each time he took her, more memories from that long-ago night coalesced inside his head. They twisted and formed and raced through his mind with a force that left him breathless.

She had taken him then as she was taking him now: eagerly, heatedly, calling out his name in that broken little voice filled with need.

Pulling back, he turned her, ignoring her frantic little mewls of denial, and lifted her to the desk.

"Lie back." His own voice bordered on demented. "Lie back, Crista. Give me what I need. Now."

She fell back, her hair fanning out around her sweat-dampened head as her hands reached back and gripped the edge of the desk.

Dawg spread her legs slowly as he lifted them, arranging her feet at the lower edge of the desk and staring at the swollen, wet folds awaiting him.

He bent forward, his eyes closing as his tongue took a slow, greedy lick through the narrow slit.

Crista jerked beneath him, her hips lifting, a low wail leaving her lips. The sounds coming from her throat were making him crazy.

"The sweetest pussy in the world," he told her gently as he leaned back, smoothed his fingers over the wet curls and stared up her. "Will you have it waxed for me, Crista? Will you have all those pretty curls removed so I can taste your skin, lick all your juices, and show you how sweet and hot it can be when nothing hides you from me? Will you do that for me, sweetheart?"

He pulled the tube of lubrication from the opened bottom drawer as he let the fingers of his other hand smooth over the drenched curves.

"Dawg." There was an edge of hesitancy and feminine distress in her tone. But her hips lifted to him, her body unconsciously seeking more.

Moving slowly, Dawg spread an application of the lubricating gel on his fingers, let it warm, then lowered his lips to the succulent flesh before him, while his slickened fingers moved to the sweet portal lower.

She cried out his name again as he pressed against the entrance to her anus. Her hips jerked, lifted, and a ragged cry filled the air as he pierced the narrow channel.

His tongue flicked around her clit, then he drew it inside his mouth as the second finger penetrated her tight rear.

God, she was fucking hot. She twisted beneath him, her juices spilling from her. His cock was aching like an open wound, and his balls were drawn so tight against his body that they were in agony.

"Answer me, fancy-face," he groaned, lifting his lips from her sweet pussy and staring up at her as he worked his fingers inside the tender back hole. "Will you do that for me? Have your pussy waxed. Make it all slick and soft for me."

He reach back to the drawer and drew out the small butt plug he had taken from the package earlier. She liked that edge of pain. She liked the burning pleasure that seared her nerve endings and made the need for orgasm an erotic agony.

"Yes," she hissed. "Anything. Anything you want."

He drew his fingers from her rear.

"No. Don't stop," she pleaded raggedly. "Not yet, don't stop."

"Shh, baby. I'm not stopping. I'm going to make it better." He lubricated the tapered toy. "So much better."

He straightened, lifted her legs, and drew them together before pressing them back.

Her eyes snapped open. Nearly black in arousal now, they watched him warily, knowingly. She knew what was coming. She had seen the toys, knew he wouldn't wait long before using one of them.

He pressed the narrow tip against the tiny puckered opening.

"No," she whispered. "Not the toy. I want you there."

His cock jerked as a grimace tightened his face.

"I'll be there later, sweetheart," he promised. "I want you to know what this is like. Filled from one end to the other. So hot and tight that you won't know where pleasure ends and pain begins, because it's all going to be so damned good that you can't stop coming."

The toy eased inside her, stretching her, causing her to arch and whimper with sensation as he watched the pleasure contort her face.

Dawg worked the toy inside her, easing it in, watching as the little hole spread to accommodate the toy and finally tightened around the narrower base. He watched as the muscles of her rear tightened and flexed as she fought to adjust to the stretching. Heard her muttered moans as he picked up the little remote that would activate the vibration inside it.

Placing her feet back on the edge of the desk, he pressed the switch and growled as she jerked, bucked. Her hips began to move, swaying and jerking as the plug began to not just vibrate but also flex inside her.

Her eyes flew open. Between her thighs, her juices began to build on the soft folds and silky curls. Her body flushed, her nipples tightened.

"Oh God, Dawg." She arched to him as he stepped closer, his dick gripped in his hand, the heavy crest tucking against the flexing opening. "Oh God. Fuck me. Fuck me, Dawg. Before it kills me . . ."

Dawg had to fight for control. The feel of silky wet heat on the crest of his dick had his teeth grinding together as he fought for control. Just a little more control. Just another minute to relish her surrender, her pleasure.

But she was so fucking hot. And he knew how tight she was, how hungry her pussy was when she was aroused. And he needed. God help him, just for a little while, he needed . . .

What had he done to her? Crista could feel the insidious vibration in her rear, the slow flex, an easing, then a stretching that began to make her insane for more.

Her eyes slitted open; she couldn't manage to lift the lids fully, sensuality made her gaze heavy, made her body weak and melting. But she was able to watch Dawg.

His broad hands held her legs up beneath the knees. His eyes were centered between her thighs, to the spot were the head of his cock was tucked at the opening to her vagina.

She could feel him, a heavy presence at the entrance, hot and thick and ready to fill her.

"Dawg," she whispered his name, a sigh of pleasure, a questioning breath as he paused.

Thick black hair fell along the sides of his face, straight and raven black, framing his savage features.

"Taking you is like losing myself," he groaned roughly. "I feel you clasping my dick, Crista, but I feel you pouring into my soul."

Celadon green eyes, so light they were like pale green ice, burned now. They flickered with a darker edge, gleamed with carnal knowledge.

Crista whimpered at the words as well as the look.

"Don't do this," she whispered tearfully, seeing the dark longing on his face, not the need to share, but the need to possess more than just her body.

He shook his head roughly, his lips pulling back from his teeth in a silent snarl as his hips moved, the broad head of his erection working inside her, stretching her, burning her.

"Did you walk away—" A hard breath hissed between his teeth. "Did you leave without looking back?"

She shook her head. She couldn't do this. She could let him have all of her.

"Answer me." He paused, the head of his cock filling her, teasing her. Daring her. "Did you look back?"

"Please, Dawg . . ."

"Tell me."

Another inch. The movement he made didn't ease his cock inside her, that additional inch was taken with a hard flex of his hips and a destructive flame along the tender nerve endings it stroked.

"Yes," she cried out. The words falling unbidden from her lips. "I've always looked back."

His hands clenched on her legs.

"You didn't forget." His voice softened then, his cock shifted and moved inside her, stroking her, taking her by the smallest degrees with each movement.

She couldn't hide from him. She wanted to. She needed to.

"I never forgot." A tear fell from the corner of her eye. "I never forgot you, Dawg."

Her heart never forgot. Her soul never released the memory of his touch, his hard voice whispering at her ear, his hunger, or her need for him. Her love. The soul-deep, unquenchable agony of loving him.

"Don't cry, fancy-face." His voice was graveled now, thick and rough as she felt the agonizing pleasure beginning to engulf her. "I'll take care of you."

Each inch of his erection inside her was like a brand laid to the tender muscles. A brand of fiery sensation and exquisite pleasure.

Crista arched, driving him deeper inside her, feeling the piercing, burning sensation of being doubly penetrated, exquisitely stretched.

"There, sweetheart." He wrapped her legs around his hips as he leaned closer, his head lowering to her nipples, adding to the ecstatic pleasure already gripping her by drawing one tight bud into his hot mouth and suckling it deeply.

His hips were moving, his cock thrusting slowly, working into her with each thrust as the overwhelming sensations of heat, stretching, and brutal pleasure began to build inside her.

It was always like this with Dawg. The world centered to two beings, time stopped, nothing mattered but this, with him, the feel of him fucking her, owning her.

He owned her.

He thrust inside her, and she arched to take him deeper.

His lips, teeth, and tongue consumed her nipples, one then the other, and her hands threaded into his hair to hold him closer.

"So good," he whispered. "So sweet and tight."

Her body reflexively tightened further around him, muscles contracting, her soul glorying in the harsh male groan that whispered around the nipple his mouth returned to.

"Beautiful." He buried his head between her breasts, the rhythm of his hips increasing, and she spurred him on with her cries and her pleas for more.

"Mine!" he snarled, and she exploded around him.

Her orgasm tore through her as his thrusts became harder, deeper. He pounded into her, shafting her with surging strokes and fucking into her with an ever-growing greed.

"Damn you." He bit her shoulder, his hands gripped her hips, and as the climax began to ease, she felt the powerful first spurt of his semen blasting into her.

She arched violently through the second release. Tightening on him to the point she could feel every throb, every pulse, every ripple of Dawg's release inside her. And she felt another part of her emotional defenses collapse.

Dawg once again held her heart.

Sixteen

Two days later, Dawg admitted what he should have known eight years ago. Crista Ann had managed to wrap herself around his heart in a way that he knew he would never manage to escape. He could feel the bonds tightening as he pulled the pickup into the parking slot directly in front of the small, exclusive spa that had moved into downtown Somerset.

Beside the truck, Rowdy pulled up on his Harley and helped the little wildcat he was engaged to from the back. Beside Rowdy, Natches pulled his Harley in and waited.

"This is insane," Crista muttered in the passenger seat as she stared mutinously at the front door of the spa. "It's going to hurt."

"I'll kiss it all better tonight." He turned to her, letting her see just how much he was anticipating kissing the delicate flesh between her thighs and easing the memory of any discomfort she would feel with the waxing he had had Kelly schedule for her.

Her arms crossed over her breasts defensively.

"How did I let you talk me into this?" she snapped, only half-angry. The other half was uncertainty, perhaps a little embarrassment.

"Because I'm persuasive?" he asked with a waggle of his brows.

He had done his best to be persuasive. For hours. Licking, kissing, tempting her with the knowledge of how much better it could be, making her so hot, so damned desperate, she would have agreed to anything.

Her lips twitched then, a sensual smile of remembrance tugging at the lush curves as a faint blush stole over her cheeks. And his chest clenched. Right there in the front seat of his pickup, Dawg felt his heart swell with an emotion so unfamiliar he knew it was fucking love. It was strong enough, hard enough that he reached up and rubbed at the center of his chest to ease the constriction.

"You were very persuasive." She sighed, staring back at the spa morosely. "And you know I'm going to be very put out when I'm finished."

A goofy smile tugged at his lips, and his heart raced.

"I'll take you someplace special when you're finished," he told her then. "Someplace you'll enjoy."

She glanced at him from the corner of her eyes.

"How special?"

"So special I've never taken another woman there," he promised, watching her gaze jerk away, that hint of hesitancy that tensed her slender frame.

She was scared of whatever he made her feel, and he couldn't blame her. He had blackmailed her, and he would keep blackmailing her until he knew she belonged to him.

She cleared her throat delicately. "Fine. But it better be worth this." She gathered her purse from where it sat behind his seat and stared him fully in the eyes as she turned back to him. "And it better not hurt too bad."

"You'll love it," he promised her. "Just imagine me doing it."

She looked scandalized. "Oh Lord, don't go there, Dawg. This is going to be hard enough." She pulled at the door latch quickly, escaping before he could say anything that would deepen that blush along her cheeks or give her eyes more of that confused, uncertain look.

He had a feeling Crista had once believed that she knew him. That she could predict him. He could have told her that wasn't going to happen.

He moved from the truck as she and Kelly headed into the spa, meeting Natches and Rowdy at the front of his truck and staring around the street curiously.

"We picked up a tail," Natches said quietly, his dark green eyes glancing to the gray sedan that had pulled in farther up the street. "She pulled in behind you after you hit the city limits."

Dawg glanced up the street, his gaze narrowing on Greta Dane. Normally when a woman looked at man with an expression as cold and hard as flint as Greta was giving him, it tended to make the balls draw up in fear.

Thankfully, Dawg wasn't prone to allow such things to affect his private parts.

"Something's up," he murmured, turning back to the other men. "Have you heard from Cranston?"

"Nothing." Natches shook his head as he crossed his arms over his chest and tucked his hands by his sides. "We picked the bulldog up there just inside the city limits, and she didn't bother to try to hide it."

Dawg rubbed his hand over his chin. "Stay here. Let's see what I can find out."

He stepped to the sidewalk and strode quickly to the little sedan Greta was driving. As he neared, the window rolled down, and Greta's pinched expression increased. She was also nervous. She tucked a cigarette between her lips and lit up as he neared the car.

"What's up, Greta?" Dawg leaned against the pickup next to her and stared back at her quizzically.

"Cranston's orders," she informed him waspishly. "Unlike some people, I'm a team player."

Dawg tilted his head and smiled slowly. "Are you implying I don't play well with others, Greta?"

She drew on the cigarette again before flicking the ashes to the portable ashtray in the middle console.

"I'm not implying anything, Mackay. I'm stating a fact."

The stare she leveled back at him was suspicious, chilling in its complete lack of emotion.

"So you were ordered to watch me?" he asked her.

"No, I was ordered to follow your girlfriend." Her own smile was nothing short of relish. "I didn't ask why."

Bullshit.

Dawg stared back at her, his gaze narrowed, his body prepared. Somehow, Cranston had focused on Crista. This wouldn't be a good thing.

"Have fun keeping up with us," he told her then, returning the smile with interest. "I'd make sure I wasn't easily shocked, though. After we leave here, we're heading into the mountains. I have a blanket in the truck, and we're stopping for a light little picnic lunch that my favorite restaurant is currently putting together for us.

Then, since it *is* private property, I thought I might introduce my girlfriend to a little fresh-air lovin'. Now, I don't mind a little exhibitionism every now and then, but you should be prepared. It could get rather hard-core."

He watched her face flush. The hardened agent could kill a man without a thought, but the subject of sex seemed to make her jumpy as hell.

"I'm sure I'll survive," she gritted out.

Dawg nodded slowly and smiled again. "I'm sure you will, sugar. Just to be on the safe side though, I think I'll have Natches go with us and sit with you for awhile. Some things just shouldn't be done alone, ya know? And Natches, he makes damned good company in such situations."

Her gaze flickered over to Natches and Rowdy as Dawg turned as well. Natches grinned slow and easy. He might not know what the hell they were talking about, but even from there, Natches would have seen the hard flush on Greta's face.

"You sic that perverted bastard in my direction, and I'll shoot him," Greta warned him then.

Dawg shrugged. "He'll survive. You're not allowed to kill him, and a little bloodshed between friends . . ." He smiled again. "Could get interesting." He straightened and dropped the smile. "You talk to Cranston, tell him I'm waiting to hear from him, sugar. Soon."

He didn't give her time to reply, but he was guessing she was on her cell phone even as he strode back to where Rowdy and Natches were waiting on the sidewalk in front of his truck.

"She's watching Crista," he told Natches softly as Rowdy listened in interest.

"Bad news." Natches grimaced as he lowered his head as though to check the tips of his cowboy boots.

"How long does this female stuff take, anyway?" Dawg glanced at the doors to the spa, knowing damned good and well he wasn't waiting inside the building for Crista to finish. No way, nohow; all that estrogen could be fatal.

"Wax, trim, and style," Rowdy mused. "You're looking at three hours."

Dawg leaned against the truck. "You two can just stand here and wait it out with me," he decided.

Natches grunted. "I had things to do, Dawg."

"Get over it. God only knows what Cranston has up his sleeve, and I'm not standing outside this place by myself."

"Hell. I'm getting the shit jobs and none of the pleasure," Natches cursed. "This growing-up crap you two seem so intent on is starting to piss me off. I think I'll go talk to Agent Dane for a while instead. She's always good for a smirk or two, if nothing else."

Casting Rowdy and Dawg both an irate look, Natches ambled from his slouch against the hood of the truck and headed for Agent Dane's vehicle.

The agent in question lit up again as she watched Natches warily.

"Do you think he's really pissed?" Rowdy drawled as Natches neared the woman's car.

"With Natches, who the hell knows anymore." Dawg shook his head wearily. "That boy didn't come out of Afghanistan easy. He was going to stay with the bum shoulder despite his CO's advice until the Marines booted his ass out."

Natches, already an excellent shot when he went into the Marines and an instinctive hunter, had been quickly inducted into training as a sniper/assassin. Dawg suspected his cousin had more kills to his record than he was admitting to, and secrets that only Dawg could guess at.

"You two didn't do anything easy," Rowdy said then. "I thought the agreement was that we'd go in, do our duty, and come home without changing who or what we were."

Dawg had a feeling Rowdy wasn't talking about the lack of need in sharing his pretty fiancée.

"Hey, you started it," he said anyway. "Getting all possessive and snarly over Kelly the way you did."

Rowdy snorted at that. "Don't play dense, Dawg, it doesn't suit you."

Dawg grimaced. "We were more suited to some things than you were, Rowdy. You just didn't want to see it."

"Killing?" Rowdy asked. "You were never suited to that. You or Natches."

"You just didn't want to see it." Dawg stared his cousin in the eye then. "Killing wasn't the draw, though. It was taking out the monsters. And that was something Natches and I both were ready to do before we were out of our teens."

Dawg's and Natches's fathers were bastards. But most of the men out of that family were bastards. Literally. Good ole Grandpa August had sired sons from one end of the nation to the other. He had paused in Somerset long enough to fake a marriage to Ellen Mackay and give her a daughter and three sons. Then he had nicely informed her that the marriage was illegal because he was already married, and then he had disappeared.

Ellen Mackay had taken the August name from her sons and given them hers instead. Four kids that she had raised herself with little help, and she had died knowing that out of all those kids, only one of them had a sense of decency. Ray Mackay had been solid as the earth. The rest? Hell, the rest of them were as black-hearted and mean as the old man himself.

As Dawg understood it, his cousins in Texas hadn't fared any better. Their father, Joe August, the legitimate issue of old Nate August, had been pure evil. The hell he had visited on his sons had nearly destroyed them. It was only by a miracle that they had survived both during and after the torture they had endured.

"I saw Johnny's mother and Natches's dad with their heads together outside the courthouse yesterday when Kelly and I were driving through. They looked like they were brewing up trouble."

Nadine Mackay Grace and Dayle Mackay were vipers apart; when together, the destruction they could cause had destroyed more than one life.

"Hell," Dawg cursed. "Dayle's already disowned Natches. What more could he do to him?"

"I just wish I knew for sure it was Natches they were targeting." Rowdy sighed. "I don't know what the hell's up, Dawg, but it's not feeling good."

Hell, no, it wasn't. Dawg could feel his teeth clenching and his neck itching. Those two things were a surefire warning that shit was coming down.

"Fallback position?" Dawg murmured.

"I have you covered," Rowdy answered.

Dawg had explained Crista's presence at the warehouse as well as the risk that Crista could be identified as part of the group attempting to sell the missiles.

Their fallback position was clear: Rowdy and Natches would hold the line, while Dawg pulled Crista into the mountains to an old, hidden hunter's cabin they had found years before as teenagers. No one knew about the cabin but the three cousins, and it would be the ideal place to hide Crista until they figured out the best way to protect her. Or until Alex and his group returned from wherever the hell they were.

"I'm going to put out a call to Alex's contact," Dawg muttered then, hating the need for that. He had hoped to be able to avoid contacting Alex. "We need to let him know Crista could be in trouble before it's too late."

Rowdy nodded, then glanced back to where Natches leaned against the sedan farther down the street, obviously arguing with Agent Dane.

"When was the last time you saw Natches argue with anyone?" Rowdy asked.

Dawg glanced at his cousin and grinned. "The last time Greta spoke to him."

"Interesting."

"Damn interesting," Dawg agreed as he pulled his cell phone from the holder at his belt and flipped it open. It took only a second to hit the speed dial number that connected with Alex's contact.

"Leave a message." The voice was cold, hard.

Dawg said one word. "Crista." Then disconnected the call. Within hours Alex would know things had the potential to go from sugar to shit with his sister in a very short time.

And then he propped himself against the hood of the truck and glanced at the front door of the spa. Crista was inside, possibly getting the intimate waxing he had spent so long that morning talking her into.

His body tensed, lust rose sharp and painful inside him, hardening his dick in an instant.

God help Cranston if he messed with Dawg's fun later that evening. He had waited years, hell, Dawg felt as though he had waited all his life for this. The man or woman who dared to mess with it would pay. Painfully.

• • •

Being intimately bald was a curiously disconcerting feeling, Crista thought as she rode beside Dawg several hours later toward the surprise he had promised her.

In the backseat, a covered wicker basket emitted the succulent scent of fresh fried chicken from beneath the large checkered tablecloth secured over the top of the lid.

There was also a new addition to the back of the truck. On the rack hanging on the window stretched a rifle. It hadn't been there when she had gone into the spa, but it was there now.

And Dawg was testy. He kept checking the rearview mirror, taking turns, and using back roads she hadn't known existed.

"Are we being followed?" Not for the first time, she turned and looked behind them.

"Yep." Taciturn and too soft for comfort, his tone did little for the nerves beginning to build in her stomach.

"I don't see anyone."

"They're staying far enough back to stay out of sight," he said as he took another turn. "I'm just getting far enough ahead of them to pull over and trash their tracker." A grin stretched his lips. A dangerous grin. "I want to get them good and lost first."

"There's a tracker on the truck?" Her voice shook, but hell, it wasn't every day she realized she was being tracked. Being followed would be bad enough.

"Hang on," he warned. And not a moment too soon. The truck came to a rocking stop.

Jumping out, Dawg strode quickly behind the truck, bent from sight, and seconds later straightened and ran back to the driver's side. Jumping in, he threw the truck in gear, flashed her a smile that was less dangerous and more filled with fun, before tossing an electronic disc out the window and speeding away.

Crista stared around the area they were in. They were deep in the mountains, and evening was coming on. Even she couldn't find her way back to town from here.

"You're going to let someone get trapped in these mountains in the dark?" she asked carefully. "Who is it?"

"A friend." He chuckled.

"You're going to get a friend lost in these mountains?" she asked in disbelief. "Dawg, your friends don't get lost that easily," she pointed out.

"Most don't." He nodded on another low laugh. The playful grin on his face reminded her of a little boy into mischief. "This friend is city, though. Don't worry, Natches is riding close to her ass, and he'll take care of her."

"Natches?" She wouldn't trust Natches in a well-lit room filled with saints, let alone on a dark mountain. "You're leaving some poor, unsuspecting woman stuck here with Natches? What did she do to make you angry?"

That canceled out any bad-guy types.

"She's spying on me." The flash of his teeth against his sun-darkened skin was playful and sexy. "For some reason, the special agent in charge of the arrests last week has a tail on you, sweetheart. Usually, I wouldn't care, but I have plans today. Plans that don't include watching eyes."

His brows waggled over the top of his dark sunglasses.

Plans that didn't include watching eyes? Crista felt her heart race further than it was already after he mentioned that she was being followed rather than him.

"Why is she interested in me?" She could feel the fear clogging her throat.

"I don't know yet." He shook his head briefly before turning back onto one of the wider country roads and accelerating along the blacktop. "I tried to call her boss, but he's not taking his calls right now. He'll let me know eventually."

"He knows I was there," she whispered. "Are they going to arrest me?"

"No one is going to arrest you, Crista," he growled. "I have another call out to Alex. A contact number I doubt you had. He should be calling us soon. Until then, we're just waiting to see what's happening and playing with the fools sent to watch you."

"Your boss doesn't trust you anymore then," she said worriedly. "They could arrest you, too, Dawg."

"Stop worrying."

Stop worrying?

"One of us should worry here," she gritted out. "Dawg, if he's got someone watching me, then he thinks I was involved."

"If he had proof, he would have had you arrested at the spa. He wouldn't have someone watching you. Not to say that he's not suspicious. But Cranston doesn't make a move without proof. He doesn't have proof."

Crista bit her lip, chewing at it worriedly as she watched the road ahead of her.

"You sound certain." She needed him to be certain.

"I know Cranston. But I am interested in what is going on. Natches should be able to figure that one out; then we'll figure out where we go from here."

"The note was in the Rodeo," she whispered. "I left it there. I know it was in there. I was going to look for it, but you kept dragging me away from it." And then it had blown up.

"Don't worry about it." His voice became more clipped as he turned up another road, a graveled road rather than dirt.

Pristine white fences ran along the side of the road. A few dozen cattle meandered in thickly grassed pastures, their heads lifting curiously as the truck sped down the road.

"I do worry about it. That was the only proof I had."

Dawg knew that. Just as he knew that proof was safely locked away in his safe.

It was hidden. Just in case. But damn, telling Crista he had it all along was going to piss her clean off. That wasn't what he wanted today.

He would tell her tomorrow. He wasn't letting anything interfere in his appreciation of her slick, honeyed flesh when the time came.

Just a few more hours. Six hours at the most, and the sensitivity of the delicate flesh that had been waxed should be back to normal. The spa, Kelly swore, had the best technicians in the business, and the emollients they used after the waxing soothed the irritated flesh immediately.

He would tell her about the note tomorrow. The letterhead of the delivery company, the date, and note would help. Unfortunately, it hadn't been signed by the delivery person. At least the handwriting on the note definitely wasn't Crista's.

That added to the fact that even with Natches's contacts, computer abilities, and general sneakiness, he couldn't find so much as a spare penny in Crista's name in the house she shared with Alex or anywhere related to her. And he had spent the better part of the past days searching for it.

Crista wasn't the money girl, the lone female that had taken the buyers' million dollars, supposedly in the thieves' interest.

The men in custody hadn't named her, but Dawg hadn't been

able to interrogate them, either. And he was damned sure it wasn't Crista.

Where had that trust come from? That question rolled through him as he passed the cattle guard in the road that led to the property he had been working on for years now.

The land, over two hundred acres of woodland and pastures, was bordered by an arm of Lake Cumberland. The sprawling two-story log cabin he had begun building the summer before sat on the rise overlooking the lake, surrounded on three sides by fir, oak, and maple trees. The ranch yard was surrounded by the same white fences that stretched along the road. Stables sat a quarter mile to the left, and the barn and tractor sheds to the right. All the buildings were placed so that they were protected on three sides by the dense woods that surrounded the area.

The little coves of cleared land that had been created inside the tree line gave the land a natural, peaceful appearance. It also pleased his need for space and privacy.

This was Dawg's. Bought by the money he saved while in the Marines and then the ATF, along with part of the profits from the lumber store in the past four years. It wasn't bought from his father's inheritance, and it wasn't tied to memories of his parents.

It was his. Just his. Just as Crista was.

"Stop worrying." He glanced at her and saw the frown on her face. "No one knows we're here. Hell, no one in Somerset but Natches, Rowdy, and Kelly even knows about this place."

"Where are we, anyway?"

"Jabez. We're still in Pulaski County. You can see the lake from the back, but it's a small distance to it."

Dawg stepped from the truck before opening the back side door and dragging out the picnic basket.

"You coming?" He looked over the top of the sunglasses, and that look sizzled. "There's a nice little clearing out back where we can picnic. I'll show you the house first, though."

Crista stepped from the truck and stared at the house. The dark logs helped it blend into the trees around it, as did the dark brown color of the tin roof. A porch surrounded it, as did a balcony on the top floor.

"I'm having a hot tub installed on the balcony outside the master bedroom on the back." He swept his hand toward the house as he met her at the front of the truck. "When the inside is finished, I'll probably bring the *Nauti Dawg* out and tie her up to the dock where I managed to buy permission to build on the shoreline."

"Are you trying to become domesticated, Dawg?" she asked as he opened the wood gate and ushered her into the ranch yard.

He could still hear the nerves in her voice, her fear. The knowledge that Cranston now suspected her had thrown her. But there was no guilt in her eyes or her expression. Confusion, fear, yes. But it wasn't blazing; it was subdued. Whether Crista wanted to admit it or not, she trusted him.

"Come on into the house." He unlocked the front door, pushed it open slowly, and checked out the open, airy rooms before leading the way inside.

The walls were unpainted. The floors were unfinished. The stairwell wasn't banistered, and the upstairs wasn't much better. It was, as he liked to tell Rowdy and Natches, a work in progress.

Kind of like Crista. He looked at her as she stared around the entryway nervously and smiled. That same smile that seemed to worry Natches so much. Possessing her heart might not be easy, but he was damned determined to do just that.

Seventeen

Dawg's house was incredible. The large entryway held a curving staircase to the second floor and an open hall that looked out over the unfinished balustrades. There were no doors on the five entrances on the second floor, but sunlight spilled from the windows on the front section and bathed the hall as well as the foyer in myriad sunbeams from the tall windows that looked out on the graveled road.

To her right, a large, open entrance led into what she assumed would be a living room with another entrance to the far end into another room. On her left, farther along the foyer, was another wide entrance into a dining room. Crista moved forward hesitantly, staring into the room and seeing the two sets of French doors that led onto the wide porch wrapping around the house. At the end of that room was another entrance that led into what was clearly a kitchen.

"Come on, I'll show you around." Dawg led the way into the dining room, then into the kitchen. "The foyer opens up to a back hall." He pointed out another door as they entered a large kitchen. "There's a pantry, a washroom, and a small spare bedroom along the hall as well as an office that opens into the living room."

Nothing was finished. By the look of the drywall and the dust along the floors, it hadn't been long since it had been installed.

"I'm surprised," she said as he gave her a quick tour of the house, upstairs and downstairs. "You've managed this without a hint of gossip."

He flashed a grin as they stepped from the stairway back into the foyer. "That wasn't easy, either. I bought the land about three years ago through a third party, and I've had the work done in stages, through the same people. Once it's complete, we'll file the proper deeds, etc., through the county. But it's mine, regardless."

"So why hide it?" she asked as they moved back into the kitchen.

Dawg moved to the roughly framed center island where the picnic basket sat on the strip of plywood covering the top frame. He braced his hip against the side of it and looked around silently for long moments.

"Pure spite, probably." He sighed, shaking his head ruefully. "The relatives seem to delight in knowing every damned move I make, so it's become a game to do things they don't know about and rub their noses in it."

"What about the house your parents left you?" Crista had seen the outside of that property several times. The front of the house was all that showed at the bottom of the mountain it had been built into. Dawg's father had been said to be one of the premier architects in the country for such buildings.

"The place makes me damned claustrophobic." He grimaced. "I'll probably sell it eventually."

"Once you've milked your relatives of all the satisfaction you can squeeze from them?" She smiled in turn.

A wry smile curled his lips as he stared back at her.

"We're not exactly a close family," he admitted. "Nadine Grace and Dayle Mackay are thorns in my side, not to mention Natches's and Rowdy's. If they could destroy Uncle Ray, they'd do it in a heartbeat. Unfortunately for them, Ray figured out how to protect himself early from them. They were snake mean even as kids, from what I understand."

"Except Ray." Crista had heard that herself. Of all the older Mackays, Ray was the only one spoken of kindly.

"Except Uncle Ray." Dawg nodded, his expression flickering with affection. "Ray raised Rowdy right, and Rowdy helped raise Natches and me until Ray could get his hooks into us. Neither one of them gave up on us. Rowdy held us together."

"Even to the point of drawing you into the sharing?" she asked.

A bark of laughter left his throat then. "Come on, we'll talk while we walk."

Dawg held his hand out to her, waiting, watching as she gazed at it a second before lifting her smaller, more delicate hand to his. Dawg twined his fingers with hers, watching as her paler, softer hand meshed with his.

It looked right. It felt damned right. Damn her. She had his guts and his heart twisted in so many knots he knew he would never be free of her.

As he led her from the house and into the tree-shaded backyard, Dawg found himself feeling emotions he hadn't expected. Aside from the protectiveness he felt, there was a well of heated hunger, fierce possessiveness, and a gentleness he had never felt toward another woman.

"You and Alex are pretty close," he said as he let her spread the tablecloth on the thick, well-cut grass at the edge of the small clearing that looked out onto a private natural cove the land created for the lake.

"We had to be," she said as she tucked a thick strand of hair behind her ear and smoothed out the tablecloth.

Dawg set the basket in the center before lowering himself on the cloth and leaning back. Crista seemed more hesitant, sitting rather than stretching out, but at least she sat close enough to him to assure him that she wasn't running from him.

"Your parents were pretty distant around people," he said as she set out the small covered platter of still-warm chicken and began unpacking the side dishes.

"They were like that with Alex and me as well." A little frown pulled at her forehead as she spoke. "They planned Alex's birth, but I was kind of a surprise." The curve of her lips was tipped with an expression of subtle bitterness. "They didn't want me. They gave me to Alex to raise pretty much. Mom was only concerned with pleasing Dad, and he was only concerned with her and his moneymaking schemes."

Chester Jansen had always been certain a fortune awaited him just around the corner. He had searched for gold, for artifacts. He had nearly destroyed his small business playing the stock market, and he had constantly been taken in with fly-by-night moneymaking schemes.

"Alex did a good job raising you," he pointed out.

"He did. Alex was already ten when I was born. He had learned to take care of himself, and he applied it to taking care of me." She nodded as she arranged the chicken and side dishes before setting two china plates between them and pulling out the glass carafe of sweet iced tea and unscrewing the lid that covered it before pouring the dark liquid into drinking glasses.

"Neither one of you turned out too bad." He accepted the glass she handed him, then watched as she began opening the food and placing the serving spoons into it.

"We survived." She shrugged, glancing at him warily again. "He warned me about you when I was sixteen, you know."

"Really?" Dawg drawled. "I'll have to discuss that with him. What warning did he give you?"

"To stay away from the Mackay cousins." She flashed him a teasing smile. "He said the lot of you were bad news to any girl who wanted love rather than nasty games."

"And you didn't want nasty games?" He smiled back at her wickedly. He had a feeling that some of those games she would have taken to like a natural once she had gotten older. She sure as hell took to them now.

She ducked her head for a long second before lifting it slowly and staring back at him in determination. "I didn't want to be one of the Nauti Boys' Toys. That's what your women were called."

"But you wanted to be my woman?" He needed to know. He needed to hear her say it.

Crista dragged her gaze away from Dawg's and stared across the clearing to the serenity of the small cove they faced. Water lapped against the rocky shore with a soothing rhythm.

She *had* wanted to be Dawg's woman. Even then, ten years before, at a time when she had no concept what it meant to be anyone's woman. Her fascination for him had been soul-deep, and it had culminated in one heated night that had threatened to destroy her soul.

"I wanted to be your woman," she admitted on a sigh. She hadn't lied to him to this point. Lying was something she hated. She had hated it as a child, and as an adult, she hated it even more.

"What changed that, Crista?" he asked her then, his voice insidiously soft, gentle. "We had one night together, and instead of slapping me with a frying pan the next morning, you ran."

She shook her head. Over the past few days she had figured that one out for herself.

"I was too young for you, Dawg," she finally admitted as she turned back to him. "We both knew I was too young for you. I couldn't handle what I felt for you along with what I thought you wanted from me. It was too much."

"And now?"

"And now you're blackmailing me." And she loved him more now than she had then.

"If I hadn't blackmailed you?"

There was something in his voice that pulled at her then. Something she was certain she would see in his eyes if she pulled the dark glasses from his nose.

She reached out and did just that. Slid them from his face as he watched her, met his darkened gaze and felt her heart trip in her chest.

He was staring at her like no other man ever had. Equal parts hunger and pain.

If he hadn't blackmailed her?

"I would have caved eventually," she whispered, caught, held by that look in his eyes. "One of those nights that I was driving around the marina just to see if you were there, I would have weakened. I would have walked out to your houseboat, and if you had been alone, I would have come to you."

She had been weakening, and she knew it. Tempted by his smiles, his teasing, his determined irritation each time she rebuffed him.

"You came to the marina just to see me?" He reached out, his fingertips smoothing over her collarbone and sending heated spirals of need crashing through her system.

Crista licked her lips, and for once, she didn't fight the need welling inside her. She didn't fight the love she knew no other man would ever possess.

"Often." She fought to overcome the breathlessness, the racing of her heart. "And I'd stop and see the lights on in the *Nauti Dawg*, and I'd have to make myself stay in my car. I'd have to fight the need to go to you."

"You should have come to me." His hand cupped the back of her head, and he pulled her to him. "You should have let me love you, Crista."

Crista's senses exploded when his lips touched hers. It wasn't the fiery, hungry kisses she was used to. It was a slow, tender exploration. It was letting her get used to the feel of his tongue against her lips before he slipped inside. It was sharing the taste of himself even as he drew hers in. It was heated, sensitizing, it was a kiss that drove the breath from her lungs and left her moaning with the need for more.

Her hands braced on the cloth beneath them as her hair enveloped them, hiding their faces, their kiss, shielding them in a veil of intimacy as his lips pulled back just enough to cause her eyes to open as a whimper of denial left her lips.

"I would have pulled you inside," he whispered, his lips brushing hers as he spoke. "I would have locked out the world and drawn you to my bed. I would have made certain you never wanted to leave it again."

"I don't want to leave it now." She couldn't hold the words in.

A distant part of her brain cursed her foolishness, cursed her weak heart and the part of her soul that had never released the memory of his kiss, his touch.

She watched as Dawg's eyes dilated, darkened, then he was stealing her kiss. He ravished her lips, ate at them, and grew greedy on the taste of her. His tongue licked, his head slanted, and the kiss deepened as fireworks exploded through her body. Brilliant heat. Flames licked over her flesh and seared her nerve endings.

When he drew back, all the way back, they were both breathing hard and fast and fighting for control.

"Not yet." His voice was a graveled sound of need. "Too fucking soon. You have a few hours before you can take it yet."

"There are other ways." She leaned forward, touching her lips with his again, and saw the surprise in his eyes. She whispered wickedly, "Come on, Dawg. Show me how nasty you can get."

Show her how nasty he could get? Oh, she had no idea the fantasies he had of getting nasty with her.

"What about lunch?" He glanced down at the food she had laid out.

"Fried chicken tastes better cold," she reminded him, and Dawg watched in eager anticipation at the slow little lick her tongue made at her lips. "We can always eat later."

Repacking the food was a simple matter of snapping the lids

back on the containers and resetting them in the basket. The basket itself was set to the side. Dawg found himself moving, forcing her down to her back as he came over her.

"I won't be nice," he warned her. "You might want to reconsider that little dare you just made."

Letting loose his fantasies could have disastrous results. Because he had a lot of fantasies.

"It could get worse than a spanking and a butt plug that vibrates and ripples?" She stared up at him in amused disbelief, even as her hands pulled his shirt free of his jeans.

She was wild, wanton. Dawg could see it in her eyes now, and he wondered if he hadn't somehow sensed that wildness inside her years before.

He held back, feeling her slender fingers pulling at the buttons of his shirt, releasing them one by one as she stared up at him with a challenge in her eyes.

He wondered how far she would go. How wild she would let herself get before she pulled back. And maybe a part of him had to know. He had no desire to share her, but that didn't mean his sexuality had dimmed in any way. He liked his sex lengthy, hard, and nasty. Crista couldn't have a clue exactly how hard and nasty he could get with her. But he could show her. He could show her, and try like hell not to scare her off while he was doing so.

Because scaring her was definitely something he didn't want to do. But he wanted her. All of her, in ways that had his cock pounding in agony at the thought of it.

"I could definitely make it compete with the butt plug," he assured her with a smile as her fingers smoothed the shirt back from his shoulders.

Dawg shrugged the material away, feeling the summer breeze as it whispered through the trees and caressed his naked flesh. It was nowhere as sensual as the feel of Crista's fingers working at his belt, drawing the leather free of the buckle before pulling at the metal button that held the band secure.

"You steal a girl's breath with your wicked ways, Mr. Mackay," she drawled teasingly, that hint of Southern belle deliberately thickened as his zipper rasped lower.

Dawg felt helpless above her. He stared into her chocolate eyes, certain he should be doing something himself. Kissing her soft lips, drawing her clothes from her body, but it was all he could do instead to maintain the strength in his arms to hold himself above her.

His jeans were loose now; her silken hands gripped the waistband and began drawing it from his body.

"That's only going to go so far," he warned her with a grimace. "We still have to get rid of the boots, sweetheart."

She smiled, a reckless, heated smile that had his balls drawing tight in anticipation.

"Lie down," she ordered softly, her palms pressing into his abdomen. "Lie down, Dawg, and we'll see if we can't get rid of them."

He lay down.

Giving a woman control had never been his strong suit, but he gave it to Crista. Because watching her, feeling her touch, was like being warmed in the winter. It wrapped around him and eased him into the sensuality rather than allowing him to throw his partner into it.

She cast him a heated look from beneath her lashes as she moved to his feet and removed his boots, then his socks. Then, like the wanton he dreamed of, she gripped the waistband of his jeans and began to drag them and his briefs down his legs.

It was agonizing, watching her undress him, seeing the pleasure in her eyes and knowing how hot it made her. As she tossed his jeans to the bottom of the red checked cloth he was lying on, his brow arched.

"You're still dressed, Crista."

She looked around as though gauging the privacy of where they were. As he started to speak, her hands gripped the hem of the little shirt she wore, and she drew it over her head.

She wore nothing but a thin lace bra beneath it. One that framed her perky breasts and almost revealed her tight, hard nipples.

Watching him with slumberous, sexy eyes, she rose slowly to her feet and dropped the cotton capris as she pushed her sandals off her feet.

"Leave the panties on." His voice was harsh as her fingers hooked into the little elastic band of the thong she wore.

Her lips tilted again. Knowing, sexual.

"What about the bra?"

"Lord have mercy." He sighed. "Take it off."

She released the clip between her breasts slowly and let the cups fall away from the hard-tipped mounds before shrugging it from her shoulders.

And there was no mercy to be found. There was sunlight spilling through the trees overhead and washing her creamy flesh in golden rays of heat.

When she came to him, Dawg couldn't help but suck in his breath at the complete sensuality of her flowing movements. She wasn't embarrassed. She wasn't playing coy. She was hungry, and she was going to feed on the sexual, sensual intensity blazing between them.

Her lips came to his. Her hands gripped his wrists, holding them at his head as her breasts brushed over his chest. Her nipples were like fiery brands, her lips as they sipped at his, nipped, laved them with lust, were extensions of the hunger raging between them.

Dawg's cock was so hard, so fully engorged it was painful. Each brush of her nipples against his chest had him flexing, his body raging to take control of the sex play and to bury his dick as deep inside her as he could get.

"You're riding the line, fancy-face," he growled as her lips pulled back, the curtain of her hair embracing them in an intimate world all their own.

Crista felt Dawg's wrists flex beneath her hand and glimpsed the powerful muscles of his biceps as they rippled.

"I'm not riding anything yet, Dawg," she reminded him teasingly, her head lowering so her tongue could lick at the powerful cords of his neck.

Her hands smoothed along his arms as she braced herself on her knees on each side of a powerful thigh. His cock pressed against her hip, his hard chest stroked her nipples with each breath. And beneath the lace of her panties her pussy was creaming furiously.

"Keep it up, and you're going to be riding more than you should be handling for another few hours," he warned her tightly, his hips flexing beneath her, pushing his cock more firmly against her hip.

The heavy male thigh she straddled shifted as well, bringing a gasp to her lips and a surge of sensation to the swollen clit it pressed against.

"Other ways," she whimpered. There were ways she was dying to try. Long-dreamed-of acts she needed to experience with him.

"Other ways." His voice was filled with challenge. "Better get started on those 'other ways,' fancy-face. I'm a dying man here."

He was sexy as hell, too. Stretched out on the overlarge picnic blanket, his eerie green eyes gleamed back at her from behind lowered lashes.

Crista lowered her head again, her lips and tongue finding a flat, hard, male nipple and working it in her mouth. A muted groan came from his chest. His arms moved as though to reach for her.

"Stay for me." She pressed his arms back to the checked cloth. "Just a little longer, Dawg. Let me have this."

She needed it. Needed him. Needed to taste and explore and fill her senses with him.

"Crista, sweetheart, you're killing me here." He was breathing rough and heavy, but his arms stayed in place as her lips moved to the opposite nipple and tormented the pebble-hard flesh.

Giving it a final lick, she moved lower. Her hands stroked his heavy thighs, inside and out. Her lips kissed, her tongue licked a sensual, meandering path down his chest and firm abdomen.

Hard muscles flexed beneath her lips. His thighs bunched; the thickly crested head of his cock gleamed with moisture as her fingers finally gripped the stiff shaft.

Crista knelt between his thighs and stared up at his body, tracking the damp flesh and finally meeting his narrowed gaze.

"I get to have dessert first," she said with a slow smile.

Her head lowered, her tongue licked over the straining crest, curling over it as a low, hungry growl rumbled in his throat.

"Sweet Crista," he groaned. "That sweet little tongue is like fire."

Dawg's hands knotted in the cloth beneath him. He was dying. Stretched out on a rack of sensation that had sweat building along his body and his balls tight with anticipation.

He watched as she smiled again. A drowsy, sexy little smile a second before her lips opened and she took the pounding head of his dick into her tight mouth, sucking it slow and easy. Her fingers caressed and stroked, tortured and tempted, until his hips were thrusting into her grip, fucking her lips as the heat built around them.

"Come here." He reached for her. He'd be damned if he would take the torment alone. "Turn around here, darlin'."

Her lips never left his cock. But her body turned and sweet, lace covered flesh came closer to his hungry lips. For the first time in his sexual life, Dawg found himself without patience, without careful deliberation.

One hand gripped her leg, lifting it over his head before both hands gripped her hips. Fingers gripped the lace and drew it slowly from the newly waxed flesh between her thighs. Dawg stared up at the bare folds, luscious pink and gleaming with her juices. Sweet, soft little droplets hugged her flesh and had him licking his lips in anticipation.

"Oh yeah." He sighed, pulling her closer. "Come here, baby, let me show you how good it can be now."

It was one of the sexiest things she had ever envisioned.

Crista caught her breath as Dawg licked over the saturated folds between her thighs. The protective curls that had once covered her there were gone, and the sensations were enough to make a woman insane.

There was nothing now to insulate her from the rasp of his tongue or the soft licks he bestowed upon her. His caresses only made her hotter, only made the need rising inside her bloom to desperation. To greed.

He licked and sucked with gentle movements, never abrading the sensitive folds but soothing them, whispering over them, consuming them as her mouth sucked greedily at the head of his cock. She was determined to make him just as desperate for satisfaction as she was becoming.

She swore the breeze whipping around them was spiked with fire now. Dawg held her hips easily, controlling her frantic need for movement against his mouth. His tongue burrowed through her slit, licked and moved to curl around her clit.

He stroked, sucked, and lashed at the fiery little nubbin with hungry licks and greedy suckling lips until the inferno inside her began to blaze out of control.

Strong fingers separated her rear cheeks and caressed the narrow cleft there.

Breathing was impulse; the cries that tore from her throat as she sucked Dawg's cock were involuntary. All she knew was the heat racing through her veins, the flames licking over her flesh, and the ache building with each lick of his tongue between her thighs.

The taste of male passion and heated flesh filled her senses. The feel of his tongue rasping, thrusting, and licking overwhelmed her.

Nothing mattered now but the pleasure. Her pleasure. His pleasure. The race to release and the need for completion. It was a like a fever in her blood, that need that consumed and overwhelmed everything else.

Her fingers stroked and pumped the stiff flesh of his cock. She sucked at the throbbing head. Her tongue lashed and stroked and tasted the heated male passion, while his tongue drove her to distraction. Stroking and thrusting and fucking inside her as his fingers caressed and pressed against the tender opening between her rear cheeks.

She was swamped with pleasure. Taken by it. Her hips writhed above him as he held her to him, thrusting against his tongue and driving it deeper into the aching core he possessed.

Her cries and his groans filled the clearing.

His fingers pierced her ass and her pussy simultaneously. His lips surrounded her clit, drew it in and sucked it with wicked force.

Crista cupped the fingers of one hand around his balls, fondled and caressed as the other hand stroked the steel-hard shaft and her mouth sucked the head with hungry greed.

His fingers pumped inside her, fucking her with strokes that, combined with the heated suckling of his mouth around her clit, threw her into an orgasm that would have had her screaming, should have had her screaming. But Dawg's release had him arching, pressing his cock deeper into her mouth and filling it with the creamy essence of his semen.

They collapsed long seconds later, Crista's head pillowed on Dawg's thigh as he turned to her, his lips pressing into the inside of her knee as they fought for breath.

"I won't let you go," he finally told her, his voice dangerously calm, stunning her as the words reached her ears. "No matter what you do, Crista, I'll never let you go again."

Eighteen

He remembered.

As he felt Crista's orgasm shaking her body, the memories washed over him like a wave of crashing emotion. How she had found him in that damned ditch, the truck he had been driving then so damned stuck his liquored mind couldn't figure out how to get it free.

Her voice had been soft, filled with pain, and it had soothed the ragged edges of fury tearing at his mind. He had let her lead him from the truck to Alex's car, and as she drove them to the marina, the scent of her had wrapped around him like sunlight.

He had made her laugh.

He leaned close to her and said something about Alex letting her out to play with the big boys, and she had laughed at that.

Once they got to the marina, she had kept him from falling from the docks into the dark water below. Leading him to the *Nauti Dawg*, she kept up a steady, whispered conversation. Teasing, her voice urged him on and made his dick so damned hard he had been amazed. He'd thought he'd drunk enough whiskey that night to keep from getting a hard-on for days.

But he had been hard for Crista.

And once he got her into the houseboat, getting her into his bed hadn't been that hard. She had wanted to make certain he was safe. That he was comfortable.

He had fallen back on the couch, and she eased his boots and shirt off. As he struggled with his pants, she helped there, too, even as she blushed to her virgin roots. And as she began to move away from him, he had cupped his hand around her head and had drawn her lips to his.

From that moment she had been his. His in a way that no other woman had been. She had taken to his touch as though she had been created for him alone. And perhaps, in a way, she had been.

Now, eight years later and nearly two hours after the memory had seared his mind, he walked behind her, back to the houseboat, the still-full picnic basket in his hand and Crista's stiff shoulders in front of him.

She had clammed up the minute he had made his declaration.

"We need to talk," she had stated as she rose from beside him and began looking for her clothes.

"So talk." Dawg had sat up, draped his arm over his upraised knee, and watched her struggle into her clothes.

She had shaken her head angrily. "Not here. I can't do this here."

And now, he was more than interested in whatever the hell had her so damned mad.

He had fucked up eight years ago; he admitted it. But not to the extent she thought he had. Half-formed thoughts had slipped past his lips, unfinished. The possessiveness he had felt rising inside him then had shocked him, left him reeling and off balance.

Now, eight years later, he was reasonably more mature, but he still felt like he was in over his head with Crista Ann Jansen.

As they stepped onto the deck of the *Nauti Dawg*, Dawg unlocked the door and ushered her in as he lifted his brow at her continued silence.

She had barely spoken in the truck. The closer they had come to the marina, the quieter she had become.

"Here we are." He placed the basket on the table and turned to face her, crossing his arms over his chest and tilting his head.

Her gaze flickered around the room before coming to rest on him. Her lips parted, and at the same second, a hard knock sounded on the glass door behind her.

Crista jumped as though a gunshot had sounded rather than the sound of knuckles against glass.

"Who is it?" he barked out.

"Dawg, I have Cranston with me. Open the damned door." Natches's voice was anything but happy.

Pressing his lips together, Dawg stalked to the door and whipped the panels to the blinds back to see Cranston's stocky form standing behind Natches.

Grimacing, he opened the door again, watching from the corner of his eye as Crista turned to the visitors with an edge of curiosity.

Timothy Cranston stepped into the room, his briefcase clenched in his hand, his gaze going straight to Crista. Dawg closed the door, watching as the special agent watched her with an intensity that had a frown pulling at his brow and Crista's.

"What's going on, Natches?" Dawg didn't bother to soften the suspicious tone of his voice.

"You're not going to believe this, Dawg." Natches's smile was cynical, cold. "I've had a few hours to digest it, and I still don't believe it."

"Cranston?"

The special agent was still watching Crista, his gaze narrowed on her as she stared right back at him, a challenge glittering in her brown eyes.

"She's about the right height. Right eye color, right hair. But I'll be damned if you're not right about the differences."

Dawg felt his body tense as Cranston walked slowly around Crista then.

"Did you turn your boat into a auction block, Dawg?" Crista snapped irritably as the agent tracked every curve and hollow in her body.

"There's a difference in the curves. You were right there, too," he muttered.

"Natches," Dawg bit out warningly. "What the hell is going on?"

Dawg could feel the warning tingle in his gut, the itching at the back of his neck. The way Cranston was watching Crista was getting his hackles up and pissing him off. And it wasn't doing much for her, either. She flashed him a hard look, a warning to do something about the bulldoggish little man who kept watching her like a strange little puzzle he was trying to figure out.

"You're not going to believe it." Natches shook his head. "I'm still not certain I believe it."

"Why not explain it and give us the chance to believe it, Natches," Crista retorted with mocking sweetness as she edged away from Cranston and moved closer to Dawg.

It was the first move she had made toward him since their time in the clearing. Crossing the last few feet to her, Dawg wrapped his arm around her waist and pulled her to him, ignoring Cranston's sardonic look and Natches's quiet reflection.

He could feel Crista's fear in the face of Cranston, though. She knew who he was; she knew the danger he could represent to her. A danger Dawg swore he was never going to let touch her.

"Does this have anything to do with Agent Dane attempting to follow us earlier?" Dawg asked.

"Plenty." Cranston's bright brown eyes gleamed merrily as he ran his fingers over his short gray hair and flashed them a victorious smile.

Victorious. As though a battle had just been won.

"You going to explain it to us anytime soon?" Evidently, there wasn't a pending arrest in the works. Cranston wouldn't have made the mistake of trying to bring in Dawg's woman without help.

Timothy grinned cheerfully. "You know, my wife, Angie, she's always telling me I need to get to the point faster. But sometimes . . ." He stared back at them with a scary sort of playfulness. "Sometimes, you just have to have fun getting there, don't you Dawg?"

Dawg glanced at Natches. His cousin had lowered his head and was shaking it pitifully at Cranston's theatrics.

"Dawg, who is this person?" Crista finally asked.

She should have stayed quiet, he thought with a silent groan.

"That's right." Timothy stepped forward, his palm outstretched. "We haven't met, have we, Miss Jansen. I'm Timothy Cranston, Special Agent Timothy Cranston, with the Office of Homeland Security. I'm Mr. Mackay's boss."

"Homeland Security?" She looked up at Dawg, moving slightly away from him. "I thought you were with the DEA."

Cranston chuckled at that. "Oh, my, no. Your friend Dawg is with the ATF, though attached temporarily to OHS. He didn't tell you that?"

Crista let Timothy shake her hand, but she was watching Dawg, her expression tightening in anger.

"He didn't mention that."

"That's Dawg for you." Timothy nodded as he stepped back. "He's good at keeping secrets, aren't you, Dawg?"

Dawg sighed. "Get to the point, Timothy."

Cranston rubbed his hands together in anticipation once again.

"Now, what Dawg probably didn't tell you as well was that the night he broke several federal laws and dragged your pretty butt out of that warehouse, we were in the process of arresting a small team of former military assholes who thought they could hijack several experimental missiles while en route to Fort Knox before continuing on their way to a storage site. We managed to round up the thieves as well as one very sly little mercenary middleman who was buying those missiles for a high-level terrorist." He looked at Crista with sudden sharp curiosity. "He didn't tell you that, did he?"

"He didn't." Crista moved farther away from Dawg.

Timothy nodded in satisfaction as he flashed Dawg an approving look. "I'm disappointed in you, son, but glad to see you still know how to keep your mouth shut."

"Timothy." Dawg wasn't happy, and he wasn't pretending.

Crista had put several feet between them and was now watching Dawg and Timothy as though they had sprouted horns and fangs.

"Okay, here we go then." Dawg watched as Timothy tossed his briefcase to the table and rubbed his hands in that gleeful manner he had. The man was positively bubbling with satisfaction. It was enough to send a chill racing down Dawg's spine.

Timothy was no one's vision of a special agent in charge of any investigation, but that was exactly what he was, and he was damned good at his job.

"Yesterday afternoon, after your good friend and cousin here was regaling the customers in that little diner in town about how your girlfriend stalked out on you, and possibly was on her way to Virginia, she supposedly walked into the detention center where our hijackers are being held and requested a visit with the leader of our merry little bunch of thieves, Camden Cole. Our boy Camden lives just outside Fort Knox. Someone checking in as Miss Jansen here met with Mr. Cole, discussed friends and family for a few minutes, gave Mr. Cole her love, then left."

Timothy opened the briefcase and began pulling photos free. "Meet Camden Cole."

Crista moved closer to the table, her eyes locked on the picture of the stern older man. Hazel eyes stared back with cool detachment in a face as unemotional as a robot.

"I know him." She was shocked that she did know him. "He worked for the electric company. He was at the house just after my parents died. Alex had requested a new meter be installed."

"Bingo." Special Agent Cranston beamed at her as though she had answered a particularly difficult question. "That was just a few years ago, wasn't it?"

Crista nodded slowly as Dawg stared at her in surprise. He had been unaware that she had been in town at that time, she had made certain of it.

"Alex asked me to come in and take care of a few things while he was out of the country."

"So, yesterday, while Miss Jansen was supposedly on her way to Virginia, she shows up at the detention center." Another picture slapped down in front of her, causing Crista to freeze in shock.

"That's not me!" But it looked like her. The hair, the profile, even the clothes.

"So Natches spent a considerable amount of time informing me after Dawg got my agent lost in the mountains this afternoon."

Crista stared back at him as she felt fear beginning to build inside her. "I was with Dawg yesterday. All day."

"And Natches was in town spreading tales of your desertion." He shook his head sadly and cast Natches a chiding look filled with mockery.

"Sometimes you have to tell a few lies to get to the truth." Natches's smile lacked any humor.

"We were in the office after we found the attempted break-in," Dawg reported. "I kept her up there until well after closing."

"Yeah, Natches was telling the customers about that one, too." Cranston nodded. "He hinted you blamed her for the break-in?"

Dawg grunted as Crista stepped back and stared at the three men.

"Who is in the picture?" she asked.

"Looks like you." Cranston gazed back at her blandly.

The patently false look of innocence would have been amusing at any other time.

"Crista, look closely at the rest of the photos," Natches said softly.

Crista moved back to the table as Cranston laid out half a dozen glossy color and black-and-white photos. There were none that showed the woman's face clearly. Most were in profile, and all looked remarkably like her.

"I have clothes just like these," she whispered shakily, feeling Dawg move closer to her, his hand settling comfortingly at her back.

The neat, almost businesslike outfits were identical to those hanging in her bedroom closet.

"Agent Dane checked your home and confirmed that these same clothes were hanging in your closet." Cranston nodded.

"You were in my home?" She stared back at him in shock. "Without a warrant?"

"Honey, it's a criminal investigation; of course we searched the house with warrant in hand. The clothes are now in custody and on their way to the lab for tests."

"What kind of tests?" Shock filled her voice now, not just her mind.

"DNA tests, little girl." Cranston frowned. "We're looking for DNA other than yours. Criminals don't always think about the many ways DNA can be found. A stray hair, sweat, sometimes blood from something as innocent as a scratch. We're hoping our boy here left something."

"Boy?" Dawg latched onto that word before Crista could make sense of it.

"Natches caught it." Timothy shook his head. "Right here."

He pulled one of the pictures free and handed it to Dawg.

Crista stared at the picture. It was a full frontal shot, though whoever was posing as her had turned their head to the side, allowing hair identical to Crista's to cover their face.

It took a minute, but she saw it. She blinked, certain she wasn't seeing clearly. The breasts were covered in the soft, chocolate brown silk of the blouse the other woman was wearing, draped over the mounds that were approximately the size of Crista's. But with one difference. In this picture the soft material of the blouse had gaped where a button had come undone and revealed a very hairy portion of flesh beneath the breast.

Crista blinked and looked again. Male chest hair?

"We went over the other pictures once Natches caught that." Cranston said. "And he found a few other anomalies. Such as this."

The next picture had a red-marked circle around a dark spot on a smooth, creamy, hairless arm that appeared female.

"This picture was taken by another agent in France, where our young person here met with Akron Svengaurrd, the mercenary that brokered the deal on the missiles."

Once again, there were no facial features, but Crista focused on the red circle that pointed out a blemish of some sort.

"I'll be damned," Dawg muttered, his voice suddenly heavy, bitter. "I can't believe it."

"He disappeared just after the missiles were stolen," Natches said then. "Remember? We wondered where the hell he had gone? He also knew Cole, he worked for Cole's father for a while on their farm near Frankfort. We cleared him on the investigation here because the connections were all superficial. Hell, Cole had a lot of acquaintances here in Somerset."

Crista stared hard at the picture, certain she was missing something. Then she saw it, remembered it. A small blemish, more a birthmark, on a friend's wrist.

"Johnny," she whispered, seeing the familiarity in the curve of his face then, in the way he stood, even dressed as he was in her clothes. "It's Johnny Grace."

"He visited the detention center deliberately," Natches said then. "To implicate Crista. Every move he's made has been made to implicate her, to distract Dawg, and possibly me as well. He had to cover himself, and this was the best way to do it. He thought you and Crista had argued, and she was heading to Virginia. The detention center is on the way, a short little detour that she could have reasonably made. Bam, she's arrested, bad guys thinks she has the money, good guys crucify her. And Johnny was damned good; those fucking mercenaries really thought he was a she. They would have killed Crista first chance they had to arrange it."

Behind her, Dawg was dangerously silent. Crista swore she

could feel the fury whipping through the room now, from Dawg as well as Natches.

"He made friends with Crista first thing when she returned, because he knew her history with Dawg, and he knew Dawg's fascination with her. He was one of the few people that could have known what happened when she left eight years ago," Natches bit out.

"Yeah. He worked at the clinic when Crista had the miscarriage. An orderly or something," Cranston added.

Crista felt her world crash around her then.

The silence in the room suddenly became heavy, tense, and filled with danger. She didn't dare look at Dawg; she couldn't. She could barely breathe, could barely form a thought.

"Cranston, I'm going to murder you." Natches sighed then. "We had an agreement."

Cranston's gaze was going between Dawg and Crista then.

"Agreements are for men I can trust, Natches," he said mockingly. "You two broke trust with me in your attempts to hide Miss Jansen's presence at that warehouse. Consider this your slap on the wrist."

Nineteen

Something was breaking apart inside Dawg. He could feel it. He fought it, he tried to force the pieces of his soul back into shape, but they continued to break away, piece by piece, destroying him in the process.

Cranston was a smart man. Once he glimpsed Dawg's expression, he excused himself and left. Quickly. It would have been laughable if it weren't for the fact that everything inside Dawg was silently howling.

And she hadn't said a word. Not a word. Even after Natches left, she stared at the carpet and avoided his gaze.

Dawg wasn't a man prone to tears. He hadn't cried since he was five, but at this moment, he wished he hadn't forgotten how to shed tears.

Because he wanted to shed tears. For his child, for what had been lost before it had even been born. For the woman who had fled the pain, and the man who hadn't had a clue the pain he had inflicted in one night of pleasure.

It had been a son. She had been carrying his son, and for some reason, some quirk of nature, it had been taken from her. Sweet God! Had been taken from them both.

The file held the facts on more than the miscarriage. It was her life for eight fucking years.

Every move she had made in the past eight years was there, as well as her living arrangements with the two men in Virginia and their sexual orientation.

They were homosexual. The two men were lovers, and Crista, from all accounts, rather than being a third to the little love nest, had been treated more as a little sister. A sister that needed protecting, to be cared for.

Neighbors had been questioned regarding Crista, as had her former boss. Everyone had given her glowing recommendations and stressed how dependable, reliable, and kind she was.

One elderly lady had told the agent, posing as a prospective employer, that Crista Jansen was a wounded little bird when she first arrived with Mark Lessing and moved into his apartment. Cranston had related that piece of information with curious satisfaction.

As he read, grief swelled in his chest with each word and the implications of what he had done to her. Agony pierced his heart, his soul, and ripped through his mind.

Crista had run from him, lost their child, then left town, barely healed from the miscarriage. She had immediately enrolled in business school. She had dated rarely, never seriously, and photos of those men were included in the file. An accountant, a banker, the vice president of a manufacturing firm. All three men were suave, sophisticated, and about as dangerous or sexual as a neutered house cat.

Crista had worked hard, played rarely. She had volunteered several weekends a month at a local hospital in the pediatrics ward, and everyone loved her.

And she had been alone. She had left Somerset after losing his baby. After he had taken her with drunken lust and committed the unbearable sin of having forgotten that night. Except in his dreams. Dreams where she had tempted him, tormented him. Loved him.

No wonder he hadn't forgotten about her. No wonder he had dreamed of her for eight long years and with her return had focused on her with something bordering obsession.

And it was no wonder she had refused every advance. No wonder she had avoided him every chance she had. She should have shot him. He was amazed Alex hadn't done the job for her.

"Did you want the baby?" His baby. His child. Grief nearly ripped his guts from his body at the thought of that child that had never drawn breath.

"More than my own life." Her voice was harsh, thick was unshed tears as his own throat closed against the pain.

"You could have told me." He would have claimed her, claimed their baby. He would have held her, protected her, shared her grief.

"I was too young for you." Pain haunted her voice and his soul. "I didn't run because of the miscarriage, or because of the threat of Rowdy and Natches. I could have handled informing you that wasn't going to happen. But I couldn't handle what you made me feel that night."

Dawg lifted his eyes from the folder, and he wanted to howl at the pain he saw in her eyes.

"You loved me, even then." He knew it, knew it in his soul, and that knowledge was killing him. She had loved him, endured this alone, and he hadn't even remembered the night that had created their child.

"I loved you," she whispered. "I've always loved you, Dawg. But what happened between us . . ." Her hand lifted, then dropped helplessly. "What you made me feel. I couldn't handle it. I craved it. I cried for you for months after I left, but I couldn't come back."

"Why?" His voice was stark, chilling.

"I told myself it was because of Rowdy and Natches. I told myself I couldn't handle having my heart broken when you refused to give up that lifestyle, but when I returned last year and saw you the first time, I knew better. I couldn't come back because I knew you would end up owning my soul. And if that happened, I wouldn't be able to just walk away. I'd hate it. I'd end up destroying myself over it, but if you had pressed, I knew I couldn't have refused anything you wanted."

Facing that fact had been the hardest part of the last few days, and Crista knew it. Knowing that in her heart she had wasted eight years of her own life running from herself hadn't been easy.

"Were you relieved you had the miscarriage, Crista?" he asked, his voice bleak, shattered.

She hadn't expected that question from him. She had expected recriminations, a suspicion that she had deliberately gotten pregnant, but she hadn't expected this.

"I nearly died, Dawg," she cried hoarsely. "I wanted to die."

His head lifted from the file, his expression so stark, so furiously intent, that she felt her chest tighten with pain.

"Why did you want that baby so bad, Crista?" he asked her then.

Suspicion. She heard it in his voice, but all she saw in his face was the same expression she had seen the night she found him drunk, his truck in a ditch and his drunken bitterness pouring from his voice as he cursed his parents.

"Because it was our baby," she answered simply, tearfully. "A part of you and a part of everything I felt for you. And it was innocent, Dawg. No matter how frightened I was, or what you wanted, it wasn't our baby's fault."

Sweet God, his eyes were wet, so dark now, haunted and rife with agony as he stared back at her.

"Would you have told me about our baby?"

How to answer that one? She felt like a criminal on trial now, and Dawg was her judge and jury. The way he watched her terrified her.

"No." She wasn't going to lie to him, not now. "But Alex would have. He was already set to tell you when I miscarried. I was—" She bit her lip as she glanced away for long seconds. "I was too scared, Dawg. I don't know if I could have survived your denial of our child. You didn't even remember the night we spent together. I knew you didn't. You would have never believed I was carrying your baby."

He stared down at the file, closing it slowly and pushing it away. The heaviness in his expression broke her heart. His brows were lowered, his features tight with the grief she had felt the minute she realized she was losing his child.

"I would have believed you," he finally said, his voice rough, harsh, as he lifted his head and stared back at her, his green eyes dark with sorrow. "Don't you know, Crista? I would have used any excuse to claim you."

She had to turn away from him. Her hand pressed to her lips as pain tore through her chest. She couldn't breathe, she couldn't stop the tears that flooded her eyes. She had to hide from what she saw in his eyes then. The shutters were removed, the distance he always forced on himself was stripped away, and the loneliness and the pain glittered in the light green orbs.

And she couldn't face it. She couldn't face the fact that she had added to it.

A second later his arms were wrapping around her, pulling her against his chest, surrounding her with a warmth that she had only known when she was in his arms.

"I would have destroyed us both," she whispered tearfully, her hands gripping his hard forearms as her head lowered. "I would have made us miserable."

"Shh. Don't, Crista," he whispered against her ear. "Don't blame yourself. We both grew up, baby. But the thought of you going through that alone. Carrying my child, losing it." One hand lifted to her face as he turned her, his opposite arm wrapping around her and holding her to him as he wiped the tears from beneath one eye. "It tears me apart."

Crista tried to shake her head.

"Don't." He stopped her, sighing heavily as his forehead rested against hers. "You've been scared to even tell me, Crista. You've held back, you've let yourself hurt and not even considered telling me, haven't you?"

"I was going to tell you when we got back here." She swallowed tightly. "I couldn't hold back any longer, Dawg. Loving you terrified me, until I awoke in your arms and realized I've always loved you. And I've been dying inside without you all these years. Never knowing, always wondering what if. The wondering was killing me. Being without you was breaking my heart more every year."

She stared into his eyes, and they broke her heart. His expression was twisted into lines of grief, his brows heavy with the internal pain she could glimpse in his eyes.

"I won't let you go, Crista," he whispered then. "Not now, not ever. We're going to get through this investigation, find out what the hell Johnny is pulling, and then we're going to figure this relationship out. Just you and me."

"I should have told you." She reached up, cupped his cheek, and ached at the pain in his face. "I shouldn't have run from you, Dawg."

She admitted that now, though it was something she had known, even then. Running away from him hadn't been the answer. Running away from herself had, in ways, been even worse.

"No more running," he told her softly, gently, his lips lowering to hers, taking them in a kiss that had her breath hitching in her chest.

The sheer gentleness rocked her mind. The way his head tilted, the lingering emotion and banked passion seemed to sink into her soul and leave her fighting for breath in a way that the raw lust never had.

When he pulled back, grief creased his expression and sheened his eyes as well as lust. Lust and hunger and need so powerful now it stole her breath.

"If I start now, we won't stop. Let's see about our lunch, sweetheart, figure some of this out, and later . . ." His eyes were heartbreaking. Filled with pain and need. "Later, we'll pick this up."

Crista inhaled roughly and tried to pull her thoughts back into some semblance of order. She tried to give him the time he needed, and she knew he needed time. She could see it in his face, in his bleak gaze.

"I can't believe Johnny is involved in this." She shook her head, wondering how many more times Dawg could handle the betrayals from the family that should have stood by him.

He had Rowdy and Natches and Rowdy's father, Ray, but Crista had seen how alone he was other than those three. He had few friends; he trusted no one but the cousins he had grown up with and the one uncle who had stood by him.

And no one held him.

"Oh, I could believe just about anything out of Johnny," Dawg bit out, slowly drawing away from her and heading back to the table where the picnic basket still sat. "He's definitely his mother's son."

Dawg's heart was breaking for the things they had both lost because of his ignorance—for his child, for the woman he loved before he knew what love was. He wasn't that same immature man any longer. He had been too damned rock dumb to go after what he wanted, even though he had sensed what Crista would mean to his future. He wasn't dumb anymore.

"Why would he do this, though?" Crista set the basket on the far end of the bar before moving into the kitchen and pulling ice from the freezer for the tea that had been packed with the food. "He's your cousin. When I left Somerset, Johnny followed after the three of you like a shadow."

Dawg shook his head. "Johnny followed us like a shadow to

see how much trouble he could brew up. We knew he was gay even then, and he was terrified we'd tell on him. Not that we cared either way; it was his damned troublemaking we couldn't stand. His and his mother's."

Crista frowned heavily as she filled the glasses with ice.

"I always remember how nice Jcohnny was." She bit her lip as she lifted her gaze to him, and Dawg wondered if he had ever seen that look in anyone else's eyes. It wasn't pity; it was compassion and anger for him. She was angry on his behalf, because she loved him. Even now, after everything he had done to her.

His chest clenched at the thought. She had even said the words, and this time, it wasn't just a hazy memory. She loved him, and he'd be damned if he was going to spend precious time distrusting her.

No, she wasn't part of the Trinity, but she was a gift from God himself. The days he had spent with her, despite the problems that had arisen, had been freer, happier than any he might have known in his life.

"Johnny's a deceptive little bastard. He likes to draw you in, and every second that he's playing the concerned buddy and dear friend, he's looking for ways to slash your throat. He learned the art at his mother's knee, and after the death of his father, she had free rein to reinforce the lessons."

"His father, Ralph, was one of my dad's few friends." Crista's lips tilted sadly. "Mom hated Nadine, though. She hated to even see her come into the store."

Dawg nodded in response. "Everyone liked Ralph. If he had lived, he would have divorced Nadine eventually, but maybe Johnny would have had a chance."

"How do you think he got mixed up in this thing with the missiles?" She frowned then. "And don't think you're not going to pay for lying to me about drugs."

"I never said it was drugs, Crista Ann; you assumed." He sighed.

"You could have corrected my assumption."

His grin was still tinted with the grief that lingered in his gaze, but at least a measure of amusement tipped it now, Crista thought.

"Johnny makes a habit of making friends with military types," he told her. "They feel sorry for him at first, until they realize it's lust and not hero worship he's displaying. Somehow, he finally hooked up with someone dumb enough to get pulled into one of his schemes or let out the information, and he used it. Either way, as soon as Natches and Cranston have the information together and a warrant, he'll no longer be a threat."

She paused, staring back at him as disbelief slammed inside her head.

"What are you talking about? Aren't they arresting him now?"

"Not without enough proof. We don't have enough yet." Dawg set plates on the table as she continued to stare at him in horror.

"But it was him. We all recognized him, Dawg."

He shook his head, his expression weary, bitter. "Doesn't matter, Crista. Any decent defense lawyer would have him out of jail within an hour and a lawsuit against the arresting agents not long afterward. We need proof, not the testimony of two cousins who have every reason in the world to want to crucify him."

The bitterness in his voice wasn't one of hatred but one of disillusionment.

"I'm sorry." She fought to rein back her anger. "Family should stick together, not try to destroy each other."

She couldn't have survived childhood without Alex. Her brother had been her rock, her anchor, and later, her best friend. She couldn't imagine having him hate her enough to try to destroy her or anyone she loved.

"Yeah well, that's in a perfect world, sweetheart." He shook his head as though shaking away his own regrets, then flashed her a smile that was at once teasing and filled with hunger. "Let's eat our lunch. We're hanging around the marina for the rest of the day, until Natches gets back to us. Once we've decided what to do to, things will move fast enough. Let's enjoy the quiet time we have for a while."

As he said that, a knock sounded at the door.

Crista's lips twitched as she glimpsed three shadows, two taller, the other petite and delicate.

"Hell!" Dawg pushed his fingers through his hair and stalked to the door.

Ray Mackay, Rowdy, and Kelly were waiting on the other side. Kelly was concerned, but Ray and Rowdy were pissed off.

"God bless Ralph Grace's soul." Ray shook his head as Dawg closed the door behind him. "He's turning over in his grave."

"Easy, Uncle Ray. We'll get things worked out."

Crista heard the tone Dawg used and wondered at it. He was comforting his uncle rather than accepting any comfort.

"I'll work it out," Ray snapped. "With the business end of my rifle. You think you're the only Mackay who knows how to shoot a gun?"

"Dad." Rowdy glanced at Dawg, and Crista saw the worry in his eyes. "Let's see what we can do to help rather than shed blood here."

"Seems like shedding blood would be the best help." Ray grimaced, though he moved to his nephew, slapped his shoulder in that gesture of male camaraderie, and shook his head in disgust. "Dawg, son, one of these days, you're going to have to learn: give those damned people an inch, and they take a mile. I can't even convince Natches of that, not all the way down. You thought they'd back off when you let that land go. I told you Johnny would never stop."

Bitterness pierced Ray Mackay's voice as well, and Crista began to glimpse the family dynamics that were rife with pain and anger.

"I'll get the land back when they arrest Johnny, Uncle Ray. My lawyer will make certain of it."

Crista watched, confused, as Kelly walked over to her and leaned against the bar beside her.

"Johnny's mother managed to win over half the property in Dawg's father's estate," she told Crista softly, obviously seeing the confusion in her face. "It was a prime piece of property and borders the land Dawg bought to build the house on. She and Johnny have gloated over it ever since. Just as Dawg gloats over the fact that he owns the rest of that valley and they have no idea who bought it out from under them."

"This is insane," Crista muttered. "How could they steal his inheritance? Didn't his parents have a will?"

"A will Nadine protested based on several letters Dawg's father sent to her stating that Dawg didn't deserve it, and how he wished Johnny had been his son as well. They read those letters in the courtroom. I was there when it happened. I swear, Crista, you could see something break inside of Dawg then. For years, there was so little softness inside him that he would have terrified you."

It terrified her now. It would have destroyed most men.

"Johnny's a dead man walking," Kelly said then, her voice steady, saddened. "Rowdy, Ray, or Dawg won't touch him, but Natches . . ." She turned and looked Crista in the eye, her own gaze heavy with remorse and fear. "Natches will kill him. He's closer to Dawg than he is to anyone else. He won't let this go."

And that would destroy Dawg.

Crista stared at the three men as they moved into the kitchen, and she could hear the worry in Ray's voice as he asked about Natches.

"He'll be fine, Uncle Ray." Dawg was assuring his uncle, but Crista could hear the worry in his voice, too.

"You know he didn't start building that house until you moved back to Somerset, don't you, Crista?" Kelly asked then.

Crista stared back at her in surprise.

The other woman's face was reflective, her gaze assessing.

"I hope you love him as much as I think you do, and that doesn't even compare to how much I know Dawg loves you. Don't betray him." Kelly's voice hardened then. "Betray him, and you'll make some very bad enemies."

It was a warning, and one Crista took no offense to. She shook her head as a smile tipped her lips.

"Kelly, I'd die first," she said softly. "I didn't wait eight years to grow up and come back to him, just to betray him. You can forget the warnings, because they're not needed."

A bright smile tipped Kelly's lips then, and a hint of teasing laughter filled her eyes.

"We're going to be great friends then," the other woman declared. "After all, we need each other to talk trash on them. Trust me, you'll have days you'll swear you should have shot him rather than loved him, but it all balances out good. Rowdy and Dawg are too much alike. There are days I swear I'm going to shoot Rowdy, but I know I could never live without him, so I resign myself to dealing with it."

Crista let her gaze linger on Dawg again. He stood with Rowdy and Ray at the other end of the kitchen. They were talking in low voices as they fortified themselves with the beers Dawg had taken from the refrigerator.

His eyes met hers, and the corners of his lips tipped into an encouraging smile at he nodded at something Ray said.

"Dawg's different with you, Crista," Kelly said then. "Calmer. Not as prone to stand distant and apart from the others. He was doing that before you returned. Slowly drawing away from Rowdy. It was breaking Rowdy's heart."

As she watched Dawg, she could understand why he would have been drawing away. Rowdy had a father who loved him, a family, and a woman to fill his heart. Dawg understood what he was lacking in his own life, just as Crista had always known what was lacking in hers.

"Rowdy was loved," Crista murmured then. "He had something Dawg knew he needed as well."

Kelly glanced at Dawg, then back to Crista as she nodded slowly.

"The change didn't come after he blackmailed you. It came with your return. Dawg knew what he was missing, and he thought he'd never find it. When you came back, the part of him that knew how to love reawakened, Crista. Don't doubt that. And don't doubt for one minute that he would give his soul to protect you."

As she would give hers. No. She amended that. She no longer had a soul separate from Dawg's. It was melded with his and had been for over eight years.

"Let's get more plates and get them fed," Crista said then, calculating the amount of food sitting on the table and how far it would go. It should just stretch.

"Good idea. Food usually settles Rowdy's bloodthirsty instincts." Kelly sighed. "He's ready to help Ray kill Johnny."

He wasn't the only one.

As they gathered around the table, Crista continued to watch the three men, drawing in impressions and letting the final pieces of the puzzle that represented Dawg fall into place.

His bond with Rowdy and Ray extended to Kelly, but there was no lust, no hint of desire, when he looked at the other woman. Crista saw friendship, affection, but nothing more. As she watched, she realized that one of her greatest fears had been that of seeing Dawg stare at Kelly with arousal.

She knew the games he had played in the past with his cousins and found it hard to believe they could step away from it so easily. Even for love.

But it appeared that at least Dawg and Rowdy had done just that. Crista wasn't uncomfortable when Rowdy looked at her; she saw no interest other than the casual interest that would have been expected.

Dawg teased Kelly, laughed with her, but he didn't desire her.

Watching the interplay made her realize exactly what she had missed in the years she had been away, but they weren't years she would regret. She had matured, grown up, learned something of herself and of the world around her. Enough to know where home was and who her heart belonged to.

Dawg belonged to her. She felt it, where she had feared it before. Just as she belonged to him.

"What do you think, Crista?" Dawg's voice drew her back from her thoughts and had her staring back at him. She blinked and refocused to see the heat stirring in his light green eyes and the heavy interest in his expression as he watched her.

"About what?" she asked.

"About taking tomorrow morning to head into town for some fresh baked goods. After all, as far as Johnny knows, none of us know what the hell he's up to. How do you feel about shaking him up a little bit?"

She stared at the three men and one woman watching her expectantly and felt shock rise inside her.

"I think you've lost your minds," she retorted in disbelief. "Don't you think that once he realizes I never left Somerset that he's going to get suspicious? That he'll figure out that you're onto him?"

The smile Dawg gave her was frankly terrifying. It was filled with expectation, anticipation, and a gleam of dangerous determination.

"That, fancy-face, is exactly what we're counting on."

Twenty

"I don't like it!" Crista exclaimed again, hours later, after the houseboat had cleared out and she followed Dawg upstairs, where he carefully pulled a panel from the bedroom wall and displayed more weapons than she wanted to think about.

Lord, the man was an armory by himself.

"It's perfectly safe, sweetheart." He was using that conciliatory tone that he had used downstairs.

She hated it then, and she definitely hated it now. It smacked of patronization, and that was something she had never tolerated well.

"Don't you sweetheart me," she told him fiercely. "And don't bother patronizing me now that you can't blackmail me any longer, Dawg. That's only going to piss me off."

"And blackmailing you didn't piss you off?" His eyes crinkled with amusement, amusement overlying pain, as he glanced around the opened panel and pulled free several handguns and clips.

Crista stared askance at the weapons. She recognized the Glock handguns; Alex had several similar ones. That didn't mean she liked them or the necessity of having them.

"At least I understood the blackmail," she snorted. "I would have done it myself if I had the chance."

He paused, his brows arching, as he laid the two handguns on the dresser and reclosed and locked the panel as he stared back at her in interest.

"You would have?" His gaze heated, filled with arousal, as she watched his body tense in preparation.

Crista frowned back at him fiercely. "Don't go there, Dawg. We're going to talk about this."

"Of course we are," he assured her smoothly as he sat down on the bed and patted his knee. "Come here, fancy-face, and tell me what you would have done if you could have blackmailed me."

Her lips pressed together firmly, controlling the amusement that would have slipped free.

"I wasn't talking about blackmailing you." She crossed her arms over her breasts and glared back at him. "Dawg, Johnny can't be completely sane—"

A bitter bark of laughter left Dawg's throat. "Crista, sweetheart, Johnny isn't insane. He's highly intelligent; he graduated only one point below valedictorian. Just under Natches, who claimed that honor during their high school graduation. He's not crazy; he's a highly intelligent menace who will cut your throat if you turn your back on him. Just like he did the driver of the military transport carrying those missiles."

Crista stared back at him in horror. "They killed him?"

"The lone female of the group sliced his throat open. We suspect, based on the video and voice box in the cab of the transport, that he knew her. Or him, as the case may be. We know Johnny has portrayed himself as female through this whole deal. As you."

"He set the explosive in my Rodeo then?" she whispered.

Dawg nodded heavily. "He's the only one with a motive, Crista. Killing you would have made it look like a hit by the mercenaries and placed all guilt on you. He would have gotten away with the money, and the mercenaries would have been in prison scratching their heads."

"What about friends of the men you arrested?"

He shook his head as he reached out and drew her to him, pulling her onto his lap.

Crista leaned into him, her head resting on his shoulder as her arms looped around his neck.

He kissed the top of her head before he answered her. "The mercenary and his team didn't have a name for the woman, only a description, which they gave. No name, and the physical features of the face, though similar, weren't yours. The buyers aren't talking yet. Cole knew your name, but only after Johnny visited in the detention center. In the small talk, Johnny told him to get fucked, pretending to be you. He had the money and he was free; Cole wasn't. That would have drawn those mercenaries right to your door. They learned different during the interrogation Cranston and Natches led after Johnny's visit. We suspect even they weren't certain exactly who they were dealing with. Johnny's slick like that, Crista. He always was. I'm just surprised that he could actually kill in cold blood. I didn't expect that out of him."

Neither had Crista. But she had a feeling Johnny had disappointed Dawg as well. For all Johnny's faults and his mother's influence, Crista had the feeling that Dawg had managed to hold out a measure of hope for his other cousin.

"He was the one who told Natches's father about the sharing, when we were teenagers," Dawg said then. "I thought Dayle had killed him when we got to the house with Uncle Ray. Natches's mother had called, calm as hell, and told Ray he needed to come for Natches before Dayle killed him. There was blood everywhere, and his father was still trying to beat the hell out of him. He was in the hospital for a week and refused to admit his father had done it. He still has scars on his back. And Johnny cried when we confronted him. Blubbered like a baby and swore he hadn't meant for it to happen. That he had been playing, poking at Dayle because he was always so critical of him."

Dawg's voice echoed with that past horror.

"He meant to do it?"

"I don't know," Dawg mused. "To this day, I still don't know. But I suspect he knew what would happen. We all knew not to push Dayle where Natches was concerned. He took great pleasure in beating the hell out of him whenever he could justify it."

Crista blinked back her tears.

"And your father?" She already knew part of Dawg's history, had known it even before that first night she had spent with him.

"He wasn't as violent as Dayle." He shrugged negligently. "And I knew how to fight back. Natches never fought back, and I never understood why."

"Because of Janey." Crista lifted her head and stared up at Dawg, suddenly suspecting why Natches had never fought back.

"Janey?" he asked.

"Natches's sister."

"I know who Janey is, but what does she have to do with this?"

"Maybe he didn't fight back because he was afraid Dayle would turn his aggression on Janey. Maybe he was trying to wait until she was old enough to run if she had to."

Janey was a lot younger than Natches, at least ten years younger. She would have been ten or eleven when Natches was publicly disowned so long ago.

"Maybe," Dawg said thoughtfully before sighing heavily. "God help the bastard if he ever hit her, though. Natches would murder him."

"Do we really have to do this, Dawg?" she finally asked on a sigh. "Push Johnny like that? It could be dangerous."

"Only for Johnny." His voice darkened, sending a shiver up her spine at the danger that filled it. "Mark my words, Crista, I won't let him get away with this. He knew what he was doing when he decided to frame you. And he should have known what would happen if I ever figured out what was going on."

She parted her lips to argue further but found herself instead flat on her back on the bed and staring up at Dawg in surprise.

"Enough about Johnny," he growled. "And I've waited long enough to collect on that little tease by the lake earlier."

"Tease?" she gasped in mocking offense. "That was no tease, Dawg Mackay. You weren't exactly groaning because you didn't get to come, you know."

"It was a tease, pure and simple." His hand pushed the hem of her camisole top up over her stomach. "All I got to do was lick that sweet pussy while you drove me insane with your mouth. I need more. Sweet heaven, Crista. I need so much more of you."

Her shirt was pulled slowly from her and tossed to the floor.

"Keep your arms there." He pressed them against the mattress, above her head, as she had done with him earlier beneath the wind and the sky. "Let me unwrap you, Crista. My own special present. I must have been a very good boy at some point to deserve this."

Her throat tightened at the emotion in his voice, at the tenderness in his touch, as he released the catch of her bra and drew it from her as well.

His hands cupped her swollen breasts, his thumbs raking over her nipples as his gaze darkened at the sight of the flushed tips.

"Would you have nursed our child?" he asked her, his voice incredibly deep, filled with regret and hunger, pain and longing.

"Yes." Crista arched into his touch, feeling her nipples tighten further as his finger and thumb gripped the pebble-hard tip.

"Would you have let me watch?" His head lowered, his lips feathering over her collarbone as Crista arched to the heated caress.

"Yes." She moaned the word.

His fingers were tormenting her nipples, making her wild for the touch of his lips, lips that were moving slowly over one flushed mound, his tongue licking at her flesh as it came closer to the aching tip.

"I love your breasts. How they feel, how they taste. How hard and hot your little nipples get for me." His hands cupped the mounds again, plumping them, lifting one closer to his lips as his tongue arrowed on the stiff peak.

When his mouth covered it, Crista was on the verge of begging. Once the heat of his suckling mouth and the lash of his tongue took possession of it, she was begging.

"Dawg. Please." Her hands fisted in the blanket beneath her. "More. Harder."

His touch was light, tender. She needed hard and hot. She needed the hunger she could feel barely leashed inside him. A hunger that was tearing through her, clenching in her pussy, spasming her womb.

"Harder, darlin'?" He licked over her nipple. "I don't want to rush this. I want to build the burn inside you. I want you ready for anything, for everything I can give you."

And she remembered exactly what he could give her when he touched her slow and easy. When each deliberate caress built the fire inside her to the point that pleasure bordered pain, and pain became a sensation so erotic that even the most wicked acts were the ones that brought the greatest pleasure. The most sensation.

"We'll both remember this, Crista. Forever," he swore. "Neither of us will forget."

Because they were both aware, connected now in a way they hadn't been before.

Crista stretched before him, her hips lifting from the bed as he gripped the band of her soft capris and drew them from her legs. His palms smoothed back up her legs, over the narrow band of her panties, and drew those from her as well.

Her eyes opened, her sight dazed as she stared down at him, watching as he spread her thighs slowly. His gaze became heavy lidded, drowsy with sensuality.

"Such a pretty pussy," he groaned, his thumbs moving into the indention between her thighs and the tender folds of her sex. "Soft and pink. Your juices glistening on it."

And they were. Already the silky wash of her arousal was gleaming on her flesh.

He didn't stop to touch or to taste though. Instead, he pulled himself on the bed beside her, leaned over her, and kissed her with all the pent-up lust she saw glowing in his gaze.

One large hand gripped her wrists as she tried to lift her hands to touch him. He anchored them to the bed above her head and ravished her lips. His tongue twined with hers, tasted her mouth, and caressed her lips. His free hand caressed her breasts, her belly, her thighs. His fingers plumped her nipples, gripped and teased them, and fanned the flames glowing from them.

Crista writhed beneath the caresses. His calloused palms stroked over nerve endings that grew hypersensitive. His nails raked over her belly. And all she could do was endure it.

He held her easily beneath him, his hands and larger body controlling her writhing undulations. She was losing thought, losing control. The need for his touch overrode everything else.

Finally, as his lips lifted from hers, his hand strayed lower than her belly. Crista's eyes drifted open again, meeting his a second before his hand delivered a heavy caress between her thighs.

"Oh my God. Dawg." She jerked beneath him, her hips arching sharply at the small, heavy pat that landed on the swell of flesh on each side of her clit.

"Not too hard," he growled. "Your flesh is so sensitive. So silken and unused to being bare."

Another pat, kissing cousin to a gentle little slap, was delivered to the flesh again. A little lower, rocking sensation through the damp folds and vibrating inside her pussy.

Her clit swelled tighter with each heavy caress, the fierce throb become nearly painful as her sharp moans filled the air.

"So sweet," he crooned, his voice a black velvet rasp as her thighs fell farther apart, opening for his touch. His fingers slid through the slick cleft, parting the plump, swollen folds before circling her aching clit.

"Dawg, please," she cried out softly. "Don't torture me."

"No torture, sweetheart, just pleasure," he promised, his fingers glancing over her clit before leaving the wet flesh and moving once again to her breasts.

He moved lower along her body. His lips slid over her neck, her collarbone. He caught a hard nipple in his mouth. He sucked it deep into his mouth, his tongue lashing at it, his teeth scraping it as Crista's hands tore loose from his hold.

Her hands twined into his hair. Crista arched closer, her head falling back in pleasure while his hands twined into the long strands of her hair and pulled at them firmly. She pulled at his in turn, the action instinctive, the driving need for orgasm rising inside her.

Dawg was determined in his pace. His caresses were slow and easy, building the flames burning in her womb with deliberate strokes and heated caresses.

He didn't give her a chance to catch her breath between levels. There was no chance for thought, no chance to regain control.

Before Crista realized where the caresses were leading, she was already ensnared. As his lips began to kiss a careful path down her torso and over her stomach, her thighs were parting farther, her knees bending, making room for his broad shoulders between them.

Release would come now, she was certain.

He could do to her what nothing or no one else could. Pleasure ricocheted through her body and ensnared her in a web of love and lust so intense she knew she would never break free.

His tongue licked over the newly bared flesh, and she knew why he wanted her to experience this pleasure. It was incredible. His tongue touched nerve endings she never knew existed. Each sip, each delicate rasp of his teeth and suckling kiss had her burning hotter, brighter. She could feel her juices flowing from her, moving from her pussy, easing into the narrow cleft of her rear as his fingers began to follow the path they made.

Minutes later, as his tongue finally delved into the narrow slit of her pussy, she felt the cool, slick lubrication on his fingers as they pressed against her rear entrance.

She knew that feeling. It was more than what he had done in the office; she could feel it. No toys were going to take her body this time.

The control, each deliberate kiss and caress, had been for one purpose. To one end. To claim every part of her.

"So sweet." His voice rumbled against the ultrasensitive flesh he was caressing with lips and tongue. "Like sweet, warm syrup."

His tongue pierced the snug opening as his two fingers penetrated her rear entrance and sent pleasure tearing through her system.

"Oh God. Dawg!" She screamed his name as the dual caresses had her trying to writhe, trying to escape the incredible sensations rocking through her body.

Heat and lightning, fiery flames licked over her flesh and burned beneath the skin. It was incredible. The pleasure was like being stretched upon a rack of impending ecstasy and tortured with the knowledge that rapture awaited.

Breathing was nearly impossible as she reached for it. Her legs strained with the effort to get closer. To drive his fingers deeper, then his tongue deeper. To make him, force him give her what she needed to release her from the almost painful pleasure searing her body.

She tried to tighten her legs, to close them just enough to tighten the sensation on her clit, to give that final pressure she was certain she needed to find her orgasm.

Below her, Dawg chuckled, a rough rasp of arousal and pleasure vibrating through her as his tongue licked with wicked strokes into the snug entrance to her pussy.

His fingers moved farther back. Stroked. Thrust.

"You're killing me!" Her fingers dug into the mattress, her hips lifted, fighting to get closer, only to have him ease the pressure she so desperately needed.

A ragged cry tore from her throat as a rumbled sound of pleasure whispered over her pussy.

"It's okay, fancy-face," he assured her erotically before his tongue licked around her clit again and his fingers flexed in her rear. "I'll take care of you."

His lips covered her clit. He drew it into the heat of his

mouth and suckled her, drew on her until she was screaming for relief. His tongue rasped over it, and she begged. As release built in her womb, he eased off, his head lowering, his tongue licking through her juices once again and denying her the relief she was begging for.

"Damn you! Stop teasing me." She reached for him, her fingers locking in his hair and clenching as another heated thrust filled her rear.

"I want your ass, Crista," he groaned, his lips pressing against her thigh before his teeth scraped over the flesh there.

She trembled, remembering the act, knowing what it would do to her, knowing how it would bind her to him. The ultimate submission. He had muttered those words as he took her there the first time. His.

Crista stared back at him as he moved, rising to his knees, spreading her thighs farther apart as his fingers slid from her rear.

"Dawg?" Crista shuddered, watching as he pulled her hips closer and pushed her legs back.

She watched, shocked, torn between feminine fear and erotic thrill as she saw him spread a heavy layer of lubrication over his cock.

It glistened, thick and powerful. Heavy veins pulsed beneath the flesh as the engorged crest visibly throbbed. Crista swallowed tightly. It looked huge, too large, too hard to breach the narrow opening it was tucking against.

"Dawg." She lifted her eyes back to his, mesmerized by the eroticism in his expression and the darkening of his light green eyes.

"Are you mine, Crista?" he asked, his voice rasping in the back of his throat as his cock pressed against her, into her.

"Always." She couldn't deny what her soul had always known.

A whimpering cry left her lips as he shifted his hold on her and let her legs fall to his chest while one hand gripped her hip, the other gripped the shaft of his cock.

Crista felt the invasion, slowly, a penetration that sent sensation shattering through the tender nerve endings. Her anal entrance began to stretch, to open beneath the blunt force of his erection.

"Oh God! Dawg, I can't stand this." Her body undulated involuntarily as her hands fisted into the blanket beneath her.

Flames were licking around her rear as the flesh parted. Pleasure and pain, submission and seduction. It was ownership. Not of her mind or really of her body. Ownership of her sensuality, of her pleasure. The intimacy was one so binding that even eight years after he had first given it, she had never recovered from the effects of it on her soul.

He was branding himself onto her soul and into her body.

Her lips opened on a soundless scream as the thickly flared head cleared the entrance, then forged inside once again. He buried his cock head inside the clenching tissue, groaning as she cried out his name in shocked pleasure.

Dawg paused then, his breathing rough, rapid, as sweat trickled down his chest and his eyes lowered to the tender opening he was taking.

"So hot and tight," he groaned, moving again, slow, shallow thrusts that worked his cock deeper inside her by small degrees. "It's like being held by flames, Crista."

Or taken by flames.

Her head thrashed on the bed as his cock moved deeper inside her ass, stretching her, revealing nerve endings so sensitive that the slam of sensation echoed into her clit. She was surrounded by a pleasure so intense, so forceful, she wondered if she could survive it.

"You're burning me alive." The hoarse snarl of his voice as the final inches of his erection burrowed into her anus had her womb contracting with an impending orgasm.

It was so wickedly erotic. It was the most forbidden, most submissive act Crista could envision, and it was overriding her sanity.

Control was a thing of the past. Dawg held the control. He held her. He shifted and moved, pulling nearly free before surging forward again. He stroked and caressed and set aflame nerve endings that hadn't flared to life in eight years.

Crista arched to him, her hips twisting in his grip as the need began to spiral out of control. She needed it hard and deep. She needed him to . . .

"Fuck me." She didn't recognize her own voice as the shattered plea filled the air. "Please, Dawg. Harder. Fuck me harder."

Her lashes lifted, her gaze hazy as she tried to focus on his face. A hard grimace twisted it, pleasure racking his features as he shook his head, sweat beading and dripping down his forehead as his hands clenched on her hips and his cock throbbed inside her ass.

"Harder," she whispered again, tempting him with a flex of those inner muscles, tightening on his flesh and feeling the pleasure spasm through her as well.

"Fuck. Crista," he groaned, panting with the pleasure, just as she was.

"I need you." She swallowed tightly. "All of you. Fuck me harder, Dawg. Give me what I need."

His hips jerked, dragging his erection back before pushing it inside her with a longer, harder stroke. As he did, one hand moved from her hip to tuck between her thighs.

Broad male fingers slid through the slick essence that gathered there, found the weeping center, and two digits thrust inside heavily.

He moved then. Thrusting hard and heavy as Crista's eyes widened, her gaze dimming as ecstasy began to wash over her.

Her orgasm came fast and hard. With his fingers stroking strong and sure inside her pussy, his cock burying repeatedly inside her ass, there was no holding back. The dark eroticism and extreme pleasure was too much.

Crista heard her own cries with a distant wonder. They sounded shattered, agonized. Beneath that sound was Dawg's. His harsh male groan as he buried deep inside her rear, his seed spurting heavily inside her, would always follow her.

His broken "I love you, Crista. God help me, I love you" threw her orgasm higher, shattering her soul with the ragged edge of hope and pain she heard in his voice.

He jerked against her, spilling his semen into her rear before giving a final groan and easing slowly from the tight clasp she had on him.

Crista whimpered at the added sensation. The feel of him slowly leaving her, his cock easing from her, his fingers caressing away from her pussy were nearly painful now in their intensity.

They were both sweat-soaked as he eased on the bed beside her and pulled her to his chest. His lips pressed against the top of her head in a kiss that had her chest clenching in emotion.

Beneath her cheek his heart raced, just as hers was racing, and his lungs heaved for breath.

It was like this, every time. It wasn't just the exertion of the sex but the intense emotions that tore through them and left them weak and shaken.

"I love you, Dawg," she whispered when she could finally find her breath and her senses. "I've always loved you."

Twenty-one

Graceful Sweets and Bakery sat just off North Main Street outside the old town center. The house Johnny Grace had bought sat on the plot of land beside the house that Crista had inherited from her parents.

The two-story brick home sat amid a perfectly manicured and landscaped lawn. Summer blooms grew in abundance around the property, wooden archways held trailing vines and climbing roses, and the front porch was home to cement urns filled with sweetly scented flowers.

Crista walked to the wide front door. The sign hanging on the door claimed, Open to Fulfill Your Sweetest Needs.

"This is a very bad idea," she muttered, not for the first time, as Dawg gripped the door latch and opened the door.

Instantly, a profusion of scents wrapped around them. Baking breads, sweet icings, and tempting delights. Crista inhaled unconsciously and felt her sweet tooth awaken with a vengeance.

Johnny had always kept her supplied with sweets. For the past year, she hadn't had to buy so much as a loaf of bread because of his generosity. Payment for betraying her? A guilty conscience? Betrayal and anger began to burn brighter inside her. It made her chest ache with the knowledge that Dawg had dealt with this most of his life.

"Crista." Johnny's voice greeted her with an edge of concern as she stepped into what had once been an open living room and dining room. It now held display cases of profuse sweets and breads.

There were other customers. Johnny had a steady clientele that kept him busy through the day.

He stepped away from the register cabinet, a frown pulling at his brow, as he glanced at Dawg behind her.

"Natches said you had left town." His gaze was filled with concern. "Is everything okay?"

He gripped her hands before kissing her cheek. Reacting normally was the hardest thing Crista had ever done. She wanted to rage; she wanted to cry. For all his problems with the Mackay family, she had always enjoyed Johnny's company.

"Everything's fine, Johnny. Natches misunderstood a slight argument Dawg and I had. Nothing to be worried about. But I have been missing my banana nut bread. Do you have any made?"

Johnny glanced over her shoulder once again, his gaze flickering with indecision.

Crista glanced back. Dawg hadn't taken off his dark glasses, and he looked mean enough to bite nails in half. She butted her elbow into his tight abs with a warning look.

Customers were watching the scene curiously, a spate of whispers breaking out as Dawg looked down at her and rubbed at his hard stomach almost absently.

"I always have your bread, Crista." Johnny's voice could have held nerves, anger, or fear. It was hard to tell.

He turned and moved back to the main display case. Lifting the hinged glass door to the long case, Johnny grabbed a wax liner, lifted a small loaf of banana nut bread from the case, and pushed it quickly into a white wax bag he used for the breads.

"Here you go," he said, moving to the register, his expression emotionless, his gaze flickering between Crista and Dawg. "Anything else?" His gaze lingered on Dawg, and Crista swore she saw hatred glittering in the depths then.

"I tried to tell her she could get the bread somewhere else." Dawg spoke up then, his tone taunting. "It's a nice place you have here, Johnny. Real nice. I'm glad to see your little court battle paid off."

The money and land they had won during the estate battle with Dawg had evidently paid for the store.

"Dawg," Crista chided, hating the need to maintain a semblance of compassion toward Johnny. She could feel the animosity that began to thicken between the two men. She pulled some money quickly from her purse to pay for the bread, wanting only to get out of there, to breathe without the stench of Johnny's betrayal choking her.

Johnny held his hand up, forestalling the payment, his gaze hardening as he stared back at her. "For old times." He smiled tightly. "But please, call before coming back. I'll make certain I have my assistant working that day. I don't need Dawg in my shop, if you don't mind."

Behind her, Dawg clicked his tongue mockingly. "Johnny, we're family, man. Surely I'm allowed in the store after paying for it? I can't believe you'd be so coldhearted."

This was Dawg at his most taunting. This, Crista had seen before. He was pushing Johnny, trying to make him angry, trying to make him strike out.

Johnny stared back at her instead. "Call first, Crista," he reminded her. "I'm sure you understand the reasons why."

The customers milling around the store were watching in interest now, the gossip mill gearing up for a spate of talk that would go on for months.

"I understand, Johnny." She kept her voice soft, but inside, she ached. And she felt her anger beginning to build.

This store Johnny took such pride in. The big house his mother had built, their airs and certainty of their place in society had been bought with the pain of Dawg's childhood. They had added to his father's cruelty to Dawg and exacerbated memories that haunted Dawg even now.

Crista stared at the loaf of bread in her hand, then back at Johnny. Her expression tightened as she laid it back on the counter.

"On second thought, Johnny, I think I don't need this after all."

Surprise filled his gaze as he looked at the sheathed loaf of bread, then back at Crista.

"Are you sure, Crista?" It could be paranoia, but she was certain she heard a warning in his tone. She was choosing Dawg's side rather than staying neutral, or far better, choosing Johnny's side.

Crista's lips thinned as she stared back at him, seeing now how easily he could have portrayed her. They were the same height, close to the same build. It wouldn't have been hard for

Johnny to fake the curves that her body held, dress in her clothes, and pretend to be her.

Getting her clothes and putting them back wouldn't have been hard. Her house sat right beside his, and he could have copied her key the few times she had left it with him, times such as when the cable repairman had been expected and she had to work.

"I'm sure, Johnny." She stepped back from the counter before turning and glancing at Dawg. "I'm ready to go now."

She didn't wait for him. She turned on her heel and moved purposely for the door, feeling Dawg moving protectively behind her. It was the oddest feeling, knowing he was there without even looking, feeling his warmth surrounding her even when he wasn't touching her.

He reached around her as she neared the door and opened it quickly. Standing back to let her through the exit, Dawg glanced back at Johnny. He should have smirked. He could have antagonized the little bastard further, he thought.

But as he stared at Johnny, all he felt was pity. He was too much like his mother, too easily influenced by his need for petty power and his drive to have more than he worked for.

Dawg saw the hatred in Johnny's eyes. He saw the resentment and years of pent-up aggression caused by the fact that only once in his life had he ever gained the upper hand on Dawg. That once being the court battle Dawg had nearly lost.

Rather than saying anything more, he merely shook his head, sighed at the weariness of the fight that had waged between him and Johnny since childhood, and left the small store Johnny had purchased from the ill-gotten gains of betraying blood.

Leaving the building, Dawg followed Crista to the truck, feeling the heaviness in his chest and regrets that he knew were better left forgotten.

He knew, to the bottom of his soul, that his own father would have preferred to have left his estate to Johnny and his mother. But it was Dawg's mother who had foiled those plans.

For all her paranoia and suspicious tendencies and cold, emotionless demeanor, Brenda Mackay had understood family loyalty. She might not have been able to keep her husband from beating the hell out of her son when he was younger, but she had counseled Dawg on the best ways to avoid Chandler's temper, and she had made certain that in the event of their deaths that Dawg's inheritance would be preserved. Had it not been for her careful wording of their wills and her wishes clearly stated, then Dawg would have lost everything.

He helped Crista into the truck, seeing the anger building in her eyes and the flush on her face as he closed the passenger side door and moved to the driver's side.

As he pulled himself into the truck and started the vehicle, he glanced over at Crista again and found himself uncertain what to say.

He had accepted the animosity between Johnny and him years ago. He found himself rarely surprised by his cousin until he learned he had actually killed. He had also refused to explain or make excuses for his own behavior where the other man was concerned.

Now he found himself wishing he could find the words to explain it to Crista. She was hurt and angry. Johnny had been her friend.

For the first time in his life, he was involved in a situation that couldn't be won, no matter what he did. He couldn't influence Crista's decision. This wasn't a war that he could win with a gun, his fists, or his money.

When he was younger, his fists had protected him. Once he joined the Marines and entered the shadowed world of an assassin, he had learned his gun could handle the monsters of the world. Monsters that killed and maimed. But the job had taken a toll on his conscience. In ways, Dawg often thought the bullet he had taken to the knee had been a blessing.

When he returned home, he returned to enough money to ensure that lawyers could fight his battles and the things he needed would be taken care of.

Fists, guns, or lawyers weren't going to change what Crista was feeling now: the betrayal, the anger, the knowledge that she had trusted someone who had been using her.

He drove to the lumber store, silent, glancing at her, wishing now that he hadn't made the decision to confront Johnny in such a way. He didn't want Crista as hard or as cynical as he had become.

It would be over soon. Cranston would pick Johnny up by evening on terrorism and selling military weapons charges. After that, maybe he could breathe easy. She wouldn't be safe until then. Johnny knew she hadn't left town, knew he was trapped; Dawg had seen it in his eyes. The agents watching him would follow him, but until he was behind bars, Dawg wouldn't, couldn't breathe easy.

"I'm sorry," he finally breathed out roughly as he pulled into the side parking lot of the store. "I shouldn't have made you do that."

She surprised him with an unladylike snort and a flash of defiance in her eyes.

"If that mousy little bastard thought a loaf of bread was going to make up for impersonating me, then he has another thing coming. Just as you do if you think I need you apologizing for your cousin's stupidity."

His brows lifted in surprise as he pushed his glasses down his nose and stared over the lenses at her.

Her lips tightened as she glanced away, then back to him.

"I always thought maybe the problems between Johnny and you, Rowdy, and Natches were because of his sexual preferences. I felt sorry for him. He was so much smaller than the rest of you and always seemed so upset because he wasn't a part of the fun." She shrugged uncomfortably. "I knew about the court battle, how he and his mother tried to steal your inheritance, but I thought it was an attempt to get attention more than anything else."

Regret flickered behind the anger in her gaze.

"It may have started that way," Dawg allowed. "When we were much younger. The problem with letting Johnny in on the fun was that he tended to carry tales. Rowdy was pretty safe from it; Uncle Ray didn't have a heavy hand. Natches and I paid enough times for Johnny's inability to keep those secrets, though. So we kept our distance from him."

She grimaced painfully. "Fathers should be understanding," she whispered. "A heavy hand only breeds resentment."

"Or hatred," Dawg pointed out cynically before shaking his head and staring through the windshield to the metal side of the lumber store. "It's not worth discussing at this point. I'm just sorry you were dragged into it, Crista."

"He did it to hurt you," she said, drawing his gaze back to her. "He impersonated me, drew me to the warehouse, and then walked into that detention center dressed as me to ensure my arrest. He did it just to hurt you."

Dawg had already figured that one out, but he found himself hurting because she had realized it. His chest tightened, and his heart actually ached.

Reaching out, he let the backs of his fingers caress her jawline, feeling the warmth of her flesh, seeing the acceptance in her gaze.

"I wouldn't have had you arrested," he finally said softly. "If you had walked out the night I blackmailed you, I would have let you leave, Crista. I had the note you left in your car. I knew you were innocent."

"Do you think I don't know that?" She caught his hand and held it to her cheek. "I always knew that, Dawg. Maybe I just needed the excuse to step out of the past and reach for what I wanted."

He pulled the glasses from his nose and laid them on the dash, all the while staring at her, memorizing her features and the emotions that filled her gaze.

It was love. He could see the love. It was the same look Kelly gave Rowdy, the way Maria stared at her husband Ray. Inviting, dark, filled with acceptance and with some emotion that defied description.

Love was such a tame word for what he felt and for what he saw in her eyes.

Dawg swallowed convulsively, suddenly uncertain, thrown off balance by her. Hell, she had always managed to do that to him, even eight years before. Made him feel like an inexperienced kid who didn't know how to get a girl.

"I want to give you another baby." He grimaced as the words tore past his lips, and her eyes widened in surprise. "No, listen." His fingers covered her lips as they parted. "I know you're not ready right now. I want to marry you, Crista. I want my ring on your finger. I want you by my side. But I want to give you another baby, too. I—" He broke off, his lips tightening at his own inability to put his feelings into words.

Hell, he wanted to bind her to him; it was that damned simple. He wanted to make certain she could never walk away from him again, that she never wanted to walk away from him again.

"Dawg," she whispered, her hand reaching out to him, lying

along his cheek at he stared back at her, desperate for all the things he had lost after she left town. "I won't leave you again. Ever."

Something inside him loosened at her words. As though a coil of dread had been tightening in his chest, her words released it, lifting a part of his soul that he had never known was restrained inside him. Heat rushed through him. Not just arousal and lust, but emotions that swamped him, that dazed him.

He was harder than he had ever been in his life, and yet inside, the hard core of anger, cynicism, and regret was melting.

There was nothing he could say. There was only one way to combat the unfamiliar morass of emotions tearing through him now.

He reached for her. His arms surrounded her, pulling her across the console until her rear rested in his lap, her head at his shoulder, and his lips were covering hers.

An inferno of hunger exploded in his veins. His flesh prickled with heat, and his kiss grew ravenous. He couldn't get deep enough, couldn't taste her or touch her enough.

Her lips parted for him, took him, as his fingers threaded through her hair and cupped the back of her head to hold her in place. Not that she was fighting the kiss. Hell no. Her hands were in his hair, tugging and pulling, as her tongue met his, licked and stroked and drove him crazy with the fierce, passionate battle they were waging.

She was summer lightning, striking hot and swift to the center of his soul. She was a hot summer day and a cool, easing breeze all at once.

"God, you make me crazy for you," he groaned, his lips moving over her jaw to her neck. "I forget where the hell I'm at and don't give a damn who's watching."

And he didn't. The employees' parking lot was fairly sheltered, but it was in no possible way private. Dawg was a desperate man, though. The emotions welled inside him, the hunger for Crista that he knew would never be sated, and his hands couldn't touch her enough.

His head lifted, his gaze lowering as he pushed his hand beneath the hem of yet another of those damned snug tank top things she wore. The ones that smoothed over her breasts and skimmed over her belly just a little too snug to make grown men comfortable.

He watched as the rough, dark flesh of his hand touched her smooth, creamy belly above the low-rise jeans she wore. Crista wasn't bone skinny, rather nicely rounded, and those curves made him crazy.

His hand moved up her belly, pushing her shirt farther up until he could cup one lace-covered mound of her breast.

"Cameras," she suddenly moaned, shuddering as his fingers gripped a hard nipple and tugged at it slowly.

"Huh?" His attention was riveted on that hard little nipple, his mouth watering to taste it.

"Dawg!" Laughter and arousal filled her voice. "You parked under the security camera."

His eyes jerked up, moved to the window, and up to the camera's eye pointing down on the truck.

"Shit," he muttered.

Laughter bubbled from her lips as she pulled her shirt down, hiding the succulent, tempting little berries he was dying for.

"You're a bad boy," she accused, scrambling from his lap and trying to straighten her clothes and her hair. Laughter gleamed in her eyes and curved her luscious lips.

"Hell, you sound surprised." Dawg sighed as he shifted in his seat and tried to relieve the pressure of his jeans against his cock. That portion of his body was so engorged now it was painful.

"Never surprised." She shook her head with a soft laugh as she flipped down the visor, smoothed her makeup beneath her eyes, and fluffed the silk of her hair before checking her shirt.

After adjusting the neckline, she flashed him a teasing glance, then pushed her door open and jumped from the truck. Damn her. She knew what she was doing to him, Dawg thought, and he couldn't help but grin as he forced himself from the vehicle and hit the automatic lock on his key chain. The truck lights flashed as the small beep assured him it had locked.

"Come on, you little tease." Moving around the truck, his arm slid around her waist as they headed for the employees' entrance. "I'll lock us in the office and have my wicked way with you there.

"I don't think so. You have orders to finish, and you still haven't made up the list for the winter inventory yet. You need to get a jump on the larger stores and plan your displays."

He scowled down at her as they moved for the office steps.

"I don't do winter displays. They cost too much, and they're not effective."

"Only because you're the one doing them," she stated. "I've been watching your displays, Dawg. They aren't effective because you have no idea what women are looking for."

"I know what women want." He frowned down at her, wondering then if somehow he had been ineffective with those explosive orgasms he'd been giving her.

"What women want in a bed and what they're willing to buy in public are two different things." The laughter in her voice warmed him, made him grin. "Trust me. I've got you covered on this. We're going to have incredible winter displays. Just wait until you see the Santa Claus I'm thinking of bringing in. And I found some incredible wrought-iron arches at a steal. Very classy, and for the most part unavailable in this area. I want to buy the distributor's stock in whole, to make certain the larger stores don't get one up on us."

As he listened to her, he was tempted to shake his head. She had plans, and he'd be damned if he disagreed with her. At the rate she was going, she would end up making his father roll in his grave at the success of it.

"I need you to check with Jim Bedsford and see what happened to the Connelly order, now that I think about it." She frowned as they entered the office and she moved to the desk. "I nearly forgot, with everything that's been going on. Layla had to reimburse him for a fourth of his order when it didn't arrive on the site. He's pretty upset over it."

Dawg took the inventory order and frowned down at it. He had worked damned hard to get Connelly to let Mackay's handle the supplies for the apartment complex he was building.

"Damn," he growled. "I'm going to have to work today."

Soft laughter and feminine warmth whispered around him then.

"You and me both. Now go take care of Bedsford. And if I were you, I'd seriously consider replacing him."

"With who?" Dawg grunted.

His gaze met hers. She was confident, certain.

"Layla's husband, Jamie. He has experience, and he spends half his time here with Layla anyway. Might as well put him to work."

And she was right, damn her.

He grunted noncommittally, knowing damned good and well he'd end up doing it.

"Stay out of trouble," he warned her before pressing a hard kiss to her lips and heading for the door. "And don't leave the store with anyone but me. You're not safe until Cranston has Johnny picked up. Promise me, Crista."

"Yes sir," she snapped teasingly. "Any other orders, sir?"

He turned at the door and lifted his brows. "Be naked when I return?"

"Only in your dreams." She rolled her eyes and waved one hand back at him. "Bye-bye, Dawg. Catch you at lunch."

He chuckled as he left the office, amazed now at the feelings running through him. He was still so damned hard his jeans were uncomfortable, but that knot of discontent, which had followed him all his life, was easing. Because of her.

Shaking his head, he moved quickly down the stairs, threw Layla a wave, and made a mental note to talk to her about her husband before heading to the back of the store. Bedsford was obviously going to have to go; Dawg just wanted to find out first why he was sabotaging the supplies Mackay's Lumber was in charge of.

Twenty-two

Summer displays were as important as winter and Christmas displays, but a hell of a lot harder without the time it took for preparation.

Crista spent the first several hours staring out the tinted windows that overlooked the floor of the store, her gaze narrowed as Layla worked at the desk behind her to get a count on the proper items they were going to need to create the design Crista wanted.

The front of the store was important. At the moment, it was all parking lot. There were no fenced areas for the summer displays and landscaping. Nothing for shoppers to get curious about as they drove in front of Mackay's to reach the large grocery store and outdoor strip mall housed farther up the road.

"Do we have the gazebo plans at least?" Crista asked Layla.

Dawg had ordered only a small amount of the gazebos, which were steady sellers through the past few years.

"We have several plans." Layla moved to the lateral files on the other side of the office. "I put them in here after the last gazebos shipped in. The supplier sends the plans or they'll build them for you. It would be incredibly cheaper if Dawg would pay a few of the younger workers to put in some extra hours to put them together."

She pulled a file free and laid the first plan out on the coffee table. "These are the ones that are selling best at the moment."

The smaller gazebos had a two-seat swing with a bench on the other side. Crista stared down at the design, pursing her lips thoughtfully. "We have the swings?"

"Plenty of those." Layla nodded. "And we could get the flowers you were talking about within three days. There's a local greenhouse owner I know who would make certain Mackay's has only the freshest blooms. They'll train the employees to care for them and check them every few days. What we don't sell, we don't pay for. Especially the perennials, flowering bushes, and trees, because they can be planted in the fall and sold to landscapers the next spring."

Crista made a few quick notes on the clipboard she carried, around the sketch she was making of the outdoor display she wanted.

"Are your boys working this summer?" she asked Layla.

Layla shook her head quickly. "They haven't applied for anything yet. They have summer classes at the college, so it would be hard for them to work most places right now."

"Could Mackay's hire them for evening work and weekends?" she asked. "We'll need someone to build the gazebos and to put the displays together. There're a few of the girls working the floor right now that I have in mind for the gardening section, but I'd like to get this taken care of first."

"That would work perfectly for them, Crista." Layla nodded.

"Let me find Dawg." Crista turned and looked out over the floor once again. "He was supposed to be talking to Bedsford about the Connelly order."

"I saw him in the lumberyard before you called me up here. They were loading the items missing on the inventory sheet. He called Connelly and got an agreement to hold off on buying the items elsewhere if Dawg would take care of the orders personally. I heard him arguing with Connelly on his cell phone," Layla admitted with a shy grin. "Dawg can be persuasive. I'd guess he'll go after Jim around closing instead. The lumberyard is pretty busy right now."

How many orders was Bedsford messing up in the meantime, Crista wondered, a frown working at her brow at the thought of the other man.

She knew Jim Bedsford, not well, but she knew him.

Her heart jumped in her chest then, an odd memory flashing in her head. She had seen Johnny and Jim one night. It had been late, after she got off at the diner. Jim had been getting into Johnny's car, but she hadn't seen Johnny. Oh Lord, she had seen a woman.

A woman with long hair and shadowed features. It had been too dark to see much, but it had felt odd, out of place, because she knew Johnny was gay. She thought he had loaned his car to a friend; he did that sometimes. She had borrowed it herself once.

It had been Johnny, dressed as her, and Bedsford had known it.

Jim was a bit taller than Johnny, broad, with a barrel chest and a perpetual scowl on his pitted face. He had been discharged from the service for medical reasons, she had heard, though there had been no specifics.

"I have to find Dawg," she whispered, her heart in her throat.

Layla looked back at her in surprise. "He should be finished in the lumberyard by now. He's probably on the floor. Is something wrong?"

"I need to talk to him about the outside display so we can get started on it," she said. She also needed to talk to him about Bedsford and Johnny. "Could you stay up here and watch the phones while I'm gone?"

Layla nodded. "I have Crystal watching the floor right now. That won't be a problem."

"I'll be right back."

Crista left the office quickly and moved down the metal steps. Her gaze scanned the rows and aisles as she headed across the floor toward the end of the building where the lumber and building displays were arranged. Some of the stock was kept inside for small purchases, while the majority of it was kept in a covered hangar behind the store.

As she entered the lumber section, she paused, frowning when she didn't see Dawg. Turning up one of the narrow aisles, she walked quickly toward the back of the store, then headed toward the other side when one of the stock boys mentioned seeing him in appliances.

Damn it, they needed a few walkie-talkies. She didn't have her cell phone on her, and right now she could have used a clue as to where the hell he was. She made a quick note on her clipboard to have him set up a system for the employees. It would also make helping customers much easier.

"Bradley." She stopped in appliances by one of the young stock boys loading a washing machine onto a metal roller cart. "Have you seen Mr. Mackay?"

"He just went back outside." Bradley nodded his shaggy head toward the employees' door that led to the side parking lot.

"Thanks, Bradley." Nodding quickly, she moved for the door, pushing it open and stepping outside as she shaded her eyes to stare around.

"Hello, Miss Jansen, can I help you?" Jim Bedsford stepped from between several delivery trucks, tossing a cigarette to the ground as he stared back at her with a heavy scowl.

"I was looking for Dawg." She gave him a cool smile, fear suddenly lashing inside her. "Perhaps he's inside."

"He's in the lumberyard." Jim moved closer. "He fired me, you know."

Crista froze as he blocked the way around the side of the building.

"I'll discuss it with him." She attempted to bluff her way back to the door.

"Miss Jansen, open that door, and I'll shoot you."

She turned back slowly, her eyes widening at the sight of the black barrel beneath the dark ball cap Bedsford was carrying in one hand.

She glanced up at the camera. There was no way to tell that the man was carrying a weapon.

"You're going to come with me, nice and easy like." He smiled coldly. "We need to talk."

"Dawg will know who I left with, Jim," she warned him. "Dawg will know."

"Don't try to run your mouth at me, bitch." His voice didn't raise or lower, it remained cold, vicious. "Just get in the fucking van and stop arguing with me before I have to kill you. I don't want to hurt you, but I'm not above it."

Crista stared around the parking lot desperately.

"If I have to kill you, then I'm going to have kill Dawg, too," he pointed out in what she assumed was a reasonable tone. "It won't be hard. He's not the only Somerset boy who went through stealth training. Or the only one who can play assassin. Now, are you going to cooperate, or do I have to get pissed off?"

Dawg would miss her soon. Crista looked up at the camera desperately, her fists clenched by her sides as she moved out of the range of the blinking eye and realized that the monitor probably hadn't even picked up Bedsford. But he would know, she told herself. Dawg would know, and he would come for her.

"I don't want to hurt you." He opened the door to a small panel van and pushed her in before following her. "Get in the driver's seat. We'll drive out of here nice and easy."

"Why are you doing this?" Crista moved into the driver's seat and took the keys with a shaking hand. "I'm sure you could find a job somewhere else, Jim."

A rough laugh met her words. "Hell, you think this job means shit to me?" He sat on the floor behind the passenger seat, the gun held firmly in his hand and leveled at her. "Lady, I couldn't give a shit about this job except for the fact that it helped us keep an eye on Dawg. We needed to know what he was up to, so I worked here and kept up on things. Kept him busy where I could."

"We?" She pulled from the parking lot, praying someone had seen her, that someone would know who she had left with.

"Come on, you're not a stupid bitch," he clucked in amusement. "Johnny knew this morning that he'd been set up by Natches. Someone figured it out. He did a damned good impersonation of you until Dawg hooked up with you and was able to track your movements. We just needed a little more time, and we would have had the money while those nasty little terrorists would have believed it was you. Even those yahoos who helped steal the missiles didn't know who Johnny was. Or you, for that matter. Until the other day."

"He told them who I was?"

Bedsford laughed again. "Walked right into the detention center and flashed your ID and signed your name. They all know who you are now. I don't think Dawg's going to be able to keep you safe. The men who helped Johnny steal the missiles think you have them. The men who paid half down on a shipment they're never going to get think he's you." His smile was satisfied. "You're dead, no matter what."

He wasn't going to let her go. Of course, Crista had figured that one out already.

"So why not just shoot me now and get it over with?" Her hands clenched the steering wheel hard as she turned down the road leading to the highway.

She didn't believe in going easy. She had one chance, and it would be risky. At the end of the lane was a traffic signal. It was green right now, but if she timed it just right, she might have a chance to escape.

Her heart was racing, fear thundering in her head as she drew closer.

"You know, I won't mind blowing your head off if you try something crazy." The gun shifted in his hand, the barrel pointing up as she brought the van to a stop as the light turned red. "Wouldn't it hurt so much less to just go along with me and pray your boyfriend rescues you?"

He couldn't rescue her if he didn't know where she was or who had taken her. And he couldn't rescue her if she had a bullet in her head.

She glanced at the gun again, then up at the scowl on Jim's bulldog face.

"Dawg will kill you," she told him, knowing he would. But she would still be gone if she didn't do something. Fast.

Johnny's warning look earlier in the day had assured her that she had taken the wrong side. He would show no more mercy toward her than he had the transport driver whose truck he had hijacked.

"Dawg won't kill me if all he has to do is clear your sweet little name and I'm nowhere to be found," he grunted. "Look bitch, we just have to do one more thing. That's all. If you're missing when it goes down, and we fly out of here, then we're in the clear, no matter what you say. Your word against ours, plain and simple. And it won't matter anyway. Johnny's going with me to Nicaragua. I have some friends there. Some contacts."

"Are you crazy, Jim?" she asked as she pulled onto the highway, amazed at the man's gullibility. "Do you think Johnny did this just so he could escape to some damp jungle? He has no intentions of leaving Somerset with you or of letting me go."

"I don't really care what he does with you." There was a shrug in Jim's voice. "And he promised. We're going to take the money and set up in a nice little hacienda there. We have it all picked out."

Crista blinked in surprise, directed a look back at him, then jerked her eyes back to the road.

Bedsford was in love with Johnny? She could hear it in his voice. It softened, and the scowl was no longer on his face. His expression radiated with emotion, and his dark brown eyes gleamed with purpose.

"Johnny couldn't live without being close enough to his cousins to throw their failure in their faces," she whispered painfully, knowing she was driving herself to her own funeral.

"Turn at the next light," he ordered. "We're going to head out of town. I'll let you know when to turn again."

"We're not going to Johnny's?"

"Why would I do that?" Jim asked her as though surprised. "That would be like hanging a sign on his door. We're going to meet him somewhere else. That's all."

"Where he'll kill us both." She was certain of it. "He killed the driver of the transport truck for no reason, Bedsford. He's not going to let you live. Or me."

"Johnny loves me." The belief in his voice terrified Crista.

"Johnny loves the money his mother gives him, trying to steal more from his cousins, and convincing everyone how socially acceptable he is," she said. "He won't see that destroyed. And he won't allow either of us to live."

Her eyes scanned the road frantically. At each stoplight she searched for someone she knew, anyone who could help her. And no one met her eyes. Time was running out, and she knew it.

Jim chuckled at her assessment. "When I came back eight years ago, Johnny was a mess over his uncle's death and what Dawg had stolen from him. Chandler Mackay tried to do right by Johnny. He knew Johnny was smarter, better than his son was. And Johnny knew how much Chandler wanted to make certain he was rewarded for being the son Dawg wouldn't be. Dawg stole that inheritance, Miss Jansen. And I built Johnny back up. I helped him regain his confidence and his sense of place in the world. He loves me. And he will leave with me. What his mother or the Mackays have is nothing compared to what I can give him in Nicaragua."

"A country filled with war and death. With insurgents, rebellions, and terrorists?" Crista shook her head. "He will never leave Somerset for that, Jim. You know he won't."

"If you don't shut up, I'm going to blow your head off right here in the middle of town." Once again, his voice only became harder, darker. Vicious. There was no conscience there, no regret, and no second thoughts.

Crista inhaled roughly, then flinched at the sound of a cell phone. It wasn't hers. No, she couldn't be that lucky. Hers was back at the office.

"Hey, baby," Jim answered the call, his voice gentling. "I'm heading to the meeting point. Do you have everything ready?"

Crista gripped the steering wheel harder, knowing she couldn't go much farther. If she actually managed to let him get her out of town, then no one would ever know what happened to her.

She stared at the traffic around her, in front of her. There was one more stoplight. If she timed that one right and ran it—

A car pulled in front of her, and from the backseat, a hand waved. Crista focused, nearly whimpering in relief at the sight of Rowdy Mackay.

She didn't know who was driving, but Rowdy was in the backseat. He was holding up fingers. Six fingers. Pointed around her.

Six. Six people following them. She didn't dare nod, couldn't do anything to draw attention to herself. She checked the rearview mirror but didn't see Dawg. He would be there, though. If Rowdy was here, then Dawg was close.

Rowdy held up a piece of paper then.

"Do as he says!" The thick black wording glared back at her.

She lifted one finger from the steering wheel to indicate she understood.

"Don't worry, Johnny. I'm watching her," Jim assured him. "We'll be there soon, and everything can proceed as planned. Just make certain you're ready."

She glanced back at him. He kept his eyes trained on her, his scowl firmly in place.

She turned back. Rowdy was holding up another note.

"You're covered!"

She lifted her fingers to indicate that she understood. Then he turned around; the car changed lanes again and let the van pass them.

She was covered. She inhaled slowly. Deeply. Dawg wouldn't let anything happen to her now. She just had to stay calm.

"I love you, baby. Just stay cool. Another fifteen minutes, and we'll be there." Jim's rough voice softened, almost making Crista ill. And it had nothing to do with the obviously sexual relationship between him and Johnny. But how could a man love anyone that much and be a killer?

Jim shifted then, moving between the seats and glancing out the front window. He looked around with quiet satisfaction, checked the rearview mirror, then moved to the back of the van to look through the dark, tinted windows.

"Excellent," he grunted. "See, we got away free and clear, Crista. Dawg didn't even know when you left. I wonder if he's even realized that you're not at the store any longer."

"He'll know." He would have known within minutes.

Jim laughed. "He doesn't know shit. I made sure of it. He had such a mess to untangle in the lumberyard that he's probably still trying to figure it out. I planned this very carefully, you know."

Not well enough. Crista stared straight ahead and tried to concentrate on just breathing. Dawg was close; she could feel him. Everything would be okay. She repeated it to herself over and over again and prayed she was right.

Dawg kept the van in sight from the backseat of the bright red extended-cab pickup truck Cranston and Dane had been waiting in outside the front of the store.

He was sweating. He could feel the moisture rolling from his forehead and dampening his back. He had promised to keep her safe. He remembered that. As they drove to Johnny's, he had promised her that nothing would happen. They were just going to let him know they were onto him, make him mess up. Everything was going to be just fine.

He should have known better. God help him, he should have figured out a year ago that he couldn't tempt fate that damned far. He should have known Johnny had an accomplice. Someone close to Dawg. Someone who had somehow figured out he was working with the ATF.

That someone was Jim Bedsford. Ex-military with contacts that Dawg was certain extended into the law enforcement community. Jim had been involved with Special Forces and deep cover investigations during his time in the Army.

"Someone messed up on this one," he commented as though he weren't imagining drawing someone's blood for the mess-up. Particularly Cranston's.

"We have her covered, Dawg," Cranston assured him, not for the first time. "We have a tracker on Alex's vehicle as well as that purse we found in Grace's house. His tail verified he left the house by the back door dressed as Crista, and he's driving Alex's car. We won't lose him."

Surveillance video on the detention center had managed to identify the car Johnny had been using to visit his buddies. Alex's car was supposed to be locked in the unattached garage behind the house he and Crista had grown up in. Johnny had her house keys and the keys to that garage and to the car.

"Do you know how many different ways I'm going to kill you if you do, Cranston?" Dawg asked him softly.

Cranston cleared his throat uneasily. "I don't have a worry, Dawg. We have it covered."

"Grace just turned off the highway and headed up a hunters' road to the lake," Greta Dane reported. She pulled up a map on the laptop she held on her lap, the moving red dot indicating the car Johnny was driving.

"Natches, are you getting this?" Dawg asked over the speaker line set on his cell phone.

"I have it here, Dawg," Natches said softly. "He's heading toward the old Bridgeland hunting cabin. I'll circle around and get in place. Don't worry, Bro. I'll cover her."

Dawg heard the complete unemotional determination in Natches's voice and felt the tight knot of fear begin to uncoil in his belly. Natches's loyalty was unquestioned, as was his ability with the rifle Dawg knew he kept close by.

"I'm heading there," Dawg told him. "Don't take any chances, Natches. I don't care if Bedsford and Johnny both lose gray matter. Keep Crista safe for me."

"No fears, Bro."

Dawg knew that tone of voice. There was every chance in the world that Bedsford and Johnny would end up with a bullet in the head anyway.

"Natches, you follow fucking orders," Cranston snapped out furiously as he flicked Dawg an enraged glare in the rearview mirror. "We need those two alive."

The call disconnected.

"Damn it, Dawg," the special agent snarled. "If those two end up dead, I'll take it out of your hide."

"If those two end up dead, I won't lose a single night's sleep over it," Dawg growled in return. "Don't fuck with me, Cranston. You knew Bedsford was involved in this, and you didn't deign to tell any of us. And don't bother denying it."

It had taken Dawg a few minutes to put it together, and if he hadn't known Cranston as well as he did, he wouldn't have suspected it. But he did know Cranston. Throw a wild card in the mix, and he was killer-cold. Cranston wasn't cold. If he wasn't driving, he would be rubbing his hands together in glee.

"How did you figure out Bedsford was involved in this?"

Cranston cursed under his breath. "He's related to the dead transport driver, Private Dwayne Stockton. There were cell phone calls to Bedsford in the weeks before he was killed."

"And I didn't know this why?" Dawg had to force the words past his lips and his hand off his weapon.

"Because he was working for you, and I decided to wait before informing you of the fact."

Son of a bitch. "You thought I was involved."

"I didn't believe you were involved, but I had to be certain. By the time I was certain, Miss Jansen was involved, and I had to decide the best way to handle it. I handled it by watching your back and hers until I knew what was going on."

"The van is turning off," Dane said softly. "Natches has directed our men in front of him using an alternate route. Grace is in place, and Natches has him in sight."

"Turn right at the next road," Dawg directed them, hating the thought of losing sight of Crista in that damned van. "The next road will keep us parallel to him and put us in place to move on foot to the cabin."

The Bridgeland hunting cabin had more than one dirt track leading to it due to the four-wheelers often used to access it.

Dawg wiped his hand across his brow, his gaze locked on the van ahead of them until Cranston made the turn. The coil of fury and fear iced in his gut then.

Dawg pulled his handgun from the holster at his back and checked the clip. Replacing it, he pulled the extra clips from the supply Cranston had tossed in the back, checked them quickly, then loaded the bulletproof vest before pulling it on and strapping the sides in place.

God bless Layla Matcher's heart. If it hadn't been for her

standing at the window and seeing Jim Bedsford forcing Crista into that van, then Dawg would have never found her.

Cranston had been watching for Johnny Grace in the main customer parking lot. It was evident that no one had expected Bedsford to move this fast or to do so without Johnny physically backing him.

"Bedsford had the contacts for the black market buyers," Cranston told him. "We found that out only in the past twenty-four hours. The Swedish mercenary making the buy finally made a deal with the federal prosecutor. He didn't have Bedsford's name, but he had enough information for us to ID him. He spent his time in the Army making contacts in the black market and setting up weapons deals."

"You should have been on the ball, Cranston." Dawg strapped a backup weapon to his ankle and stuffed several spare clips for it into another pocket of the vest. "You fucked up."

"Information was slow coming in." Cranston shook his head. "Our sources do have other things they're working on as well, you know."

"You fucked up. And if Crista gets hurt, then you've really fucked up. Because I'll kill you."

Dawg didn't let free the fury burning in a small corner of his mind. He kept it bottled, kept it contained. He couldn't afford it now, not when logic and clear thinking alone were going to get Crista through this.

His cell phone beeped.

"Give me the goods," he answered with the order to Natches.

"I'm positioned in one of the pines beside the cabin on the side Bedsford's van will have to use. Johnny's here in full Crista disguise. Hell, Dawg, he looks hot." There was murder in Natches's voice. "Want me to draw a little blood?"

"Hold tight. Cranston has a transmitter in that damned pocketbook Johnny's carrying as well as in the wig. I'll be in place before Bedsford gets there. We'll go in together."

"Here." Cranston tossed him an earbud. "We're close enough to use these. Tell Natches to put his in place now. Don't fuck with me, Dawg. This is a team play, not a vendetta."

"Use the earbud, Natches." Dawg grinned back at Cranston through the rearview mirror. The sight of that smile had the special agent's gaze flickering.

Attaching the communications device, Dawg activated it, then tested it quickly before disconnecting the phone. Cranston and Dane were both similarly wired as, Dawg assumed, the rest of the team was.

"Now, we're all here," Cranston spoke into the device.

"Now I can tell you I'm going to kick your ass personally when this is over, Cranston," Natches spoke through the ear receiver. "Didn't I warn you about pulling surprises on us, man?"

Cranston grunted. "Keep your finger off that trigger, Natches, and your eyes on Grace. Let's at least get a little evidence against these bastards before we start shooting. If you don't mind, that is?"

"And if I mind?"

Twenty-three

Natches kept his sniper rifle trained on Johnny and his finger on the trigger. That finger twitched. He wanted to kill the bastard so damned bad it was all he could do to hold back. It ate at his gut with a power that nearly gave him indigestion.

Johnny Grace. He was a first cousin. He had been raised with them when he was younger, until he, Rowdy, and Dawg figured out that Johnny was more like Natches's father than the gentle, smiling father Johnny'd had.

Ralph Grace, before his death, had managed to keep his wife and his son in check. After his death, though, Nadine and Johnny had revealed the vicious, evil streak they possessed.

He caressed the trigger of his rifle as he trained his sights on Johnny's forehead. Fucking bastard. God, how he hated Johnny. It was a hatred that nearly rivaled the hatred he had for his own father, Dayle Mackay.

As he stared through the rifle sights, he didn't see the image Johnny was trying to impersonate, that of Dawg's lover, Crista Jansen. No, he saw Johnny. Just Johnny. His beady little eyes narrowed as he leaned against Alex's car, his arms crossed over his fake breasts as he watched the dirt road he expected Bedsford to use.

Natches knew he should have expected this. He should have known Cranston was hiding shit; it was what Cranston did best. And to be honest, he had suspected it; he just hadn't put two and two together fast enough.

Because he had been too damned busy holding back a more personal fury.

It was bad enough that Rowdy had to be so damned possessive over Kelly, but now Dawg had to go and do the same thing with Crista. That lack of connection was affecting him. He was beginning to feel disassociated, cold. That tight knot of bitter ice inside his soul that he had fought all his life was hardening now.

Rowdy and Dawg had grown up, and they had grown away, though he was certain they didn't see it that way. Since Rowdy had taken Kelly, Natches had tried to share time with Dawg and Rowdy rather than women. But hell, women took up time, and Kelly was as spoiled as any female ever had been by Rowdy.

Sometimes, Natches thought they lived in each other's pockets, and now Dawg and Crista were taking the same route. And Natches was left standing on the outside, watching, wondering, and regretting.

He had thought the sharing would continue. He had let himself care for Kelly, let her into his heart, believing that when Rowdy came home that he would be a part of the intimacy, only to find out that Rowdy had found a core of possessiveness somewhere.

And Dawg. Dawg was doing the same thing. No other man would touch Crista without finding himself wishing he had held back. And Dawg was a mean bastard when he was riled.

And this was why Natches hadn't connected Bedsford and Johnny. Because he was too busy adjusting to changes that he hadn't expected, too busy trying to find a way to keep the ice around his soul melted.

He wasn't succeeding. A testament to that fact had his finger aching to twitch just enough to put a bullet in the back of Johnny's head.

Johnny had instigated every beating, every humiliation, every vicious attack Dayle Mackay had ever made against Natches. He had carried rumors to his father, and in many cases, proof of Natches's supposed crimes.

Sharing his women. Drinking too young. The instances were too many to name and too dangerous to remember right now.

His shoulder ached like hell as he stood amid the thick branches of the pine tree, his rifle resting on one thickly needled tree branch as he bent to keep Johnny in sight.

The bullet that had taken him out of the Marines hadn't

completely taken him out of the game. Once an assassin, always an assassin. Once a man deliberately set his sights on another man and pulled the trigger, then it was a part of him forever. He might walk away from it, but he could never escape it.

Natches hadn't wanted to walk away or to escape. He just hadn't had any other choice.

"Natches, we're moving into position." Dawg's voice came across the receiver in his ear. "Bedsford should be driving into the cabin yard any second."

Natches lifted his gaze from the gun sights and stared down the road.

"In sight." The van was pulling up the dirt track, bouncing over the ruts as the driver obviously took her time.

Crista was driving. Natches's gut clenched at the fear she must be feeling. She was depending on them to protect her, trusting Dawg and him to make certain nothing happened to her.

"Natches." Dawg said his name, nothing more, but he understood the message in it. The plea that Natches keep her safe, no matter the cost.

"I have her covered, Bro," he said quietly. "No fears."

"Natches, we need those two alive," Cranston repeated. "We need them all alive. Don't you pull any shit on me."

The corners of Natches's lips kicked up in amusement. It was a good thing he liked Cranston.

"Do your job; I'll do mine," he said softly. "Crista is priority. Period."

Cranston cursed, but Natches could have sworn he heard Dawg's breath of relief.

He'd die for Dawg and Rowdy. Without them, he wouldn't have survived past his teens. He was irked at the direction their lives had taken; at times, he was damned pissed off over it. But he understood it. Rowdy especially. Rowdy had never known the darkness that Natches and Dawg had lived through. And even Dawg, who had known the pain but not the pure evil that Natches had experienced.

Kelly and Crista had healed Rowdy and Dawg. He couldn't blame the two women for not seeing the loneliness it had caused in Natches.

Loneliness doesn't kill, though. It aches, it taunts, but it doesn't kill. He could survive loneliness.

"Van in sight." Natches came to attention as the white panel van drove into the cabin's yard.

He wrapped the strap of his rifle around one hand, held it steady against the branch, and caressed the trigger with the other. He'd have to take Bedsford out first, then Johnny, if it came to killing.

He would protect Crista. Rowdy and Dawg had protected him, saved him. He could do no less for them now.

Crista pulled the van to a stop beside Alex's car and stared at the vintage '67 navy blue Camaro. She stared at the car and would have winced at the fury Alex was going to experience if he ever learned his baby made it out of the garage he kept it locked in.

He was going to explode all over Johnny Grace with a force that would strip the man's flesh from his bones and make him pray for forgiveness.

If Johnny managed to live past Dawg, that was.

"You know, Johnny just signed both your death warrants with that car, right?" she asked as Bedsford straightened behind her. "Alex will hunt you to bell and back."

"He'll have to find us first." The side panel door opened, and he turned back to her with a wave of the gun. "Come on, lady. Let's get this over with so we can get the hell out of your fine little county."

Crista moved stiffly from the driver's seat, her gaze on the gun in his hand before moving past it and stepping out into the dirt clearing to face Johnny.

She stared at him, her gaze going over the clothes he wore. One of her best dresses. The wig was a near-perfect match to her hair, and with the makeup he had used, his features were almost similar.

And he was leaning against the Camaro, a wide smile on his face as she watched him silently.

"You did good, baby," Johnny told Bedsford quietly as the other man moved to him.

Johnny lifted his face and gave Bedsford a quick kiss while keeping his eyes on Crista.

"Poor Crista." Johnny sighed as Bedsford moved away from him. "You should have kept your distance from Dawg. I could have helped you out a bit here if you had. Besides, torturing my cousin was one of the points of this game that I enjoyed the most."

"How sad," Crista whispered, meaning it. "You've spent your life coveting everything Dawg is and has rather than building your own life. Why?"

His eyes narrowed on her. "Because it should have been mine. Haven't you figured it out yet, Crista? I actually thought Dawg would have figured it out, but he was never smart enough to put two and two together."

She stared back at him, old gossip whipping through her mind as she traced his features, his build. He looked like his mother, nothing like his father, so it was impossible to tell.

He chuckled, a low, frightening sound. "You remember, don't you? After Ralph Grace died, the rumors began slithering through the county like snakes that refused to die. Mother was pregnant when she married Ralph. Unfortunately, Ralph wasn't the father, no matter how much he thought he was."

It was sickening.

Crista glanced away from him, her eyes closing momentarily at the thought of those old tales.

"Yes, Chandler Mackay was my father." He sounded girlishly pleased at relating that information. "I was actually born first, by a few days. Brenda Mackay, Dawg's mother, knew, of course, and used it to force our father to sign it all over to Dawg in his will. The stupid bitch, she should have taken her little bastard and left then rather than hang around and steal everything that should have been mine."

Crista felt her knees weaken at the fury in Johnny's voice.

Incest. Chandler Mackay, it had been rumored, had been sleeping with his sister for years before she married Ralph Grace, and then again, after the other man's death. There were those who swore that Chandler Mackay had had a hand in Grace's death himself.

She turned and looked at Bedsford then, watching as his gaze roamed around the area, eyes narrowed, as though searching for something.

"Your boyfriend here thinks you're going to run to Nicaragua with him, Johnny," she said, more to distract Bedsford than anything else. "I told him you would never leave Somerset or

Dawg. What would be the point of all this if you couldn't torture him with it?"

A self-satisfied smile shaped Johnny's lips as Bedsford turned to him.

"Our plans may change now that I have you here." He shrugged his shoulders as though it didn't matter. "Why leave Somerset when, like you say, I can stay here and torture all parties involved?"

"So you definitely intend to kill me." She prayed Dawg was close. Surely if he was here by now, he would have done something.

"I really don't have a choice, sweetheart." He sighed, shaking his head in mock compassion.

"That wasn't the plan, Johnny." Bedsford stared at him in shock. "We can't stay around here now. There's no way the Mackays won't know we were involved."

"They won't know anything, Jim," he promised, reaching out to touch the scowl on the other man's face. "Settle down, lover. Everything will work out perfectly. You'll see."

Crista saw it coming, and she was certain Jim should have, most likely did. The hand holding the gun twitched as his scowl deepened, but Johnny's other hand came up too fast. The gun he held exploded. The bullet tore into Bedsford's chest, straight through his heart, and left him staring back at Johnny in shock.

He fell to his knees, his hands reaching out to Johnny as Johnny stepped back; then Bedsford toppled over to the ground.

Crista stared in shock, her eyes locked with Jim Bedsford's surprised, agonized gaze as it slowly dimmed and grew cold.

"That was unfortunate." Johnny sighed.

Crista lifted her head, only then noticing that Johnny wore clear latex gloves over his hands.

"He loved you," she said, knowing it didn't matter. Nothing mattered to Johnny but destroying Dawg.

"Of course he loved me." Johnny rolled his eyes at the declaration. "He adored me. I worked hard to make certain he did. But I no longer need him. This way, I don't have to split the million dollars, and I don't have to leave Somerset for fear of him growing a conscience over his cousin's death. Jim was a bit of a whiner. He didn't like killing the boy."

"Dawg knows you're involved in this, Johnny. If you kill me, he won't need the law on his side. He'll take you apart. You know he will."

"A million dollars can buy a lot of protection. And Dawg and Natches aren't the only ones who know how to hide and fire a rifle, Crista," he told her with amused unconcern.

Johnny couldn't know the evidence the agents had on him; if he did, he wouldn't be so certain. All she had to do was be patient; Dawg would be there. Johnny wouldn't expect that. As far as he knew, no one would even consider suspecting him of impersonating her.

"And Alex? Do you think he won't take up where Dawg might fail? This isn't going to go over as easy as you think it will, Johnny."

He was silent for long moments. Moments that seemed to drag out, to stand still as the forest around them held its breath. Silence descended in the clearing as the smell of blood and death began to fill Crista's head.

She could feel herself shaking, shuddering.

Where was Dawg? Rowdy had promised he would be here, that they were watching her, following her. A chill of fear raced through her body, causing her to clench her teeth to keep them from chattering.

"I've had this planned for a long time, Crista." He sighed. "Though I hadn't intended to kill you. Only make certain you were arrested for my crimes." His smile was maniacal. "That would have destroyed Dawg. He's really in love with you, you know that? He nearly drank himself to death after you left eight years ago. Of course, he didn't remember the night you spent with him. And"—his smile became demonic—"he didn't know about your miscarriage either, did he? Does he know now?"

"He knows." Her throat was so tight she felt as though she were strangling. "What you don't understand, Johnny, is that he knows you were involved. The Homeland Security agents know its you; Alex will know. You are not going to get away with this."

"No one has enough proof for anything." He waved her warning away. "No one can touch me, Crista. I made sure of it. When your bodies are found, it's going to look like you had a disagreement and killed each other. And of course, I'll give a statement that Jim confided his affair with you to me. Too many people are aware that we were at least friends. I have it all worked out, sweetheart." He moved then, sliding to the side as he waved the gun toward Alex's car. "Move on over here now."

Crista moved slowly, praying. Dawg had to be close by. She could feel him, feel eyes watching her, just as she was certain Jim had until she distracted him. Before Johnny killed him.

"There you go." Johnny smiled back at her as he bent and lifted Jim's gun from the ground. "Now, all I have to do is put a bullet in your heart, place the weapons appropriately, and drive out of here. It's all over now."

"Like hell!" Crista snarled. She wasn't going to make this easy for him.

Everything seemed to happen simultaneously then. Crista threw herself in front of Alex's car, hitting the ground as she heard a bullet ricochet off the metal. Then the forest seemed to come alive with gunfire.

She rolled to her back, watching as Johnny took the first bullet to his head, the second, third, and fourth to his chest. His body jerked violently as blood sprayed around him.

"Crista!" Dawg's voice screamed out her name. Then he was there, his arms coming around her, jerking her to the other side of the car, his hands running frantically over her. "Are you okay? Crista, baby, answer me." She stared up at him, dazed, feeling the blood racing through her head, pounding into her brain as shock began to shudder through her.

"Oh God," she whispered, feeling the darkness edging around her. "I'm going to fucking faint."

His face swam in front of her vision as her lashes fluttered.

"You faint on me, and I swear to God I won't fuck you for a week," he snarled, his voice low, his expression violent. "Don't you dare, Crista Ann."

Won't fuck her for a week? Could she make it a week? Could she keep the darkness from spreading through her?

She smiled, feeling amusement thread through the darkness.

"It's okay. Week works." And she gave in to it.

There were no wounds. The only blood on her was what had splattered from Bedsford. She was dusty, her arms scraped from throwing herself to the ground, and tears tracked her face.

She was pale, but she was breathing.

Dawg clasped her to him, burying his face in her hair as he

realized he was shuddering and tears were escaping from between his lashes as he rocked her against his chest.

She was alive. Dear God, she was alive, she was safe. She was safe, and nothing else mattered. He pulled her as close to his body as he could get her, feeling the silent sobs that racked his chest.

He had no idea how much he had loved her until he saw that gun leveling on her. Until he saw the moment that Johnny was actually going to pull the trigger. His world had narrowed down to one thing. To stopping it. No matter what it took. No matter how much blood Johnny shed or whether or not Cranston had his suspects.

Then the forest had exploded with gunfire.

"Dawg, man, is she okay?"

Alex? Dawg lifted his face from her hair and stared at the camouflage face paint, the fear in the other man's gray eyes, and the savage contours of his expression.

"What the fuck are you doing here?" Dawg snarled, his hand pressing Crista's head closer to his chest. "Where the hell were you when he was pointing the gun at her chest?"

Alex's smile was tight as he sat back on his heels and indicated the four other similarly painted and dressed men around him. "Recording this little event for the authorities," he stated. "Tyrell had point; he put one of the bullets in Grace's head. I suspect Natches can take credit for the other one. Mark." He waved his hand to the hard-eyed soldier at his side. "Crista stayed with him and Ty in Virginia. When you called the emergency number, it went through Mark. He pulled in some friends while I ditched a mission in Afghanistan. We pulled in here at midnight last night after Mark managed to get the information on the op here and we followed Johnny in."

"You moved fast." Dawg inhaled roughly, his hand pressed at Crista's back, feeling each breath.

"I had a feeling she was being pulled into something last time I talked to her." Alex sighed. "I had everything in place just in case."

"Everything but the emergency number," Dawg snapped. "Son of a bitch, Alex, don't you think she needed it?"

"If she had it, she wouldn't have gone to you," Alex told him then. "I wanted her where she needed to be."

"She didn't come to me, you stupid bastard." Dawg was enraged. "She nearly got her ass killed in a warehouse during the attack we made on the buyers and sellers of those stupid fucking weapons. Grace set her up, Alex. She almost died there."

Alex paled. "She didn't call you?"

"Not even on a fucking dare." Fury was pounding through him now. "You're a lucky bastard I managed to save her ass. Otherwise, I'd have to kill you now."

"Hell, I didn't know she was that damned stubborn." Alex rubbed his hand over his face, smearing the face paint he wore as he stared around the clearing. "I'll have to have a talk with her about that."

"The hell you will." Dawg gathered her closer as sirens wailed along the rough track leading into the cabin yard. "Tell me there's a fucking medic here somewhere?"

"Ty." Alex turned to one of the two men standing behind him. "Get your pack and check her out. Where's Cranston?"

Alex rose to his feet, his in-charge voice echoing through the area as Cranston cursed in the background.

Tyrell Grayson came down on his knees beside Crista, his fingers going to her neck, his expression concerned.

"She lived with you?" Dawg snarled. "Slept with you?"

Hard lips kicked up in a grin. "Mark and I babied the hell out of her," he said then. "See if you can do near as well."

Dawg's gaze sliced to Mark Lessing. Both men were dangerous, as dangerous as Alex and just as hard. There wasn't an ounce of softness in them.

"Thank you." He had to force the words past his clenched teeth. "For taking care of her."

Ty nodded sharply. "That's us. Protector of broken hearts. Take better care of her this time, or we're going to break your bones."

It wasn't a threat, it was a warning. An unneeded one at that.

"She's good." Ty finally nodded sharply. "She'll wake up with a headache, probably. I've never seen her faint, but I know tension gives her killer headaches. I'd be more comfortable if you'd let them transport her to the hospital and keep her overnight though, just to be sure."

Dawg nodded as Natches and Rowdy flanked him then.

"I see you don't need our help." Ty stood to his feet, staring down at Crista with the first flash of softness that Dawg had glimpsed in him. "She's a damned good woman, man. And she's grieved for you for far too long. See if you can't make up for that now. She deserves it." He nodded before giving Dawg a chance to say anything and turned away.

"My bullet hit Johnny's forehead at the same time someone else's did," Natches informed him. "Same place, same time. Those boys aren't slouches."

Alex's team was slowly disappearing into the forest as Alex kept Cranston busy.

"Alex recorded everything." Dawg stood, lifting Crista into his arms as the ambulance Cranston had had standing by pulled into the lane. "Cranston has what he needs. I have what I need."

Crista, resting against him, safe, unharmed. And hell yes, he would make damned sure he made up for those lost years. Just as soon as he had her checked out at the hospital and she was capable of taking his loving.

Wait a week as he threatened? There wasn't a chance in hell. The minute he could get inside her and assure himself she was still his, unharmed, safe and sound, the better. He wouldn't breathe easy until then. Hell, he didn't know if his heart was going stop racing like a runaway horse until then.

"She did good," Natches murmured. "Made them talk. And when she realized Johnny was ready to shoot, she fought. She's strong, Dawg."

"Yeah. She is." He kissed the top of her head as the EMTs jerked the gurney from the back of the ambulance and another raced toward them. "And she's safe. That's all that counts."

Twenty-Four

"Look, I'm just fine." Two days later, Crista paced the living room of the houseboat and glared at Dawg as he sat back on the couch. "I want to go back to work."

"Not yet." He was as uncompromising as he had been hours before when she tried to leave for the lumber store.

"I have to get those displays set, or its going to be too late."

"Layla and her brood are taking care of it." He picked up his glass of sweet tea and drank from it casually as his green eyes stared at her from over the rim of the glass.

"I'm bored." She propped her hands on her hips and faced him, heating up at the way his gaze went over the shorts and loose T-shirt she wore. "I don't like being cooped up for no reason. I'm not a damned invalid."

But she could have been. Or worse.

Dawg set the glass carefully on the end table, forcing back the remembered horror of the day he nearly lost her.

"Dawg. Would you please put that glass on the coaster beside it," she bit out. "That is why I put it there."

He smiled blandly and placed the glass on the protective coaster before staring back at her.

He had noticed her hard nipples an hour before. The way she watched him expectantly, obviously more than ready to be touched.

He'd held back since bringing her home the day before. Despite his own arousal, his anticipation, and the need to take her, he had forced himself to control the need.

She had to come to him. He'd blackmailed her, more or less forced her into his bed, and despite the fact that he knew she loved him, he needed her to reach out for him.

"What do you intend to do today, then?" Her gaze flickered to his lap and his obvious arousal.

"Whatever you want to do. As long it doesn't entail leaving the marina," he inserted as her lips parted in reply.

A frown creased her brow as her lips tightened.

She had no idea how little he wanted to share her with the curious employees and customers at that damned store. He didn't want anyone else around her right now. He wanted to stare at her, hear her voice as she spoke to him alone, and let himself believe she was safe.

He had nightmares now. He'd spent four years in the Marines, two of those years training as an assassin, and he'd brought no nightmares home with him. But now, demons chased him through his dreams. Demons intent on forcing him to relive the day he had nearly lost her. Forced him to face the horror of his life as Johnny's bullet pierced her chest.

He could handle the nightmares. He couldn't have lived through the reality of it.

"Stop looking at me like that." Her soft voice drew him back from the nightmares. "I'm fine."

She was still bruised. Her arms were still scraped. There was a scratch on her cheek. He stared back her, refusing to forget what he had nearly lost.

"Yes, you're fine." He nodded as he stretched his arms on the back of the couch and let his gaze linger over her body.

Hard nipples pressing against thin cotton. He wondered if her pussy was wet. Silken bare flesh glistening with feminine cream. The thought of it had his mouth watering.

"Your business is going to fail at this rate," she warned him, but he saw the softening of her body, the almost imperceptible shift of her thighs, her accelerated breathing.

"So?" He licked his lips at the thought of tasting her.

"Could I convince you to go in later?" The insinuation in her voice had his brows lifting as he met her gaze.

"I'm easy," he assured her. "If you have something to bargain with." He made certain his gaze let her know exactly how he liked bargaining.

Crista almost smiled at the look. She had known when she awoke in his arms, his erection prodding her rear, but Dawg was in an unusual mood. He wasn't intent on relieving his arousal. For some reason, he was making himself wait. As the morning progressed, she began to figure out why.

He wanted her as bad as she wanted him. But Dawg needed acceptance. He needed her to come to him. The past hour had been a battle for that as she pushed him, tested his resolve, and only became more aroused as he held back.

What would he do once that control slipped? Once the hunger had him by the throat, how much more intent would he become?

She didn't want slow, easy sex. She didn't want foreplay. She wanted affirmation. She wanted him hard and deep inside her, pounding into her pussy and marking her with his hunger.

She wanted Dawg wild. She wanted all that hunger and all that emotion washing over her like a tidal wave.

But he wasn't going to be pushed into taking it.

"Yes, I've heard you're easy." She nodded sagely, hiding her grin at the frown that snapped between his brows.

"Easy for you," he amended with scowl.

"Really?" She lifted her brows in disbelief. "You're being very stubborn today."

"You're just not convincing me the right way." His lips twitched in amusement, though his gaze was intent and hot.

"Really?" She shifted, her fingers playing with the hem of her T-shirt as she stared back at him beneath her lashes. "What would it take to convince you, Dawg?"

He swallowed tightly as she eased the T-shirt higher. She wasn't wearing a bra. She hadn't bothered after her shower in the face of Dawg's stubborn refusal to go to the store.

His hands tightened on the back of the couch.

"Do you know what I used to dream, Dawg?" she whispered as her fingers played over her stomach.

"What?" His gaze was locked on those fingers, his own fingers caressing the back of the couch in reflex.

"I used to dream that you came to me. That you walked into the apartment I shared with Mark and Ty. They would be gone.

You'd step into the door, take one look at me, and then you took me. Against the wall. My legs wrapped around your hips as you pounded into me."

She pulled the shirt over her head and tossed it to the floor before her hands moved to her shorts. She got as far as pushing the elastic band over her thighs before he moved.

His shirt ripped over his head and flew to the side. Before she could do more than breathe in roughly, he was on his knees in front of her, pulling her thighs apart and burying his lips between them.

"Fuck it," he snarled. "I'm a wimp. No control."

She would have gone to the floor if he wasn't holding her up. His tongue slid through the narrow slit of her pussy, licking as he moaned before his lips surrounded the hardened bud of her clit.

She wanted hard and hungry, and he was going to give it to her. She could feel it.

Her back met the wall before she realized he had maneuvered her the few steps to it. Her shorts were on the floor, and Dawg lifted her leg, laying it over his shoulder as his head dipped and his tongue drove inside her sex.

"Oh God!" Crista's head hit the wall as she shuddered at the feel of his tongue fucking inside her.

His lips moved, slid back to her clit, while his fingers took the place of his tongue, and she was melting around him.

"I have to fuck you," he muttered, licking around her clit, sipping at it, kissing it. "You're killing me. I can't wait a week."

"Don't wait a minute," she moaned, pulling at his shoulders. "Fuck me, Dawg. Now."

"Soon."

"Now."

He replaced her foot on the floor and rose to his feet, but his hands pressed to her shoulders.

"Suck my cock," he ordered roughly. "Let me watch you suck me."

Crista went eagerly to her knees, her hands surrounding the thick, hard flesh as she covered the head hungrily. She wasn't teasing. She was too desperate now, the heat rising hard and fast inside her, burning her alive with the need to feel him inside her.

She sucked at the engorged crest, her tongue flickering over it as her hands stroked the throbbing shaft. She loved having him in her mouth, feeling the hard throb of blood pounding through it, tasting the sharp saltiness of pre-cum on her tongue.

He was fucking her lips with shallow movements, his hands tangling in her hair, his head thrown back in pleasure. His thighs were rock hard, his abs flexing tight as the fingers of one hand curled around his balls.

"Fuck. That's good," he groaned. "You suck like a dream, Crista. So fucking good."

His voice was rasping, sending a thrill of sensation racing down her spine at the pleasure it contained.

Her tongue probed beneath the crest before curling over it, her mouth sucking him deeper as she stared up his broad chest.

Sweat beaded on the hair-spattered flesh, glistening on the teak skin and catching on the short curls. She mouthed his cock head, moaned on it, and then cried out in impending ecstasy as he pulled her to her feet.

"Against the wall," he bit out, his lips pulling back from his teeth as he stared back at her with fiery lust. "Oh, baby, I can take you against the wall."

One arm wrapped around her hips as he lifted her, the other easing one leg around his hip as her other leg followed on the opposite side.

A second later, Crista cried out sharply, pain and pleasure whipping through her at the fierce, hard thrust that sent him burrowing through the snug tissue of her pussy.

"God, yes!" His hands gripped her rear as he rocked against her, stroking her internally, sending cataclysms of sensation to attack her nerve endings. "You're so fucking tight, Crista. So hot and sweet."

"Do it again," she moaned, her hands gripping his shoulders, nails biting into his flesh as he pulled back. "Take me hard again."

He retreated, nearly sliding free of her grip before shafting inside her with a quick, forceful thrust.

"Oh God, Dawg. I love that," she cried out hoarsely.

"Love that, do you, sweetheart?" He retreated again, plunged inside her again, stroked the internal blaze higher until sweat soaked their bodies in an effort to regulate the body heat.

There was no regulating the hunger building sharp and fast inside them. Crista could feel her juices flowing between them in response to the pleasure. Dawg's cock was fierce, thick inside her, stroking once-hidden nerve endings and burning her with the liquid-hot lust building harder inside them.

"Want more?" His hands tightened on her rear, his fingers sliding inside the narrow cleft until they met the damp entrance there.

He stroked, he played. He let his fingers dip inside her as his cock pounded inside her pussy. Tingles of sharp heat, hard thrusts that sent shocking waves of sensation tearing through her womb.

It was too much. He began to thrust faster, harder inside her with deep, plunging strokes that sent waves of sensation, violent pleasure, and emotion clashing inside her.

"I love you." She couldn't hold the words back. "I love you. Always loved you. Dreamed . . ." Tears filled her eyes and fell to her cheeks. "Oh God, Dawg, I dreamed . . ."

"And I dreamed, Crista," he groaned, his lips moving to her shoulders, then her neck, as his hips thrust and surged, filling her with his cock in quick, hard strokes. "Dreamed of loving you. Holding you. Always loving you."

Emotion fueled pleasure and fueled lust. The conflagration that resulted had them both crying out. Crista's wails mixed with his harsh, male groans as ecstasy began to explode inside them, then around them.

She felt the hard, fierce jets of cum exploding inside her. He felt the tight, heated clasp of her pussy gripping him like a fiery fist, flexing around him and throwing him higher into his own release.

Long minutes later, they found themselves on the floor, breathing hard, their bodies still tangled together, arms wrapped tightly around each other.

"Leave me again, and I won't fuck you for a week," Dawg mumbled against her ear.

"Forget about fucking me again, and I'll shoot you myself." She gave him an unladylike snort, then smiled at the slow stiffening of his cock inside her.

"I didn't forget the first time," he whispered then. "I just didn't want to accept that I had been so damned stupid. You lived in my dreams, Crista. Every night you were away from me, you lived in my dreams. And in my soul."

She leaned back and stared at him, seeing the intensity in his eyes, the light green seeming to glow inside his dark face as the sensual fulfillment relaxed his features.

"No more dreams," she whispered. "Just this."

"Just this."

This being more than love, more than lust. It was the dream, the hidden wish, and the fulfillment of two hearts meeting, two souls merging.

"I love you," she whispered. "And I'm looking forward to many many naughty nights in your arms, Dawg."

"Many," he promised. "Many naughty nights in my heart."

There, in the center of the room where it had all begun eight years before, the future began. For Dawg and Crista.

Weeks Later

Natches listened to the sounds of the night. It was late Summer. The lake was filled with those determined to take advantage of every second of the final days of summer.

Kids laughed, parents chided, teenagers dashed about the docks, and the sound of boats returning for the night filled the air with life.

And if he listened closely, really closely, he thought he could hear the sounds of pleasure coming from the boat beside his. He'd moved from his place beside the *Nauti Boy* after Kelly moved in with Rowdy. He'd parked the *Nauti Dreams* on the other side of Dawg's boat instead.

There was no place left to move to avoid the late-night whispers of passion and pleasure that sometimes flowed from the two boats.

He slouched further in his chair and stared out over the lake from the upper deck of the boat and considered his options. There weren't a lot.

He was sure sick of bullets chasing him, though, sick of toting a sniper's rifle, and sick to damned death of the lovey-dovey kissy-faced shit going on around him. His two cousins and their women, monogamous and proud of it.

He finished his beer at the thought of that, then opened another. There wasn't much danger of getting drunk; he didn't keep the hard stuff on the boat, so that kinda canceled out becoming oblivious.

Hell, he could move into town. There was an apartment over

the garage, and he was spending more time there anyway. Anything to get away from the monogamous bliss settling in on the back side of the Mackay docks.

He breathed out roughly. They weren't the hell-raising, high-living, hard-loving trio they used to be. The Mackay cousins were no more.

And that made for a very, very lonely night.

Nauti Dreams

Tippytoes, for everything you've done,
thank you.

Prologue I

Iraq

Five Years Ago

"Little American whore." The kick was harder this time, aimed at the tender flesh of Chaya's stomach, driving the breath out of her and causing her to send a tortured cry through the small cell she had been tossed into.

Her cry. She knew it was her scream, strangled and agonized, but it no longer sounded familiar to her. Reality had receded the day before, and it hadn't yet returned.

She had been dragged from her car just outside Baghdad, blindfolded, and shoved into a van. And that had been a walk in the park compared to the hours since.

"How much easier would it be, whore, to simply give us what we need?" The muzzle of a handgun caressed her cheek. "You could die then. Quickly. There would be no more pain. Wouldn't that be nice? No more clamps attached to tender parts of your body. No more electricity. No more kicks. All you need to do is tell us who contacted you. Tell us the information they have."

The voice was an insidious whisper inside her head as she felt herself crying. Curled in on herself, shuddering with sobs.

Oh God, please don't let them hurt her anymore. She could feel the bruises along her body now, the swollen tenderness of her nipples, the fragility of bones that couldn't take much more abuse without breaking.

They hadn't broken her yet. Had she managed to convince them she didn't know? That she was unaware of the illegal weapons pipeline they were buying their guns and explosives through?

That she knew nothing of the information she had been sent to retrieve about the spy within Army Intelligence providing access to those weapons?

And what did she do with the information that only one person had known where she was headed and why?

"So easy," a voice crooned, and she focused on the accent. It wasn't Iraqi, she knew Iraqi. It wasn't Afghani. There were tonal differences in the voices, even when speaking the same language. She knew the difference. This voice was a whisper of something else. Someone else. She knew this voice.

Another blow landed and a scream tore from her as the toe of the boot connected with her ribs. Terror washed through her like an oily, dark wave of suffocating heat. They would break them next. If her ribs broke she wouldn't have a chance of escape. Naked, bruised, and hurting, hell yeah. She could escape given half a chance. But if they broke her ribs? If they caused internal bleeding? She would never make it.

"Maybe we will get to keep this one awhile," the voice mused, laughter filling the tone. "I think maybe she enjoys our caresses, yes?"

No. No. She shook her head, dry heaves shaking through her, torturing her as the spasms ripped through her body.

"You do not like our touch?" False sympathy filled the voice as he bent to her again. "Maybe we use you and fill your belly with seed. We take your brat then and place it in a pretty stroller filled with explosives and park it in front of your White House. Who can resist a baby's cries, eh?"

She fought to breathe.

Reality. Reality was birth control that had been administered before this mission. Reality was backup, somewhere. Her team didn't want to lose her or the information she had, but they could only rescue her if they knew she was missing. If the officer she had discussed the trip with had reported that she hadn't returned.

Reality was, she was beginning to suspect that officer may well be the leak they had been searching for in Army Intelligence.

Reality. She had to hold on, just a little bit longer. She had to find a way to escape, a way to get that information back to her superiors despite the disillusionment and the betrayal that seared her soul.

She felt a hand on her thigh, moving along the back of her leg, fingers touching her, probing.

Rage and terror blazed through her mind. Kicking out she fought to avoid the touch, tried to hurt or to maim, to piss him off enough to keep him away from her. She would prefer to be kicked. She would prefer the broken bones.

"Tell us, Greta." The voice sighed then, resignation in his tone as she heard the shuffling around her. "Raping you would not be a pleasant experience for some reason. And raping you broken and unable to fight holds even less appeal. But if you do not give me what I need, I will spread you out here and I will let these guards use you. They will use you over and over again, until your body is so defiled that even your own people will know nothing but disgust for you. Is this what you want?"

The false gentleness in his tone built the fear inside her. He was going to do it. She knew he was. She had known all along that he would take this step. What better way to torture a woman? When the electrical clamps to her nipples and clitoris hadn't worked, he had gotten more inventive. His men hadn't raped her, but the painful device he used had.

She couldn't bear more pain.

"Such a beautiful woman." He sighed.

Saudi. The accent was Saudi. She couldn't see him, her eyes were so swollen now she doubted she could see daylight if she was in it. But the accent, the voice.

"Nassar," she whispered, dazed, sobbing. "*You* betrayed us, Nassar?"

And it only supported the fact that the man she suspected of betraying the Army was a traitor. Her husband. Nassar was his friend. His contact. And so, obviously, his coconspirator.

Silence filled the void for long moments. Nassar Mallah. She remembered him now. He was a contract agent for the CIA and one of their most trusted moles. Handsome, charming, his black eyes always twinkled with humor and a smile always curved his lips. She had never guessed, never known he was a traitor.

"Ah, Greta." He stroked her cheek again, but she had distracted him. He was no longer stroking the abused flesh between her thighs, no longer threatening to open her again, to destroy her with a helplessness she couldn't accept.

"Why?" Shudders were working through her, and she knew she was finally going into shock.

Or perhaps they had meant to kill her slowly like this.

"Kill her." She felt him rise to his feet. "Use her however you please first, but when you leave this cell, she is to be dead."

"No. Nassar," she cried out his name weakly. "We trusted you. We trusted you."

"No, *you* trusted me. Fool that you were." She heard the shrug in his voice. "Enjoy your last minutes, Greta. I doubt they will spend much time enjoying your broken body. But, with these four, you never know."

The cell door clanged shut. Her fingers tightened around the makeshift knife she had managed to sharpen against the stones earlier. It was gripped in her hand, tucked along her wrist and hidden beneath her body as they dragged her from the pallet.

Reality was, she was going to die here and she knew it.

Pop. She heard the sound, but it didn't make sense. She heard someone grunt, heard something fall.

Several more of the hollow, wet pops and more shuffling.

She knew that sound. Bullets. She couldn't see, but she knew the guards were dead. Frantically, she scrabbled at the floor, found one of them, and raced to tear his shirt off his torso. Buttons. God she hated buttons. She worked them loose with stiff, swollen fingers as she heard shouts, screams, and grunts outside the cell door.

The shirt came free, and she dragged it off his body before shoving her arms into it and wrapping it around her. There wasn't a chance she could rebutton it. Pants. She needed pants.

She was frantic. She worked fast, struggling, panting, trying to ignore the pain searing her body as she worked boots and pants off the guard.

She belted the pants on, feeling their length and filth around her. But they covered her. She would have to do without shoes.

Gun. She had the gun in her hand, and she couldn't fucking see. She was crying, her tears burning the cuts on her face, burning her eyes as she crept to the cell door.

It swung open, sunlight piercing her eyes for too long, shadows enveloping her as she brought the gun up while trying to strike out with the small wooden stake she had managed to hone.

"Chill!" The voice was American, harsh as strong hands gripped her wrists, tore the gun and the stake from her hands and moved quickly behind her. "Extraction in progress," he hissed.

Backup. He was reporting in. Extraction. SEALs? Were they SEALs?

"You got me, Faisal?"

Hands were roving over her quickly.

"SEALs?" She gasped out.

"I only wish," he snarled in her ear, his voice deep, like aged whiskey and soothing to her shattered senses. "Try one lone fucking sniper and a teenage kid with more guts than good sense. Can you run?"

His arm was around her, holding her against him. He was warm and protective. Was he protective or did she just need to convince herself that he was? Did she need this to survive the events of the past twenty-four hours?

"I can't see." And she wanted to see him. Wanted her senses in order, her thoughts clinical, as sharp as they had been yesterday.

"I'll lead, you run?" The suggestion was almost a croon, his voice almost tempting.

"I'll run."

He had her on her feet. Her bare feet. But she would be okay. She would run, anything to escape this cell, the hands touching her body, the voice at her ear, sinking into her head.

"Small cell here." He rushed her into the heat and blinding light. "I think we got them all, but I'm not betting on it. We have bogeys heading in a few miles out and tight quarters to hide in."

He was talking to her as he ran. Ran hard and fast, holding her against his side and taking most of her weight as she forced herself to keep up with him.

"Nassar?" she questioned roughly. She hoped the bastard was dead.

"Rode out in the only gun jeep," he informed her. "Gave us our chance."

Nassar got away. But she had the information, had what she needed to fry his and her husband's asses, and she would do just that.

"I need a radio," she gasped. "I have to report in before he gets away."

"Fuck that." Hard, scathing, the voice was nonetheless comforting. It was American. Southern drawl, Kentucky if she wasn't mistaken. "Look, little girl. I'm on a short leash here and ammo is tight. I'm a Marine sniper with no backup or comm until closer to extraction, or until the extraction team comes searching for me. I wouldn't even be here if your friend Faisal hadn't sent out a Mayday on shortwave and connected with my only comm. We gotta boogie and boogie hard, or both our asses are grass. Those bad boys back there are sure to make fine lawn mowers, too."

They were running uphill. He was barking commands. Gathering his guns, his pack. Getting ready to run again.

"Where are we?" She was fighting to breathe, to keep up.

"Bum-fucked nowhere." He was running full out and wasn't close to being winded. "I have a hole a mile out. You're gonna have to hang on for the ride, sugar, 'cause we don't get there, we're all dead. And dead and me don't get along."

"She live? She live?" Young, Iraqi, the boy's voice was frantic as the man paused for just a second. She knew the voice. Faisal was one of her informants. The young boy's courage was incredible.

"She lives, now boogie your ass, boy."

"Boogie my ass, Natchie," the boy claimed. "Boogie boogie."

"Damned kid." But there was affection in his voice. That affection, that sense of protectiveness that seemed to surround her, dug into her, made her chest ache from more than the run.

How long had it been since she had felt protected? Had she ever? But she did now. With this stranger's arm tight around her waist, half pulling her, half carrying her. Rescuing her. And Chaya had never been rescued in her life.

They were running full tilt. She couldn't see, her feet were bleeding, and her bruised ribs were in agony. But she was free. Reality was, she was free, and with just a little tiny miracle, she could stay free. But she knew those arms wouldn't always be there. That strength wouldn't always surround her, and she spared just a moment to regret that.

• • •

Natches rushed the mile to the hole he had made the night before after Faisal's shortwave coded message had hit his radio. He'd made the holes, prepared them, and then went after the girl the boy had seen hauled into the dump of a terrorist camp. A small enough camp, out of the way, populated by barely a dozen hard-eyed, fanatic bastards and one little American blonde.

Hell, who had been dumb enough to lose her? She was an agent, he could tell from the automatic stamina pushing her. She didn't have the strength to crawl on her own, but her legs were moving and she was fighting to help him as much as she could.

Faisal was easily staying at his side, his dark face creased with worry at the sound of gunfire behind them. They were out of sight as they rounded the low, rolling hill, and the hole was just ahead, covered deep with stripped trees and wrapped with dead brush. A natural part of the landscape.

"Get in the hole." He lifted the first cover and pushed Faisal into it with the supplies he would need in a smaller pack.

He threw himself and the girl into the second hole and jerked the secured covering over them as the sound of a helicopter began to hum from the direction of the terrorist base.

Of course, there had to be a fucking helicopter, he thought as he lifted himself enough to stare through the natural break he had created to see if they were followed. Fuck, he didn't need this.

The hole was deep enough to sit in, the upper natural covering strong enough to hold a tank, maybe. They were secure as long as the bastards didn't have dogs. It wasn't very long, wasn't very wide, but it was the best he could do on short notice.

"Do you have extraction coming soon?" Chaya rasped.

He glanced back at her and winced. She was curled against the dirt wall, eyes swollen closed, her lips dry and cracked. She looked vulnerable, but the woman had a spine of steel.

"I have a tracker on me. They'll find me when they get in close enough. When I wasn't at the first extraction point, they'll have followed the beacon I have on me."

Her lips twisted mockingly. "Are you sure? Collateral damage is the motto these days, you know."

Fuck wasn't that the truth. "Every good redneck knows you always have a plan B," he assured her. His team was all the plan

A or B that he needed. Most snipers worked alone, but on this mission, he was numero uno and he knew it. They needed him too damned bad to allow him to become damaged.

She breathed out wearily as he pulled a canteen from his pack and uncapped it. "Here. Drink slow." He lifted the water to her lips, staring at her face as she sipped.

"I have some salve and bandages for your eyes," he said. "Bastards always go for the eyes first, don't they?"

She gave a small, bitter laugh. "At least second."

He pulled out the medical kit, smoothed the salve over her eyes, then secured bandages over them. She had the face of an angel, he thought. Fine bones, delicate cheekbones, pretty sensual lips, he bet. Right now they were bloody and swollen.

"Old lady at home makes that salve," he told her. "Bastards caught me last year, just about tore my eyeballs out before I escaped. When I went home on leave, she made the salve and made me promise to keep it with me."

"Kentucky," she whispered as the helicopter swept overhead.

"Lake Cumberland." He gently touched the scratches on her face with the salve.

She was a slender woman. Dirt caked her hair and smeared her face, but he bet she was a beauty before Nassar and his men got hold of her.

"You're New England." He nodded at her accent. "Damn pretty area. Damned pretty girls."

Her smile was tired. "There's one less now."

He sincerely doubted that. "Did they rape you?"

He was surprised at the fury that threatened to drown his common sense. Of course they raped her. They were known for it.

She shook her head and grimaced mockingly. "*They* didn't."

"*Who* did?" He smeared the salve over her swollen lips as he caught the emphasis.

"Nassar has some interesting toys." She grimaced. "But he was tired of using them. His little buddies were going to do the deed when he left. Thanks for the timing by the way."

Natches sat back on his haunches and listened carefully for noise outside. There were no caves in this area. The next hill over had several. The area he had chosen was no more than a flat, uninteresting gorge. Nothing but some scrappy foliage and dead brush. The perfect place for a hole. They would check the area, but they would be more eager to hit the caves a mile away.

"Faisal, your goat herder friend," he explained softly. "He saw Nassar bring you in. He's also got a handy-dandy military shortwave and an American Army sergeant for a buddy who taught him a little bit of code. That code caught me on my way back. I sidetracked to rescue you. All the guys at home are gonna be slapping my back for this one. I might even get a street named after me."

Her smile was slower. Dazed. She was slipping away from him and he couldn't allow that. "Faisal's a good kid," she whispered, her head nodding to the side.

"Wake up there, girl."

"Chaya. My name is Chaya." Her voice was soft, sweet. He liked her voice.

Damned pretty name for a damned pretty woman. He touched her cheek again.

"Talk to me, Chay. Tell me where you're hurt. I need to fix as much as I can just in case we have to run."

"Feet. Bruised ribs, possible concussion. No internal bleeding, no broken bones."

She was drifting away from him.

Natches leaned in and touched her lips with his. Her head jerked back as she gasped. But her hands reached out for him, her fingers—slender, fragile fingers—clenching his wrists, tightening, as though she were afraid to let go of him, before she did just that. Slowly. Hesitantly.

"There, awake now?" He moved to her feet, pulling one into his lap as he dragged the medical kit closer.

"Why did you do that?" She sounded shocked, but awake, aware.

"My kisses are potent," he bragged shamelessly, desperate to keep her grounded and aware. "They wake all the girls up."

He used a penlight to check her feet carefully, always listening, always tracking the sound of the helicopter overhead and the vehicles now moving through the ravines.

He peeked over the edge of the hole but couldn't see anything moving near enough to be deemed a threat.

He smoothed the salve over her feet, then pulled his shirt and T-shirt off. He tore the T-shirt into strips, padded her feet, then wrapped them with stretch gauze.

"All the girls like your kisses, do they?" She still sounded awake.

"They beg for my kisses." It was nothing less than the truth, but as he stared at this woman, so strong, so determined, he wondered at the women he had known before. Would any of them have found the strength to make it this far? And he knew they wouldn't have. But this one, this one would never join in the Mackay games as the others had.

"Conceited." Her smile was tired, and worry lashed at him.

She was sheet white, pain and shock setting in now that she was still and no longer enfolded in complete terror. He couldn't risk shock. Not yet.

He dug in the med pack again and pulled free the potent pain pills he carried. "Take this." He pushed it into her mouth and lifted the canteen to her lips again.

She sipped and then leaned her head back against the dirt wall behind her.

Silence filled the hole for long moments. Her breathing was short and erratic, and every few seconds she would flinch or grimace just enough that he caught the wary movements in her expressions.

He wanted to hold her. She was almost broken, maybe not physically, but mentally at the least. She had endured this far, he had to get her just a little further.

"The trucks are getting closer." There was weariness in her voice, but no fear yet.

"They'll search for a while. I'm good at this. Don't worry."

He checked on Faisal's hole. It was silent. Faisal knew how to hide; it wasn't his first time, probably wouldn't be his last. He had everything he needed to stay secure as long as no one identified the hiding place Natches had made.

"How did they get you?" he finally asked her when she said nothing else.

"Dragged me out of my car outside Baghdad, threw me in a van, beat the shit out of me, and played with some torture." She shrugged, but he heard the echo of horror in her voice.

"What do you have that they want?"

She was an American woman and she had enough strength to strip a dead man and get his clothes on in the time it took him to pop a few heads and get to her location. She was an agent; he knew that from the comment she had made about needing to let someone know about Nassar. That was going to take a few hours at least.

"I don't have anything anyone wants," she said tiredly. "I'm a relief worker. I was working in Baghdad."

"Don't pull no shit with me, sugar."

"Then don't pull none with me. You know how it goes." She copied his accent exactly. "I have to get out of here."

Yeah, he knew how it went. She couldn't disclose and he shouldn't be asking, but he was a nosy bastard and that was the truth.

"Won't be long now. I've already missed my bus," he stated. "When I'm not at extraction, they'll send a team out for me. I'm important, you know."

"Obviously more important than I am." She sighed. "Can I take a nap?"

"No naps." The helicopter was getting closer. He hoped Faisal had his deflecting blanket over his head. "Come here; we gotta hunker down."

Fear flashed across her face for just a second as he unfolded the light, silver-backed blanket and pulled it over their heads, tucking it in carefully around them. So much as a foot sticking out from beneath it would allow any heat-seeking equipment to pick them up.

He had no idea what that helicopter was packing, and he wasn't taking any chances.

He was wrapped around her like a possessive lover now, and he could feel her fear as easily as he could feel the heat building beneath the blanket.

"You know, if I was back home, the ladies would be purring at being here with me," he pointed out to her as he smiled against her head. "They like my hard body. They think I'm sexy."

A nervous laugh parted her lips as he rested his cheek against her hair.

"I can't see if you're sexy," she reminded him, and he hated that quiver in her voice.

"Oh, you're missin' out." He sighed pitifully, his voice whisper soft. "I'm damned fine, Chay. Green eyes and a nice tan. I got hard abs. Black hair. The women drool over me."

He smiled, listened carefully, and was thankful to feel a small measure of the fear ease from her. He didn't consider himself particularly handsome, but he knew what the ladies said. He had to distract her though, and this was all that mattered.

"Conceited, too." Her hands were clenched tight around his lower arms, broken nails digging into his flesh.

"Hell yeah, I am. I'm spoiled as hell."

"So what are you doing here?"

"Playing? Escaping the marriage market?" He held her closer as the sound of the helicopter hovering overhead had her shuddering against him. The camouflaged top of the blanket, added to the dead brush secured to the narrow timbers above them, would hide them from sight. He had a moment to worry about Faisal, then pushed it away. If they were caught, they were probably dead anyway, despite the extraction team that he knew would be barreling its way to him.

He had pictures, layouts, troop movements, and hidden terrorist bases. He'd been out in bum-fucked nowhere for six weeks now after completing the primary mission he had been sent on to aid in the extraction of another captured agent.

That agent had been rescued. So why hadn't a team been sent out for this one?

"They're getting closer." Her voice was a breath of terror.

"No worries, baby. By nightfall, we're going to be safe and sound and celebrating with some homemade shine I'm saving just for the end of this mission. I'll get you drunk and seduce you."

"Seduce me?"

"Oh yeah." He held her closer. "I'll lay you down and kiss every bruise, then lick all the hurt away. I'll lave those pretty, tender nipples, and when I go lower, you'll forget all about the pain."

"Ego." She was shuddering in his arms at the sound of the vehicles moving into the ravine.

"Truth." He kissed the top of her head. "When I'm finished, this will all seem like a very bad dream. Distant and gone away. It will be just me and you, sweetheart. Sweaty and hot and doing things that might make both of us blush."

"I bet you don't blush." She buried her face in his chest at the sound of voices shouting in Arabic.

"I bet you could make me blush." He kissed the top of her head and smiled, triumph singing through him at the feel of the light vibration of the radio at his thigh. "You gonna make me blush tonight, sugar? I just got signal." He took her hand and laid it against the radio. "Five minutes and hell is gonna sweep through here. Five hours and I'm going to make you blush."

"You can't." He could have sworn he heard tears in her voice.

"Making you blush would be my sole aim in life," he murmured. "I promise, baby, I can do it."

"I'm married."

August, Four Years Later

Chaya Greta Dane found the tracking device that had been left beneath Dawg Mackay's vehicle on the side of a dirt road so deep in the Kentucky mountains that she knew she would play hell finding her way out.

She blew out a hard breath and shook her head. The Mackays weren't stupid, but sometimes her boss liked to pretend they were, and that was a very big mistake, especially in light of the fact that Cranston really wasn't a fool.

She stared around the area before brushing back her dark blond hair and resigning herself to the inevitable.

Dawg Mackay had led her on a merry chase, and he had known exactly what he was doing. Through twisting hollows, up steep mountain roads that barely passed as trails, and into the thick forests that surrounded Lake Cumberland like a protective lover.

She would find her way out, eventually, but there was no doubt she was stuck for the night. Her satellite phone wasn't cooperating for some reason, the cell phone had no reception, and night was coming on.

She straightened from the crouch where she had found the locator another agent had placed beneath the Mackay vehicle, propped her hands on her hips, and stared around the thick forest surrounding her.

It would have been enjoyable if she'd been prepared. Simple things like enough water to get her through the night, a sleeping bag maybe. She did have her weapon. And her thoughts. Too many thoughts the longer she stayed in Somerset—the longer she was around Natches Mackay and all the memories she tried to push behind her.

She shook her head and reached inside her back pocket for the habit she had picked up again in the past few months, only to find the cigarette pack she had stuck there earlier empty. Great.

Shaking her head, she wadded up the pack and tossed it into the back of the borrowed jeep her boss had had waiting for her just outside of Somerset, after she had reported the direction Dawg and his lover, Crista Jansen, had been heading in.

Crista Jansen looked too damned much like the woman brokering a missile sale between hijackers and terrorists to suit the Department of Homeland Security. It had been her job to follow Crista, to keep an eye on her and whoever she met with.

Knowing Dawg Mackay, Crista Jansen was meeting with nothing less than every inch of that Kentucky native's hard body. Dawg wasn't a traitor. He wanted those missiles as much as they did, and it was apparent he believed his woman was innocent.

But, hell, everyone thought the person they loved was innocent. Human nature had a tendency to overlook the truth whenever it wanted to. She had learned that lesson herself, the hard way.

Always the hard way. And look at what she had lost. Sometimes Chaya wondered if she hadn't lost her soul in a desert so bleak it sucked the spirit out of a person.

She snorted at that thought as she kicked at a clump of grass and leaned against her car, determined to enjoy just a few minutes of being unreachable by her boss, Timothy Cranston. No doubt he was frantically calling both the cell and sat phones. And here she stood, breathing in the fresh mountain air, feeling the peace of the place wrap around her, sink inside her.

Beseeching her to relax. To remember. To remember one night. One man. Urging her to close her eyes and to remember his touch. A touch filled with tears and her sobs, but also with his gentleness, with the warmth of his kisses, the heat of his possession. A night she only remembered in her dreams.

Her lips kicked up in a grin at the thought. Yeah, relax and drop her guard. Hadn't she done that before? And hadn't she paid for it? Hadn't she lost everything she loved in life because she had trusted the wrong person? And here she was, a part of her wishing, regretting things she knew she had no right to regret.

Strong arms that didn't hold her through the night. A voice like aged whiskey that didn't rasp her name with heated passion at his release. Hands, calloused and possessive. And she regretted, because that illusion was the most dangerous one she could ever reach out for.

A second later an unexpected sound had her jerking her weapon from the holster at the small of her back and taking aim at the front of the car.

She knew who it was. She took the precaution of waiting, watching, but the sound of the jeep rolling up the mountain was unmistakable. Powerful, a hard, male throb of power that her piece-of-crap borrowed jeep didn't have.

At least he was driving up in front of her rather than slipping through the trees and taking aim. He could have taken her out before she knew what hit her. And he would. No matter how well he knew her, no matter the short history they had shared so long ago, he would put a bullet between her eyes as fast as he would an enemy combatant if he felt she was a threat.

She held the Glock comfortably, confidently, as the wicked black vehicle pulled over the rise. If a jeep could strut, it strutted up the mountain and caused her to grit her teeth. Cranston could make her crazy running her in circles, but he couldn't give her a vehicle decent enough to make those circles in.

Tall tires, gleaming paint job, and a black pipe bumper. A winch at the front, the top pulled back, the man behind the wheel staring back at her from behind dark glasses, hiding those incredible green eyes.

But nothing could hide his somber expression as he jumped from the driver's seat, the engine still idling, throbbing. Like the rumble of a monstrous cat.

This was the dream, and the illusion. And somehow she had known he would be here. Here, in the mountains that bred him, as strong, as secure, as dangerously primitive as the man himself. As dangerous as the regrets that whispered through her as she watched him.

Chaya licked her lips slowly, staring back at him, trying not to notice the smooth, corded grace of his body. The way his jeans hung low on his hips and drew attention to his thighs. The way his gray T-shirt snugged over taut abs. The aura of power and male grace that seemed to ooze from the pores of his heavily tanned skin.

The wind ruffled through his overly long black hair, whipping it across his forehead and along the nape of his neck. Those thick, tempting strands had her hands itching to touch them, her fingers curling into fists to restrain the need.

Hell, she needed that cigarette bad now. She'd been working with him for months, and she still couldn't dampen the sickening nerves, the pain each time he came near her. The need. Oh God, the need wrapped around her until sometimes she wondered if it would eventually drive her insane. The need to touch. Just one more time, just one touch, one kiss, one more night to hide within his arms.

Instead, she tucked her weapon back into its holster and shoved her hands into the pockets of her jeans as she watched him. The way he moved. The intensity in his forest green eyes, the knowledge in his expression. There was always that knowledge, the words that whispered just below the surface, the memories that never really went away. The hunger that never really receded.

Natches moved lazily to the front of the jeep and leaned against the heavy bumper. He stared at her, unsmiling, as he crossed one booted foot over the other and eased the dark glasses from his face.

Piercing green eyes tore into her senses, scrambled her brain and had her heart throbbing like a schoolgirl's. Summer's heat rushed around her then, stroking over her body and reminding her, always reminding her, of things she shouldn't let herself remember.

"Busted." He lifted his brows mockingly. "Want to tell me why you're following my cousin and his woman?"

Her lips parted as she fought to drag in more breath. He could do that. Make her breathless. Make her want. With only a look, he made her feel like a virgin on the verge of her first kiss. And that was very dangerous. He was dangerous. In more ways than one.

"You're not answering me, Chaya." He was one of the few people who dared to call her by her given name rather than the name she used in the agency. Greta. It was nice and plain and unassuming. But he had to call her Chaya instead. He had to remind her of who she had once wanted to be rather than who she was.

She licked her lips again, fighting for her composure.

"You'll have to ask Cranston." She was not taking the blame for this. "His orders. I just live to obey them." That was nothing less than the truth in the past few years. He controlled her. For now.

Natches shook his head, straightened, and moved closer. Standing her ground wasn't easy. She wanted to run. She wanted to run to him, touch him, stroke all that hard, dark flesh, and let the intensity of these dangerous desires free.

She wasn't married anymore, she reminded herself. She had been reminding herself of that for years.

She watched him, wary, suspecting the danger that lurked beneath that easy smile. *Suspected* nothing, she *knew* it lurked there. She knew she was facing a man who at one time had been a cold, hard killer. He had been taken into sniper training within six months of his enlistment with the Marines and within a year was ranked as one of their most proficient assassins.

And now he was retired. Bum shoulder. He liked to grin when claiming the injury that pulled him out of the Marines. She doubted a single cell on his body was "bum."

"You know, Chaya . . ."

"My name is Greta," she grated out. "Use it, Natches." She had to find some kind of defense against him. The name Greta reminded her, kept the memories of the one mistake that had shaped her uppermost in her mind.

"Chaya." His lips caressed the words as he drew closer, within a breath of her, forcing her to stare up at him. "Darlin'. Cranston's gonna get you in a shitload of trouble. You know this, right?"

Oh God, if she didn't know it before, she was finding out now. She had thought working with Cranston would make her life easier, that the team that worked stateside only would ease her slowly away from the horror of the past and allow her to step out of the world that had begun to smother her.

"Take it up with Cranston." She forced the words from her throat as his hand curled around the side of her neck and the dark, sexual light in his wicked eyes began to gleam with intent.

That touch, just like that, the implied power and gentleness of that hold, had her knees weakening. She was a trained agent; she wasn't supposed to let emotion or lust cloud her judgment. But right now it was clouding her entire mind.

His fingers flexed against her neck, the power and strength in his arm echoing along her nerve endings. Pleasure corrupted her normally logical thought processes and eroded the control she had fought for over the years.

Suddenly, she was in the dark, fighting to breathe through the agony of a hell she couldn't accept, holding on to only one thing. Holding on to Natches's touch.

She couldn't let herself hold on to that memory.

Chaya didn't bother to struggle. She could see the desire already burning in his eyes, and she knew she didn't have a chance against him if those luscious lips actually touched hers. She would be lost in him, and she couldn't afford to ever lose herself again.

"Don't kiss me, Natches. Don't do that to me. Please."

He froze, those fingers contracting on her flesh, stroking cells that hadn't known a man's touch in so very long.

He had no idea how hard it was to turn away, to walk away. How she ached at night, tossing and turning in her bed, the thought of the promise in those cat's eyes of his burning through her soul. She wanted him with a strength that terrified her.

"Give me one reason why I shouldn't," he said, his voice low as those fingers stroked against her flesh. "You're not married anymore, sweetheart."

His gaze wasn't mocking now; it was somber, intense. The memories flashed in his eyes as well, and she couldn't bear it. It connected them, made it so much harder for her to break away, to hold herself steady as she fought through the never-ending abyss of emotions that threatened to swamp her.

"Because I can't handle you, and we both know it. Have mercy, Natches. Don't you have enough women in your little stable? You really don't need me."

And there was no way she would survive it. He was wild, intense, the most wickedly alluring man she had ever met in her life. And he wasn't the man for her. She wanted him until she ached with a force that tore at her soul, and she couldn't allow herself to have him. This man, the one who fired her soul, who made her dream when she had no right to dream.

"That's not a good enough reason."

She gasped as his lips covered hers. Sensation exploded through her body; pleasure rippled and waved over her nerve endings and began to burn along her flesh. This kiss, this man, he was like nectar, like a drug she couldn't get out of her system.

She gasped harder as her weapon dropped to the ground and she felt Natches's hands tugging at her shirt, baring her, allowing the warmth of the sun-filled air to touch her flesh.

She told herself the perspiration was from the heat of the day, but she knew better. It was from his kiss.

Oh God. His kiss. She flattened her hands against his chest to push him away, but he wasn't budging. His hands stroked up her back, beneath her shirt, then around, the pads of his fingers at the tender swells of her breasts, covered by nothing more than lace.

Chaya struggled with the war waging within her now. Her body, eager, desperate, it knew this man's touch, knew his possession. Her heart, her head, was screaming out in warning.

And her body was winning.

"Ah, Chay." He nipped at her lips. She loved that sexy little sting and lifted closer, begging for more. "There you go, baby. Show me how you can burn again."

She breathed in sharply as his hands slid to her hips, gripping them and lifting her until she was sitting on the hood of the jeep, then lying back, his big body pressing her down as her hands tugged at his shirt.

She should be pushing him away, not baring that gorgeous body.

But that was what she was doing. Baring all that hard, delicious muscle. Feeling the rasp of crisp chest hairs against her palms, the dampness of his sweat beneath.

She twisted under him, feeling his knee press between her thighs, and saw stars explode behind her closed lashes as he pressed against the sensitive flesh between her thighs.

"Hell yeah." He groaned against her lips as he worked her jeans loose. "Burn for me, Chaya. Just a little bit. Burn for me wild and sweet, sweetheart, just like you do in my dreams."

His voice was rough, tight with arousal, and she knew it could become guttural. That his drawl could slur his words and make him sound drunk with passion. She wanted that sound. She wanted him drunk on *her*.

"Natches!" She cried his name as his hand pushed beneath her open jeans and his fingers found her. Found the slick, too-thick layer of juices that prepared her for him, that betrayed her need.

That need was killing her.

She twisted, arched to him as his lips slid down her neck to her breasts. His teeth rasped the tender tip of a nipple as his free hand pulled the cup of her bra beneath the swollen mound.

Then his mouth was covering it, his lips closing on it, sucking it inside with tight, hard pressure that sent sensation ripping to her womb.

Long, broad fingers speared inside her vagina, drawing another cry from her. Flesh unused to any touch but her own since he had taken her so long ago. Too long.

She came instantly. The stretching heat, the feel of his mouth sucking her nipple, his tongue lashing her, it was too much. She exploded in a prism of light and color, his name on her lips and in her heart.

Oh God, she was never going to be free of him. And in this moment, exploding around his fingers, she wondered if she ever wanted to be.

She struggled to open her eyes, then lost her breath as she watched him. He pulled his fingers free of her, lifted them, and tasted her. Right there, beneath the sun, the breeze whipping around them, he opened his lips and sucked the taste of her from his fingers.

"Natches." She could barely do more than breathe his name when his face suddenly stilled, his head lifting, like an animal scenting danger.

"Son of a bitch Cranston." He was jerking her bra in place and pulling her shirt down when she caught the sound of a helicopter coming closer.

Pulling back from her, Natches let her fix her jeans, his green eyes filled with mocking amusement as the helicopter flew around the sheltering trees and came over the clearing.

It couldn't land, but she knew who it was. The Department of Homeland Security had found her. They had nearly seen more than she could have safely gotten away with.

Natches drew farther back from her, his expression hardening. "Come on. I'll lead you back to the main road. Then you can call Cranston and tell him to meet with me. I've had enough of this crap. It ends now."

What was going to end now she wasn't certain, but she was more than ready to get the hell out of there, away from him. Let Cranston deal with him, because she knew, as sure as she was standing there she knew, there wasn't a chance in hell that she could handle him.

One

Somerset, Kentucky

October, One Year Later

Natches Mackay sat silently in the jeep and watched as Chaya Dane hauled her luggage into the hotel she had reserved in town. The Suites were just that. A nice hotel that offered a variety of live-in suites with a bedroom, a small living room, and a kitchenette for those required to be in town for an extended stay.

Chaya was registered for a two-week stay but the luggage she brought wouldn't have kept one woman for four days. A single large suitcase, an overnight bag, and a laptop case. She was definitely traveling light.

Eyes shaded behind the dark lenses of his sunglasses, he rubbed the short growth of beard at the side of his jaw and considered this new development.

It had been a year since she had been in town. A year since he had pulled the trigger and buried a bullet in his first cousin's head. And seeing her again brought the memories he tried to suppress back in vivid detail.

Johnny Grace had been a disgrace. He had masterminded the hijacking of a missile shipment as well as the sale of the weapons, and attempted to place the blame on a young woman who his other cousin Dawg Mackay was in love with. To add insult to injury, he had then attempted to kill her when he found out Dawg was onto him.

Saving Crista hadn't been easy, and Natches had known, as he drove to the rendezvous point where Johnny Grace was meeting his lover and coconspirator, that Johnny wouldn't leave there alive. It was a promise Natches had made to himself. Rowdy and Dawg were family, like no one else was. If it hadn't been for them and Rowdy's father, Ray, Natches wouldn't have survived the turmoil of his own life when he was younger.

People who knew the Mackays knew you didn't strike out at one of them. All of them came running if you did. And Rowdy's and Dawg's wives, Kelly and Crista, were strictly hands-off. It was hands-off or Natches would go hunting.

Johnny should have known better. He should have known Natches would be waiting with a bullet for him. But the little fucker had been convinced he could pull it off without anyone being the wiser.

His death had ended the investigation. The missiles had been recovered, the prospective buyers had been arrested, and all was supposed to be right in this little part of the world. Not that Natches slept any easier at night, but he had found a measure of peace. That peace had been hard-won over the past five years, and he had been enjoying the hell out of it.

Until last year.

He watched as Chaya disappeared into the hotel. Chaya was the pet agent of Timothy Cranston, the special agent in charge of investigations. She was his gopher and shit wrestler, and as much as it grated on Natches to see her following the snide little man's orders, he had still considered her rather intelligent. Smart enough that he had tried to stay the hell away from her.

Maybe she wasn't as smart as he had thought. Because she was back here, and he'd be damned if any of his sources had warned him of an operation going down here.

What that operation was, either no one knew, or no one was telling him.

He rubbed at his lower lip and stared at the hotel entrance she had disappeared into. She hadn't looked happy to be back—she'd looked worn, tired, as though she had slept about as much as he had in the past year. Which amounted to less than nothing. And she looked damned good enough to eat. Unfortunately, she wasn't much into being a snack for him.

So why was Miss Dane currently taking up residence in his fair town again? It had to be under orders, because he'd warned her, she wasn't safe here, least of all from him. If she wanted to keep to that cold, lonely bed of hers then she should have found another town to sleep in.

He was brought out of his contemplation when his cousin Rowdy pulled his pickup in beside the jeep. On the other side, Dawg pulled in, his black dual cab taking up space and rumbling like the powerful machine it was.

He glanced to each side, taking in his cousins as they moved from the vehicles. The wind shifted through Dawg's black hair, which wasn't near as long as he used to wear it, but Rowdy's hair, an identical black, was longer.

Married life was keeping them decent in too damned many ways. Dawg had a decent haircut, and Rowdy let his grow out. Dawg was broader than the other cousin, a few years older. They were both just as damned powerful and irritating as they ever were.

And irritating they could be. Married and shackled and tied so damned tight to their wives that if a man just breathed in those women's directions, their hackles rose. But they still came when he called, and the thought of that tugged at something inside him. One of those bits of emotion that he fought to keep buried and hidden.

As they came up beside his jeep, Natches opened the door and stepped out slowly, his gaze still centered on the building. He'd called the little girl on duty at the front desk before he arrived to make certain Miss Dane was given the proper room.

One that looked right out on the parking lot. He wanted her to see him, wanted her to know she was being watched.

"What's brewin', Natches?" Dawg leaned against Rowdy's gray pickup, his arms crossing over his broad chest.

Natches lifted a brow as he took in the pressed jeans and white shirt his cousin was wearing. It was a damned far cry from the holey, scruffy appearance his cousin had before he picked back up with Crista Ann Jansen last year.

"Snazzy-looking duds there, cuz." Natches grinned. "Crista iron those for you herself with her own little hands?"

Dawg scowled back at him, but his light green eyes, nearly a celadon in color, flared with impatient arousal at the mention of his wife.

"Dry cleaners," Dawg finally growled. "And I don't think you called us here to discuss my laundry."

"Watch him, Natches." Rowdy grinned, his dark green eyes, sea green, crinkling at the corners with mirth. "Dawg's been a hair upset over the laundry. Crista put her foot down over the wrinkled, hole-ridden T-shirts he likes wearing to the store. She won't let him play the disinterested owner anymore."

Dawg grunted as Natches smirked absently and glanced back toward the hotel.

"That call you made earlier sounded kind of important, dumb ass." Dawg sighed as he addressed Natches again. "What the hell is going on?"

Natches turned back to him, glaring at his cousin for the nickname that was becoming more frequent.

"You keep calling me 'dumb ass,' and I'm going to split your head open for you."

Dawg grunted and it was his turn to smirk. "I think it suits you. You go moving out of your houseboat, for solitude over that damned garage, and start working like a man who's grown some principles, and I start worrying about you."

Natches's nostrils flared as anger began to churn inside him. Damn Dawg. He didn't need his damned advice or his snide-assed comments, which pretty much described the reason why his cousin was calling him names. Because he refused to listen to either.

"Cranston's running another op in town," he told the other two men before he let that anger take hold. The rest of the accusation he ignored completely.

He didn't need to get pissed right now. He'd spent a lot of years trapping that emotion so deep inside him that it didn't burn in his gut anymore. Keeping it there was important. Keeping it there kept breathing certain and Natches's conscience clear.

"What the hell does that fat little fucker want?" Dawg straightened and glanced toward the hotel with obvious animosity. "Is he in there?"

"No. Not yet. Miss Chaya Greta Dane is there right now, and if my guess is right, she's watching us right now from room three oh four. Do you think maybe she's figured out we're onto her?"

"How did you find out?" Rowdy was watching Natches.

Natches hated it when Rowdy watched him like that. Like he knew something, or saw something Natches didn't want seen.

"Anonymous tip." Natches grimaced. "And that ain't no joke. A call to my cell phone an hour ago—untraceable so far—letting me know she had hit the county line and was here for DHS. If Cranston's lost more missiles, boys, I might have to kill him."

He was joking. Kind of.

"We haven't heard anything." Dawg rubbed at his clean-shaven jaw as he glanced toward the window of Chaya's room.

She liked to go by the name Greta, but hell if that name suited her. With her multihued blond hair and exquisite features, she was as exotic as a tropical flower. *Chaya* suited her. The name rolled off the tongue, and in the darkest nights, as he jacked off to the image of her in his head, the name sounded like a prayer as he spilled his release into his hand.

"I've not heard anything from my contacts either," Rowdy murmured. "Not even a whisper that a DHS agent was coming to town."

Which meant Cranston was keeping whatever he was up to very close to his chest. And that was a very bad thing. When that rabid little bastard kept his mouth shut, then things were about to get ugly.

The thought of that had him glancing toward the hotel again. Chaya was a hell of an agent, but her heart wasn't in it. Natches had seen that the year before. She hadn't wanted to be in Somerset, and she hadn't wanted to play Cranston's games.

"She was supposed to have resigned," he murmured, his eyes narrowing against the bright autumn sunlight overhead. "Turned the papers in just after the op here was what I heard."

He was unaware of the curious looks his cousins gave him. Rowdy glanced at Dawg questioningly, but all his cousin had in reply was a brief shrug.

Natches never cared enough about anyone except his cousins, their wives, his sister, and Rowdy's father, Ray, to check up on them over anything. He often claimed when it came to people, he wouldn't stop the train from wrecking, because it was too damned amusing to sit back and watch the cars piling up.

He hadn't been nearly so amused by the role Cranston had forced Miss Dane into though. He had placed her in danger, and that had pissed Natches off. Just as Cranston had placed all their asses in the fire.

"What do you need from us?" Rowdy turned back to his younger cousin, his chest tightening as it always did whenever he stared at the other man too long.

Natches was almost cold now. It had been coming for a while, but sometimes he feared that cold had taken full hold of him, and chilled him clear to his soul.

Natches seemed to shrug at the question, as though he either didn't care, or wasn't certain what he needed.

"Doesn't little Lucy Moore work here?" Dawg asked then. "She works registration, doesn't she?"

Natches nodded at the question. Lucy was a third cousin on his mother's side, a sweet little girl, but sometimes she was a little too smart for her own good. She had put Chaya in the room he wanted her in, but she had been curious as to why he wanted her there.

"Then just wait till she leaves and slip into her room. Check her shit out and see if she's as anal as she used to be with her notes," Dawg suggested.

Natches glared at him. "She's not stupid, Dawg. Those notes, if she has them, will be locked tight in that laptop and none of us are hackers."

"Slip in and seduce the information out of her." Dawg grinned at that one. "You're good at that shit. Get her to talk, then send her ass home."

It was an idea, except he knew something they didn't know. Chaya didn't have a home.

"What the hell is up with this, Natches?" Rowdy questioned him then. "You knew her before she came here; don't deny it. Now she's back with no clear reason why. Maybe she's back to see you."

Natches shook his head slowly. No, she wasn't back to see him. He came with memories, and Natches knew exactly how that worked. Those memories were too painful, and they were rife with too much emotion for Natches or Chaya to willingly touch them with a ten-foot pole.

"She's not here for me," he finally said, wondering at the regret that pricked at him. "This is an op, boys. Anonymous call, pretty agent, and no agency gossip. Cranston's trying to pull something over on us and I want to know what the hell it is."

Chaya stared through the filmy curtains at the three men gathered in the parking lot. There weren't a lot of cars parked out there, and it was as plain as the dark glasses on Natches's face that they were there because of her.

For a moment, just a moment, she could hear screams in her head. Desperate, clawing sounds that ricocheted inside her, shredded her hard-won composure and had her swinging away from the sight of Natches to pace through her bedroom.

It wasn't just her own screams she heard in her head. The feel of flames licking at her, the horror and stench of death poured into her senses and left her shaking.

She had to swallow tight, clench her fists and force herself away from the memories just as she had to force herself not to return to that window and stare at the men who occasionally glanced up at her room.

They already knew she was here. So much for the element of surprise where Natches was concerned. She had hoped to surprise him with her appearance, hopefully throw him off balance just a little bit.

She snorted at that before pacing back to the window, drawn, despite her best efforts, to the sight of him.

Natches Mackay. He was almost a legend in the Marines. He had been inducted into sniper training right out of boot camp. Within four years he had a kill ratio that made her flinch at the thought of it. Then, in a trick of fate or, as Timothy liked to say, a trick of Natches, a stray bullet had slammed into his shoulder, taking him out of the game.

For years it was rumored Natches had never regained the ability to handle a sniper rifle again. Last year, they had learned differently. Natches was just as silent, and just as deadly, as he had ever been.

She flinched as his head turned and he stared back at her. Surely he couldn't see her behind the filmy curtains, but he knew she was there. He knew which room she was in, and he knew once she saw him out there, she wouldn't be able to look away.

"Put your head down! Close your fucking eyes, Chaya. Ah God. Sweet mercy! Don't look, baby. Don't look."

She closed her eyes. The feel of him lying on her, holding her down despite her struggles, her screams, still brought her awake at night.

Very few people in the world knew that she and Natches had a history. She prayed that only she and Natches knew, because if

Timothy had managed to find out exactly what happened before she came to DHS, then he would never let her go. And he would have the edge he needed to pull Natches into Homeland Security rather than merely using the Mackay cousins as contract agents whenever he could manage to trick them into it.

She opened her eyes and stared out the window again, those dark glasses shielding his eyes, his too-long black hair pulled back at the nape of his neck, the savagery of his features more pronounced than it had been the year before.

He always looked like a dark avenging angel to her. But now, he looked like a savage warrior. She knew if he pulled those glasses off the forest green eyes would be piercing, dark, and filled with knowledge and anger.

So much anger. And she couldn't blame him. Not in the least.

"You've done it this time, Chaya," she murmured into the silence of the room.

And she had. She had allowed her boss to blackmail her into another mission that threw her directly in Natches's path. Big mistake. Very big mistake.

Rowdy strode into the upstairs office of Mackay Lumber and Building Supplies and glared at Dawg as his cousin pulled a beer from the fridge and threw himself in the big leather chair behind the desk.

"Someone needs to let me in on the secret," he snapped as he slammed the door closed. "What the hell is going on? Or has gone on?"

Dawg slouched back in the chair and tipped the beer to his lips thoughtfully. A long drink later he sat the bottle on the desk and stared back at Rowdy.

"Now see, I was hoping you would have the answers to those questions." He wiped his hand over his jaw before shaking his head in obvious confusion. "He was actin' stranger than hell with her last year. Every time he got around her he was pokin' at her or watching her. Don't you think she's a little plain for him?"

Rowdy moved to one of the comfortable leather chairs across from the desk and lowered himself into it as he considered Dawg's question.

"She has pretty hair." He finally shrugged, his expression creasing into male contemplation.

"She's homely," Dawg grunted.

Rowdy snorted at that. "We've been saying that about every woman we've come across since Kelly and Crista got their hooks in us. Admit it, Dawg; we're prejudiced."

Dawg glared. "I know a pretty woman when I see one. Just because you're blind as a bat doesn't mean I am."

Rowdy shook his head. "She looks okay, I guess. Can't tell much with those loose clothes and the way she scrapes her hair back from her face."

"She smokes." Dawg tapped the desk with his fingers, his expression worried.

"You're nitpicking. What's the real problem, Dawg?" Rowdy leaned forward, watching his cousin carefully. "It's not like you to nitpick."

Dawg's lips tightened, then pursed thoughtfully.

"Natches brought a woman out of the Iraqi desert with him on that last six-week mission he took. You know he was always goin' off on a hit and taking his good ole easy time loping back to extraction so he could spy a little on the enemy?"

Rowdy nodded.

"Word got around. Natches managed to hook up with an Army Intelligence agent. Female. Beaten, tortured. He pulled her out and the extraction team picked them both up. After that, no one's talkin'. Something happened after that, Rowdy. Something that made Natches darker than ever."

"Female agent, beaten and tortured." Rowdy frowned. "She didn't have time to break his heart, Dawg. A lot of shit happened to all of us in the Marines. That wasn't a pleasant place to be."

Dawg shook his head. "No. Something bad happened out there that Natches doesn't talk about, and I think she was there. Natches knew her the minute we met the team Cranston brought in last year. That night he went on a drunk like I ain't seen since he busted up his daddy's restaurant for him."

Rowdy leaned back in his chair and grimaced at that information. He hadn't been a part of that mission. His damned cousins seemed to think he needed a vacation after dealing with the serial killer who had tried to kill his wife.

But Dawg was right, something had changed in Natches last year, something that had bothered both of them for a year now.

"Is he in love with her?" Rowdy mused.

It was damned hard to imagine Natches in love with any one woman. He seemed to like them all equally. But there had been something different about how he acted last year outside the spa in town.

Dawg and Rowdy had met with Natches there, while Kelly and Crista went in for their woman stuff. They hadn't felt secure enough to leave the women unguarded. And Greta Dane—no, Chaya, Natches had told them her name was really Chaya—had been there following Dawg and Crista.

Natches hadn't been able to stay away from her and neither of them acted just normal around each other.

"She's on an op," Dawg muttered. "I can feel it. Something's getting ready to go down and she's going to pull him into it."

"Hell." They didn't need that. Rowdy knew Natches. His cousin could be as impulsive as hell, and he rarely thought to cover his own damned ass until it was too late.

Rowdy pushed himself to his feet and paced the interior of the office. He knew the operation that had played out the year before and it still kept him awake at night.

"What was left untied?" He turned to Dawg. "The operation last year, the money Johnny got as a down payment on the missiles, was it found?"

"Not hardly," Dawg grunted. "Cranston was pulling his hair out by the roots when it didn't show up."

Timothy Cranston, that rabid little bastard of an agent in charge. He should be shot with his own gun. Rowdy had had the extreme displeasure of meeting him several times. He still didn't like him.

"Who else would have helped Johnny, Dawg?" Rowdy asked then, his voice heavy, his chest still tightening, even after all this time.

Johnny had been their cousin, and he had used them all. He would have killed them all if he could have. He had definitely planned to kill Dawg's wife, Crista. Him and his lover, Jim Bedsford.

"They picked up the team Johnny used to steal the missiles," Dawg said. "Johnny and Bedsford are dead, and only they knew where the million in down payment was hidden. Hell, what's left to find?"

"We've missed something," Rowdy suggested then.

"What the hell could we have missed?" Dawg cursed. "His agent is back and Natches gets an anonymous call informing him of that fact? Doesn't make sense, Rowdy. If the girl came back to get hot and sweaty with Natches, why the call?"

Rowdy frowned at that. If it hadn't been for the phone call, he'd have assumed that getting hot and sweaty was exactly what was on Miss Dane's mind. But why would someone call and warn him?

Rowdy felt the hairs at the back of his neck lift in warning, and he rubbed at them in irritation.

"Yeah, that's my answer, too," Dawg admitted. "My neck is tingling like hell. Something's getting ready to go down."

"And Agent Dane is putting Natches right square in the middle of it," Rowdy realized. "So we cover him?"

"And cause him to shoot us?" Dawg snarled in disbelieving amazement. "You know how much he likes shadows, Rowdy. We try to cover him and he'll try to kick our asses."

That left one last option. "I have some contacts I can call on." Rowdy was pulling the names up in his head as he spoke. "I'll see what I can find out."

Dawg nodded. "I'll do the same on my end. Call some of the old agents from last year's op and see what they have to say."

"Someone has to watch out for Natches," Rowdy insisted. "At least check up on him."

Dawg stared at him askance. "Fine, you do it. You've had Kelly longer than I've been with Crista. I kind of like my body in working order right now."

"You and me both."

Dawg breathed out roughly. "Flip for it or take turns?"

Rowdy dropped back in the chair. "I guess take turns." He was imagining the pain once Natches caught them. He was hell in a fight, and he would definitely fight.

Dawg slunk down farther in his chair. "I should kill Cranston."

Rowdy grunted. "Give Natches time; he'll do it for you."

And that was what they were both afraid of.

Two

The next morning Chaya met with the team that had been pulled in to work the investigation Cranston had managed to get operational status for.

The six men were older, late thirties to early forties, and would blend in well. Their various covers worked for the area and would provide rationale for their seeming nosiness.

That would work in her favor, Chaya thought as she headed back to her room after the first, early morning meeting. They would gather bits and pieces of the gossip drifting around about the events of last year, and then Cranston could begin a list of persons of interest and the questions Chaya would ask.

They were working in the blind though, and she knew it. The problem was they had been working in the blind for five years. It had to end here. She just couldn't do this much longer. The reason she was back this time was Cranston's bribes. Her resignation was still awaiting the stamp of approval.

Gritting her teeth at the thought of Cranston dragging his feet on her resignation, she swiped her key card through the security pad and waited for the light to flicker to green before pushing the door open and stepping through.

She allowed the door to close slowly behind her. She shrugged her jacket from her shoulders, unclipped the holstered weapon she carried just behind her hip and smoothed her free hand down the side of her skirt. She wished she had worn jeans.

She dropped the jacket and weapon on the table, just inside

the small suite, then turned and moved for the bedroom. The door was open, and when she stepped inside, she felt her heart catch in her throat.

Natches.

She swallowed tightly as she caught sight of him, sprawled out in the easy chair by the window, long jean-clad legs stretched out before him as his hand lifted.

She felt the flush that suffused her features as she saw the heavy, latex vibrator in his hand. The molded penis was her toy of choice, especially when visions of this man drove her crazy with need.

She hadn't managed to get over him, no matter how hard she tried.

Swallowing tightly she watched as he tilted the erotic toy toward his face and inhaled slowly.

She swore her knees nearly went out from beneath her, and arousal, sharp and hot, shot through her core.

"You amaze me," he said then, reaching out to lay the toy on her pillow. That wasn't where he had gotten it from. "You bring a toy to do a man's job, knowing the man is more than willing to provide the service. Where does that make sense, Chay?"

She braced one hand on her hip, the other on the doorframe and stared back at him, forcing her features to bland interest even though she knew she was eating him with her eyes.

"Considering the fact that the man offering comes with strings, I decided it was the safer option."

He would always demand more from a woman than was comfortable. More than Chaya had been able to consider in the past years.

He chuckled at that, his forest green eyes roving over her, taking in the skirt, the silk shell she had worn beneath her blazer, and the pumps on her feet.

Maybe she should have worn stockings rather than panty hose? She had a feeling he knew exactly what she had on beneath her skirt.

"Everything in life comes with strings, darlin'." He shrugged and looked entirely too comfortable in that chair.

Shaking her head, Chaya stalked across the room, not thinking—she never thought when it came to Natches—to jerk the incriminating dildo from her pillow.

"Oh, you didn't do that." He laughed. It was the only warning she had before he was behind her, one arm going around her waist, the other catching her wrist and the toy as he rolled her to her back.

Her little screech didn't even slow him down. His legs trapped hers as he came over her, and he ignored her hands as she pushed at his hard stomach.

She could have made him let her go. She knew how. But God, she couldn't consider it. Besides the fact he would find a way to block her, she had no doubt in her mind that he would come up with a way to make certain she regretted it.

"These games are beneath you, Natches," she snapped, wishing she didn't sound so breathless.

"No, the games aren't, but you are." His brows arched, a smile curved his lips and humor flashed with suspicion in his gaze. A gaze turning hot with arousal as she glimpsed the thick wedge at the front of his jeans.

"Let me go, Natches."

He lifted the dildo and stared down at her. "How do you use it?"

Her flush became hotter. "Duh. Figure it out."

He leaned closer, his lips turning into a wicked smile now. "Do you suck it first? Do you taste yourself on it and remember how much I loved going down on you and tasting all that hot cream?"

That hot cream as he called it was flooding her vagina, saturating her panties. Was there anything more wicked than this man? Anything that tempted her past her pain more than he did?

"You're insane," she whispered, weak now. She could feel the weakness flooding her, the need. The need that had forced her to use that toy just that morning.

"When you suck it, do you think of me?"

She fought to breathe as he brushed the head of the toy over her cheek.

"Let me watch you use it."

Shock rounded her eyes, had her fighting to swallow.

"Are you crazy?"

"Oh yeah. Because the minute it sinks past those pretty pink lips I'm going to remember the feel of your mouth on my dick. I might come in my jeans. I don't think I've ever done that."

Her heart was going to beat out of her chest. Her breasts were swollen and sensitive now, the nipples pressing hard into her bra and the thin material of the top.

"Come on; let me see." He smiled, so wicked, so erotic, as he brushed it against her lips. "Let me see and remember, Chay. Just for a minute."

She knew better. She had known better than to return to Somerset. The minute she did, she knew exactly what Natches was going to do: He would destroy her with her own desires.

Her lips parted.

A tight, erotic grimace contorted his lips as he stared down at her, at the toy within touching distance of her lips, and sparks of anger filled his gaze.

The next second it was his tongue filling her mouth. His lips covering hers. She didn't know what he did with the toy; she didn't care. He was kissing her again. He was possessing her lips, eating at them, and she was eating back.

He always tasted so good, so dark and male. Her arms wrapped around his neck, her fingers spearing into his hair as she felt him jerking her skirt over her thighs, his fingers pressing her legs apart.

He was going to take her. She could feel it. She wasn't going to escape this time. Last year he had been kind, even for him, and let her go. This time, he wasn't letting her go.

"Natches." She breathed his name out in protest as he tore his lips from hers, pressed kisses along her neck, moved to the heaving mounds of her breasts.

Her nipples ached for him. For his mouth, his tongue.

"I should spank you," he growled. "Damn you, Chay. You knew better than to come back here. I know you did."

Yes, she had, and she'd had no choice but to return. But she would have anyway. She knew she would have, because the fight to stay away from him had been too hard. It had been more than she could bear.

One more assignment. Just this last operation and then—they would have time then. Not now.

She shook her head as she arched to him. Now wasn't the

time. She couldn't divide her attention like this. She would end up getting killed.

His mouth buried between her breasts, his tongue licking, stroking as she moaned his name. She needed. Just one more taste of him, then she would be strong.

"Damn you." Suddenly, his head jerked up. "Why are you here, Chay?"

She shook her head. She wasn't drawing him in to this. It wasn't happening.

"Just questions," she panted. "Follow-up. I have to follow up."

She was going to have to do some heavy talking if he ever found out where those questions would lead.

"Liar." The accusation was soft, wickedly knowing. "You can't lie to me, Chay."

He pressed her legs apart with his and the toy; he still had that damned toy. He stroked it over the damp cotton that shielded her from him.

"Let's play a game," he whispered. "I ask a question, you tell the truth, and I give you something you'll really like."

"Kiss me, Natches."

As he had once bragged, his kisses were potent.

He leaned forward, brushed his lips against hers.

"Scared?" he asked softly, his eyes knowing.

"Let me get drunk on you," she urged. "Just kiss me."

"Just kiss you?" The head of the toy pressed more firmly against her hungry core. "But, Chay, you're so wet and so wild beneath me. Let's play my little game first."

She arched and cried out as he pulled back.

"First question." He licked over the top of a breast revealed by the material he nudged lower with his chin. "Did DHS send you here?"

Okay, that one was easy.

"Yes," she answered carefully.

A soft approving murmur against the curve of her breast and he was nudging the cup of her bra lower to lick at her nipple. Heat sizzled in her veins and sent her hips thrusting, grinding against the toy he held pressed to her panties.

"Good girl," he murmured. "Am I involved?"

Was he? She didn't think he was. He shouldn't be. She could be honest there.

"No." She lifted her hips again, wanting more. Damn him, she was honest. Reward time here.

He nipped at her nipple and nearly sent her into orgasm.

"Why are you here?"

Her lips parted to answer, to spill her guts just for another taste of the pleasure he could give her.

"Follow-up." She moaned.

"Hmm, Chay, my little liar." He pulled the toy back. "Come on, baby; fess up."

Her eyes opened as she stared back at him, aching, hurting for him.

"Follow-up," she repeated, the tormented whisper dragged from her throat. "It's the only reason I'm here." And it was partially the truth. Enough of the truth, and all he needed to stay safe.

He knelt above her. She watched hungrily as, tossing the toy aside, he loosened his belt, unsnapped his jeans, then lowered the zipper slowly. She licked her lips, her hands poised to help him, to catch the heavy length of his erection when it was free. To taste it. To fill her mouth with it.

"Why are you here, Chay?" She barely missed the hardening of his voice.

"Follow-up." She felt dazed, off balance, impatient. Like an addict anticipating a fix.

And just that fast he rolled away from her, moved to his feet, and was fixing his jeans, his expression still, silent with anger.

Damn. There went the fix. Her body was screaming out in protest, reminding her how mean she was being to it. How long had it been now since she had known his possession? Five years, two months, three days, and how many hours, she thought morosely.

"I guess that means I don't get any more rewards." She sighed as she adjusted her skirt and top. She didn't bother to roll from the bed. "Lock the door behind you if you don't mind. I may need some privacy after you leave."

He glared at her. The next thing she knew, the thin cord was jerked from the base of the dildo and as she watched in horror, he tore it in half.

"Oh my God. Natches, you didn't do that."

"If you need privacy, then by God you can make do with your

fingers. That's what you've reduced me to." He tossed the pieces to the floor. "When you're ready to tell me the fucking truth, you know where to find me."

With that, he stalked out of the room. She stared at the floor in disbelief then at the door as the echo of the main door slamming penetrated her mind.

He broke her toy and left?

She was going to kill him.

Three

Somerset and Lake Cumberland appealed to Chaya in a way that had surprised her. Arriving ahead of the Homeland Security team, in advance preparation more than a year ago, she had been taken aback by the friendliness of the citizens and the relaxed, peaceful atmosphere of the mountains surrounding the town.

There was serenity here. Not that there wasn't crime, or criminals, of course. The theft and attempted sale of the missiles last year was proof enough. No, it was something else. There was a quiet, easygoing feel to the area, and she had loved it.

She had missed it since the team had left last year. She had missed the community, and she had missed Natches. Unfortunately, she had missed Natches more than anything else.

And Timothy had known Natches was her weakness. That was the problem with having a boss as manipulating and calculating as Timothy Cranston. He knew the agents under him to their back teeth. Their strengths and their weaknesses. And he didn't have a problem using both to his advantage.

Hell, she was supposed to be out of this. Right now, she should have been apartment hunting or something. She should have been getting her head straight, because it was something she hadn't managed to do in five years.

She had managed to quit smoking again. It was a nasty habit, and breaking it hadn't been easy. Timothy alone was an excuse to smoke. She bet half of his agents had picked up the habit only after having been assigned to his team.

This operation had obsessed Cranston though, worse than Chaya had ever seen him obsessed. Those missiles in the wrong hands would have been disastrous. And knowing that it had been Americans behind the hijacking and attempted sale had enraged Cranston. Finding out it had a connection to a much older investigation had made him rabid. They were so close he claimed, so close to finding the bastards he spent every waking moment of his life chasing.

He had pulled every string he could find and had broken more than one rule in that investigation last year. One of those strings was pulling in two ex-Marines onto the team. Locals known for their wild reputations and their ability to gather and filter local gossip. Dawg and Natches Mackay. And there had been the added benefit for Timothy of finally finding Natches Mackay's "weakness" as he called it.

And that one she had to roll her eyes at. She was anything but his weakness. Natches wanted her. He would spend the night in her bed in a heartbeat and she knew it. She could have him. On his terms and by his rules. And that would mean dragging him into an investigation he had no business being a part of. That, she couldn't find it within herself to do.

As she pulled her rental car into the parking lot of the local diner that the Mackay men were known to frequent, Chaya checked her weapon and breathed out a sigh of frustration.

She hated this. Hated the deception and the need for it. And even more, she hated being under Natches's radar once again. Especially after he broke her toy. And here she was on assignment. It wasn't as though she could just go out and buy a new one.

She checked her rearview mirror and there he was. That wicked black jeep pulling into the back entrance and stopping, the man behind the wheel watching her from behind dark glasses.

He hadn't approached her since he had stomped from her hotel room days before. But he had been following her since she left the hotel that morning. He had hung back, stayed distant just as he had the year before. He just watched, and just made her as nervous as hell.

Parking the sedan, Chaya gathered her purse and the heavy file she'd brought with her before stepping out into the crisp autumn air.

She could feel his eyes on her back as she moved to the entrance of the diner. Intense, blazing. The feminine core of her had been reawakened by that look over a year ago, and now, after knowing his touch again, it didn't seem inclined to go back to sleep.

She pushed her way into the diner and stood for a moment, getting her bearings as all eyes turned to her. Suspicious, curious, amused. She latched onto the amused gaze of Sheriff Ezekiel Mayes before striding across the large room.

His hawklike eyes followed her progress through the room as he rose slowly to his feet. The dun-colored sheriff's uniform showed off a body in peak condition for a man of thirty-six years. Dark brown hair was military short and emphasized the strong planes and angles of his masculine face.

"Agent Dane." He nodded as she took her seat and laid the heavy file on the table in front of her, then he returned to his seat.

"Thank you for agreeing to meet with me, Sheriff." She tried out her best business smile, but at the narrowing of his eyes, she assumed it hadn't gone off quite as planned. "I know it was short notice."

"I wouldn't expect anything less." He picked up his coffee and took a drink before setting the cup on the table and motioning to the waitress as she moved by. "Becca, we'll need more coffee over here."

"Gotcha, Zeke." The waitress gave Chaya a quick, suspicious look before moving away.

"Have you had lunch yet?" he asked Chaya then.

"I'm fine. I just have some questions I needed to ask and a few things I'd like to go over with you before we head out to begin these interviews."

Why Timothy had arranged for this sheriff to tag along with her she wasn't certain. Ezekiel Mayes was nobody's fool. He'd spent five years as a homicide detective in Los Angeles before returning to his hometown and running for sheriff. He was suspicious by nature, perceptive, and when he had learned an operation had been conducted without his knowledge by the DHS last year, he had been in D.C. screaming in the faces of men with enough power to scald Cranston's ass.

Mayes had some small amount of pull there, Cranston had learned, and he knew exactly how to wield it. Proof was in the fact that she was working with him now.

Oh what a tangled web we weave, when first we practice to deceive. The quote whispered through Chaya's mind, and not for the first time. Cranston was playing a very dangerous game here, and Sheriff Mayes was but one of the potential enemies that he could make.

"Coffee, Zeke." Becca, the waitress, set the cup down before turning to Chaya. "You need anything else?"

"No, thank you." She shook her head, wishing she could find a way to still the nerves in her stomach as she lifted the coffee to her lips.

Becca nodded and moved off, but the sheriff's gaze never left Chaya.

"Cranston's sunk to a new low." Mayes leaned back in his chair and regarded her with sharp golden brown eyes.

"Cranston's always finding new lows." Chaya shrugged. "What has he managed to do this time?"

"He sent a pretty little girl to do a man's job." He grunted in disgust. "The Mackays are none too happy with DHS right now, and neither is the local law enforcement around here. You don't pull an op like you did last year and not inform the locals without stepping on some toes."

"We weren't required to inform anyone of our operation here. We were required to reacquire those missiles, Sheriff, not make nice with the local law enforcement. And my gender has nothing to do with my ability to conduct this end of the investigation."

He grunted at that. "Yeah, two years in military intelligence and five with DHS. You have a hell of a record under your belt, don't you?"

She did, and it was one she was proud of, sometimes, she assured herself. When she needed something to find a source of pride in, then it worked.

"I'm not a green agent, Sheriff." She leaned back in her own chair and stared back at him. "Nor am I out of my element here. You have enough pull that you were able to make certain you were contacted and included in any further investigations. I'm fine with that. But you don't have the power to give me orders or to direct these interviews. Are we clear?"

His gaze flared with anger for a moment, then the amusement was back. "Just your little lackey, huh?" he murmured, glancing over his shoulder at the sound of the bell over the door tinkling merrily to announce another customer.

Chaya sighed. It was Natches. She could feel him now.

"Shall we get down to business?" She picked up the list of interviewees that she had chosen to visit that afternoon. "Here's the short list of people I need to see today. I assume we can have this completed before too late tonight."

Mayes took the list and studied it with a frown. "This isn't the full list."

"I'm not required to give you the full list," she told him, feeling Natches moving in closer, hearing him as a chair scraped across the floor just behind her.

The sheriff's lips twitched as he continued to study her.

"You like to live dangerously, don't you, little girl?"

She barely contained her flinch. She had heard those words before, and the hell she had lived through afterward still haunted her nightmares.

"I live as I must." She shrugged. "Another of those details that I'm not required to discuss with you. Now, as you are the first on my list to be interviewed, shall we get started?"

There was a snort of a laugh behind her. The sound had her hackles rising and a curl of anger prickling inside.

Before Mayes could answer, she turned slowly in her chair and looked back at Natches. He was no more than four feet away from her, staring at her from behind those dark glasses.

"Your presence really isn't required at this time," she told him quietly. "Your turn will come."

She refused to let him intimidate her. If he managed to throw her off balance now, then she was lost. She would never be able to complete her assignment as needed.

He didn't smile; he didn't speak. He just stared at her until she turned her back on him again and shuffled through the papers in her files for the information she had tagged regarding the sheriff.

"You've been sheriff for how long now?"

"Almost six years." Mayes was definitely amused now. "They

voted me back in for some reason. Personally, I think folks around here consider me a bit of an easy mark, don't you think?"

That was definitely a jibe at the man behind her. Chaya was well aware of the fact that the sheriff and the Mackays had gone head-to-head several times last year over Dawg Mackay's activities.

"I wouldn't know the reasons why." She smiled tightly. "Johnny Grace was a popular citizen in town though. You had known him for a while?"

Mayes nodded slowly. "I'd known him all his life, Agent Dane. I only spent eight years away from home, not a lifetime. Johnny and his parents are well-known to most people in Somerset and the surrounding towns."

"Yet you had no suspicion he could have been involved in the hijacking of the missiles?"

"Those missiles were taken in another county, close to an Army base." His voice was clipped now. "I had my eyes open for them, but there were those who neglected to inform me that they could be in my county." And that was a jibe at Chaya and DHS.

He was professional enough that his animosity didn't show, but she could feel it.

"Sheriff, I'm not your enemy, nor was I the head agent in that investigation. You're snapping at the wrong agent here," she assured him. "I want to complete this and head home as quickly as you want me out of your county."

Mayes tilted his head to the side. "Now, what would make you think I want you out of my county? Unlike most people, Agent Dane, I enjoy a good comedy every now and then. And this situation appears to at least have an element of amusement within it."

The bell tinkled at the door again. When Chaya lifted her head to glance at the mirror placed next to the register behind Sheriff Mayes, she felt like cursing.

The Mackays were amassing. The tall, broad forms of Dawg and Rowdy Mackay were reflected in the glass as they moved across the room. They all but swaggered. Dressed in jeans and light T-shirts, Dawg wore a denim jacket, Rowdy wore a leather jacket. Both were suspicious and more than a little intimidating as they joined Natches at his table.

When her eyes met Sheriff Mayes's again, the amusement in them had thickened.

"What about known associates of Grace's?" she asked him then, lowering her voice further. "Did you have any reason to suspect them after the operation completed last year?"

This was the wrong damned place for these questions. She knew it, and she could see the knowledge of it in Mayes's eyes. She had tried to warn Timothy, several times, this man was no one's fool. Timothy had arranged this meeting here specifically to allow Mackay involvement.

The sheriff leaned closer. Bracing his arms on the table, he stared back at her warningly.

"Are you sure you want to finish this here, Agent Dane?" he asked her, his voice official, cool.

"This is as good a place as any, Sheriff. If you could answer the question please."

"I'd have reason to suspect half the county then," he told her. "If you want to discuss specific suspects though, we're going to do it elsewhere."

That was good enough. That was the best answer she would get right here and now—that Mayes did suspect various parts of the Grace and/or Mackay family. She had spent most of her life learning how to read people, and despite the chill in the sheriff's face, she could read that much in his eyes.

"At the time of the operation were you aware that Natches and James Mackay were involved in the operation?"

Sheriff Mayes snorted at that question. "If there's trouble to be found, then James Dawg Mackay and his two cousins are always bound to be close by." He flicked a mocking look behind her shoulder. "They're trouble like that. You'd do well to remember it."

"But you didn't answer the question," she reminded him softly.

"I suspected they were in up to their necks in something, I just didn't know what." He shrugged easily. "Remember? No one informed me anything was going on."

"But you knew enough to begin your own investigation and to contact several members of the FBI as well as a contact you made within DHS and the Department of Justice?"

She handed him the memos that had made it into Timothy's hands. The sheriff's phone records clearly revealed the calls that were made, but not which agents took those calls.

His lips tipped knowingly. "I'm a suspicious bastard; what can I say?"

"And who did you speak to at that time?"

He smiled at that. "Names elude me, Miss Dane. I just asked to speak to an agent, and they plugged me into someone."

Chaya stared back at him suspiciously. He wasn't even bothering to disguise the fact that he was lying to her.

"And what did they tell you?"

"They told me to mind my own business in my own little corner of the world," he continued to lie. "What were they supposed to tell me?"

Chaya held back her own grin though she inclined her head in acknowledgment. Truth be told, she didn't want to know his contacts and she didn't give a damn. Timothy was dying to get his little hooks into them though.

Behind her, silence reigned.

"One last question, Sheriff. Can I trust you?" she asked, allowing her own suspicions to enter her voice now. He was a friend of the Mackays; the people of Somerset were his people. She needed to know, to watch his eyes, hear his voice, to determine how far she was going to trust him.

His eyes narrowed on her again before he leaned forward carefully. "Agent Dane, I'm a duly sworn officer of the law, and this is my home. You can trust me to cover your back. You can trust me to make damned sure any suspicions you have are held in confidence. I might not like what you are or what your team did here last year, but I don't have to like you to do my job. Are we clear on that?"

"And should *friends* of yours question you regarding the interviews we're about to make? Will your loyalties then be torn? Because I have to ask you to step aside if they will be. I can bring in another agent to provide backup."

He frowned, his jaw clenching. He knew the out she was offering him, and it was one Cranston hadn't approved. There was no reason to drive a wedge between this man and the Mackays. It was his choice. And she would leave it up to him.

"You're insulting me," he bit out. "And pissing me off at the same time. I just told you my loyalty is to the law. Period."

"Excellent." She closed the file and flashed him a cool smile.

"Shall we go then? I'd like to start with the first name below yours on that list if you don't mind."

His lips tightened, but he jerked his hat from the side of the table and slammed it on his head before rising to his feet.

Chaya gathered her file together, looped the strap of her purse over her shoulder then turned to face three sets of Mackay eyes on her.

Light green, emerald green, and behind dark glasses she knew were the deepest, darkest forest green eyes she had ever seen. They mesmerized, sank into the soul and left their impression forever after.

"It was good to see you boys again." She smiled tightly. "Maybe next time we'll have a chance to chat for a while."

Dawg and Rowdy ducked their heads, but Natches's expression never shifted, his eyes never left hers.

"Greta, you don't want to be here," Dawg finally muttered as his head lifted, his expression concerned. "Let this go. Make Cranston send someone else to do his dirty work."

"But, Dawg, you know how convincing he can be," she reminded him mockingly. "I think you and I both know I'm rather stuck here. And I do have a job to do. Good day."

She nodded to them, then moved past the sheriff, who had stood back, watching the confrontation. Natches's eyes still followed her, silent, aware.

Did the memories bring him awake at night in a cold sweat? she wondered. Did he even let himself remember?

She tried not to remember, but she did. Too often . . . Remembering was a weakness, because each time she allowed herself to remember hell, then she was also reminded of ecstasy. And she wondered if hell wasn't safer.

"You want to tell us what's doin', bro?" Dawg stared across the table at Natches as he sipped at the coffee he'd finally ordered.

"Nothin's doin'," he replied, flicking his cousin a mocking look.

"Take the glasses off, Natches," Rowdy finally bit out.

And he didn't dare. He'd been out of the game too long. His eyes showed what he knew his face didn't, and when it came to Chaya, they showed even more.

There were secrets he kept, secrets he was determined to keep. And Chaya was one of them.

"I have you, Chay. Hold on, baby. Just hold on. I have you."

He almost flinched at the memory. The smell of gunfire, of violence and blood, filled his head, and the sounds of her screams. Screams so horrifying, so filled with rage and pain that he hadn't known how to live with them in his head.

"I need to roll." He pushed the coffee cup back and dug into his jeans for a few dollars to pay the bill.

He didn't have time to fuck around here. Chaya and Zeke were on the move, and Natches was very curious as to the names on that list she had shown the sheriff.

He was very damned curious as to why she was here to begin with. He had the official line. He had the rumors and he had the suppositions his contacts had come up with. None of those satisfied him. None of those reasons kept his hackles from rising every time he thought about it, or every time he saw Chaya.

He tossed the money on the table and started to rise.

"I don't want to make a mess of this diner, cuz," Dawg said then. "And if we fight, you know there's gonna be a mess. Sit your ass down here and tell us what the hell is going on. Let us help you, Natches."

He stared back at Dawg, then Rowdy. He could see the concern in their eyes, the worry that he was riding that line again. He had ridden that line a lot in the past. The one that separated common sense from pure, bloody violence.

What the hell was wrong with him? He couldn't make sense of it. He hadn't made sense of it in seven years and it still didn't make sense. When Chaya was anywhere near, he didn't know himself. He didn't know who he was and he didn't understand the needs that tore through him, nor did he understand the extreme possessiveness.

In one hot afternoon in the Iraqi desert while he waited for the calvary to ride in and listened to the enemy get closer, he had found something he hadn't expected to find.

There, buried in a hole, he had held a woman, and somehow that woman had slipped inside his soul.

How did that happen? In such a short time, how did one woman change everything a man knew about himself?

"I'm married." She had whispered the words, and they had been filled with pain, with a knowledge he couldn't have guessed at, at the time.

And what had shocked him clear to the bottom of his soul was that it hadn't mattered. As he held her, he'd known that marriage wasn't going to stand in his way. She was his, and that feeling had seared his soul.

And he had found a core of possessiveness that he hadn't imagined lived inside him. That possessiveness had shocked him clear to the center of his being, and still had the power to throw him off balance.

"Natches." Rowdy's voice was warning. "Don't walk out that fucking door."

Natches shook his head and followed the woman he couldn't stay away from. He had to follow her. He had to know what the hell she was doing and how much danger it was going to place her in.

"It's okay, I have you, baby."

He held her as she sobbed. Broken, horrific cries that ripped at his guts and flayed his soul as he carried her through hell. The smell of blood and death and broken dreams surrounded them, and all he could do was hold her.

As he left the diner he didn't feel the late autumn air, he felt the heat of an Iraqi summer, the sun blazing down on Baghdad as fire blazed at their backs. He didn't hear the traffic around him, or Dawg's voice behind him. He heard her screams. He heard her pleas as she begged him, pleaded with him to let her die, too.

"Natches, enough of this shit!" Dawg and Rowdy caught him as he neared his jeep, gripping his arm and swinging him around. "Damn it, what the hell is going on with you? You're starting to worry us, man."

They were defensive, ducking instinctively, knowing his habit of swinging first and asking questions later. But Natches didn't swing.

He knew these two men. Knew them almost as well as he knew himself, and he knew they wouldn't let it go.

Shaking his head he pulled the glasses from his face and stared back at them. And he knew what they saw. Both men stepped back, staring back at him in surprise. He saw those eyes in the mirror every morning since Chaya's return last year, and he saw his inability to control the need riding him more every day.

"My fight," he told them both. "There's no room for all of us here. I guess I finally grew up, huh?"

It was a reminder that as Dawg and Rowdy had matured, as their hearts became involved with their women, rather than just their cocks, their possessive instincts had kicked in. No one touched what they claimed themselves. They didn't share their women anymore, not even with each other.

And they didn't need to be involved in this. He knew Dawg and Rowdy, and he knew that knowing the truth would do nothing but worry them more.

They thought they knew Natches. That was the mistake most people made. They thought they knew him, understood him. They thought they could predict him, and they had found out they were wrong.

He turned away from his cousins, ignoring the worried looks they gave each other, and jumped into the jeep. Chaya's rental car was still sitting here; that meant they were in Zeke's official SUV. That wouldn't be hard to find.

Chaya would never be hard for him to find, no matter where she was or how she tried to hide. He had proven that to her. And now he was paying the price.

He had let her leave a year ago. He wasn't willing to do that this time around. He'd find out what the hell she was doing here. Then, he'd find Chaya.

He pulled from the parking lot in a squeal of tires and a grinding of gears before shooting out into the alley and heading for the main road. He didn't know the names on that list she had given Zeke, but he'd find out tonight what was going on there. Until then, he'd shadow her and see if he couldn't figure out what the hell was going on.

Because he knew she wasn't supposed to be here. She wasn't supposed to be with Homeland Security and she wasn't supposed to be in Kentucky.

So why was Chaya Greta Dane doing exactly what she wasn't supposed to be doing in a place she wasn't supposed to be?

And why the hell did he let himself care?

Four

Ezekiel Mayes was leaning against his car as Agent Dane pulled from the restaurant parking lot, and he waited. He had just dropped her back at her car, and knew he wouldn't have to wait long; he was just curious who would show up.

He wasn't left in suspense, and he had to hide his smile as the black jeep pulled in behind his SUV and Natches stepped out of the vehicle.

Those damnable glasses covered his eyes. The black lenses were a shield between Natches and the world, Zeke often thought. And damned if he could blame the other man. Natches hadn't exactly skated through life. Some years, Zeke knew, he'd hung on by his fingernails alone as his father tried to destroy him.

Last year, Zeke feared, had been a breaking point for Natches. The day he had taken a bead on his first cousin Johnny Grace and pulled the trigger.

Natches had been one of the finest snipers the Marines had possessed. Often working alone, without the benefit of a spotter, completing his missions, then hanging around to gather intel. Four years in the Marines and he had nearly been a legend by the time an enemy sniper had taken his shoulder out.

If that was what happened. Zeke sometimes wondered. Natches wasn't a man one could slip up on, even from a distance. He had instincts like the sheriff had never known in another man. Instincts honed in the Kentucky mountains and in his father's home.

An ex-Marine himself, Dayle Mackay was one hard-bitten son of a bitch. If ever a man deserved a bullet, then it was Dayle.

"Figured you'd show up eventually." Zeke sighed when Natches didn't speak. "I wasn't able to get any info, if that's what you want to know."

"Why is she here?"

"Follow-up is what I was told." Zeke shrugged; he didn't believe that one either. "They're still missing the million. I guess the government has to line their coffers somewhere, huh?"

He tipped his hat back and stared up at the setting sun as Natches stood still and silent. What the hell was he thinking behind those glasses? Reading Natches Mackay was like trying to read ancient script. Pretty much impossible.

"Who is she questioning tomorrow?"

Zeke shook his head. "Hell if I know. Said she'd give me the names when we meet up in the morning. I couldn't get shit out of her."

She was as closemouthed as Natches was, and almost as wary. But where the man was stone-cold and silent, Zeke had seen nervousness in the agent. She had known from second to second exactly where Natches was behind them, when he would round a curve, or where he would park. That little girl had been so attuned to the killer shadowing them that Zeke had been amazed.

"Would you tell me if you had?" Natches asked him then, his big body shifting dangerously as he pinned Zeke with that shielded gaze.

"In this case, yeah, I'd tell you." He nodded. "Because I want an end to this as well, Natches. What went down last year has ripped through this town like a plague. Homegrown fucking terrorists? God help us all. People are scared to trust their neighbors here now. And that bothers me. That bothers me real bad."

Pulaski County was his home, his county, his watch and his responsibility. It was one he took seriously, and until last year, he had thought he was doing a damned fine job at keeping out the worst of the evil the world had to offer.

Terrorists. Son of a bitch. It was bad enough when the bastards were foreign, almost fucking conceivable. But homegrown? A man you'd known all your life?

He and Johnny Grace hadn't been friends, but if anyone had asked him if the boy could kill, he would have given an emphatic no. And he would have been wrong. If anyone had told him Johnny had been conspiring to steal and sell missiles that would be used against his own nation, Zeke would have denied it to the last line.

Johnny had been strange. He'd been a little off in left field sometimes, but Zeke had never imagined what his smile hid.

"She's after more than the money." Zeke breathed out heavily at that thought. "There's something more important here than that."

"Like?"

"Like hell if I fucking know," Zeke cursed. "You Mackays tell me what the fuck is going on after it's done the hell over with." He flicked Natches a glowering look. "If you had been honest with me from the beginning, we wouldn't be standing here now, would we, damn it?"

"That or we'd be standing over your grave." Natches shrugged. "We were almost standing over Dawg's and Crista's. I didn't like that, Zeke."

The understatement was almost laughable. When Johnny Grace had taken Dawg's lover and tried to kill her, he had signed his death warrant with Natches.

There was nothing Natches cared for outside Rowdy, Dawg, and Rowdy's dad, Ray Mackay. Unless it was his sister, Janey. Zeke had never figured out for sure if he gave a shit about the girl or not, but he knew he'd hate to test that boundary. Natches might act like she didn't exist, but Zeke was betting the other man kept very close tabs on the girl.

"What are you going to do here, Natches?" he finally asked. "Don't get between me and the law, man. I'd hate to have to butt heads with you. But I will."

Natches's lips quirked humorously. "I'll stay out of your law, and you stay out of my way. Other than that, I don't know what the hell to tell you."

Frustration gnawed at Zeke then. He really didn't need this. Natches was, Zeke often thought, the most dangerous man he knew. He wasn't given to strong temperament, he didn't hold grudges. But Zeke had a feeling that spilling blood didn't bother him overmuch either.

"We don't need another killing like last summer, Natches," he warned him. "You didn't have to kill Johnny. You could have wounded him and left enough to question. Then we wouldn't have these folks running around now."

Natches didn't stiffen. There was nothing in his demeanor to indicate a change in mood. But the air around them seemed to crackle with tension and rage.

"Killing him was better than sex." Natches's smile was cold enough, hard enough, that Zeke wondered if he should feel an edge of fear. There was something completely unaffected in that smile.

"Better than sex with Agent Dane?" Zeke had a feeling he had just taken his life in his hands with that question.

Natches stared back at him, his expression closed. Tight. For a moment, Zeke thought he would speak, thought something would finally pass by that tightly shielded expression of his. Instead, Natches turned away, jumped back into the jeep, and shoved it into gear before pulling away with careful restraint.

Zeke slowly let out his breath, unaware that he had been holding it after asking that last question. And he had no idea which way the answer would have gone.

"You didn't have to kill Johnny. You could have wounded *him and left enough to question."*

Zeke's accusation didn't sit well with Natches, no more than his response had. That killing Johnny had been better than sex. Hell, killing that little bastard had set up a sickness in his gut that he couldn't seem to get rid of. Not regret. There was no regret. It was Johnny or Crista, and Crista had been innocent. No, it was something else, something Natches hadn't known since he had taken a bead on Nassar Mallah, the traitor that had kidnapped Chaya in Iraq, and blew his damned head off. It was a knowledge that he was truly becoming a killer.

Didn't matter the why of it, didn't matter that it was monsters he was killing. What made him sick to his soul was that he no longer felt regret. He hadn't regretted Nassar, and he hadn't felt any regret over killing family.

He was afraid he was turning into the same sick bastard his father was, and that terrified him. It terrified him almost as much as the knowledge that through the day, something had shifted inside him where Chaya was concerned.

He wasn't letting her walk away again. Not without having

her. Not without fucking this hunger in his gut out of his system so he could survive the next time she decided to run out on him.

It was time to do something about her.

Natches drove through the darkened streets of Somerset, made a left onto the interstate and headed to the hotel Chaya was checked into.

Tonight, he wouldn't be staring into her darkened window, wondering why the hell she was there. Tonight, he would find out exactly why she was there, and what she wanted in Somerset. He could guess until hell froze over, but if Timothy Cranston was heading this little operation that was obviously being conducted in his town, then God only knew exactly what was going on.

At least it had nothing more to do with the Mackays. Or not his end of the Mackays. He'd held back the past week, watched, gathered his own information. Had he learned this operation targeted his family, then he wouldn't have hesitated to snatch Chaya and make damned sure Cranston understood it wasn't happening.

Rowdy, Dawg, Kelly, Crista, his uncle Ray, and his sister. They were his family, and he'd not allow pain to touch them any more than it already had. The information he had attained so far assured him the Mackays weren't targeted. Anyone else was fair game, and he was willing to help.

And he couldn't stay away from her much longer. He'd never been able to stay away from her for long.

As he drove toward the hotel the memory of her rescue whispered through his mind. She'd been hurt, abused, and terrorized, and married. And when she had learned her husband had been the reason for her capture and torture, she had cried in Natches's arms, while in the hospital in which she had been recovering. And she had begged him to help her.

He forced those memories back. He hadn't cared that she was married even before they learned her husband was a traitor. She was his; it was simple. Then he had learned it wasn't that simple.

She'd walked away from him. Disappeared as though she had never existed, and for years he hadn't known where she was or how to find her. Until she'd arrived in Somerset on the operation to locate the missiles.

And what the fuck had she done when that mission was over? Run. She had run from him again without looking back, without acknowledging a damned thing that had happened in that fucking desert.

And he had let her go.

He pulled into the hotel parking lot and spotted her immediately where she stood, propped against the trunk of the rented sedan.

Her arms were crossed over the light blazer. She wore another silky top beneath it. Those short little thin-strapped tops were making him crazy. Jeans hugged her legs; the top of them rose barely to her hip bones, where the top she wore beneath the dark blazer barely met the band. And she wore boots. It was one of the first things he noticed last year; she wore leather boots. He surely did like a woman who wore boots. And boots on Chaya looked damned good.

He pulled up beside her, then he reached over and unlatched the door before swinging it open.

"Get in." He didn't ask. He'd gone too far to ask. He could feel the dominance, the possessiveness rising inside him, fighting against the restraint he was attempting to maintain.

She slid warily into the jeep and closed the door behind her before hastily locking her seat belt.

"Where are we going?" Her voice was soft, just a bit nervous, reminding him of that hidden hole and the darkness and the intimacy that had wrapped around them.

"Someplace where we can talk."

Where they could talk. Chaya stared out the windshield as Natches drove, his command of the vehicle confident, but obviously restrained. She could feel the fine thread of tension moving through him, the obvious control he was exerting over it.

And she knew what he was like when that control slipped. When the restrained man became the dominant lover. When he became a force she couldn't deny.

"What do we need to talk about, Natches?" she finally asked as he turned onto the main road and headed in the opposite direction of the marina.

"We're not going to the boat?" The *Nauti Dreams* had been his home last year.

"Winter's coming on." His voice was as frosty as that season. "I moved out to the apartment over the garage last year anyway. Damned lake is getting too busy."

There was leashed anger in his voice, a temper she didn't want to chance right now. She had heard of his dangerous temper, the cold, lashing rage he could project, but she had never experienced it herself.

Chaya couldn't imagine where she had found the courage tonight to actually get into the jeep with him. At one time she was known to have nerves of steel. Now she could feel the wariness moving through her. Not fear, but something female, something that recognized Natches as perhaps more man than she could handle.

Sometimes, Chaya reasoned, a woman just knew when she had too much man on her hands. Too much lust, too much strength, too much hunger. And all that described Natches only too well.

"You've been watching me," she finally stated. "Why?"

He removed the glasses from his eyes slowly. How he managed to drive wearing the dark shades she hadn't figured out. But when he looked at her, it happened again. The same thing that happened every time she stared into the perfect forest green of his eyes.

The breath seemed to rush from her lungs, nerve endings heated, and between her thighs she felt a flood of liquid warmth she couldn't control.

"You shouldn't have come back," he finally said as he turned and took a side road that led to his garage. "You should have resigned from DHS like I heard you had and gotten the hell away from Cranston."

"What does that have to do with you watching me here? You knew there would be further questioning conducted in Somerset, Natches. Did you think it was really over? It won't be for Timothy until he finds the money and Johnny's coconspirator."

"You're so certain he had one?" He shook his head at that. "Johnny didn't share that easily, Chaya."

"Unlike the Nauti Boys," she murmured.

She knew the rumors that the cousins shared their lovers and wondered at that, because Rowdy and Dawg seemed more than possessive over their women.

"Long ago and far away," he muttered.

There was something in his voice that had her gaze sharpening on him. An ache of loss, of regret. Something that assured her he was right. Whatever sharing may have gone on in the past, it was over now. Her question, though, was how much he regretted it.

Silence descended then. Chaya watched as the darkened scenery sped by and they drew closer to the garage and the apartment over it.

"Here we are." He pulled in behind the garage and parked the jeep beneath the wooden steps that led up to the second floor.

The light on the overhead porch threw a glimmer of golden rays below to add to the subtle landscaping lights behind the shrubs that grew close to the building beneath the porch.

Chaya moved from the jeep and watched warily as he waited for her at the front of the vehicle.

"Have you had dinner?" he asked, placing his hand at the small of her back and giving her a firm push to the steps.

"Sheriff Mayes and I ate after the last interview," she told him, feeling his hand tense at her back.

She swung her head around to try to see him in the dim light. She could have sworn he growled something not quite complimentary where the sheriff was concerned.

"Keep going, Chay." He crowded her, pushing her up the stairs, his larger, broader body making her feel too feminine, too weak.

She was a trained agent, or she was supposed to be, but every time she was around Natches the agent became overwhelmed by the woman.

He was her weakness; she had figured that out at a time when she hadn't needed to know it. And the certainty of it had only grown.

She stepped onto the landing and stood aside as he unlocked the door, stepped in, and looked around before turning back to her.

"Come on in."

Her heart nearly strangled her as it raced in her chest and jumped to her throat. She stepped inside, staring around the starkly masculine area as she felt her palms dampen.

Here, she was in his territory, completely surrounded by Natches. She stepped farther into the room, then paused at the mantel over the gas fireplace. A smile tipped her lips. There was a picture of Faisal, the young goatherd who had managed to contact Natches on a shortwave radio channel to inform him that a female agent was being held and tortured in the desert.

He was her savior as well that day. Faisal had covered Natches while he pulled her out of that dark, hellish cell. She knew the extraction team that had picked them up had made certain Faisal made it back to his goats.

"I talked to him a few months ago," he told her. "He said you were still sending messages and money."

She nodded slowly. She couldn't protect him; all she could do was try to make things easier.

"He makes a monthly trip past one of the bases in the area. I make certain he has something waiting for him there."

She could feel him behind her as he asked, "Do you ever talk to him?"

Chaya lowered her head and shook it. "No. I don't contact him personally."

She couldn't. She'd tried several times, had actually gone so far as to purchase the phone cards and send him her number. She knew he had his own cell phone now. One he was very proud of.

She turned back to him. "Do you talk to him often?"

He nodded, the movement sharp. "His family was killed just before your rescue. I've been trying to make arrangements to get him over here. I haven't had much success yet."

Yes, she knew that, just as Cranston did. It was one of the promises versus threats he had made to force her into this operation. Cranston would make certain Faisal would be given his entrance into America, if this operation completed to his satisfaction.

She felt a chill race over her head at the thought, then down her spine. Then it sort of went over her body as she forced herself to move away from Natches. Once Natches knew who DHS had targeted, he was liable to kill her and Cranston.

"What do you want from me, Natches? You know I can't give you this mission or Timothy's suspects; so what's left?" She stared around the large living room with its heavily cushioned furniture and male accoutrements.

There were pictures of Natches and his cousins Dawg and Rowdy. A few that were taken while he was in the Marines with buddies. There was a picture of Natches with Faisal.

A table had been set up at the side of the room with a jigsaw puzzle. Hell, she didn't know people still did those.

There were some oil lamps on a table and a heavy lamp on

the end table next to the couch. The kitchen and living room were separated by a bar. There was no dining room, but the kitchen was large enough for the heavy oak table that was set to the side of the room.

She assumed the doorway off the living room went to a bedroom, but she wasn't checking that one out.

And as she stared around, she realized Natches hadn't answered her.

She turned back to him, watching nervously as he strode past her and moved into the kitchen, his expression stark, furious. This was it and she knew it. Natches wasn't going to let her avoid the past any longer.

"I'd have followed any other agent," he finally growled, pulling out a beer from the fridge and unscrewing the top with a quick jerk of his hand.

Broad, long fingered. Those hands could make a woman think of heaven even as hell moved in around them. And she knew they could make a woman fly, steal her senses and her thoughts with their touch.

Would he ever want to touch her with those hands after Timothy's operation finished here in Somerset?

"I didn't think I'd see you back here," he said, staring back at her with a hint of sensuality, a hint of anger.

"Cranston has a way of convincing agents to do his dirty work for him." She shrugged with a mocking smile. "Come on, Natches, you know how it works. The follow-up was important. He wants that money and he wants to make certain no one else is involved here. That's all."

"Are you investigating my family?" Short and to the point. And here was where things were about to get sticky. Because she couldn't lie to Natches. He had saved her, not just once but twice, and then he had held her and let her fly while she found her sanity once again.

"As far as Cranston is concerned, everyone is suspect," she reminded him dryly. "You're all on my list to question."

"Why did he send you?" He lifted the bottle to his lips and drank, his gaze never leaving hers, the dark green depths dragging her in and leaving her breathless.

She was an agent, fully trained to ignore sexual need or even fear during a mission. But she couldn't ignore Natches. He made her weak, made her need, and he made her fear herself.

"Because it amused him?" She lifted her shoulders as though she didn't know and didn't care. "He was pissed over my attempted resignation and decided to play with me. Cranston's good for games like that."

"Cranston's good at games, period." Natches finished his beer, then tossed the bottle in the trash as Chaya watched him closely now.

He ran a hand over his face before staring back at her.

"Do you have any idea how much I missed you?" he said, his voice soft. "How much I ached for you last year?"

Chaya backed up a step, her movement jerky as she tried to look everywhere but at Natches. She didn't want to talk about last year; she didn't want to talk about five years ago. She wanted this over with. She wanted to run and hide, to bury her head in the sand and pretend this mission and this man could be ignored.

"That wouldn't have been very wise then, and it wouldn't be now," she answered, her throat tightening as she watched him, as she watched his expression flicker with primitive lust.

He wasn't going to just let her go this time, and she knew it. He was going to force her to face everything she didn't want to face, and she didn't know if she could do it.

Chaya shook her head at the look. "Don't, Natches."

She couldn't handle his touch, not now, when this entire mission hinged on betraying him. She wasn't cold-blooded enough; she wasn't the agent Timothy thought she could be.

"Don't." He shook his head wearily before running his fingers through his thick hair and staring back at her with an expression of torment. "How long is it going to lie between us like a double-edged sword, Chaya? When are you going to forgive me?"

No. Oh God, she couldn't deal with this. Her throat tightened and closed with pain and fear as she saw the determination in his eyes.

"I don't want to talk about that." She gave her head a hard jerk. "We can argue over this operation or Cranston or anything else. But not that." She had to fight her tears, her sobs. She had to fight the memories that wanted to return in a rush of agony.

"Damn you." He was across the room before she could avoid him. His hands gripped her arms as he jerked her against him, and she felt the heat of him, felt the weakness that threatened to flood her as she dragged in a hard, gasping breath.

"Five years." He moved, forcing her to back up as she stared up at him in shock. "Five fucking years, Chay. How much longer do we have to suffer for something that neither of us caused?"

"No." Her cry sounded too close to hysteria. "Stop, Natches. I can't discuss this. I won't."

"She was a beautiful little girl. I saw her pictures later." His voice was agonized, tormented.

Chaya heard the pain-filled moan that left her throat. Even when she was being tortured, she hadn't made a sound like that.

"He stole her." He groaned the accusation as she felt his forehead press against hers. "She was safe with your sister, wasn't she, Chay? If he had just left her there."

"Don't do this."

"She looked like you. She had your smile and your hair. Your innocence."

"Stop it!" She screamed the words at him, tearing from his embrace as she pressed her fist against her stomach and swallowed back the sickness rising in her throat. "You didn't know her. You didn't raise her, and you didn't love her. And it's none of your damned business."

Beth. Sweet Beth.

"She was three years old, and your husband had her flown to Iraq. While you were being tortured, she was landing at the airport in a military transport believing she would see her mommy again."

Her heart felt as though it were shattering in her chest now, and she didn't want to collapse from the pain of it. She had lost everything in that damned desert. She didn't want to remember it, and she didn't want to think about it or talk about it. Especially not with the man who had been there to witness it, who had held her back, who had covered her with his own body to protect her while her child died.

"Why?" She turned on him, tears she swore she wouldn't shed escaping now. "Why are you doing this to me? Do you think I don't know what happened?"

Her voice was rasping. She sounded nothing like herself. She sounded like the demented creature she had been the day she lost Beth.

"Army Intelligence didn't know he had your child." His expression looked as agonized as hers felt. "They didn't give the orders to bomb that hotel, did they, Chay? Someone else did. Something fucked up like it always fucks up, and your baby was killed."

She shook her head. Her body shook. Tremors raced through her as she stared at the ceiling. But she didn't see the ceiling; she saw the missiles, ribbons of steam flowing behind them, the hiss of flight, the fiery destruction with impact.

"I know who killed her," she whispered. She had always known.

Her husband. Beth's father. He had killed their child just as surely as he had ordered his wife's torture and death. But she knew even more than that. She knew there had been others, those who knew what her husband had done, and they had struck out. They had killed her child when there had been a chance of saving her.

She lowered her eyes back to Natches and saw the pain, his eyes so dark with so many emotions. Grief and sorrow and need.

"You hold her between us as though it were my fault," he said then, his voice graveled, accusing. "As though I ordered the attack or I arranged her death, Chay."

Chaya swallowed tightly and turned away from him again. She didn't know which way to turn, which way to run. She wanted to run. She wanted to escape the shared memories, and she wanted to escape her own loss.

Natches had been with her when they had learned where Beth and Chaya's husband, Craig, were staying. The suspected headquarters of a terrorist cell. He had raced after her when she went to rescue her child. He had thrown her to the street, held her down, and tried to shield her eyes as missiles slammed into the building.

"I held you when you identified her. I held you then, and I held you through the night. Did you think I wouldn't hold you longer, Chay, if you had given me the chance?"

Five

Craig Cornwell had been a major in Army Intelligence and a traitor. He had been selling secrets to Iraqi terrorists, and when he'd known he would be identified for it, he had arranged for his daughter to be brought to Iraq, believing he could hold her for Chaya's cooperation in helping him escape.

He couldn't have known the cell he was tied to had already been targeted and that their headquarters would be taken out so violently.

Natches stared into her face now, paper white, her golden hazel and brown eyes dark with the memories that tore at him as well. And he wanted to howl out in rage, in agony. Because he felt the need to wipe the horror from her. To tear aside that wall she had placed between them.

"I don't blame you." She tried to tear herself from his hold again. "I never blamed you for her death."

"You blamed me for saving you instead," he snapped, fury rising inside him at the thought of losing her like that. "Is that what you wanted for me, Chaya? For us? To have it all end that way?"

And despite his anger, he could only touch her with tenderness. He lifted his free hand, brushed back the hair that fell over her forehead, and he ached.

"There was no us."

She only infuriated him with that statement, because he knew better. He'd always known better. From the moment he'd torn into that fucking cell and seen her struggling to drag that dead guard's clothes on, her eyes swollen shut, lips bloodied, and courage shining in her face, he'd known there was going to be an "us." It was just a matter of time.

And later, buried in that hole, waiting on extraction, he shouldn't have been attracted to her. She had been in shock. She had been hurt and fighting so valiantly to stay conscious. And in such a short time, she had dug her way inside him. Into a place he hadn't realized existed within the killer he had been shaping himself into.

He'd breathed in her pain when she'd realized her husband had betrayed her to the enemy, that he had betrayed his country and their marriage. And he had soaked in her pain the night she'd lost her child. He'd stroked her trembling body as she'd begged him to hold back the horror of what she had seen. He had taken her, amid both their tears, and the next morning, when he'd awoken, she had been gone.

He released her now, grimacing, feeling his flesh tighten over his muscles, as though something within him stretched dangerously, confined by his own skin and growing impatient.

"I guess there wasn't, because you were gone the next morning," he bit out.

"And you were gone that night when I returned," she snapped back, anger trembling in her voice, anger and something else. A finely threaded emotion that had his gaze sharpening on her pale face. "You didn't come back."

Natches stared back at her, his eyes narrowing. Had she come looking for him when he had believed she was gone?

"I was called in that afternoon for a mission. It was a quick strike; I was flown directly to my drop-off. I returned three days later, and you had left Baghdad," he told her.

He remembered his rage. He had torn apart his quarters with it, and then he had torn apart the hotel room they had shared. The MPs sent after him hadn't fared very well either.

As he stared at her now, he remembered all the reasons why he had gone insane over losing her. The lush lips, the stubborn angle of her chin. The way she knew how to smile, the feel of her coming alive against him. He had known all that before the day she had lost little Beth. He'd known it because he had spent two weeks haunting that damned hospital, teasing a kiss out of her, a laugh. Knowing she was married, knowing she was bound to a traitor.

And she had known. She had known, and like a flower opening to the sun, she had slowly begun opening for him.

She shook her head now, her eyes, that deep golden gaze locked with his, the color shifting, shadowed with so much pain. "Timothy said he checked. He was there that morning I went in to finalize custody of Beth's remains."

She crossed her arms over her breasts as though she were hugging the pain inside herself when all he wanted to do was wipe it from her. "He wanted me to leave immediately to take Beth home, then join DHS. I wanted to talk to you first." She shrugged stiffly. "You were gone. He said he checked to see if you were on a mission and you weren't."

Lying bastard. Natches grunted at that. "DHS ordered the mission. They had a line on Nassar Mallah. I went out after him. When I finished and returned, you were gone."

Chaya bit her lip as she moved across the room and lifted herself heavily onto one of the stools that sat at the counter. She looked tired; she looked hopeless. And that look tore at his heart.

"Sounds like Timothy." Her voice was nearly toneless. "But it didn't matter, not really. I couldn't function then, Natches. Not for either of us."

God he wanted to hold her now. What the hell was it about this woman? She was inside him, and five years of fighting it hadn't managed to push her out of his soul.

Was it love? Hell if it felt like anything he had seen out of Dawg and Rowdy. He didn't feel gentle. He felt like he wanted to devour her from head to toe. He wanted to roll around in oil with her. He wanted to lift her to that counter and spend hours eating the tastiest flesh he'd ever found between a woman's thighs.

She was hurting, enmeshed in memories that he knew had to be ripping her guts to shreds. The sight of it made him crazy. He would do anything, say anything, to ease her pain, but by God she wasn't hiding from him anymore.

She held that past between them like a spiked shield, and he'd had enough of it. Five years. He'd let her torment him through endless, aching nights. He'd suffered every nightmare he knew she suffered, and his pain for her sliced through his soul with each memory.

"You've had long enough to begin functioning then." He had to force himself to stand back from her, to not touch her.

She looked lost, lost and lonely, almost as broken as she had looked the day they told her her husband was the traitor who revealed her to the terrorists who had kidnapped her.

He watched as her shoulders straightened then, her chin lifted. He didn't know what the hell she had in her mind now, but he knew exactly what she intended to do, and he'd be damned if he would let her.

She was not walking out on him again. Not like this. This was the closest he'd managed to get to her since the night her daughter had died. And then, it had been comfort, not need, not hunger. She had needed someone to hold on to. Someone to take her away from reality while she found a way to handle the coming grief.

He'd given her that. He wasn't willing to be that someone to her again though. He wasn't a warm body to hold back the pain, and damn her to hell, he was sick and damned tired of being relegated to her past. A part of a memory she desperately wanted to forget.

"I would have divorced him for one night with you." And all the need, the hunger, the driving, aching desperation he felt himself was echoed in her voice.

Her declaration surprised him though. And he could tell by the tone of her voice that it filled her with guilt.

She turned to him then, her gaze haunted. "Using the excuse that our marriage had been lost before then doesn't help. I took vows, and I meant them. But I was going to leave him, even before I knew he had betrayed me. I was going to leave him, Natches, and I made that decision because of you."

He could feel the "but" coming, and he knew it was going to piss him off. He could feel it in the tension gathering in the air around them.

"He was a bastard," he snarled before she could say anything more. "You knew it, even if you didn't have proof of it."

He had known it. Any man who allowed his wife to face danger alone deserved to lose her to another man. Women were precious. Women who loved, who honored their vows, were more precious than the finest gems. And Chaya would have honored those vows until the ink dried on the divorce papers. He knew it. And sometimes he wondered if he hadn't hated that part of her.

"That doesn't excuse it," she said, staring at him from where she sat, her expression somber, her gaze flickering with guilt. "I wanted your kiss, Natches. I wanted you; I wanted your touch and your voice whispering all those naughty little secrets you used to whisper to me when I was in the hospital. I wanted it. I was married, and I ached for it. And I paid for it."

It took a moment, one long, disbelieving moment, for that comment to soak into his head and light the spark of his normally rational temper.

"Son of a bitch." He stared back at her in complete amazement. "I'll be a son of a bitch. You've let that bastard steal your soul even from the fucking grave." His voice rose as he spoke. "Is that how you're blaming yourself now, Chay? That Beth was taken from you because you wanted me?"

Anger poured from him as he watched her flinch, saw the truth in her eyes. Stubborn pride lined every curve of her body. She actually believed what she was saying. Believed every word of it.

"I don't expect you to understand," she whispered, her voice hoarse.

"I understand this, by God. If you were my wife, Chaya—my woman—you'd never, fucking never, be on a mission without me. You'd never face danger alone, and you'd never know a night that I wasn't in your damned bed. How long had that bastard been out of your bed?"

"That's not the point." Her voice trembled. He could see the fear in her eyes now, a fear that made no damned sense because she had to know he would never, never harm her. But damn her to hell, he was so furious with her that he wanted to slam his fist into a wall to relieve the rage burning inside him.

"The fact that he was fucking every trainee he could get his hands on didn't matter either, I guess," he sneered, furious, consumed by that fury as he realized the ways she had made herself pay for her daughter's death. And her hunger for him. "The fact that he managed to get your baby on a plane to Iraq without your knowledge because he was fucking your sister before the two of you left didn't matter either, did it?"

Her face only tightened further. Her eyes raged though. He saw her eyes; he saw the banked fury, the agony that she tried to dim, tried to hide.

"Did it matter, Chaya?" He strode to her, his fist slamming into the top of the bar as she flinched from the sound of his voice and the crack of his flesh against the Formica. Hell, he cracked it again, and he didn't even give a damn. "Answer me, damn you!"

"That was no excuse," she screamed back, shuddering from head to toe, everything he needed to hear, everything he wanted to know, in her voice now. She wanted. Just as he did, she ached and she hungered for what was between them, and she was too damned scared to take it. "That didn't give me the right—"

"No, it gave *me* the right."

Before he could stop himself, and God knew he didn't want to stop himself, he jerked her into his arms and slammed his lips down on hers.

He wanted to be gentle. She deserved it. She deserved sweet, liquid kisses. She deserved gentleness and warmth, and all he had was hunger, lust, and heat.

All he had was the need to taste the passion without the grief. The woman without the pain of loss.

And he had her. He felt the first resistance, shock and surprise. Her hands pressed against his shoulders, then her fingers curled. A second later, she made that whispery, whimpering little sound of surrender that he had only ever heard from her lips.

They parted beneath his kiss, opened to the stroke of his tongue, and a second later, a firestorm of need rocked through his body.

She kissed like a wanton, like a woman whose need for pleasure had grown to the same torturous depths his own had grown to. Satin-soft lips slanted beneath his; her tongue met his, licked and consumed and had him strung as tight as a banjo string within seconds.

It wasn't enough. The kiss was only the tip of the iceberg. He needed so much more from her. He needed more than he had known in that fucking desert, more than he had fantasized of over the years. He needed her rocking in his arms, lifting to his thrusts.

He groaned into the kiss, lifted her closer, felt the soft swell of her stomach cushioning the hard-on raging beneath his jeans, and knew he couldn't live without tasting more of her.

She was like a drug in his system, impossible to get rid of. And there were times he wondered if he didn't embrace this particular addiction. Her lips moving beneath his, her moans filling his head.

He fought back a growl as she tore her lips from his. He needed more.

"I need more of you." Her lips were on his neck, biting, sucking, kissing, as her hands lowered to his belt. "I need to taste you, Natches. Taste you all over."

"Ah, hell." Her fingers were lowering the zipper, parting the material, and shoving it aside to release the fully engorged, throbbing length of his cock.

As he watched, she went to her knees. How many times had he dreamed of this? Dreamed of her taking him like this.

"Damn you." He flinched in agonizing pleasure as her lips parted and took him.

She was too hungry for preliminaries, and that only made him hotter. The head of his cock disappeared into her eager little mouth and immediately set flame to wildfire.

It flashed through his body, drew his balls tight, then had them knotting with ecstasy as her nimble little fingers began to caress and play with them.

And she sucked. She sucked his cock into her mouth, nearly to her throat, and drew on it, milked it until he was growling with pleasure. Her free hand wrapped around the shaft, stroked, tightened on it, and drove him crazy.

His hands were in her hair, his hips moving, fucking her mouth, and he loved it.

"Is this how you used that little toy, Chay?" The thought of that damned dildo infuriated him. "Did you think of this, baby? Of me inside your mouth, fucking those sweet lips?"

He had been dying to do just that, and she had filled her mouth with something else? Damn her. Not again. Never again.

She moaned around his cock head, and he nearly came from the pleasure of it. Sensation rippled through the shaft, into his balls, and up his spine. Holding on wasn't going to happen for long. He could feel the cum boiling in his balls, knew he wasn't going to be able to hold back.

"Damn you. Suck it, baby. Show me how you sucked that damned toy and thought of me."

His teeth clenched as she moaned again, her mouth tightening, her tongue stroking and licking and drawing him so damned tight he felt as though he were going to break.

He was going to come. Ah, hell. Close. So damned close.

A second later he jerked back, fury pulsing, raging through him. Chaya fell back with a cry as he pushed her to the side and jerked the gun from the top of the couch where he had placed it and cursed furiously.

The door had crashed open, Dawg and Rowdy rolling into the apartment like pure vengeance itself as Natches stared back at them in unholy fury.

"What the fuck are you two doing?" He barely had time to pull his finger back from the trigger as the men rose from the floor, their own weapons lowering.

Sometimes some information just took a minute to process. His head was still filled with the sweet scent and the heated feel of Chaya's mouth.

And rather than searching for her own weapon, what the hell was she doing? Laughing. He glanced at her in disbelief. She lay on the carpet behind him, their bodies sheltered by the couch, which faced the door, and she laughed.

Her lips were red, her face flushed, and she was laughing with such damned amusement it made his back teeth clench.

And pure fury was burning in his brain, demanding he take action now. That he kick them out of his apartment with his foot up their asses for daring, even daring, to interrupt his pleasure.

The bastards were shadowing him.

There was no other explanation for their presence or the lock that had been torn free of the door. He only barely remembered hearing and ignoring their knock. He hadn't cared enough to answer the damned door because his head had been ready to explode with ecstasy.

He slowly fixed his pants and tightened his belt. He laid the gun on the counter cautiously, watching as Chaya stared at him in something akin to wary surprise as she climbed to her feet, her eyes still bright with her laughter. He was glad someone was amused.

"Natches." She laid her hand on his arm, her voice shaking as she obviously fought back more of those feminine, joyous giggles. "It's just Dawg and Rowdy."

She was staring at him now in rather the same way he would eye a rabid animal. And she had good cause to watch him just that carefully.

He turned back to his cousins, her hand still on him, and he was loath to break that contact. It was the only reason he wasn't charging them now. The only reason any of them were still standing rather than busting the walls of his apartment with their heads.

"You broke my door," he said carefully, staring at the two men as they watched him just as carefully.

Dawg sniffed, blushed to the roots of his black hair, cleared his throat, then glanced at the door and the lock that had ripped from the wall. "Yeah. Well. We were just coming up for a beer. Thought you could use some company and thought we heard fighting. Right, Rowdy?" He nudged Rowdy.

Dawg was obviously lying through his teeth, and Natches knew it. He turned to Rowdy then, forcing his fingers not to curl into fists as Chaya kept her hold on his arm.

Her grip had actually tightened in response to the flexing of the muscles beneath her hand.

"Right, Rowdy?" Dawg hissed again. Under other circumstances it might have been comical. Dawg was bigger, heavier, and his fist was a damned sight harder than Natches's. Sometimes. But it was obvious he didn't want to return to his wife bruised.

Natches turned to Rowdy.

And Rowdy grinned, because he knew. Natches saw in his eyes the knowledge that Chaya held him back, that Chaya could always hold him back.

"Nah, we were freezing our butts off outside because we thought Agent Dane might have a little more up her sleeve than a few questions." Rowdy's grin was cocky, which only pissed Natches off further.

Dawg winced. "Dumb ass," he muttered to Rowdy.

"Thanks for the vote of confidence, guys," Chaya laughed, and Natches felt her move.

"If you try leaving this apartment, then I'm kicking their asses the minute you walk out the door," he warned her.

She paused, and when he glanced at her, he could see the caution in her eyes again. "There are two of them, Natches."

"And I have pure mad on my side. Want to take bets who will win?" He made damned sure she saw nothing but determination in his gaze.

"Looks like you're going to have to head to the *Dreams* tonight anyway." Dawg cleared his throat, and it might have placated Natches, seeing a hint of nerves in his cousin, if the amusement hadn't been so bright in his green eyes. Dawg was clearly enjoying the fact that he had interrupted something here.

"I need to get back to my hotel." Chaya stepped back, and Natches let her.

He was careful to keep his expression bland as he glanced at her. She might try to run, but she wasn't going far. Hell, she was going to finish what she started before the damned interruption, and he was going to make sure of it.

"We'll, umm, fix the door." Dawg smiled, clearly enjoying the fact that, for the moment, Natches was leashed. "You go ahead and take Miss Dane back to her hotel, Natch. We'll have that beer at the boat."

"If I see you on my boat tonight, I'm going to shoot you, Dawg," Natches warned him, and he was afraid he just might be serious. "You can try the beer tomorrow afternoon, not a moment before."

Natches moved too fast for Chaya to avoid him this time, his fingers curling around her upper arm before pulling her with him to the door. "And make sure you nail the door tight. Some bastard walks in and steals my beer, and I'll kill you for sure."

"Natches, I'm not going to that damned boat," Chaya protested as they neared the door. "I have a job to do. You're taking me back to my hotel. Period."

"Sure I am," he agreed.

She almost paused, would have if he hadn't tugged her after him. "You are?"

Had he agreed too easily? He almost smirked.

"Sure I am. Sometime. I'm sure you'll need more clothes in a few days." He hardened his voice, firmed his grip, and ignored her curse.

She could bitch until hell froze over, but they weren't finished. Talking, fucking, he'd take either one he could get, or both, but tonight, he wasn't letting her go.

Dawg rubbed at the back of his neck as he heard Natches's jeep drive off, and he turned to Rowdy slowly. His cousin had a thoughtful expression on his face.

Rowdy was a thinker. He always had been. He rarely jumped into anything impulsively, unlike his two cousins. He always weighed the evidence, the pros and the cons, and sometimes he could be damned scary in his predictions.

"You could have backed me there, cuz," he finally sighed when Rowdy stayed silent.

When his cousin turned to him, it was with a smirk that almost had Dawg bursting out in laughter.

"Why bother?" Rowdy grinned. "She has a chain around his neck thicker than a junkyard dog's. He wasn't about to jump into a fight. That boy doesn't want a bruised body right now either, Dawg. We both know that one well."

Damned if they didn't.

Dawg remembered a time when a good fight and a good drunk was almost as good as sex. Now, since Crista, a fight, with the bruises, busted ribs, and/or swollen lips, was something he avoided at all costs. He liked the feel of Crista's hands on his body, demanding and wild as she moved against him. The thought of losing so much as an ounce of that pleasure to pain was intolerable.

Evidently, Natches was already considering that fact. Dawg chuckled at that thought as he moved to help Rowdy with the door.

"She's still not pretty," he told his cousin. "But at least I didn't smell the smoke."

Rowdy grunted. "Smoke wouldn't have mattered to Natches, Dawg," he pointed out.

And that was the damned truth. Even last year, when she was lighting up every time Natches came around her, their cousin hadn't been able to stay away.

"She's still not pretty," he said again.

"What's your problem with her looks?" Rowdy paused as they propped the door up and Dawg went in search of a hammer and nails. "He won't have to use a bag for her head. Hell, Dawg, I don't care what she looks like. Natches isn't ice anymore. He was scaring the shit out of me with that cold attitude of his. We're not far from losing him forever, if you haven't noticed."

And Dawg had noticed. Natches had been drawing further and further away over the years. He pulled the hammer and nails from the kitchen drawer and moved back to the door.

Her looks shouldn't bother him, and Dawg knew it. Crista had just torn into his butt the night before over a similar comment.

"It's not just her looks," he finally admitted.

"Then what is it?"

"It's her eyes. Look at her eyes, man. They're dead inside. That woman isn't even alive, and you can see it in her face. Her expression and her eyes. She'll destroy Natches."

Rowdy was quiet for long moments then. The sounds of the hammer striking wood and the four-inch nails sinking into the frame were the only comment Dawg received.

Finally, the door was secure, and Rowdy was just staring at it.

"She's not dead inside," he finally said, his voice soft.

"Same as." Dawg shrugged. "You didn't work with her last year. She's cold inside, man. She can get nervous as hell, she can get scared, and she did a fine laugh tonight, but there ain't no love in her for anyone."

Rowdy shook his head at that. "There's too much emotion." He looked at Dawg then. "Just like Natches. And she's determined to hide it. You can't see past that need we both have to keep protecting our little cousin, Dawg. Sometimes I think we forget he's all grown-up now."

"And just as alone as he ever was," Dawg growled.

Rowdy shook his head. "Not anymore."

Six

He didn't take her back to the hotel, just as he'd told Chaya he wouldn't. She didn't remember Natches being *this* damned stubborn. Not that he couldn't give the proverbial mule a run for its money. But practically kidnapping her wasn't something he had done before.

"Why bring me here, Natches?" she asked him as they stepped into the comfortable living area of the boat, and she stared around in interest.

"Because we're not finished." He closed the door, locked it, and reset the security system.

She felt her heart race at the sound of the muted little beep from the security console. Somehow the boat seemed much more intimate than the apartment had. It wasn't just that the space was less open and smaller; it was as though a part of Natches himself was infused within the interior.

Dark browns and desert tones made up the color scheme of the furniture. The carpet was a creamy white. Small dark maroon pillows rested at the arms of the couch, and a rug of the same color was laid at the door. Heavy desert brown shades covered the windows, and the splash of golden light that fell from the table lamps softened the room.

The kitchen was separated by a combination table and bar. Laminate flooring stretched to the curved metal staircase at the far end of the kitchen and beyond, to what Chaya assumed were the bedrooms.

She turned back to Natches when he didn't explain further, and watched him warily. He reminded her of a caged beast straining against his restraints. It was there in the wild glitter of his dark green eyes, in the taut planes and angles of his face.

"Why the hell did Cranston have to send you here?" he finally asked, the guttural tone of his voice causing her to flinch.

"That was my question as well." She shrugged, watching him carefully as he strode past her to the refrigerator in the kitchen. "His answer was that I was his best bet. He didn't tell me what the bet was though."

"Driving me bat-shit crazy?" he asked as he twisted the cap off a beer and tipped it to his lips.

Watching him drink from the longneck bottle was sexier than it should have been.

"Probably." She finally admitted there was a chance that that was exactly why Timothy had sent her rather than another agent. "He wasn't pleased with you or Dawg last year. And he does enjoy his petty little revenge games."

Actually, he normally had a solid reason for those games, they were just irritating as hell.

But the real conversation she and Natches were having was beneath the actual words, thrumming with tension.

Chaya couldn't forget. Anytime she was near Natches, every time she was within touching distance, the memories and the pain returned. And the need. The same need that had his erection buried between her lips earlier. The need to touch and be touched was stronger than the pain.

It had been five years. Losing Beth had nearly driven her crazy, but the years had helped her to sew closed the ragged wound that loss had left. She still cried sometimes; she still ached most of the time. But she had learned to go on. Beth was gone; there was no way to bring her back.

But Chaya had always known that Natches was still alive. And the guilt she felt at the thought of going to him had always held her back.

While Natches had been teasing her in that hospital, seducing her, making her laugh, her daughter had been in danger. While she had made plans for a future that didn't include her traitorous husband, her daughter had perhaps been crying for her mother. And while she had been laughing with Natches, someone had been planning to bomb the building Craig had taken their child to.

Hunger, guilt, anger, and need vied inside her now just as they had for the past five years. They twisted inside her, making it impossible to see past what she had lost long enough to decide what she was running away from. And now she had no choice but to face it.

Whoever that faceless organization was that had managed to authenticate a strike code on that hotel in Iraq, it had to be stopped. It was too dangerous, its influence becoming too corrupt. There were moles in Army Intelligence, and Cranston had traced them to the op here.

"I'm going to kill Cranston when this is over." Natches set the beer bottle down on the bar, his heavy-lidded gaze moving over her again.

That look made her sizzle. Chaya could feel all the nerve endings in her body coming alive. That look could make women across the world weak in the knees. He could bottle it and make billions.

"Good luck." She shoved her hands in the pockets of her jeans to keep them from shaking. To keep herself from shaking.

"Take your clothes off."

Chaya blinked back at him, certain she hadn't heard what she knew she had heard.

"Do you think it's just that easy?" She shook her head and wished it was. "Sorry, Natches, I'm not here to be your toy. I'm here to do a job."

"So you can do both now." He grabbed his beer and finished it before tossing it in the trash can in the corner. "You can be Agent Greta Dane during the day and my toy at night. I promise you won't be in the least neglected, Chaya."

Oh, she just bet she wouldn't be. And when the time came that Timothy decided to let them all in on the little game he was playing, what then? Would she be cast aside as all his other playthings had been?

"You have plenty of other toys, Natches; you don't need me." She wanted to sound flippant, uncaring, but she could feel the ache building inside her.

Five years. It had been five years since he had taken her. She had been so filled with pain then that she hadn't been able to appreciate the pleasure that had torn through her.

But she remembered it. She remembered his tears mixing with hers as he kissed her, just as she remembered how easily he had coaxed more than one explosive orgasm from her.

She watched him uneasily. He wasn't just going to take no for an answer, and she didn't know if she had the strength to hold back if he touched her again.

And he was going to touch her. She pulled her hands slowly from her jeans pockets as he advanced on her, his expression predatory.

"Natches." She whispered his name in warning.

"There's the door; run, little rabbit," he suggested, his voice wicked as he nodded to the door that led to escape. "Go ahead. Or do you have the courage to actually take me on without excuses?"

Her fingers curled against her palm as he challenged her. The chance to touch him again, to feel whatever it was she had felt that night that she hadn't been able to forget. She hadn't been able to touch another man after that.

"That so isn't going to work," she retorted and wished her voice sounded stronger, wished it had more conviction.

She could feel herself preparing for him despite the protest. Her breasts were sensitive and swollen, the nipples throbbing. And between her thighs, she could feel herself dampening, her clit engorging.

She wanted. She ached. She had been aching this past week with a strength that had forced her to masturbate several times. And it hadn't been enough. It was never enough when she thought of Natches.

"You want me." He was too close now, standing in front of her, forcing her to look up at him.

He was so wicked. A rogue. She had called him that once, and he had laughed and winked as he agreed with her.

"Does just wanting make it all right?" she whispered, catching his wrists as his hands settled on her hips. "Wanting isn't always enough, Natches."

"It'll be enough for tonight." There was no plea in his words, just pure demand. "I'm not asking for forever, Chaya. I wouldn't dare."

And before she could question the angry tone of those last words, he was kissing her. His lips covered hers, his tongue pushed between them, and he was taking what he wanted. There was no question of giving it to him, because he didn't ask for a damned thing.

This wasn't the teasing seducer she had known five years before. This was a conqueror. This was a man who refused to ask. He knew what he wanted, and God help her, he seemed to know exactly what she needed, too.

Chaya felt the world tilt around her; she could have sworn the ground shook. Whatever it was, it was Natches holding her, his lips on hers, his muttered, hungry moan vibrating against her lips as his mouth slanted across them and his tongue tempted and teased hers into an excited, erotic duel.

It was fire and lightning, this kiss. It was being awakened from a lifetime of nightmares and finally given light. It was like being reborn.

Chaya heard herself cry out, felt her arms latching around his neck, her body arching to him, needing more. More contact. More touch. Oh God, she couldn't get enough of him, and the need would destroy her. This need rocked her to her very core, to the center of that lonely, almost broken, spirit that had sent her running before. Because she couldn't face losing anyone else. She couldn't face losing Natches, too.

She trembled as she felt his hands caressing her, running along her back, pushing beneath her top and touching bare flesh. He moved against her, pressing his thigh between hers, rocking her against him.

She felt the delicate, sensitive flesh between her thighs flame. Wicked, greedy wildfire swept through her, and nothing mattered but more. More of his kiss. If she didn't get more of his kiss, she would lose her mind from the need. More of his touch. She wanted to be naked in his arms. Naked and shuddering and surrounded by Natches. Surrounding him. Burning as she only burned in her dreams.

"There, Chay." He pulled her closer, one hand on her butt, forcing her to ride the hard muscle of his thigh as she ground herself against him. "See how good it is, baby? Remember how hot it is?"

Oh yes, she remembered. She remembered begging him for more, screaming for more. The memories were hazy because the pain had been overwhelming that night. But she remembered enough to know why she had ached in the darkness of the night after she'd left Iraq. She remembered enough to know that, once he took her, she was never going to be the same again.

No more sleepwalking. She had existed the past five years, forcing herself through each day, refusing to acknowledge that a part of her, that hidden, feminine core of her, was right here. In Natches's arms.

"Natches, let me breathe. Let me think," she gasped as his lips slid from hers—lazy, confident—and nibbled at her jawline. Her nerve endings rose up in a crescendo of pleasure.

"No thinking allowed." The rasp of his day-old beard sent shards of the most incredible pleasure washing through her body. "Now, let's get these damned clothes off."

It was sexy. It was erotic. It was the most gentle act of sexual intensity that she could have imagined. He pulled her arms from around his neck, then, staring down at her, his forest green eyes darkening to moss, his palms touching her flesh along the way, he slid her blazer from her shoulders and over her arms.

Chaya stared up at him, unable to break the contact, the connection. He had done that before, she remembered. Stared at her, watched her eyes as he undressed her.

"This isn't a good idea." She tried to protest, but it sounded more like an invitation. It was an invitation. Everyone knew Natches did anything anyone else considered a bad idea. And the more erotic, the more wicked, that bad idea was, the faster he was there.

"Who needs good ideas? Come here, baby. Let me see those pretty breasts just one more time. Lift your arms for me." He pulled the hem of her shirt up and over her head, off her arms. It dropped to the floor as a hungry growl left his lips and long, thick lashes feathered over his eyes.

When he looked at her like that, she melted. Then she felt his hands at the belt of her jeans.

She was naked from the waist up, or practically naked, because the bra she wore didn't hide much from view.

"Natches, I don't think I can stand through this."

And she didn't. Her knees were weakening. She could feel her legs turning to mush, right along with her objections. This was Natches. Wicked, erotic Natches. His kisses were a flame that burned to the icy core of her. His touch was an inferno, warming her from the inside out.

And she needed to be warm. Just for a little while. She needed to be warmed by him, just one more time.

As his lips moved over her neck, her arms found strength. As his hands pushed beneath the waist of her jeans, she struggled against him, pushing at his arms.

"Easy, Chay."

"Not easy." She nipped at his neck, clearly surprising him as she tugged at his T-shirt. She wanted him bare as well. She wanted to feel him against her, bare flesh to bare flesh. She needed it.

He whipped the shirt from his body and tossed it aside as her hands went to his belt. Shaking, uncertain, her fingers pulled and tugged at it.

"There you go, Chay. Get naughty for me."

She tore at the metal button, then eased the zipper over the hard, throbbing length of his cock. She moved it down slowly, working it over the stiff ridge as a hard growl passed his lips.

He wanted her naughty? She wasn't naughty; she was starving for him. Five years of pent-up hunger blazed through her, erupting from a well of need that she'd had no idea existed within her.

Those distant memories from five years before didn't compare to this. The feel of his body, so large and broad, hard and muscular, bending to her, almost protectively. His lips on her neck, teeth rasping. His hands working her jeans over her hips as hunger seemed to permeate the air.

Chaya could feel perspiration gathering on her body, the heat building inside them, flowing around them, as she pushed at his jeans, frantic to get to the heated flesh of his cock.

"There you go, sweetheart; burn for me," he growled as his hands slid around to her rear, clenched, then lifted.

He raised her along his body, dragging her from her goal as a protesting cry fell from her lips. A second later, she felt the cool top of the low counter, heard a chair falling to the floor as he kicked it out of the way, and then Natches was kissing her again.

She couldn't get enough of his kisses, or his touches. She couldn't kiss back enough, couldn't touch enough. She was consumed, inside and out, by a need so fiery she didn't have a hope of controlling it.

"Here, get these off." He pulled away from her, despite her attempts to draw him back and the mewling sound that fell from her lips.

His hair was tangled, mussed from her fingers and framing his roguish face. Dark eroticism sharpened his features, his eyes. His bare chest was sheened with sweat, the hair prickling her fingers as she ran her hands down it.

She ached for him now. Ached with a power that had her arching as she fought to breathe, as he pulled the boots from her feet and tugged her jeans down her legs.

She was naked but for the bra and panties. Scraps of material that did nothing to shield her from his eyes. And he was looking. His gaze went over her slowly as his hands smoothed up her legs, her inner thighs, parting them as he centered on the wet core of her body.

"You still shave?" He ran the backs of his fingers over the damp cotton that shielded the swollen folds of her sex.

Chaya swallowed tightly. "Wax."

Pleasure and anticipation tightened his features, and the look caused her womb to clench in response. He was aroused, dangerously aroused. She could see it in his face, feel it in his body.

"Five years." His voice was guttural. "I've dreamed about that one night, Chay, for five fucking years. Tormented by it. Driven fucking crazy by it."

Her lips parted at the intensity behind the words. To be wanted like that. She had never been wanted so desperately by a man as Natches wanted her. And only once—five years before—had she felt this kind of desire for a man.

Five years. Too long. Too many memories, too many dreams and fantasies to fuel this hunger.

"I—I ached. Every day." The words came from her, unbidden, the strain from the attempt to hold them back causing a sob to pass her throat. "Natches—you're going to destroy me."

His fingers hooked in the band of her panties, and he drew them slowly over her hips with the soft command "Lift."

She arched her hips, watching his eyes, his face, watching the hunger grow in him and feeling it grow in her.

He dropped the scrap of material to the floor, a grimace contorting his features as he forced his gaze from the glistening flesh between her thighs and stared back at her.

Chaya felt caught, trapped, and it terrified her. The power this man held over her. How was she supposed to fight this? Control this?

"Now for this." His fingers moved to the front clasp of her bra.

Chaya's breath caught in her throat as he flicked the tiny clasp open, then peeled the cups back from her breasts and pushed the straps over her shoulders. Her fingers dug into the countertop as she leaned back at the urging of his hands against her shoulders.

"So pretty." His hands framed the swollen mounds, his fingers dark against her lighter flesh as he lifted them, caressed them.

Calloused fingertips stroked over the hardened nipples. Her womb convulsed, and she felt the damp warmth of her juices spilling from her.

"Natches." She arched to him, distant memories of him bending to her, taking her nipple in his mouth, flashing through her mind a second before his actions followed her memories.

And the reality was better. She arched and cried out at the feel of his mouth, hot and hungry, devouring her nipple. His tongue lashed at it, rasped over it as he suckled, sending exquisite sparks of pure sensation exploding through her system.

"Oh God, Natches." Her head fell back as she felt her arms weakening.

As though he knew, sensed her inability to hold herself up to him, one arm curved around her back, tightened, and allowed her hands to lift from the counter as he lowered her, her arms curling around his shoulders, her nails digging into his flesh.

His mouth was so hot, his tongue like a brand burning across her nipple. First one, then the other. He sucked at the hard points greedily as she became lost in a vortex of pleasure she knew she could never escape.

"Ah, yes, that's my Chay." He ran his tongue in the valley between her breasts.

She shivered at the caress, her thighs tightening on his, her hips undulating at the subtle pressure of his cock head against the slick folds of her sex.

She needed him there. She needed him to take her. Hard. Fast. Deep.

"I missed this," he crooned as his lips began to kiss a path down her stomach. "Missed touching you, feeling you against me."

Her back arched as a tremulous cry tore from her.

"Do you remember it, Chay? So hot it burned us alive? So much pleasure we thought we were dying."

She remembered it. She remembered all of it. Like an inferno blast that she had convinced herself was no more than her need to escape her pain. It had been so much more though. Because it was hotter this time, the ache deeper. It was Natches. His touch was like an addiction, and the need only grew the longer the separation. There was no going cold turkey. No escaping the effect of it.

"Ahh, so sweet." His tongue licked over the top of the mound between her thighs. So close to her clit. So close she could feel the heat of it, anticipate the wild ecstasy it could bring her.

When it came, it shattered her. Because it was even brighter, hotter, than she remembered, the pleasure swirled through her fear and dissipated it. The need for control evaporated. She was lost in the pleasure, and there was no other place to be. No other place she ever wanted to be.

His tongue slid around her clit, and he groaned against it.

"So sweet, Chay. You taste like summer."

Her hands speared into his hair, the thick, silken strands twining around her fingers as she fought to pull him back to her.

And he chuckled against her flesh, a dark, greedy sound. His tongue licked slow and easy through the narrow slit so rich with awakened sensations. Nerve endings came fully alert, too close to the surface of her skin, reveling in his touch again.

She called out his name, her voice hoarse with need, begging him to take her. His hands pushed her thighs farther apart, his head dipped, and his tongue filled her. Ecstasy nearly shattered inside her. So close. She was so close.

"Please." She moaned, feeling her release, so close, almost there. Oh God, she needed to come. She needed that wild explosion tearing through her, the release she had only known one other time, had only known with Natches.

"Are you mine, Chaya?" His voice was a dark, seductive croon, pulling her in as he licked again, drawing her taste to him, stroking her into an abyss of sensation and pleasure.

She would give him anything for this. Be anything he wanted as long as she had this.

"Yours." She was barely aware of the word tearing from her lips. "Always yours, Natches. Oh God, I've always been yours."

He paused, a short moment of stillness that her breath caught, then his lips surrounded her clit, drew it into the suckling heat of his mouth, to the licking tip of his tongue, and he pushed her over that edge.

She felt the explosion rip through her, drawing her up, arching her against him as a throttled scream left her lips and she dissolved into him.

She melted. For a moment, just for a moment, she felt herself sinking into the very pores of his flesh, and understood that this was where she belonged. This was the addiction that was Natches. To belong to him so deeply that she was a part of him.

And it lasted for an endless moment. Then he was lifting his head, pushing her legs apart, and before the final wave of release washed through her, he began working the hard length of his erection inside her.

"Look at me, damn you."

Chaya's eyes jerked open at the command. Dazed, almost unfocused, she stared up at the dark vision of every woman's sexual fantasy come to life.

Black hair framing savage features, green eyes almost glowing in his sun-darkened face, nostrils flared in desperate hunger as his lips drew back from his teeth.

Raw erotic pleasure tore through her at the sight. This man, this sexual intensity, centered on her. On plain Chaya Dane, and God only knew Natches was more man than she had any hope of controlling.

And there was no need to control him now. Pleasure swamped control. There was no thought of control, only sensation—the feel of him working his cock inside her, the thick crest parting tender tissue as perspiration began to form on his shoulders and chest and run in small rivulets along the center of his body.

"Look at me, Chay." His voice was deep, hoarse. "Let me see you, baby. Let me see if I'm making you feel good. Does it feel good, Chay?"

Feel good? He was destroying her with pleasure. Her lips parted to tell him, but all she could do was moan his name and stare back at him. And feel him. Feel him stretching her, burning her. She was locked in a grip of ecstasy—it thrummed through her veins, heated her blood and tormented her nerve endings.

"Look at me, Chay." His voice hardened when she would have closed her eyes.

Forcing them open, she stared back at him. His jaw was clenched, sweat dripped along his forehead and down his face. His shoulders bunched, and she felt his thighs tighten as he pulled his erection back, then worked it into her farther, deeper, taking her until she was trying not to scream, until she was burning around him, and with a strangled groan, he buried himself full length inside her.

Hard hands clenched on her hips as he penetrated her fully, and some dark emotion in his eyes flared.

"Has there been anyone else?" She watched him speak, heard the words and tried to make sense of them.

"What?"

"Other men. Has another man taken what's mine, damn it?" Pure male dominance flashed in his expression, in his eyes.

Another man? She shook her head; she couldn't bear another man's touch. Didn't want it. Never, ever thought of it.

She shook her head again. "No one. No one but you . . ." She wanted to tell him she only wanted him, only needed him, but as the words tried to slip past her lips, he moved.

As though the admission broke the last of his own control, he was moving inside her, plunging, fucking her with fast, furious strokes that threw her almost instantly into orgasm.

It was like that with Natches. So wild there was no hope of holding on. So hot there wasn't a chance of not burning alive.

She arched and cried out his name. Her eyes closed, her neck lifted, and she felt him tighten, heard his hoarse exclamation before she felt him spill inside her. Heated, fierce jets of semen spurted into the quaking depths of her vagina and pushed her into another, destructive release, and to an edge of fear. Just the tiniest spark of concern because she knew there was something she should have remembered, something she should fear in this pleasure. A pleasure that left her sated, filled, and somehow, she knew, irrevocably bound to Natches in a way she never had been before.

Seven

Natches wasn't certain what brought him awake just after daybreak. The sun wasn't shining through the windows yet, and there was a light chill to the air.

At the end of October, it could get cold on the water. His bed was warm though, and he was drowsy and seeking the touch of Chaya's body when it hit him.

She wasn't in the bed.

He listened carefully and couldn't hear her moving on the houseboat or in the shower. Irritation washed through him instantly, as well as a healthy dose of anger.

He sat up in the bed, his eyes narrowed against the gloom that filled the large bedroom as he glanced at the clock.

It was barely seven, too damned early to be up and moving around unless he had actually intended to be at the garage that day. Which he hadn't. He'd intended to spend the day happily rolling around the bed with Chaya.

As he moved to flip the blanket back, he saw the paper on her pillow and picked it up before reading it silently.

Am meeting Sheriff Mayes this morning. I have work to do.
Will call you this evening.

She would call him this evening?

He crumpled the note slowly in his hand, and for just a second, only a second, a grim sort of humor touched his mind. How many times had he either written or stated that sentiment, never to return?

Oh, if she thought for a single damned minute she was getting away that easily, then he'd just have to show her different. He'd let her go twice. *Third time's a charm, sweetheart,* he thought furiously. This time, she was stuck, and he'd make certain she understood that. Clear to her soul. No matter what it took.

Stomping from the bed, he headed for the shower. If he knew Zeke Mayes, and he did, then sweet little Chaya's day wasn't going to begin until after ten. Zeke had his rounds to make, his paperwork to do, and then he headed to the diner for breakfast around nine thirty or ten. Plenty of time for Natches to get ready and reach Chaya's hotel. He'd drag her back to the houseboat and show her exactly how this relationship was going to work from here on out.

He paused as he stood beneath the shower spray. Relationship. Hell, he'd never had a relationship. Until now. Until Chaya. He'd never kept a woman around long, never wanted to, but he was starting to suspect he wanted to keep Chaya forever.

He finished his shower, dressed, and was downstairs in the living room pulling on his boots when a fist landed in imperative demand against the door.

His head jerked up, then he lowered and shook it in resignation. He knew that knock.

Pushing to his feet, he stalked to the door, pulled the shade back, and glared at Dawg as he slid the door open.

"Isn't Crista draggin' your ass to the lumber store?" he smirked. Dawg's wife kept him on a very short leash. Dry cleaned and pressed clothes that looked presentable rather than day-old and holey. A decent haircut. But the scowl on his older cousin's face hadn't changed by much.

"Crista's not feeling well this morning." Dawg shrugged as he stepped into the boat. "Where are you headed off to this early? I thought you took Fridays off from the garage now."

Natches watched curiously as Dawg prowled the living room and the kitchen.

"When did you start checking up on me?" Natches leaned against the wall and crossed his arms over his chest as he watched Dawg.

"When you came back from Iraq and started actin' brick dumb." Dawg grunted as he turned to face him. "You know, I always wondered what the hell made you so much harder while you were gone. What did she do to you? Screw around on you? And you're heading right back into trouble with her?"

Natches stood still. "You don't want to go there, Dawg," he told him carefully. "Chaya's not the reason for however the hell I was acting or whatever I may have done. I didn't poke my nose into your hijinks with Crista, so I'd suggest you stay out of my relationship with Chaya."

"Relationship?" Dawg narrowed his eyes on him. "You've never had a relationship in your life, Natches. Are you sure you know what the hell you're doing here?"

Natches uncrossed his arms enough to scratch at his jaw and remember the fact that he had forgotten to shave. Again. But his cousin's attitude was bothering him more than the growth of beard on his cheek. Dawg had been acting strange ever since he had learned Chaya was back in town.

"Did you know what the hell you were doing with Crista?" he finally asked. "Come on, Dawg; you blackmailed her into sleeping with you. Did I give you grief over it?"

Dawg grimaced at that. He stood there in his jeans, shitkicker boots, and that perfectly pressed long-sleeved shirt of his and glared at Natches again.

"Why is Agent Dane back here anyway?"

Natches shrugged. "Tying up loose ends is what I hear. What do you hear?"

"I hear Cranston's running another op," he snapped. "And Agent Dane is smack in the middle of it. Did she let you in on that little piece of information?"

"We didn't exactly get around to discussing it," Natches informed him. "First you and Rowdy broke down the door to my nice warm apartment, and once I got back here, I wasn't exactly in the mood to fight with her. What the fuck is your problem anyway? You're acting like a worried father. I didn't exactly stay out past curfew." He smirked at the thought. "Man, Crista is so domesticating you that it isn't even funny."

And damned if a flash of pride didn't hit Dawg's expression, rather than anger at what he would have once termed an insult.

"Look," Natches breathed out in irritation. "I know you and Rowdy have been following me around like a spy after secrets. You can stop now, okay? I'm a big boy. I do real good on my own."

"Until Agent Dane hit your life?" Dawg snapped. "I've been doing some checking. Before that bullet took out your shoulder, Natch, you were self-destructing like hell. Taking every mean-assed suicide assignment you could find. Why? And why the hell did it come around just months after you rescued some blond agent from a hellhole in the Iraqi desert? Tell me that agent wasn't the same one messing your head up now."

Natches was quiet for long, silent seconds. He stared at his cousin, promising himself he wasn't going to lose his temper. If he lost his temper, then he'd miss Chaya. And on top of that, he and Dawg would end up whipping on each other with enough force to leave both of them bruised and limping for days. Nope. Wasn't going to happen.

"Lock up when you leave." He turned and walked out the door before stepping from the small deck onto the floating walk.

He heard Dawg curse behind him, and he ignored it. His cousin was fishing, and Natches wasn't biting. It was Dawg's favorite means of getting answers from Natches, and it used to work. Piss him off and get him fighting. He didn't give a damn what he said to Dawg or Rowdy then. He would just spill his guts right there in the middle of a fight.

Natches grinned at the thought. Hell, those were the days. Before the Marines, when they were young and wild and filled with too much damned ego. Long ago and far away. More than eight damned years ago.

As he dug his keys out of his pocket and moved from the docks to the parking lot, he glanced back down the marina, flashed Dawg a smile, and lifted his hand in farewell. His cousin was standing there with his hands propped on his hips, and even from where he stood, Natches could see the scowl on his face.

Dawg had never liked Chaya, and Natches knew why. His older cousin had spent too many years trying to protect his younger cousins. Seeing Chaya again last year had ripped Natches's guts out. It had torn into him knowing she wasn't ready to push past all that pain inside her yet, knowing it wasn't time to claim her. And unfortunately, Dawg had witnessed Natches's struggle; he just hadn't been positive who the woman was.

Sometimes it concerned Natches, the way he knew things

about Chaya. Knew when to push her, when to just hold her. It was in her eyes, those needs she had, swirling in the golden depths. And the harder she fought it, the more she needed.

Last night, she had been like a firecracker ready to explode before he had even touched her. Those pretty golden brown eyes had been frosty, her expression closed, every line in her body straining to hold distance between them. Because what she felt scared her, scared her all the way to the bottom of her soul, and she knew it.

He unlocked his jeep and pushed the key in the ignition as he considered that, and the implications of it. Maybe Dawg had reason to worry, because Natches had a feeling he was only just beginning to realize how far over his head he was with Chaya. He was very much afraid that he just might love her.

Dawg watched Natches drive away and shook his head before jumping the short distance between Natches's deck and his own. And Crista was waiting for him, standing in the door, watching him curiously as he cast another scowl back at Natches.

"Well, you're still in one piece anyway." She looked up and down his body, her eyes twinkling in her still-pale face.

"You should be lying back down." He let his gaze sweep over her now, his heart softening in his chest even as his cock hardened in his jeans. Damn what this woman could do to him.

"I'm feeling a little bit better." She shrugged, looking away from him before turning and moving back into the houseboat.

"It's too cool outside for you to be standing in the doorway like that." He closed the door before frowning.

Maybe it was time to move out to the house. It was almost finished. He could push the contractors and get the carpet laid sooner than the spring date they had quoted him. A little extra money and they'd come out sooner. It hadn't been too cold last year, but still cold enough that she had insisted on wearing too many clothes. And the walkway had gotten icy a few times. He didn't want to risk her falling into the water.

He made a mental note to call the contractors later that morning, deciding he didn't want to spend another winter on the water. Summer and fall would work if they decided the house didn't suit them to live in year-round.

"I'll be fine, Dawg."

He grunted at that as he moved to the refrigerator. "You ready for breakfast yet?"

She was silent; he turned back to her, and he swore she was more pale than she had been moments before.

"I think I need to go lie back down." She headed for the stairs.

"I think you need to see the doctor." Something snapped inside him then. Fear. Dawg had rarely known fear, but he had never seen Crista sick either. "Call him this morning, Crista."

"I'll be fine." She shook her head as she headed up the stairs, her voice strained.

"Like hell," he muttered, moving behind her and catching up with her as she was pulling the blankets over herself.

Sitting next to her, he touched her forehead. She felt clammy, but she wasn't running a fever. She was pale though, and that worried him.

"It's just a bug." She sighed. "Everyone's sick at the store, Dawg. Just because you can't catch a virus doesn't mean the rest of us can't."

She sounded jealous, and he had to grin. "We'll get you nice and healthy before no time," he promised her. "Just living with me will rub all those good healthy genes off on you."

She snorted at that. "Go away and let me sleep. And you need to check the deliveries this afternoon. Don't forget that."

He frowned. "I'll have Layla's husband check them. I'm staying here with you."

"Hmm." She looked up at him, her gaze sharpening for a moment. "Why are you so upset over that woman staying the night with Natches?"

She didn't sound jealous; she sounded concerned. The question had him rubbing at the back of his neck in irritation.

"She's up to something. That's Timothy Cranston's little pet, Agent Greta Dane. I don't like it."

"Is that all?"

"She's too damned plain," he muttered, knowing she wouldn't understand any more than Rowdy did.

Her lips quirked in amusement. "You're not the one sleeping with her; so why should you care?"

He glared at the dark carpeting on the floor before lifting his gaze back to her. "I don't know. It bothers me."

"She's actually a very pretty girl," Crista told him. "It's not her looks that bother you."

A frown snapped between his brows. "I know a pretty woman when I see one."

And she smiled at that. A smile he didn't quite understand. It was patient and amused and made him grit his teeth.

"You know, it's mothers who are supposed to protest the girl's looks, not fatherly cousins."

Her comment had him staring at her in disbelief.

"You're crazy."

And she shook her head. "You have to let them go sometime, Dawg. Natches is all grown-up now. Let him try his wings a little bit. It might not be as bad as you think." She was on the verge of laughing at him.

"You obviously have a very strange virus," he grunted, put out that she was laughing at him, that she just didn't understand what he didn't understand himself. "Go to sleep."

She didn't protest. She just yawned a little and pulled the blankets closer to her chin. "It's cold in here."

Yeah, maybe it was time to move to the house. He was definitely calling those contractors. Then he was going to make another call and find out just what the hell Agent Dane was doing back in town.

Chaya made sure she spent no more time in her hotel room than she had to. She was betting Natches was a very early riser. She showered, dressed, dried her hair, and pulled it back into a ponytail, and within an hour she was out of there. And not a moment too soon. When she pulled her rented sedan onto the interstate, she swore that she saw Natches's jeep headed toward the hotel.

She glanced at her watch and breathed out roughly. She had an hour to kill before meeting the sheriff at the diner. That was going to be a long hour, considering the fact she had to make certain to avoid running into Natches.

And who the hell was she kidding? An hour later, she pulled into the diner and stared at the wicked black jeep sitting beside the sheriff's cruiser, and clenched the steering wheel of her car.

He was in there, waiting on her. She had run out on him this morning, terrified of what had happened the night before, leaving only a note. At least she had left a note this time, she assured herself. She had told him she would call him this evening, hadn't she?

She jerked her case from the seat beside her and pulled herself out of the car. She forced her chin up, stared around the parking lot, and glimpsed both Rowdy's and Dawg's vehicles as well. Didn't any of those damned Mackay men work? Surely they had something better to do than to harass her this morning?

Evidently they didn't.

As she entered the diner, she flicked a look at the table beside the one Sheriff Mayes was sitting at, and restrained the urge to grimace. Three Mackay men sipping coffee. Rowdy looked amused, Dawg looked pissed, and oh boy, Natches looked ready to hit the damned roof.

Sheriff Mayes, that bastard, didn't even bother to hide his laugh as she walked in.

She moved through the diner, thankful there were very few customers, and stopped in front of Natches. "Are you following me today as well?"

He tipped the glasses he wore lower on his nose and glanced up at her from over the dark lenses. She almost flinched at the anger burning in the forest green depths. He was livid.

"I'm going with you," he stated. "As soon as you tell Mayes over there that's the deal."

Shit. That wasn't the deal. That was expressly—with an unqualified no—forbidden.

"I can't do that, Natches." She forced herself not to show her own nervousness, or a reaction. She couldn't, not here. He would take any weakness and run with it.

"You don't want to do it like this, Chaya," he warned her then, and she could feel her stomach tightening in dread.

"I don't have a choice." She refused to glance at the other two men for their reactions. "This is my job, Natches, and you're no longer a part of that team."

And then he smiled. She could feel her throat going dry, and she swore she could feel her stomach drop with pure female terror. This was one full-grown, pissed-off alpha male, and she was going to pay. She could feel it clear to her bones.

Not painfully. Not in bruises, in blood, or in insults. But, oh boy, was he going to get her for this one.

"Well, Natches, I guess she's not as easy as we all thought she was." Dawg leaned back in his chair and shot her a tight smile. "Natches seemed to think you could see reason, Agent Dane. He even said you were smarter than to say no to him."

She turned her gaze to him, keeping it cool, detached.

"Oh, I see reason quite well, Mr. Mackay," she assured him. "And if I had my preferences, then his company would be welcome. Unfortunately, Special Agent Cranston made his wishes clear before I arrived. And in this case, that prevails."

Natches muttered something uncomplimentary about Cranston that she highly agreed with.

Dawg shook his head, his smile jeering now. "Loyalty, Agent Dane? Where's your loyalty? To your own butt or to those who can watch your back?"

"Enough, Dawg." Natches's voice was hard with warning.

"Let her answer the question, Natches." Dawg held her gaze. "I'd like to hear her answer."

"I'll tell you what." Her smile was benign, emotionless. He didn't like her. He'd never liked her, and she didn't give a damn. "Why don't you go? Then you can share that federal prison with me when Cranston finds out about it. I hear big, tall guys like yourself are really popular there. You're cute, James Mackay. They like cute rednecks with attitude there. Consider them a challenge, you know."

Rowdy snorted, and she could have sworn Sheriff Mayes was choking behind her.

Dawg's eyes narrowed. "You're playing in the big league here, little girl. You don't want to keep this up."

"I said enough, damn it!"

Even Chaya flinched as Natches's hand hit the table and he came halfway out of his chair. She stared at him, shocked, surprised as he and Dawg both seemed to hover over the table, almost nose to nose.

"Watch it, kid," Dawg snarled. "I still remember how to wipe the floor with you."

"And I still remember how to lock both your asses up in the county jail." Sheriff Mayes, his voice hard, commanding, stood by the table now. "Come on, Agent Dane, before you cause these two to fight like the hellions they used to be rather than the grown men I thought they were."

Chaya stared at Natches, amazed, disbelieving as he straightened, his body tense, his expression furious.

"If you get in a fight, I'm not going to be happy with you," she stated coolly.

"About as happy as I am with you right now?" he snapped.

"Try even less so." She lifted her chin a notch and reined in her anger as she turned to Dawg. "And if you don't back down, I'll have a talk with your wife. I have a feeling she's more inclined to act decent than you are at the moment. I wonder how she would feel if she were to find out about this little fiasco this morning?"

"Don't you threaten me with my wife." He glared back at her, but some of the heat seemed to leave his voice.

"Then don't push me, either of you. Because I could get sick of dealing with thick-skulled rednecks really fast. Unlike you, Dawg, I don't bite and snarl; I get to the heart of the problem and the solution. When you're willing to tell me what your problem is, then we'll talk. Until then, stop sniping at Natches, or I'll talk to Crista at first opportunity. Good day, gentlemen."

She turned on her heel, ignoring their surprised looks before joining the sheriff at the door and leaving the diner. And here she had hoped the most she had to deal with was a pissed-off Natches. Now she had a pissed-off Natches, a mad Dawg, and a laughing Rowdy. Her day couldn't get worse.

Dawg sat back down in his chair and scowled at the door while Natches slowly took those damned glasses off and glared at him.

"Son of a bitch, I'm going to kick your ass," Natches cursed.

Dawg sneered back at him. "Yeah right. Go right ahead. You think I didn't see your balls shrink when she gave you that cold little look? You ain't kickin' no one's ass today."

He was pissed. Pure pissed. Son of a bitch, she threatened to tell Crista on him? Like he was a little boy acting bad, and she was threatening to tell Mommy? How the hell old did that mouthy little agent think he was anyway? And he really wanted to beat Natches's ass, too. Snarky little upstart. He never could take advice worth a damn.

"What the hell is your problem?" Natches dug a few bills out of his pocket and slapped them on the table for the coffee. At least he was paying this morning instead of mooching off the rest of them. "Why can't you get the hell off her case?"

"Because she's lying to you," he snarled back, keeping his voice low, anger egging him on. "I don't know what the hell she did to you in Iraq, and I'm getting to where I don't give a damn. But right now, she's lying to you, and those lies could get you killed. And she's fucking plain."

Natches snapped back, blinked, and stared at Dawg as though he didn't know him. He glanced at Rowdy, but Rowdy seemed pretty interested in something he had found on the ceiling and refused to look over. Natches shook his head, as though befuddled.

Watching Natches, Dawg knew he was acting like a damned bastard, and he couldn't help it. Hell, he knew a lie when he saw it, and this whole setup Dane was involved in was a lie.

"Look, Natches, man," he breathed out roughly. "You're getting in over your head. She's up to something; I can fucking feel it. Like an itch at the back of my neck every time I see her. She's trouble, and she's going to get your ass killed."

That was the problem. That gunsight between the eyes thing. Sometimes, Dawg swore he could feel someone with a gunsight between Natches's eyes, taking aim, getting ready to fire. And it was worrying the hell out of him.

"Rowdy, take him home to Crista," Natches said, his voice hard, and that was a bad thing. Natches might shoot him himself now. "Tell her he needs help fast. Before I kill him and make her a widow. Understand me?"

"Sure, I'll get right on that." Rowdy nodded slowly, pulling his gaze from the ceiling to stare at both of them. "While I'm doing that, why don't one of you mosey over across the street and ask Aunt Nadine why the hell she's been watching us all so close through the window from that shop?"

They turned. Across the street, in the wide shop window, stood Nadine, hatred flashing in her expression before she turned and stalked away.

"Shit," Natches cursed. Just what he needed, the damned Mouth of the South running her vicious mouth now.

Dawg muttered something Natches was sure he didn't want to understand, and Rowdy stood slowly to his feet.

"Dawg's right about one thing," he said. "There's trouble

here, and it's starting to circle around your Agent Dane. But he's wrong about something, too."

"Yeah? What?" Natches snapped.

"She's not plain. She's actually kinda pretty. Dawg just can't see past Crista. Or his own daddy complex."

With that, he walked away from the table and out of the diner. Natches sat back down slowly. He still wanted to kick Dawg's ass. He stared back at his cousin and scowled.

Dawg glanced out the window, to his coffee cup, then sighed. "Do you really think she's gonna tell Crista about this?"

And he'd be damned, but Dawg was worried.

Eight

"Hello, Mr. Winston. Thank you for agreeing to talk to me." Chaya sat down on a worn, faded couch inside the single-story weathered house on the outskirts of Somerset.

Clayton Winston was a widower, and his son was a traitor. His son, Christopher Winston, had been arrested along with the Swedish mercenary and his merry band of men during the raid on the warehouse containing the stolen missiles.

Mr. Winston was stooped, his face lined with grief and pain. Rheumatoid arthritis had a cruel grip on his joints, and heart disease was draining him fast.

Sheriff Mayes stood on the other side of the room, watching Winston silently, his expression compassionate, somber.

"I didn't raise Chris to be a traitor," the old man sniffed. "He's still my son, but he wasn't right to do that."

He rubbed his grizzled cheek with a shaking hand before taking a handkerchief from his pants pocket and wiping his eyes. Those pale blue eyes were swimming with tears.

"I'd offer you some coffee or something," he told her. "But the cold makes it harder to move in here."

"I'll get the coffee, Clay." Mayes headed for the Spartan kitchen.

"Good man, Sheriff Mayes." Clayton nodded. "Better than his daddy. His daddy was always more concerned with getting elected again than he was with doing what was right. Zeke knows that, too. He makes up for it."

"Don't be talking about me, Clay," Zeke called from the kitchen. "I'll tell Miss Willa on you."

Clayton's smile was sad. "I like to brag on the boy. He's a good boy."

"Sheriff Mayes is a very kind man." Chaya nodded, her heart aching for the man sitting across from her.

Clayton Winston had served two tours in Vietnam. He had a medal for bravery and a file filled with commendations. Chaya's heart broke for him as she thought of the son that had turned his back on the life his father had believed in.

"You wanna talk about Christopher, I guess." His voice roughened. "How's he doin'? They moved him to that place in D.C. where they said I could come visit if I wanted, but I wasn't able to go see him. And he can't take calls." He hunched his shoulders as despair flickered in his gaze.

Chaya's lips parted to answer him when a knock sounded on the door.

"I got it, Clay." Zeke moved from the kitchen, casting Chaya an impatient look as he moved to the door.

"Hey there, Zeke. Fancy seeing you here." Natches pushed past him and moved into the room. "And Agent Dane. You're looking nice today."

Chaya rose slowly to her feet. "Natches, you're not supposed to be here."

She had to speak between clenched teeth. She couldn't believe he had barged into this interview.

"That's my fault." Clayton's shaking hands reached out to Natches as Natches knelt beside his worn recliner. "I called him when gossip came around you was askin' questions. I asked him to be here."

Chaya's lips thinned. Sitting back down slowly, she glared at Natches. "You didn't mention that to me," she stated, her voice clipped.

"We didn't get a chance to discuss it. You left." The accusation in his voice had her breathing in deeply.

"Natches can stay if that's your choice." She turned back to the old man, watching how he held on to Natches's hand with his gnarled fingers.

"Another good boy with a lousy sire." Clayton's voice trembled. "I used to sneak him sweets when ole Dayle wasn't lookin'."

Chaya watched Natches's face, his eyes. This old man meant something to him, and there were few known people that Natches cared for.

"Natches, get in here and help me with the coffee," Zeke snapped.

"I'll be in the other room, Clay." Natches rose to his feet, staring down at the grizzled, gentle giant who watched him fondly. "I'll hear every word. Okay?"

Clayton nodded as Natches threw Chaya a hard, warning look and moved back into the other room.

"Do you think I'm going to accuse you of anything, Mr. Winston?" she asked him softly. "That's not why I'm here."

His lower lip trembled for the briefest second before he seemed to suck it back in and his shoulders squared.

"Christopher's my boy. What he became, it's on my shoulders, Agent Dane. I realize that. But—" He lowered his head and shook it. "Sometimes I don't think as clear as I used to. I asked Natches if he minded being here to make sure, if I was arrested, that my cat was taken care of."

The cat was curled along the back of the couch and blinked at her lazily. The cat looked as old as Clayton Winston, and as tired.

"I'm not here to arrest you, Mr. Winston, for no reason," Chaya told him gently. "I'm not here to accuse you of anything, because what your son did was his choice. You chose to defend your country, sir. Your son made other choices. I'm trying to find out why he made those choices and who else may have influenced him there. That's all."

From the corner of her eye, she watched as Zeke walked out with two cups. He sat Chaya's coffee cup on the table in front of her. The other, a closed thermal cup, he put in Clayton's hand.

"It's just good and warm, Clay. I put ice in it, just like you like."

Clayton nodded, and Chaya's throat tightened with emotion. She couldn't remember an interview she had ever done that was quite like this one. Natches and Zeke were as protective over this old man as a mother with a child.

"Clayton, I told you Miss Dane would take good care of you," Natches told him from the doorway.

"He did." Clayton nodded. "But I feel better, Natches, with

you and Zeke here. If she has to arrest me, then old Hisser here might go hungry; we can't have that." He reached up and stroked the cat's tail as it curled over his shoulder, and Chaya wanted to cry.

"Mr. Winston, I just have a few questions. If you prefer not to answer them, or if Mr. Mackay feels it's not in your best interests to answer them, then I want you to know now that there will be no repercussions. I'm not here to see you hurt further. I merely need to clarify some things and make certain I didn't leave any loose strings."

Clayton nodded to that as he lifted his cup, both hands wrapped around it, and sipped from it.

This man, so patriotic and kind, was facing what had to be his greatest nightmare. The questions Cranston had given her weren't recriminating or accusatory. They were simple—asking about Christopher's friends, if he was part of a hunting group, or if his friends were military. She asked him about his son's teen years, his friendships then. Strangely, he and Johnny Grace hadn't been friends. Yet he had ended up involved with Grace in the theft of those missiles.

"Christopher was always preaching about America and politics and how all this nation lives for is money." Clayton shook his head wearily. "Said we needed a revolution to wake the people up. That boy, he never understood." A tear tracked down his cheek as he stared back at her. "I lost friends and a brother in Vietnam. I was willing to give my life to provide this great nation for him, Agent Dane. Many, many great men shed their blood for my boy, and I never realized how little he appreciated that sacrifice. I raised him wrong. I should be in that cell." His chin wobbled. "Locked away like that, and I can't even hear his voice, see if anything of my boy remains." Another tear fell as Natches moved forward and took the thermal cup before Clayton dropped it. "I didn't teach him right," he whispered. "And I'm sorry about that."

Chaya had to blink back her own tears. Ignoring Natches and Zeke, she reached out, covered the old man's hand, and waited until he could focus on her.

"Mr. Winston, your sacrifices and the sacrifices of your friends ensured his choice. What he did with that choice is on his shoulders, sir, not on yours."

"You believe that?" he whispered.

"I believe that with all my heart. You, sir, are, and have been, one of our nation's greatest assets."

"You're not going to arrest me?" he asked then.

"Not in a million years," she whispered. "But I am going to arrange that phone call for you. I promise you that. I'll make sure you get to talk to your son."

It wasn't for the son, who she'd just as soon see flayed alive. It was for the father. The soldier who had saved countless others, who had given all but his life for the freedom his son had never cherished.

Clayton blinked and his eyes filled with tears again. "I'd like that," he whispered. "Just for a minute. To hear my boy's voice."

She nodded to that and rose, making another promise to herself. When this was over, if he could make the trip, if he wanted the trip, she would make certain he got to see his son. And she would make damned sure that son showed him the respect this man deserved.

"She's a good girl, just like you said, Natches." Winston looked up at Natches, a shaky smile crossing his lips. "Don't you let this one get away. She's tough enough to put up with you."

"That she is, Clay." He gripped the other man's shoulder gently as he stared back at her, and she didn't want to feel the warmth that bloomed through her at that look. "That she is."

Chaya straightened and nodded, heading for the door.

"Agent Dane."

She turned back to Clayton as Natches moved aside behind her.

"Yes, sir."

He frowned, his rheumy eyes thoughtful as he rubbed at his whiskered chin. "I just thought—Christopher, he wasn't friends with Johnny a'tall. Or that Bedsford fella. But he mentioned some friends once, called 'em by something. Called 'em his compatriots, said they were starting their own club or some such stuff. Freedom boys or something. I don't remember right off."

"If you remember, could you contact me? Just let the sheriff know, and I'll come right over."

He nodded to that. "I'll think on it. See what I remember."

"Good-bye, Mr. Winston."

"And you'll remember to get that phone call for me?" His

voice was filled with hope. "Just for a minute. Just so I can hear his voice one more time."

She was going to cry. Oh God, don't let her cry here, in front of this proud old man.

"Department of Homeland Security will be contacting you tomorrow, Mr. Winston. I promise."

He nodded again, reached for his coffee cup, and brought it to his shaking lips. She wanted to howl at the unfairness of it, and she couldn't. All she could do was walk out the door and move to the sheriff's car.

"I'm going to stick around and make sure Clay gets dinner." Natches caught her arm and pulled her to a stop. "I'll see you tonight."

She shook her head. "Not tonight."

"Like hell. Tonight, Chay, and that's final. I didn't know Miss Willa wasn't coming over here every evening to take care of Clay's dinner, and I have to fix that now. But you can bet on the fact you will be seeing me this evening."

She pulled away from him and followed Zeke to his car, getting in and slamming the door behind her as she continued to fight her tears. She would rather interrogate a roomful of terrorists than ever have to face that old man with so much as one more question regarding his son.

She was losing it. There was a time when she could have questioned him and pushed back her sympathy, her compassion. It was what she had been trained to do. She was an interrogation specialist. She knew how to do her job without worrying about the consequences.

At least, she used to know how.

"One more to go," Zeke said as he got in the car and looked over at her. "I believe it's the widowed mother of another of those boys."

She nodded. A man who had paid his mother's bills, bought her food, and took care of her, and now his mother was suffering.

Her fingers curled into a fist, and fury spiked hard and hot inside her.

"No. We're finished for the day."

Zeke paused as he slid the car into gear. "It won't be any easier tomorrow, Agent Dane. Trust me, I can tell you that one for a fact."

She stared out the window, ignoring her own reflection, afraid of what she might see. She knew tomorrow wouldn't be any easier.

"I've interrogated dozens of terrorists. I've interrogated suspects' families. I've been a bitch and remembered what I was fighting for, for years now." She was twenty-eight years old. She had come into Army Intelligence right after boot camp and worked her way up. She knew what she was doing, she knew how to do it, and she couldn't stand the thought of one more parent forced to face the choices his child had made.

"Yeah, I hear you're real good at your job," he murmured.

"Am I?" she whispered, refusing to look at him as he pulled out of the driveway.

The yard around the Winston house was overgrown. Clayton Winston's only son used to keep it mowed and trimmed. The trees needed trimming, and there was no one to do that now.

"You know, you didn't make the choices those boys made any more than Clay did," Zeke told her as they headed away from the house. "It's our job to stop them, your job to make sure we stop all of them. It might hurt like hell; it might cut us up until nothing helps but a shot of whiskey and a tear or two. But we do what we have to do."

"For as long as we can stand to do it," she said softly. "Take me back to my car, Sheriff. I told you; I'm finished for the day."

She returned to her hotel and ordered a bottle of wine. She showered and changed into a robe and curled up on the couch, where she put in a call to Cranston. Two hours later, suffering the effects of a furious, heated argument over the phone call she had promised Clayton Winston, she'd arranged it. At noon the next day, he would have ten minutes with his son.

The bastard. Christopher didn't deserve to hear his father's voice. Didn't deserve to know that the man who had lost a brother and countless friends in the service of his country still loved him.

It would bring Christopher Winston more comfort than it would bring his father, but even a small amount of comfort was reason enough.

And what of the widow? she asked herself. What was she going to promise her? What about the wife and two small children of another man they had taken? A man with a promising career, who had laid it all on the line to betray his country.

She pushed her fingers through her hair and fought the scream welling in her throat. What about those children who had lost their daddy and didn't understand why? The wife whose eyes were haunted in the surveillance pictures, who hid in her home and tried to ignore the gossip swirling in this small town?

She rose to her feet and paced to the window. She stared out at the darkness falling over the mountains, the lights of the city around her, and she could feel the tears inside her.

When had she ever cared before? The men they had arrested had made their own decisions, yet she was beating herself up over the fact that she had to question their families.

It wasn't those men facing the consequences of what they had done to their families, staring into their haunted eyes. It was her. Her and the people who had loved them.

As she stood there, she heard the door to the suite open. Through the reflection in the glass, she watched as Natches entered the room, and she had to clench her teeth to hold back a sob.

His expression was somber as he crossed the room, his gaze dark, concerned.

She expected him to castigate her for questioning Clayton Winston. For making his pain worse. Instead, she was shocked as he came to her and turned her against his chest.

"It's okay to cry, Chay," he whispered at her ear. "Clayton wouldn't think less of you for it. And neither would I."

She shook her head, but she felt the tears building in her chest. Crying didn't help. It wouldn't bring back Clayton Winston's pride in his son, and it wouldn't ease the pain of a widowed mother or a family damaged by betrayal.

This beautiful town. These people that she had somehow let into her heart right along with Natches were tearing her apart.

"He deserved better," she whispered, holding on to Natches, desperate to find some way now to control the emotions she didn't know how to handle. "This is why I hate you," she cried out. "I get around you, and I start feeling. I start laughing over two nitwits who broke into your apartment because they thought I was going to somehow hurt you. I cry over old men who deserved better but are a whole lot better off knowing the truth. And I start aching for things I never needed before. I hate you for this."

She was shaking in his arms, felt them tighten around her as she dug her nails into his back and held on for dear life.

"You love me, Chay," he whispered against her hair, his voice quiet and deep. Secure. Damn him, he was always so secure, always so confident, and at this moment she felt as though she was struggling just to hold on to reality.

"You make me feel too much," she whispered. "Make it stop, Natches."

Make the pain go away.

She shook her head against his chest and jerked away from him.

"I didn't mean that." She had done that to him once before, asked him to take away the pain. She had never forgotten the way he had looked at her. The regret in his eyes, the sorrow. Because it wasn't him she was asking for; it was solace.

"Chay, come back here." He pulled her back to him, one hand holding her head to his chest as his arm wrapped around her. "Do you think I mind being your shield against the world, or the pain?" He tipped her head back, forced her to look at him, and her vision blurred with tears. "Sweetheart, my shoulders are broad enough for your tears, your fists, or those sharp little teeth. However you need to hold on to me. I'm here."

"What about you?" Her voice shook now, almost as badly as Clayton Winston's had trembled earlier. "Always a shield and never shielded, Natches?"

He chuckled at that, his gaze gentle. "Is that what you think?" He touched her cheek, ran his thumb over her lips. "That I have no shield? Don't you know, Chay? You've been my shield since the day I met you, whether you were here or not. The memory of your laughter, your tears, the memory of your touch and your kiss. You changed me, Chay, and I think it's only fair that I'm changing you as well."

Changing her, and that change was destroying her. Before he could say anything more, before the tears welling inside her could fall, she reached up, grabbed his head, and fought for his kiss.

She needed this. She needed to feel him burning inside her, just one more time, because she could feel parts of herself unraveling that she didn't know how to handle.

She was being attacked by emotions she had promised herself since she was a girl she would never feel. All her life, she had maintained distance, but distance wasn't possible with Natches.

He lifted her off her feet as his lips controlled the kiss despite her battle to lead it. He chuckled at her attempts to nip his lips, and nipped hers in turn. He slanted his lips over hers, pushed his tongue inside, and lit a fire in her that she knew would burn her to ashes.

She was tearing at his clothes as he laid her on the bed and stripped her of her robe. She couldn't get him undressed fast enough.

She fought him as he wrestled her to the bed, his lips and tongue burning over one nipple, then the other. He sucked one into his mouth, lashed at it with heated licks of his tongue, and filled her with passion.

She had never known passion until Natches. She had never known this heat, this fire that became a void of loneliness and loss when she walked away from him.

How had she ever walked away?

She twisted beneath him, gasping, crying his name.

"I need . . ." She arched as his teeth raked the hardened peak, and he growled against it. "I need you, Natches."

"I'm right here, Chay." His voice was deep, rough. It grated across her senses and made the pleasure deeper, hotter. Because she knew he felt it. Knew he was as lost in it as she was.

"Now." Her head tossed against the mattress as he held her in place, his lips sipping at her flesh, his tongue licking it. "Don't make me wait."

His hand cupped between her thighs, heated, calloused flesh meeting swollen, wet folds.

She arched and cried out as two fingers thrust inside her, throwing her higher, deeper into the maelstrom overtaking her.

And she let it have her. She let him have her. She arched, pulling at his shoulders, feeling him come to her. Thick and hard, his erection worked inside her, stretching her, easing her, building sensation and emotion into a kaleidoscope of color and pleasure.

When he was buried to the hilt, his breath rasping, his expression twisted in lines of hunger, she felt his desperation to meld with her inside her very pores.

"Hold on to me, sweetheart." He shifted and knelt in front of her, gripping her hips and pulling her to him until her rear rested on his thighs, his cock buried full length inside her.

Her hands grabbed his wrists as his smile, strained with need, seared into her brain.

"You hold on tight now," he crooned. "I'm going to make you scream."

He braced his hands beside her on the bed as her legs curled around his hips. And he began to move. Hard, driving thrusts that buried his flesh inside of her. Again. Again. Sending lightning crashing across her nerve endings, fire building in her womb.

She held on and, as he promised, she screamed. She exploded around him, her back bending, her hands gripping his wrists, and heard his cry echoing around her. Heated warmth filled her as he began to ejaculate, deep, fierce throbs of his release sending her arching into more pleasure.

He destroyed her. And he remade her. And when the final tremors eased, he pulled her into his arms as a tear fell from her eye. Just one tear, she told herself. She could afford to shed just one.

And that one tear seemed to last forever.

Nine

Rebuilding her defenses against Natches wasn't going to work. He bullied her into returning to the houseboat for dinner with him, then he made certain she was too exhausted to return to her hotel that night.

She fell asleep in his arms, drained emotionally and physically, and knowing that if she wasn't very careful, Natches Mackay could destroy her.

The next morning, as she had the morning before, she slipped out of his bed and off the boat. Her cab was waiting at the marina office, and as she opened the back door and glanced behind her, she saw him. Standing on the top deck of the *Nauti Dreams*, fog whispering around him, his chest bare. She wondered for a second why she bothered to try to run. And why it was so damned hard to face him after the wild loving he gave her.

It was a problem that followed her through the day, just as Natches followed her from one interview to another.

The first two interviews didn't matter. They were surface tests, no more. Former friends of Johnny Grace who had already been cleared in the investigation. But she had to make it look good. Timothy had an idea of who was of major concern, and as the day progressed, Chaya became more nervous over that particular interview.

Because Natches was following them in his black jeep, watching her, always there.

As they pulled into the driveway of Nadine Grace's home at

about three o'clock that afternoon, Chaya felt like drying her sweating palms on her jeans before getting out of the car.

"You sure about this?" Sheriff Mayes stared at the house, his expression concerned, before glancing at her. "Johnny was her son. The only person in this town she really liked. She's not going to be polite."

Oh, there was someone else in town Nadine had liked, and the thought of it sickened Chaya.

"I'm not here to win a popularity contest, Sheriff," she told him as she gripped her briefcase and opened the car door. "I'm just here to get answers."

"And rile the Mackay cousins up?" he asked as he exited the vehicle. "I ain't seen those two as pissed off at each other as they were yesterday morning in years. I'll end up having to lock them up tonight if they get into a public brawl."

She flicked him a disagreeable look. "They're not going to fight."

"And how do you know this? They nearly tore up that diner about two years ago or so. I had them in a cell for a weekend, and trust me, that's not pleasant."

She rolled her eyes. "To start with, Dawg's not going to risk making his wife that angry. And Natches wasn't nearly mad enough to fight yet. Dawg won't push him that far either."

Mayes shot her a disbelieving look but didn't say anything more as the front door jerked open.

"Zeke. That's a Mackay whore, and I don't want her on my property." Nadine Grace's pretty face was twisted in fury, her green eyes blazing with rage. "Get her out of here."

Slender, still attractive at fifty, and filled with anger, the other woman glared daggers at Chaya.

"I wish I could, Mrs. Grace." Zeke sighed, glancing at Chaya as she stared back at the other woman coolly.

"Mrs. Grace, I'm Agent Greta Dane, Department of Homeland Security." She pulled her badge folder from her jacket and flashed the ID at the other woman. "Mackay whore isn't my title today. Catch me tonight though, and you might hit it right."

Nadine's nostrils flared as though picking up a disgusting scent. "Get off my property."

"Sheriff," Chaya said to Mayes. "Please have Mrs. Grace detained and brought to your office. We'll change this from an interview to an interrogation. I'll call the main office and apprise them of the situation." She didn't take her eyes off Nadine Grace.

"Now, Agent Dane, we don't want to do that." He sighed.

"Of course we do." She smiled tightly. "If she doesn't want to cooperate, then I don't have to be nice. Do I?"

The other woman was nearly shaking with rage now. Her gaze was spitting fury, her face pale with it.

"Nadine, just a few minutes of your time, and then we can leave," Sheriff Mayes assured her. "Agent Dane has a few questions. That's all."

The woman was going to crack her jaw, she was clenching it so hard.

"You have ten minutes." She turned away from the door, her dark blue dress swishing about her legs as she stalked into the house.

Chaya stepped inside, instantly shivering at the stark white walls and furniture. The place looked like an ice cave, there was so much white.

"Take your damned shoes off," Nadine snapped, glaring at them from the living room as she took a seat on the white sofa.

Chaya glanced at the sheriff before putting her briefcase down and tugging off her boots. Mayes followed suit, but clearly didn't like it.

She padded into the living room and took the chair facing Nadine as she pulled a recorder from her case and laid it on her knee. Nadine spared a look at the small device, her lips curling into a sneer.

Chaya turned it on, stated the date and time.

"For the record, you're Nadine Mackay Grace, mother to Johnny Grace," she stated, then stared back at Nadine.

"I am," she snapped.

"Mrs. Grace, were you aware, at the time, that your son, Johnathon Ralph Grace, was involved in terrorist activities?"

Nadine's eyes narrowed. "He was not. Johnny wasn't involved in anything of the sort."

"There's clear evidence that he not only masterminded the theft of several government missiles and guidance chips, but he also murdered the driver transporting those missiles. He contracted and brokered the sale of those missiles. He shot and killed Jim Bedsford, his lover and partner, and attempted to kill Crista

Jansen. Were you aware of those activities before or during the time they were taking place?"

Nadine was breathing roughly, her fists clenched on her knees, her face splotching with a furious flush. She wasn't nearly as pretty now as she had been when they had entered the house.

"I don't have to answer these ridiculous questions," she snarled.

"We can answer them here, or we can answer them under more formal settings," Chaya told the other woman. "If you would like to contact your lawyer, we can Mirandize you and take you into the sheriff's office for interrogation. Why waste time, Mrs. Grace?"

"My son did none of that," Nadine retorted, her voice harsh. "Those cousins of his, they did it all and they framed him. Those bastards made it look like he did it so they could kill him."

And Nadine knew better. She was lying through her teeth. Chaya stared back at her silently, her eyes holding the other woman's for long seconds before Nadine looked away and pretended to blink back tears.

What was she lying about though?

"Mrs. Grace, were you aware of the theft of those missiles at any time before your son was killed?"

"No." She shook with fury as she answered the question, but once again, she couldn't hold Chaya's gaze. She turned to the sheriff. "Isn't this enough yet?"

Chaya ignored Mayes and continued to stare at Nadine until the other woman glanced back at her.

"Did Johnny tell you where the money he gained on deposit of those missiles was hidden?"

"No." Like an animal, Nadine's lips curled back from her teeth and her eyes glittered with malicious glee.

"Who would he have told?"

"No one. He didn't do it."

"You're saying the Mackay cousins framed him?"

"That's exactly what happened." Nadine's teeth snapped together.

"Why would they do that, Mrs. Grace?"

"They always hated Johnny. He was always smarter; he always did what was right. They hated him for it."

"Was James Dawg Mackay aware Johnny was also the biological son of his father, your brother Chandler Mackay?"

"That's a *lie*." Nadine nearly screamed the word, hatred burning hard and bright in her eyes.

Chaya watched her carefully now. "Mrs. Grace, we have a recorded statement of your son bragging about those crimes. Just as he admitted to being the son of Chandler Mackay, your deceased brother. DNA testing from blood collected after his death and compared to James Mackay's, proves this to be the case. Are you stating, for the record, that your son was not conceived in an incestuous relationship between yourself and your deceased brother, Chandler Mackay?"

This was the part Chaya hated. The part she had argued and fought Cranston over for days before leaving for Somerset.

Nadine was silent. She drew in a hard, deep breath.

"I want to call my lawyer now," she stated.

Chaya flipped off the recorder and placed it back in her briefcase before standing. Sheriff Mayes followed suit, his expression granite hard as he glanced at Nadine Grace, then to Chaya.

"You do that, Mrs. Grace," Chaya told her softly. "And when you do, perhaps you had better warn him to advise you on your rights should you lie under oath. Because the next time we question you, you will be under oath."

"There won't be a next time," Nadine spat back at her.

Chaya smiled and walked back to the front door, where she put her boots back on before straightening and staring back at the other woman.

"There will be a next time, Mrs. Grace. I'd contact that lawyer if I were you. You're going to need him."

She didn't give the other woman time to protest but stepped out of the house and moved toward the sheriff's cruiser. Natches was still sitting on the other side of the street, staring at her, his expression hard but thoughtful as she and the sheriff got back into the cruiser.

"Would you like to tell me what the hell was going on in there?" Sheriff Mayes asked her carefully, coldly. "No matter what he did, Agent Dane, she was still his mother. And you showed no respect for that."

No, she hadn't, and it didn't sit well with her, but she knew

Timothy's suspicions and she knew the evidence he had amassed so far. At this point, she couldn't afford to worry about respect.

"Sometimes, Sheriff, we all have to do things we don't particularly like, as you reminded me yesterday," she finally answered, glancing at him as he reversed out of the driveway and passed Natches's jeep. "Have you ever had to arrest a friend? Did the fact that he was your friend sway you from your sworn duty to arrest him?"

He spared her a brief, flinty glance. "No, it did not."

"The fact that she's a mother can't sway me from mine, and there's a difference between her and Clayton Winston," she informed him. "Johnny Grace killed an innocent soldier, stole those missiles and their guidance chips, and negotiated a rather low price for them. The money is missing, and pertinent information regarding the whole deal is missing. He had another partner. Nadine Grace was lying for her son; Clayton Winston didn't. And I want to know what she was lying about."

"And you think it was his mother helping him?" He clearly didn't think it was, but then neither did she.

"What I think doesn't matter. I have a clear set of questions for each person I'm interviewing. Those recordings will be transferred to DHS, where they will be gone over by the experts there and determinations made as to who will be pulled into formal interrogation. DHS won't let this go."

Sheriff Mayes wasn't stupid. He wasn't letting it go either, but he clearly wasn't saying anything more.

"Who's next on your little list then?" he finally asked.

"Wenden Frakes," she answered.

"Shit," he breathed out. "Johnny's uncle."

"Ralph Grace's half brother." She nodded.

"Just what I need," he growled as he made another turn and hit the interstate. "Wenden Frakes pissed off. That's just gonna round out my day."

Wenden Frakes wasn't pissed off. And he didn't end up pissed off. He was feeding cattle when they arrived and agreed to talk to them after a careful silence.

His answers were cautiously worded, his expression disagreeable, but he didn't give them any trouble. Didn't like that little bastard Johnny, he declared. Everyone knew he was Chandler Mackay's kid because everyone knew Nadine Grace was doing the nasty with her brothers. Not just one brother, he stated, but both Chandler and Dayle Mackay.

When they left the Frakes farm, the sheriff heaved a hard sigh. "We're going to the Mackay Marina, aren't we?"

Chaya almost felt sick inside. "I don't have a choice, Sheriff."

Sheriff Mayes shook his head. "I sure hope you know what you're doing."

She didn't. She only knew the list, the questions, and the vague sense of disquiet slowly stealing over her. Timothy had plotted out each person to question and the order of the interviews. He knew something; he was pushing someone, and she just couldn't figure out whom. She knew she was growing more and more concerned though. And by the look Natches had flashed them as they passed him, he was growing angrier with each visit they made today.

As the sheriff turned into the Mackay Marina, Chaya drew in a slow, control-restoring breath. Natches had guessed where they were headed, too, because there was Rowdy Mackay at the front of the marina office, his wife standing beside him.

They watched as she and the sheriff stepped from the car and Natches drew the jeep into the parking space beside them. Chaya paused. She had no intention of fighting him over this one.

"What are you doing, Chaya?" His voice was harder now, suspicious.

"My job." Turning to him, she tried to push past the ache in her chest as she saw the suspicion in his eyes. "They're just questions, Natches. That's all. I swear."

"Why?"

"Clarifications. Making certain DHS has everything. Timothy isn't targeting Ray Mackay; I can promise you that much."

"Who is he targeting?" Ice formed in his tone.

She shook her head, aware of the sheriff watching them in interest. "I don't know. All I have are the questions. That's all."

He didn't say anything for a long moment. His arms crossed over his chest as he glanced to the marina, then back to her. "Just questions? Or accusations?"

"Questions, Natches. And the questions aren't in the least accusatory."

He glanced to the marina office again, and she followed his gaze. Ray Mackay stepped outside, his broad form powerful, his gaze piercing, and his expression confident. Everything about him the same as she remembered from the year before. This was the man who had practically raised Natches, the man who had sheltered him through what had obviously been a hell of a childhood.

"He's a good man," she said softly, turning back to the angry man watching her. "I would never take that from him. And I wouldn't let Cranston do it either—not without warning you first. Not without fighting him every breath of the way."

He finally nodded, his arms uncrossing before his fingers curved around her arm and he walked her to the marina.

"You young fools." As they reached him on the stoop, Ray shook his head before smiling back at Chaya. "Nadine's done called everyone in the county, spitting out poison. I figured you'd be here sometime today."

"Hello, Mr. Mackay." She extended her hand in greeting, pleased when he took it in a firm grip. "I just have a few questions if I may. Alone, please."

"Not a chance in hell," Rowdy objected.

"Son, I don't need you watching my back." Ray glared back at his son with fatherly reproof. "Put your back down, and keep Natches and the sheriff here company. Me and Miss Dane here will just have a little chat in the office."

"Damn it, Dad—"

"And don't curse in front of the women. I taught you better than that." Ray glared back at him before turning to Chaya and inviting her into the marina office. "Come on in, Agent Dane. These boys can stand out here in the sun and let off some steam while we talk. It's the best thing for them."

She liked him. She had liked him the year before, the few times she had seen him. He was protective of his son and his nephews. He had protected them as well as he could when they were children, and he continued to do so after they were grown.

Ray Mackay, for all intents and purposes, didn't have just one son, he had three.

"Right back here." He opened the office door as his wife stood by worriedly. "Maria just made fresh coffee. Would you like some?"

"No thank you." She felt like slime as she took the seat he offered her and waited as he closed the door and moved behind his desk.

Then he was staring back at her with too-perceptive blue eyes and a concerned expression. "You're sure making a mess of my boys." He sighed. "I heard Dawg and Natches almost came to blows at the diner yesterday. And Natches is fit to be tied right now."

Chaya nodded. "I know. It couldn't be helped."

Ray Mackay was what Chaya had always thought a father should be. At fifty-nine, he was trim, his hair black and silver, his face weathered. And kind. He had a kind face, and that just made her feel worse.

She pulled the recording device from her briefcase hesitantly.

"I need to record this," she told him.

He nodded in agreement.

She turned the machine on, stated the date and time, and looked up at him. "Your name is Raymond Douglas Mackay. You were Johnny Grace's uncle. Brother to his mother as well as to Chandler Mackay."

"I am." He nodded.

She swallowed tightly. "Were you at any time aware of Johnny Grace's illegal activities here in Somerset or outside the county?" She watched his eyes, and he didn't turn from her, didn't flinch.

"No, ma'am, I didn't know Johnny was capable of such activities."

She nodded to that.

"Mr. Mackay, as stated by Johnny Grace, he's the half brother to his cousin James Mackay. A product of the incestuous relationship between his mother and her brother Chandler Mackay. Did you know this?"

"I suspected a time or two," he said softly. "My brothers and sister weren't my concern after I left my mother's home, Agent Dane. I lived my life, and I stayed out of theirs."

She nodded again.

"Would his mother be capable of aiding him in those illegal activities?" she asked him.

"His mother would have aided the devil himself if it meant destroying Dawg. If it meant destroying any of those boys outside there. She hated them. Even more than Dawg's and Natches's fathers hated them."

"Was she also sleeping with her brother Dayle Mackay? Would he have aided her and/or her son in those activities?"

Ray stared back at her silently for long moments. "I'd like to say no," he finally said.

"But?"

"But I learned with Johnny that nothing is impossible. Honestly, I wouldn't know, Agent Dane. Dayle's ex-Marine, always seemed damned patriotic to me. He preaches about it, argues politics, and votes in every election. Hates foreigners, and my first thought would be he'd never betray his country. But after Johnny . . ." He shook his head. "What the hell do I know?"

"There's a million dollars in cash missing, and connections Johnny or Jim Bedsford couldn't have had aided in the near sale of those missiles, Mr. Mackay. Who would have helped him?"

Ray scratched his cheek as he thought, then finally shook his head. "I just don't know. Things like this don't happen around here, Agent Dane. Somerset is a quiet little town, and this whole thing . . ." He shook his head again. "It's spooked a lot of folks. Hell, I think it spooked me."

"Wenden Frakes, Ralph Grace's half brother, says Johnny spent a lot of time on the lake last summer. Did he use any of the boats off your marina?"

"Not one of my mine." He shook his head firmly. "I didn't let Johnny Grace rent out my boats for no reason. He had a tendency to tear them up. Those boats are hard to replace. Besides, Dayle had a boat he kept out at his cabin farther up the lake. Johnny used it some, I think."

She nodded again and flipped off the recorder. She had what she needed here.

"Thank you, Mr. Mackay," she said when he stared back at her in surprise. "I know the questions weren't comfortable, and I apologize for that. They weren't questions I chose; I want you to know that."

Ray leaned back in his chair then and watched her with the narrow-eyed intent of a man who knew people and, sometimes, knew them too well.

"Dawg says you're cold," he stated then, surprising her. "That you're just using Natches for whatever DHS has going on here. Is that true?"

Chaya slid the recorder back in her case before lifting her eyes to Ray. She let him hold her gaze, just as he had allowed her to hold his. "Natches is my weakness, Mr. Mackay," she finally admitted. "And he doesn't take no for an answer sometimes."

"That doesn't answer my question," he said, his voice gentle as he smiled back at her. "Are you using my nephew, Agent Dane?"

"No, Mr. Mackay. I'm trying to protect your nephew."

And to that, he nodded slowly. "And I believe you. Now I think you have some bridges to repair outside. Rowdy's got a slow burn. He doesn't do mad easy, but he's getting close to mad. Dawg is ready to fight. And Natches will stand between them and you, but I'd hate to see that happen. Fix it, if you don't mind."

"And I'm supposed to do that how?"

"By being honest, Miss Dane. As honest as you can be. Those three boys ain't no one's dummies, no matter what that Cranston fellow wants to think. And after today, they're going to block you unless you're smart enough to work with them."

"And if that threatens Natches?" she asked softly.

"Then now's the time to warn him." He rose from his seat and watched her with that fatherly look that demanded action. The right action. "Let him help you, Miss Dane. You'd be amazed how easy he can be to get along with then."

And he was right. She couldn't tell them the truth, because even she didn't know the whole truth. But she could tell them enough to perhaps get them to back down. Because they had to back down, just for a little while longer.

He stared at the caller ID on the phone before answering it, his jaw clenching in anger.

"Yes?"

"They were here." Nadine's voice was shaking with fury. "We have to do something now."

His lips thinned. "Settle down. Now's not the time to do anything, peanut. We sit back and let her ask her questions. She can't hurt us."

"She knows something," Nadine hissed. "I could tell. And she'll get what she needs. If she finds out, she'll fry us."

"If you don't calm down, you'll fry us. You don't know anything, remember that. Johnny was a good boy and you're his mother. Period."

"They recorded Johnny bragging about belonging to Chandler. They did DNA tests. That bastard Dawg gave them blood and they matched it. They know it's the truth. If they keep digging, they'll find the connection."

Now that piece of information was worrisome. He hadn't expected that. He'd managed to keep that information buried for too many years, he didn't like it coming out now. Didn't it just figure that Johnny had to brag? As though it were something to brag over.

"The connection is hidden, peanut. Take one of your pills and calm down. As soon as I can I'll be there and we'll talk. We'll figure this out. Until then, remember, they can't get anything unless you tell them." He hoped.

"Do something," she whispered. "You have to do something before they question anyone else. They've already been to Wenden's and Ray's. If they keep digging, they could dig up something else."

If Johnny had revealed the truth about Chandler, God only knew what else he had let out. He grimaced at the thought of that. Hell, he had thought Johnny was smarter than that. He hated being wrong.

"I'll be there as soon as I can," he promised her again. "If they show up again, don't answer the door. Pretend you aren't home. I'll check into things and I'll have something when I get there."

He heard her breathing, heard the little sigh of relief.

"Will you stay the night this time?" she asked then, that little whisper of hope bringing a smile to his lips.

"I'll try to arrange it. I'll call you when I'm coming. Promise you'll stay calm, peanut."

"I promise. Until you get here."

"Until I get there."

He disconnected the phone, tapped his finger against it thoughtfully and began to make plans. It was sooner than he liked, but it was time to start cleaning things up.

Ten

Natches caught her as she came out of the marina office. His fingers latched around her arm and before she could do more than breathe a protest he began dragging her toward the *Nauti Dreams*.

He had no idea what the hell was going on here, but he was getting ready to find out. She wanted to question the rest of the damned town, that was fine and dandy by him, but when she started questioning family, then he expected answers.

And when she started dealing with that rattler Nadine, then he sure as hell expected those answers to be forthcoming.

"I don't like being dragged around like a child, Natches," she told him as he pulled her onto the deck of the boat and unlocked the door.

He pulled her into the houseboat, slammed the sliding door closed behind him, then stalked to the kitchen for a beer.

All shit aside, he'd seen a new side of Chaya today. For the first time, this morning, he'd seen the agent. Steel eyed, her demeanor cold, she refused to back down. And rather than turning him off as it should have, it had made him hard. Because he knew the woman underneath, liquid hot and burning for him alone. Dawg called her plain, and he'd wanted to smash his cousin's face in for the comment despite the fact that he knew, had seen, the metamorphosis she somehow managed to undergo.

The agent, with her hair slicked back into a ponytail, her eyes cold and hard, her expression emotionless, blended into the background for most people. Not plain, but easily passed by for some reason. Natches had always seen the woman beneath that look though, because he knew her, in all her expressions, in many of her moods, and he knew there was nothing plain about her.

She was complex, complicated, and sometimes too damned sharp to suit him. And she was good at hiding. Hiding herself as well as her secrets.

He turned back to her after downing half the bottle of beer he'd pulled from the refrigerator, remaining silent as he watched her.

Dressed in jeans because she knew they made folks more comfortable and a light sweater beneath a dark blazer. And those boots. Those boots made her legs look longer, made them sexier. The gray sweater brought the soft golden highlights in her eyes free, and softened her delicate face.

And when she crossed her arms over her breasts and glared back at him, his cock throbbed in anticipation.

"The Mackays are going to have to keep their noses out of this," she snapped. "You and Dawg following me around town all day, then showing up here. What the hell did you think I was going to do anyway? For God's sake, Natches, you know how an investigation works. There are questions afterward, loose ends to tie up and, considering there's a million dollars missing and possible coconspirators, facts to find. You don't just drop a case like this."

He didn't say anything. He finished the beer, tossed it in the trash and narrowed his eyes on her once again.

And it infuriated her. He could see the mad rising in her eyes. The distant expression he referred to as her "agent face" began to peel away. A light flush worked over her cheeks, her lips lost that thin, cool little line and the lower curve became almost lush, definitely sensual.

Here came his Chaya, the woman.

"Timothy's playing a very neat little game," he said then. "I can see it in every move you're making and I know you can, too. He gave you orders I'm not to accompany you on these interviews? Have you asked yourself why?"

"Probably because you're too damned nosy and you don't know how to stand down," she muttered.

He almost grinned at the accusation.

"Because he knows he's going to be poking in my business," he informed her. "Whatever the hell he has going on here is going to piss me off and he doesn't want me to know about it until he has no other choice."

"This does not concern Ray Mackay, Natches," she told him again, and he saw the truth in her, felt it. "Are you going to go off the deep end when I question Dawg? Rowdy? What about Crista Mackay? Are the Mackay cousins going to close rank against me then?"

He paused and stared back at her. Is that what she really expected? That he would side with his cousins, with anyone, against her? Hell, he had risked his damned hide for her in Iraq, not just once but twice. Did she think he would do any less for her here?

"I have a job to do, Natches. I don't have the option you chose last year of telling Timothy Cranston to get fucked. And to be honest, this time, I don't want that option. I want to know who the hell thought they could get away with murdering that kid that drove the transport vehicle. I want to know how Johnny Grace got away with nearly killing Dawg's woman. And I want to know why the hell this little town is suddenly a beehive of terrorist activity."

His brows almost arched at that statement. The last year, he and Dawg had admittedly been concentrating on their own lives. Had they somehow managed to miss something going on that they should have seen?

"I haven't seen many terrorists this week, Chay," he finally stated, tilting his head and watching her curiously. "Is there something here that I should know?"

She inhaled slowly. "Last year you had nearly a dozen terrorists near or around Somerset. The Swede that laid that down payment on those missiles wasn't a happy little camper after his arrest, and he has friends. Friends who most likely are sitting right here just waiting to see who they should target to get that money back. A million dollars is a hell of a lot of money, Natches, even in today's economy."

His brow arched. "That was one of your flimsier excuses," he told her. "Try again."

Chaya stared back at him, recognizing the slow, lazy drawl as it passed his lips. It wasn't what he said, it was how he said it. It was the dangerous throb of suspicion just beneath the careless tone, the warning that he wasn't buying whatever she was selling. And she had warned Timothy he wouldn't. No matter the truth of it, Natches knew there was more going on. Somehow, the list of names she had interviewed today, in that little group, she had managed to tip Natches off, and it wasn't just her questioning of Ray Mackay.

"Someone in Somerset was helping Johnny," she told him. "Someone who had more contacts than Jim Bedsford could have managed. Bedsford was a front, Natches, nothing more. Someone else was pulling the strings."

He leaned against the low counter, crossed his arms over his chest and stared back at her with those frighteningly observant eyes of his. Sometimes, she swore he could see clear down to her soul with those dark green eyes.

"What's your proof?"

"Bedsford's contacts couldn't have gotten him and the Swede together last year for that missile deal. That group doesn't deal with penny-ante thieves. They're too slick for that no matter how impressive the merchandise. Someone else brokered that deal, someone from Somerset. Someone Timothy's been chasing for years. That's all I know."

"The deal in Iraq?" he asked her then. "The one Craig was involved in? Does it tie in?" The illegal transfer of arms and information to terrorists, and the unsanctioned attack on the hotel, the explosion that killed her daughter.

She flinched at the question and forced back the more personal aspects between herself and Natches now. There were things they had to deal with, later. Right now, she had to deal with this, and she hated it.

"It ties in," she told him. "It also ties in to several other thefts the public is unaware of, that were made too close to Somerset. Those thefts go back further than Iraq and the threads of suspicion lead right back to Somerset."

"So you're here to do what? Avenge Beth?" He shook his head wearily as he pushed his fingers through his hair and stared back at her. She could see the memories in his eyes, too. The loss. The pain.

"I'm here to ask the right questions and see if I can't force them into making a move. Timothy has other agents watching persons of interest." She held her hand up as he started to speak. "I have no idea who they're watching. I'm here to ask the questions; they're here to see who moves after I ask those questions. This isn't about Beth, Natches. It's about stopping it."

"So he's put your ass in the line of fire and he's hoping to catch whoever puts you in their sights?" he bit out. "Son of a bitch, Chay. He's working you. He's using your baby and your pain, and he's working you."

She didn't like to think of it that way, but she inclined her head in agreement, because there was always the risk of that. Timothy was definitely capable of it.

"He's hoping to catch whoever he's watching through the questions he's sending me to ask. He's spent years investigating this, Natches. He's not going to stop now." She sighed.

"And you think he didn't expect me to get involved?" He threw her a disbelieving look as he paced to the other side of the room and turned back to face her, his hands propped on his hips, his expression forbidding.

"I was told to keep you as far away from this as possible. He knew you wouldn't stay away from me, but he was hoping you would stay out of the rest of it."

"And here I thought you were more intelligent than that. Hell, I thought Timothy was," he growled. "Do you believe that bullshit, Chaya?"

"No. But I'm asking you to do it anyway," she told him. She didn't want him involved in this. She wanted him as far away from Timothy Cranston's games as possible. She knew how Timothy worked. He lied and he connived and manipulated everyone to get what he wanted, the way he wanted it. She didn't want Natches pulled into the webs Timothy created.

"All I have to do is ask the questions," she repeated. "The danger is limited, Natches, and he's watching whoever he suspects."

"He suspects someone he knows I'll try to protect, or he wouldn't have sent you." He snorted. "And that one, I have to admit, has me as confused as hell. Because Timothy knows me, too, and he knows there's few people here that I'd protect."

"No one you would protect could be involved," she argued. "Rowdy, Dawg, Ray, or their wives? For God's sake, I know for a fact they aren't under suspicion. Do you think I didn't do my own damned homework? Do you think I would let him try to crucify someone I believe is innocent?"

"Timothy wouldn't try to crucify someone who's innocent." Natches shook his head as he stared at her from across the room.

He looked dangerous, too controlled, too suspicious.

"Timothy's a lot of things," he continued, "but he doesn't do witch hunts. Whoever he suspects, you can bet they're guilty, he just needs the proof of it. And he'll sacrifice anyone or anything for that proof, Chaya. Even you."

He had already sacrificed her, and she knew it. He couldn't have guessed that Natches would give a damn about her if his cousins turned against her. And it appeared that was exactly what was happening.

And perhaps Natches wasn't standing by her. He was angry, she knew that. Suspicious.

She turned away from him and moved to the sliding doors, staring beyond them to the nearly deserted boathouses. Summer was over. There were very few year-round residents here. And she didn't blame them. It was colder than hell on the water.

"Dawg, Rowdy, and Ray aren't under suspicion. Neither is Crista. I have Timothy's word on it," she told him quietly. "According to him, he doesn't want you involved in this because you draw too much notice and you're too temperamental where the Mackays are concerned. The questions he has me asking involve family, connections between Chandler Mackay, Nadine, and Johnny Grace. I record the answers and send the recordings via FTP back to him."

She didn't know what Timothy was looking for, and she was beginning to wonder if it even mattered. Timothy knew who he was after by now. The questions had begun changing, taking a new direction, leading her straight into the heart of too many family secrets. At this point, he was merely playing a delicate little game designed to catch his quarry faster.

"I want to see the names and the questions before you leave each morning."

She swung around. "I have direct orders that you're not to see anything." And she followed orders. The agency had been her life for the past five years. It had held her together when nothing else could have.

He smiled.

Chaya felt her stomach tighten as he moved across the room. Clothes did not hide the shift or power of the muscle lurking beneath them, nor did it hide the sheer arrogance of the male animal she was now facing.

"I said, I will see the names and the questions before you leave my bed each morning," he growled, his eyes darkening, his expression forbidding, and for the first time in ten years, Chaya faced a force that had her swallowing back her nerves.

"Or what?"

"Oh, Chay, sweetheart," he crooned. "Now we just don't wanna go there, do we? We wanna wake up in that big bed of mine, nice and warm every morning, and work this out together. Because, if we're not working this out together, then we're going to be fighting. Yelling. At odds. Out of sorts. And if we're out of sorts, then bad things might start happening. I might follow you into these places where you're questioning folks. I might make things rather hard."

She stared back at him in confusion. "Why? I swear, your family is not involved in this."

"Something more important than family is involved here," he said then.

"What?" She threw her hands up in disbelief, amazed that Natches could find anything more important than family. From what she had seen since coming to Somerset, he wouldn't just die for them, he killed for them. "What could be more important to you than your cousins or your uncle?"

"You."

She blinked up at him, and she swore she felt the very air around them become thicker, still, heavy with tension.

"You don't mean that." She shook her head slowly. He had to be lying to her. He loved his family, he was loyal to them, loyal enough that he would lie to her.

It broke her heart, but she accepted it. She had no other choice.

"You don't have to lie to me," she whispered, moving around him as she put her hand to her brow and eased her palm over the perspiration forming there. "I know you have priorities."

"I'm glad you do. And I thought you knew, Chay, I don't bother to lie to anyone. Wastes too much of my damned time."

She held her hand up while keeping her back turned to him. She couldn't handle this. If he needed this bad enough to lie to her, then fine. He could have it. It wasn't enough to tip Timothy off, and she knew Natches was going to do whatever the hell he wanted to do anyway.

"You can see the list and the questions," she whispered, picking up her briefcase before turning to face him. "I'll meet you at the hotel in the morning."

A sharp laugh left his throat. "Bullshit. You're not leaving me. Not again, Chaya. I'll tie you to the damned bed at night."

"And I'm not going to stand here and let you lie to me to protect your family." Something was building in her, shimmering like a bloodred cloud in front of her vision as she watched his eyes go from dark to light, watched moss green go brilliant green, like a forest in spring.

"You actually believe I'd lie to you like that?" He glowered back at her. "Baby, I don't have to lie to you to get that list, those questions, or anything else I need out of you. All I have to do is get you beneath me."

And it snapped in her head then. Chaya felt herself almost sway in shock. He hadn't used a condom last night or the night before. He had been bare, his semen spurting inside her, sending her crashing into another wave of release even as a part of her mind had whispered the warning. Each time, and her emotions had been in such disarray that she had ignored the implications.

She wasn't protected.

"Not without a condom you won't be." Her head snapped up, her vision clearing as fear surged through her. "And not without the truth between us."

"What the hell do you mean by that?"

"The truth? It's a fairly easy concept . . ."

"I mean the condom." His hand sliced through the air. "I'm safe, Chay, and you know it just as well as I do. I may have played some games in my life, but I always protected myself."

"This isn't about STDs," she snapped. "I'm not protected, Natches. I went off the agency-sanctioned shots last year when I thought I was resigning and didn't have time to restart them. You need condoms. I can't believe you didn't use one last night."

Natches stared back at her. From her eyes, to her stomach. Back to her eyes and her stomach again as he swallowed tightly.

She wasn't protected? He'd filled her more than once with his release the night before, pumping into her, crying her name, feeling her so sleek and hot, milking it from him.

Use a condom now? The first time he'd taken her, there'd been nothing between them either, and he remembered that last mission, wondering about the agency protection she used. Wishing she didn't. Wishing he could fill her with his baby, to give back to her everything she had lost.

He blinked now, feeling the sweat that gathered on his back, the sense of hunger that suddenly raged through his body. He'd rationalized those thoughts as insanity years before. Her grief had marked him in a way he hadn't expected, couldn't have been prepared for, he had told himself.

But now it wasn't grief. He was staring at her belly, seeing her growing round with his child, and the hunger for it grew.

"Are you okay?" Her eyes narrowed on him as he jerked his gaze back to hers. "I'm safe right now, Natches, but that doesn't last long. Get the condoms. And stop lying to me. We'll get along much better that way."

"No." He shook his head slowly, barely able to believe that word had slipped past his lips. They were numb, his throat was tight, thick with so many emotions he didn't know how to make sense of them.

"Why?" She had a death grip on that briefcase and one on his soul. Hell, even he hadn't known the grip she had on him until now. "Is the truth so damned hard?"

"The truth is easy." He had to fight to hold himself back, to keep from latching onto her, to keep from devouring her. "I meant, no condoms."

Chaya went silent. Even her thoughts seemed to stop in shock as she stared back at Natches. He couldn't have said that. He didn't just say that.

"I see." She wet her lips. Had he changed his mind that quickly? Was she misunderstanding something important in this conversation? "If you don't want to have sex with me, I can understand . . ."

"I want to lay you down and lick every inch of your body. I

want to bring you over me and watch you ride me. I want to fuck you so many ways, so many times, that neither of us can find the energy to crawl from the floor let alone the bed. Oh, baby, wanting you is like a sickness with me, and it never fucking goes away."

"Oh." Her heart was racing. Each word out of his mouth had her skin sensitizing, her clit swelling. "Then what do you mean, no condom?"

He stalked to her then. Slowly. His expression was more savage than she could ever remember seeing it, his eyes bright, his lashes lowered over them. He looked dark. Dangerous. And something in that look terrified her.

"I mean, if you don't want my baby, then you better get your ass to a clinic and take care of the birth control yourself." His hand flattened on her stomach as she stared back at him in a shock so deep, so overwhelming, she wondered how she was standing upright. "Because I'm betting I have the fastest, slickest little soldiers in the state of Kentucky. Just a breath of a chance, sweetheart, and you're pregnant." His expression, his eyes, grew taut with possessiveness. Possessiveness and lust. "And I could very much get into making damned certain they have every chance."

Chaya felt herself swaying. She could feel the blood draining from her face, even as it began to thunder in her ears.

She could feel Natches's hand on her belly, his eyes boring into her soul, as though will alone, and nothing more, could make her conceive.

And it didn't make sense. She couldn't understand this. He couldn't be serious.

"Why?" She forced the word past numb lips. Why would he want to tie himself to her like that?

"Ah, Chay," he whispered, his expression gentling, just a bit, just enough to force her to trap a sob in her chest rather than give rise to the cry that seemed to echo through her soul. "Sweetheart. Don't you know I'd give everything I possess to hold you to me? And the thought of giving you my child, of watching that pretty belly grow large with my baby, makes my dick so damned hard I wonder if it's going to push straight past the zipper of my jeans."

She felt the briefcase drop from her fingers as she stared back at him, searching his eyes, searching for the lie. There had to be a lie there. But lying didn't make sense. She knew Natches. Knew he would never, ever risk a child of his so cavalierly. He was so damned protective over family that even Cranston feared him. He would kill for them. He had proven it.

"Chay." He breathed her name against her lips, and she felt herself weaken. Her knees. Her soul. Something inside her, something she needed for protection, to hold back the dreams and the loss and the years she had run, even from herself, began to crack. "Let me have you like that. Just us. Just the chance that we could dream together like that."

Eleven

Natches could feel himself shaking inside, a need, a hunger he couldn't control, didn't want to control, rising inside him.

Chaya. Just her name invoked the power to make his knees weak, to make him hard, to make him want to believe in miracles and to reach for them.

The boy inside him that had once screamed out in the darkened forest, howling in fury at the loneliness, the pain that melded through his body, howled out now in hope.

Because Chaya was here. For such a brief moment in time in a foreign desert, in a hostile land, Natches had known peace. One night, so far away that it felt like a dream, he had held her in his arms and knew she belonged to him. No matter what happened, no matter where life took either of them, he had found the one person that was his alone.

Chaya.

He stared into her eyes. Honey eyes. Eyes that drew him in and promised him life, promised him joy. He could find joy with her. He found joy with her.

"You're not serious," she murmured, her voice as dazed as he felt lowering his hand once more to her stomach. There, his child could be growing even now. Sheltered in the warmth of her body, growing strong and sure.

Sweet God—the prayer slipped into his mind unbidden—*let my child rest there.* Within the woman who held his soul.

"I'd die for you," he said softly. "I'd kill for you, Chay. And I'd go to my knees for you."

He had never willingly gone to his knees for anyone, man or woman, no matter how many times his father had tried to force him there.

She blinked back at him. Those clear golden eyes of hers flickering with dreams that she fought to keep buried, with hope that he knew she tried to hide.

She was his hope, but he knew, to the bottom of his soul he knew, he was hers as well.

"Natches." She shook her head, her lips parted, fully, lush now with the arousal he knew was moving through her.

It made her wet, just as it made him hard, the thought of coming together, bare, unprotected, spilling into each other to create something new. Something innocent.

It shouldn't have been that way. He knew that. Hell, the last thing he needed to think about with his childhood was a kid. But a baby with Chaya? Something to bind her to him forever, just as he would be bound to her.

Family was his salvation. His uncle Ray, his cousins, they were all the family he'd had. He'd never had his own. Until now, he hadn't wanted his own.

"You want me like that, Chay, don't you?" He lifted her shirt, flattened his hand against the bare skin of her stomach and watched her eyes.

It was Chaya's eyes that held her secrets. There, they flickered in those honeyed depths, the soft golden brown color warming him no matter her mood.

"Bare, Chay." His jaw clenched at the hunger. "I want to pump inside you and feel you reaching for me. Milking me. That sweet hot body taking my seed and nourishing it."

Her face flushed instantly, hot, as her eyes flickered with fear and with dreams.

"I want to watch your stomach grow round with my baby. I want to lay my head against it, feel our child move within you."

She trembled, shuddered, and her eyes darkened as they always did when she began to surrender to him.

He wanted that surrender.

Before his knees gave out on him he swept her up in his arms, ignoring her little cry of protest and he carried her through the boathouse to the stairs. Up the rounded staircase, to the bedroom, to the big bed that awaited them, the sun-drenched warmth that welcomed them.

"We can't just decide to make a baby." She was breathing hard, rough as he set her on her feet and pushed her blazer over her shoulders.

"Of course we can," he crooned, knowing, as he had always known, how much she loved that sound. When his voice roughened, deepened. She shivered in response to it. A sound he had never known how to make, had never given another woman.

"It's completely irresponsible," she protested, but it was a moan, filled with surrender as his hands stroked down her arms then gripped the hem of her shirt.

"It's every dream I've ever had," he told her as he tore the shirt from her body and cupped those pretty breasts as they filled the lace of her bra. "I want to watch you nurse our child here." He kissed the full mounds as they spilled over the cups of her bra. "Chay, you know you want it, don't you, baby? Bound to me? You won't be able to just walk away anymore. Think of it, sweetheart. No more reasons to run, and every reason to lie in my arms night after night."

It was her nightmare and he knew it. He used it shamelessly, because he also knew it was her weakness. His Chay. So tough, so determined to never lose again, to never hurt as she had hurt before. To never risk having what she cherished most taken from her.

She had run from him, because she couldn't face losing him. He'd figured that out about her. Knew it about her. Just as she surely knew he wouldn't allow her to run any longer if she ever returned to Somerset.

The running was over.

"Natches, this isn't a good idea." She was thinking. He could feel her thinking.

His lips moved to hers. He sipped at her lips as a breathless moan passed them. He stroked them with his tongue as he nearly tore his shirt from his own body. He caught that lush lower curve between his lips and laved it, nipped at it, and watched her lashes flutter over eyes gone dark with hunger.

No thinking right now, he decided. That sharp little mind of hers needed to rest; it needed to be stroked and loved, tempted and teased. And he was just the man to do it.

He loosened her belt, aware of the weight of her weapon at her hip, and almost grinned at the thought of it. His woman was a tough little warrior. She would walk by his side. She wouldn't put up with his moods, and she'd tell him like it was. Always. The thought of it turned him on even more. She was a fitting mate for the darkness inside him, because she lightened it.

He released her jeans, slid the zipper down, and, as he released her lips, slid his palm beneath her panties to the sweet, rich flesh beyond.

So hot it almost burned. Swollen, slick with her sweet juices. His mouth watered at the thought of tasting her again. Of burying his tongue inside her, and lapping at her like hot, delicate candy. Like nectar. Like life itself.

"There, baby, let me have you," he urged as she shook, trembled, her nails digging into his shoulders as he held her to him. "Remember how good it is? How hot?"

He worked her jeans and panties over her hips, careful to keep in contact with the wet folds between her thighs, his finger caressing, his palm grinding against her clit.

And she was burning for him. Her hips shifted, moving against his hand, grinding her clit against his hand as he eased her to the bed.

Her cry of protest flamed through him as he moved his hand, but the taste of her exploded against his tongue as he pressed a kiss against the swollen little nubbin of her clit.

As he kissed, licked her gently, he worked her boots from her feet and finished undressing her. When she was soft and hot and naked, stretched across his bed and immersed in her arousal, he paused long enough to jerk his boots off and finish undressing himself. When he turned back to her, his sensual little kitten was on her knees, gold eyes glittering with hunger now, her features flushed, desire raging in her eyes.

This was the woman he dreamed of. The woman who had taken him to heaven that night so long ago.

His head went back as she came over him, her lips on his, her hands sliding over his damp shoulders, nails raking as he ran his hands up her back and prepared to hold on for the ride.

He remembered Chaya, wild and hungry, too long ago. He had ached for that woman, needed her as he'd needed nothing else, tempted and teased her, and here she was. The balm to the wounds that had festered inside his soul.

Chaya felt Natches ease back on the bed for her, felt his hard, muscular body laid out for her, hers for the taking, and it was like coming home. Like being in the cold and then sinking in front of a fire that filled the soul.

Natches's fire filled her soul. And he offered it to her willingly. A sacrifice to the unbearable hunger raging inside her now, untamed, breaking free of the fear that had housed it for so many years.

Oh God, how had she stayed away from him? Five years. She had been without him for five years and each day had been an eternity of need and loss that she hadn't realized, until now.

"God, Chay," he growled, a deep, rough sound that stroked her senses as his hands stroked her back. "There you go, baby. Come to me."

She nipped at his lips, caressed them, and let him devour her. He didn't let her control the kiss; he never would, she knew. He was powerful, dominant, but he gave his body freely, and tonight she intended to take. And take.

She trembled at the thought of taking all of him. Of giving all of herself. And she knew that was exactly what she was doing, giving herself.

Lifting her head she stared down at him, at those wild green eyes, the way his thick black hair fanned out from his savage face. The way the muscles flexed in his shoulders and arms, the perspiration that trailed down his neck. And she had to taste it.

She lapped at it with her tongue, filled her senses with the taste of him, and gloried in the sound of that rough male groan.

"I missed you." The whimpering sob shocked her as it fell from her lips, pressed to his flesh. "Oh God, Natches. I needed you. I needed you until I burned. Until I thought I'd die without seeing you, hearing you."

His hands flattened on her back, held her closer.

"I was right here, baby."

Right here. In his bed, waiting for her.

Sleek and hard and hungry.

Her lips slid from his neck to his chest, feathered over hard male nipples before her teeth raked first one then the other. He jerked beneath her, and she thrilled at the evidence of his pleasure.

Another thing he gave her freely, his pleasure. She didn't have to worry about how to please him, because every touch she had ever given him, he had urged her on, relishing it.

"Ah, Chay, sweet baby." His hands slid to her sides, to the curve of her breasts, and the backs of his fingers caressed them with subtle heat.

He wasn't stingy with his touches or his words.

Chaya luxuriated in the generosity. His heat, the friction of his hair-roughened male chest against her swollen nipples. The feel of his muscles tightening, his breath rasping in his lungs as her lips slid lower.

She took quick, heated kisses down the center of his body, moving with slow, delicate greed to the thick, steel-hard shaft that reached up his lower stomach, eager for her touch.

Natches shifted, his hands pulling at her hips as her head went lower. And she remembered that. Remembered how she had taken him in that humid little room in Iraq. The night her tears had mixed with her release, and they had drunk from each other.

She tasted the head of his cock, her tongue licking over it, curling around the engorged crest as the shaft jerked in response.

Natches lifted her leg as she slid into position, pulling her hips over his face and blowing a heated breath against the wet folds of her sex.

A whimper fell from her lips, because she knew what was coming and she couldn't wait. She lowered herself to him, feeling his tongue slide through liquid heat and tender tissue to burrow inside her vagina. Her lips opened over the head of his cock, her hands stroked the heavily veined shaft and Chaya let herself be taken, even as she took.

She worked her pussy on the thrusting tongue tormenting her with wicked pleasure. And with her mouth, she tormented in turn, crying out with delight, with need that bordered on pain.

His hands stroked over her rear, between the full curves, and teased the delicate flesh there as he worked his tongue through the slit of her pussy, circled her clit, and rubbed at it erotically. Stealing her mind.

She couldn't allow him to steal her mind. Not yet. She needed to stroke him, touch him. She needed to pour the past five years of loss and loneliness into every touch. Then she needed to take him as she had dreamed of taking him. Riding them both into ecstasy.

Before he could stop her, not that he tried hard, she swung away, lifting herself from his lips despite his growl of displeasure and her own aching regret.

She couldn't touch him as she wanted to if he stole her strength as she was doing so. When Natches touched her, she melted. Tonight, she wanted him to melt.

And Natches was melting. He stared down his body, strung tight with the most incredible pleasure. Pleasure that went beyond pleasure and bordered on agony of sensations. Chaya knelt above him, straddling one hard leg, rubbing the slick heat of her pussy against it as she worked her mouth on his cock head.

Sucking and licking, moaning in pleasure as her honey gold eyes darkened further and glittered with the needs rising inside her.

God he loved this. Seeing her like this. The agent disappeared beneath the woman's demands as those demands took over.

She sucked greedily at his cock head. Her hands stroked the shaft of his erection and his balls as they drew up tight at their base.

He was in an agony of sensation now. Her hands were silken heat, her nails rasping, her mouth. . . . Sweet heaven, her mouth was like ecstatic fire licking over his flesh as her heated, wet pussy rubbed against his leg.

She was pleasuring him as she pleasured herself. Taking him and twining deeper into his soul as she did so.

Chaya lost herself in each touch, in each taste of Natches's hard body. As though she had been born for this, to belong to him.

Drawing back she licked the hard crest one last time before allowing her tongue to taste the thick, silken shaft. Heated iron met her lips, silken heat stretched tight. Heavy veins throbbed with anticipation just beneath the flesh, and with each lick, she swore his cock grew harder, pulsed harder.

"You're killing me." His voice was graveled, thick and rasping as she kissed the base then licked the tightly drawn sac below.

He flinched, jerked, and moaned hard and low.

Chaya clenched her legs around the hard thigh rubbing against her pussy and knew she was drowning in this pleasure. She was sinking into a sensual storm and had no idea how to save herself. She didn't want to save herself. She wanted to ride the waves. She wanted them cresting over her, surrounding her, swamping her.

She lifted her head and dragged herself over him, embracing his muscular hips with her thighs and lowering herself onto the rigid, heated flesh rising to her.

"There, Chay. That's it, sweetheart; take me. All of me, Chay. It's all yours."

She stared into the narrowed bands of green as he watched her, his expression twisted into lines of savage lust and determination.

She couldn't keep from sobbing at the pleasure. The feel of him penetrating her slowly, taking her as his hands moved up her back, down her arms, then his hard fingers linked with hers.

"Take me, Chay," he demanded. "This ride is all yours, baby."

He was barely buried inside her, his cock throbbing, eager to take her.

"Ride me, Chay, like we've both dreamed."

She straightened, flung her head back at the incredible pleasure racing through her, and she took him. Slow and easy, then with quick, shallow strokes. Her hips twisted, rose and lowered and she lost that final piece of herself.

Nothing mattered but the pleasure. Nothing mattered but the sensation of flying within his embrace, knowing he was there to catch her if she fell, that he would hold her if she faltered, and he would give her the reins when she needed them.

She needed them now.

Holding on to his hands she took him to the hilt, feeling all that wild heat and hardness penetrating her, stretching her, a burn that was pleasure and pain, and she gloried in it.

She twisted against him, and she rode him as he lifted beneath her, driving his erection deeper and harder inside her. Perspiration gathered between them. It rolled down her shoulders, ran in rivulets down his chest. Slick and heated they clashed together, twisting and thrusting, strokes that speared straight to her soul as the driving rhythm grew, deepened, heated until she was exploding, flaming out of control and screaming out his name.

Deep wracking shudders jerked her body tight as her womb spasmed, her vagina convulsing, milking around him as his hard, throttled shout was followed by the deep, heated spurts of his seed inside her.

Chaya's eyes jerked open, met his and locked. She felt his cock jerk inside her, felt each pulse of his release, and felt her body heat and shudder further at the feel of it. That final hard orgasm rippled through her as his gaze held hers, as his soul wrapped around her. Forcing her to see, to know, nothing in life could be as good as right here, in his arms.

As the final, desperate tremors washed through her, she sank slowly against his chest, just fighting to breathe, to make sense of the woman she became when Natches touched her. Because it wasn't the woman she had known before she met him five years ago.

It was as though he had opened something inside her during that time in a cramped little hole in the desert. He had rescued her. He had protected her. And as danger swirled around her he had teased her and made her want to fight at a time when it felt as though the fight had been sucked out of her.

And that was how he made her feel now. Like fighting. Like tearing down the obstacles she knew stretched between them, and she knew it could be done so easily.

She could betray Natches, or she could betray the rules she had lived her life by. And at this moment, she knew the choice she was going to make. No matter what tomorrow would bring, she chose Natches. The naughty dream that haunted her, the man who owned her soul.

I love you. She mouthed the words against his chest because she couldn't bring herself to say them yet. As sanity began to whisper through her mind once again, that one shred of fear remained. She had only told one person in her life that she loved them, and that tiny vision of purity was gone now, jerked from her so brutally that she had feared she wouldn't survive it.

That edge of fear still held its grip on her, strangling her with the words that wouldn't whisper past her lips and bringing tears to her eyes as she held on to Natches tighter.

"I love you, too, Chaya," he said, his voice rough. "It's okay, baby, because I love you, too."

Twelve

Somewhere in the darkness of night, she had to have lost her ever-loving mind. And finding it again didn't appear to be an assignment Natches was going to allow her.

"Look, you have the information, the interview files, and the recordings," she told him the next morning as the first rays of the sun began to peek over the tops of the mountains. "I need to return to my hotel room—"

"And check out," he interrupted her, his voice controlled, mild, as he went through the files she had transferred to his laptop. "You'll move into the apartment with me. Dawg and Rowdy should have the door fixed by now."

She inhaled deeply. "That's not going to work right now, Natches."

He lifted his head slowly. It was a curiously dangerous movement the way he did it. The calculated restraint in it had her holding back the shiver that would have worked up her spine.

"Why? Because you won't have a chance to rebuild all those nifty little defenses you keep between us?" he asked, his mocking smile grating on her temper.

"Because I won't have the investigation compromised any more than it has been already," she told him. "I'm sharing information with you despite direct orders to the contrary. Do you have any idea how many years Cranston could put me behind bars for that?"

He merely grunted at that and turned back to the file.

"I'm meeting Mayes in just a few hours. I need clean clothes, and I have my own notes to put together as soon as Cranston sends the new list of interviewees this morning. I can't do that with you breathing over my shoulder."

"You might as well give it up now," he murmured. "You're not driving back to that hotel alone and you're not staying there alone. You don't want to stay at the apartment, that's fine. I'll stay at the hotel."

He said it absently, his eyes narrowed on the laptop screen, as though simply because it was his decision then it was a foregone conclusion that it was happening.

"Natches, you seem to be forgetting something here," she told him coldly. "This is my investigation and my job. I don't need your help doing it."

"So you keep tellin' me." That smooth southern drawl deepened, causing her to wince. This wasn't the sexy, lazy drawl. This was the cool, velvet drawl of a man who had no intentions of backing down.

"Do I poke my nose into your garage?" she finally snapped. "Do I tell you how to fix cars or how to deal with customers?"

He lifted his head and stared back at her. "Not yet."

That shut her up and she hated it. Turning her back on him she propped one hand on her hip as she nibbled at her thumbnail and glared at the covered window.

Despite Cranston's orders to keep the Mackay cousins out of the investigation, she would have cheerfully told him to shove it if she thought the investigation would proceed better with Natches involved. Unfortunately, she had a feeling she knew exactly where it was headed, and she didn't need Natches there for that.

She had read his file so many times she had nightmares about the childhood he had endured. His father was ex-Marine and a sorry bastard. Dayle Mackay was a bully, heavily muscled; he had nearly beaten a young Natches to death more than once. Natches's back still held the scars of the most brutal beating that he had taken, at the age of twenty. The night his father had disowned him, he had beaten Natches to the floor then ripped his back to shreds with a lash. All because Natches had refused to allow his father to strike his sister, Janey Mackay.

"You'll only complicate matters for me at the moment, Natches. As well as bring Cranston out of the woodwork." She turned back to him as he lifted his head once again and stared back at her. His forest green eyes were mocking, his smile knowing.

"It's not happening, Chay." He closed the files out before leaning back against the couch and watching her with hooded eyes now. "From this moment on, just call me your shadow. Because doing this alone isn't going to happen."

"I have the sheriff with me. Most of the people I'm talking to seem to share a dislike for you, Natches. It wouldn't be conducive to my investigation if you're there."

He just smiled. A patient, questioning smile as though he were trying to figure out exactly why she was still arguing with him.

She propped her hands on her hips and glared back at him. "Okay, let's try it this way. You are not accompanying me on those interviews. Period."

"It makes me hard when you get mean, Chay," he drawled. "Come over here and sit on my lap while we discuss it." He patted his knee invitingly and she wanted to kick herself for almost moving toward him.

"You're just being an ass now, Natches. Stop it and let me do my job. I can be amazingly adept at that when I don't have to deal with men who think they can do everything better than I can." She smiled with false sweetness.

"It's hard to watch your back when you're concerned with watching where you're going." He shrugged. "I watch backs real good. Ask the Marines, they loved me."

Of course they had, he had been a suicide mission waiting to happen for over four years and probably would have taken another tour if a sniper hadn't taken out his shoulder.

There was talk that Natches had arranged the hit, that he knew it was coming and managed to deflect the damage. Chaya knew better. Natches didn't play games. Oh, he may well have known the danger was there and that the shot would be taken. His instincts were so well honed that he had probably felt it coming and, yes, deflected the damage. But it wasn't arranged. Natches was too honest for that, too in-your-face to ever play those games.

"I don't need you to watch my back here," she told him. "That's the sheriff's job. You have no place in this assignment, and you don't need to be involved."

And he just smiled. Again.

"Damn it, Natches. You're not even a contract agent on this assignment. I am not letting you butt your nose into it."

"Are you ready to go pick your stuff up at the hotel this morning? You can pack while you're waiting on Cranston's e-mail to come through."

He was as immovable as the mountains surrounding them. Stubbornness defined his expression and the cool green of his eyes, and had her gritting her teeth to hold back her anger and her desperation.

Was it too much to ask for just a few hours to think? To clear her head enough to make sense of what she had done the night before? Was that too much to ask for? Evidently it was as far as he was concerned.

"You are not returning to the hotel with me. I know how to pack on my own." There was no getting out of moving in with him, and she knew it. But at the moment, that was as far as she was willing to go. "You can give me that redneck pride and stubborn look until hell freezes over, but I'm a fairly competent agent, Natches. Until Cranston begins sending names that might actually trip some tempers in your fair little county, I'm doing this by the book. Period. And my book says I follow orders. And those orders say no Mackay cousins involved. Period."

Frustration flickered in his eyes—and an edge of anger—as he rose from the couch, standing to his full, impressive six feet two inches. And he glared at her. Natches's glaring was sexy as hell, but it was also damned intimidating.

"You don't know this town or these people," he argued again. "You don't know which questions will trip tempers, and from the looks of the previous questions, tempers were more than likely tripped further than what you believe. This isn't the city, Chay. It's Kentucky."

"You make it sound like another planet." She rolled her eyes at his tone. "They're still people, Natches."

"Are they?" he growled. "One of the good ole boys you questioned can shoot a deer from over a half mile out and his hunting rifle is sighted for even farther distances. How much easier would it be to take out one lone little agent?"

"And now you stop bullets, too?" She widened her eyes in mock surprise. "Why, Natches. Why didn't you tell me sooner that you were freakin' Superman?"

She watched him grind his teeth, the bunching of his jaw muscles, the flattening of his lips. Yeah, it was sexy as hell, but pretty damned intimidating.

"I was a Marine assassin," he snarled. "Do you think I won't feel those sights on you before some stupid bastard takes the shot? I know what it feels like, Chay, and you don't want me going hunting if something happens to you, because the first son of a bitch I'd look up would be Timothy Cranston."

Chaya almost took a step back at the banked anger in Natches's eyes. She wanted to tell him yes more than anything. But if she gave in to him now, then she may as well turn the entire investigation over to him because she would completely lose control.

"And do you think I don't know when I have gunsights leveled on me, Natches? Do I really look that fucking green? That I'm not aware of when I'm pushing too many damned buttons?"

"International fucking terrorists are not damned pissed-off rednecks," he almost yelled. "No rules here, Chay. No warning. No instinct, unless you're one of them."

She held on to her own temper by a fingernail.

"My strength in these interviews is the fact that you aren't with me, and though you've been shadowing me, you're far enough away that most people are more amused than concerned. You'll hamper my ability to get the answers I need, Natches, and that will only hinder the investigation."

"And you think people aren't going to know you're living with me?" He crossed his arms over his chest and glowered back at her.

"Where I sleep isn't as big an issue as you sitting there terrifying everyone I question or having you chauffeur me from place to place. If we change the process at this point, we hamper it."

"And what the bloody hell does that have to do with me returning to the hotel with you this morning?" His voice rose slightly, just enough to assure her that his patience was reaching its limit.

"Because I need a few minutes to think if you don't fucking mind," she yelled back at him. "Excuse me, Natches, but you have my brain in so many damned pieces it resembles a puzzle right now."

"He does have that habit." Dawg stepped in as he slid the sliding glass door open and stared at Chaya, who fought to pull her anger back and adopt the cool, unaffected appearance she gave everyone but Natches.

And evidently, she was failing, because he was staring at her as though he didn't know her. His eyes narrowed, his celadon green eyes, so light they were almost colorless, watching her curiously.

"What the hell do you want?" Natches growled at his cousin. "You know, Dawg, this nosy attitude of yours is really starting to piss me off."

"When hasn't it?" Dawg finally shrugged. "I just thought I should let you know that I have a call coming in about a half hour on that project we were working on. I need you there."

Natches glared at his cousin. The project was this damned assignment Chaya was on, and it was obvious Dawg was hesitant about including her in on it.

"Yeah, I'm sure he has information now regarding your little project," she snorted knowingly as she stomped across the room and pushed her laptop back into the case before collecting the keys to her sedan, which the sheriff had had delivered to the marina the evening before.

As if she didn't know what the hell they were talking about. She wasn't a moron, and she didn't enjoy being treated like one.

From the look on Natches's face, he was still intent on following her though.

"Don't turn this into a battle, Natches," she told him fiercely. "Not yet. Not now. Being your lover is a far cry from being your lapdog. I don't heel worth crap, and you should know that right up front."

"Like I didn't figure that shit out in Iraq." Throttled male irritation spiked his voice and almost had her grinning.

Dawg didn't bother to hide his smile.

"Damn, son," he drawled at Natches. "I think you're losing this battle. Do you need any pointers? Advice?"

"So says the man who blackmailed his lover." Chaya rolled her eyes. "Really, Dawg, I don't think Natches needs any advice from you. It could end up getting him arrested."

Dawg scowled as he turned to Natches. "Not like you to tell tales, cousin."

"He didn't tell the tale. I believe it's become something of a local legend. I've heard about it from several sources, Dawg. Small-town secrets and all that." She smiled grimly.

"Go home, Dawg." Natches hadn't taken his eyes off her nor had his face lost the edge of irritation burning into anger.

Dawg grinned. "But this is more fun. Crista's sick again this morning. That virus is kicking her ass for some reason, and she ran me off."

"Then go to work." Natches and Chaya snapped the order back at him simultaneously, causing him to chuckle.

"Sorry, kids, but this project is kind of important right now and I've been working long and hard on it." He turned to Natches. "You know where I'm at when you two get this ironed out. Try not to take all day though, because Crista's getting put out over my absence from the store. Like she can't run it better than I do anyway—when she isn't sick." He shook his shaggy head as he turned to the door, slid it back open and stepped outside.

When it snapped closed again, Chaya pushed her fingers through her hair and stared back at Natches, aware that if she gave in to him now then she may as well turn every ounce of independence she possessed over to him.

It wasn't that he was controlling, there was a difference between protective and controlling, she was finding. Her first husband, Craig, had been controlling. Natches was protective.

"I'll follow you back to the hotel." He grimaced, adding, "Then head back here. I'll meet up with you at the diner."

"No, Natches. I don't need a bodyguard."

"What's wrong with having a damned partner? Hell, Chaya, I'm not asking for anything you can't give me here."

She had never had a partner though. She had worked independently within a team, but she had never had a partner.

She shoved her hands into the pockets of her jeans and breathed out roughly. "You can follow me back to the hotel if you need to, but not to the room. I need to take care of checking out, and I have an early meeting scheduled in one of the other rooms with the other agents working the case. I'll be lucky to make it to the diner on time this morning."

She rubbed at her neck as she stared back at him, watching his expression settle a bit, though not by much. He still wasn't comfortable with this.

"I'm not used to a partner either, Natches. I'm used to working alone—you know that. But I'm trying. I really am."

And she was, but she needed this morning to get a grip on

herself and what was changing in her life. He was changing things inside her that she had never imagined she would allow.

"You're too damned independent sometimes, Chaya." He stalked across the room and pulled her into his arms. One broad hand cupped the back of her head, his head lowered, and his lips covered hers.

Instantly, heat rose within her. Her breath caught and the passion that raged through her with each touch began to burn across her system.

"That's why." He pulled back, his gaze so intent, so filled with emotion that she felt her chest clench at the sight of it. "Because I've never known what you make me feel, Chay. And losing it would destroy me."

Those words haunted her that morning. She parked at the hotel, feeling his eyes on her as she entered and got the paperwork started for her checkout.

She moved from there straight to the meeting in one of the other agents' rooms, thanking God there were donuts and coffee because she had refused the breakfast Natches had offered her. Her nerves had been strung too tight, her senses too off balance to eat that early.

As the meeting wound up and she saved her notes to her laptop, she was looking forward to finally getting to her room. She would have an hour, maybe, to shower and get her thoughts in order before checking for Cranston's e-mail and making her notes for the interviews.

That hour didn't help though. As she stored her luggage in the rented car and stared back at the hotel, she felt the old fears rising inside her again. The same fears that had kept her from staying the year before. The ones that had kept her chasing danger rather than making a trip to Somerset long before any missiles had been hijacked.

That fear of loss.

As she slid into the car, she thought about living versus losing, and realized that if she didn't manage to lose Natches, then it would be the first time she had managed not to lose someone she loved.

She had lost her parents in her teens. Not to violence or to death, but to sheer disinterest. Her socialite mother and career-intensive father had no idea what to do with the little girl that always needed a hug or a kiss.

Her sister—she had thought she'd managed to maintain that relationship, before she found out Craig had been sleeping with her. The woman she would have trusted above anyone, the one she trusted her child with, had been sleeping with her husband.

Not that there had been a relationship between her and Craig for years. After Beth's birth, Craig had drifted away, and Chaya had slowly realized she didn't even miss him. When she had been called out on that last assignment in Iraq, she had already informed her superiors that she wouldn't be remaining after the assignment finished. She was resigning to stay home with her daughter. Beth was only three, and she needed her mother.

She forced back a muted sob at the thought of her little girl, her laughing eyes, her rounded, pretty face. Beth had been her life. And within a few short hours after her rescue, Natches had become her heart.

That betrayal was the one she had fought to forgive herself for. While her daughter was in danger, Chaya had been flirting with another man. Natches had sat in her hospital room, teased her with kisses, brought her flowers. He had slipped candy to her and he had made her laugh. And during that two weeks when she had been unable to contact her sister, Beth had been in Iraq with Craig.

She had been falling in love, and Beth had been in danger.

She hated herself for it. She had screamed out so many times in the darkness of the night, sobbing, begging for a forgiveness she couldn't give herself.

And now what was she doing? She laid her hand against her stomach and tried to fight the panic building inside her. Was she risking the life of another child?

She shook her head. She couldn't do this. First thing this evening she was stopping at a drugstore and picking up the condoms herself. It was her choice, Natches had warned her. If she wanted them, then she would have to remember them. She would have to remember them because she didn't know if she could face the consequences.

But a child. She had always wanted to be a mother. To make

a secure, happy home filled with laughter and love, the very things she had never seemed to find until she had found Natches. Or he had found her.

And he wanted a child with her. The playboy of Somerset, the wildest, the most wicked of the Nauti Boys, and he wanted to keep her. He wanted to laugh with her, and he wanted to raise babies with her.

It was inconceivable.

Shaking her head, she started the car, then looked up in surprise as the sheriff's cruiser, followed by Natches's jeep, blocked her in.

Frowning, she opened the door and started out of the car.

"Get your case." Natches jumped from the jeep and in two short strides was pulling her away from the car before reaching in and grabbing her briefcase. The door slammed behind her as Sheriff Mayes went to the ground, rolled onto his back and wedged himself beneath it.

"Move." Natches was dragging her away from the sedan.

"What the hell is going on here?" Jerking her arm out of his grip she looked from him to where Sheriff Mayes's long legs stuck out beneath her vehicle.

Her gaze jerked up once again as three other vehicles pulled in. Dawg, Rowdy, and Ray Mackay jumped from their pickups and moved quickly to the car.

"Have you checked under the hood yet, Zeke?" Dawg called out.

"Get your asses out of here. I have an explosives squad on the way. Don't you touch that car."

Male voices were filling the area as hotel employees and a few guests began to move from the building.

The sheriff rolled out and jumped to his feet. "It's here," he snarled. "Get the hell away from the car. Now!"

Chaya started in shock as Natches all but lifted her off her feet and pushed her into the jeep, forcing her to crawl over the console as he moved in behind her. With a jerk and a squeal of tires, the jeep raced a safe distance from the car, then with a hard twist of his wrist, Natches turned it in a quick half spin to face the vehicle as Chaya stared at him in complete disbelief.

"What the hell is going on here?"

Natches turned to her, dangerous. Here was danger. Forest green eyes were the color of moss, savage planes and angles marked his expression, and rage flickered in his gaze.

"You lost an agent this morning," he bit out, his voice dangerously soft.

Chaya stared back at him in mute shock.

"What are you talking about? They were all at the meeting just an hour ago. I left them there."

"Kyle Denton made it about three miles out of town before his car exploded. It took out a nice chunk of the interstate and the back end of the eighteen-wheeler he was driving behind. There's nothing left of him but fucking pieces. The minute Mayes learned it was Denton, he called me and we rushed here. Now tell me Chaya, who the *fuck* is Cranston after here?"

Chaya felt her face go numb with grief and shock. She had just spoken to Kyle. He had told her about his engagement, to his third wife. He was barely forty. He had laughed about her showing up late and the news that she was moving into the boat with Natches. Accusing her of going above and beyond the call of duty.

He had a daughter in high school. She had worked with him for years. He was going to retire after this assignment. Go into private security, he had told her once. Plenty of money and none of the hassles. A man made it to forty, and he wanted a chance to enjoy just a few years danger free.

And he was gone.

"There is a bomb under your car that was not there this morning," he told her then. "Dawg and Rowdy checked that car before we went out to it. I checked it before you got into it; do you remember that, Chay?"

She nodded slowly staring back at him as she tried to think, to figure out where and how and why.

"Someone planted that bomb after you arrived here. Are you still safe, Chay? Did you check that motherfucking car before you got in it?"

She licked her lips slowly. "I ran the transmitter over it. I always do that. I did it this morning. I used the mirror in my bag to look beneath it."

"But it was hidden," he snarled. "Do you realize that? A pro put that bomb in there, sweetheart. Tell me, Chay; do you realize that?"

His voice was rising, his hands tightening on her shoulders until she was afraid he might start shaking her.

"Natches, I am neither a moron nor a candidate for suicide," she informed him coolly. "I didn't find the bomb, which means it was well hidden and expertly placed. And someone has already taken out one of the other agents, so this assignment is severely in danger." She pulled her cell phone from her bag, flipped it open, pressed the secured speed dial and waited while he glared at her.

"Cranston," Timothy barked into the phone.

"We just lost Denton to a car bomb. We're compromised."

"Are you with Mackay?"

"Natches, yes." She stared back at Natches.

"Keep your ass there. I already have calls out to the other agents to park their vehicles immediately and contact the sheriff for pickup. I just received word myself. I'm on my way."

He disconnected and Chaya slowly flipped the phone closed.

"Who is he after?" Natches snarled again.

"Military intelligence and DHS have tracked the persons responsible for the hijacking and theft of military weapons, including those missiles, across the nation to a paramilitary group. Freedom's League. Five years ago, Freedom's League was hijacking and stealing weapons in Iraq as well. Their members are military and ex-military. They steal the weapons by hijacking them one at a time here and there, or in large shipments. Some they sell, evidently to fund other missions they undertake.

"It was Freedom's League members I was investigating when I was captured by Nassar in Iraq. It was those same members that executed a false order for those missiles to be launched on the hotel Craig and Beth were staying in when he was trying to escape. They've managed to infiltrate the military to a degree that DHS is now desperate, and Timothy is rabid to capture one of their generals.

"The League is located in the eastern, southern, and western states, and their leaders are well trained and well organized."

"I didn't ask you what. I asked you who," he snarled back, so furious she flinched.

"I don't know who," she screamed back at him, her fists striking his chest to get away from him, to escape the ragged pain she could see in his eyes, that she could feel in her heart. "If I knew who, I would have killed him myself, and Cranston knows it."

She jerked around, staring out the windshield, watching as the other Mackays, the sheriff, and several deputies worked to tape off the area and roll other vehicles away from her rental car.

"All I know is that one of the head members of the League has been tracked here, through the operation with the missiles. The Swede attempting to buy the missiles finally made a deal with the government. In exchange for a lighter sentence, he gave them the information he had on this one buy. The League was involved and he was contacted by someone he trusted and had dealt with in the past. He wasn't originally contacted by Johnny Grace. He didn't know his name, didn't have a description, all he had was the fact that his contact had been in the military, and he was based here in Somerset, working within the League to gather the funds and the arms to launch a future revolution in America."

She watched as Dawg and Rowdy rolled another car out of the way. The agents who were still at the hotel were now marking their vehicles, but it looked like four were out.

"You're in danger, Chay," he told her, his voice throbbing with his anger. "They obviously know why you're here and who you're after."

She shook her head. "That's not possible. I don't know who. I don't think Timothy knows. He makes his list night by night, his questions as well, based on the answers I pull in from each interview. You know how this works," she repeated. "It's not an easy process, and this link is the only one Timothy has managed to find in five years. If we can manage to identify one of the head members and take him alive, then we can bust the organization."

"Until they re-form?"

"But even that takes time." She turned back to him, staring into his tormented eyes, seeing the same fears that plagued her. The fear of loss. "Sometimes, even a lifetime, Natches. We fight one battle at a time, as long as we can fight, then we turn the rest to the new generation and pray they're as diligent. What more can we do?"

Thirteen

Four of the six agents' vehicles had been wired, Chaya's among them. Three of the four, including Denton, were assigned to watch the subjects after interview. It was obvious someone was getting spooked, and Chaya couldn't figure out how.

"The only questions we asked that could have possibly tripped anyone's radar were the ones involving the Mackay family," Chaya told the sheriff and Natches that afternoon as she sat in the back of the cruiser, headed for the last name on that morning's list.

Timothy Cranston had called and ordered the interviews for that day be completed. Natches hadn't been pleased, and Chaya knew he was only biding his time. She could feel the temper rising inside him as they drove toward one of the more popular nightclubs—or bars, as Natches called them—in town.

The sheriff pulled into the parking lot, and from the corner of her eye, she caught his grimace as he glanced toward the Harleys parked close to the building.

"Biker bar?" she asked him.

"We could only get so lucky." He shook his head as Natches moved from the front of the car and opened the back door for her.

"Ever been in a honky-tonk, sweetheart?" Natches asked her then.

Chaya stared around the parking lot and shook her head. "What's wrong with honky-tonks?"

"The question is: What's not wrong with them?" The sheriff

sighed as he jammed his hat down on his head, his expression intimidating. "Who's on the damned list for this place anyway?"

She pulled the small notebook from her pocket and glanced at the name. It was cute. "Rogue Walker."

She nearly bounced into Natches's back as he came to a hard stop, turned, and stared over her head at the sheriff. Swinging around, Chaya got a glimpse of complete male horror a second before it was gone.

"It's a cute name," she announced.

"Lord have mercy on us," Sheriff Mayes muttered before Natches gripped her arm and led her to the door.

"Try not to piss her off," he suggested.

Chaya would have grinned at the suggestion if her nerves weren't still rattled over Denton's death and the bombs they had found in the vehicles the agents drove. Someone was definitely trying to send a message. That person didn't like the questions and was going to put a stop to them.

"The file Cranston sent stated that Ms. Walker—"

"Don't call her miz nothin'," Natches interrupted. "Call her Rogue. Period. Don't comment on her clothes, her hair, or her motorcycle, and no matter what you do, don't even hint at mentioning her past employment."

Chaya stopped and stared up at him with a frown. "She was a schoolteacher; what's so bad about that?"

"Lord help us if you ask about it," he muttered. "Let's get this the hell over with. If fists start flying, get back to the cruiser. We'll be right behind you."

Oh yeah, she just bet he would be. He was probably praying for a fight to get rid of some of that testosterone.

Shaking her head, she followed him into the bar and picked out the subject immediately.

Dressed in black pants, boots, and a snug vest, Ms. Rogue Walker was tipping a beer to her lips and glancing to the door in boredom.

Long golden red hair cascaded down her back in thick ringlets; pale creamy flesh was accentuated by the black attire and gave her an almost feyish appearance. She was slender but curvy. Full breasts pressed against the front of the vest, and deep, pretty violet eyes widened before a sharp, disinterested mask descended over her face and she turned away.

Interesting. Chaya looked back at Natches. "A former conquest?"

"Even I wasn't that damned brave," he growled. "Now get this over with so we can leave."

"Fine, get a beer, park your butt at the bar with the sheriff, and leave me alone."

He grabbed hold of her arm, keeping her from turning away as his head lowered, his eyes darkening in irritation. "Not gonna happen."

"Better happen." She smiled tightly. "Or else? I can do 'or else' really well, Natches, and I can make it stick. This is the wrong place to decide to take over, and it's definitely the wrong place for a public quarrel." She jerked her arm out of his hold and tried to tamp down the adrenaline still racing through her. It made her cranky and it made it more difficult for her to hold on to the patience she knew she needed right now. "I'll just be a few minutes. You can see me perfectly fine while having a beer."

"And when I get you home we're going to have a talk about this 'do it your way' crap," he said, scowling. "First thing."

"Fine." She nodded. "First thing. I'll be ready for you. Are we doing it naked or clothed?"

Before he could do more than narrow his eyes on her, she turned and moved down the bar to where Rogue Walker was watching the confrontation with interest now.

"I wondered when you would get to me," she said as Chaya stepped to her.

Her voice was beautiful. Chaya cocked her head to the side and stared at the petite woman. She was a few inches shorter than Chaya's five feet seven inches, and much smaller boned.

"Do you sing?" Chaya asked her as she lifted herself onto one of the barstools and turned to face the other girl.

"In the shower," she said suggestively, running her eyes over Chaya. "Want to hear me?"

Strange, Rogue Walker's file hadn't said anything about an alternate lifestyle. Or a lover of any type.

"Natches gets jealous." She sighed mockingly.

Rogue rolled her eyes. "As many games as that man played before he left for the Marines, he has no right to jealousy."

"Does any man?" Chaya countered.

Rogue laughed, a soft, amused sound. "No, they don't, Agent

Dane. But I'm sure that's not why you came here to talk to me. I assume this has something to do with that little bastard Johnny Grace?"

Chaya pulled the digital recorder from her jacket pocket and laid it on the bar. "I need to record this," she told the other woman.

Rogue shrugged. "I sound like crap on it, but whatever." She lifted the beer to her lips and sipped as Chaya set the recorder and stated the date, time, and subject.

"For the record, your name is . . ."

Rogue stopped her by laying her hand over the recorder and staring at her hard. "I imagine you know my full name?"

"I do."

"State it and we're going to fight. My name is Rogue Walker, period. Understood?"

Chaya inclined her head. "Understood."

"And don't state my age, please." Her smile was all teeth. "If you don't mind."

Chaya didn't know the game this girl was playing, and she didn't care. When Rogue lifted her hand, Chaya continued, as requested, and received Rogue's affirmation that she was aware she was being recorded.

"For the record," Rogue drawled mockingly. "I thought Johnny Grace was a teeny-tiny little maggot that needed to be blown away, so you're looking to the wrong person if you think I was helping him."

"Who would have helped him?" Chaya kept her voice low enough to keep those around from listening.

Rogue shrugged. "His uncle Dayle. He's a son of a bitch, but I'm sure Natches told you that. He wouldn't have helped kill soldiers or steal weapons though. Dayle Mackay likes to knock the women around, and he likes to run his mouth about politics, but he wouldn't sell missiles to terrorists unless he had them rigged to blow them to hell and back."

"What about Johnny's mother?"

Rogue sneered maliciously. "The only thing that bitch knows how to do is fuck her brother. Johnny got drunk one night right before he died and decided I should know that. Dayle tells her what to do, and she does it. She doesn't make many moves without Dayle's permission."

"But Johnny did?"

Rogue stared across the bar as she tipped the beer to her lips and narrowed her eyes thoughtfully. Finally she set the bottle back on the bar and shook her head.

"I would have said no, but it appears he did." She shrugged again.

"Why would you have said that?" Chaya asked.

Rogue pursed her lips. "Johnny was a weaselly little thing. He craved male attention and approval. I wouldn't have thought he would have done that, simply because his uncle Dayle would have been disappointed in him. And he couldn't have borne that. It was bad enough when Dayle found out he was gay."

"What happened when his uncle found out he was gay?"

Rogue tapped a fingernail against the bar, frowning down at the movement for long moments. "Johnny didn't walk for weeks," she finally said. "I kind of felt sorry for him, went to the house to check on him." She shook her head on a bitter laugh. "Dayle had beat him from head to toe. Johnny was in a dress, stockings, and a wig. Said it was his punishment." Disgust marked her expression. "Damn, sometimes I wonder why I don't just go ahead and move back to Boston. You know better than to get involved with people there."

Chaya glanced around the bar. There weren't many customers, but those who were there seemed to keep an eye on Rogue. And Chaya.

"Did Johnny spend much time in bars?" she asked the other woman then.

Rogue shook her head. "Not really. Johnny was the home-and-hearth type. I guess that's why it surprised a lot of us when we found out what he'd done. He didn't seem the type."

"And you don't care that you're telling me all this?" Chaya injected. "Getting people around here to talk hasn't been easy. Yet you're more than willing."

Rogue smiled. A wicked upturn of Cupid's bow lips, and eyes filled with cynical amusement. "Lady, this county holds no love for me, or me for it." Bitterness flashed in her eyes. "The only difference between me and the fine upstanding citizens of this town is that I tell the truth as I see it. Let's see. Example. I bet a half dozen spiteful little bitches are going to tell you, if they haven't already, how hard they partied with Natches the weekend before you lit back into town." She smiled gleefully. "I can tell you Natches hasn't snacked on any homegrown offerings since he came back from the Marines. Now, the good sheriff over there? Widowed at a young age, he sampled the fine pleasures of one Janice Lowell just last week. And from what I hear, he's a real go-getter. An all-nighter." She leaned over and waved at the sheriff over her shoulder.

Chaya glanced back and was surprised to see Sheriff Mayes watching the other woman with narrow-eyed disapproval.

"He does the whole good-cop routine so well." Rogue sighed elaborately.

"What else can you tell me?" Chaya asked her then.

"I can tell you a lot of women want to claw your eyes out. Weekend gossip is so much fun. And I can tell you that one of your agents—" She paused and shook her head, the brittle amusement dropping for a second. "Hell of a way to go. I heard he was killed this morning and several others almost went up in flames as well. What do you want me to tell you, Agent Dane?" The mocking, devil-may-care grin was back.

"Who was pulling Johnny's strings? Even better, who set the bombs?"

"If I knew, I'd be barbeque, too." Rogue grimaced. "All I hear is a little gossip here and there." She shook her head, the tiny bells at her ears chiming softly. "The Mackay family is damned weird though. Ray, he's a good guy, so are Dawg, Rowdy, and Natches. I didn't know Chandler before he died, thank God, but I know he and Dayle were having one major fight the night Chandler and his wife were killed. And I know Nadine Mackay Grace and Dayle like to get the nasty on a little too often." Her smile was all teeth; her eyes were bitter and much too cynical. "If I had known anything more, trust me, one of the Mackay cousins would have known, because there's nothing in this world I would have loved better than bringing down Nadine Grace."

"Why?" Sometimes that was the most important question a person could ask.

Rogue picked at the label on the bottle of beer, then reached over and turned the recorder off.

"Interview over," she said softly.

Chaya picked up the recorder, transferred it back to her

pocket, and watched Rogue expectantly. "Just between us girls then," she told her. "What did Nadine do to you?"

Rogue glanced at where Natches and the sheriff sat, then turned her eyes back to Chaya. Somehow she wasn't surprised to see the hollow pain reflected within them.

"She helped create me," Rogue said then, her voice low and haunting. "One of these days, I'll get to remind her of that. Create a monster, and it can come back and bite you in the ass. Isn't that true, Agent Dane?"

Chaya nodded slowly. "That's very true, Rogue. Very true."

"Natches, you're making a mistake here," Zeke muttered as they watched the two women. They couldn't hear the words, but a look told a thousand tales. "You need to pull her out of this."

Rogue, the one woman who men in three counties feared on a daily basis, almost blushed, and she softened. She looked younger; her gaze twinkled in humor. Then her expression shifted again, sorrow, and then bitterness. Natches swore that in the years he had known her, which hadn't been many, he'd rarely seen anything but hard, mocking amusement in her eyes.

As he watched Chaya though, his chest clenched. He'd been ready to tie her to his bed and force her out of this. Make her swear she would duck and hide until this was over and let him deal with the mess Cranston was creating.

But as he watched her, he remembered crashing into that filthy little dirt cell in Iraq. The smell of blood and death had filled the cramped area, but there had been Chaya, crouched, a gun in her hand, dressed in her tormentor's uniform.

Her eyes had been so swollen there had been no way she could have seen out of them. Her feet had been ragged, though he hadn't known that at the time. She had been so bruised and mauled, he'd seen his own life flash before his eyes. Because he couldn't have left her, and there hadn't been a chance he could've carried her out of there.

But she had run. There had been no tears, only strength. No excuses, no recriminations. She had fought to live and fought to fight, and it was those qualities that had first stolen his heart.

And he thought he could take that from her now?

"That's not my job," he finally murmured.

"It's your job to protect her, damn it," Zeke cursed.

And to that, Natches nodded. "It's my job to watch her back while she does her job. You don't change what you love, Zeke, or you never loved it to begin with."

He had fallen in love with the agent. Strong, independent, fiercely determined. Take those things away from her, and she wasn't Chaya. She wouldn't be his heart or his soul, and that he couldn't allow.

Natches escorted Chaya back to his houseboat after the interview, the tension burning hot and heavy through them.

"The boat has been checked thoroughly," he told her as they walked along the floating docks toward it. "Alex hit town a few hours ago. He and his team went over it from top to bottom while we were on our way in."

Alex Jansen was Special Forces and worked closely with Cranston. Chaya had worked with him several times. He was also Crista Mackay's brother.

It was already dark and growing bitterly cold for the season. The wind off the water felt like ice and cut through Chaya's thick jacket like the sharpest blade.

She felt cold from the inside out. As though icicles were growing in the pit of her stomach and freezing her with fear.

What the hell was going on in this beautiful little county? A place where young men were punished in such horrible ways for their sexual preferences, where young women, like twenty-four-year-old Rogue, were more cynical than women twice their ages. And agents, good men, family men, were being targeted to die in an inferno.

"Alex and his team are at Dawg's right now." Natches's voice was low, restrained. "We'll wait till later to meet with them. After you've had a chance to rest and eat. You haven't eaten today, Chay."

Was that concern in his voice? God, she didn't want to hear the gentleness in his voice when she knew he was furious. Probably furious with her. She was furious with herself. She hadn't taken the proper precautions. Somehow, she had missed something during the interviews she had conducted. An expression, a flash of maliciousness, a lie. There were always signs. Always. It was always there, in the eyes, in the small shifts of the face, and she had missed it. And because she had, Kyle was dead.

Cranston had arrived in town as she left the bar. The text message had flashed on her phone, warning her that he would meet with her the next morning. On Natches's houseboat. She hadn't told Natches yet.

"Come on, baby." His voice was a breath of warmth against her ear as he unlocked the door and they stepped into the heated interior.

After locking the door behind them, he slid her jacket from her shoulders and unclipped her weapon from her side.

"You need a shoulder harness for this." He laid the holstered gun on the jacket at the end of the couch.

Chaya stared at the gun for long moments. She hated it. She hated carrying it, she hated being tied to it, and she hated the life she had led for the last five years. God, the last ten years. The only part of her life that had seemed worthwhile was the time with Beth. And with Natches.

She shook her head. "They aren't comfortable."

She wanted to turn to him, she wanted to beg him to hold her, to take away the pain, and she couldn't. She was the agent, this was the life she had chosen. What right did she have to burden him with her regrets now? He would only feel as though he should fix it, somehow drag her from it, and now she couldn't let it go.

"Chay." His arms came around her as she felt her throat tightening with emotion. "I have you."

His head rested against hers, and his warmth surrounded her.

"I need a shower." She pulled away from him. "Do you want to order dinner? I could probably fix something when I get finished."

"How domestic." He let her go, though his tone grated on her nerves, that hint of knowledge, patience, and just a tinge of condescending male. "I do know how to cook, Chay," he told her a second later as he breathed out roughly. "I've been doing it for a while now."

"Since your father threw you out of your home." She turned on him, feeling it burn in her now, that icy rage. Nearly everyone she had spoke to knew about it, mentioned it, seemed to wallow in the dirty gossip and nasty stories they thought they knew.

"It was never my home," he said simply. "It was a place to crash for a night or two."

He said that so simply, as though it didn't even matter.

"The scars on your back? He beat you senseless . . ."

"Yeah, well, he managed it that time." His grin was smug if tinged with bitterness. "He has a few scars on his back now though. What the hell is this, Chay? I was barely twenty years old. We got into a fight over my sister and ended up fistfighting. He had the bigger fists at the time. Too bad, so sad. I survived it." He shook his head and stared at her in confusion. "If you want to crucify Dayle Mackay, I'll be the first in line to help you, but that's not what this is all about."

No, it wasn't. It was about the fact that he had every intention of jerking her out of that bar. That he had informed her, quite bluntly, that they would be discussing it when they returned here.

Well, she was ready to discuss it now.

"You haven't yelled at me yet, and I'm sick of waiting on it." Her hands were shaking with nerves, with reaction. "Go ahead and do it and get it over with. I should have come straight back here this morning, right? I should just let you take care of all the pesky little details of my job and of protecting me. Go ahead. Say it." She waved her hand back at him as she felt the tears trying to fill her eyes. "Get it off your chest."

She was yelling. She was irrational. She had never been irrational in her life but as Natches stared back at her with that expression of patient male understanding, she wanted to scream. Men didn't understand. They didn't feel the same things, they didn't hurt the same way. They didn't fear the same things. And she knew damned good and well he hadn't understood anything when they entered that bar.

"So. Let me get this straight." He crossed his arms over his chest and tilted his head, watching her curiously. "I should be chewing on your ass for doing your job? Despite the fact that it just impressed the fucking hell out me. Kind of like it did in that damned desert. Now, suddenly, I'm supposed to change everything about you that made me so crazy about you to begin with?"

"You didn't want me to go," she snapped back. "You were ready to tie me up and drag me back here."

He infuriated her as he nodded slowly. "Yes, I was. Until I remembered this is who you are. You couldn't walk away now even if I demanded it. No more than I could. I don't want to change that part of you, Chay."

She pushed her fingers through her hair and turned her back on him.

"Why aren't you angry with me?" She turned back to him a second later. "I could be carrying your child and I went out there anyway. I finished those interviews knowing someone wanted me dead."

"And I made sure you did what you had to do, while I watched your back," he said simply. "Chay, I don't want a lapdog. If I wanted a woman willing to say yes to everything I wanted I could have had it two hundred times over by now. I want you."

"Why?" She clenched her fists at her side as that anger poured through her. "Why do you want me?"

"Hell, do I have to have a damned reason?" he fired back. "For God's sake, Chay, because you know how to stand up to me? Because you know how to live? You know how to love."

"I don't."

He stopped. "You don't what?"

"I don't know how to love, Natches." She felt the tremors shaking through her body then. Deep, hard shudders, the ice building, tightening inside her until she wondered if she could ever be warm again.

He smiled then. That slow, wicked smile that sent a flame shooting through the ice and a ragged tremor of response ripping through her senses.

"Well, I guess that's why you need me then."

"Why?" She did need him. She needed him until she couldn't breathe without the thought of him. And she still couldn't fathom how to deal with it.

"To show you how to recognize all that love burning within you," he answered.

He moved to her, stalking across the room until she had to look up to hold his gaze, to stay connected to the only security she had found in all the years she had lived.

"Where?" She needed to know where it was, how to open it, and how to set it free.

"Ah, Chay," he whispered, framing her face, his lips brushing against hers. "It's all just right here, baby. Burning inside you. All you've got to do is let it burn."

Fourteen

Natches wanted to kill. As God was his witness, the moment those shattered honey gold eyes locked with his after they entered the houseboat, he wanted to kill.

He wanted to make her dead husband, Craig, die again. He wanted to make Nassar Mallah suffer. He wanted to beat Cranston to a bloody pulp and he wanted to rip whoever had dared to kill Denton, limb from limb.

He wanted their blood to wash over his hands, but even more, he wanted to ease the haunting pain from Chaya's eyes.

"Look at you," he said, keeping his voice low and gentle. "Running on nothing but coffee and a few donuts. Shaking in my arms and staring at me so fiercely. I bet if your eyes hadn't been swollen shut when I rescued you, I would have seen that same will to fight in them then."

"Don't do this." She shook her head. "I'm not what you see. I'm not that strong."

He flashed her a wicked smile, because he knew better. A smile as smug and confident as any self-appointed sensualist had ever given a woman. And it succeeded in bringing a flush to her face, a glitter of anger to her eyes.

"You think you know everything." She pushed at his chest, as though he was actually going to let her go now. "Let me go."

He laughed at that. "Baby, I watched your back and let you fight. I took you into the baddest honky-tonk in three counties and sat at the bar like the good little boy I was told to be. This is my territory now. I don't have to be a good boy here."

"As if you've ever been a good boy," she snorted and tried to twist in his arms.

Natches chuckled at that. "I've always been a good boy with you, Chay. I let you run every time you wanted to run, remember?"

"You're not letting me run now," she snapped. "And all I want to run to is the damned shower."

He held her easily, letting her twist, letting that sleek little body stroke and rub against his. His cock was rock hard, it had been ever since he had watched her in that damned bar.

He'd wanted to wrap her in his arms and rock her, and at the same time he wanted to fuck her until she knew to the bottom of her soul exactly who she belonged to.

"Yeah, but I'm tired of being a good boy today." He grinned and dipped his head, stealing a kiss before she could do more than gasp in protest.

As she struggled, he managed to wrestle her shirt off her. She had changed clothes at the hotel, but he realized her luggage was likely up in smoke somewhere. The bomb squad had set several of those suckers off just to match the debris with the dead agent's car.

The thought of how close she had come to going up in flames as well had his hands trembling as he held her hips against him and took another kiss. A deeper kiss.

Hell, if he didn't forget the bone-chilling fear he felt when he realized her car was rigged to blow, then he might disintegrate from the inside out.

"Natches." Her voice was more a breathy moan now. "You have to stop this. I have to think."

"No thinking allowed here."

He let her struggle, let her twist until she turned and met the edge of the bar that separated the living room and kitchen. And then he pressed her shoulders down.

He wasn't going to go for slow and easy tonight. Slow and easy would come later. Right now, he was burning alive for her.

He loosened her jeans and dragged them over that very shapely ass. The prettiest ass in fifty states he swore as he hurriedly released his own jeans and freed the tormented length of his erection.

Fucking her was ecstasy, and he couldn't do without it much longer.

"What are you doing?" Breathless, hot, her voice washed over him. She wasn't protesting, she was losing herself in it, just as he always lost himself in her.

"We're trying to make a little Natches, remember?" He tucked the head of his cock against the swollen, saturated folds of her pussy before pressing into her.

Damn. It was like pressing into a living flame. Natches groaned, feeling sweat coat his flesh as she burned him alive. He worked his cock farther inside her, feeling her tighten around him, feeling the delicate muscles of her vagina milking and caressing his sensitive flesh.

Nothing was this good. There was no pleasure on earth that could ever be as good as taking Chaya like this. When she reached back for him, her short, neat little nails digging into his thigh, he gave her more. Slow, easy strokes that buried him inside her a little at a time. Gave him a chance to relish every ripple of response around the ultrasensitive head of his cock.

"Damn you, Natches," she cursed him even as she tugged at his thigh, trying to force him deeper.

Her voice was thick, a feminine little growl of demand that had him grinning with the pleasure of it.

"What? You want me to stop?" He stopped. Buried halfway inside her, his cock head throbbing, dying for more.

"You're insane," she cried out.

"Hmm. Good thing one of us is sane then." He leaned forward and laid a row of kisses between her shoulder blades. "Our kid needs at least one sane parent. You be the sane one." He pressed in farther.

He felt the wash of her juices and had to grit his teeth to hold back his release. His balls had drawn tight against the base of his shaft, electric sparks of sensation racing from them with the need to come.

"Oh God, Natches, we can't keep keeping doing this." She was breathing hard now, panting little breaths that assured him that she was as far gone to the pleasure as he was.

"Doing what?" Sweat trickled along his temple as she burned him clear to his soul.

"Talking babies."

His hips shifted and he drove another inch inside her, quick and hard, and gritted his teeth as she arched, a hungry little moan begging him for more.

"The thought of giving you babies makes me harder," he panted. Hell, the thought of her breathing made him harder. He stayed hard between each release at just the hope of having more of her.

"Everything makes you harder," she gasped, and he had to laugh.

"Everything about *you* makes me harder." He drew back, the head of his cock poised just inside her liquid heat before he forged inside again.

A throttled, feminine wail filled the air as he took her again. Pushing deep inside her, pausing and drawing back, only to push inside her again. Impaling her with slow strokes, then one fast hard thrust that pinned her to the table and had her trying to scream his name.

"Did you get those condoms today?" He could barely think, let alone talk. But it was the love play she needed tonight. That, and the slow realization that it was going to happen. She was going to belong to him. All of her.

"Damn you," she cursed, but there was no anger, an edge of laughter, maybe.

"Oh, man, that's too bad, Chay." His hands clenched on her hips as he drew back.

"Natches, don't you dare stop," she cried out, panic filling her voice. "Oh God, please, don't stop."

There wasn't a chance.

He thrust inside her to the hilt, snarled at the pleasure that bordered pain as he forced himself to stop, to hold deep inside her. To feel her.

She was close to orgasm. Her pussy was clenching around his shaft, stroking the sensitive head, rippling over him like a thousand hungry little fingers caressing him at once.

"You feel so good." He leaned into her, kissed the shell of her ear then drew the lobe between his teeth to worry it erotically. "So tight and hot around me. I could stay inside you forever, feeling you come for me, over and over again, Chay."

He could feel the perspiration coating both their bodies now. Her nails were digging into his thigh, a sharp little pain to keep him centered amid the pleasure.

"Are you ready for me, Chay? I'm going to take you hard. I'm going to take you so hard and deep you'll think you're dying. Then, before the last tremor is gone, I'm going to take you again. Over and over again, until you feel all that love burning and heating inside you. You hear me, sweetheart? We're going to find all that love."

She cried out his name. The sound of her voice, dazed and thick with the pleasure he was giving her, was almost, just almost, enough to send him over the edge right then. He had to clench his teeth, had to fight to hold back his release. But he knew holding back wasn't going to happen for long.

Gripping her hips firmly, he began to move. He started slow and easy, but slow and easy wasn't what either of them needed. She needed to burn through her pain and he needed to guide her through the heat. He needed to feel her come apart around him, shattering with the ecstasy as she shattered with hers.

Within seconds, the thrusts built. He was slamming against her, burying his cock inside her with blinding, furious strokes as she begged for more. For harder. Harder, stronger, until he heard her wail fill his head and felt her pussy, like a fist tightening on his cock, milking it, pulling his release from him, tearing through him with fire and lightning.

"Ah hell!" He barely recognized his own voice. "Chay. Ah God, baby, yes, take it. Take all of me."

He poured himself into her as he felt the contractions of her pussy spill her release around him. Deep, violent spurts of semen tore from the head of his cock, the racing pleasure tearing through his body as he thrust against her, buried himself deeper, and felt stars exploding in his head as she cried out his name.

He collapsed over her, his knees weak, and damn if he wasn't starting to feel as exhausted as she had looked earlier.

The contractions flexing around his cock were easing, and as he kissed her shoulder, he smiled.

"You know what, sweetheart?" he drawled.

"Hmm." She was boneless beneath him, sated, relaxing.

"You know you are *so* pregnant now, don't you?" Pride flared deep and strong inside him, and he swore he was growing hard again. "See? I told you, the thought of making babies with you just makes me harder."

No sooner had Chaya showered and eaten the impromptu meal Natches had waiting for her than his family converged on them. Rowdy and his wife, Kelly; Dawg and his wife, Crista; and their uncle Ray and his wife, Maria. And Crista's brother, Alex Jansen.

Chaya knew Alex Jansen fairly well—he was better known as Timothy Cranston's muscle, though Chaya doubted the Mackays knew that. And from the warning look he had thrown her, he didn't want it known, either.

Oh, how tangled this little web was becoming. She knew Alex could report back to Timothy and cause her more trouble than she wanted to face, but she also knew the man's incredible loyalty to his little sister, Crista.

Which way would Alex's loyalty swing in this one though?

As the men converged on the beers Natches had stacked in an ice-filled cooler and the women came bearing snacks, sandwiches, and chips, Chaya got a look into the relationships between the Mackays, their wives, and the uncle that had more or less raised all of them.

Ray Mackay was the complete opposite of his brothers or sister. He loved his son and his nephews, he was incredibly protective over all of them, and the loyalty and warmth seemed to extend around Alex as well. And maybe even Chaya herself.

He had hugged her as he walked in, patted her shoulder, and told her not to worry, the Mackays were going to take care of everything.

She'd wanted to grin at the proclamation, but she had a feeling he was entirely too serious.

Now, as she sat back and watched the men going through the printed reports Natches had taken from her laptop, she had a moment to worry about involving any of them. If something were to happen to even one of them, it would affect the whole family. And it wouldn't just affect them; it would devastate them.

"The subjects you questioned were all ex-military members." Rowdy cast her a narrow-eyed look from across the wide table as he laid down the file he had been going through. He flipped two files toward her. "Hollister Mcgrew."

Chaya stared at the picture clipped to the corner of the file. Hollister Mcgrew's pitted face, framed by limp brown hair and sporting a bullish look, stared back at her. He and Johnny had been reported to have been friends in high school, and later had run and drunk together in many of the local bars before Hollister signed up for the Army.

He wasn't gay, actually considered himself quite the ladies' man, despite his rotting front teeth and sour breath. His honorable discharge from the Army had been medical. Hollister hadn't handled the Army well.

"George Mack." Rowdy tossed out another file.

Pole skinny with straight, thinning brown hair and dirt brown eyes. For a few years, he and Johnny had been best friends, until George had joined the Navy. As with Hollister, George lasted only the first tour before receiving discharge, though his had been less than honorable. He'd nearly ended up in Leavenworth.

There were others. Many of them were rumored to be involved in drugs, grand theft, or burglary. The few who weren't ex-military, such as Rogue Walker, a former friend of Johnny's, were persons of interest who may or may not have had information tying Johnny to other persons of interest.

"Johnny was the one who admitted to masterminding the whole deal," she pointed out, playing devil's advocate.

"None of them had the brains or connections to have helped Johnny put everything together, nor could they have kept their dirty little paws off a million in cash," Alex stated. "They are the pawns. Who's the king?"

That was a good question. Chaya pushed her fingers through her hair in frustration. That one she hadn't figured out yet.

"They have ties to others as well," she stated. "The mayor and chief of police. George Mack is Mayor Sunders's second cousin. Hollister worked for Sunders as a handyman for several weeks. The same pattern follows for everyone I've questioned. I received three to five names each day as well as their most likely locations or residences. And the questions."

"The questions aren't that hard," Dawg snorted. "And it's damned easy to lie."

"And sometimes, it's damned easy to see that lie." She shrugged. "I've been trained to see the lies. I'm an interrogation specialist, Dawg. This is what I do well."

She had been lied to quite a bit during the questioning, and the knowledge of that had gone into the notes she sent to Cranston each evening. The same notes everyone here now held.

"There's no one here Johnny would have trusted," Ray told them all as he looked through the files. "He was a strange boy, but trust wasn't something he gave easily."

"Trust was something he traded with," Natches said, his voice curiously bland. "Johnny only trusted his mother and Dayle. And we know Nadine would lie out of her ass if it got her something she wanted. Dayle's no better."

That was his father, but there wasn't so much as a hint of emotion in his voice.

"Cranston's arriving here in the morning," she told them. "I received his message before we returned to the boat. I'm hoping he'll have more answers."

"I'd suggest he come bearing answers." Natches's more dangerous drawl was back now. If Timothy didn't have answers, then he was going to have to deal with more than one pissed-off Mackay.

"Several of these boys were military, too," Alex noticed. "The team we captured after Johnny's death was all ex-military. Penny-ante troublemakers, none of them did well there, but thought they were Rambo once they came home.

"The group we're after, Freedom's League, uses such men to help steal the weapons they've targeted. But the League has never attempted to sell something so powerful to terrorists before.

"The few times they managed to steal weapons of any strength, DHS was there to stop the sales. Smaller caches the agents allowed to slip by as they worked to identify and capture those heading the militia group.

"If the League was involved, then it would have been a hit. They would have taken out the Swede and his group, and they would have used men better able to pull the operation off," Alex stated.

And Crista agreed with that—to a point.

"Except the Swedish broker has, according to evidence he turned over, worked with the contact in this area before. The missiles went cheap. Two million?" She scoffed. "Give me a break, they could have gotten twenty million for them. And that was the intention. The broker was only buying the rights to transport and arrange auction on the missiles. And that was what Johnny didn't know. He thought the missile sale was a done deal."

"Which means someone was pulling the strings somewhere else," Natches mused, sitting back in his chair and staring at the papers on the table before lifting his eyes to Chaya.

She saw the bitterness now, the anger.

"Each step we take points in that direction," she agreed.

"Fucking Somerset, Kentucky, a hotbed of illegal militia sales and homegrown terrorism." A cynical laugh passed his lips. "Son of a bitch, boys." He looked to his cousins. "Have we been sleeping or what?"

Chaya shook her head, aching for him. This was his home, and she knew his love for the mountains, the lake, and even in some part, the people.

"Somerset is only one of many small towns," she told him. "The guerilla militias can grow and thrive in such areas, because of their family and community ties. They know who to target, who they can trust and who they can blackmail. Most of them are harmless. Good ole boys plotting to defend God and country against aggressors. They have ties to military personnel, gain a few weapons here and there, and it makes them feel safer. Doesn't make it legal, but they feel safer. Then, every now and then, you get something like FL. And they twist it, pull in those once harmless groups, and suddenly they have an army with ties all across America. If we could capture the person or persons pulling the strings here in Somerset, then there's a chance we could take the entire network down."

"And you think asking a few dipshits some sticky questions is going to do this?" Dawg flipped his hand over the files in disgust. "I didn't see a damned thing in there about Freedom's League or a network of homegrown terrorists."

"You didn't read her file," Natches told him quietly, his gaze still locked with hers. "I did."

Chaya pressed her lips and dropped her eyes. She had asked the questions she knew could come back on Natches and his father. How loyal was he to his father? He claimed he wasn't, but family ties often had strong undercurrents. And Natches wasn't always as easy to read as he pretended to be. In some areas, his secrets went far deeper than most people could imagine.

"The questions Cranston is sending to me now are becoming more specific. Centered on Johnny, his friendships, and his ties. And there are certain threads that bind each one. Johnny's parentage." She watched Dawg's jaw bunch. "His loyalties. His friends. Who he associated with the most, because within those groups, we'll find the contact we need."

"Not in that group of names you won't," Rowdy snorted. "I've gone over these files, Agent Dane. There's nothing here to identify any kind of leader of a homegrown militia network. These people are misfits. They can't decide where to use the bathroom next and you expect me to believe they're part of some growing grassroots terrorist group?"

"I'm more inclined to believe they're the pawns of such a group," she snapped back. "I've worked this case for five years, Rowdy. I know the signs. And they're all here."

"Who in Somerset could organize and lead something like this?" Dawg looked to the others then his eyes flashed with anger as he leaned toward her. "Fucking Mackays. Me, Rowdy, Natches, we could do it," he snarled. "Is Cranston after our asses now?"

She shook her head.

"Bullshit." His hand slapped the table. "There's no one in this county with more expertise in military, paramilitary, or plain dirt-assed killing than the three of us."

A sniper assassin, an explosives assassin, and Rowdy, one of the Marines' finest commanders. They'd all left the military early. For Dawg and Natches, after one tour, both with medical discharges. Rowdy had taken two tours and signed out. No sooner had they returned than the League had begun growing within the area.

"I investigated that option myself," she told them, staring back at Dawg coolly. "You don't have the ties nor do you personally have the temperament needed for such work."

He almost gaped back at her, rising halfway from his chair as Natches stood fully to his feet.

"Don't tell me I don't have the temper for it, little girl," he snarled. "That piddling-assed little car bomb that took out your agent looks like a firecracker compared to what I'm capable of."

"Back off, Dawg," Natches warned him.

"Leave him alone, Natches. I can handle it." She smiled back at Dawg tightly as his wife came up behind him, her eyes sparkling in anger as she glared at Chaya.

" 'That piddling-assed car bomb,' as you call it," she bit out, "had a signature. We've tracked it before."

"I don't leave fucking signatures," he snarled.

"Exactly. You don't. And that alone is your signature," she told him. "Don't play dumb, Dawg, just because you don't like me." Chaya came to her feet, her hand gripping Natches's wrist. "You, Rowdy, Ray, your wives, and your closest friends were investigated first. Thoroughly. I headed that investigation. I know how thorough it was, because I knew none of you were evil. Snarky, damned mean when you need to be, and so damned arrogant you make a woman's back teeth clench. But you're not traitors, and you're not terrorists. And I proved it."

"She's right." Alex spoke up, drawing their gazes. He was leaning back in his chair, his gray eyes lit with amusement. "You'd make lousy terrorists, and you made lousy soldiers. I believe that's why the Marines let you all go so easy, because you don't follow orders worth shit." He leaned forward and smiled placidly. "But they think I do. And Chaya knows her stuff. She's not the only one who's been working this case. Now, if we're all through playing these little power games, maybe we can get back to work here and figure out who the hell Timothy is chasing. Just in case he hasn't figured it out himself."

Natches stared back at Dawg, furious, bordering enraged, but the rage wasn't directed at his cousin. It was building inside him, threatening to burn out of control, because of his own suspicions. No, his own certainties.

He let Chaya pull him back to the chair and ignored her worried looks as the work continued. Finally, she moved away from them as Alex filled them in on the Freedom's League and their ties. It was information she already knew in abundance. She knew it, because that damned organization had killed her daughter.

He watched as she moved to the living room, sitting outside the group of women. Finally, Maria drew her forward, her smile kind. Maria was the kindest damned woman Natches had ever known until his cousins began falling in love. They had chosen women with those same qualities.

Finally, Chaya and Crista were talking. Natches watched

them, noticed Dawg watching them, and caught his cousin's eye. They were going to have to talk about this, and soon. He couldn't figure out Dawg's problem with Chaya, and he was beginning to not even care what the problem was. It was going to stop.

Finally, as the hour grew later, they stood and stretched, shook their heads and admitted they would have to wait on Timothy. Natches stayed silent, watchful.

Chaya was exhausted and he led her to bed, tucked her against him, and waited for her to go to sleep. While he thought. And all the thinking in the world wasn't helping him to make sense of the knowledge brewing in his gut, or the anger tormenting his mind.

Thinking was only making it worse.

Fifteen

Natches left Chaya, exhausted, sleeping peacefully in the bed he'd dreamed of her sleeping in.

When he'd returned from Iraq, he had thrown the bed he'd partied in for so many years right into the lake. He'd come in at night, taken one look at it, and something inside him had shattered.

The man who had slept in that bed wasn't the same man who had returned to it. The man who had returned belonged to someone now and was no longer the man that bed represented.

Before he left, he'd been the bastard everyone thought he was and had been on a fast track to self-destruction. It was why he joined sniper training; it was why he worked without a spotter; it was why he had become one of their most proficient killers. Because life didn't matter to him—not his, and not those he was sent to kill.

To the man he had been, happiness was something others felt. All he had felt then was the rage, the bitterness, the knowledge he was tainted by the blood of an incestuous, child-beating son of a bitch. And the fear that somehow, part of Dayle Mackay lived inside him. And then, he had seen true strength. He had seen a woman who should have been weeping in horror, in fear, and she had stood strong. She had lifted her chin defiantly and she had kept fighting.

And in those two weeks of recovery, she had let him hold her when she cried, when she learned the husband she thought she could trust had betrayed her and his country. He had teased her into laughter days later, and stolen a kiss. He had watched her eyes sparkle and his soul had claimed her.

And she had changed him. In that short time, she had erased the man he had been, and shown him the man he wanted to be. A man who was worthy of a woman that strong.

He stood on the deck now, leaning against the rail and staring into the dark water stretching out behind the boat, and realized that he had grown up long before his cousins had realized it. Maybe it had begun before Chaya, but he just knew it had cemented with Chaya.

He had bitched about the sharing that didn't continue after they came home, but only because to not bitch was to reveal too much. And he didn't want to explain Chaya. He didn't want to relive in words what he couldn't forget in his memories. And he couldn't betray Chaya by taking another woman.

He'd let others think he had. Hell, he even watched Dawg take a few, but he hadn't been tempted to join in. He hadn't wanted to be tempted to join in. Chaya had been so firmly entrenched in his head and in his heart, that no other woman came close to the memory of her.

She loved him silently, as though she was afraid that to love him any other way would break her.

And his heart broke. As wild, as vicious, as his life had been at one time, it was nothing compared to the loss Chaya had suffered in the space of a few seconds. The death of her child, the knowledge that the father of that child had betrayed them both.

He breathed out heavily, tightening as he felt the boat rock, felt a presence behind him.

He knew who it was. He knew Dawg wouldn't be asleep any more than he was tonight. Not with the events that were beginning to reveal themselves and the knowledge of the danger surrounding all of them.

He stood still, staring out into the water until a longneck beer was thrust in front of his face. His lips quirked as he took the bottle and glanced at the man who leaned against the rail beside him.

Dawg. They nicknamed him that for a reason. He never let things go. He chewed and chewed on a problem, worried it and fought with it until that problem either evaporated or bowed before him. He was as stubborn as the damned wind.

Natches took a long drink of the beer and waited.

"You changed," Dawg finally said quietly. "Others didn't see it like I did when you came home. You played a good game of pretending you were fucking the girls, of being as wild and woolly as you always were, but you weren't."

Natches stared at the bottle as he shook his head. "No," he finally admitted. "I wasn't."

"You had no intention of sharing Kelly with Rowdy even if it had been what he wanted, did you?" Dawg grunted. Rowdy would have killed both of them if they had touched Kelly.

"Neither did you unless Rowdy really still needed it." Natches brought the beer to his lips thoughtfully. "Your game was just as good."

Dawg sighed, the sound rough, worried. "I don't have a daddy complex," he finally growled. "What I've got is a complex against games. Cranston's games and Agent Dane's, especially after what I learned tonight. She almost destroyed you once . . ."

"She lost her daughter in a missile attack against enemy headquarters in Iraq five years ago. That was the false order initiated by the League. I suspect to keep their own activities secret. Beth was three. Her father was military intelligence and slipped her into the country after he deserted to the other side."

Silence filled the void as Natches held the beer loosely between his palms. "It was two weeks after I rescued her from the terrorists who had taken her while she was on assignment. Terrorists her husband betrayed her to. Nassar Mallah raped her with a baton, Dawg. He beat her face until her eyes were swollen shut. He kicked her and beat her until I wondered how she was still standing when I broke into that fucking dirt cell. But there she was. She'd torn the clothes off the guard after I took his head off; barefoot and in shock, she was ready to run."

Dawg breathed out a vicious curse. A sound rife with the horror Natches described, the images blooming between them, steeped in blood.

"We hid in a hole I'd made, and I activated the beeper for extraction. My team was waiting not far out, and I knew it, but too far to wait on them to rescue her. I bandaged her feet there, I covered her eyes, and in that dark little hole, I gave her my soul." He lifted the beer to his lips and finished it before turning to stare at the cousin that was more a brother, who was almost a father to him. "Cut her again, and we're finished. As friends, as family. Do you hear me, Dawg? That woman owns me, and she always will. You cut her again, and we're finished."

Dawg stared at Natches. Between them a lifetime of memories and trials, tears and brawling male adventures stretched. He'd have sworn years ago that nothing could come between him and his cousins. But as he stared at Natches, the youngest of the cousins and the one most scarred inside, he saw something he'd never imagined he'd see.

He was used to seeing Natches as the battered kid he was always helping to rescue from Dayle Mackay's brutal fists. Then as the wild, too charming, troublemaking hellion he grew up to be. Then they went into the Marines.

And he guessed they really had grown up. Except Dawg hadn't wanted to see it in Natches. He hadn't wanted to see the horrors his cousin had survived when they were separated. And now, he saw it. But he saw something more. There was a core of pure hard steel inside him. That steel had pulled the trigger and killed another cousin to save Dawg's heart. That steel faced him now, and damned if Dawg would have blamed him if Natches had already decided to cut him out of his life.

Natches had given him and Rowdy a loyalty that, Dawg didn't realize until this moment, he hadn't given his cousin in return.

"Fuck." He sighed, wiping a hand over his face. "I didn't mean to cut her, Natches. Son of a bitch, if I didn't want to hate her though. And I was wrong."

Natches continued to stare out on the water, and it broke Dawg up inside, seeing the pain on his cousin's face. Hell, he'd have killed anyone else if they so much as thought to cut that little agent as he had. The Mackay cousins stuck together, it was that simple.

"I'd have never let anyone else do it," he admitted, and it wasn't easy. "We might fuss a little between us, Natches, but you know that."

Natches nodded then. "It's the only reason we're talking now, Dawg. It's the only reason my fist hasn't gone down your throat and my boat is still here. Because I know that."

Dawg almost felt a spurt of fear. How had he let his enmity, his fear for his cousin almost bring them to that point? *Fucking dumb redneck,* he thought to himself. That was how. Sometimes, he was still the dumb redneck he had been when he was young.

"She's not plain," he finally grated out. "But she's tough. And whatever she's dragging you into scares the shit out of me because you're not sharing it with us. And I know you, Natches. I know you know what's going on. You're protecting her from us when you don't need to and risking yourself. And *that's* what's pissing me off about her."

He watched as Natches lowered his head, his gaze slipping to his cousin's bare back, and he still flinched. After all these years, so many years, as the moonlight washed over the scars on Natches's tough, sun-bronzed flesh, fury still spiked through him.

Natches's father had done that. That mean fucking bastard had lashed Natches until he nearly killed him. He'd broken his rib, got him down, and then beat the living hell out of him. When Dawg, Rowdy, and Ray had burst into the house, Natches had been curled in on himself, nearly unconscious, his back in ribbons, and Dayle still laying the fucking lash to him.

And Dawg had sworn that night, sworn to God, it would never happen again. That no one, fucking no one, would scar Natches like that again, physically or mentally.

And still, something had had almost as profound an effect on Natches as his father had. A woman's pain. A woman's scars.

In that second, he realized that was what pissed him off now. Once again, Natches wasn't watching his own back. He was more concerned with someone else's safety, someone Dawg didn't know and was too damned wary to trust.

"Natches, stop looking at the fucking water, man. Tell me what the hell is going on. I watched you tonight going over those files. You put something together, and you're still trying to protect the rest of us. Let us help you. We didn't take that from you when we were in trouble. Don't do it to us now."

Whatever it was, Natches had figured it out slowly, because he hadn't hit the roof, he hadn't dug out his sniper rifle, and Dawg and Rowdy hadn't heard the rage. Natches was easier to figure out when he hit a hard, fast rage. The slow ones, those were damned scary. And Natches was in a slow-building rage.

As he stared at Natches, the boat rocked again. Dawg looked

up as Rowdy crossed the deck now. Their boats were close enough to jump from one to the other. Rowdy wasn't being cut out from this late-night conversation and Dawg could tell from Natches's grimace that he knew it, too.

"Beer's in the cooler," Natches said softly, finishing the one Dawg had handed him. "Get me another while you're at it."

He turned and lobbed the empty bottle into the trash can at the corner of the railing.

At least Dawg didn't have to look at those fucking scars anymore. The sight of them just pissed him off, even now, so many years later.

Rowdy got the beers and moved to them, his expression still as he handed them over.

"You two going to fight?" he asked, and his gaze narrowed on them. "I'm not up to refereeing tonight, I'll tell you."

Dawg snorted. "No, I've just been trying to convince knucklehead here to tell me what the hell is going on with his woman and that damned Cranston. My neck is starting to itch damned bad. It's keeping me awake at night."

"Natches will tell us when he needs to." Rowdy shrugged, but Dawg heard the question in his voice as well.

"Your neck itches," Natches said then, his voice eerily quiet. "Have you felt the sights between your eyes yet? Playing with you, targeting you, just waiting, because the time isn't right yet?"

Dawg froze. His gaze slashed to Rowdy's and saw the same shock in his face that Dawg felt.

"What the fuck are you talking about?" Rowdy snarled.

Rowdy rarely cursed, Kelly just didn't like it, and he tried to clean his mouth up. For a Marine, that was some hard shit to do. And the fact that he was slipping told more of his fury than anything else could.

Natches lifted his head then and stared at the mountains around them. The grief they saw on his face then, the heavy, quiet sorrow had Dawg's guts cramping with dread. Because he knew. God help him, he was terrified he knew exactly what was getting ready to come out of his cousin's mouth.

"It's Dayle, isn't it, Natches? That's who Cranston is after; he's the one who was helping Johnny. That's why he's playing games with you, and with your agent." In a heartbeat, Dawg knew the truth.

Natches grimaced, a tight, mocking smile twisting his lips before he tilted the bottle to his lips and drank. In seconds the bottle was empty and crashing into the trash hard enough to rock the can as Dawg and Rowdy flinched.

Natches stared at the can, wishing he could free enough emotion where his father was concerned to just get mad. Just mad. Just enough to rage at the injustice of life that allowed something as rabid as Dayle Mackay to sire a child.

But he couldn't. All he could feel was that cold, hard core of knowledge inside him. The same one he had felt when he realized Johnny Grace was as dangerous as a rattler coiled to strike. His fingers itched to caress his rifle, to take out the threat, to make certain, damned certain the bastard couldn't strike at Chaya, Rowdy, or Dawg. Or, God forbid, Ray.

Dayle couldn't touch his sister, Janey, at least. She was away at college, far, far away; Natches had made damned certain of it.

"He's been playing with me," Natches commented. "Not right now, but often enough. He must have been busy this month, I haven't felt his gunsights in a while. But right after I terminated Johnny, I felt them. I felt them hard enough that I wondered if he'd finally made his mind up to do it."

"And you didn't say anything?" Rowdy growled, furious. Natches could hear the anger in his tone.

Natches shrugged. "I know how to give back. I let him feel *me* for a while." And it had amused him. Just as he knew it had amused Dayle when Natches felt those sights between his eyes. Once a sniper always a sniper, but once an assassin, a man always knew when it was turning back on him. Dayle amused Natches for the most part with his games. He didn't know how to target, didn't know any more than an experienced hunter knew. The wind positioning was never exact. He was always too far off. But he liked to pretend he could kill his son. The mess cook turned gourmet cook who thought he was a general in a revolution. It was so fucking laughable Natches still had trouble believing it.

Dayle Mackay had the temperament for what he was doing though. He'd learned enough in the Marines to know how to be hard. He'd made connections, and he'd kept those connections. And Natches had known, as he'd read those reports, as he had begun to put the pieces together along with the mental snapshots of the past few events that had tied in. Natches had known.

"How long have you known who Agent Dane is chasing, Natches?" Dawg asked.

Natches could feel his anger, too. Protective, that was Dawg. And he knew Dawg would never forget the night Natches hadn't been able to protect himself. The night he had nearly let his father beat him to death, to protect his sister. And he would have done it again. If Ray hadn't found a way to make certain Dayle was too scared to leave so much as a bruise on Janey, Natches would have let his father kill him to protect her.

Because no one in the damned county had the balls to stop it. They were terrified of Dayle Mackay. Bullying, cold, mean to the fucking bone. And a fucking gourmet chef on top of it. It was almost enough to leave a man rolling in laughter at the thought of it. Dayle Mackay could make a meal that would leave a man crying in joy at the taste. And he could beat a man to a bloody pulp with the same cold precision.

"I knew before she arrived." Natches finally shrugged. He hadn't wanted to admit it to himself. He'd refused to even consider the suspicion. But he had known. The day Johnny had died Natches had stared into his father's eyes across the town square and Dayle had known who had killed Johnny. And Natches had known, in that one instant, who had helped Johnny. Hell, helped him nothing. Johnny hadn't masterminded that little deal, Dayle Mackay had. And now Natches had to deal with it.

"Cranston has Chaya playing a smoke game, and I know it. Not enough to cause Dayle to target her, but enough, he's hoping, to make Dayle mess up just enough to rain down the wrath of Timothy Cranston on him. The wrong phone call. The wrong meeting with the wrong person. Just enough to pull him in on suspicion of terrorist activities."

Silence surrounded them. Natches didn't feel the chill of the night on his skin, he felt the chill of betrayal in his gut. And of fear. Because the one thing he hadn't considered until tonight, until that bomb had taken the other agent out, he hadn't considered the risk to Chaya.

Dayle had no problem whatsoever targeting her. Killing her would kill Natches, and figuring that out wouldn't take rocket science, especially not after the past few days.

"I'm moving the boat tomorrow," he told them then. "I'm going to dock her behind the garage for a while."

"The hell you are." Rowdy faced him, cold, hard. "We stick together, Natches. He'll expect you to separate yourself from us. We don't separate."

Natches shook his head. "Kelly and Crista . . ."

"Are just as fucking innocent in this as that woman you have in your bedroom now," Dawg snarled. "I might not like the situation, damn it, but I'll be damned if you'll pull away from us like that. There's safety in numbers, man. And right now, Dayle isn't going to take that risk here. We'd all know who did it. We know his style and his signature, he can't take that risk. You make yourself a target, and he can take you out easy."

Natches scratched at his cheek and gazed out into the night. That was the only insurance Natches had ever had against his father's wrath. He'd rubbed Dayle's nose in it, too. He couldn't take Natches out without the whole damned town knowing it. And a part of Natches had never really believed his father would try to kill him, until recently.

Hell, he should just pack himself and Chaya up and leave. Making a life somewhere else wouldn't be that damned hard. Except there was no way in hell she would go for it. She was an agent, and she didn't break her word, she wouldn't betray DHS that way. She would resign, and that was a given once this assignment was finished, if they survived it.

"Have you discussed any of this with Chaya yet?" Rowdy asked.

Natches shook his head. He had only let himself believe it tonight. "She's sleeping."

She was curled in his bed, safe and warm for the moment, where he needed her to be always. Safe and warm, and sheltering his child under her heart.

"She's pregnant." He let the words slip past his lips.

He knew she was pregnant. He could feel it clear to his soul. The moment she told him she wasn't protected, that knowledge had slammed clear to his gut.

Silence again. Rowdy's eyes widened and Dawg's seemed to bug out.

"She's what?" Dawg wheezed. "What the hell? She's not been back here long enough, unless . . ." He let it trail off.

"It's mine." His child. Boy or girl, it didn't matter, it wouldn't matter. "She won't admit it, but I know she is, Dawg. The first time, she wasn't protected and I didn't give a damn." But now, fear sliced inside him. His baby rested inside her, barely more than an instinct, and already that child was in danger. "I haven't given a damn since."

"Damn," Rowdy breathed out roughly. "Okay, another reason why you don't go running off solo. Your ass is staying here. And so is hers."

"You're risking your lives," Natches told them both. "Kelly and Crista need you two. This is my fight."

"He wants me to kick his ass," Dawg snapped.

"No, he wants a cold bath tonight, and I might oblige him by tipping his ass over that rail and into the lake," Rowdy said with a healthy dose of disgust. "Get over yourself, Natches. Later today, we tackle Cranston. That little bastard has gone too far this time. He should have contacted us to start with."

"He did."

Dawg and Rowdy stared back at him in surprise. "When?"

"The anonymous call the night Chaya came into town. I finally recognized the voice despite his attempts to disguise it. It was Cranston. That was his warning."

"Then he needs to brush up on his social-fucking-skills." Dawg's smile was one of those nerve-racking curves that always denoted trouble. "And I'll just enlighten him on that little tidbit when we get hold of him."

Natches stared at Rowdy, then at Dawg, and shook his head. He hadn't wanted them involved, but hadn't they always been? Dayle would never be satisfied if he managed to take Natches out, because he hated his nephews with the same consuming fury that he hated his son. And his brother Ray? His hatred for Ray ran so strong and so deep that Natches had worried for years that Dayle would strike back at him.

"We meet back here in the morning, then tomorrow night," Rowdy told them both as he moved to the rail of the boat. "We hash this out then and figure things out. And we do this together." He stared back at Natches, his gaze hard, determined.

Natches nodded. There wasn't a chance they would let him do it alone, he knew.

He watched as his cousins, his family, jumped from his boat to Dawg's. Dawg headed inside while Rowdy made the jump to his own houseboat, his shadow barely visible even under the clear sky and nearly full moon.

He stared up at that moon, and before he headed back inside to Chaya, he whispered another prayer. This one for protection. God, don't let him lose Chaya, because he knew beyond a shadow of a doubt that he would never survive it.

Chaya smiled as she felt Natches move silently beside her in the big bed, then gave a little shiver as his cool body curled around her.

"You're cold," she murmured, not quite awake, not quite asleep, but content to drift where she was, content and peaceful.

"You gonna get me warm." His voice washed through her, just a little rough, tinged with masculine amusement.

"Hmm." She shifted against him, her legs rubbing against his hair-roughened ones as a sense of completeness began to make itself known.

She shouldn't feel comfortable. She shouldn't feel like she was home in his arms, because she hadn't known what home felt like until Natches.

"I'm really cold," he murmured, rolling her to her back as her lashes lifted and she stared into his shadowed face, glimpsed his quick smile.

She loved his smile, though she hadn't seen it nearly enough since coming to Somerset. She wanted to see it every second of her day, she realized. A smile on his lips and in his eyes.

She let her hands slide up the arms braced on each side of her body, until they curved around his neck. She was ready for his kiss when it came, and he had no right to claim being cold, he was an inferno, heated and hungry.

His kiss sank into her, his lips slanting across hers as he moved over her, sliding between her thighs and nestling the head of his erection against the slick folds of her sex.

"You feel warm now, Natches," she whispered, feeling the need beginning to grow inside her again.

As he slid inside her, thick and hard, her breath caught in her throat and her back arched, taking more of him, taking him deeper and fighting to hold him tighter. Though she was stretched so tight around him that a thought couldn't have slid between his flesh and hers.

"Downright hot now." His breathing was rough, his hands demanding, gentle, as he stroked her body, his head bending until his lips and tongue could play over her nipple.

"Yeah, you feel kinda hot," she gasped, then moaned as he suckled her deep and thrust heavily inside her. "Oh God, Natches, what are you doing to me?"

But she knew what he was doing to her. Binding her so tight to him that there was no way to escape, no way to protect herself.

"Loving you," he murmured against her nipple before kissing it softly and turning to the other tight peak. "Can't you feel me loving you, Chay?"

She could. Thrusting, sliding so deep and warm inside her, like a dream. He was taking her like a slow, lazy dream, making every stroke memorable, every touch burning inside her heart.

"Keep loving me." She almost sobbed the plea, and she bit his shoulder as he raked his teeth over her nipple, sending sensation after sensation shooting clear to her womb. "Don't stop, Natches. Don't stop loving me."

"Not gonna happen," he groaned. "Always love you."

And she had known it, just as she had known she felt the same. She mouthed the words against his arm, felt him nip the curve of her breast, and the pleasure began to spiral. His thrusts became harder, deeper. They stroked, penetrated, and filled her with ecstasy as she flew in his arms.

Her hips lifted, her legs wrapping around his hips as she held on for the ride of her life. Each time with Natches was better than the last. Each touch, each kiss, each heated thrust inside her body bound her more tightly to him. And when she exploded, felt him explode and felt their release mingling, she knew his intentions of binding her even closer would only give them more to share. There was no way of binding her closer; he already was her soul.

Each spurt of silky release flowing into her had her crying out though. Her name on his lips, his name sobbing from hers as he finally collapsed against her and rolled to his side.

He still held her. He didn't let her go, just tucked her closer to him and let their breaths ease as drowsiness stole over her again.

"I love you." She whispered the words to herself.

Or so she thought. Natches felt his heart expand, nearly tearing from his chest at the sleepy, almost unconscious words.

I love you. Such a simple statement. Yet, those three little words embedded inside him and filled him with determination. He wasn't going to lose her. He'd kill again first, and just as with Johnny, he would never regret it.

Sixteen

Timothy Cranston, a.k.a. the rabid leprechaun of DHS, strode into Natches's houseboat as though he owned it. He was followed by the other five agents assigned to the Somerset case, and they looked harried, sleepless, and concerned.

Behind them strode Sheriff Mayes, and he looked ready to explode with fury. His golden brown eyes were sizzling with anger and his tall, hard body was tense with the effort at maintaining self-control.

"What happened?" Chaya stood from her seat at the table, her eyes going from Timothy to the sheriff.

"Someone tried to kill Rogue Walker last night." Zeke's voice grated with fury. "And they almost succeeded."

"Damn!" Chaya turned away, scrambling through the files laid out in front of her, looking for information. "Rogue didn't know anything. She would have told me if she did."

"Maybe she just didn't know she knew anything," Natches suggested as he propped himself against the edge of the table and sipped at the coffee cup he held.

His green eyes were like flints of ice as he watched Timothy. "Isn't that how it usually works, Timothy? It's what a person isn't aware they know that always trips them up. Or what someone suspects they know?"

"Rogue knew something," Timothy growled. "She rides with that damned group of troublemakers on a regular basis. Several of them were tied to Grace and Bedsford."

"By association only." Natches shrugged, but Chaya caught the calculated drawl in his voice. "Hell, arrest the whole town and pull them into interrogation. Everyone but everyone associates eventually here."

"This little town of yours isn't as closed off as you want to think it is, Natches," Timothy snapped. "The tourism rate is incredible. Lake Cumberland is one of the greatest draws in the area."

"So now we're looking for tourists?" Natches lifted his brow and Chaya almost winced.

He'd been cool and focused all morning, going through the files, making notes, answering her with short, brief replies.

"I hate Mackays." Timothy sighed.

"Yeah, especially when they're self-proclaimed generals of a homegrown militant group." Natches grinned tightly, then reached behind him for the files he had stacked there, and threw them to the table. "Try those boys and see if you come up with more than I did."

Chaya stared at him in shock.

"What are you saying, Natches?" Timothy stilled, the agents around him adjusting their posture, their hands in close proximity to their weapons.

Natches laughed at the moves as Sheriff Mayes angled himself to cover Natches if needed. Interesting. A man Chaya would have sworn didn't uphold loyalty over the law, yet he was silently aligning himself with Natches.

"Stop baiting him, Natches." She turned back to him, narrowing her eyes at the gleam of anger in his gaze. "We want to keep Timothy calm, remember? I'm certain his secretary wasn't able to slip his meds in his coffee this morning, so let's not tease him."

It was a running joke that his secretary needed to dose his coffee with sedatives. He was so hyper sometimes he drove the rest of them crazy.

"Look at the last file." Natches shrugged as he finished his coffee and set the cup aside. "You'll see what I mean."

Chaya hadn't seen the files. Natches had been up working before she awoke, and he had stayed distant, refusing to discuss whatever he was working on.

"You're not dealing with clumsy, drugged out hometown boys

here," Natches informed them as Timothy pulled out that bottom file.

Chaya barely managed to stifle her gasp.

"You're dealing with men who have had a dream all their lives," Natches stated mockingly. "Instead of sending Chaya in and risking her neck on this fool's errand you gave her, you should have come to someone who would know."

Dayle Mackay. There were three pictures on the front of the file. Dayle Mackay, Chandler Mackay, and another man who Chaya knew was suspected to be part of Freedom's League. These were obviously the men they had needed to target.

"Chandler wasn't in the military," she said, her voice low, shocked.

"Nope, Chandler liked to play war games though. His pansy ass was too important to risk, big-shot architect that he was. But he liked to show his kid how tough and strong he was, usually with his fists, though his wife did have a measure of control over him.

"Now, good ole Dayle Mackay, there's another story."

Natches had once thought he had pushed that part of his past behind him, that he had conquered that hatred, that bitterness. Maybe he hadn't fully managed it, he thought as he watched Cranston read the file.

"Dayle didn't care who he beat up on, or how bad. And he kept his wife sedated enough that she didn't really give a shit either. He married money, confiscated the money on her parents' deaths, and let her live to watch all his glory plans move right along. General Dayle Mackay. That's what he calls himself in private. But then, he always has, so it wasn't easy to put it together at first."

He moved aside as Chaya shifted closer to him. Hell, he'd thought he could have a life with her, and now that was being tested in the worst possible way. The son of a traitor? She had been married to one traitor already; he was pretty sure she wouldn't want another in the family.

"The other files, those are the men I remember from years back who made late-night visits, sat and drank his fine wine and talked about the golden future they could create."

He had been a kid then. Those memories were always rife

with pain. Natches had been a nosy kid, and sometimes he had been caught being nosy. And he'd paid for it.

"They're all right here together," Timothy exclaimed as he pulled free one of the few pictures Natches had stolen out of the house before his father had disowned him.

"That picture was stolen by accident." He grinned. "I used to steal family pictures, not that we had a lot. His wife, Linda, she tried taking them for a few years, but finally gave up. She liked being sedated better."

Natches looked at the picture. Six men. Dayle, Chandler, and the men he remembered visiting when he was younger. And one woman. Nadine Mackay Grace between the two Mackay brothers, their arms around her as they grinned for the camera.

His mother, Linda, wasn't in the picture. Just those hard-eyed men and the sister the Mackay brothers had used for their own pleasure.

Natches moved back to the coffeepot, feeling the need to slip away, to hunt. His rifle was clean and ready, ammunition prepared, his knapsack was packed. He could leave at a moment's notice and no one would have a clue where he was going. Or that the need to kill the man who sired him was eating him alive.

"Delbert Grant is your explosives expert," he told them. "He was in town a few weeks ago. He's been out of the service a hell of a long time. But his son was with him; I guess every man needs an apprentice."

Natches almost snorted at the thought.

"How do we get the evidence we need against them?" Timothy mused as he turned to his agents, and Chaya moved to Natches.

He tried to pull away from her again, to ignore her gaze.

"Don't. Please." She stared up at him, then laid her head against his chest and he wondered if his heart was going to shatter in that moment.

He couldn't stop himself from touching her, from letting his hands flatten against her back and feel her melting against him.

But he stared over her head and watched as the agents went through the files, comparing names, associations, and placing each one at specific points of operation.

They weren't incredibly wealthy men. They were plotters,

planners. They were bullies and self-appointed saviors. They were the worst kind of enemy.

"This one has a boat on the lake." The sheriff tapped the file of one of the more well-to-do members of the group. "He has a group out here several times a year. They don't cause trouble, but they give you a clear feeling of trouble."

"Uncle Ray wouldn't let them dock here," Natches told them.

Timothy's head raised at the mention of Ray's name. "Where are your cousins? And Jansen? They're not around this morning."

He stroked Chaya's back as she turned in his embrace to watch Timothy. She was still relaxed against him, conforming to his harder, larger body, as though her petite frame could cushion him against any of this.

"They're around," he said softly.

Chaya tensed at the sound of his voice. Soft, almost gentle. A lazy drawl that held no warmth, no comfort.

Chaya watched as Timothy narrowed his eyes on them, taking in their position, the way Natches held her against him. It was an unmistakable picture and the special agent's gaze flickered with knowledge.

"Yeah, that's what you wanted, wasn't it, Timothy?" Natches asked, and Chaya forced herself to remain silent, to keep her eyes on Timothy. "You sent her in here stirring the pot so you could draw us out and make us do your work for you."

Timothy exhaled roughly, ran his hand over his balding head, and gave Natches a wary grin.

"I knew if anyone could do it, you boys could." He finally shrugged. "I was getting nowhere. All we had was the Somerset connection and Johnny's connection to your dad and your uncle."

"Don't," Natches snapped. "Never title those two with those names again. You call them by name; you don't relate them to me."

Cold bitter rage cut through his voice then, and Chaya felt her heart breaking. She had to blink back her tears, and watched as Timothy lowered his head and ran his hand over his face before nodding sharply.

"Yeah, you're right." The agent sighed. "They don't deserve it. You're a fine man, Natches, you and your true uncle and those cousins of yours. You're damned good people. I'm not fighting you for that. Nor am I going to argue over the stench the other two have cast on the rest of you. But we have to deal with this now." His fingers flicked to the files Natches had produced in the early hours of the morning. "We can't arrest them without proof." He looked at Chaya. "And we don't have anyone tying them close enough to Johnny Grace yet."

"You will have," Natches stated. "When you're fishing for the big bass, Cranston, you just have to have the right bait."

"And who's the right bait?" Cranston asked him warily.

"I am."

Chaya felt her heart nearly stop in her chest as fear began to drive a spike through her soul. She twisted around, ignoring his attempt to hold her in place, and stared into the hard, savage expression that had settled over Natches's face.

This wasn't the man she knew. The man who teased or laughed or even the man she had known to be angry. This wasn't anger, it wasn't even rage. It was pure icy terror packed into six feet two inches of tight, hard Marine assassin. This was the man who had killed Johnny Grace the year before, the man who left Timothy Cranston sweating in fear for months after that operation. And seeing the icy, frozen core of that man sent a tremor of wariness through her.

And he knew it. His gaze licked over her, icicles and cold fire, causing a shiver to race down her spine.

"You're the wrong bait." Chaya had to force the words past her throat. "He knows we're together; he knows I'm an agent. He won't go for it."

"Sure he will," Natches drawled, and God she hated that sound. There was nothing warm or comforting in it.

"How do you figure?" she bit out, pulling farther away from him to stare back at him angrily. "He'll know it's a trick. A trap. He'll never mess up like that."

"Keep looking in those files," he told her then. "Check out Fletcher Linkins. We were in sniper training together."

Her gaze moved to the files and then back to him. "Good ole Fletch is dead, did you know that?" He directed the question to Timothy.

Timothy nodded. "Car wreck while he was on leave about four years ago."

"He didn't wreck his car," Natches snarled. "He was killed. I went looking for him after I returned home. I wanted to know why a fellow sniper took a bead on me and tried to take my head off. He was already dead when I found him. Because he had failed the mission the Freedom's League gave him to kill me. Check his link to good ole Dayle."

Timothy shook his head. "Why target you?"

"Because I was helping Chay in Iraq." Natches smiled tightly. "I was investigating the orders that sent those missiles into that hotel and I was the one that took out Nassar for torturing her. They wanted me out of the way. They didn't want me tying the threads together, because then I would have known."

"And you didn't know what was going on in Iraq until Chaya came back this time," Timothy mused, nodding his head. "It makes sense."

"Dayle's involved in this up to his eyeballs. He's connected with the men in that photo, and those men are all connected in various ways to military intelligence and/or DHS. They're not wealthy, they're not powerful, but they're going to be. If they're not stopped."

Chaya wrapped her arms across her breasts and listened as Natches and Timothy discussed how to trap them. She watched Natches, and she knew he'd already decided exactly what he was going to do. He was only going through the motions here, letting Timothy get his say in. He was patient, controlled, and Timothy had no clue that Natches was already formulating his own plans.

It was the reason why the other cousins weren't here. It was why Alex wasn't here. Because they were already working their end. He'd already discussed it with them.

The knowledge of that had her jaw clenching as she stared at him, willing him to meet her eyes. When he did, she wanted to flinch. Because she could see beneath the ice, and she could finally see the pain building inside him.

Finally, Timothy and his agents were gone and Natches was locking the door behind them. He stood still as he set the security system, his gaze focused on the digital settings, glaring at them, trying to push back the need to destroy something.

He'd mastered those uncontained rages years ago. The ones that left every stick of furniture around him in slivers. The ones that left his hands bloody from ramming them into the walls.

He breathed in deeply and caught Chaya's scent. A fresh, clean smell that almost, just almost, pushed past the putrid scent of betrayal in his mind. The smell of his own blood, his own pain.

"You lied to Timothy," she whispered then.

Natches turned back and watched her. Dressed in his T-shirt and another pair of borrowed leggings. He was going to have to remind Dawg to check on her luggage, see if she had any of her own clothes left.

"Why did you lie to him, Natches?" Her voice was soft, and the sound of it tried to ease the ragged edges of his soul.

"How do you know I lied?" He crossed his arms over his chest and stared back at the woman who held his soul with such silken bonds that he knew he would never be free.

And he felt just as unworthy of those bonds now as he had in Iraq. Not that it was going to stop him from tying her to him, and better she learn what he was now, rather than later. But sometimes, in the darkest reaches of his soul, there were moments that he cringed at the thought that he was dirtying her.

"I'm a trained interrogation specialist, lover. That's what I do. Remember?" Her smile was just as hard and just as tight as his had been earlier. But that word on her lips. *Lover.* Hell, no one had ever called him "lover," even teasingly. It was such a simple word, and often used so carelessly. But it wasn't a word Natches had used, or had used for him. And it sank inside him, tried to warm him in all the places he had gone cold and hard. For years, he had existed on autopilot, a Marine, a man who knew he had no true home, no family other than the cousins and uncle who still yet belonged to others. Nothing was his alone.

Until Chaya. And here he stood trying to protect that one precious thing in his life, perhaps two, and he could tell she was going to fight him tooth and nail. Just as his cousins fought him.

He shook his head and moved into the room, staring around it, and realizing why he had moved from the houseboat to the garage apartment the year before. This wasn't a home. He hadn't wanted it to be a home.

"Natches, you're not talking to me." His head jerked around at the slightest thread of fear in her voice.

She stood across the room watching him, her arms wrapped across her breasts as she stared at him. And those pretty eyes, such a warm, sweet honey color, seemed to spill inside him.

"He was part of the reason your daughter was killed." He

spoke the words slowly and watched her flinch, watched her and made her accept that betrayal. The group Dayle Mackay was a part of had found a way to authenticate a strike that had never been approved. The strike that had killed her child.

"You weren't." She swallowed tightly as he watched her battle her tears.

He had only seen her cry once, and God help him, those tears followed him in his nightmares. Wrenching sobs tore from her soul as he held her safe beneath him, forced her head to his chest and watched that hotel explode.

And that night, the first time he had loved her, the night her daughter had died, he'd had to tear his gaze away from her, turn his back on her and clench his fists to keep from going after Dayle Mackay then and there. Killing him would only solve a part of the problem. Just one part out of a dozen. But he wanted to kill.

Because he remembered her screaming sobs as he dragged her back to the small hotel where he stayed sometimes. There he had held her, rocked her, loved her, and he let silent tears fall from his own eyes.

"His blood is mine." He turned back to her and shook his head as he felt the chill inside him.

"And your blood?" she whispered as she moved to him, took his hand and placed it on her stomach. "You're blood is here, Natches."

He caressed her stomach through the clothes; he couldn't help himself. Her heated flesh met his calloused hands, and as he did when he held her at night, he imagined he felt life there. Hope.

He shook his head and wanted to pull away from her, but he couldn't force himself to.

"And when this is over, you may curse the night you allowed me to come inside you." He found the strength to pull back from her, to walk away.

"You son of a bitch!" He didn't get far before her fingers gripped his wrist and she jumped in front of him. "Excuse me here? But are you daring to walk away from me?"

He dragged his fingers through his hair, a frown jerking between his brows at the anger on her face, the accusation in her eyes.

"I have things to do, Chaya."

"And of course you're not going to do the 'partner' thing you've been preaching about here and tell me what the hell they are. Right, Natches?"

He nodded slowly. "That about sums it up."

She looked as though he had slapped her. Natches stared back at her in confusion as she backed away from him, her face paling.

"So much for all my courage and strength that you so highly respect," she sneered. "I guess, once again, I'm delegated back to the weak little woman who has to be protected. Right?"

"This is my fight," he bit out.

"Because it's your blood?"

"Fucking A," he snarled.

"Well, excuse me, Mr. Mackay, but there's a damned good chance I'm carrying your blood inside me, so I think that makes it my damned fight as well."

And how the hell was he supposed to counter that argument?

"It doesn't work that way, Chay." He tried pure male dominance and decisiveness.

"Because you decree it?" Her eyes were fiery now, not just in anger, but in confrontation, in determination.

Hell, he was getting hard. He could feel his arousal stretching to life, the ice that had encased his emotions beginning to melt as she glared back at him.

"You can decree to hell and back, Natches, and it's not going to do you one damned bit of good. You dragged me into this relationship, you're the one that made damned sure my soul was so tied to yours that I couldn't breathe without feeling you, and then you did everything in your power to help create life from it. Damn you, you're not backing away now."

"Backing away was never in the cards." He lowered his head and growled the words at her. "Did I say you could leave this relationship?"

Her eyes widened and disbelief filled her face. And that made him grow harder, because the disbelief was filled with scornful amazement.

"Oh my God, you take the cake." Her hands went on her hips, and his cock just got harder still. "I can't believe your complete arrogance."

"You should, you've dealt with it before." He wasn't budging.

If he told her what he had planned, then she would just stick her nose into it. Her nose was far enough on the chopping block; he wasn't going to allow it to go any farther.

"You are not doing this without me!" The words were said with such snap that his brow lifted mockingly.

"And you're not going after him with me." She'd lost enough in her life; he wasn't going to allow her to lose any more. Not her life, or their child's. And he knew that child was there, resting securely within her. He intended to make damned sure he kept that child safe. The child and his or her mother.

"I've worked this case for five years," she said furiously. "Five years, so you could come in with your lies and your damned charm and force me out of it? 'Oh, Chay, I just admire your courage and strength,'" she sneered, her face twisting in fury. "Fuck you, Natches."

"And I didn't lie." His voice rose, unintentionally, fueled by the anger and the arousal rising inside him. "Do you think I don't admire it? That I'd want to change a damned thing about you? I'm not trying to change anything, damn you, but I will protect you."

"Screw your protection."

He clenched his fists, not in rage, but to keep from touching her, to keep from jerking her to him and taking all the wild passion, driving into it until they both forgot the pain and the danger moving in on them.

"Chay, don't push me on this," he growled back. Damn her, she was tearing him apart inside. He could see the betrayal in her eyes, the hurt, and he hated it. "This isn't a fight you can be a part of."

"And it's not a fight I'll let you push me out of," she yelled back.

Turning, he watched as she stalked to the table and snapped her laptop shut. She gathered the files, stuffed them with the laptop in her case, then jerked her boots from the floor and sat on the couch.

"What the hell are you doing?" He grabbed the boot from her hand and held it out of her reach as she came off the couch, fury stamped on her flushed features. "You're not leaving here."

"The hell I'm not." When she couldn't jerk the boot out of his grasp, she pulled the case on her shoulder and moved to the door barefoot.

"You can't go outside without shoes. It's cold out there." He parked himself in front of the door as she stood before him, breasts heaving, her little fists clenched at her side as though she were actually going to use them on him.

"Better the cold outside than the cold in here." She slapped his chest. "Now get out of my way."

"Chay, you don't want to keep this up," he grated out. "Calm the hell down."

"Don't you tell me to calm down, Natches Mackay." A finger was in his face, pointing too close to his nose as he looked at it, then slowly looked up at her.

"Put that finger down, Chay." There was something about that finger in his face that made every male instinct inside him stand up in outrage.

"Make me." That finger jabbed into his chest. "Come on, tough ass. Make me. You've cheated everywhere else in this relationship, you might as well cheat here, too. What are you going to do? Tie me to the bed? Because damn you, that's the only way you'll keep me here."

Seventeen

There was something about that finger in his chest and the complete and total fury transforming Chaya's expression that did it to him.

"It" being completely wiping his mind of everything but possessing her. "It" being imagining her on her knees, naked, nipples tight, hard, and red, while he fucked that sarcastic little mouth with shallow thrusts.

"It" being owning her soul because she owned his. He knew, even as he stood there mad as hell and fighting it, that there wasn't a chance in hell he could keep her if he did this alone. And that just made him madder. Just made him hornier.

"That finger is getting ready to get you in trouble," he warned her softly.

Her lips flattened, then she did something he would have never imagined. Something that had his eyes widening in shock. She lifted that cute little hand and her middle finger shot up like a flag.

She didn't have to say a word. Her expression said it all as she turned her back to him and began to move through the living room. Probably heading to the back deck door.

Oh, that was just too bad.

He jerked his boots off and let them thump to the floor as she reached the kitchen. And she kept going. His shirt came off as he moved after her, and he tossed it to the couch.

And she knew. She threw a look over her shoulder and almost

managed to run a step or two. Before she made it past the table his arm hooked around her waist and he dragged her to the stairs.

And like the little hellion she was, she fought him. She kicked, she wiggled, she snarled, and he swore she bit his shoulder. But she wasn't fighting hard enough. All that heavy breathing wasn't just because she had her mad on. Hell no, she was as wet as he was hard, and he was betting his cock on that fact. Because that was the portion of his body that was going to fall off if he didn't get it inside that hot little body of hers. Fast.

He couldn't remember a time that he had been so enraged and so aroused at the same time. He could feel his muscles pumping with blood, his dick throbbing like an open wound, his balls tight with lust.

She wasn't getting by with a single bout of anything today. Double helping, he thought. He was going to have that wet, impudent little mouth, and he was going to have that slick, heated little pussy, and when he was finished . . . hell, when he was finished, he was going to figure out how to give her what she needed and keep her safe at the same time.

But he didn't have to tell her that yet. Hell no. She was spitting mad and clawing at his shoulders, cursing him even as he tossed her to the bed and stripped his jeans off.

Chaya tore off the shirt she wore, then the bra. She was certain the strap snapped at some point. As Natches stepped out of his jeans, she wiggled out of the leggings and panties and she was waiting on him.

His shoulders were scratched from her fury, and she was certain she would be reasonably sorry for that later, but right now, smug possessiveness curled her lips instead.

"I marked you," she snarled at him as he stepped toward the bed.

He smiled. A slow, lust-worthy curl of his lips that had a fist punch of reaction jerking in her stomach.

"That's okay, baby, because I'm sure I'll mark you, too, before the night's over."

She crawled to the edge of the bed and licked her lips, staring up at him from beneath her lashes and waiting. Anticipating.

"I thought of you every time I used that toy." She taunted him now and watched his eyes flare with wicked heat. "I sucked it until

I could take it to my throat, and thought of you. I heard your groans in my head and I moaned around it as I touched myself."

"To your throat?" His voice was a raspy, guttural growl.

"To my throat. And I moaned." She licked her lips as she lifted one hand from the bed and let it run down her body. "And I touched myself." She touched herself now. Her fingers slid through the slick juices, circled her clit, and her lashes fluttered in pleasure.

"Did you come?" He was closer, coming closer, his hand circling the thick shaft as the engorged crest tightened and throbbed in hunger.

A small bead of pearly pre-cum dampened the tiny slit, drew her attention and her hunger.

"I came," she teased him. "I came and I moaned, and it wasn't enough. Because it wasn't you."

And she had needed him. Needed him until parts of her had felt barren and lost.

He came closer, the head of his cock almost within reach.

"You're going to take me to your throat, Chay," he warned her, his voice so rough, so deep it caused her knees to weaken, her heart to pound in her chest.

"Make me, Natches." She smiled, then her breath caught as she raked her finger over her clit, and knew he was aware of the pleasure she was bringing herself.

One hand snaked out, catching her hair, tangling in it as he held her still. Her tongue swiped over the broad head and she moaned at the rich earthly taste of the liquid bead on her tongue. Passion infused with lust. A storm, heat and lightning. It filled her senses and drenched her fingers with her response.

Then his cock was filling her mouth. Thick and iron hard, the head throbbing violently as he pushed inside her. Chaya moaned and heard his answering growl as she did what she promised. She took him to her throat, her tongue rippling beneath the underside as she relished the taste of him.

One hand gripped his shaft, stroking it fiercely, determined to rip his control from him the same as he had managed to rip hers. Damn her, she had never given anyone, man or woman, the finger. That was what he did to her. He made her crazy. He made her insane to have him, made her want to fight and love him.

And God help her, how she loved him.

"Damn you," he snarled as she lifted her lashes and stared up at him, taking him as deep as she could as she touched herself, stroked herself. "Your mouth is illegal, Chay."

She would have smiled, but she whimpered instead. Because she needed him, hungered for him. Because she wanted to taste his release, glory in it.

She sucked him harder, flicked her tongue over the head as he fucked into her mouth, and swallowed him deep.

"Hellion." He pushed the fingers of both hands into her hair, tightened and pulled, and she moaned again, knowing the sound was vibrating against his cock head and glorying in his response.

"Sweet Chay." Sweat drenched his face, his shoulders. It ran down his neck in tiny rivulets and dampened the hair that fell over his face.

He looked like a pirate. He felt like a pirate, because he had stolen her heart and her soul and she didn't want them back. She just wanted his in return.

"Sweet." He groaned, his lashes lowering, a dark flush on his cheeks as his lips appeared heavier, fuller, more sensual. "Sweet Chay. Suck it, baby. Suck it deep."

She drew him deep, moaned, licked, and felt the warning throb of his impending release. His abdomen tightened, sweat rolled down it, and a second later his head tilted back, his jaw clenched, and her name tore from his throat as he exploded.

Hot, rich, a taste of salt and man and the storm rising and he was filling her mouth with it, making her drunk on him. She took each furious blast and whimpered in loss as he pulled free of her.

"Enough." He pulled her hand free of the pulsing flesh of her pussy a second before her own loss.

Her eyes snapped open. "I was ready to come," she almost howled as he flipped her to her back.

"Yeah. I know." His grin was pure wicked male. "If you want to come, baby, all you have to do is ask nicely."

"Asshole!" She grabbed his hair as he moved between her thighs and pulled. Pulled until his lips were buried in the tormented flesh and her legs were wrapped around his shoulders.

"Oh God. Yes. Damn you, Natches." She arched, her shoulders grinding into the mattress as his tongue dove deep inside the clenching depths of her core.

And he licked. "Oh yes. I love it. Love it when you do that." Her head thrashed; her fingers dug into his hair.

He licked and lapped inside her like he was eating candy and loving every minute of it. She was dying. Right there in his arms, she was dying and she didn't know how to stop it. She didn't know how to handle the burn or the violence of her response to his touch.

She was twisting against him, mewling in need as his hand landed on her rear. The rough little caress only made her burn brighter.

"More." She twisted. She arched. "Oh God, Natches. More."

He gave her more. More of the rough caresses, the heated little smacks over her butt, and more of those delicious licks inside her. Then outside her. Then around her clit. He sucked the little bud into his mouth, and she exploded into fragments.

She screamed his name, pulsed and shattered, and before she could catch her breath, he pushed her legs apart, rose above her, and buried his cock inside her.

Full length. One hard thrust. He pushed inside her with hungry demand, her name on his lips as he began to thrust hard and fast. Stroking and fucking inside her and sending her crashing into wave after wave of fiery release.

And he didn't stop. She was burning, drenched in both their perspiration when he pulled free of her, flipped her on her stomach, and lifted her rear.

And he was pushing inside her again.

"Take all of me." He groaned, coming over her, his fingers lacing with hers as he held her beneath him. "Feel me, Chay. Feel all of me and I know I belong to you."

Her head tipped back as his teeth scraped her neck and he surged inside her again. Again. He pounded inside her until she shattered, flew, until she swore her soul left her body and merged with his as she felt the violent, harsh pulses of his semen shooting inside her.

If she wasn't pregnant yet, she knew she was now. She could feel it, that bonding, a connection she had never believed she could feel with another human being. And yet, with Natches, he had given her no choice. He had stolen her heart. Made her a part of him, and now, the fight was over for it. That didn't mean he was getting his way though.

"I love you," she whispered as he collapsed over her, his head lying against her shoulder, his eyes opening to meet hers as she turned her head to stare back at him. "With my soul, Natches Mackay, I love you."

Natches sighed heavily as he forced himself to pull from her, grimacing in pleasure at the heated friction along his cock.

Lowering himself beside her, he pulled her into his arms and pressed his lips against the top of her head.

"I love you until, sometimes, I wonder if I can breathe without you now," he told her then, staring into the sunlit expanse of the bedroom as he caressed her back with one hand.

She was still and silent against his chest, though he knew that indomitable will of hers was still firmly in place. She was the strongest person he had ever known in his life, and he wanted nothing more than to allow her to be weak.

And that was the redneck in him, he knew it was. The man who wanted to protect his woman against any and all threats. To be a partner until danger rolled around. But he had chosen a woman who refused to hide from danger.

That courage she possessed terrified him.

"Dayle Mackay is dangerous," he said softly, staring at the ceiling now, his brow creasing into a frown as he let the memories of his childhood wash over him.

He didn't do that often. The past was just that, it was the past. When he had met Chaya, seeing her courage and her will to laugh had somehow helped him to dull those memories, but nothing could eradicate them.

"Dayle wanted a carbon copy of himself in a son," he stated. "A bully without a conscience, and one he could control. He didn't have much luck with me. I was a smart-mouthed little bastard eaten up with rage. I defied him every chance I had, and I gloried in it, even when he was taking his fists to me."

That had been his relationship with the man he refused to call father.

"You're not facing him alone." Her voice was soft, sweet, it was tinged with emotion and struck a bolt of feeling inside him that had him closing his eyes against the strength of it.

"There's no other way to face him, but alone." He sighed. "That's what it's come down to here, Chay. Just me and Dayle. I've avoided him, I've put it off. Hell, I should have just killed the son of a bitch before I met you, like I wanted to. But Uncle Ray would have felt as though he failed to raise me right, and Rowdy and Dawg, well, they would have had something to say about it."

Not much. But they would have said something, Natches thought.

He should have felt an edge of sorrow, hell, he should have felt guilt over the fact that it would be that easy to kill a man. But Dayle Mackay wasn't a man—he was a monster.

Yet, he still hadn't killed him, and Natches was never certain what stopped him from doing it. Maybe because until now, Dayle had never really done anything evil, even though Natches had known he *was* evil.

And he wasn't going to kill him now. Not unless Dayle gave him no other choice.

"You can give me the silent treatment until hell freezes over." She lifted her head and stared him in the eye. "But you're not doing this alone."

He, Dawg, Rowdy, and Ray had come up with the plan while Chaya slept. Their voices quiet to keep from disturbing her, their minds made up.

Natches knew the one thing Dayle had always wanted from him. Loyalty. It came down to something that simple. From the time Natches had been small, Dayle had been enraged at his affection for Ray and the two cousins he hadn't even known until they started school together. They had been instantly drawn to each other. And Natches had begun slipping away from his own home and sneaking to Ray's.

He and Dawg had been fascinated by Ray Mackay's gentle if sometimes gruff demeanor.

"If you're with me, he'll never talk," he told her, keeping his voice firm, keeping himself strong. "You're not a part of this, Chaya. There's no way to make you a part of this."

He watched her as she laid her head on his chest, her eyes glittering with tears. And Chaya didn't cry easily. She didn't use tears to get her way; she didn't pull any of the female tricks to force a man's agreement he had seen over the years from other women.

Kelly, love her heart, she shamelessly used tears whenever she felt Rowdy was being too stubborn. Shamelessly because she and Rowdy both knew what she was doing. It wasn't a game to her so much as a way to get past Rowdy's sometimes stubborn mind-set. She was sweet and innocent, and sometimes she didn't understand the evil that existed in the world. Though he knew she would argue that sentiment.

Crista was stronger, but still, she was so completely female that Natches could only grin at the battles Dawg fought with his wife. She led the big, tough Dawg around with a crook of her finger and managed to get past even his most stubborn decisions. Like running the lumber store himself. Taking responsibility for it. Dawg was turning into a real businessman, courtesy of one little stubborn female.

Chaya, Natches knew, would never be like Kelly and Crista. Not that there was anything wrong with either woman. It was just both of them saw the world as it existed around them; they didn't know the darkness that existed beneath it. And Dawg and Rowdy would kill anyone that tried to show it to them.

Chaya was different. She knew the evil. She had lived with it. She knew the darkness, because she had spent years navigating it. And she knew him. And because of that, she was going to be hell on his nerves and he knew it.

"You better find a way to make me a part of it," she stated. "Because you're not doing it alone."

He wanted to grin at the tone of her voice.

Turning her onto her back, he stared into her eyes and laid his palm on her lower stomach.

"Do you know I swore all my life I'd never allow a woman to have my child?" His fingers caressed her belly where he knew their child lay.

"Don't use that against me, Natches. That's dirty."

He shook his head. "I'm not doing that, Chay; I'm trying to make a point here."

"You're point being that I'm risking our child if I try to help you. What about you? If anything happens to you, who is going to help me raise our baby? Who's going to teach him how to be a man?" Her eyes didn't glitter with tears now, they glittered with anger.

His lips quirked at the sight of that anger.

"If anything ever happens to me, you'll be taken care of," he told her. "Just as Kelly or Crista would be taken care of if anything happened to Rowdy or Dawg. But that wasn't my point."

"Then get to your damned point so I can tell you how much of your time you've wasted. I'm keeping track of it by the way."

He had no doubt in his mind that she was.

"My point was, Chaya, until you, I never dreamed I'd find a woman strong enough to make certain my child was protected. Even if it had to be protected against me."

Her eyes widened then, and Natches forced himself to face the fear that had followed him most of his adult life.

"They say blood will always tell," he told her. "Dayle Mackay uses his fists at the slightest provocation. He's one of those men that should have been sterilized before he had a chance to breed. To make certain that kind of mean wasn't hereditary."

"Are you crazy?" She jerked away from him then, her expression incredulous as she rolled from the bed and stared back at him furiously. "You just wasted a half hour of my time with that crap?" She was almost snarling now. "Get your ass out of the bed, get dressed, and tell me what the hell you have planned before I have to shoot you."

"You're strong enough to stand up to me, Chay. But I don't know if I'm strong enough to keep from murdering Dayle Mackay if you have to see the monster that sired me."

There, it was out. He said it. That was the end of the subject as far as he was concerned. He rolled from the bed himself and jerked his pants from the floor. When he straightened, he stared back at her, feeling that inner rage flashing through him.

"Cranston needs that son of a bitch alive," he told her. "I don't want to take away from your courage or your pride, Chaya, but this is my battle, and it's my fight. I won't have the control to keep from blowing his head off if he strikes out at you. And he will. Just to test me. Just to make sure he has what he wants, he would do it."

"Like hell," she bit out. "Natches, what could he want that would make him so stupid? He's worked with the League most of his life from what I understand. He's been damned good at what he's done. What could he want so much that would make him mess up to that extent?"

Chaya was furious. She stood her ground in front of him, glaring back at him, enraged that he would try to protect her when he needed her.

"My soul," he said bitterly. "What does any monster want, Chay, but your soul?"

"Natches . . ."

His hand went over her mouth, and when she stared into his eyes, she saw something that almost terrified her. Something more frightening than the icy rage she had seen before, something more destructive than mere fury. She saw a feral determination, animalistic, almost uncontrolled as he stared into her eyes.

"If he so much as breathes violence in your direction, so much as curls a finger to touch you, *he will die.*" Natches's lips curled back from strong, clenched teeth. "If he breathes the same air you're breathing, so much as dares to step in your direction, I won't bother to think, I won't bother to try to control my rage. Is that what you want?"

She swallowed tightly, the anger draining away to be replaced by a sorrow so strong it nearly stole her breath as her hand lifted and she touched his face. "What did he do to you?" she whispered.

"He created me," he stated coldly. "Now, he's going to have deal with me. But if DHS wants him alive when we're finished, then you'll stay out of it. Otherwise, I'm not making any promises."

Eighteen

With Cranston aware of what they were looking for, it didn't take long to get the files of the men in the photograph with Chandler and Dayle Mackay, or to find the connections that brought them together.

They were in the same Marine Corps unit for nearly eight years. They had stayed in touch afterward. Hunting trips. Fishing trips. Covers for their own dreams of glory as they drew in more and more recruits after they left the service but stayed involved in various military groups.

They had no true power backing them, individually, but they had gained it as a group. Here and there. Drawing in like-minded soldiers, at first, discharged soldiers, and slowly working their way up until their recruits were coming in from active service.

They had them tied in together. They connected the dots through the day until Cranston was certain it was only a matter of time before they had those responsible for the strike order in Iraq that had killed Chaya's child. But to ensure their arrest and the complete disclosure of all their members, they needed something more to bring Dayle Mackay in.

Natches would get them more. And Chaya was terrified how he would manage that, and what it would do to his soul.

Letting go of the fight over his decision to meet with Dayle Mackay by himself wasn't easy for Chaya. But she'd seen that the more she argued with him over it, the more determined he became.

Redneck pride and stubborn will. She'd heard about it; she'd just never seen it. Not that he was a whole lot different from any other man of his kind. It just rankled more perhaps because he was hers.

And that was the part that was driving her crazy. He had charmed her, seduced her, loved his way right into her soul, and now he was shutting her out.

She looked over at him from where she sat at the table. Stretched out on the couch, one arm behind his head as he supposedly watched television.

He wasn't watching that droning news report any more than she was. He was wired, tense, waiting. Whatever Dawg and Rowdy had done that day evidently wasn't going to have immediate results.

As she watched him, her cell phone beeped imperatively at her ear.

"Dane," she answered the call, watching as Natches tensed further.

"You want to tell me what the hell your boyfriend's cousins are up to?" Cranston snarled in her ear. "They just had a rather heated, if amusing, argument in the parking lot of Mackay Lumber. It seems they've had a bit of a falling out with their cousin over a fucking picture he found."

God, what were they doing?

She lifted her eyes as Natches sat up and turned to face her. His eyes narrowed as she stared back at him.

"I don't know," she finally answered. "And he's not talking."

"Agent Dane, we don't need fuckups here," Cranston bit out. She could imagine him scowling, his face wrinkling like an irate bulldog's. "Find out what the hell is going on."

"And you expect me to do that how?" she asked him, still watching Natches, fear building inside her. "Do you have the details of the conversation?"

"Oh, something along the lines of wiping their hands of him forever because he destroyed evidence against someone. A picture. One that implicated someone they didn't name, but anyone with a brain could put it together."

She licked her lips nervously as Natches rose slowly to his feet and walked toward her. Her teeth clenched as he slipped the wireless unit from her ear and brought it to his own.

"Chaya's rather busy right now, Timothy," he said quietly. "Try again later."

He disconnected the call and tossed the unit to the table.

"Don't answer it." He pointed his finger to the ringing phone, then turned and walked into the kitchen.

And Chaya had had enough. She stood to her feet, gathered the files she was working on, and pushed them into her case. Shutting her laptop down, she pushed it into the case as well and carried it to the door.

"Walk out that door and I'll tie you to the bed." His voice never rose.

"I'm sick of that threat now." She sat down on the chair and pulled her socks on her feet before pulling her boots to her.

He pulled a beer from the fridge, opened it, and moved back to the living room, where he sat down on the couch and watched her, his green eyes intent, his expression carved from stone.

"I'm not Crista or Kelly," she told him. "I won't be pushed behind you and protected, nor play the helpless little woman. If that's what you think, then you should sit down and rethink your options. That one isn't working."

She pulled the first boot over her foot.

"He'll be calling sometime tomorrow," Natches stated. "Alex will be contacting Cranston tonight. At present, this marina, as well as the lumber store, is under surveillance by three of the men in that photo." He pointed to the picture laid out on the table. "If you walk out of here, you compromise me, is that what you want?"

She let the boot fall back to the floor.

"What have you done?" she whispered, staring back at him as she felt her chest clench with dread. She remembered the year before, the operation that had very nearly ended with Crista Jansen's death because Dawg had played games with Johnny Grace. And now, Natches was setting himself up as a target.

"Everyone knows the Nauti Boys always stick together. Nothing comes between them. Now something has; there's a division. Nadine glimpsed it that morning Dawg and I were arguing at the diner over you. Remember?"

She nodded, remembering the morning she had threatened to tell Crista on Dawg.

"They've seen us arguing more than once here lately, over

you and this investigation. That worked in our favor. Now it appears that Dawg and Rowdy are arguing between them because I destroyed a picture that implicates someone in the investigation. And Dawg's letting his opinion that 'blood will tell' be known."

Chaya shook her head slowly. "What kind of blood? What does he mean, 'blood will tell'?"

"Meaning, Chaya, that evidently, when it comes right down to it, my loyalty is to the bastard that sired me rather than the family that raised me."

"And you've kept me in the dark about this for what reason?"

"Hoping I could keep you out of it?" He arched his brow mockingly. "I'm telling you, because I've decided there's no other choice. Have you considered how someone found out who your agents were and managed to plant highly professional explosives on their vehicles?"

"Cranston suspects a leak," she whispered. "He's been going over the files. So have I."

Natches shook his head. "There's no leak, sweetheart. You were all staying at the Suites. You met there, in one particular room for a meeting most every morning."

"How did you know that?"

"Because dishonorably discharged Private Michael Wheeler works there. And he's very good friends with Dayle Mackay. Look at the files on the men who have joined the ranks of the League. Most are dishonorably discharged for abuse, ignoring the chain of command, sex crimes. Those who weren't in the military are malcontents with a bitch, nothing more. Except maybe dreams of glory. Once I determined who at the hotel could have gotten in a position to watch you, it was easy to figure out. That's where Cranston made his mistake. He was afraid blood would tell, so he sent you in so he could watch me, see which way things would swing before he pulled me in."

"He was afraid you would protect Dayle Mackay."

"Just as his agents were. Just as his agents no doubt discussed in that room after you left each morning. The room could have been bugged, individual rooms could have been bugged. Who knows? But Dayle found out what was going on, and he knew Cranston was onto him; otherwise they would have never struck out at the agents."

She nodded slowly. She had argued this with Cranston, warning him to bring Natches and his cousins in on this phase of the investigation, but he had refused. Now she knew why.

"What are you doing now?" she asked.

"Letting blood tell." He shrugged. "Dayle's going to think about this. He's going go think about that picture, think about what I could know, then he's going to call me. The break he's been waiting for. A sign of loyalty to him rather than to my cousins or my uncle."

"Or your country."

"Or my country," he agreed. "We'll set up the meet. Alex will cover me; he's a hell of a sniper. Dawg and Rowdy will back me up from a safe distance, and I'll get the information DHS needs."

She shook her head. "That's not going to work. Any defense lawyer in the nation will blow you off the stand if you testify against him. With your family history, it will never work."

"It's the only chance we have," he told her.

"You go in wired . . ."

"Won't work; he'll check me for a wire, Chay. He's not incompetent, he's proved that already."

"A different sort of wire." She leaned forward intently. "A cell phone, Natches, the receiver inside it will stay activated whether the cell phone is turned on or off. It's new. Something he won't suspect. You carry it right on your belt, in clear view. He'll never know."

He stared back at her silently.

"It's not even something our agents know about. Cranston had a friend of his working on it. It works; we've tried it out several times. Reception is perfect. We could get the meeting recorded, get our evidence, and fry him and Nadine and all his friends."

"Do the agents working with you know about it?" That was the risk, Natches thought. If this was something the other agents had known of, or discussed, then Dayle could already know about it and suspect.

But Chaya shook her head quickly. "I'm telling you, only three of us know about it. Cranston, me, and the electronics expert Cranston works with on the side. He's not even agency. And I know Cranston has it with him. He's just been waiting for a chance to test it."

It could work. He narrowed his eyes, watching her silently for long moments. If it didn't work, if reception didn't go through, if the electronics failed, then what the hell. Nothing lost. Except blood. If DHS couldn't make the charges stick on Dayle, then Natches, as much as he was finding he hated the thought of it, would take care of things himself.

His home had been torn apart in the past year because of Johnny and Dayle's crimes. Once news had leaked of the activities some of their citizens had been involved in, the town had been left in a state of shock. It was time for it to end, one way or the other.

"This could work, Natches," Chaya urged him softly. "We can have the van in town before daylight if I contact Timothy now. I'll call Alex; he'll be able to get to Timothy without anyone else knowing. Everything can be ready and waiting before Dayle ever calls you."

What was there left to lose? If it worked, then he wouldn't have to face Chaya after shedding more blood. Despite what he had told Sheriff Mayes—that killing Johnny was better than sex—he admitted now it had put a mark on his soul. Not a regret, but a knowledge that he sometimes found himself shying away from.

If he killed the man who sired him, what example then was he laying for his children? Children who would grow one day to no doubt hear the tale. Some secrets you just didn't keep when everyone pretty much knew everyone else.

"Call Alex." He finally nodded. "I'll get a message to Dawg and Rowdy. They can slip over without the eyes watching ever suspecting a thing. We'll get things ready to go."

Chaya felt her heart almost explode in joy. He wasn't dismissing the idea, he was embracing it. He didn't want her involved, but he was willing to allow her to back him, and that concession, she knew, hadn't been easy for him.

Being with Natches wasn't always going to be easy, she had found that out. When he decided something, he could obviously get incredibly stubborn about it, even with her. But he could listen to reason. That was all she asked of him, to listen to reason.

"Look at your face." His lips quirked with a hint of amusement as he reached out and touched her cheek. "You'd think I just gave you diamonds."

Chaya shook her head slowly. "Something better than diamonds, Natches."

"What could be better than diamonds?"

"Your trust."

Natches stared back at her now, almost confused. Chaya's eyes were shining, the golden brown a rich honey color, filled with warmth and some strange glow of happiness. Hell, a man would think he had just given her the crown jewels or something.

"Chay." He shook his head, letting his fingers trail down her cheek before pulling back and continuing to stare at that strange sight. "Baby, you've always had my trust."

"Not all of it, Natches." She shook her head. "Not when it came to being here for you, with you. It's something you don't even fully allow Dawg and Rowdy."

He frowned at that. "I discussed this with them. We made up the plan together."

"And then you sent them away," she told him. "You gave them just enough to satisfy them, just enough to make them feel as though they were a part of it, but you were still going in alone."

"I'm still going in alone," he warned her, making certain she understood that. "You're not going in with me, Chay."

"But I'll be there with you," she whispered. "And I'll be close. I'll know you're safe, and you're willing to allow that risk, so I can make certain you're safe."

"Hell." He rubbed at his jaw roughly. "Like you'd back down." He glowered back at her. "You'd give me a run for stubborn any day, do you think I don't know it? You just came up with a solution I wasn't aware of. I'd have figured something out before the meeting."

It wasn't that big of a deal, he kept trying to tell himself. He'd walk into the meeting, see what the hell was going on, get some information then hand Dayle Mackay over to Timothy Cranston and DHS. It was that simple. But he didn't intend to take any chances with Chaya's life.

"And let me tell you something now," she said then. "Earlier, you said he created you. Dayle Mackay didn't create you. You made yourself. That's all any of us do."

Natches shook his head at that before reaching out and dragging her from the chair to his arms.

"You're a dangerous woman," he told her as he held her against him. "And maybe you're right. Either way, I'll be the one to bring him down. Now make that call to Alex and get your plan set up. I don't want Dayle calling before you have everything ready."

He let her go and watched as she moved across the room to retrieve the wireless earpiece to her laptop.

"Just in case the cells aren't secure enough at the moment." She frowned as she sat down in front of the laptop. "I prefer not to take chances."

She sent the encrypted e-mail quickly. A short, terse request for a new cell phone and accompanying accessories. Cranston would know what she was talking about.

Within minutes, his reply came through. An affirmative and already in place. As usual, Cranston was moving ahead of everyone else, she thought with a smile as Natches read the message over her shoulder.

"Bastard," he muttered, but there was that vein of amusement again.

"What time are Dawg and Rowdy supposed to be here?" she asked as she rose to her feet and moved to him, eager, almost desperate to touch him now.

She needed him, a part of her was so hungry for him, to be held by him, that she wondered if she could bear to wait even as long as it would take to undress.

He caught her immediately, his arms, so strong and sure, wrapping around her, lifting her to him. "We have plenty of time," he promised. "God, Chay, I'd steal time if I had to for this."

He tumbled her to the couch, coming over her as his hands pushed at the cotton leggings she wore and stripped them from her.

His lips came over hers, his tongue delving deep, tangling with hers as her hands tore at his belt, at the fastening and zipper of his jeans.

It was always like this with Chaya. Wild and explosive, so searing that sometimes he wondered if he would survive it. And always desperate. As though a part of him couldn't believe she was actually here, in his arms, a part of his life.

He'd let her run from him for too many years. Trying to let her have the time and the space she needed to come to grips with everything that had happened in her life. And he wondered if that hadn't been a mistake. For both of them. The years they had lost could never be returned. But they would ensure that he cherished every moment he had with her.

As he stripped off her clothes, then tore his own off, he stilled, staring down at her, naked and aroused, her body flushed and heated as he spread her thighs and moved slowly between them.

Her breasts were swollen, her little nipples peaked and hard, reaching out to him, eager for his hungry mouth. He took first one, then the other, sucking at the sweetness of her flesh and the tight warmth of the tender peaks. He kissed the curve of her breast, then her shoulder, as he rose over her.

"I love you, Chaya," he whispered in her ear as he began to press his cock inside her.

Instant, silken heat began to enclose his sensitive cock head. Liquid fire tightened around it and sucked him inside, inch by inch until he was gritting his teeth against the pleasure consuming him as he buried himself full length inside her.

It was like living in ecstasy, the moments that he was a part of her. The way she took him, so freely, without hesitation, giving every part of herself to him whether she realized it or not.

He had always known it. Whether it was one of the kisses he stole, or now, buried so deep inside her that he didn't know where he ended and she began, he could feel her soul clasping him. Just as surely as the depths of her pussy encased him, her soul encased him as well.

Natches sheltered her beneath him, held her to him and began to move, to thrust slow and easy inside her. Each penetration dragged a hard breath from his chest and caused her to breathe in roughly. She trembled beneath him, shuddered with the pleasure he gave her. She made him feel stronger than he knew he was, more powerful than he had ever imagined he could be.

"Oh God, Natches. It's so good." Her breathless cry sent a surge of pleasure racing up his spine.

"Hold on to me, Chay." Her arms were already wrapped tight around his shoulders, her nails digging into his flesh. He carried her marks every time he took her, and he gloried in it.

His head lifted so he could watch her face as he took her. Watch the flush that washed over her expression, the perspiration that gleamed against her flesh.

Nothing in his life had ever been so beautiful as Chaya in her passion. And nothing, no one, could strip his control from him as she did.

He moved against her, harder, deeper. He groaned out at the tight clasp, the feel of her pussy tightening around him, trying to hold him inside her each time he withdrew. The feel of her pleasure mounting, the convulsive clench of silken muscles around him, her rising cries, the demand in the return thrust of her hips.

He was losing control. He could feel it. His muscles tightened as he fought to hold back just a little bit longer, to feel just a little bit more of her pleasure.

Then she melted beneath him, around him. Her hips slammed into his and her cry filled his ears, and holding on was impossible.

Her name was on his lips as he thrust inside her again, again, lost in the release rising inside him until he buried inside her one last time and felt the hard, forceful jets of his release throbbing from his cock.

Nothing had ever been this good in his life. Nothing else had ever filled him, fulfilled him, as Chaya did.

"I love you," she whispered at his ear. "God help me, Natches, I love you so much."

And those words, they completed him.

Nineteen

Natches moved the Nauti Dreams from her berth beside his cousins' houseboats and pulled her into a spare slot at the other end of the marina. To preserve the illusion, he had told Chaya. His expression was still, too still and too quiet, as though he were with her in body only.

Chaya leaned against him as he maneuvered the craft from the second-floor control room. He sat back in the custom leather captain's chair, guided the huge craft into the empty slot, and watched as two of the marina's part-time workers secured her to the dock.

It was dark; clouds rolled over the moon and blocked the stars as a cold wind whipped around the glass-enclosed control room.

"When this is over, we'll find a house," he said as he stared off into the mountains surrounding them. "I think a baby needs a real house."

Chaya pressed her lips together and found the ache and the panic building inside her at his voice.

"A baby just needs a home, Natches," she told him softly. "And two parents."

What he was getting ready to do wasn't without an element of danger. Chaya had read Dayle Mackay's Marine file. He had been a mess cook with control issues. He used his fists indiscriminately, not caring who he hurt, or how he hurt them. But he was proficient with weapons, namely, a knife. His hand-to-hand skill rating was high, and from everything else she knew about him, he didn't have a conscience.

But it wasn't the thought of the physical danger that had him staring off into the distance; it was who he was going up against. What he was going against. The man who should have been his father.

"I was seven the first time he locked me in the closet," he said. The lethal throb of cold determination in his voice had her hands tightening on his shoulders from where she stood behind him.

"He kept me in there until I thought I was going to die," he said. "Almost two days. No food, no water. When he dragged me out, I was almost senseless with fear. After I managed to get cleaned up and he gave me a drink of water, I lied for him, just like he wanted me to do before he put me in that closet. And he told me, 'Loyalty, son. That's all I want from you. Just be loyal.' "

Natches couldn't even remember what his father had needed him to lie about at the time. Something inconsequential. It always was. Just something to prove his loyalty.

"And what did you want?" she asked him.

Funny, he could hear the ache in her voice for him, just that easy. As though he were that much a part of her, that he knew how much she ached as he talked.

He had never felt another person the way he felt Chaya. The way he had always felt Chaya.

"I caught Faisal's transmission the day they brought you into that camp," he said instead of answering her question. "I checked the area, desperate for a place to hide you, because I just knew I was going to pull out a mess when I went in for you. The caves were a no go. It was the first place they would have checked. There was no other cover, no other place to hide but a hole."

Chaya felt her heart clench as he caught her hand and pulled her to his lap, surrounding her with warmth when she wanted to surround him with it.

"I made that hole. I was going to shove you in it and try to find cover above you. I hate closed-in places, Chay. Dark, small places. That was always my weakness."

His cheek brushed against her hair.

"You were in that hole with me," she whispered.

And he nodded.

"I couldn't leave you in there by yourself. You were all but blind, hurt. When I killed Nassar later, Chay, I think I scared myself, because I enjoyed it. I saw you, so brave and strong, and trying so hard to fight when you should have been leaning against me, crying, doing something other than storing your strength in case you had to go down fighting. And you would have gone down fighting."

She felt his heart beat beneath her cheek and held on to him, because he had forced himself into that hole with her.

"I was losing it," she told him then. "Before you pulled me out of there. I was ready to break, Natches. And in that hole, when I heard them coming for us, I was screaming in my head until you kissed me." That kiss had pulled her back, it had saved her. "You made me strong. Because of you I was able to run. You held me up, you almost carried me. And because of you, I was able to stand the darkness in my own mind, and the fear that they were going to hurt me again. I didn't want to hurt anymore. And when I lost Beth. You kept me sane. With your touch, with your kiss, with all the wild pleasure you poured into me that night." She stared up at him, seeing his somber expression, even in the dark, her heart breaking for the man who had forced himself into that hole with her, and was now trying to face his own nightmare. Alone.

His expression was shadowed, dark, but his eyes were alive. And they brought tears to her eyes. Fierce, shockingly determined. He would do whatever he had to do to make sure Dayle Mackay never hurt anyone he loved, ever again.

"Clayton Winston called while you were in the shower earlier," he said. "He got to talk to Christopher. Then DHS called him back. They've arranged transportation through a private broker to D.C., where he can see his son in a supervised visit."

Chaya closed her eyes, thankful Cranston had followed through with that.

"Clayton's dying," he said. "Doctors don't think he'll see the year out. He needed this before he passes on."

"And what do you need, Natches?"

It felt like an epitaph, the way he was talking, as though he wouldn't return to her, and she refused to consider that.

"Come on." He lifted her from his lap and drew her through

the doorway into the bedroom. There, he closed the door to the control room and locked it with a flick of his fingers.

"You didn't answer me." She turned to face him in the darkness of the room. The drapes had been drawn that morning and the room was almost pitch black now.

He turned on the low lamp by the bed and turned to face her.

"You're coming back to me," she whispered, her breath hitching. "Don't you look at me like that. You're going to be covered, and you're coming back to me."

And tears filled her eyes, because she couldn't imagine anything less.

"I'm coming back to you," he promised her. "One way or the other, I'm coming back, Chay. But how will you see me, how will our child see me if I come back with blood on my hands?"

His father's blood. She could see it in his face, his uncertainty that he could leave Dayle Mackay alive.

"Bullies are weak," she told him huskily. "You get what DHS needs and they'll break him. I swear to you, Natches, they'll break him and they'll put the rest of that group away for good. You'll win."

She knew they would. She was the interrogation specialist, but she only interrogated subjects of interest, she didn't interrogate suspects, nor did she interrogate suspected terrorists, homegrown or foreign. There was a division for that, men and women who made her worst nightmares seem like a picnic in the park.

He nodded. The confidence, the sheer knowledge in his eyes that he would do whatever it took to protect what belonged to him, humbled her. He tried to be a shield between the world and those he loved, always trying to protect them, to make certain danger never touched them. And he never expected, never asked, for the same, though he knew Dawg, Rowdy, and Ray Mackay had always been there for him. He had never asked.

"We're good to go then." He nodded before moving to her, his lips settling on hers like a promise. A gentle, forever promise, as sweet and heated as a dream.

"We're good to go." She nodded, and she pushed back the fears. She would cover the angles, she would create a bubble around him that could do nothing less than protect him from any outside forces.

But inside that bubble, Natches had to face the knowledge that he wasn't just betraying a monster. He also had to confront that last glimmer of hope, that the monster had a soul.

Monsters didn't have souls though, Natches assured himself as the meeting with his cousins and Alex Jansen drew to a close.

Not for the first time, he found himself amazed at Chaya's knowledge, and her ability to find workable solutions to the problems that were going to face them when it came to executing the plan they had conceived.

Illegal wiretapping was nothing new, and Cranston wasn't above using it to make certain a plan was coming together. A call had been made to Dayle Mackay by one of the men watching the Mackay cousins, informing him of the division between Natches and his cousins over an old picture, evidence against a citizen of Somerset in the stolen missiles case, and Natches's refusal to give the authorities pertinent information where that citizen was concerned.

And Dayle had been interested.

Natches listened to the other man's voice on the digital recording Alex had slipped in to him. The smug certainty in Dayle's voice—that, finally, blood had thickened in Natches's veins and become more substantial than water.

He turned his back on his cousins as the recording played, kept his expression calm. This wasn't a Mackay he was going after; it was just another monster. Just as it had been in the Marines. It wasn't a person. It was a target, nothing more.

"Moving the *Nauti Dreams* was also noted," Alex told them all softly and switched to the recording of another call. Natches's phone call to another marina and the arrangement of transportation for his houseboat was given as well. With each call, Dayle became more confident, more certain that his son and cousins were finally making the split he had been waiting on.

"That's my boy," Dayle mused softly, smugly. "I knew it wouldn't take long."

"What about the woman? The agent with him?" the voice on the other end questioned him. Daniel Reynolds was one of the men in the photo, one of the fanatical leaders of the future revolution.

"Women are easy to get rid of," Dayle snorted. "An accident, a few little drugs popped into her drink, and she does the bar on a Saturday night. Natches'll drop her."

"She's still an agent."

"And she doesn't have the information he has," Dayle pointed out. "No doubt, that relationship will terminate soon enough, on its own. I'll call him soon."

"Are you certain about this?" the other voice pushed determinedly. "We can't afford to mess up."

Dayle laughed at the question. "Trust me, Daniel, I know my son. I knew it was just a matter of time. The boy's a killer. He was a killer in the Marines, and he'll always be a killer. That kind of cold only adheres to its own kind. He'll come in."

"Very well," Daniel agreed. "Arrange the meeting and contact us when you've finished."

The sound of the recorder disengaging flipped a switch in his mind. Cold. Hard. Yeah, he was a killer. He turned slowly to meet his cousins' eyes.

"Chaya, do you still have those files?" He knew she did.

"They're upstairs in my case." She moved for the staircase but not before she cast him a suspicious look.

As she disappeared upstairs he looked at his family. His cousins and the man he called friend.

"This might not go as easy as she thinks it will," he told them quietly. "If anything happens to me, you take care of her and my child." He looked to Dawg and Rowdy. "Give him what Uncle Ray always gave me, and make it stick."

Dawg and Rowdy glanced at each other.

"Man, this is going to be a walk in the park," Dawg protested. "Alex has point, your woman has your wire, DHS in the van, and me and Rowdy in place. Nothing's going to happen." Dawg's gaze sharpened. "Unless you do something dumb. You gonna do somethin' dumb, Natches?"

Natches's lips quirked at the question. "Have I ever done things any other way, cousin?"

"Hell."

"He's going to do things right, or he'll find me standing beside him."

Natches jerked around, frowning at Chaya, who didn't have those files in her hand. But her hand was propped on her hip and her expression was something just this side of pissed off.

"Isn't that right, Natches?"

He inclined his head smoothly. "I'll play by the plan," he promised her.

But he knew Dayle. And he knew Dayle would never play by any kind of rules. This was it and he knew it. When he walked out of that meeting, one way or the other, it was going to be over.

And she didn't believe a word he was saying.

"Here's the cell phone." Alex pulled the phone out of his pocket and handed it across the table. "Cranston's proud as hell of this little puppy. He said not to break it; it's the only prototype they've managed to complete successfully."

Natches lifted the phone from the table, flipped it open, and checked it for anything that Dayle could use to identify it as a wire rather than a phone.

"It even makes phone calls," Chaya told him with a hard smile.

"Cranston has the van parked in town, one agent inside. As soon as he has the location point he can park it within half a mile and still receive clear reception," Alex informed them. "As far as any listening ears at the hotel could know, he's raging over Natches's refusal to join the team or to help Agent Dane complete her mission. He's making plans to pull out of Somerset once she contacts him."

"Which will be tonight," she told them. "I'll contact Cranston and inform him that he should pick me up in the morning and that I'll be returning to D.C. with him."

"That's when I assume Dayle will make his call." Natches nodded.

"I'll need to activate the cell phone to your number rather than using your own cell," Chaya told him. "We want a recording of it. Calls will transmit with no possible trace outside the half-mile limit."

"We'll be ready to move when Cranston gives the order." Alex nodded to Dawg and Rowdy. "We'll have everything in place and ready to move."

"And he'll have his own watchers," Natches warned them.

"He has six we've identified, and we'll have men covering them. We'll allow them to stay in place until the last minute before taking them out."

It was a damned good plan. Natches nodded to the three men

as he curled his arms around Chaya and pulled her back against his chest, one hand against her lower stomach as he stared back at his cousins, his look intent.

They knew. Brief nods assured him they knew. If anything happened to him, then Chaya was to be protected, just as he would have protected one of their wives, one of their children.

They had made that vow long ago and far away. Three boys that should have been brothers, that had wished they were. They had become brothers. And they had made that vow, what belonged to one was the others' to protect. That simple.

Chaya felt his hand on her stomach and stared at Dawg and Rowdy fiercely. No matter what Natches wanted, he was to be protected. Their gazes flickered to her, then back to Natches, and she hoped, she prayed that the nod they gave was an affirmative to that silent demand.

The Nauti Boys were thick as thieves, it was said. Their loyalty was to each other and to family alone. That bond would protect Natches.

"We're out of here then." Alex got to his feet and looked to the back of the boat. "Damn, that water's fuckin' cold tonight."

"And Kelly and Crista have electric blankets and hot coffee waiting on us. That's the best you're going to do tonight, Alex," Dawg informed him.

"Yeah, the two of you curl up with a warm body, and I get stuck with an electric blanket," he grunted. "I always get the short end of the deal with you boys."

"Yeah, and we'll remind you of that one of these days."

They disappeared along the hallway, silence slowly descending through the houseboat. There wasn't a splash, a dip of the boat, or a slide of a door to indicate they had left.

"Come sit with me." Natches drew her to the couch, but rather than sitting, he stretched out on the cushions and drew her into his arms.

"Just sit?"

"Just let me hold you." He tucked her close, his body warm and hard, strong and secure.

"Stop making this feel like a funeral, Natches. Nothing is going to happen."

He chuckled at that, then sobered. "You know, Chay, the last time I spoke to him I was twenty. I had cracked ribs, one was broken, my mouth was full of blood, and I could have sworn I was dying. I told him, as Dawg, Rowdy, and Uncle Ray dragged me off of that floor, that the next time I spoke to him, I'd kill him."

He'd spat his blood on the bastard's shoes and made a vow, and Dayle had laughed at him. Natches had never forgotten that gloating laugh; he had heard it again tonight.

"And you're not going to kill him," she told him.

"Yeah, I am." Natches smiled as she stiffened in his arms, and at the thought of what he was going to do to Dayle. "Betraying him to DHS will be the same as death for him. It's the ultimate revenge for me. Because I'll know, every day, that he's breathing; we'll both know I beat him."

He held that inside him, though he knew clear to his gut that things weren't going to be that easy. He was a Marine. A sniper. An assassin. He'd always worked alone, without a spotter, sometimes without extraction. Because shit happened after blood was shed, and when shit happened, information came out. He'd learned to go with his gut. To know when to run and when to hang around. And when something wasn't going to go as planned.

This wasn't going to go as planned.

And if it all went to hell and back, then he wanted this night. He wanted to hold her, he wanted to talk to her.

His hand slid along her stomach once again.

"If our child is a boy, I want to teach him to play baseball," he told her softly.

She laughed at that. A soft, amused little sound that had a smile curling at his lips.

"If it's a girl, you'll be a tyrant."

A girl? A frown drew at his brows. A daughter, with her mother's hair and eyes and, God help him, Mackay blood. He shuddered. "I'll lock her up until she turns fifty."

"You will not." Her hand covered his, her fingers twining those of his other hand as it lay on her thigh.

"I promise you. Till she's fifty. That girl will be wilder than the wind and harder to control than a green mule."

She looked up at him, the dim light in the room catching the sparkle in her eyes, the love, the concern, the fears that would ride her until this was finished.

"She'll be a lady." The sound of her laughter was almost a giggle, because she knew better, just as he did.

"Wild as the wind," he argued again.

"And a boy wouldn't be?" She reached up and touched his face, and that touch, tenderness and warmth combined, was another memory he stored inside him.

"Boys are different," he told her.

She frowned, just as he knew she would. "How do you figure?"

"Boys are born to be wild."

"And girls are born to tame the wind," she said softly. "What are you doing, Natches?"

He knew what she was talking about. Why was he just holding her, just talking, just building memories?

"I'm creating my shield." He lowered his head and kissed her lips. "You're my shield, Chay, you just don't know it. Soft and sweet, born to tame the wind and to tempt my dreams. When I walk into that meeting, I want to carry this with me."

"Why?"

He was silent for long moments, wondering if there was any way to make her understand.

"So I won't kill him," he finally admitted. "Because this memory and all the others will be wrapped around me, and I'll remember what you're fighting for and how important keeping him alive really is. You're the only thing standing between him and death, Chay. Just this, and knowing he's more important to your fight than he is to mine."

"Then I'll be your shield," she whispered, turning, facing him, embracing him. "Always, Natches, I'll be your shield."

Twenty

He didn't make love to her that night. He waited until the sun rose and carried her to the bed. There, he stripped her slowly, gently, and gazed at the woman splayed out before him.

Sweetly rounded breasts, her nipples hard and red. Her stomach was smooth, only slightly rounded. There was no sign yet that his child rested there, but he knew it did.

Sweetly curved thighs, and between them, silky bare flesh.

The hours he had spent holding her, kissing her, stroking her, had stoked the fires inside them to a burning simmer. Something Natches had never known before. It was the first time in his life he had ever spent time just holding a woman, just stroking her, just laying velvet kisses wherever he could reach.

He'd been hard for hours. He could have fucked her ten times over in the time he had taken just loving her on that couch. But he wouldn't have traded it for anything he'd known in the past. Each touch, each kiss, each little laugh, sigh, and whispered love word had bound them closer together.

She had felt it. He felt it. He knew there were silken-wrapped chains in his soul now, and they led back to her. The burn was now a flame though. Natches smiled down at her, wild, wicked hunger raging inside him.

He'd been born as wild as the wind, and like the wind, he had torn through his own life, whipping around it without direction, shearing his own dreams as he moved, until he met Chaya.

And she had been born to tame that wind inside him. Not the

man, she made the man wild, made him hungry. But the rage, the burning fury that had driven him before that day in a dry, hot desert, was now tamed, held in the hands of one tender woman.

"Are you going to just stare at me all morning?" She stretched beneath his gaze, her eyes flickering to where he stroked his cock, anticipating, holding back that final moment when he would have to let her go.

"Would you let me?" He smiled, using one finger to trace a line from between her breasts to the silken, soft mound between her thighs.

"If that was what you wanted to do." She lifted her hands and let her fingers trail along the path he had made. "I didn't take you for a watcher, Natches. Though I'm sure we could adapt if that's your kink."

If that was his kink? He almost laughed; he did smile. God, he loved her. Smart mouth and all.

"What if it is my kink?" He lifted his brows curiously. Not that it was, but he could play with her. That was the joy with Chaya, she enjoyed playing. Even patched and healing in that hospital in Iraq, she had enjoyed playing with him.

"Isn't it too bad you broke my vibrator then?" She let her fingers whisper over her mound before returning, stroking along the top of the glistening slit.

Hell, he'd come in his own hand at this rate.

"You would have let me watch?" He hadn't anticipated that.

"Oh, I would have," she whispered, letting her finger dip into the folds, her hips arching as he watched. "I would have shown you how I survived five years without you. I would have let you watch, and let you hear me crying because I couldn't reach the same peak you could bring me to. Would you like to see that?"

See her cry? God no.

"I'd finish you, baby," he promised her. "I'll let you show me how you do it, then I'd show you how it's done." His wicked smile drew a light vein of laughter from her, a twinkle of the same wicked hunger to her eyes.

"Then show me how it's done." Her fingers lifted from her flesh, dewy with her juices and he couldn't help himself. He snagged her wrist and brought her fingers to his lips.

Her taste exploded against his tongue. Sweet and earthy. Nothing tasted as good as Chaya's passion. He covered the tips of her tasty fingers, licked them clean, and watched her eyes darken as he caressed the sensitive tips with his tongue.

"I'll show you exactly how it should be done," he murmured. "You should be savored."

He stretched out between her thighs, pressed them wide, and blew a breath across the dampened flesh, his gaze lifting to her as a tremor shook her body. "Savored in the most delicious ways. With a kiss." He covered her hard little clit in a heated kiss, nudged it with his tongue, and felt it throb in anticipation.

"Just a kiss?" Her voice was hoarse with pleasure now.

"Hmm. A kiss wasn't enough?" He kissed the silken folds, drew the taste of her juices onto his tongue, and hummed in appreciation.

"Not enough." Her hands were in his hair now as she tried to press him closer.

"A taste?" He dipped his tongue inside those luscious folds, licked softly, slowly, felt the soft flutter at the entrance of her core and the echo of the clenching need building in the muscles there.

"Taste isn't enough." She writhed beneath him, her hips arching, pressing her pussy closer to his mouth as he kissed and licked and listened to her cries of pleasure building in his head.

Making love. He'd never made love before Chaya, but that was what he was doing now. Making love to her. Loving her with everything inside his soul.

"Kissing or tasting?" His own voice was ragged now. "Demanding little thing, aren't you?"

He lifted his head, smiling back at her as she watched him, lashes lowered sensually, a sheen of perspiration on her face now.

And those sweet, lush breasts. They were swollen, her nipples hard, tight, and flushed with need. He couldn't help but lift one hand, slide it over her stomach, and cup one of those sweet mounds as he went back to kissing, tasting. And licking. He licked around her clit. He laid little kisses on it, pursing his lips and drawing it inside the heat of his mouth until she unraveled beneath him, arched and cried his name in release.

Before the tremors finished sweeping through her, he jerked to his knees, lifted her legs until they lay against his chest, and began working his cock inside her.

Fuck. She was tight. So hot he had to clench his teeth, tried valiantly to think about car motors, anything, everything but the destructive, velvet grip encasing his cock.

And nothing worked. Nothing filled his mind but the scent and the feel of her. Her voice crying out his name, her hands gripping his wrists as he held on to her hips. Until he was buried fully inside her, balls deep in the sweetest, slickest haven a man's soul could ever find.

"Natches. Oh God, it's so good."

Good wasn't even a description. There was no description for this pleasure; it defied any poet's ability to voice it. He tightened, arched deeper inside her and felt the sweat running down his chest as sensation upon sensation whipped over his body, dug into his nerve endings and filled him with ecstasy.

His head lowered until he could kiss her ticklish little ankle, before she jerked, a panting little cry falling from her lips.

He glanced up at her and grinned before licking over the side of her foot. And she moaned, her foot flexing as he lifted one hand from her hip to her foot, and as he began to thrust, let his teeth bite down, just below her big toe.

Chaya screamed with the sensation. He bit her. Bit her foot and thrust inside her, once, twice, and she was coming again. Exploding into a million brilliant fragments as his hips moved harder, moved faster. He was pounding into her, his expression tightening, sweat rolling down his neck as she felt herself flying from one peak to another, then joining him as his release flowed into her.

She watched him, the way his eyes narrowed on her, became sensual and heavy a second before they closed and a shudder wracked his body.

"I can't get enough of you," he breathed out roughly as he collapsed over her, allowing her legs to embrace his hips before sliding to the bed. "Every time, I only want you more."

Running her fingers through his hair she smiled. "Good. Because I can't get enough either."

He rolled to his back, dragging her to him until she was draped over his chest, weak and exhausted and knowing there was no time to sleep.

They lay like that, their hearts finally easing in their chests, their breathing returning to normal.

"When you leave the boat, don't look back," he told her.

"Don't stop, don't pause. You're a woman walking away from something she can't deal with."

"I know how to do my job." But her voice caught on a sob. Walking away from Natches without looking back?

"I know you do. But it won't be easy, Chay. And you can't pause. You have to keep going."

She nodded against his chest.

"I have a duffel packed for you. Some clean clothes Dawg brought over in a plastic bag last night. Your other clothes. You'll take your briefcase, but only your laptop inside it. They can tell by the way you carry it, the way you move, the way it hangs from your shoulder or your hand if there's anything more in it."

She nodded again.

"When it happens, when I meet with him, you're not to come near until he's cuffed. Do you understand?"

His voice was so hard, his tone cool, but she could feel the emotions coursing beneath the surface. As able as she knew she was, she had also come to realize something. He called her his strength, but she could also become his weakness. Just as he could become hers if anyone ever wanted to hurt him to strike back at her.

"Not until he's cuffed," she agreed, praying she could keep that promise.

"Let's get you ready to go then." He lifted her from his chest and moved from the bed with her.

Standing beside it, he touched her face and gave her a hard, lingering kiss.

"When I get you back here, you're not getting out of the bed for a week."

"At least a week," she promised, standing still as he moved back and stared down at her.

"I don't like this," she finally told him. "You shouldn't be alone with him."

His smile was tinged with bitterness, but no regret. "I won't be. Remember? You're my shield."

And she had to be content with that.

"Go shower. I'll get your things together."

And then she would leave him alone. Alone to think, alone to remember, and Chaya knew it. Just as she knew there was no other way to convince the monster that Natches was alone.

Leaving him this time was breaking her heart.

Twenty-one

Natches gave Chaya time to get started up the boardwalk before he stepped onto the deck of his houseboat to watch her leave.

Instantly he felt the rifle scope between his eyes, which meant, hopefully, he was drawing it away from Chaya. He smirked at the would-be assassin, daring him to take the shot, knowing none would be taken. But he was smart enough, instinctive enough to feel it.

Then he turned his gaze back to Chaya, keeping his expression carefully mocking, as though watching her walk away meant nothing to him.

It wasn't forever, he reminded himself. Hell no. After this, he was never going to watch Chaya walk away from him again, he would make damned sure of it.

Shaking his head as though amused at something, he turned and walked back into the living room and closed the door behind him.

Chaya's cell phone was tucked at his belt; it was turned on. According to her, even disabling the battery wouldn't disable the wire.

All he had to do now was wait for Dayle Mackay to learn Chaya had left and to call. And he would call. Cranston was betting against it, as was Alex. Three against two, because Dawg, Rowdy, and Natches all knew Dayle would call.

He didn't have to wait long. Two hours that he spent pacing

the living room, going over the plan, trying to make certain he'd considered every angle, and the cell phone rang.

He unclipped it unhurriedly and flipped it open before bringing it to his ear.

"Yeah?" As though he didn't know who the hell it was.

"We need to talk, son." Grating, smug, Dayle's voice came over the line clearly.

Natches stayed still, his fists clenching. He took the phone from his ear and flipped it closed, disconnecting the call. He didn't want to appear too eager, did he? He had to swallow back the urge to throw up at the sheer confidence in Dayle's voice.

How could anyone deceive himself to the extent that Dayle had, believing he would ever carry the right to call Natches "son"? Even with the slight evidence Dayle had been given, how could he ever imagine Natches would have a desire to speak to him? To kill, yeah, killing him might assuage a hell of a lot of anger, but in the long run, it would only end up pissing Natches off more.

Natches liked to think he wasn't a man who fooled himself easily. He'd thought Dayle wasn't. It seemed he was wrong, because a half hour later, the phone range again.

"What the hell do you want?" was his answer.

"We need to talk," Dayle repeated, his voice throttled, anger evident in it.

"About what? Your treasonous activities? They've already caused me enough problems if you don't mind," he sneered. "If you're going to save the world, try to do it without involving me. Okay?"

Save the world his ass. He almost choked on that one. Damn, he'd thought he was a better actor than this.

Dayle said nothing for long moments. "Some information is dangerous to have, Natches," he finally replied.

"Yeah, so pull the damned trigger next time I step outside, why don't you? That would just solve all our problems."

Dayle chuckled. "That sixth sense of yours has always been good. Come to your aunt Nadine's house, Natches. One hour. Just give me a few minutes to talk to you; that's all I'm asking for. Believe it or not, we might have a few things in common."

Uh-huh. They sure did. His blood and the fact that Natches really wanted to spill it.

But he stayed silent.

"I can't imagine we have anything in common," he finally stated. "And I doubt Nadine would let me in the door."

"One hour, Natches." Dayle's voice gentled, and it sounded sickening. "I'll be there waiting for you."

This time Dayle disconnected.

Natches flipped the phone closed and returned it to the clip on his belt. He checked the clock. It was barely nine and he needed a beer. Hell, whiskey. The bastard was driving him to drink.

He pushed his fingers through his hair and walked upstairs. He buckled the black leather chaps he used for riding the Harley in winter over his jeans and pulled on the heavy boots he wore when riding the powerful machine.

The leather jacket, scuffed and beaten, was pulled from the closet and thrown to the bed as he moved to the dresser. He tucked a knife in the side of his boot. Picking up the jacket, he walked downstairs and pulled a beer from the refrigerator.

Hell, he wished Chaya was here. He'd lie on the couch with her again, hold her, and reinforce the shield. His lips quirked at the thought of that. It had taken him long enough to get beneath *her* shields, but once he had, the woman he found beneath there was more than a match for him. And he liked that; he liked that fine.

He finished the beer, tossed it in the trash, and moved to the couch to wait. He'd wait that hour before he left the houseboat. There was no sense in arriving early, or even on time. He may as well make an entrance when he arrived. He and Dayle Mackay had never pretended to stand on ceremony with each other.

He pushed his fingers through his hair and thought of the team moving into place. They knew where Dayle's spotters were; that would make it easier. Natches knew Alex and his team—they didn't make mistakes. And Dawg and Rowdy were black death when they wanted to be.

He waited. He didn't pace; instead, he sat on the couch and stared around the living room. He thought of the house Dawg had nearly completed farther in the mountains. There was land close to him, and it wasn't but a few miles from the house Rowdy and Kelly were building. He could buy that land, build him and Chaya a home. A place to love and to raise their babies.

Lots of bedrooms, he thought. He wanted to fill her life with babies and with laughter. Both their lives. He wanted to be the husband he'd dreamed of being with her, the father he'd never had.

When the clock showed five minutes past the hour, he stood and left the houseboat. He paused on the deck as though considering turning back, then shook his head and moved to the docks, striding quickly to the small metal building Ray had allowed them to set up to park the Harleys in. He took his time getting it out and checking it over.

Half an hour and he was on the road. He didn't rush, there was no need to. Dark glasses protected his eyes from the cold wind, but it ruffled through his hair, clearing his head.

He pushed thoughts of Chaya and babies as far back in his mind as he could, though he admitted, that wasn't far. Hatred, a child's rage and pain, and the fear of the dark that kid had known. He erased it from his mind. It was just another mission he told himself. Except this time, he wasn't going to kill.

He pulled onto the side of the street before Nadine's driveway forty-five minutes past the deadline and parked the Harley before cutting the motor and stepping off. Far enough away that he'd be surprising them.

He'd passed the dark panel van parked on the street, blending in with the SUVs and pickups it shared space with. Wasn't Nadine nice? Why, she had bought her a nice little place in the middle of town. Made things so much easier. But it didn't make this any easier.

Stepping up to the door, he didn't bother to knock. He pushed open and stepped into the living room before coming to a rocking stop.

"You're determined to make me puke this morning," he stated as he watched his aunt jump from Dayle's lap and Dayle pull his hand slowly from beneath the silk dress she was wearing.

Nadine didn't even bother to flush. Actually, she let a nervous little smile touch her lips; it was almost welcoming.

What dimension of the twilight zone did he step into? Natches wondered as he lifted his brow and closed the door.

"We thought you weren't arriving." Dayle rose to his feet, adjusting the polo shirt he wore and the creased slacks.

He looked as powerful as he ever had. Six feet plus, wider than Natches, broader. Older, Natches reminded himself as he hooked his thumbs in the top of the chaps he wore and stared at the man who dared call him son.

"I didn't think I was either." He shrugged and stared at Nadine as she twisted her hands together nervously and glanced between Dayle and Natches. "What's her problem?"

Dayle smiled. "She wants to welcome you home."

"Really?" Natches arched his brows. "How interesting. Last I heard, she wanted to gut me for popping Johnny's head off for him. Changed her mind rather fast, didn't she?"

She paled, swaying as Dayle put his arm around her and whispered something in her ear before nodding toward the back of the house. Giving him a grateful look, she accepted his kiss on the lips before moving through the house.

Natches shook his head. "You know, that relationship you have going on there never did make sense to me. She had her brother's kid, and you're not the brother. No wonder Johnny was so screwed up. Now she just wants to welcome me right into the family as though she never hated my guts? You two been doing hard drugs or something?"

"You always were a smart-mouthed little bastard," Dayle snapped irritably.

"Yeah, I do good at that." Natches grinned in pride. "So, what the hell do you want and how do I return things to where you ignore me rather than harass me?"

Dayle grimaced, his lined face tightening into displeasure as he pushed his hair, still thick and barely graying, back from his forehead.

"Little whelp," he muttered. "You don't even look like me. If it wasn't for those eyes of yours I'd swear you weren't even mine."

"Maybe Chandler was my daddy as well as Johnny's," Natches mocked. "From what I remember, it could be possible."

"I thought of that," Dayle snapped. "Even had the paternity test done. No such luck, you're mine. And now it's time we both come to terms with that."

"And how do you suggest we do that?"

"You know what I am, what I'm a part of." Dayle sighed. "I always knew you'd remember it."

"Is that why you hired Linkins to try to kill me in Iraq?"

Dayle shrugged again. "It wasn't an easy order to give. And I have to admit, I wasn't disappointed when it failed."

Natches forced himself to keep from curling his fingers into fists.

"The strike order on the hotel where Chaya's husband and child were?" he asked. "Another attempt?"

Dayle's eyes widened, then narrowed. "That had nothing to do with you or the girl. I didn't find out about your relationship with her until later. And I didn't give that order, that came from one of our founding members based there at the time. Craig Cornwell was working for us. We had no idea he was working for the enemy, too, until then. We couldn't risk his capture. He would have talked."

"I want to know how the hell you managed it. A strike order, authenticated and radioed to the planes. That seems pretty much impossible."

"Orders get messed up sometimes." Dayle shrugged. "The commander only knew the orders he received. We just had to get them through the proper channels. As I said, Iraq wasn't my call. I'm a recruiter, that's all."

"You're not a very good recruiter," Natches informed him. "I've been checking up on you a bit. Dishonorably discharged, malcontents, some of your boys aren't even in the military. Those that are still there are just a breath from being tossed into Leavenworth."

"Because they know where our leaders are taking us," Dayle snarled. "Someone has to pave the way. The revolution is building, Natches. You can be a part of it. You can be at my side as a general and a leader now that you've disassociated yourself from Ray's little bastards."

And here it was. Natches grinned in full-throttled smug triumph. "What makes you think I've done that?"

Dayle tensed. "My reports are that you're arguing over information you're refusing to turn over to DHS. That you're protecting me." Pride flared in his eyes.

Natches let himself chuckle at that one. "Nah, not really. They're just a little ticked off at me right now because I wouldn't let them in on the fun. No, sorry, Dayle, I'm here to bust your ass."

Dayle froze, his eyes narrowed. "You're not serious."

"Yeah, I am." Natches grinned. "Real serious. See, those

guys you had targeting me in their gunsights? Dawg and Rowdy have them already. Go ahead. Try to call one of them."

Dayle pulled his cell phone from his belt and punched a number in. Listened. Tried another. Another. Yeah, Dawg and Rowdy were black death when they wanted to be.

"I'd say there's some blood fertilizing a few areas." Natches nodded. "It was a good try though. Too bad you didn't pay attention to the fact that I don't even fucking hate you. I just basically want to see you locked up until hell freezes over, knowing I put you there."

Yeah, this was better than a bullet. He watched Dayle pale, watched his shoulder twitch as he prepared to go for his weapon.

Natches went for his first. He pulled the Glock from the back holster beneath his jacket, holding it comfortably on his father.

"Did you really think you were going to convince me to help you do anything?" Natches asked him. "I ask again, are you on hard drugs?"

Dayle's lips thinned as he watched Natches lean against the wall, the gun held easily, pointing directly at him.

"You can't prove any of this."

" 'Course I can. I'm wired." He shrugged.

Dayle grinned at that. "Not here you aren't, Natches. Any wire you wore was jammed the minute you walked in."

"Cell phones aren't jammed, are they?"

Dayle glanced at his cell. "Yours isn't open though."

"Doesn't have to be." He shrugged. "I got ya. DHS has ya. Busted, old man."

"I don't think so."

Natches swung around, the gun barreling on Nadine's voice as he felt his stomach drop.

Janey. For a moment, fear had nearly paralyzed him, the thought of Chaya uppermost in his mind. But now, the fear nearly burned through his mind. Chaya could have worked with him; she would have known what to do. But it wasn't Chaya Nadine held by long, thick black hair. It wasn't Chaya who stared at him from dazed, confused eyes.

"Insurance." Dayle sighed. "Put the gun down, and hand me the cell phone, please."

Natches watched as Nadine leveled her own gun at Janey's head.

"I'd love to kill her," she told him vindictively. "Pop her little head right off, just like you did Johnny's."

Natches lowered the gun, shifted away from the wall and forced Nadine in a better alignment with the window as he came closer to her.

Be in position, Alex, he prayed. God help them all, he better be in position.

He pulled the cell phone from his belt and tossed it to Dayle. He almost winced as Dayle cracked it against the table, busting the frame before he dropped it into the vase of water that held fresh flowers. So much for Cranston's new toy.

"The gun, Natches." Dayle waggled his fingers demandingly. "Let's not . . ."

Pop.

Nadine went down, dragging Janey with her as Dayle jumped him. The fist that plowed into Natches's jaw felt like a jackhammer. He went backward, the gun flying, clattering to the floor before he righted himself and faced an enraged Dayle.

"Just like Johnny," Natches snarled. "What now, bastard?"

"Now I beat you to fucking death like I should have when you were a snot-nosed kid," Dayle snarled.

Natches laughed as he shed his coat, feeling the blood pump through his body, adrenaline racing through his veins.

"I'm not a kid now, old man," he sneered. "Come and get me. We'll see who ends up with the busted ribs this time."

The second Chaya realized Nadine Grace had a hostage, and who it was, panic nearly flared in her throat.

"We have a hostage situation." She spoke quietly into the mic at her cheek that connected her to the team surrounding the house.

Alex was the closest in position, stretched out on the roof across the street, hidden from view by the branches of an aged oak growing beside it.

"Alex, confirm visual."

"Confirmed. Target acquired."

She heard the pop of the sniper rifle, her eyes widening as Cranston began to curse and order all agents to converge on the house.

"All agents, be advised, don't interfere. Cover only. This is Natches's fight."

"Are you insane?" Cranston turned back to her, his eyes bugging out of his head. "Natches will kill him." He pulled his own mic closer to his mouth. "All agents, detain—"

"No." Before Cranston could stop her she pulled the plug on his communications unit and stared back at him furiously. "Stop fighting me so I can get to Natches. We cover him, that's it. This is his fight, Cranston. No matter what."

"And if his father manages to get a killing blow in? What then, Agent Dane?"

She breathed in roughly. "Then I'll deal with it, Timothy. It's his fight. It's his pride. I won't take it from him."

He cursed again, turned from her, and a second later they were running from the van to the sidewalk, racing to the two-story brick house that sat peacefully amid the residential street.

Neighbors were stepping from their houses as the sheriff's car sped down the street, sirens wailing. And she wondered how Timothy had managed to keep Zeke from coming in sooner.

They rushed the house. Dawg and Rowdy with their black law enforcement vests made it there first. The door splintered as they went through it, and stood blocking the living room, staring back at Natches and Dayle Mackay in shock.

They were brutal. Fists were slamming into faces. Natches's jaw and lip were bleeding; Dayle probably had teeth missing though. He was bleeding profusely from the mouth, stumbling back as Natches buried his fist in his ribs. And from the grunt of pain, it wasn't the first time.

Dayle went to one knee, staggered, and then pulled himself back up. Lowering his head he charged Natches. A second later, he came up on his tiptoes, a wet groan leaving his throat as Natches buried his fist in his stomach and threw him back.

"Have you had enough?" Natches's drawl was lazy, that dangerous sound Chaya swore she was going to make sure he never uttered again.

"Son of a bitch," Dayle wheezed and charged again.

The blow to his ribs took him to his knees.

"We can keep this up all day," Natches informed him, stepping back as Dayle rolled to his side. "Come on, old man; pull your ass back up. I don't think you're bleeding enough."

Nadine was sprawled where Alex's bullet had left her, and as Chaya watched, Alex stepped into the hall from the back and lifted Natches's sister into his arms. Her eyes met his, and she almost backed up at the emotion in Alex's face.

"She's been drugged, Alex," Natches told him, still watching Dayle as he held his ribs and groaned weakly. "Get her to the hospital, now."

Alex moved as Timothy barked orders into his radio, calling for a unit to meet Alex on the street for the drive into the hospital.

Zeke stepped into the house, and he, too, watched as Natches moved farther back from Dayle Mackay.

"I think his rib is broken, maybe several of them," Natches informed them cheerfully as he gripped Chaya's arm and began to move her back. "Take care of this, boys. We'll see you in a few days."

"She can't leave." Timothy was nearly hyperventilating now. "You need to be debriefed. We have fucking red tape to get through and questions that need answering. Get your ass back here, Natches. Agent Dane."

Natches turned back to him, stared at him, and Timothy went quiet.

"You remember that talk we had last year, Timothy?" Natches asked him.

Timothy glared back at him.

"I see you do. Cut the red tape. You have the damned recording if your phone worked. Debrief him." He shoved his finger in Dayle's direction. "Arrest him, get him the hell out of Somerset and keep him locked up. Because if I have to deal with you one more time, in my town, I might break a promise I made to myself and Chay about no more killing. You don't want that."

"And Timothy." Chaya stood her ground when Natches would have dragged her out of the house. "Don't forget your promise to me. I did my part. I expect yours as a Christmas present. As we agreed."

He rubbed his balding head, squinted at her, then sighed. "By Christmas."

She nodded, then turned and let Natches lead her from the house. The street was filled with vehicles. He wrapped his jacket around her, lifted her to the back of the Harley, and seconds later they were maneuvering through the crowd converging on the Grace home.

It was over. She wrapped her arms around his waist and leaned against his back as they hit the interstate and headed back to the *Nauti Dreams*.

"You promised me at least a week in that bed of yours," she reminded him. "How are you going to keep your cousins away from us?"

"I have my ways." He turned, flashed her a wicked smile and a wink. "Don't worry, baby. I have my ways."

Epilogue

Enter At Your Own Risk
No Knocking
No Visitors
GO AWAY

The sign blocked the entrance to the *Nauti Dreams* for two weeks. It had gone up a week after Dayle Mackay's arrest, and Chaya and Natches stayed secluded.

Rowdy and Dawg shook their heads as they passed by and heard the male laughter, the feminine giggling, from inside. They swore Natches and Chaya were going to starve before they came out, but they both had to admit, the sound of Natches's laughter from inside that houseboat lightened their hearts.

Finally, the sign came down though. As October turned into November, and the chill wind turned icy on the lake, Natches stepped from the *Dreams.*

Dressed in jeans, zipped only, no shirt, and socked feet, he inhaled the scent of winter coming and wrapped his arms around the real dream in his life as she stood in front of him, bundled in a quilt, drowsy and sated from the early morning loving they had shared.

Excited by the knowledge they carried.

Natches had slipped from the boat the night before and made a trip to the pharmacy. This morning Chaya had taken the pregnancy test he had brought home, and it was positive. She was having his child.

"You're going to teach him to play baseball then?" she asked, a smile teasing her lips as he kissed the curve of her neck.

"Of course," he drawled. A silky, rich, lazy sound that she already loved. "And if we have a daughter, I swear, Chay, I'm locking her up till she's fifty."

"If you lock her up, she won't be able to find a Harley-riding hellion to steal her heart," she teased, laughing.

"My point exactly, sweetheart. My point exactly."

Before Chaya could reply, Dawg stepped out of the *Nauti Nights*, pushed his fingers through his mussed hair, and threw them both an irritated look.

"Take your mushy crap back behind closed doors," he grumbled, the scowl on his face boding ill for daring to get in his way.

Chaya watched him in surprise as Natches arched a brow.

"Problems, Dawg?" he asked.

Dawg grunted. "I'm calling her brother; maybe he can force that hardheaded little minx to listen to reason. She sure as hell isn't listening to me."

"About what?" Chaya asked him.

"She needs to go to the damned doctor," he snarled. "Three weeks now and she's sick more often than not. She's tired all the damned time, and she refuses to go to the doctor. Just looks at me like she wants to rip my head off or something."

Worry strained the thin, tight-lipped expression on his face.

Chaya grinned and he glared at her. "She's sick."

"It's normal." She rolled her eyes at his look.

The thought of it still cracked her up. Crista Mackay had been complaining of her ailment the night she, Kelly, and Maria Mackay had been at the boat.

"The hell it is. She never gets sick."

"She does if she's pregnant."

Natches tensed, but Dawg froze. He stared back at her, his lips parting, then closing a second before she swore he almost stumbled as he stood still staring at her.

"She's what?"

Chaya frowned. "I thought she knew. With the morning sickness—she said it wasn't fair you weren't sick, too." She had known, hadn't she? Chaya asked herself. "Doesn't she know?"

Dawg lifted a hand toward the door, and she swore it was shaking. Then he turned back to her and swallowed tightly.

"Damn." His voice was almost weak. "Are you sure?"

Chaya stared back at him in surprise. "Sure she's pregnant?" She laughed. "No, but Natches bought no less than three of those tests he slipped out last night to get. We won't need the last two. You're welcome to them."

Dawg's gaze sharpened. "You're . . . ?" He couldn't seem to say the words.

"Pregnant?" Natches drawled in amusement. "So the test says."

Dawg looked back inside the houseboat, looked to Chaya, then at Natches, and she swore he paled.

"What if she has a girl?" he almost wheezed. "Oh hell. A Mackay daughter? Natches, what will we do?"

"Lock her up till she's fifty." Natches laughed as Chaya butted her elbow into his tight stomach. "We'll lock them up till they're fifty, Dawg, because I don't think I would survive it."

"A baby?" Dawg shook his head, blinked, then without another word, turned and went back into the houseboat.

"A dollar says she's dressed and headed to the doctor in the next hour." Natches chuckled.

"Two says he borrows the test," she countered.

An hour later, Dawg barged in, ignoring the fact that the door was closed and drapes were drawn. He even ignored Natches's curse as he tried to fix the quilt around Chaya's naked body.

"I need that damned test."

He was definitely pale. And his hands really were shaking.

"Get up, Natches. This ain't no time for that crap." He all but lifted Natches from the couch as Chaya dissolved into laughter. "Get the damned test already."

"You owe me, Natches," she called out as he laughed and headed upstairs for the pharmacy bag. Then she looked at Dawg again.

He was pacing. Dressed in jeans and a dark blue shirt, the ends hanging over his jeans, barefoot and decidedly worried, he paced the living room and stared at the stairs.

"Wish he'd hurry," he growled.

Chaya held the quilt tight around her. She knew Crista had miscarried their first child several years ago, something Dawg hadn't known about until Crista'd returned to Somerset the year before. If Dawg's demeanor was any indication now, he was terrified. A terrified Nauti Boy. She would have had to see it to believe it.

"She'll be fine," she said softly then.

He turned back to her, his light green eyes pinning her, his expression intense. "Damned right she will be," he snarled. "I'll make sure of it. Hurry, Natches," he yelled. "Damn it, I don't have all day."

Natches was grinning as he came back down the stairs, tossed the bag to his cousin, and watched as Dawg rushed from the houseboat.

"Do you think he'll survive it?" He chuckled, returning to the couch and wrapping her in his arms.

"As long as it's not a girl," she snorted. "You guys deserve girls. A half dozen of them at least."

The wounded-male look he gave her had her giggling. "That's just wrong, Chay. On so many levels." He sighed. "A daughter would make me old before my time."

"That's okay." She nipped his chin and touched his cheek. He was her nauti dream; she wasn't going to allow that. "I promise I'll keep you young."

He smiled at that and caught her lips in a heated, hungry kiss. Because it was the truth. Loving Chaya would always keep him young. And maybe, just maybe, it would give him the strength to survive if God decided to start laughing at the Nauti Boys and actually gave them daughters.

Christmas Day

"Now, you can't look," Chaya reminded Natches firmly as he kept his back to the door of the houseboat, his forest green eyes watching her with amusement and love.

There was nothing she had ever known that had prepared her for the full extent of Natches's love. He could drive her crazy, make her insane with his arrogance and male dominance, but there was always a smile, always a kiss, and he always held her. It was like nothing she could have imagined.

"We could be in bed, cozy and warm," he suggested, his brows waggling. "We could try out those new presents I bought you."

She blushed. He'd bought her a small cedar box and more vibrators than one woman could use in a lifetime.

"Later," she promised, ducking around him to stare out of the door to where two figures were making their way along the dock to the houseboat.

She checked Rowdy's and Dawg's boats. The men were coming out, their wives with them.

Dawg was still in shock that Crista was pregnant and had kept that news from him for over a week before Chaya had unintentionally dropped the bomb. He barely let Crista walk on her own now. The other woman swore it was all she could do to keep him from carrying her every step she needed to make.

Rowdy wasn't much better. It seemed all of the women who belonged to the Nauti Boys were pregnant within weeks of one another. And each one of their men would go pale at the mention of having daughters.

"Now, remember, keep your back turned." Chaya opened the door, the cold wind swirling in as Dawg, Crista, Rowdy, and Kelly stepped inside.

"He looks impatient, Chaya." Kelly laughed, her gray eyes twinkling as she looked at Natches's back.

"Why are they here?" Natches almost turned around, but Chaya was ready for him. She pushed his shoulder back.

"Stay," she ordered laughingly.

"I'm not a dog," he grumped. "It's Christmas day."

"Here are Ray and Maria." Rowdy opened the door, and Ray stepped inside, beaming.

The others knew the surprise coming, just as they knew how hard it had been for Timothy to arrange it. But he had come through, just as he had promised he would.

She looked down the dock again, feeling her hands sweating. They were getting closer.

"Natches?" She turned to him.

"Can I turn around yet?" There was a grin in his voice.

"Not yet." She wiped her hands down the sides of her jeans and looked around at the others helplessly. Maybe she had gone about this the wrong way.

Ray winked at her. "Grandsons are good things to have," he told her.

"Yeah, and you get three of them." Natches laughed. "Come on, Chay. Let me turn around."

The other two guests stepped onto the deck of the boat as Chaya slid the door open to let them in.

Timothy stood beside the young man Natches had been trying so hard to get out of Iraq. Faisal was older now, twenty, but his smile was still bright, if a little nervous.

He was wearing jeans and a white shirt beneath the leather jacket Chaya had asked Timothy to get him. His eyes glittered with warmth and excitement as he stared around the room at everyone.

"Chaya." Natches's voice was a warning now as he felt the tension gathering in the room. "Who's visiting?"

She smiled at Faisal before moving in front of Natches.

"I love you," she told him, staring up at him. "I've loved you forever."

"I'll love you past forever, baby," he said shamelessly. "Now what the hell is going on?"

She breathed in, then nodded to Faisal.

His smile lit up the room. "I wish to you, Natchie, a merry Christmas."

Natches froze. His eyes widened, shock spreading over his face as he turned slowly.

He stared at the young man and saw the boy he remembered. Courage and strength still lined Faisal's face and filled his eyes, and his smile was still wide, friendly. He was a man now, but Natches saw the boy who had aided Chaya's rescue in Iraq. The kid who had risked his own life to protect an American.

"Mr. Cranston. He says I'm an American now." Faisal stared at Natches, that hint of nervousness back. "That you wanted me here."

There was a hint of question in Faisal's voice when Natches didn't speak. He couldn't; his throat was tight, so many emotions tearing through him now. Chaya would have died if this young man hadn't gotten a message out that she had been captured. She and Natches would have both died if Faisal hadn't covered them, if he hadn't helped Natches rescue her.

There would be no light in his world if it hadn't been for

this boy. No Chaya, no life growing within her. There would have been nothing but the killer he had been slowly turning into.

Natches blinked back the moisture in his eyes, then moved to the boy. Before he knew his own intentions, he wrapped his arms around the kid and hugged him quickly and tightly before grasping his shoulders and pushing him back.

"Hell, Faisal, you grew up on me, kid," he said huskily. "Why the hell did you go and do that?"

Faisal's grin was filled with warmth. "Timothy Cranston. He says you have a baby coming. Maybe a little girl that will need a brother such as I. I could be a very good brother, Natchie."

A little girl. Natches felt his stomach clench in fear.

"Nah, a boy. You'll have to help me teach him how to fight."

"This I can do." Faisal nodded, clapping Natches on the shoulder, his nerves receding. "I will do this, Natchie. I . . ." He looked around. "This is your family that you told me of? Damned Dawg and Fucking Rowdy?"

Dawg and Rowdy glared at Natches as he cleared his throat. "Just Dawg." Natches almost laughed as he nodded to his cousin. "His wife, Crista. Rowdy and his wife, Kelly. And Uncle Ray and Aunt Maria."

"Your uncle Ray, too, son." Ray stepped forward and shook the boy's hand before patting him on the back. "We're all your family."

Faisal's expression clenched then, emotion working through him as it was through Natches. Hell, Natches'd come to think of Faisal as an adopted cousin, or even a son. He hadn't imagined the young man he had turned into, but that would work, too.

"My family?" Faisal asked, turning back to Natches to be certain. "They are my family as well?"

"Adoption papers." Timothy slapped them into Natches's hand. "We began the process when you first started harassing me for it. I'm on suspended leave, I'll have you know, for pushing this through."

"For this and several rules he broke in a certain arrest." Chaya glared at him. "Timothy, you need to settle down and stop making everyone crazy."

Timothy's smile was all teeth. "Maybe I'll move to Somerset. Fine little town. I could have a hell of a lot of fun here."

Natches ignored the sniping as he stared at the papers.

"Faisal Mackay," he said, looking up at the boy. "This works for you?"

Faisal's smile was filled with excitement. "Mackay, it is a good name. Strong. And filled with family." There was hunger in the boy's eyes as he stared around the room. The hunger for family, for roots. "If it pleases you, Natchie, it pleases me."

"Hell, I got a nephew." Dawg grinned. "He can work at the lumber store."

"The marina would be better," Ray argued. "He'll like the lake."

"He can make up his own mind." Natches clasped the boy's arm and felt Faisal's fingers curl around his, too, as he grinned down at him. "But he gets to work in a garage first."

Natches turned to Chaya, pulled her to his side, and felt the warmth of family surround him. Even Timothy, the rabid little fucker, was grinning.

"I hid your presents in the back," Chaya told Faisal. "Both of your presents." She looked to Timothy. "Merry Christmas, Timothy."

He scratched his cheek and frowned at her. "I didn't get you anything." Out of sorts, that was Timothy, clear to the bone.

"Yeah, you did." She smiled softly and looked around the room at the family she had. "You gave me everything, Timothy."

She surprised him with a kiss to his cheek, then moved from the room to the back of the boat, where she had hidden the other presents from Natches. The rest of the family's were beneath the tree, and now it was time to add to that family.

She turned back when she reached the hall, a grin touching her lips as the cousins began to argue around Faisal again about where he could work. The young man looked ecstatic, excited, nervous, and filled with hope.

With hope. That was what they all had now, what Timothy had given to them.

As the agent turned to her helplessly, she winked at him and smiled before entering the room that held the presents.

Life was exceptionally good. Natches's sister would be here within the hour to open presents, then they would move to Dawg's and Rowdy's boats, and eventually to Ray and Maria's for a family dinner and more presents.

Janey was settling in slowly, finally finding a balance, and Faisal was now safe and where he belonged. With the family that would ensure his future. She and Natches had a life now. Warmth. Family.

Finally, Chaya had found home.

Lora Leigh lives in the rolling hills of Kentucky, often found absorbing the ambience of this peaceful setting. She dreams in bright, vivid images of the characters intent on taking over her writing life, and fights a constant battle to put them on the hard drive of her computer before they can disappear as fast as they appeared. Lora's family, and her writing life co-exist, if not in harmony, in relative peace with each other. Surrounded by a menagerie of pets, friends, and a teenage son who keeps her quick wit engaged, Lora's life is filled with joys, aided by her fans whose hearts remind her daily why she writes. Visit her website at www.loraleigh.com.